Praise for the Saga of Recluce

"Modesitt has established himself with his
Recluce series as one of the best nineties writers
of fantasy. The fantasies are characterized
by a highly developed and consistent
system of magic."

—*Vector*

"L. E. Modesitt, Jr., never fails to deserve praise."
—*Analog Science Fiction and Fact*

"Unique and refreshing."
—Robin Hobb, author of *Fool's Quest*

"My favorite thing about L. E. Modesitt's books
is that . . . I enjoy rereading them as much
as I enjoy them the first time."

—*SF Revu*

TOR BOOKS BY L. E. MODESITT, JR.

L. E. MODESITT, JR.

THE MONGREL MAGE

TOR®
fantasy

A TOM DOHERTY ASSOCIATES BOOK
NEW YORK

THE MONGREL MAGE

A Tor Book
Published by Tom Doherty Associates
175 Fifth Avenue
New York, NY 10010

www.tor-forge.com

Tor® is a registered trademark of Macmillan Publishing Group, LLC.

ISBN 978-0-7653-9469-9

Our books may be purchased in bulk for promotional, educational, or business use. Please contact your local bookseller or the Macmillan Corporate and Premium Sales Department at 1-800-221-7945, extension 5442, or by email at MacmillanSpecialMarkets@macmillan.com.

First Edition: October 2017
First Mass Market Edition: October 2018

Printed in the United States of America

0 9 8 7 6 5 4 3 2 1

For Brooks
And his knack for getting the conventional
done unconventionally

CHARACTERS

Beltur	Orphaned mage
Kaerylt	White mage, Beltur's uncle
Sydon	White mage, Kaerylt's assistant
Denardre	Prefect of Gallos
Wyath	Arms-Mage of Gallos
Margrena	Healer
Jessyla	Healer, Margrena's daughter
Athaal	Black mage, Elparta
Meldryn	Black mage, baker, Athaal's partner
Cohndar	Senior black mage, Elparta
Felsyn	Black mage, Elparta
Lhadoraak	Black mage, Elparta
Fhaltar	Captain, City Patrol, Elparta
Osarus	City Patrol Mage, Elparta
Waensyn	Black mage from Fenard
Jhaldrak	Councilor for Elparta
Veroyt	Chief Assistant to Jhaldrak
Helthaer	Marshal of Spidlar
Nakken	Majer, Marshal's chief of staff
Vaernaak	Commander, Spidlar
Jenklaar	Majer, Spidlar
Waeltur	Majer, Spidlar
Laugreth	Captain, Second Reconnaissance Company
Gaermyn	Undercaptain, Second Reconnaissance Company
Zandyr	Undercaptain, Second Reconnaissance Company, son of Trader Alizant
Toeraan	Captain, Naval Marines
Alizant	Trader in spices, Elparta
Alastyn	Son of Alizant, older brother to Zandyr
Aliza	Daughter of Alizant
Eskeld	Trader, Elparta
Jorhan	Smith, Elparta

NORTHERN

CANDAR

Gulf of Candar

Gulf of Murr

RECLUCE

EASTERN OCEAN

The WORLD

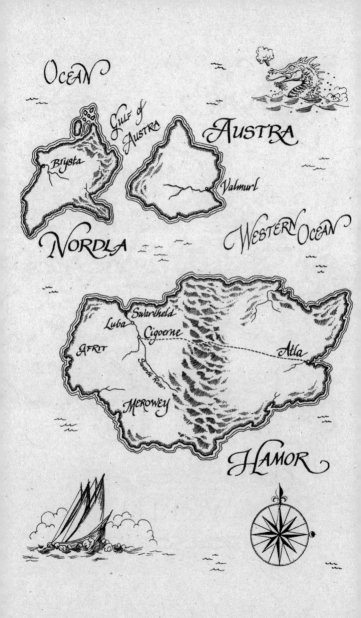

OCEAN

Gulf of Austra

AUSTRA

Briysta

Valmurl

NORDLA

WESTERN OCEAN

Swartheld

Luba

Cigoerne

AFRIT

Atla

Swarth River

MEROWEY

HAMOR

NORTHERN OCEAN

Gulf of Murr

Land's End

Black Holding

Extina

Alberth

Reflin

Cape Devalin

Spidlaria

Lydiar

SPIDLAR

Quend

Kleth

Alaren

East Horns

Elparta

Tyrhaven

Rytel

SLIGO

Lavah

Mattra

Feyn

CERTIS

Jellico

MONTGREN

Wandernaught

Enstronn

Passera

Weevett

Vergren

Clarion

Sigil

Yryna

Fenard

Fyven Freetown

Nylan

SouthPoint

Tellura

Hydolar

OHYDE RIVER

FREETOWN

Meltosa

(Lydiar)

KYPHROS

HYDLEN

Renklaar

Dasir

Telsen

RECLUCE

Tikoya

Arastia

Asula

Pyrdya

Lythga

Sunta

Farhkaar

STURBAL

HIGH DESERT

FAIRHAVEN RIVER

Ruzor

Worrak

EASTERN OCEAN

C. Hibbell 1995

THE MONGREL MAGE

I

As Beltur walked along the stone walk on the south side of the causeway extending from the gates to the city, he glanced down at young Scanlon, walking beside him, half wishing he hadn't needed to bring the boy with him, but there was no help for that, not if he wanted to keep the burnet he was seeking from spoiling too soon. Satisfied that the ten-year-old was having no trouble keeping pace, Beltur studied the low-lying fields that stretched almost a kay eastward from the main gates of Fenard before reaching the outer walls. Supposedly, the water gates in the outer walls and levees could be opened to allow the river, such as it was, to flood the fields, making them impassable to an armed force.

The only problem, reflected Beltur, was that much of the time, the Anard River was little more than a stream, unlike the River Gallos, into which it flowed all too many kays to the northeast. He'd never quite understood how a cubit or two of water over the paved causeway and the fields would be much of a deterrent to a determined army, but then no one had asked him, and it was unlikely anyone who mattered would, or that they'd listen to a third-rate mage.

In the meantime, he needed to see if he could find enough burnet—just because Salcer hadn't gathered enough before he'd left, and there was no one else to gather it. *Not that the great white mage Kaerylt could be bothered, nor even Sydon.* Beltur swallowed his resentment, if he dared to do otherwise, especially given that Kaerylt was not only a powerful mage, but also his uncle and the only one standing between Beltur and his possible conscription as a battle mage for the Prefect's army. The very fact that the Prefect needed so much burnet meant trouble, since his principal use for it was as the main ingredient in a balm used to stop blood loss, and stockpiling the ingredients for that balm was a good indication that someone anticipated significant losses of blood.

As for Kaerylt getting the burnet himself, well, if Beltur were to be fair, he had to admit that it wouldn't have been the best idea to let his uncle or even Sydon anywhere near herbs, given that they both carried so much chaos that their touch would wilt the herbs largely to uselessness. *But then, while yours has much less chaos, you still carry enough to spoil the herbs.* It would just take longer, Beltur knew. Which was why Scanlon was accompanying him to the old herbalist's gardens.

Beltur took a deep breath and kept walking, thinking of the old rhyme.

> *Blood from the blade, screams in the night,*
> *Bind him with burnet, in dark or in light,*
> *So blood doesn't flow*
> *And order won't go.*

Although it was early morning, with the sun barely above the low rolling hills farther to the east, Beltur had not only to squint against the light, but to blot his forehead. The summer day was going to be hot, as were most of the days leading to harvest, and the stillness of the air made it seem even warmer than it was. He had no doubt that he'd be soaked through with sweat by the time he and Scanlon returned, since Arylla's cottage and gardens were more than a kay from the nearest gate in the outer walls.

"Why couldn't we have hired a cart, ser?" asked Scanlon.

"Carts and horses cost silvers. Walking doesn't. If you want your coppers, don't complain."

"Yes, ser." Scanlon shifted the empty cloth bag from one shoulder to the other.

Roughly a half glass later, after walking from the outer gates along the wall, Beltur rapped on the weathered door of the small cottage, whose gardens spread behind it under the old outer wall of Fenard. The gardens contained no trees. By edict of the Prefect, no trees were permitted within half a kay of the wall, despite the fact that all that lay between the outer walls and the city walls were fields and pastures.

The door opened, and a wiry woman stood there, wearing brown trousers and a patched brown tunic. Beneath short brown hair strewn with occasional gray, black eyes focused skeptically on Beltur, looking up at him just slightly, not exactly a surprise because Beltur was somewhat on the short side, and more than a head shorter than his uncle.

"Good morning, Arylla," offered Beltur with a cheer he did not entirely feel.

Arylla looked sourly at Beltur, then at Scanlon. She shook her head. "Brinn or burnet?"

"Burnet."

"Makes no sense to me why Prefect Denardre put a white mage in charge of making balms."

"You know as well as I do, Arylla." *Because the few healers in Fenard wouldn't.* "You won't do it, either."

"I could, but knowing why he wants it, I wouldn't sleep for days." She stepped back and motioned for the two to enter the cottage, then closed the door behind them, turning and walking toward a narrow doorway at the rear of the cottage.

"That doesn't make sense to me," Beltur replied. "You aren't even a healer. Besides, how can making something that can save a man's life be chaotic?"

Arylla stopped, her hand on the latch to the rear door. "War is chaos, especially if you don't have to fight. It's not like the Marshal or the Tyrant are ever going to attack Gallos. Or even the Viscount for all his talk. As for those traders from Spidlar, they hate war. Bad for trade, they say. Anyway, I've only got enough left for one bag."

"You have more than that," pressed Beltur.

"I do. You take that, and there won't be any come next summer."

He could sense the truth of her words, and that meant Kaerylt wouldn't be happy. But then, his uncle was seldom happy, and when he was, it wasn't for long, or so it seemed to Beltur.

"You have a bag for me to put the leaves in?"

"Scanlon, give her the bag."

"You haven't touched the bag, have you, Beltur?"

"No, and it hasn't been near Kaerylt, either."

"That'd be some small help. Wait here." She paused after opening the door. "And I'd thank you not to touch anything." Then she stepped outside, leaving the door half open.

As he waited, Beltur was glad they were inside, because the cottage was cooler than outside, if not by much, and they were out of the sun.

"She never lets us go with her," said Scanlon.

"No. Herbalists are like that." Except Beltur knew that Arylla had no problem with Scanlon, just with Beltur. She was protective of her plants and bushes. He couldn't blame her.

"Brinn costs more, doesn't it?"

"Usually."

"Why doesn't Mage Kaerylt want more of it?"

"It's not what he wants. It's what the Prefect wants." And burnet was easier to grow or find than brinn, and a great deal less expensive. "The Prefect most likely has all the brinn he needs." *Enough for his officers, at least.*

Scanlon did not ask any more questions.

Beltur waited and watched as Arylla cut the burnet, easing the long leaves with their ragged-looking edges into the bag. Despite her deft movements, the wait seemed to stretch into what seemed to be almost a glass, but was undoubtedly only a fraction of that, before Beltur could see Arylla returning. He stood back as the herbalist reentered the cottage and closed the rear door.

She handed the bag, seemingly slightly more than half full, to Scanlon, then looked to Beltur. "Half a silver, and a bargain at that. You got more than half a bag."

Beltur extended the five coppers. "Thank you."

"Still doesn't make any sense to me," murmured the herbalist, shaking her head, then adding in a louder voice, "You'd best be on your way. It won't get any cooler if you wait."

In moments, Beltur and Scanlon were walking back along the dusty road that paralleled the outer wall, puffs of dust rising from the mage's white boots with each step he took. He was careful to keep enough distance from Scanlon so that he wouldn't inadvertently brush the bag of burnet. The last thing he wanted was for anything to happen to the burnet, because his uncle would immediately blame him.

When the two of them reached the open gates of the outer wall, one of the guards in the black uniform and leathers of Gallos looked at Beltur. "What's in the bag, Mage?"

"Burnet. It's an herb for healing." When the guard looked skeptical, Beltur said to Scanlon, "Open the bag a little and show the guard."

"Don't bother."

The other guard frowned. "Why the boy? The bag's not that heavy."

"Chaos wilts the herbs, and they won't stop the bleeding as well."

The second guard waved them through.

The causeway was even hotter than the road outside the walls had been, and Beltur blotted his forehead again. He hated to think what the city proper would be like by late afternoon.

Unlike the guards at the outer gates, neither of the two at the inner gates gave more than a glance to Beltur and Scanlon, perhaps because they were more interested in a peddler and his cart, and the young woman with him. Once inside the walls, Beltur glanced up at the clear greenish-blue sky, then dropped his eyes to the ancient stones of the old city wall, a wall that supposedly dated back to the time of Fenardre the Great. Certainly, he could sense the age, with the random chaos that coated the old ordered stone blocks of the wall.

With a small sigh, he turned his steps toward the Great Square, well beyond which was the stone dwelling he shared with his uncle and Sydon, Kaerylt's main assistant, and also a much stronger mage than Beltur. Then he adjusted his heavy off-white tunic, almost wishing that he didn't have to wear it, because of the early heat of the day, and because it led people to think that he was a more powerful mage than he really was, as opposed to the weak white wizard he was. *Who can sense and use a small amount of order as well.* Then again, the white tunic did mean that he was less likely to be the victim of a cutpurse or other less savory types.

From somewhere drifted the acridness of burning

wood and the more enticing aroma of fowl roasting. For a moment, he thought that it was too early for that . . . except it was already midmorning, and whoever was roasting the bird or birds wanted to have them ready by noon.

Beltur could feel his entire body tightening, the way he felt when there was a concentration of chaos somewhere nearby. He kept walking, slowly looking across the Great Square, taking in the various peddlers and their carts and stalls. His eyes paused at a stall that featured all manner of blades, mainly knives, but he realized that was because one of the older blades, an ancient cupridium shortsword of some sort, seemed to contain chaos. *For use against ordermages?* Pushing that thought aside, he kept searching, both with his eyes and senses, past a vendor with a rack of scarves, whose voice carried across the square.

"The finest in Hamorian shimmersilk scarves, all the way from Cigoerne . . . the very finest!"

"Perhaps the finest since the vanished silks of Cyad, if that," murmured Beltur to himself, as he continued to seek out the source of chaos, his eyes going beyond the silks peddler to a heavyset man with a cart piled high with melons of at least two types, who was so ordered that he couldn't possibly be the source of the chaos. Nor would a mage with that much chaos be comfortable for long near the grower.

Beltur glanced back over his shoulder and saw no one, but he could definitely sense the chaos several yards behind him, which meant that the mage was holding a concealment. The unseen mage was also fairly close. Wondering whether the mage was just moving across the square without wanting to be seen, or if he just might possibly be following them, although Beltur couldn't imagine why anyone that powerful would follow him, he said to Scanlon, "This way," and then turned to his right, away from the scarf vendor and between the stall with the knives and another stall where a wizened woman in gray was setting out cloth bags that looked to be herbal or fragrance sachets, not that Beltur could smell the fragrances amid the heavier odors of fowl and bodies.

Scanlon glared at Beltur for a moment, but kept pace with the mage.

After passing several rows of vendors, Beltur changed direction again, back toward the north side of the square and the side street that would lead to the old stone dwelling where he studied and lived under Kaerylt's sufferance—and largely did his uncle's bidding. Unhappily, the concealed chaos mage remained behind him, if slighter farther back, but still fairly close. That wasn't surprising, given that Beltur was a weak white who didn't hold that much free chaos near him, and most whites sought out chaos in sensing, possibly because many strong whites were practically order-blind. Given the power and the amount of chaos Beltur sensed around the other, there really wasn't too much else that he could do except continue on . . . and raise his feeble shields if it appeared that the mage following them was going to attack.

Still worrying, Beltur and Scanlon turned onto the street that led home, or the only place Beltur could have called home in the ten years since his father's death, since Beltur had no other relatives. He tried to stay on the east side, where there was still some shade. The street had no real name, but everyone called it Nothing Lane, because unlike Joiners Lane, Coopersgate, Baggersway, or Silver Street, there was no particular shop or occupation represented along its narrow way, among them a small inn with a sign proclaiming it was the Brass Bowl, even though most regulars called the public room the "yellow bucket," a cloth merchant, a fuller's shop, and a number of narrow dwellings including that of Kaerylt, although his could have been said to be on Middle Street as well, since it was on the corner of Middle and Nothing.

Kaerylt hadn't been pleased the one time that Beltur had referred to its location as "half-nothing."

Strangely, after Beltur and Scanlon had gone two blocks toward Middle, still two blocks from home, the other mage had stopped, then turned back toward the Great Square. Beltur wasn't sure what that meant, but he was glad the man hadn't kept following them. He blotted his forehead again. Even so, sweat was still running down the side of his narrow face and into his eyes. He took a slow deep breath and kept walking.

As the two neared the end of the second block, Beltur found he wasn't sweating as heavily. He was sure the shade helped, but he had been worried about the mage who had been seemingly trailing him. When he reached the heavy oak door, just one step above the uneven bricks of the sidewalk, he paused, then took out the heavy brass key and unlocked the door. The lock was heavy and crude, but it kept out casual thieves. Even Beltur could muster enough chaos to take care of those who were less casual, and Kaerylt never left traces—except ash—of those who were foolish enough to enter.

Once inside, he just slid the lock bolt, and blotted his forehead again. At least the stone house was cooler than outside, and would remain so until late afternoon, perhaps even longer. He motioned for Scanlon to lead the way to the storeroom, then followed, stopping outside the locked outer door. He used a touch of order to shift the stored chaos from the lock to the sealed cupridium box fastened to the rear of the door, then unlocked the door and opened it, stepping back and turning to the boy. "You know what to do."

"Yes, ser." Scanlon stepped forward and opened the second door, revealing the thin sheet of iron attached to the back side, moved forward.

Beltur watched from the hallway as Scanlon put the bag on the second shelf, beside several others there, then stepped back and closed the inner door on the small storeroom, the one place in the house that neither Beltur nor Kaerylt ever entered, unlike the larger storeroom and work spaces farther back in the house. Although the larger storeroom was also locked in the same fashion, a double door was not required.

After Beltur closed and locked the outer door to the small storeroom, replacing the chaos, Scanlon looked to Beltur, with a trace of a grin. "Do I get my coppers, now?"

"When we get to your house. Not until. The same as always."

"Mother will take them." Scanlon offered a mournful expression. "She always does."

"We'll see." Beltur hid a smile.

The two made their way from the building that was both dwelling and workplace back out onto Nothing Lane, crossing Middle Street, and hurrying slightly to avoid a dray being driven too fast by a young-looking teamster, before entering the fourth door on the east side of the lane, over which was a signboard of sorts that displayed two baskets, rather the halves of two baskets, because displaying a complete basket would have been an invitation to theft as soon as it was completely dark.

In the small room behind the door stood a sturdy dark-haired woman with a worried face, concentrating on weaving osier shoots into a small basket. She looked up.

"We're back, Therala."

Therala looked to her son. "Were you good?"

"He was quite good." Beltur nodded, then extracted the three coppers from his wallet and handed two of them to Scanlon, keeping the third hidden.

In turn, Therala held out her hand.

With a grimace and a sigh, Scanlon handed the coins to his mother.

"Your father needs help with the osier shoots."

"I'll go with him," said Beltur. "I need to ask Zandyl about a basket-weave belt."

"He doesn't like to make those." Therala shrugged. "Talk to him if you want."

"It can't hurt." Beltur managed a rueful smile, then turned to follow Scanlon, who trudged toward the rear workroom. Just before they reached the archway into the workroom, Beltur slipped the last copper into Scanlon's hand, murmuring, "Not a word."

The boy managed not to grin, then said to the man at the workbench, "Ma said you needed me."

"About—" Zandyl broke off his words as he looked up and saw Beltur. "Didn't know you were here, Mage."

"Therala said you weren't too keen on doing woven belts."

"Basket-weave anything for the right price."

"I thought a woven belt might last longer than a leather one."

"It true that you mages are hard on garments?"

"Some are harder than others. How much might a belt cost?"

"Half a silver."

Beltur nodded. "I'll have to think about it."

"Think too long, and it might cost more."

Beltur grinned. "Can't say that surprises me." He looked to Scanlon. "Thank you, again."

Then he turned and headed back toward the front room. Therala barely looked up as he let himself out and began to walk back home.

He still couldn't help but wonder why a powerful white mage had been holding a concealment in the Great Square . . . and why the man had followed him and Scanlon for two blocks from the square before turning away.

Did he think you were someone else?

Why else would anyone follow a third-rate white mage?

Beltur certainly couldn't think of any other reason.

In the meantime, he intended to clean up the main workroom, something that Sydon and Kaerylt felt was beneath them.

II

After cleaning up the workroom, Beltur went to the study, simply because it was the coolest chamber in the house. He couldn't help but pick up the thin volume bound in faded green leather—*The Book of Ayrlyn*. Kaerylt had inherited the book from Beltur's father, unlike the books on magery that had come from Goeryn, the old mage who had mentored his uncle, but his father had never disclosed how he had obtained the druid volume. That was what Kaerylt claimed, anyway.

Beltur settled down in the corner chair and began to leaf through the pages until one section struck him in a way he had not noticed before.

. . . Yet Saryn struck the gates with order and chaos, and the gates yielded, and the walls holding them crumbled, and all within perished or were scattered to the winds. Upon the plains outside of Duevek, the

city that became Sarron, Saryn met and destroyed all
the white mages sent from Suthya to best her . . .

She struck the gates with order and chaos . . . Beltur
frowned. Despite the fact that the book was a product
of druid scriveners, and doubtless not accurate when it
came to the depiction of the powers of women, even
Kaerylt had acknowledged that the description of
Gallosian history, and the treachery of Prefect Arthanos,
was in fact largely as described in *The Book of Ayrlyn.*
Yet Kaerylt had always stressed that a white mage or
any user of chaos needed to keep the use of order to an
absolute minimum to avoid weakening the chaos.

He was still pondering that when he heard the front
door opening.

Quickly, he stood and replaced the green-bound volume on the shelf and hurried out of the study and toward the small entry hall to greet his uncle and Sydon.

Kaerylt was tall, broad-shouldered, with blond hair
already silvering and deep-set black eyes that seemed
to look right through Beltur when he frowned at his
nephew, but he smiled pleasantly as Beltur approached.
"Did you get the burnet?"

"All that remained. Half a bag."

"That's all?"

"Arylla said she wasn't going to destroy her plants
to give me an extra half bag."

"She always says something like that," added Sydon,
who turned from sliding the lock bolt on the front
door.

"She was telling the truth," replied Beltur.

"As she saw it," said Kaerylt dryly. "That's what is."

"There was something I wanted to talk over," began
Beltur.

"That can wait. I need to prepare to leave first thing
in the morning."

"For where? Why?"

"Prefect Denardre wants me to do something about the trouble in Analeria, and he's paying well, which is unlike him. It will also bring in some silvers and get us out of Fenard for a while."

"What trouble?" asked Beltur. "I haven't heard about anything to the south. Well, except for the nomad raiders in the southern grasslands. They're always causing trouble. But that's nothing new."

"No . . . it's not exactly new, but this time it's the result of a recurrence of an old problem. The arms-commander in Kyphrien tried to enforce the law against women leaving their families to flee to Westwind."

"Kyphrien's not . . . Oh . . . and he's in charge of Analeria as well?"

"Brilliant deduction."

"If the women don't want to stay, why force them to? They'd only make their families miserable—and whatever poor fellow has to consort them."

"Women should listen to their men," replied Kaerylt. "If a lot of them leave, then that makes the men angry, and it's harder to keep the peace. Besides, you know how I feel about the bitches of Westwind. One way or another, they and their Legend are always stirring things up."

"There's always some belief somewhere causing trouble," said Beltur, wondering why believers in the Legend were any different from the Chaordists or the few remaining believers of the black temple.

Kaerylt looked condescendingly at Beltur. "You really don't understand, do you?"

What is there to understand? Beltur wasn't about to say that. "I probably don't."

The older mage offered a sound between a sigh and a snort. "Then let me make it very simple. If the young women and the girls who are about to become women leave, then there are more men than women. The men raid other towns or hamlets for women. The others fight back. Soon everyone is fighting. This requires the Prefect to send armsmen to keep the peace. Lots of them, and that costs golds . . ."

More than hiring poor white mages, thought Beltur.

". . . In the meantime, because the men are fighting, more women flee to Westwind. Because the Analerian men have even fewer women, they fight more. The Prefect's armsmen have to kill the Analerian men to stop the fighting. Dead men can't be conscripted, and everyone loses horses, and that costs the Prefect more golds." Kaerylt looked hard at Beltur. "Now . . . do you understand?"

Beltur had understood that much before the explanation. "Why does he need more men for the army? He's not fighting anyone."

"There are rumors that the Viscount of Certis is going to increase tariffs on goods passing through Certis. Those rumors are likely to become fact because the Viscount is short of golds."

"What about just sending goods down the River Gallos to Spidlaria?"

"The Spidlarian Council is also thinking about raising their tariffs. Just not as much." Kaerylt glared at Beltur. "Don't ask about using the Phroan River. Even getting to the river is not only hundreds of kays by wagon, but the river's not navigable except for the last hundred kays or so."

"Oh." What he still didn't see was what a white mage could accomplish. "What does the Prefect expect you to do?"

"The impossible. As usual. That's why Sydon is coming with me, and so are you."

Beltur managed not to wince.

"We'll have a squad of troopers escorting us, and the Prefect is lending us mounts. So we won't have to worry about dealing with brigands or supplies."

"But why you and not Wyath? He's the Prefect's arms-mage."

Kaerylt sighed again. Loudly. He turned to Sydon and said, "Go start packing your gear." Then he looked back at Beltur. "Must I explain everything? As arms-mage, Wyath's duties are to protect the Prefect. If the Prefect isn't going to Analeria, then Wyath isn't. He's also more interested in persuading the Prefect to have more white mages at the palace." Kaerylt snorted. "Even if we don't have as many silvers, I'm not all that interested in bowing to Wyath each and every day. As for the Analerians, the task isn't to incinerate them. It's to use magery to persuade the women to stay and the men not to fight."

"I'd probably do you more good staying here," offered Beltur. The idea of bouncing all those kays to Analeria on horseback scarcely appealed to him, nor did he relish dealing with herders or nomads.

"No, you wouldn't. You're good with delicate uses of chaos . . . and even a bit of order. You also are very organized."

Beltur knew what that meant. He'd end up cleaning up and keeping track of everything.

"Now . . . I know you don't think all that highly of Sydon—and don't tell me that you don't—but he's loyal. He works hard, and there isn't anyone better with chaos-bolts than him."

Strong with chaos and not all that bright. Beltur kept that thought to himself. "How long will this take?"

"As long as necessary," replied Kaerylt. "It could be some time. You can use one of the small duffels."

"What about the burnet?"

"Healer Margrena's daughter Jessyla will be here

later this afternoon to collect it. Margrena already paid me for it, and the Prefect will pay her for the balm. We don't make anything that way, but we also don't lose, and Margrena will owe me a favor. Just the eight bags of burnet. Nothing else."

"Yes, ser." Beltur paused, then said, "I thought healers didn't like to make balm for wound healing."

"They don't . . . as a rule. This is an exception. That's all you need to know."

Beltur wondered how Kaerylt had persuaded the healer. "I didn't know she had a daughter."

"She does." Kaerylt turned as if to step around Beltur. "I need to consider what we'll need to take."

"There's one other thing, ser."

"What?" A momentary expression of annoyance crossed Kaerylt's face.

"On the way back from Arylla's there was a powerful white mage who followed us through the Great Square until we were two blocks north of the square. He was under a concealment."

"You couldn't tell who it was, could you?"

"No, ser. He wasn't you or Sydon, or anywhere like you, and there was a lot of power, but the feel was different from any mage I've met."

"Did he see you enter the house?"

"I don't think so. He turned back after two blocks, and I couldn't sense him by the time we reached the door."

"Would you be able to tell if you encountered him again?"

"If I did sometime soon. Feelings . . . they're hard to recall."

Kaerylt frowned slightly. "You'd get better at it if you met more other mages and healers."

"Yes, ser."

"Well . . . you'd better get yourself packed. You'll

have to be here when young Jessyla comes. Sydon and I will be running other errands to get ready for tomorrow."

Beltur nodded. He wouldn't have expected anything else. He stepped back and let his uncle pass before following and then heading up the narrow rear steps to the second floor, where his room was at the back corner.

He could feel the heat even before he opened the door. Once he entered, he left the door open and walked to the single window, which he immediately opened. It couldn't be any hotter outside than it was inside, not in his room, anyway. He wished that his room had windows on two walls the way his uncle's did, because that meant there was a chance for a breeze without opening the door.

What should you take? His eyes went to the small chest that held all of his clothes, except for a set of trousers and a tunic hung on the wall pegs.

He had what he thought he'd need laid out on his narrow pallet bed in less than half a glass. By that time, Kaerylt and Sydon had left again, and Beltur made his way downstairs to the main storeroom, where he found a small duffel, which he took upstairs. Packing took almost no time, and after that, he returned to the study, where he retrieved *The Book of Ayrlyn* and began to read again.

He hadn't gotten all that far when someone rapped on the door. So he set the book aside carefully and made his way to the entry hall. Even from there he could sense the depth of order outside. He opened the door, expecting a stocky blond girl.

"Mage Kaerylt?"

"No . . . I'm Beltur. I'm Kaerylt's nephew. You're Jessyla?" Beltur tried to conceal his surprise as he looked at the redhead who wore the pale greens of an apprentice healer. She was almost as tall as he was, with eyes almost the same color as her greens. And she definitely didn't look anything like her stocky blond mother, although she was wearing the same kind of scuffed brown boots. But then, from what few healers Beltur had encountered, they all seemed to wear brown boots.

"We don't look much alike. I take after my father, she says." Jessyla's voice was firm, neither high nor gravelly like her mother's.

"That can happen. I don't look much like anyone else in the family, and certainly not much like Uncle Kaerylt. Come on in." Beltur opened the door wider and stepped back.

"Thank you." The smile that followed her words was pleasant and cheerful.

"The burnet's in the small storeroom. I'll open it for you and tell you where it is." He closed the front door.

"Tell me?"

"You'll see." Beltur didn't want to explain until she saw the storeroom. "This way." He started off down the hall.

After a moment of hesitation, Jessyla followed.

When Beltur reached the outer door of the storeroom, he used his limited abilities to force the small chaos-mass protecting the outer door back into the cupridium box, then unlocked the door and opened it.

"I wondered about the iron," said Jessyla.

"You could sense it before I opened the door?"

"It is rather obvious . . . in terms of order."

"And that's one of the things healers do."

"More likely that we're looking for wound chaos or the absence of order."

Beltur stepped back, careful not to touch the iron backing of the door. For him, it would only sting, but if Kaerylt or Sydon touched it, they'd get a burn. "You can open the inner door. You'll see all the bags of burnet on the second shelf on the right." He smiled. "If you're going to take them all, you'll have an armful."

"Mother's man Bardek will be here shortly with a handcart." Jessyla opened the inner door and stepped into the small storeroom, surveying the bags of burnet. "You do have a lot here. Not just herbs." She frowned, as if wondering why a chaos-mage would hoard herbs useful only to an ordermage or healer.

Beltur wondered if she'd say anything. She didn't. So he did. "I'd give you a hand, but that wouldn't help the burnet any. I can open doors, though."

"I'll carry it to the entry hall, and then wait there until Bardek shows up."

"How long will that be?"

"Less than a glass. It might be sooner. Bardek has his own sense of time."

Then why does Margrena even hire a man? Again, as with so many thoughts, Beltur didn't voice the first thought that came to mind. He'd learned, painfully, first from his father's switches and then from his uncle's biting words, that saying the first thing that came to mind wasn't a good idea.

"Mother said there were eight bags. It looks more like seven and a half."

"The last one is more than a half, but less than full. It was all that the herbalist had left."

The hint of a smile crossed Jessyla's lips, vanishing almost before it appeared. "You're being relatively honest."

"For a white, you mean?" Beltur grinned.

"You're not really a white. You could almost as easily be a black."

"Iron hurts when I touch it. That wouldn't work very well for a black." *Besides which, Uncle Kaerylt would throw me out.*

"That's the chaos talking. It doesn't like the iron. If you used order completely to manipulate chaos, touching iron wouldn't hurt at all."

You know this from your vast experience with chaos?
"That sounds rather . . . unlikely."

"That's how all good blacks handle chaos. Athaal says it's worked for chaos-mages in the past. The really powerful ones. They lived longer, too."

"Athaal?"

"He's a black from Elparta. A friend of Mother's." Jessyla lifted two bags of burnet from the shelf. "If you'd open the outer storeroom door all the way."

"I can do that." Beltur did so, stepping back.

He felt useless in watching as she made four trips to the front entry, and then returned.

"You want me to close the inner door, I take it?" she asked with an indulgent smile.

"I would appreciate it, thank you."

Once she had done so, he closed and locked the outer door, then eased the chaos back into the lock.

"That's a rather nasty precaution," she observed.

"It was my uncle's idea, and it is his house."

"Are all the doors trapped that way?"

For a moment, Beltur debated not answering, except he realized that she and her mother could sense the chaos anyway, assuming even that they had any reason to enter the house. "Just the storeroom doors. What Uncle has done in his own chambers, I have no idea."

The two walked back to the entry hall, where Beltur eased the front door ajar and looked out onto Nothing Lane. No sign of either a man or a cart. "How far does your mother's man have to come?" He turned to face Jessyla.

"A little over eleven blocks. We live in the northeast."

"The black corner." *Not really poor, but close.*

"It's not really black. It's just that there aren't any whites or much chaos there."

"There aren't that many near here, either. Most live in the southwest." He paused, uncertain what to say, but not wanting to seem distant. "How long have you been an apprentice?"

"Too long. It won't be long before I'm a full healer, though."

"According to the senior healers?"

"Three of them have to agree. Mother can't be one of them. What about white mages?"

"There's a set of tests. If you can do them, you're a mage. Two other mages have to witness the tests."

"And not your uncle?"

"No. He wouldn't count . . . although he's harder on me than the examiners were."

"Mother's the same way." After a moment, she asked, "Why does your uncle deal with herbs he can't use?"

"It's a way to make coins." Beltur knew because he'd asked the same question.

Jessyla frowned, then nodded. "That makes sense."

"Why do you think so?"

"Because most of those who would pay for a white mage's services would want them more for things like battle magery. Mother said that your uncle decided not to avoid that. So he'd have to do other things. What else do you do? She never said."

"Sometimes the Prefect pays him to do things. We also use chaos to clean out places that need it, barns and stables, mostly. That's after they move out things that could burn. Chaos-fire gets rid of vermin. Sometimes, Uncle will help a healer."

"Isn't that dangerous for the person who's ill?"

"I suppose so, but they don't ask him unless they think the person will die if he doesn't do something."

"Destroy wound chaos with chaos?" Jessyla's expression wasn't quite one of revulsion.

"Sometimes, it works. Sometimes, it doesn't. It's not something I've ever done." *And I hope I never have to.*

Abruptly, Jessyla looked past Beltur. "Here comes Bardek."

Beltur turned to look out the partly open door. A slightly stooped graybeard pulled a small handcart down the lane, bringing it to a stop opposite the front door. Beltur opened the door wide and stood back as Jessyla carried the bags of burnet from the entry hall to the cart, crossing the two-yard distance and back four times, before returning to the door a fifth time.

"Thank you. I enjoyed talking to you."

"You're welcome. So did I."

Jessyla's brief smile was pleasant, but nothing more . . . and brief, before she turned and hurried back to the handcart.

Beltur watched from the doorway as Jessyla walked northward on the lane beside the cart. He wished that Margrena's man had taken longer.

III

Between thoughts of what Kaerylt might expect of him and Jessyla's almost offhand comment that he wasn't really a white, Beltur didn't sleep all that well on two-day night. He even had a nightmare where Kaerylt was telling him that he'd never be more than a fifth-rate chaos-mage. He awakened early, just after the first graying of dawn. After he washed up and dressed, he took a quick look in the small mirror. He hadn't changed— the same muddy brown hair and hazel eyes, and the same pug nose. With a wry smile, he headed downstairs and was eating what breakfast there was—mostly stale bread and hard white cheese, washed down with some flat ale—when Sydon joined him.

"You're up early."

His mouth full, Beltur just nodded as Sydon sat down and cut a wedge out of what remained of the round of cheese.

Moments later, Kaerylt appeared. "Finish up. The troopers will be here before long. We need to be out of Fenard before sunrise."

"You didn't say anything about that," mumbled Sydon.

"I did. You weren't listening." Kaerylt sat down, took the remainder of the loaf of bread, and sliced off a small wedge of cheese. "The Prefect doesn't want everyone knowing he's sending three white wizards south."

"We could have left earlier," offered Beltur.

"If we left before dawn, that would be unusual enough that the other troopers here in Fenard would have it all over the city even before we departed. The Prefect would prefer not to have it known that he's sending white mages to deal with the Analerians. This way, we're just leaving early enough to make good time before the day gets too hot."

Beltur could see that. He swallowed the last of the ale in his mug, then stood. He would have preferred amber ale, but Kaerylt liked the dark chewy brew and wasn't about to indulge Beltur's preferences. Beltur had few enough coins that he wasn't about to spend them on ale when he didn't have to. A brew with more bitterness than he liked paid for by his uncle was preferable to spending coppers he generally had to hoard.

"Bring your gear down to the foyer first, Beltur. You can clean up things after that. And don't forget to sweep up as well."

"Yes, ser." He picked up his mug and set it on the wash table, then made his way up to his room.

Once there, he checked what he had packed, then put on the battered visor cap that Kaerylt had provided, most likely a castoff from a trooper, and without any insignia, then lifted the duffel and carried it down the stairs to the entry hall, where he waited until Kaerylt and Sydon left the kitchen. Then he washed the mugs and put them away, and packed what was left of the cheese round as well as the hardtack crackers into a cloth bag that he carried out to the entry hall. He wiped off the table and swept the floor . . . carefully.

Then he waited for a good quarter glass for Kaerylt and Sydon to return, which they did just about the time that ten troopers and an undercaptain reined up outside on Nothing Lane. All wore faded grays. The rankers immediately lined up the three spare mounts, one beside the undercaptain and two behind him and in front of the rest of the squad, formed up two abreast. Beltur waited until Kaerylt picked one of the spare mounts, then took one of the two remaining and immediately looked over at the way the troopers had fastened their gear before strapping his duffel—and his impromptu food sack—behind the saddle. He mounted the horse cautiously . . . and more than a little awkwardly.

Immediately, Sydon appeared. "I wanted that horse."

"You didn't say so," replied Beltur. "I've already strapped my gear in place."

"Just take the other mount, Sydon," ordered Kaerylt. "If you're going to dally around, you don't get choices."

Beltur had been half counting on that. His uncle hated anyone else to delay anything.

"Are you ready, Mage?" the undercaptain asked Kaerylt as soon as Sydon was in the saddle.

"We're ready, Undercaptain."

Without another word, the junior officer flicked the reins of his mount.

Beltur tried the same thing. Nothing happened. So he tried to apply his boot heels to the horse's flanks. That was more difficult than it looked, but he managed, at least enough so that when he flicked the reins again, the horse moved.

Nothing Lane was deserted, although a few peddlers were already setting up in the Great Square. Not a one even looked up as the troopers and mages rode past.

Obviously, they've seen early riders before.

Even the guards at the city gates paid them little attention.

Once outside the inner gates, Beltur could see more than a few people already in the fields, and by the time he rode through the outer gates, there were even more people in the fields, although he couldn't really see what most were doing because anyone who saw the soldiers quietly moved farther away from the road.

That didn't change even when they were several kays away from Fenard.

By midmorning, Beltur, Kaerylt, Sydon, and the half squad of the Prefect's troopers were a good ten kays south of Fenard on the main road south to Kyphrien, a road wide enough for the three mages to ride abreast, with Kaerylt in the middle, although Beltur knew that in several days, they would have to take another road that headed more to the southwest . . . and through the rolling hills that separated the flatter plains to the south and west of Fenard from the grasslands that comprised most of Analeria. A single ranker rode beside the undercaptain.

The greenish-blue sky was clear, and the white sun of late summer beat down on the riders. Sweat oozed from under the visored riding cap that Beltur wore and down his forehead. He had thought to bring a kerchief, but it was already soaked from blotting away the sweat.

Beltur had refrained from asking his uncle anything earlier, given how short Kaerylt had been, but after another glass of quiet riding, he finally spoke. "You haven't said much about what we're going to do . . . or how we might proceed, ser."

"You know, Beltur, you sound like a black mage, wanting a nice neat plan to follow with everything lined up in columns like a trader's bookkeeper. I'd like that, too, except it doesn't work that way. First, we don't even know which villages and hamlets have the biggest problem. We have orders to proceed to the nearest hamlet with a problem and work from there. We only know that the arms-commander in Kyphrien has reported a problem in conscripting Analerians and that he believes the problem is somehow connected to ungrateful women abandoning their consorts and fleeing to the bitches of Westwind. We need to find out if both of those reports are true before we can do much of anything."

"You don't think the reports are accurate?"

"I'm sure that the arms-commander believes what he has been told."

"Oh . . ."

"Exactly." Kaerylt's tone suggested quite definitely that any discussion of details would have to wait, either until they knew more or until they were well away from the hard-faced Undercaptain Pacek, who rode several yards ahead of them.

Not knowing what else he could ask, but feeling that their conversation should continue for at least a little while, Beltur looked to his uncle again. "What do you know about Jessyla?"

Kaerylt didn't turn in the saddle to look at Beltur. "Not much."

"She's an apprentice healer. She says it won't be long before she's a full healer."

"That's not surprising. Her mother's almost strong enough to be a black mage."

"What about her father?"

"Margrena never said anything about her daughter's father. In fact, I often wondered if she just seduced a likely fellow. With blacks and healers, you never know."

"Jessyla mentioned a black mage by the name of Athaal. She said he was a friend of her mother's from Elparta."

"He wouldn't be her father. He's a lot younger than Margrena, doesn't look to be really that much older than you. Decent sort, as blacks go. Doesn't put on airs the way some do here in Fenard."

"Who might that be?"

"I'd rather not say. I'd just say that there might be three blacks left here, and there's not much difference between them."

"What about the ones from Sarronnyn?"

"I have no idea. I'd venture there are more there, given that the marshals of Westwind don't much care for mages of any sort. The first marshal drove out the black mage who gave her victory and a daughter . . . and then she drove out the woman who became the first Tyrant of Sarronnyn, except it was called Lornth then. You should know that. It's in *The Book of Ayrlyn*."

"Ah . . . ser, it just says that Ryba dispatched Saryn to bolster the regent of Lornth."

"You have to read more than the words, Beltur. Saryn the Black had to have been more powerful than Ryba. She trained all the Westwind Guards. As soon as Ryba could, she sent Saryn off. Most likely she just thought that Saryn would do enough to weaken the rebel lords and get killed in doing it. That would have done two things at once—gotten rid of a rival and left Lornth weak for a generation or two."

"It didn't work out that way," said Beltur mildly, hoping to draw Kaerylt out, since it would make the time pass, and he might learn something new.

"No, it didn't. Instead, Candar has two lands ruled by women, and the black bitches of Sarronnyn may be even worse than Westwind. That's the problem with relying on scheming. It often doesn't work out as planned. Force is always surer."

"It kills more people, though."

"Everything a ruler does kills some people and rewards others. If he makes laws and enforces them, people die because they break them. Someone will always break the laws. If he doesn't make laws, other people die because the strongest will use force on the weakest."

Beltur knew that all too well just in living with his uncle. "How much do the Sarronnese scheme?"

"Do mountain cats have claws? Do traitor birds call attention to anything that hides?"

"That's because they want to scavenge what the cats kill," Beltur pointed out.

"The Tyrant of Sarronnyn is the same way. She'll point out things to the Suthyans or to the Prefect, even to the Marshal, just hoping to scavenge something before matters settle down. That's the way the Tyrants have always been."

"The first Tyrant didn't scheme, not according to the book."

"She couldn't. Times have changed."

"I know why you don't care for the Marshal, but you've never said much about the Tyrant."

"There's not much to say. She's likely even less trustworthy than the Marshal." Kaerylt cleared his throat. "Enough of that sort of talk. Thinking about either for long gives me a headache." Kaerylt paused, then added, "Forget about Margrena's daughter. If you want to lose what little ability you do have, Beltur, just get involved with a black. Even a healer will leach the chaos right out of you."

At those words, Sydon laughed softly.

"She'd likely do worse to you, Sydon. Where women go, you've got even less sense than Beltur."

Sydon swallowed.

Beltur managed not to grin.

IV

The remainder of threeday consisted of riding two glasses, stopping, resting, watering mounts, riding, stopping, resting, and riding. They rode through or past hamlet after hamlet, but only one place that might even have been called a village. That night they stayed at a way station, little more than four stone walls with a gate, and a small building with a large hearth, which, given the heat, no one wanted to use to fix a meal. Beltur had to ask one of the troopers for help in unsaddling and grooming his horse, but he watched carefully.

Fourday was much the same, except for the brief cloudburst that soaked everyone and then made the ride even hotter and muggier ... and, for Beltur, made grooming his mount even more difficult and sweaty a process.

A glass after noon on fiveday, the undercaptain called a halt on a low rise from which Beltur could see east to where the road they had been following split, with the wider road heading southeast toward a line of trees beyond the fields, pastures, and woodlots and the narrower road continuing due south toward a long ridge that appeared to be rocky and sparsely dotted with low pine trees. Beltur blotted his forehead and waited, grateful for the first wind he'd felt in days, warm as it was, that wafted across him from the southwest.

The undercaptain turned in the saddle and addressed Kaerylt. "Beyond that ridge is where the grasslands start. Right now, there's not much grass there. It looks like straw this time of year. Most years, anyway. There's another way station there, with a spring. Unless we run into trouble, we should make it before dark."

"Are there any towns close to the way station?"

"No. For the next day from the way station, there's very little but grass. Not much water at this time of year, either."

While the two talked, Beltur listened, but he also studied the slope down to the fork in the road, noticing that the grasses of the ground between the diverging roads appeared to have been trampled rather than just wind-blown, yet there had been no tracks to speak of on the road they had just traveled.

Before long, they were again riding, this time down a long slope toward the fork in the road. As they neared it, Undercaptain Pacek said, "Riders headed southwest, not all that long ago."

"Then they must have come from the other road," suggested Kaerylt. "Why would they come this far and then go back? Why not cut across the space between the two roads somewhere?"

"There's a dry wash that begins in another kay or so. Turns into a canyon and separates the grasslands from the better lands. Goes on for some thirty kays. Even the bottom is so rough that it's easy to have a mount break a leg."

Beltur nodded to himself.

Some five glasses later, as the sun hung just above the ridge they had crossed, Beltur could make out the walls of another way station ahead on the left side of the dusty road. Although he could easily see the tracks of the previous riders, he'd never glimpsed anyone or even seen dust rising from the road that seemed to stretch endlessly into the distance.

"The Analerians won't be at the way station, will they?" asked Kaerylt.

"No. The way stations are for the army."

"Have you ever been attacked by the Analerians?" asked Kaerylt.

"No Gallosian company has been attacked. Some squads have had trouble, but that's likely because the raiders didn't realize who they were. If there was a real attack, the Prefect might have to do something. Torch the grasslands, or slaughter their herds."

"That wouldn't be all that useful," pointed out Kaerylt.

"Well . . . long as they fight each other, we just watch."

If that's so . . . why are we here? wondered Beltur. *Or is it that the Prefect doesn't want anyone to know how badly he needs more men for his army?*

Another half glass passed before the fourteen riders rode into the empty way station, as the sun was beginning to drop below the western horizon.

"Beltur, make yourself useful," said Kaerylt. "Go over and draw up some water for the horses. If there's plenty there, use the first bucket to rinse the trough."

"Yes, ser." The last thing Beltur felt like was drawing water. His legs and buttocks hurt, and the insides of his thighs were raw. Besides, wasn't that something for the troopers to do? He eased the gelding toward the square brick walls of the well. Even before he dismounted, he could see that there was no windlass, just a rope and a bucket. He tried not to wince as he dismounted and tied the gelding to a corner post rising out of the waist-high masonry wall. Then he checked the rope and the bucket. He definitely didn't want to have the rope break or lose the bucket.

He peered down the well, but in the long shadow of the western wall cast by the setting sun, he could see nothing, although he thought he sensed water below. He slowly lowered the heavy bucket, weighted so that it would sink, until he felt it reach the water and begin to fill. Then he began to haul it up. He'd forgotten just how heavy a full bucket of water was. When he got the bucket to the top, he rested it on the flat stones of the well wall for a moment.

He started to pour the bucket of water into the trough, then stopped. He couldn't so much see as sense something like orangish-red flecks throughout the water. He set the bucket down on the wall again. "Ser!" he called to his uncle. "You should come here."

With an annoyed expression, Kaerylt handed the reins of his mount to Sydon and strode toward Beltur. "What is it now?"

"There's something like chaos in the water."

"In the water? Likely story." But Kaerylt bent over the bucket and studied it. Finally, he straightened. "There is something in the water."

"Could it be poison or something?"

Kaerylt shook his head. "It's corruption chaos. Not a lot, but it's there. Someone's likely dumped a diseased animal or parts of it into the water." He turned and called, "Undercaptain!"

In turn, Pacek scowled and then strode across the dusty ground toward the well. "What is it?"

"The water might be tainted. Are there any other streams or springs near here?" asked Kaerylt.

"No place I'd want to send anyone in the dark. No

place they could get to before full dark, either." Pacek almost glared at Kaerylt, then looked down at the bucket in the dim light. After a pause, he bent down and dipped his cupped hand into the water and brought it up, smelling it, and tasting it. "I don't smell anything, and I don't taste anything. It's good enough."

Beltur was about to protest, but held his tongue as he caught his uncle's quick sharp look.

"You have more experience with this than we do," Kaerylt said deferentially.

"Is that all?" asked the undercaptain.

"That's all."

"Good." Pacek turned and marched away.

"What do we do now, ser?" asked Beltur quietly.

"Just pour it into the trough. It likely won't hurt the horses."

"What about us?"

"It's likely not bad enough to turn your guts to water, but there's no point in risking it. I'll show you what to do after you get some water in the trough."

It took Beltur two buckets of water to clean the dust out of the short trough, and three more before Kaerylt said, "That's enough for now. Get out your water bottle."

Beltur reclaimed it from the holder on the saddle.

"Draw another bucket of water, and fill the bottle."

Filling the water bottle from the heavy bucket was harder than it looked, and Beltur ended up getting water on his trousers and lower sleeves.

"Watch with your senses."

Beltur did, sensing as Kaerylt eased a small bit of chaos into the water, except that the reddish white of magely chaos seemed as separate from the water as did the orangish flecks of chaos that had already been there.

"Now, cork the bottle and shake it gently. Keep sensing the water."

Beltur could sense that whenever the orangish flecks

encountered the mage-induced chaos, the orange flecks vanished. He looked to Kaerylt. "Thank you."

"Now that you know what to do, you can fill all our water bottles and make sure they have no corruption."

"Yes, ser."

In moments, there were five more water bottles on the top of the masonry wall.

Beltur was very careful in filling each one, and even more careful in adding chaos to the water. Even so, he had a splitting headache by the time he finished and returned the full bottles to Sydon and his uncle . . . just in time for hard biscuits and dried mutton jerky, both of which required liberal application of the just cleaned water to even chew, let alone swallow.

Seeing the expression on Beltur's face, Undercaptain Pacek said, "These are good rations, Mage. Sometimes, the hard biscuits have more weevils than biscuit."

"Weevils taste better, too," muttered one of the rankers.

Beltur wondered if a touch of chaos would rid such biscuits of vermin, without destroying the biscuit. At the same time, he hoped he never had to find out. Then he took a deep breath, remembering that he still had to deal with his mount.

V

Surprisingly, Beltur slept soundly, and while he was stiff when he woke on sixday, his legs didn't hurt nearly so much as they had, and the rawness of his thighs appeared to be lessening, or his skin was toughening. Breakfast was the same as dinner, and they were on their way before sunrise. Beltur had to admit that riding in the gray light before dawn was much more comfortable than riding in the late afternoon had been.

By midmorning the sun was as hot as it had been on the previous days, and Beltur was again mopping sweat off his face. He also noted that several of the troopers had to dismount and scurry into the chest-high tan grass beside the road to relieve themselves, in more ways than one. Neither Kaerylt nor Pacek commented on that, and Beltur certainly wasn't about to say anything.

Sydon finally asked the question that Beltur had kept to himself after more than a day of riding through the seemingly endless high grasslands. "Aren't there any towns?"

"Nearest place of any size is Arrat," replied Pacek. "We should be there late this afternoon. It's more of a hamlet than a village. There's a post there, with hot food." The undercaptain looked back ahead, not that there was anything to see, except the narrow road stretching ahead . . . and more of the brownish tan grass, bent in most places by strong winds, unlike the vagrant breezes that had too seldom graced the grasslands they had traveled so far.

After a time, Beltur turned to Kaerylt, and, keeping his voice low, asked, "Are we stopping at Arrat?"

"We're headed on to Desanyt, another day east from Arrat. It's a village, closest thing to a town around."

"Is that where there's the most trouble?" asked Beltur.

"I'd doubt it," replied Kaerylt. "It might be where there's the least." At Beltur's puzzled expression, he added, "That's not one of the places that complained about being raided. In the places where the herders have raided because they've had the most women leave, the men aren't about to say anything unless the losses continue. That means that the raiders are going after other villages. They won't raid the larger towns because they'd likely lose too many men, and they won't gain many women by raiding other bands of nomads."

"We're going there so that the Prefect can say that he's sent white mages to deal with the problem?"

"Another brilliant deduction," said Kaerylt dryly. "Besides, we have to start somewhere."

"You're hoping that our presence will stop the women from leaving and cut down on the raiding."

"It should," interjected Sydon.

"The most our mere presence will do," replied Kaerylt in the same dry tone, "is to let the towns know that the Prefect is concerned. The raiders may not even know that we're around. It may be helpful to let them know. If they see that the Prefect is concerned, it might stop the raids. More likely, they'll raid where we aren't."

"Do you think more women will leave because they'll think we'll stop the men from chasing them down?" asked Sydon.

"Both of you are equally brilliant this morning."

Once again, Beltur was reminded why he tended not to ask too many questions. Yet it seemed that a half squad of mounted troopers would be more effective in tracking down fleeing women than three white mages who didn't know all that much about the grasslands of northern Analeria. Except . . .

He nodded. With kays and kays of high grass that looked pretty much the same, it would take hundreds of troopers, if not thousands, to try to track down a comparatively few women . . . and if the Prefect happened to be worrying about what the Viscount might be doing, using troopers to track unarmed women wasn't the best use of his army. *It's not the best use of mages, either.* But then, white mages who weren't regularly paid retainers of the Prefect really couldn't afford to turn down paying tasks offered by Denardre.

In the very late afternoon, one that was hotter and drier than the previous days, Beltur caught sight of what looked to be a woodlot just next to the south side of the road, possibly two kays ahead, although that was hard to tell, given the flatness of the grasslands.

"That's Arrat," announced Undercaptain Pacek laconically.

Beltur's immediate thought was that there must be a spring at Arrat, since there weren't trees anywhere else, and he doubted that anyone would dig a well just to water trees. Even as they rode closer, though, he saw no sign of houses, just a brown wall with the trees behind it, in what appeared to be a square roughly a kay on a side. The tree trunks appeared to be very close together.

"Where are the houses?" Sydon finally asked.

"Behind the trees," replied Pacek. "They're gray thorn trees, and their lower branches fill most of the space between the trunks."

Beltur nodded. The trees formed a natural barricade, and there was nothing else that would burn, except for grass, for kays and kays, and the grass wouldn't burn that hot for that long.

"I could flame my way through that," murmured Sydon.

"To what end?" asked Kaerylt. "To obtain their hoard of gold or their beautiful women? Or perhaps to admire their magnificent structures that tower into the skies before using your last scraps of chaos to destroy them?"

Sydon started to reply, then shut his mouth.

"Are all the hamlets protected in the same way?" asked Beltur.

"Most aren't," replied Pacek. "It takes too much work and plentiful springs."

That made sense. Beltur nodded.

As they neared the hamlet, he kept watching, both the grasslands and the walls, but he saw no one. The dusty road ran parallel to the eastern wall of the hamlet, but a space of a good hundred yards separated the road from the wall and the trees. When Beltur rode past the northern wall of the hamlet, he noticed a walled enclosure located on the road several hundred yards south of the southern wall of Arrat. It did not appear to be in the best of condition, with piles of crumbled bricks at the base.

Something appeared at the base of the wall, almost as if hiding behind one of the brick piles. Beltur realized it was a dog, lean and clearly wary.

"That looks like an old way station out there," said Sydon.

"There's also a dog there," added Beltur.

"It is," said Pacek. "That's the way station for those they don't trust. The mongrel dogs sometimes scrounge there from mongrel traders. There's a barracks and stable just inside the walls for us." The undercaptain laughed. "That way, if anyone attacks, we'll be close to the gate. I've been coming here for nearly ten years. Never happened yet. The other reason is that it keeps us away from their women. They don't ever mention that, but you won't see many. Those you do see are white-haired. If you're lucky, they might only have gray hair." He laughed harshly before adding, "The food is decent, sometimes better."

A brick-paved narrow lane ran from the road to the narrow iron-bound gate barely wide enough for a single wagon. The gate itself was set between two massive brick gateposts three yards on a side that stood over five yards above the entry lane. The square crenellated wall on top of each post, as well as a number of arrow slits, suggested that the hamlet was serious about defending itself. The gate itself was four yards tall and closed. The gate remained closed as the fourteen rode from the road toward the hamlet's walls.

Pacek reined up some ten yards back from the gate, then gestured to the ranker who had been riding beside him. The trooper produced a small trumpet and played a short salute. That was what it sounded like to Beltur, anyway. Nothing happened. No one appeared at the gate.

After a time, Pacek said, "Again."

Shortly, the gate swung open, pushed outward by two young men. Beltur half expected that the heavy gate would squeak or creak, but it did neither. He could see that the pavement continued into another walled area.

A dark-haired and clean-shaven man perhaps the age of Kaerylt walked out from a narrow archway just behind the right gatepost. He wore pale or faded blue trousers, a long-sleeved tunic, and sandals. "Who seeks shelter in Arrat?"

"The troopers of Prefect Denardre."

"With white mages?"

Pacek gestured to Kaerylt, as if to suggest the answer was up to the senior mage.

Kaerylt eased his mount forward, even with Pacek, and reined up. "The Prefect has sent me in response to a request that he address the concerns of the people of the grasslands that too many of their women are fleeing to the Westhorns."

"He has not seen fit to listen to our concerns in the past."

"I can only say that he ordered us here for that reason."

"You are welcome to the quarters for the troopers. After you have refreshed yourself, you can meet with the council, if that is agreeable."

"That is most agreeable and generous in spirit on the part of the council. I look forward to such a meeting."

"We will hear what you say with interest." The councilor looked to Pacek. "You and your men and the mage and his men are welcome in the usual manner. And for the usual terms. You will sign the accounts in the morning."

"I will, as always." The undercaptain nodded solemnly. "Thank you."

The councilor turned and left by the same archway he had used before.

"The stables are through the gates and to the left at the far end of the courtyard," said Pacek. "We're supposed to stay in the area around the barracks. It's a good idea to do that."

Kaerylt looked at the undercaptain quizzically. "Terms from the locals?"

"No. Discipline from the Prefect's arms-commander if there's a complaint. The hamlet and town councils will make complaints."

"That might seem . . . difficult . . . for them," suggested Kaerylt.

"It's very easy. They keep the gates closed until they get a response. There's no water in that way station. Not anywhere else, either. Why do you think the Prefect pays?"

"Couldn't he take over the hamlet?"

"He likely could, but that would require a garrison, and garrisons are costly. Much more costly than provisions."

Kaerylt nodded. "I see."

While Beltur understood why the troopers didn't wish to upset the people in hamlets like Arrat, he was also beginning to wonder why the Prefect even bothered with trying to rule Analeria, although he knew there had to be a reason, even if it might not be the best one. He and the others followed the undercaptain through the gate and then left toward the south end of the narrow courtyard, the walls of which had no windows or other openings, except for the doorless archways into the stable and a second single and narrow gate in the middle of the west wall.

The stable was constructed largely of mud bricks, with a roof of grass thatch, but the archways were low, and all the riders had to dismount in the open courtyard and then walk their horses into the stable. Beltur couldn't help but notice that the stable floor was paved with the same kind of bricks as the courtyard, except the bricks comprising the stable floor had been coated with something like varnish, although he had no idea what substance would harden over mud brick. In any case, he was glad for the comparative coolness of the stable, and the fact it was far easier to unsaddle and groom his horse in the narrow stall.

He was just finishing when Kaerylt appeared and stood at the end of the stall, waiting. Beltur didn't hurry, but finished grooming the horse and gathering his duffel before leaving the stall, closing the half door, and then sliding the wooden bolt into place.

"You did a good job with the horse."

"Thank you, ser."

Sydon appeared, carrying both his duffel and Kaerylt's, and stood there waiting.

The older mage did not move. Instead, he cleared his throat. "Beltur . . . I have a task for you. You're good with concealments. Good enough, anyway, even if your concealments are more like those of an ordermage than I'd like . . . but then, I suppose that's also a form of concealment."

Beltur managed not to wince. He'd heard that more than once.

"After we eat, I'd like you to slip away in a fashion that doesn't call attention to you when you conceal yourself. Then I'd like you to walk around and just look at things. See if you can sense anything about the women. Don't get caught, either."

"What about me?" asked Sydon.

"You'll be with me, meeting with the council."

Sydon frowned.

"If two mages are meeting with them, it conveys greater importance. It's also less likely that anyone will be thinking about Beltur." Kaerylt gestured. "The barracks are this way." He led the two to an iron-banded heavy door set in the brick rear wall of the stable and along a short hallway, narrow and windowless, to a second iron-bound door.

Both doors, Beltur noted, were designed with slots for triple bars on the back, and the bars were there as well, resting against the inner wall in slots in the brick floor. The walls also looked to be almost a yard thick, but the edges of the bricks were rounded, suggesting that they were anything but recent.

"We have a room around that corner ahead."

As they passed a square archway, Kaerylt nodded. "That's the mess—the dining hall where we'll eat."

Beltur glanced through the archway. The chamber was oblong and contained two tables, one short and one long. There were chairs at the short table and benches at the longer one. He could smell spices and the scent of cooked meat, but not what kind.

The sleeping room for the three was simple enough. There were three pallet beds, each set on square brick posts barely a third of a yard off the floor, which was the same as the stable floor. Two high windows too small for a man to crawl in or out of provided some light and air, and there was a bar for the door leaned against the wall in the corner. Pegs sticking out of the wall beside the end of each pallet bed were for clothing.

"This is it?" asked Sydon.

"It's far better than the alternative, but you can try the way station if you wish," suggested Kaerylt.

Beltur concealed a smile. He waited for the others to pick their beds, then put his duffel on the one closest to the door.

"There's a fountain for washing in the small court-yard through the door at the end of the hall. You need to hurry if you want to wash up. I washed while you two dealt with the horses."

Dusty and sweaty as he felt, Beltur hurried in washing up as much as he could, then made his way to the dining hall, reaching it just after Sydon, who'd barely washed his hands and just splashed water on his face.

Kaerylt and Pacek were already seated at the smaller table, and Sydon and Beltur joined them. The only items on the table were four earthenware mugs, four bowls, and four spoons.

A tall and thin, almost gaunt-looking, white-haired woman walked from the kitchen carrying a large bowl to the table. She wore a high-necked but loose-fitting shirt with long sleeves over equally shapeless trousers. Both trousers and shirt were of the same faded blue as the councilor's garments. When she set the bowl before the undercaptain, she did not speak, but merely nodded and then headed back to the kitchen, returning almost immediately with a large pitcher in one hand and a basket in the other, which she set on the table and which contained four loaves of flatbread. She set the pitcher on the table and then departed, again without speaking.

A second woman, gray-haired, joined the first in serving the troopers at the longer table.

"They don't speak at all?" asked Kaerylt.

"They never have when I've been here." Pacek used the ladle that was in the large bowl to fill his smaller bowl. "The brown meat and sauce here, that's a lamb chili," said Pacek. "I'd take small mouthfuls with plenty of the bread. Otherwise, you'll think you're eating raw chaos."

"Rather fiery, I take it?" Kaerylt looked at the large bowl dubiously.

"It's their way of telling us that they're dutiful subjects of the Prefect, but that they don't have to like it. Or something like that. Also, go easy on the teekla."

"Teekla?" asked Sydon.

"The drink in the pitcher. You might call it cactus ale, except it's three times as strong."

Beltur let his chaos-order senses range over the food, but he could sense no actual chaos. After the others had served themselves, he ladled out a modest amount of the lamb and broke off a good chunk of the flatbread. He half filled the earthenware mug, then took a small mouthful of the lamb chili. For a moment, the chili didn't seem all that spicy or hot—but only for a moment. An instant later, his mouth felt as though he had chewed on red-hot coals.

He started to grab for the mug, then remembered what Pacek had said and jammed a chunk of bread in his mouth. It helped, but he could feel his entire head getting hot and feel sweat beading on his forehead. A second mouthful of bread helped more.

Sydon grinned, then took a large mouthful of the chili. In moments, he was gulping the teekla.

"The teekla doesn't get rid of the burning," said Pacek, after calmly taking another mouthful of the spicy lamb chili and following it with a modest bite from the chunk of flatbread he held. "Only the bread helps."

Sydon promptly stuffed a large hunk of bread in his mouth.

Beltur noticed that his uncle took small mouthfuls of the stew with equally small morsels of the flatbread. He immediately followed that example and discovered that the chili, while spicy hot, was indeed tolerable. After a time, he asked the undercaptain, "Is everything here in the grasslands this heavily spiced?"

"Chilies are a part of everything they cook, but here in Arrat, it's about as hot as it gets."

"Are most of the hamlets fortified in some fashion?" asked Kaerylt.

"Some are. Most aren't."

"Do you know what makes the difference?" asked Beltur.

Pacek shook his head. "The men don't talk much, and they don't answer questions, and the women don't talk at all."

Beltur could see why he had a task after eating.

"How many days' ride to the next hamlet or town after Desanyt?" asked Sydon.

"Depends on which way you go. East the road will eventually take you to Tellura. Hamlets about a day's ride apart. No towns, though. South, it's three days beyond Desanyt to Caanak. Southwest'll only take you to Kasiera and then into the foothills on the way to the Westhorns."

It only seemed a few moments longer when Kaerylt looked to Sydon. "Finish up. We need to meet with the local council." His eyes then went to Beltur. "You have chores to do while we're gone. Don't tarry here."

"No, ser. I'm almost finished." That was actually true, Beltur realized as he looked down at his bowl. He took a last mouthful of the lamb chili, then ate the last of the bread, followed by a small swallow of teekla. As soon as Kaerylt and Sydon rose, he did as well, but headed back in the direction of the sleeping room. He continued past it, making his way through the pen archway to the courtyard that held the fountain, just a simple basin with a raised circular stone spout in the middle, from which water bubbled gently.

Even without looking around, he knew he was the only one in the courtyard, yet he had the feeling he was being watched, although in the dim light of late twilight he couldn't see anyone at the second-level windows on the north and south ends of the courtyard. In the middle of the west side of the courtyard was another square archway, beyond which was a covered portico leading toward a grove of what looked to be olive trees.

He washed his hands and face again. The water did reduce the remaining feeling of burning in his lips.

Where does the water go? He could see it flow from the spout into the basin, but the edges of the basin were dry, and so were the bricks.

After several moments he discovered, using both his eyes and chaos-order senses, that the water drained through two openings in the basin into fired clay standpipes that had to connect to something under the bricks. He would have wagered that the water was being carried to the olive grove, but that was a guess.

He slowly walked back to the archway and stepped back into the hall. He looked around. He could see no one, and he didn't have the same feeling of being watched. He quickly raised a concealment. That wasn't the hard part, but moving while holding one took great concentration, because a mage couldn't see, unsurprisingly, since a concealment bent light around the mage. That meant he had to use order-chaos senses to discern where people and objects were, and he could only sense shapes through their order-chaos structure and flow. Kaerylt claimed to be able to read expressions. Beltur had his doubts about that, not that he was ever about to express such.

He walked back toward the fountain, slowly and

carefully, since the concealment didn't block sound. Nor would it mask footprints in soft earth, sand, or dust. Moving past the fountain, he headed for the open archway on the far side of the courtyard and the covered portico beyond. When he reached the covered walkway that led toward the grove, he could feel the sand under his boots, and even hear the faint gritting against his soles, carefully as he was trying to move. The buildings on each side were some five yards from the walkway's roof and pillars, and the space was bare ground.

Beltur could vaguely feel people some distance ahead, but not within the thirty-some yards where his chaos-order senses were more accurate. The roof of the covered walkway ended roughly where the adjoining buildings ended as well, but the brick paving continued for several yards into the open space. Ahead was the grove of trees, and to each side of the grove there were other structures, although Beltur couldn't determine much more than that.

What he did sense were two people sitting on a bench in front of the trees. He moved closer, quietly, moving to one side as he did, still trying not to make any noise on the scattered sand that seemed to form a thin layer over hard-packed dirt or clay. Between what he heard and sensed, and from their general bent posture and the lower level of order and chaos in their bodies, Beltur thought it was likely that two older men sat on a bench, certainly not young men.

"White mages came . . . with the soldiers."

"They come. They'll be gone tomorrow."

"Salket says the young one is powerful."

"He should worry about the older one."

"Ha . . . the young always think strength lies in youth . . ."

"The old white ones have learned stealth and treach-

ery. Let Salket think what he will. They will find nothing here, and they will leave."

"There is nothing to find."

"I said that."

A long silence followed, and Beltur froze, wondering
if either of the two had sensed or heard him.

"There will be no winds until harvest."

"There seldom are."

After another silence, one of the men said, "Fharela
is not the cook her mother was."

"She is too young . . ."

Beltur eased away, heading toward the buildings beyond the south end of the grove. The grove was larger
than he had thought, and he walked more than a hundred yards before it ended, although he could sense
that it extended even farther to the west. The nearest
structure, which might be a dwelling, although he wasn't
certain, was also to the west and seemed to be set some
twenty yards back from the trees. Staying close to
the edge of the grove, he kept moving, then froze in
place as he sensed something coming in his direction
from within the trees.

After a moment, he released his breath. The chaos
and order pattern had to be a cat, and the feline soon
turned away, most likely repelled by the chaos-mist that
clung to all white mages, even the smaller amounts that
swirled around him. Beltur continued toward the dwelling. Two smaller figures faced each other, making mo-
tions in a pattern. As he heard the whisking sound and
a muted impact, and then another whisk and no sound,
he realized they were playing basket-catch, with the
curved baskets affixed to leather gloves, and that both
had to be boys.

". . . almost missed that one!"

"Did not."

"Did so."

"Did not."

Beltur kept moving until he was past the two and then angled toward the open space between the two. He had almost reached the corner when someone stepped out of the house.

"Boys . . . it's time to come in."

From the chaos-order pattern, and the voice, Beltur was certain the speaker was a woman, most likely the boys' mother. As he concentrated, he determined that she also wore the same shapeless clothes that the older serving women had worn.

"It's not dark yet . . ."

"How come Mara couldn't play?"

"You know the rules. Besides, she's too old to play with you."

"No one comes this way from the gates. Dakar said they were from Fenard, anyway, not from the south."

"Rules are rules. Would you like to explain that to the elders?"

"No, Mother."

The two boys trudged into the dwelling.

Beltur waited, but no one emerged. Finally, he moved on, carefully making his way to the next dwelling, where he eased around to the back, only to discover that a wall enclosed a rear garden or courtyard. He could hear voices, and he moved along the wall, and then back until he found the place where he could hear the best. Even so, it was hard to make out what was being said, partly because some of the words were muffled and partly because the speakers had an accent that made it hard for Beltur to understand. For a time, the words were about the wind and weather, and Beltur was thinking about moving on when he heard something that piqued his interest.

". . . worrisome . . . Prefect . . . sending mages . . . grasslands . . ."

". . . worry too much . . . southerners . . . never raid this far . . . don't ever come north . . ."

". . . never have . . . lost so many . . ."

". . . lost scores . . . last time . . ."

". . . was then . . . way back . . ."

". . . mean they won't . . . not if they've lost . . . women . . ."

". . . horse barbarians . . . need to treat . . . better . . ."

". . . like asking . . . sun not to shine . . . wind never . . . blow . . ."

From there, the conversation turned to olives and dates, and Beltur moved on to the adjoining dwelling, which also had a walled rear courtyard. No one was there. He tried listening under several of the high narrow windows, but the voices inside were too indistinct for him to make out anything.

He tried eavesdropping at three more dwellings. At the first house, no one appeared to be there—or awake. At the second, a man was berating his wife for something. Beltur thought it was for being too hard on their son, but he wasn't sure. At the third, a couple talked on and on about the fact that the summer had been the driest in years and that the flow from the springs was lower than either could recall . . . and that it was all the fault of the black angels of the Westhorns.

People must have been going to sleep or at least not talking at the next two houses, and Beltur headed back to the barracks. He encountered, at a distance, three more cats, but no dogs, which he puzzled over.

It was pitch dark when Beltur finally returned to the barracks and the single room he shared with Kaerylt and Sydon, both of whom were sitting on the end of their pallet beds.

"You took a long time," observed Kaerylt. "What did you find out? Keep your voice down."

"Not much. That was why I was gone so long. All

the houses are almost like small forts. They only have a single door in front, and the windows are narrow and high. They all have a rear garden or courtyard, but it's surrounded by a wall. The women I saw or sensed all wore those shapeless garments. They do talk, but it's hard to understand because of their accent. I didn't see or sense any young women, but one mother said some things that suggested that girls and young women stay out of sight when strangers are around . . ." Beltur went on to relate the rest of what he had heard and observed—except for what the two older men had said. He kept that to himself, although he couldn't have said why.

"Eight dwellings . . . and you couldn't get any closer? You couldn't discover more than that?" There was a disgusted edge to Kaerylt's voice.

"Well . . . the fountain is drained to the olive grove, and there aren't any dogs, and every door seems to be kept barred all the time unless someone's coming in or going out. At least, while strangers are around."

"No one was walking around? No one?"

"I only saw the two boys playing and two old men. They sat on a bench. They talked about the weather and the wind."

Kaerylt nodded slowly. "All that makes sense . . . in its own way."

"How can that make sense?" asked Sydon.

"I would guess that Arrat is so well fortified because the grasslands raiders once attacked here, and no one has forgotten. They distrust all strangers. There are likely weapons in every dwelling. The raiders couldn't ever take it again, and the cost to anyone else to take the hamlet would never be worth it."

"But the Prefect—" began Sydon.

"It's far cheaper and easier to pay for someone else

to guard the water, and the council is likely glad to get the silvers for doing it."

"But . . ."

"Sydon . . . don't try my patience. Go to sleep. That will do you more good than anything. It will certainly benefit Beltur and me more as well."

Beltur slipped off his boots and stretched out on the pallet bed, far more comfortable than anywhere he'd slept since leaving Fenard. As he lay there, he wondered what Jessyla might be doing. Her comment about him being possibly a better black than a white still troubled him.

VI

Sevenday morning came early, but Beltur awoke more rested than he'd felt in days, perhaps because he'd slept well. Breakfast—an egg and lamb hash, seasoned with chilies, and accompanied by flatbread—was again served by older women, and all fourteen riders were outside the gates of Arrat well before sunrise, heading south into what looked to be endless grasslands.

Beltur noticed that his uncle had obtained a wooden staff from somewhere and carried it in the saddle's lance holder. So far as Beltur knew, only black mages carried a staff, and he wondered why his uncle had come up with one, especially since a regular wood staff could be quickly destroyed by a chaos flame or bolt. Even so, he wasn't about to ask.

No one said much until they had ridden far enough that Arrat had vanished in the grass behind them. Then

Kaerylt asked, "Is it always like that when you stop at Arrat?"

"Always. Sometimes the servers are even older. The only men we see are at the gates. The food is spicy, but good and filling." Pacek shrugged. "It's a far more pleasant place to sleep than at the way stations."

"Do the grassland raiders ever come this far north?"

"A few people in the towns talk about raiders. In my time, I've never seen any."

"Have any troopers had to deal with them?"

"The unlucky bastards who have to patrol the Phroan River road north of Ruzor. The raiders there are always looking for traders to rob." Pacek laughed harshly. "The pickings here are meager. Not many traders. Fewer travelers."

"And they'd likely lose more than they get in attacking a place like Arrat." Kaerylt nodded. "What about a town like Desanyt?"

"Doesn't make a lot of sense to attack there. You can see for yourself."

Beltur could tell by the way his uncle stiffened before he nodded that he wasn't satisfied with the under-captain's answer.

After that, the older white mage turned to Beltur. "You need some practice with shields."

"I thought you were worried about my problems with chaos-bolts."

"I am, but practicing with chaos-bolts in the middle of an ocean of dry grass isn't the best idea. Your shields also need work." Kaerylt eased the staff from its holder. "Sydon . . . drop back and give us some room."

"My pleasure, ser."

Beltur didn't care for Sydon's sardonic grin, but said nothing.

"Block the staff with your shields," Kaerylt said. "Don't burn it or turn it to ashes, just block it."

"Burning it is easier," said Sydon as he slowed his mount for a moment to let Kaerylt and Beltur move ahead of him.

"That's not the point," snapped Kaerylt. "It's to strengthen his shields. You can't locate and burn arrows or a lot of spears thrown at once. And trying to burn chaos-bolts is worse than useless."

From Sydon's concealed smirk, Beltur could tell that Sydon was baiting his uncle, playing on Kaerylt's short temper.

"Lift your shields," ordered Kaerylt.

Beltur did so, creating a shifting interplay of chaos, just trying to keep it strong and contained.

Kaerylt swung with moderate force, and the staff bounced off the barrier, but he immediately struck with greater force, enough that Beltur had to reinforce the place where he had struck—which was exactly where his uncle hit the third time, before striking at the side.

The blows then came fast and furious.

After half a glass, by which time Beltur was exhausted and sweat-drenched, Kaerylt replaced the staff in the holder. "That's better, but you shouldn't use so much effort. You'll not only exhaust yourself, but you'll waste too much chaos."

"Yes, ser." *That's easy enough for you to say.* Beltur blotted his forehead and then his cheeks, and wiped the sweat off the back of his neck.

When he had cooled off some, not that he was about to cool that much at any time during the day in late summer, Beltur couldn't help but think about his uncle's comment about wasting too much chaos . . . and what Jessyla had said about powerful white mages using order to control chaos. *Does it matter how I do it, so long as I control it?* Besides, if Jessyla happened to be right, and while she might have been honestly mistaken, she hadn't been lying, and it could be a better way for him.

But he'd have to be careful in practicing when his uncle wasn't around.

He took a long swallow from his water bottle, then corked it. After several moments, he looked sideways, toward Kaerylt, who had eased his mount closer to Sydon and was talking to the other mage in a low voice.

Beltur gathered the smallest bit of free chaos, trying to use order to create a lattice into which he could ease another bit of chaos. While the process was tedious, and took concentration, it didn't seem to take much physical effort. After a time, he glanced at Kaerylt, who had stopped talking to Sydon and was looking ahead, but both seemed unaware of what Beltur was doing.

Beltur worried that he had no way of knowing how strong such a shield might be . . . and he certainly wasn't about to ask his uncle, since what he was doing was totally contrary to everything Kaerylt had taught him.

Still . . .

Next, he tried to shift the pattern into interlocking diamonds. It seemed that might be stronger, but again, he had no way of knowing. He stopped when he began to feel light-headed. Using order might be easier— perhaps—but it still took effort.

He eased out a scrap of flatbread he'd saved from breakfast and slowly chewed and swallowed it. That seemed to push away the light-headedness.

By midafternoon, the flat grassy plains immediately south of Arrat had gradually given way to rolling hills, also largely covered with grass, with scattered bushes in the lower reaches between the rises. Every once in a great while there was a scattered and seemingly scrawny tree. Beltur wondered how that occurred, but supposed some bird had dropped a seed at just the right time. He'd thought about asking, but saw a frown and the concentration on his uncle's face, as if he were deeply involved.

Trying to chaos-sense something ahead? With that thought, Beltur opened himself to trying just to feel any changes in the patterns of order and chaos that lay ahead. After several moments, he realized that there was indeed something—or many somethings—just over the rise in the road ahead, little more than a kay ahead. He was about to say something when his uncle spoke sharply.

"Undercaptain, there are riders on the far side of the rise ahead. They're headed this way."

"Can you tell how many there are?"

"Around a score. It's hard to tell."

"Can you tell if they're troopers?"

"They're too far away for that."

"There shouldn't be any on this road right now, but you never know. More likely raiders." Pacek glanced around. "There's no high ground and nowhere to hide. The grass isn't high enough . . ."

Two riders appeared on the road at the top of the rise, then two more, and then others, all riding raggedly two abreast.

"I count twenty-two . . . so far," declared Pacek.

Beltur watched, but it was hard to tell because of the dust raised by the first riders. After a few moments, when the dust began to settle, it was clear that no more riders followed the first ones, at least not immediately.

"They're raiders, all right. They've got bows out."

"Do they always attack?" asked Kaerylt.

"Not always. Mostly, though." Pacek's voice was resigned. "They'll try to get us with their bows. They don't like to close because we're better with blades."

"If you look ready to fight, and we don't make any hostile moves until they do, and then they get hit with a few chaos-bolts, would they decide to leave us alone?"

"They might, especially if you can stop their shafts." replied the undercaptain. "I don't see any other choice."

"We'll see what we can do."

"We'll keep moving," said Pacek. "That'll make it harder for them to hit us."

"Beltur," snapped Kaerylt, "ride up beside the undercaptain. If my shields fail, do your best to shield the two of you." He turned in the saddle. "Troopers, close up on me, as near as you can."

"Do what the mage says!" ordered Pacek.

The Gallosian troopers and the mages kept moving at a moderate walk, and the raiders continued to draw nearer, not galloping but riding at a faster walk. By the time that the raiders were less than half a kay away, Beltur could see that each carried a bow, with some sort of blade in a waist scabbard. All wore leathers of some sort, although the color ranged from faded tan to deep brown.

Just as Pacek had predicted, the raiders began loosing shafts when they were about a hundred yards away.

Kaerylt threw up a shield some fifteen yards in front of Beltur and Pacek. Beltur could sense that it wasn't that strong, but just strong enough that the first volley of arrows lost speed and dropped harmlessly to the ground well in front of Beltur. So did the second. By then, the raiders were little more than fifty or sixty yards away, and Beltur could feel the chaos-flows as Kaerylt strengthened his shield somewhat.

The third volley of arrows also dropped out of the sky short.

"Sydon!" ordered Kaerylt. "As soon as they get within fifty yards, start picking them off with chaosbolts."

"Yes, ser."

At that moment, the raiders loosed another volley of arrows, then stowed their bows, and urged their mounts into a full gallop. Immediately, Kaerylt contracted his shields to just around himself.

Even as he prepared to lift a shield, wanting to hold off until the last moment, Beltur had a sinking feeling that his uncle and Sydon weren't going to have enough time to target all of the raiders. *Can you narrow a chaos-bolt to a point with order?*

The lead raider was closer to forty yards from Beltur when a chaos-bolt from Sydon struck him full in the chest, turning him into a half-charred figure. Two more chaos-bolts from Kaerylt blasted riders, and another from Sydon took down a fourth.

Beltur saw a bearded raider in darker leathers heading for him and Pacek. He immediately tried to focus a chaos-bolt with order . . . but the thin line of chaos merely struck the raider's curved blade. While the raider dropped that blade, a second was in his hand immediately, and Beltur threw up his shield. The impact of the raider against the shield nearly ripped Beltur out of the saddle, and he had to release the shield in order to stay mounted, but the shield had worked well enough to bring the raider's horse to its knees and stun the rider, so that Pacek only needed a single slash to finish the bearded raider.

Beltur somehow managed another regular chaos-bolt to another raider, and then a weaker one to the face of a second, enough to blind the man, and leave him easy pickings for Pacek.

Then . . . there were no more raiders.

Beltur glanced backward to see the raiding band reforming on the road behind them. None of the raiders appeared to be considering making a second attack, but they also weren't moving; they were waiting, as if to see what the Gallosians did. He also could see more than a handful of fallen raiders, and three riderless horses.

Pacek looked to Kaerylt.

Kaerylt shook his head.

"Keep moving!" ordered Pacek. "No spoils today."

Beltur looked back and to the side at his uncle, who looked pale, almost unsteady, in the saddle. "Are you all right?"

"I will be in a bit." Kaerylt's hands seemed to shake as he fumbled the cork out of his water bottle and took a swallow, then murmured a few words.

Beltur thought he muttered something about getting soft. He quickly looked away and turned to the undercaptain. "How much longer before we reach Desanyt?"

"We'll be able to see it in the distance from the top of the next rise, the one after this one. Most likely another three glasses."

"Thank you, Undercaptain." Beltur slowed his mount and then eased in beside his uncle. He kept glancing back over his shoulder, but before that long, there was no dust or other sign of the raiders, just as if the grass had swallowed them all up. Finally, he felt comfortable without turning to look behind the trailing troopers. Behind him, he could hear a few of the words exchanged by the troopers.

"Nice to have mages . . ."

". . . still wonder where they're headed . . . can't take Arrat with a score of raiders . . ."

". . . lot less'n that now . . ."

". . . maybe one of the towns east of the big wash . . . been years since they were raided . . ."

Before long the troopers lapsed into silence, and none of the three mages spoke for close to half a glass.

Finally, Kaerylt, who finally didn't appear nearly so pale, turned to Beltur. "You threw a few chaos-bolts, didn't you?"

"Yes, ser."

"What in the black demons were you doing with that first one?"

"I know I'm not strong the way you and Sydon are.

I was just trying to keep it narrow. I thought that way, I could do more. I got it too narrow, and it hit the raider's sword."

"It curved toward the iron. Iron can attract chaos if it's not strong enough," explained Kaerylt. "It was a good effort though, and it helped."

Beltur ignored the condescending tone. "Thank you. I did my best. You and Sydon must have killed half of them."

"Just eight, but with the one you killed, and the two you weakened enough for Undercaptain Pacek to take out, that was enough to make the raiders decide not to attack a second time."

Left unsaid, Beltur knew, was the fact that none of the three mages could have done nearly as much if there had been a second attack. Beltur couldn't have done much of anything, he knew.

Not quite a glass later, as they came to the top of the second rise, Pacek gestured southward and announced, "You can just see Desanyt from here. Between those two hills. The trees—they sort of make a line—are all on the edge of the stream. They call it a river, but a horse could piss across it."

To Beltur, the town looked more like a wide brown smudge between the grayish-green hills. There was also a thin line of green connecting the trees, most likely fields irrigated by the river. There were no tall structures, nor even any walls around Desanyt, and just three woodlots in places along the river, two north of the town and another to the south.

Almost two more glasses passed. During that time, the road made a gradual long curve until it headed almost due east, and the sun that hung just above the hills to the west stretched out their shadows across the road's dusty clay when the group rode past the first huts on the outskirts of the town.

Beltur turned to Kaerylt. "Ser . . . they don't have any fortifications . . . nothing . . ."

"That's not quite true," replied Pacek. "You'll see the army post before long. There's a company here all the time. But that's not the only reason. There are over a thousand locals here. Twice that in the winter. That's a lot more people than in any nomad group or raiding party. They don't take kindly to being raided. They won't trade with any group that raids them, and the next time any show up, they'll kill all they can."

"Raiding's not worth the trouble," said Kaerylt.

"But . . . if the people here are the ones who complained . . ."

"I told you." The older white mage sighed. "These people didn't complain. If the grasslands nomads lose their women, they raid other groups or the smaller hamlets and villages. That upsets trade and travel. The only way a larger town loses women is if some of the women here prefer the herding life . . . or to go to Westwind. Sometimes, it happens."

Beltur nodded, although he wasn't sure what Kaerylt said was the entire story . . . or that it made sense.

"When we reach the river," added Pacek, "we take the road south to the post."

The scattered huts set near the road with sheds beside them and plots behind them soon gave way to small cots, set with only a few yards between them. All appeared to be built of mud brick, with mud smoothed over that as a finish, and a wash, usually white and faded, over that. The roofs were some sort of thin thatching. The windows were narrow and shuttered. Beltur saw no sign of any glazing. The men and women working the plots scarcely turned their heads as the fourteen riders passed.

Before long, the road just ended at the river road, and

Pacek turned his mount south on the river road, pointing. "That's the mighty Sanyt River."

The river was wider than Beltur had expected, its greenish waters stretching five or six yards from bank to bank, and each bank was a solid earthen berm. There were cots on the west side of the road, but nothing but packed earth on the short stretch between the road and the berm, which rose little more than a yard above the level of the road. The east side of the river seemed filled with tilled plots, but Beltur couldn't determine what grew there. Ahead, he could see an open space on the west side of the river road, where there were no buildings.

"That's the market square. It's busier in the morning."

Coming north on the river road was a single cart, pulled by a single scrawny horse led by a one-armed man, who immediately moved off the road to let the riders pass. A basket crate in the cart contained chickens, at least one of which was squawking loudly.

The square was anything but prepossessing, just an open space surrounded by low buildings. There were no statues, no fountain, and almost no one there except two handcarts being readied to depart, one by a bent and graying woman, and the other by a slightly younger man. The man's handcart held a few melons, likely what had not been sold.

That portion of Desanyt south of the square was similar to the part Beltur had already ridden past. The Gallosian post was on the south side of Desanyt, set on a low rise overlooking the Sanyt River, with almost a quarter kay separating it from the dwellings to the north, dwellings Beltur belatedly realized were somewhat more capacious and better appointed than those in the center of the town. While the river road was packed clay with a trace of sand and gravel, there was a brick-paved lane from the river road to the post. The post's four brick walls stood roughly five yards high and formed a square. The only gate was in the middle of the east wall. Two guards watched from sentry boxes on top of the wall on each side of the open gate.

One of them called out, "Troopers coming in!"

Pacek led the way through the gate and then to the stables, where he reined up and turned to Kaerylt. "I'll need to report to the captain about the raiders."

"I'm also supposed to report to him," said Kaerylt dryly. "And deliver a dispatch from the Prefect."

Pacek hesitated for a moment. "Then we both should do that."

"That we should." Kaerylt turned to Beltur. "You can take care of the horses, and Sydon will carry the gear to whatever quarters we have."

That didn't surprise Beltur in the slightest.

Sydon didn't return to the stables until Beltur was finishing grooming the last of the three horses, but at least he had already carried Beltur's duffel to the small barracks chamber they were to share.

Beltur just followed the older mage.

"It's an undercaptains' room," explained Sydon as he opened the door. "They share. Or they would if there were any here. The only time that happens is when a larger force comes through."

Beltur wrinkled his nose, trying not to sneeze. "That must have been years ago."

"I know. I did use a little chaos to move out the worst of the dust."

Beltur wasn't sure whether Sydon's chaotic cleaning hadn't left things worse. "Thank you. When or where do we eat? Or should we just go looking?"

"I found the mess. They looked to be getting ready."

"I'd like to wash up."

"Oh . . . I imagine you would. There's a washroom at the end of the corridor."

Less than a quarter of a glass later, the two were waiting outside the mess when Kaerylt arrived.

"Good. You found the mess."

"How did your meeting go with the captain?" asked Beltur.

"We'll talk about that later. We'll be seated at the officers' table with Captain Lemaryt, along with his under-captain and Undercaptain Pacek. He'll want to hear from you two about the skirmish with the raiders. I'd prefer that neither of you discuss any difficulties you had."

"Yes, ser," agreed Beltur.

Sydon just nodded knowingly.

"They're already inside." Kaerylt motioned and then turned.

As his uncle led the way into the mess and toward a table at one end, Beltur saw three officers already standing there. One was Pacek, and the other two were a captain and another undercaptain. Lemaryt was graying and angular, and a good half head shorter than Beltur, but his eyes were a hard and intense gray. He studied the mages intently as they approached.

"Welcome to Desanyt Post, and our rather humble fare," offered the captain in a voice that was not quite rumbling and also gravelly. He nodded to the under-captain. "This is my second, Undercaptain Harryn."

"We're pleased to meet you both, and we appreciate your hospitality," replied Kaerylt.

"It's not like the Prefect afforded a choice to either of us, Mage." Lemaryt grinned, if briefly, showing yellowed and uneven teeth, then gestured for the others to sit as he seated himself.

In moments, a ranker appeared with two pitchers,

followed by another ranker with two platters. The pitchers ended up in front of the captain, the platters immediately behind them. Behind them was the basket of bread that had been there earlier.

"Light and dark ale," explained Lemaryt.

Beltur studied the platters, noting that one had some form of sliced meat smothered in what looked to be a milk gravy, while the second contained a vegetable combination of green beans, mushrooms, and carrots and a heaped pile of boiled sliced potatoes.

"No chilies, I notice," observed Kaerylt.

"I've told the cooks no more than four spicy evening meals an eightday. Sometimes, the spicy meals are better, but chilies all the time burn out your taste."

Beltur refrained from nodding. Even though he was the last to serve himself, there was still plenty of fowl left on the platters, and no one had touched the pitcher of light ale.

After a time, the captain took a swallow from his mug, then looked at Kaerylt. "I'd like to hear from your mages about the raiders."

Kaerylt nodded to Sydon. "You first."

"Yes, ser. There were about twenty-two of them, and they started loosing shafts at us as soon as we were in range . . ." Sydon gave a quick summary of what had happened, then looked to Beltur.

"I can't add much to that, ser, but I did notice that most of them carried two blades, and each was shorter than a real sword but longer than a dirk."

"Sabre length," corrected Lemaryt. "Go on."

Beltur added a few more sentences about the raiders walking and then breaking into a gallop, his use of chaos on the raiders, and his surprise when the skirmish was suddenly over.

"The only surprise I have," commented Lemaryt dryly, "is why it took them so long to realize attacking you was stupid." He turned to Kaerylt. "Do you really think you can do anything to stop women from fleeing to Westwind?"

"That's what the Prefect has ordered."

"He could order the wind to stop blowing, too."

"The dark angels have to be doing something to entice those women," replied Kaerylt. "Why else would they flee to a place that is colder than anywhere else in the world?"

"Why indeed?" Lemaryt offered a laugh. "And you will oppose their dark arts with white chaos?"

"As well as anything else I can think of." Kaerylt took a long swallow of dark ale and then refilled his mug. "Do the nomads fight over herds . . . or do they just feel they have to fight?"

"Both, from what I've seen. They also fight over women. The band leaders always have more than one woman, and that makes women scarce for the younger men."

"Is that common here in Desanyt and the other towns?"

Lemaryt shook his head. "That's another reason why the nomads don't attack the towns. Most of the women here carry dirks, and they can use them. We usually lose a few men every year."

"You *let* that happen?" Kaerylt's voice carried an edge of incredulity.

"A man is found in an alley with a single blade wound to the heart. No one knows how it happened. You expect me to round up every woman with a dirk?" Lemaryt shook his head. "The rankers are all told that forcing a woman here is dangerous, especially one who's already consorted. Some of them don't listen. Then, after one of them dies, the others listen for a while."

"I can't believe . . . women . . ."

"There was one young fellow, big strapping farm boy out of somewhere east of here, Tellura . . . maybe Meltosia . . . made a habit of having his way with women. He lasted a month. What was left of him wasn't . . . anything you'd want to see."

"How do your men deal with that?" asked Sydon, clearly curious, rather than confrontational.

"It's simple enough. If a woman says 'no,' she means it. If she says 'yes,' she also means that. If she says nothing, she hasn't decided, and you don't force her. Honey and silver work better with women anywhere. There are more than enough who prefer coins. It's still a hard life here in the towns. Easier than with the nomads, but women from both sometimes think Westwind might offer more."

Sydon nodded, and Kaerylt shot a hard glance at his main assistant.

Beltur took another small swallow of ale, ale that had a taste that was rather different, but not unpleasant, and another slice of the not quite gamy fowl.

"How long will you be here?" asked Lemaryt.

"Only a few days, but that depends on what I learn from the council."

"The council here doesn't have much power. They just advise the town elder. That's Jhankyr. You'd be better to ask for a meeting with him first. He might suggest you meet with the council, but you wouldn't offend him by approaching him directly."

"Thank you for the advice," said Kaerylt evenly. "Where are the problems with the women likely to be the worst, and where are they causing the most difficulty in recruiting and dealing with raiders?"

Lemaryt frowned. "Anywhere closer to the Westhorns. That's just because a runaway woman doesn't have to go as far to reach Westwind. Kasiera is a name I've heard and seen in the dispatches. It's two days from here, south and west. More west than south."

"What exactly have you heard?" pressed Kaerylt.

"Not much. Just that there are more nomad raiders around the town. That might mean that they're getting desperate."

"Or that the town was careless," suggested Harryn. "Maybe both."

"That's possible," agreed Lemaryt easily. "It's all that I've heard, though."

Conversation for the rest of the meal was more on pleasantries—and the difficulties of maintaining the post and getting proper supplies.

Beltur could tell that his uncle, while pleasant, was less than impressed with either Lemaryt or Harryn, but Kaerylt said nothing until the three left the mess and then met in the chamber given to Kaerylt.

"It's as if the Prefect doesn't even rule here," said the older mage in a low voice, as if he suspected others might be listening, even though Beltur could sense no one nearby. "The commander of a Gallosian post allowing women to kill troopers . . . and deferring to a mere town elder? That's absurd."

"What do you want us to do about it?" asked Sydon.

"Bad as it is, that's not something we can do anything about. We weren't sent here for that reason. We'll just have to deal with it. But we don't have to like it. You also had best remember that we're on our own if we get into trouble. If the locals can kill troopers without fear of retaliation, don't think anyone is going to save you."

Beltur had never thought that, even in Fenard, and he doubted that Sydon had either.

"Now, we might as well get some sleep."

That was fine with Beltur.

VII

Beltur was so tired that he didn't wake up on eightday morning until he heard Kaerylt pounding on the door, followed by Sydon's mumbled reply about it being early.

"That's the whole point of getting up early," came Kaerylt's response. "To get something done."

The two junior mages hurried, rushing through dressing, washing, getting to the mess, eating, and then following Kaerylt to the stables. There the older mage glared—again—at both younger men.

Beltur resigned himself to the tenor of the words that would follow.

"Sleeping late is for babies and old men. You're certainly not old." Kaerylt snorted. "You're coming with me, Sydon. Beltur, you need to walk into town and look around. Don't use a concealment at first. If you think people might be talking, get out of their sight, and then raise a concealment and go back and see what you can discover. Take your time, but be back here a good glass before the evening meal." The older mage handed over a silver. "If there's what passes for an inn or a tavern, and there are more than a few people there, use this and then listen. First openly, and then under a concealment."

"Yes, ser."

Beltur watched as the other two saddled and rode out. Then he walked through the stable, looking for an armsman who might be willing to talk. Before long, he found a younger trooper in a small room off the tack room, glumly polishing various items of brass, mostly wall lamps, it appeared. "Extra duties?"

"Oh . . . no . . ." The trooper, barely beyond being a

youth, took in Beltur's white tunic, and quickly added, "I mean, yes, ser."

"How long have you been posted here?"

"Not quite a season. Nine eightdays."

"Are you from Fenard?"

"No, ser. Linspros."

"That's not that far away. Almost due east of here. What, three days' ride?"

"If you could ride there straight. Can't get there that way, though. More like six days."

"Because of the big wash or canyon?"

"And the brigands that hide there."

"Linspros has to be a lot bigger than Desanyt."

"Not that much bigger. Only has three public houses. There's two here."

"Which one here is better?"

"Both are pretty poor. Brown Pitcher's got better brew. Women, if you can call 'em that, at the Brass Bowl."

"You'll spend more at the Brass Bowl," offered Beltur.

"Not me. You can't even look without paying more."

"So most of the troopers go to the Brown Pitcher?"

"Couldn't say, ser."

The way the young man said those words was almost a confirmation, but Beltur nodded. "Anything else exciting in town?"

"Watching the wind blow and the river flow, maybe."

Beltur laughed, then asked, "Do any of the grasslands types come into town often?"

"Once in a while, I hear. I can't say as I've ever seen any." The trooper frowned. "Why are you here?"

"The same reason you are. Orders. Of a sort. The Prefect sent the mage I work for here. Something about too many of the nomads fighting because they don't have enough women."

"Mages have to follow orders?"

Beltur shrugged, then offered a rueful smile. "Well . . . if we want to eat."

The trooper tried not to smile. "Suppose it's the same everywhere."

"Too often, it is." Beltur smiled again and stepped back. "Best of fortune."

"Thank you, ser."

Beltur left the stable and headed for the gate. The guards at the gate barely looked at him as he walked out. While the lane to the river road was paved, when he reached the road he discovered that there was only a dirt path beside the road spanning the distance between the lane and the first dwellings north of the post. Each step he took raised a puff of dust in the still air of the cloudless morning, a morning already too warm to be comfortable.

As he neared the houses, he could see that they were similar, but certainly not identical. As with all of the dwellings and buildings he had seen riding in, the houses were but a single story. The outside walls were smooth, mud bricks covered by a mud stucco, then painted with a white wash. On the southernmost dwelling, the wash had faded so much that the grayish brown underneath showed through in places, but the dwelling three north of that was an almost pure white, suggesting a recent refinishing. Unlike the houses on the north end of the town, the narrow windows in the ones Beltur could see were glazed, as well as fitted with shutters. Each house had a wide stoop, but no porch, and, as in Arrat, a wall extending from the rear of each dwelling enclosed a rear courtyard or garden, most likely both, since Beltur could see trees rising above the walls. He thought the trees were apricots, but wasn't sure.

As he passed the second house, he heard a woman singing, and the sound came from the rear courtyard of the third house. He tried to pick out the song, listening as carefully as he could.

"*All day I dragged a boat of stone*
and came home when you weren't alone,
so I took all those blasted rocks
and buried all your boyish fancy locks . . .
and took you for a ride in my boat of stone . . ."

Beltur winced at the last line, but kept walking, thinking. As he moved away from the singer, what puzzled him most was that the words, if he'd heard them correctly, were almost vindictive toward men, but the song was cheerful, and the singer had sung loud enough for those words to be heard well beyond the courtyard.

That doesn't sound like an unhappy woman. He considered again. *Or is she really angry and doesn't care who knows it?* He glanced back at the house. It looked much cleaner and neater than those on either side, and it had been recently given a fresh coat of whitewash.

All he could do was shake his head. He wasn't about to try to climb a wall to find out, even using a concealment. *Not yet, anyway.* He kept walking. Some of the houses were almost as neat as the white one, although a few looked run-down. He walked past six or seven side streets before he came to the market square.

He wasn't certain what to expect, given that it was eightday. The market squares in Fenard were busy on eightday because so many people worked seven days, and Desanyt seemed to be the same, with peddlers and growers setting up stalls and arranging their carts. Beltur made a rough count, and judged that there might be forty-five to fifty carts and stalls set up in the square. There was an entire row of carts filled with various melons. He recognized sweet green and yellow melons, but not the most prevalent melon, one with a yellow and green patterned skin. So he stopped and asked an older man what the melon was.

"It's a sweet canlyn. You won't find a sweeter one anywhere in the square."

"Where do you grow them?"

"My plot's next to the river, good rich bottomland there . . . Just a copper for two."

Beltur smiled. "I might be back."

"They'll be all gone if you wait too long, ser mage."

"I'll keep that in mind."

As he moved along the vendors, he did notice that while he saw several very small children, some of whom were girls, they were not with their mothers, but with either men who could have been their fathers or older women who were likely grandmothers. There were no young women, not that he could see, in the square. He looked more closely at the next two older women he passed, noting that they both wore dirks at their belts, and both wore garments that covered everything but their hands, face, upper neck, and hair.

At one edge of the square, he saw a much older man, slight of build, a tinker with a grindstone, and a small table with knives and scissors laid out on the gray cloth.

"You be needing a knife, ser mage? I've got the best you'll find this side of the great wash."

Given how little Beltur had seen, he wouldn't have doubted the man's truthfulness, even if he hadn't sensed the honesty behind the words. "Do you have a shop here?"

"Hektyl's the name. Best tinker in Analeria. Spend an eightday or so in each town, then travel on."

"Because folks don't need too many knives?"

"That'd be true. But they like to keep 'em sharp and true. That's why they come to me."

"Where were you before Desanyt?"

"Came from Arrat, and Paalsyra before that. Just a night there. Not much more than a hamlet."

"You travel alone?"

"Not if I can help it," replied the tinker with a wry chuckle. "Try to hire out as a guard. I'm fair with a blade, better'n that with my horn bow."

"How did you get to be a tinker?"

"I always liked to be on the move. Didn't like following the herds."

"Or the idea of raiding?"

"Didn't seem right to me. There was an old fellow, a tinker, too. He needed a stronger back. No one seemed sad to see me go." Hektyl grinned, showing a gap-toothed expression. "They're glad to see me when I come back, though. Claim no one else can sharpen their knives and blades like me. True in the towns, and true back there."

"Where is back?"

"Wherever the band is. You have a knife that needs sharpening?" The tinker gestured to the table. "Or another blade?"

Beltur could tell that the former herder or raider wasn't about to say more about his antecedents or their location. "I'll have to pass on that. I'm a young mage of most modest means." Besides which, Beltur had always felt uneasy carrying more than a belt knife, unlike both Sydon and Kaerylt, both of whom carried not only belt knives, but also rather long dirks.

"Your time'll come," replied the tinker cheerfully.

After the tinker, Beltur approached an older woman selling linen scarves. Although several of the scarves were quite attractive, and Beltur briefly thought of Jessyla, he doubted that he could or should buy one, since he had no idea when he might see her again, and since his reason for approaching the woman was not the scarves, but the small girl she kept with her.

"I don't have any white scarves, ser mage."

"I doubt I could afford work of your quality. Isn't it a bit warm to grow flax here, though?"

"Not if we plant at the end of winter. The weather's better for the fibers than for seed."

"I haven't seen anyone else with linen here."

"There isn't anyone else. They think it's too much work."

Beltur looked at a scarf patterned in green and brown. "That's fetching, though."

"It'd be a silver, were you thinking of buying."

Only a silver, for something that good? Then he realized most likely why scarves were cheaper in Desanyt— because most of the cost was in labor and women's labor was cheaper, much cheaper than in Fenard. Even so . . . who could afford a silver for a mere scarf? "You sell mostly to the troopers, don't you?"

"They've got the coins, those that don't drink them."

Beltur looked to the small girl seated on a small stool beside the table. "Your daughter or granddaughter?"

"Granddaughter."

"I haven't seen many younger women in the town."

"You won't. It's not seemly. Not wise, either."

"The raiders?"

"They're not a problem. There are always men who think with the wrong parts of their bodies. It's best not to encourage them. You certain you wouldn't like to buy that green one?"

"I'd like to, but I am, alas, a very junior mage of modest means." As he spoke, he glanced quickly to her belt, and the old, but clearly very usable dirk there.

The older woman just smiled.

Beltur could tell she didn't believe him.

All in all, Beltur spent more than a glass in the market square, learning far less than he would have liked, but what he didn't learn was also instructive. No one really wanted to talk about young women or raiders, but every one of them wanted to sell him something, and all of them believed he wasn't telling the truth when he claimed to be a junior mage of modest means.

From the market square he headed away from the river, along what had to be the main street of Desanyt, past what passed for a chandlery, which was open, and then a small shop of a crafter who appeared to work in silver and copper, which was not.

Ahead he saw a larger building, with half of a wooden bowl painted yellow fastened to a signboard above the entrance. Beltur had no doubt that he was approaching the Brass Bowl and that it would be closed on eight-day morning. He was right on both counts. He also observed that the one-story building extended quite a ways to the rear, suggesting there were rooms for hire, some likely for more than just sleep, at least as alluded to by the young trooper.

A block later, he came to a cross street that also appeared to have shops or other structures on it. A block later the shops largely ended, and for several blocks farther to the west there appeared only to be dwellings. Beyond that, there seemed to be a few scattered cots . . . and a great deal of grassland. He retraced his steps to the cross street with the shops, where he headed south, thinking that the other public house might be there, since a location closer to the post might be advantageous.

He saw a fuller's shop, and then a longer building that was a weaver's place. He also could smell an odor that suggested a renderer might be somewhere near. A bit further along, near where there seemed to be mainly smaller cots, he came upon the Brown Pitcher. The building had a signboard with a simple painting of a brown pitcher. The paint depicting the pitcher had been recently refreshed. That on the letters spelling out the name below had faded almost into obscurity.

Although the Brown Pitcher was actually open, and there appeared to be a few patrons, it was too early to spend time in the public room for what Kaerylt had in mind. Beltur noted its location and turned westward on the next street, more of a lane, watching and listening to see who might be about.

When Beltur returned to the Brown Pitcher some two glasses later, he had almost no better an idea about the town or its people than he had before, despite having listened outside walls, often under a concealment, and having walked most of the streets in the town. He'd heard two women complaining about having to rely on a water carrier to bring the water necessary to do their laundry, and another mother instructing a daughter on the proper way to sweep the bricks. There had been several different women singing so softly he'd not been able to make out the words, and a man yelling so loudly inside a house that while the anger had been evident, the meaning of the words had not been. He'd seen men loading and carrying, and another applying a whitewash to the mud surface of a house. He'd attempted conversation, but while those men he had approached had been pleasant, he'd learned nothing, except that no one wanted to reveal much. He'd gone back under a concealment in two cases to hear what the men said afterward, and heard only that mages should mind their own business and let honest men get on with their work.

All in all, his feet were getting sore and his throat was dry when he walked into the Brown Pitcher. He also was blotting his forehead from the near midday sun. The public room was half full, but surprisingly, at least to Beltur, only about a third of the men there were troopers, obviously those who did not have duty on eightday. By evening, he suspected most of those around the tables would be from the post. He took a small square table against the side wall. There were no chairs, only stools, and a set of benches at the one long table in the middle of the room.

Before long, a dark-haired server appeared, the first even halfway young woman he'd seen in Desanyt, although he would have judged her to be a good ten years older than he was. Despite the summer heat, she wore brown trousers and a long-sleeved and high-necked but loose-fitting tunic of roughly the same shade of brown.

"What will you have?" Her voice was rough but pleasant.

"What kinds of ale do you have?"

"Amber, brown, and black. Two coppers."

"Amber."

She nodded and was gone.

Beltur studied the public room more carefully. There were no troopers drinking alone, but two local gray-beards sat alone, each with an earthenware mug before him. The troopers talked among themselves, but rather more quietly than troopers did in Fenard, where conversations could be heard well out into the street. Then again, reflected Beltur, it was early in the day.

The dark-haired server returned and set a large brown mug before Beltur. Rather than use the silver, Beltur gave her his own coppers.

"What's a mage doing in Desanyt?"

"A junior mage goes where his senior mage tells him," Beltur replied with a smile. "He's trying to talk to the town elder about raiders, something about them raiding more for women." Beltur doubted he was saying anything that wouldn't be all over Desanyt in less than a day or two.

"Frigging raiders are always after women."

"But they leave the larger towns alone." Beltur

glanced at the dirk in the scabbard at her waist. He wouldn't have been surprised if she didn't have another one hidden somewhere else.

"They learned that was too costly a long time ago."

"Do many of the young men here become troopers for the Prefect?"

She laughed, a quietly harsh sound. "Only about half the post. The pay's better than what they can make as a gatherer or grower's helper. Less dangerous than herding."

"Are there a lot of grass cats around here?"

"Enough." She nodded and turned, heading toward a table where three locals sat.

Beltur studied the ale with his senses, but detected no signs of chaos in it. Then he took a careful sip . . . and frowned. The brew was tasty, but different. It wasn't bitter, or chewy, the way Kaerylt liked his, but . . . just different. Abruptly, he realized that it was the same ale, or something very close to it, that he'd had the night before at the post. He took another sip, puzzled.

The server reappeared. "Saw you looking puzzled over the ale. Is there a problem?"

Beltur shook his head. "It's good, but I've never tasted a brew like this."

"You probably won't. We use wild tallgrass seeds for the malt."

Beltur nodded. Why not? There was certainly plenty of grass around. "It's different, but good. Is eightday busy for you?"

"It's the only day we're open before fourth glass of the afternoon."

"So you'll be packed by third glass?"

She shrugged. "Some eightdays. More times in the winter. Glad you like the brew. Let me know when you want another."

"I will, thank you."

As the server moved away, several more locals entered the public house, followed by a group of three troopers. None of them took the tables nearest to Beltur. He wasn't surprised. Because no one talked all that loudly, he definitely wasn't learning that much by eavesdropping. Still . . . he was in no hurry to leave. The ale was good, and the Brown Pitcher was cooler than outside.

He sipped slowly. More than half a glass later, he motioned to his server and waited until she came over.

"You ready for another?"

Beltur shook his head. "One's enough for now." He handed her a copper. "I need to be going."

"Come back sometime." Her smile was slightly warmer than mere courtesy or duty.

"I just might." He stood, nodded to her, and walked from the public room.

Once outside, he stepped away from the door and walked to the adjoining space between the Brown Pitcher and the next building, a cot that had seen better days, but did not look to be abandoned. He glanced around. So far as he could tell no one was looking, and he couldn't sense anyone close to him, except those in the public room. So he raised a concealment and then moved back to the front of the building. He had to wait almost a quarter of a glass before two men approached from the south, troopers from their shapes and carriage.

He slipped into the public room, so close that the trailing trooper muttered, "Don't pull at me. I'm coming."

"Didn't touch you. You need something to drink."

"You would, too, if you'd had Harryn chewing you out."

"Don't let him get to you."

Beltur eased away from the pair and toward the long table in the middle of the room, recalling that the men

around it had been locals. He positioned himself beside
a timber post that had to be a roof support and listened.

". . . still say the river's low as it's been this close to
harvest . . ."

". . . said that last year . . ."

One man laughed, adding, "You always see the
worse, Severyn. I don't see why with that consort
you got."

". . . not your business . . ."

". . . just like bringing in tallgrass seeds to Bortaak . . .
telling him when he'd had too much to drink wasn't his
brother's business . . ."

For at least a quarter of a glass, the talk was about
the river, harvests, and other matters of interest to the
five, but not particularly to Beltur.

". . . young mage left pretty quick like . . ."

". . . and Saera was a lot nicer to him than you . . ."

"That makes three of 'em here. Two were headed
to the elder's place, Naarn said. Don't care for that
at all."

"Why here?"

". . . young mage said . . . Saera said he said . . . the
Prefect worried about the raiders losing too many
women to the mountain bitches . . ."

". . . if they'd lose 'em all, then afore long we'd not
have to worry about 'em . . ."

". . . like you'd want to be a herder . . . where'd you
get the wool for your weaving?"

"Someone would do it."

"Like your cousin Berdyn?" Low laughter filled the
table.

The conversation turned to people, and Beltur
stepped around the room, hearing little of interest. Finally, he slipped into the back room, following the other
server, a woman he hadn't seen or sensed before he'd
raised the concealment. One side of the room held

racked kegs and barrels, the other a large square device set in the middle of the hearth. Belatedly, Beltur realized from the fire chaos he sensed within it that it was a stove of sorts, on which were set an assortment of pots. Set back from the stove were two tables, but Beltur couldn't sense exactly what was on them from where he had positioned himself between two racks.

"You never said anything about that young mage," offered the shorter server to the taller one, Saera.

"What's to say? He was pleasant enough. He asked about the amber brew. He said the older mage he works for was seeing Elder Jhankyr . . . something about the raiders being short of women."

"The way they treat 'em, you wonder how they have any."

"Stop jawing," called the squat man standing in front of the stove. "More troopers just came in."

"They'll wait," replied the taller woman, the one who had served Beltur. "Where else will they go? Don't tell me the Bowl, either. They can't pay that much. Not if they're here." For all her words, she turned and moved into the public room, followed by the other server.

Beltur carefully made his way from the Brown Pitcher and toward the Brass Bowl, dropping the concealment in the afternoon shadows after several blocks.

He used the same approach at the Brass Bowl, which had apparently opened just slightly before he had arrived, since there were only seven others in the entire public room. He ordered the amber ale, this time from a hard-faced blond woman, whose voice was far softer than her appearance. Although the cloth of her pale blue garments was better than that of Saera, the cut was the same, and she also wore a scabbarded dirk. When she returned with the ale and gave him seven coppers in return for the silver, he asked, "Is it always this slow in the afternoon?"

"Until after fifth glass. Then you'd be sitting with someone."

"There aren't any troopers here."

"Ale's cheaper at the other place."

"And that's fine with you."

"Most armsmen are tight with their coins." She smiled, a clearly calculated expression. "Are mages?"

"Junior mages are careful, but not tight."

"What brings you to Desanyt? It's been years since we've seen a mage here."

Beltur repeated what he'd said at the Brown Pitcher.

"If the Prefect's paying you for this, he's wasting his coins. Most raiders are bastards. Nothing a mage does is going to change that. Smart woman comes to town or goes to Westwind."

Beltur guessed. "It sounds like you came to town."

"You're a bright one. Yes, I did. Best choice I ever made. You follow the rules here, and you're respected. It's that simple."

"Even here?"

"What I do is my choice. I could have consorted. Enough have asked."

Beltur could see that was quite possible.

"Try the ale. It's the best you'll find."

Beltur smiled and lifted the mug, larger and better formed than the one he'd had at the Brown Pitcher. He took a sip. While similar to the brew he'd had before, it was smoother, and likely more potent. "It's quite good."

"It is. I just wanted you to say it. Let me know when you're ready for another." After another practiced smile, she was headed to another table.

Although he stayed for almost a glass, and then left, after giving the server a copper, before returning under a concealment, he never heard anything more of interest, from anyone, than what the server had told him. Some of that conflicted with what his uncle had said, because the server had been more than clear that no woman would prefer the herding/raiding life if given a choice. Yet Kaerylt had said some women did. *In other towns than Desanyt, perhaps?* He'd just have to see.

Beltur was back at the post just after fifth glass, where Sydon cornered him almost as soon as he walked through the gates.

"Where have you been? Your uncle wants to see you—except we need to eat. I almost missed supper waiting out here for you."

"I've been doing what he told me. I've walked every demon-dross cubit of Desanyt and listened to more useless words than you can imagine."

"Just come on."

Beltur repressed a smile at Sydon's discomfort and hurried to keep up with the older mage as he rushed toward the mess.

Kaerylt was waiting. He glared at Beltur. "You took your time."

"I did everything you asked. It took time."

"You can tell me after dinner."

The eightday evening meal was all too similar to the one the evening before, except the meat was mutton, not even lamb, and dry and chewy, despite the gravy. Beltur wasn't so sure he wouldn't have preferred the spicy chilied lamb of Arrat.

The conversation dealt mainly with the trials and tribulations of maintaining a post so far from Fenard, and the difficulties of doing so when the locals remained largely separate and aloof. Beltur nodded and said little.

When the three mages left the mess, Kaerylt marched them to his quarters, where he immediately turned to Beltur.

"What did you find out that took you all day and

then some, Beltur? Oh, and did you spend the entire silver?"

"No, sir. There's three coppers left. I walked every street in town, listened where I could, and did what you suggested at each public house. There are two—the Brown Pitcher and the Brass Bowl. The Pitcher is for younger men and troopers. The Bowl is for those with more coppers."

"That doesn't tell me much," said Kaerylt coolly.

"All the women dress pretty much the same. Only their face, hands, and hair are showing. That's even the women who serve at the two public houses—and those are the only places where there were any younger women in public. I overheard two women talking about waiting for water from a water carrier in order to be able to do laundry . . ."

"What does—" Sydon broke off at Kaerylt's sharp glance.

"Go on," encouraged the oldest mage, surprisingly to Beltur.

"All of the women wear dirks. Even the oldest ones. And none of the men in the public houses even attempt to touch the women there. I've never seen that anywhere else . . ." Beltur went on to relate the rest of what he had observed and heard, then waited for Kaerylt's reaction.

"I have to admit that fits with what Elder Jhankyr told me," replied Kaerylt in measured tones. "Women here seem to have . . . a certain position. That may be the problem the herders face." He shook his head. "I cannot see how men in their right mind would allow it to become so, but we must deal with matters as they are and not as we would wish them."

Neither Sydon nor Beltur said anything.

As the silence stretched out, Beltur finally asked, "What are we to do?"

"What we must," said Kaerylt. "Elder Jhankyr mentioned another place besides Kasiera, a place called Wulkyn. It's the clan village of the herders—or raiders. They seem to be the same. It's the only permanent village the herders have. We will need to go there. It is a day southwest of Kasiera. We'll go to Kasiera first and see how best to approach the clan village."

If we can. Beltur wasn't about to say that. "When will we leave?"

"Tomorrow, of course. You two can go back to the room. I'll need to talk to Undercaptain Pacek and Captain Lemaryt."

"Yes, ser."

Once Beltur and Sydon were back in their quarters, Beltur looked to Sydon. "What do you think?"

"What else can we do? Besides, the raiders sound like they need a lesson of sorts." Sydon snorted scornfully.

"From just three mages and a half squad of troopers?"

"There are ways . . . You'll see."

Beltur didn't feel like arguing, but he worried about just what they might see.

VIII

By just after dawn on twoday, after an uneasy sleep at what passed as a way station on oneday night, Beltur was again in the saddle, riding beside Sydon, while Kaerylt rode with Undercaptain Pacek. Beltur was just as glad Sydon wasn't much for talking, because that allowed Beltur to try using tiny bits of order to confine chaos in various patterns, something he could do without Sydon noticing because Sydon used very little order, and at times, seemed almost unable to see or sense free order, unlike his uncle, who could use both, but who preferred dealing with chaos. Beltur had the feeling that he was getting better and quicker at creating order-based patterns to direct chaos, but he still remembered how that had not worked all that well during the attack by the raiders.

Keeping his uncle's admonitions in mind, at least in a way, Beltur kept working at using the least order possible to confine and direct the free chaos, occasionally glancing toward Sydon or Kaerylt, but neither seemed aware of what he was doing. After a time, he realized that one reason that Kaerylt wasn't interested in Beltur was because his uncle was also doing exercises, although his involved a great deal more chaos.

Why? He had no more than asked the question than he remembered how shaky his uncle had been after the raider attack. *Even he needs to practice to keep up his skills.* For some reason that offered a certain comfort.

Perhaps a glass later, he paused from his efforts and looked around more intently, although there was still little to see except the endless tannish-brown grass. Less than a kay ahead, the road began a gentle slope toward the top of a grassy ridge. Looking beyond the ridge to the west, Beltur could see a mass of clouds, the bases of which were dark, and what looked to be rain falling in places beneath the clouds.

"There's rain ahead," said Kaerylt to Pacek.

"Most of the time," replied the undercaptain, "thundershowers that far away are gone before they're a problem. Besides, there's nowhere to take cover."

Beltur didn't even have to glance around to know that. Even the low ridge ahead only showed grass and a few patches of bushes, but he couldn't help glancing past his uncle in the direction they rode, and he didn't see any sign of the storm vanishing. In fact, the clouds seemed to be darkening as he watched—and moving toward them. The riders covered another half kay before the clouds blocked the sun and the light breeze turned into a stiffer wind bearing the smell of rain, followed by scattered droplets.

Then, the clouds overhead darkened quickly, so that in moments it seemed more like twilight than midday when the rain began to pelt down with such intensity that Beltur could scarcely see beyond his uncle and the undercaptain, although they were only a few yards in front of him. He wondered how they could even see the road, but the undercaptain kept riding.

Perhaps a hundred yards short of the top of the ridge, as the rain abruptly stopped, Pacek reined up. "Column! Halt!"

Scarcely had the undercaptain issued the order when lightning flared along the top of the ridge, to the north, but close enough that Beltur could sense the cold but slender links of order and how they held far larger amounts of raging chaos—just before the thundering lash of sound washed over him.

Another flare of lightning struck, farther to the south.

Those patterns aren't that different from what you've been doing . . .

While he still held the memory and feel of the lightning, he tried to replicate it, gathering in what he could of the lingering free chaos dispersed by the lightning, then concentrating and aiming it to the north of the road and just ahead.

A flare of light blinded him, and a crashing wall of sound hammered into him. For several moments, Beltur could hear and see nothing, and when his sight returned he was so light-headed that he was swaying in the saddle. *That was too close, much closer than you intended.* He forced himself to straighten up immediately because he didn't want Sydon to notice his reaction.

"Demons! That was close!" declared Sydon.

"Too close," Beltur agreed, his voice uneven. If he'd tried to put it any closer . . . He repressed a shudder. At the same time, he realized that Jessyla had been right—that he could control chaos through order, much more chaos than he'd ever managed before. *But you'll need much better control to try that against raiders.*

He also felt tired. Not as tired as he had after the skirmish with the raiders, but tired enough that he wasn't about to try to work any ordered chaos patterns for a while.

After waiting perhaps a fifth of a glass, Pacek called out, "Forward!"

When they reached the top of the rise, Beltur half expected to see Kasiera in the distance. He didn't. What he did see was more of the rolling grasslands, and a faint line of white in the distance.

"You can just barely see the tops of the Westhorns from here," announced Pacek.

"Where is Kasiera?" asked Sydon.

"Straight ahead. Some four glasses of riding."

The sky cleared, and the sun beat down, and Beltur began to sweat, despite clothes that were still soaking, but the air was so hot and damp that the sweating didn't cool him all that much . . . and his clothes didn't seem any drier. He thought that such was to be expected in summer, then realized that it was already the second day of harvest, not that early harvest ever seemed much different from summer.

By the time Kasiera finally came into view, some two glasses later, Beltur's clothes were only damp. Kasiera was a much smaller version of Desanyt, a huddle of huts, houses, and cots along a stream far smaller than the Sanyt River, one so narrow that Beltur wondered if it didn't dry up at times. There were far fewer trees and tilled plots along the stream.

Kaerylt, who had been talking to Pacek, half turned in the saddle and addressed the two younger mages. "There is an inn, of sorts, but we'll be sharing a chamber, since the Prefect was not overly generous with coins for expenses, and the men will be in tight quarters."

"If not in the stable," added Pacek dryly. "That's still better than the way station at Arrat."

The inn turned out to be a long one-story mud brick building located on the north side of the rain-dampened clay area that apparently passed for Kasiera's main square, most likely its only square, thought Beltur, as he reined up outside the adjoining stable.

Once more, Kaerylt tasked Beltur with stabling and grooming all three mounts, and Beltur had just finished dealing with his own mount, after grooming the other two, when Kaerylt returned to the stable. The white mage glanced around, then asked, his voice low, "What were you doing on the ride?"

"Riding, and practicing my shields. You told me that they were weak and that the only way I'd strengthen them was to work on them. You said I couldn't work on chaos-bolts while we were riding through dry grasslands."

"I'm glad you listen, at least occasionally."

"I do, ser. I really do." *Even if I'm not sure that what you suggest will work for me.*

"I think you doubt me at times," said Kaerylt evenly.

"The only thing I doubt, Uncle, is my ability to do things as well as you do." *At least in the way that you suggest.*

"Did you sense anyone besides our party during the time the lightning struck?"

"No, ser. Why?"

"That last lightning bolt had much more order in it. It wasn't like the others."

"It wasn't natural?"

"It was . . . different, as if . . ." Kaerylt shook his head.

"You think an ordermage created it?"

"Probably not, but you can sense order from farther away than I can. That's why I asked."

"I didn't sense anyone else." Beltur paused. "What would an ordermage be doing here?"

"Sometimes, the druids leave the Great Forest, and some say that they favor the black bitches. That is one possibility for why more women might be leaving the herders."

"Oh. I didn't know that."

"Now you do. Let me know if you sense any strange or unnatural concentration of order."

"Yes, ser. I certainly will."

Beltur managed not to sigh in relief after Kaerylt turned away. How could he practice handling chaos with order if Kaerylt sensed the order any time he was near? Also, he couldn't help but wonder why his uncle thought a concentration of order was unnatural, but a concentration of chaos wasn't.

He took a long slow breath, then closed the stall and headed across the damp ground toward the front of the main building, following his uncle.

IX

On threeday, Beltur woke in the grayness before sunrise, burdened by a sense of worry, and, not incidentally, by his uncle's snoring. He immediately pulled on his clothes and slipped from the tiny room as quietly as he could, with little enough noise that his departure did not wake either Sydon or Kaerylt. Because he wasn't certain what had caused his apprehension, he immediately raised a concealment once he was in the empty and narrow hallway.

He first hurried to the stable, but there was no one there except a stableboy, and the mounts all appeared to be fine. After that, he returned to the inn proper and carefully made his way toward the public room and kitchen.

While the public room was empty, the kitchen was not. Beltur could sense two servers and two men dealing with pots and grates over the white-hot chaos of the bed of coals in the large hearth. One server was laying out platters and mugs on a side table, while another was doing something around the wooden rack that held the barrels of ale. As in Desanyt and Arrat, the women all wore the same concealing garments, and long dirks, but the servers the night before had included younger women—younger meaning that one had actually been perhaps only ten years older than Beltur. After easing into the kitchen, already far hotter than he would have preferred, he positioned himself beside an open window, but close enough to hear what any of the four might say.

". . . finished with those platters, Larala?"

". . . be ready before anyone shows . . ."

"What about the mages?"

"What about 'em? They need to eat, like anyone else . . . won't pay more or less. Less with the extras, I'd wager."

"You think the herders will be coming soon?" asked the server moving away from the ale barrels.

"Could be. Cyntyl saw horsemen to the west yesterday . . ."

". . . be about that time of year . . ."

"... won't come if they know about the white mages ..."

"How will they know? Besides, they can't wait for-ever for winter supplies."

"... don't have as much this year. That's the word ..."

"Always less in a dry year ..."

"Enough about weather," growled the larger man at the hearth. "Parcyn and his boys walked in."

Larala hurried from the kitchen.

The other server moved to the table with the platters, asking, "Egg toast again?"

"Scrambles, no toast. Bread and pork strips. Por-ridge."

For the next third of a glass or so, the sparse talk was about food, the appetite of the elder Parcyn, and the increasing price of firewood. Because Beltur began to worry about what Kaerylt might say when he woke, he slowly moved out of the kitchen and through the public room, avoiding the three tables with patrons. Once he was alone in the long hall leading to the room, he dropped the concealment, continued walking, then slipped into the room.

Sydon carefully ignored looking at Beltur.

Kaerylt, who was sitting on the edge of the pallet bed pulling on his boots, just glared. "Where were you?"

"I couldn't sleep. I didn't want to wake you. I was a little worried. So I went out to see what was happening in the inn and in the stable. Under a concealment."

"And?"

"The horses are fine. No one else has ridden in since we did. The servers and the cooks are worried that the herders won't come to Kasiera because we're here. They didn't say why."

"Harvest-time trading, most likely," snorted Kaerylt, as if what Beltur had reported was of little use. "It's the only time they're civil. Did you hear anything else?"

"Nothing about us or women."

"At least, you're trying to be helpful and not letting them know anything. We need to go eat before I find the town elder and see what he knows." Kaerylt looked at Sydon. "Both of you, keep your ears open in the public room." Kaerylt stood and then opened the door.

"Yes, ser," replied Beltur.

"I will," agreed Sydon, "but all they talk about is the grass, the weather, and crops."

Beltur nodded as he followed the other two toward the public room. That was certainly all he'd heard the night before.

Kaerylt took a corner table and the stool in the back from where he could survey the entire chamber. Beltur's best view was that of the entrance to the kitchen. He ordered the scrambles, whatever they were, along with a mug of ale. The scrambles turned out to be a mixture of muffin scraps, eggs, and small slices of chewy pork covered with a tangy white sauce that made the whole mélange close to tasty. The grass ale was the same as the night before, drinkable, if warmer than Beltur would have liked.

The public room was half full, and few of the other patrons were talking. Those that did kept their voices too low for Beltur to hear anything, except orders or requests to the servers.

Just about the time that Beltur finished eating, Kaerylt cleared his throat, then said in a low voice, "Sydon, I want you to ride out along the stream and see what you can. Beltur, you're to do what you did in Arrat and Desanyt, except you won't need coins when you come back here to find out what the locals may be talking about."

After leaving the other two mages, Beltur made his way northward along the street that bordered the east side of the inn, deciding against using a concealment to begin with, since he wanted to actually see the dwellings, sheds, and huts, and since anyone behind a wall wasn't about to see him anyway.

He immediately saw two men coming toward him, one leading a donkey pulling an empty cart, and the other walking beside the cart, all headed toward the square. They wore long-sleeved shirts and trousers, both a faded tan color.

"Good morning," offered Beltur cheerfully.

Both men nodded in return, but did not speak.

A block farther on, he saw a gray-bearded man apparently repairing a shutter over a window that was definitely not glazed. The man took a quick look in Beltur's direction and then glanced away.

A block farther north, Beltur saw a youth walking swiftly toward him in the direction of the square and the river. Despite the heat, the youth wore tan garments similar to those of the men. Beltur immediately moved so that he came face-to-face with the young man, barely more than a boy. "I've heard that the herders might be arriving sometime soon. Do you know anything about that?"

"They always come in early harvest." The youth did not quite meet Beltur's eyes.

"Do they stay in the town?"

"No, ser mage."

"Do they ever . . . take consorts from Kasiera?"

"No girls here are that foolish, ser."

"Do they take women?"

"No raider is that stupid. If you would excuse me, ser, I need to join my father in our field."

The youth practically ran from Beltur.

A half block farther north, Beltur thought he heard voices from behind the rear wall of a small house. He angled toward the house, and when he was in a position where he hoped no one would see him, he raised a

concealment and then slowly made his way to the wall
to listen.

"... good day for laundry, don't you think little
one?"

Beltur heard no response.

The woman continued to speak cheerfully. "The sun
is out. There are no clouds, and your father will bring
us a fine melon ..."

After several moments more, Beltur realized that the
woman was speaking to an infant or small child as she
did her chores. He moved on.

Three glasses later, he dropped the concealment
after walking what seemed to be every street of Kasiera
and trudged back to the inn. He'd seen no younger
women, but more than a score of men, all of whom
were less talkative than the youth he'd confronted. He'd
also listened at more than a score of rear walls, invari-
ably to women and children, and heard very little of interest, although he would certainly convey those few
tidbits to Kaerylt.

As he entered the front of the inn and glanced through
the archway into the public room, he could see only a
handful of men, all older, at the tables. He kept walking toward the room, but passed it without stopping
when he sensed that no one was there. He raised a concealment before leaving the inn and walking across to
the stable, where he hoped to find the troopers, possibly talking.

There were only three, standing in a corner. Beltur
moved close enough to overhear and began to listen.

"... glad I'm not riding out with the undercaptain ..."

"... cooler watching the gear ..."

"... be out there tomorrow ..."

"... won't get any answers traveling from small
towns to smaller towns ..."

"Undercaptain thinks they want to go to Wulkyn."

"Never heard of it."

"It's where the raiders' clan leaders gather. Another day southwest of here."

"Ride into a raider village? Sowshit . . . rather take a mount to the Westhorns and beg mercy from the black bitches."

"Either way your stud days'd be done, Vaergas." A raucous laugh followed.

"What's so friggin' important about raiders looking for women?"

"What's important is that the friggin' Prefect thinks it's friggin' important."

"No . . . what's friggin' important is that we don't lose our asses to what the friggin' Prefect thinks is friggin' important . . ."

All three troopers laughed.

"You got the bones?" asked one.

"Here?"

"Why not? We can hear anyone coming. Under-captain doesn't care so long as we're watching the gear . . ."

As the three settled into their game, Beltur left and made his way out of the stable and around to the rear looking for somewhere he could practice, releasing his concealment once he was behind the stable and where no one was near. Beyond a rubble heap consisting mainly of broken chunks of mud bricks he spied a tumbled-down set of sod walls perhaps three yards on a side, the tallest part of which was only shoulder-high. There was no sign of a roof, but with so few trees near or around Kasiera, someone had likely long since made off with any usable wood.

He nodded to himself. Sod wouldn't catch fire.

His first effort was to gather free chaos using what felt like an order-lattice shaped into a cone. He was surprised that it seemed so easy, but when he tried to focus that chaos into something like an arrow, it just seemed to dribble out of the cone and land in a sizzling heap on the ground . . . well short of the sagging sod wall.

He tried again . . . with exactly the same result.

He didn't want to use his own personal chaos to throw the gathered free chaos, nor did he think that bringing the gathered free chaos into his own aura was what Jessyla had described, yet the free order didn't seem to provide any power, just structure, and the free chaos just flowed, almost like water.

Like water? Abruptly, Beltur smiled. He gathered, or regathered, the free chaos, and used the order to lift it higher and channel it. That worked, in a way, but the chaos struck the sod without much force.

His next attempt was to visualize a bow made of order, and an arrow of order holding the chaos, but with the "point" almost open. That worked somewhat better.

He had been practicing for more than a glass, finally coming up with what amounted to an order-catapult that delivered chaos with fair force—at least over a distance of twenty yards, which wasn't nearly so far as his uncle and Sydon could throw chaos-bolts, but which allowed him to deliver such bolts one after the other, for up to five or six, before having to rest, which was far, far more than he had been able to do before. At that moment, he heard horses. He immediately turned and walked toward the stable yard, where he saw Kaerylt and Sydon, along with Pacek and seven troopers. The two mages were beginning to dismount. Since no one had yet looked in his direction, Beltur quickly raised a concealment and ducked back against the stable wall, moving away from the yard and around the stable itself. *Sydon can do a little grooming for once.*

He quickly made his roundabout way back to the inn, still under a concealment, and then into the public room, discovering that another handful of men had swelled the numbers there since he had last looked. Finding a place against the wall where he could hear what was being said at two of the tables, if barely, he began to listen. For a time, he only heard complaints about the heat, the low stream level, the fact that it was looking to be a less profitable harvest, and that the Prefect had insisted on a tariff for the town.

". . . never paid a tariff . . . never will . . . Prefect doesn't do sowshit for us . . ."

". . . might have to . . . mages and troopers . . ."

He tariffs towns? Beltur was thinking that over when he heard something else.

". . . Scaryll sent word . . . two of those mages . . . out riding with troopers . . ."

". . . not good . . ."

". . . wouldn't dare attack the town . . . no point . . ."

". . . probably not . . . don't like it, though . . ."

". . . about the other one?"

". . . saw him walking around town . . . talked to a few people . . . couple of glasses ago, though."

"Don't like that, either."

"You going to do anything about it?" The man laughed. "Best thing to do is be polite and avoid them. They keep going out in the grasslands, and the herders might take care of them."

"Scaryll might think so, but they might be the ones dealing with the herders . . ."

"Better the first way . . . but it's between them . . . not us . . ."

From there the conversation turned back to comments about one of the servers and the melon crop and certain comparisons.

Beltur decided enough time had passed, and he quietly left the public room and headed for their sleeping chamber, where he sensed Kaerylt was alone. As he opened the door, he dropped the concealment.

"Where have you been?"

"Walking every street of Kasiera, talking to men who would talk, listening to women talk, eavesdropping on the three troopers the undercaptain left, and then hearing what I could at the public room." Suddenly, Beltur realized that his legs were wobbly, and that he was light-headed. He sat down quickly on the end of the pallet bed.

Kaerylt frowned. "You're looking pale."

"I've been holding a lot of concealments."

"Have you eaten anything?"

"No. I hadn't thought about that."

The older mage shook his head. "We might as well go to the public room before you collapse. I told Sydon to find you and meet me there."

Beltur had no doubt that his uncle had said for Sydon to find Beltur if he could.

Less than a quarter glass later, the three were seated around a corner table in the public room and Beltur had already drunk half a mug of the grass ale, and his light-headedness had slowly receded.

"Now that you look like you can think, Beltur, tell us what you found out."

"Well . . . no one around here really wants to talk to white mages, even young ones. But . . ." Beltur summarized what he had observed and heard in his initial meetings with the men.

"That's all?"

"I did overhear two women talking about the raiders and how there seemed to be fewer of them in the past several years, and that they didn't buy as much as they used to. When I came back and listened to the three troopers one of them said he'd rather desert than ride to Wulkyn. And a man in the public room said that you and Sydon were riding the grasslands, and that was bound to get the herders stirred up, maybe enough that they'd attack us if we kept doing it. The others thought that it was our problem, not theirs."

Kaerylt's low-voiced questions forced Beltur to go back over what he had said for another third of a glass before the older mage finally said, "Did they say more about that Scaryll?"

"No, ser. Just what I told you."

"That's not a lot."

"I know, ser, but it still took a long time." Beltur paused, then asked, "How was your day?"

"The elder wasn't much more forthcoming than the men you encountered. The herders do trade here, usually at season-turn. People almost never see them except near those times. No one here has ever been to Wulkyn. The raiders have a habit of killing people who get too close."

"So what do we do?" asked Sydon.

"The next best thing. Talk to the herders or raiders who visit Kasiera. There's a sort of agreement, like a truce, when the raiders come to trade. A band leader or someone who speaks for him comes first." Kaerylt shrugged. "If they're here, one way or another, I'll talk to him and see what I can find out. In the meantime, we'll do some more riding in places outside of town to see what we can discover. It doesn't seem likely we'll learn much more except from the herders or raiders."

Was there a hint of discouragement in his uncle's voice? Beltur thought so, but he wasn't entirely certain.

X

On fourday, immediately after breakfast, Beltur and Sydon, accompanied by five troopers, rode north out of Kasiera along a road that was barely more than a dirt path, under instructions from Kaerylt to look for any trace of raiders and herders, and anything else they could see, while Kaerylt headed southward with Undercaptain Pacek and the other five troopers.

"You, Beltur," Kaerylt had said firmly, "are to keep your senses alert for signs of excessive order. Sydon, you are to use chaos to protect the others, only as necessary. Do not use chaos against anyone unless they attack first."

Once they were well outside of Kasiera, Sydon looked to Beltur. "Do you sense any untoward order?"

Beltur ignored the belittling edge in Sydon's words. "He sensed extra order around the thunderstorm that hit us on the way to Kasiera. He thinks that it's possible that the druids from the Great Forest may be helping Westwind entice women away from the raiders. That's why he wants me to be alert to any unnatural concentrations of order."

"Why would the druids do that? What would it gain them?"

"Westwind would gain more women and greater strength to oppose the Prefect." That was a judgment on Beltur's part, because Kaerylt had never said anything to that effect.

"Do you really believe those old legends about the power of Westwind? They're just women."

"I don't notice the Prefect doing things to anger them,

and the Tyrant of Sarronnyn seems to be doing quite well. She's a woman, also, you might recall."

"That's because there's no real power west of the Westhorns. Not since Cyador fell, anyway."

"What about the druids?"

"They don't count. So long as you leave them alone, they leave you alone."

Beltur had the feeling Sydon was missing something . . . or that what Kaerylt had said about the druids had omitted something . . . or a few somethings. *What else is new?*

Some three kays north of Kasiera, the path split, one branch heading northeast, the other northwest. Sydon immediately gestured. "We'll head to the northwest."

Beltur didn't disagree, since they were looking for herders, and it seemed as though they'd more likely be to the west than to the east, although that was definitely not a certainty.

By midmorning the day was as hot as all the others on the grasslands had been, and he was sweating profusely. The only moving thing that he had seen was a long-legged antelope that had immediately fled upon seeing the riders. In moments, it had vanished over one of the low rises, and by the time the riders had reached the rise, Beltur could neither see nor sense the antelope. Given the grazer's speckled light brown coat, it could have been less than two kays away, just out of Beltur's range in sensing living order, but blending in with the tall tannish brown grass.

After another glass passed, one of the troopers called out, "There are vulcrows circling ahead." He pointed west of where the seven rode, although there was another low rise between them and the spot where the birds circled and the path-like road angled away from the vulcrows.

Sydon looked puzzled for a moment.

Beltur replied before the older mage could say anything, "That means there's carrion, there, doesn't it?"

"More than likely, ser," replied the trooper. "Could be a grass cat feeding, too. Maybe on that antelope we spooked, or another one. Vulcrows would be on the carcass already otherwise."

"What about herders or raiders?"

"We haven't seen any tracks, ser."

That wasn't exactly reassuring, given that the grass, shoulder high on the horses in places, seemed able to conceal anything that wasn't on the path that passed for a road, although Beltur had sensed nothing large except the antelope and the men and horses in his own party.

As they followed the dirt path toward the top of the rise, Beltur kept watching the circling vulcrows, noting that the path was taking them somewhat farther north of the spot the birds continued to circle. He had the feeling that might be for the best, although he still couldn't sense the vulcrows or what might lie beneath them.

When they reached the rise, he scanned the grasslands beneath the birds, a good kay away from him, immediately sensing the mix of order and chaos that indicated people, although he could not see them at first, given the variation in the height of the grass between the path and the vulcrows' target. Then he saw two, and then three more riders. "There are herders there! They must have brought down an antelope or something."

"Where?" asked Sydon.

"Under where the vulcrows are circling. They almost look like taller patches of grass." Beltur realized that two of the horses were without riders, possibly because the herders were gutting or skinning the animal. He also could make out more riders farther to the south, and they were moving toward the two mages and their escorts. As they neared, he counted ten riders, two of whom were clearly smaller. *They're women . . . or girls.* But weren't the herder women so badly treated that they were fleeing to the Westhorns?

"We should rein up," Beltur suggested, "and see what they do."

Sydon kept riding.

"Rein up!" said Beltur sharply.

Sydon did so, as did the other troopers, but the older mage scowled.

"They think the grasslands are theirs. Kaerylt said not to make trouble."

"Easy enough for him to say," muttered Sydon, barely loud enough for Beltur to hear.

The approaching party of herders slowed to a walk, then stopped, and a single rider moved ahead.

Beltur sensed chaos gathering around Sydon and called out, "Sydon! Don't throw any chaos-bolts!"

The older mage ignored Beltur and released a bolt that arched toward the lead herder.

Beltur immediately formed a small order-linked shield in front of the bolt, which flared in the air well short of the advancing herder, who immediately turned his mount and swiftly retreated.

"Why did you do that?" snapped Sydon.

"Because Kaerylt said we weren't to use chaos unless we were attacked. One man riding toward us isn't an attack. Didn't you see that he had nothing in his hands?"

"He was riding like he wanted to attack."

"If he wanted to attack, he would have waited for all the others, and they would have had their bows out, the way that other group did. Besides, some of the riders were women."

"I couldn't tell that. They all looked the same. Anyway, Kaerylt said I was to protect us. I did what I thought best."

And you're an idiot if you thought attacking them first was best. Beltur didn't speak what he thought, knowing that it would do little good. Abruptly, he worried about whether his order-linked shield had stopped the chaos from Sydon's bolt from dropping into the dry grass and starting a fire, and he immediately tried to sense where the free chaos had gone. He couldn't find any concentration. Nor was there any sign of the natural chaos that a fire would create.

For a time, he just watched as the herders rode away into the distance. Then he said, "It might not be the wisest course to follow them."

"They won't come after us," declared Sydon.

"They might not, but what if they gather more riders? Why don't we see if there's another path that leads more south that might circle back toward Kasiera?"

"That's not all that likely," muttered Sydon.

Beltur thought it was highly likely, and, although they rode more than a kay before they encountered what he was looking for, he did find it. He didn't quite breathe a sigh of relief as they turned southward, not until another glass passed, and it was clear no herders were trailing them.

The rest of the afternoon was uneventful, and Beltur quietly spent a considerable amount of time working on creating larger and stronger shields. With all the drying grass around him, he wasn't about to try to replicate a lightning bolt. He'd been fortunate enough that his small order-shield had blocked any fire from Sydon's chaos. By the time they turned back toward Kasiera, Beltur had seen more than enough of the grasslands, and he couldn't help worrying about how the herders might take Sydon's firebolt. He just hoped that his blocking it short of the rider had been taken as a warning, rather than the hostile gesture that Sydon had clearly meant.

Kaerylt was waiting for them when they rode back to the inn and reined up outside the stable. "Meet me in our room. You can tell me what you found out there. Then we'll get some dinner."

Beltur wondered at his uncle's curtness, but he just nodded and said, "Yes, ser."

Sydon didn't say a word.

Beltur was more than happy not to be stuck grooming Sydon's mount, especially since Sydon was clearly miffed at having to do it himself. Beltur did have to wait for Sydon to finish, but he kept his smile to himself, and then walked quietly across the courtyard with Sydon to the main inn building.

No sooner had the two stepped into the small inn chamber where Kaerylt sat on the end of his pallet bed than Sydon immediately blurted out, "We ran into a bunch of raiders. They attacked us. I threw a chaos-bolt. They backed off." He shot a sharp glance at Beltur, as if to suggest Beltur say nothing.

"It wasn't quite that way," Beltur said evenly. "The raiders had brought down a grasslands antelope. We neared where they were. Several of them rode toward us. They weren't carrying bows—"

"Yes, they were!" interrupted Sydon.

"The nearest one was empty-handed," stated Beltur. "So were the others, and they reined up well back of the one who rode toward us."

"Then what happened?" asked Kaerylt.

"The chaos-bolt—"

"Beltur partly blocked it!" snapped Sydon.

Kaerylt turned to Beltur. "Why did you do that?"

"You said we weren't to attack unless they did. They hadn't loosed arrows, and they didn't have blades in their hands, and there was only one rider coming toward us. Besides, two of the riders were women."

"Women riders?" questioned Kaerylt. "That's preposterous."

Beltur shrugged. "I saw them. I also sensed them. They were women."

"You must have been mistaken. The herders don't let their women ride free."

"He certainly was," insisted Sydon.

Kaerylt turned his eyes on Sydon. His voice was cold as he said, "Beltur is doubtless mistaken about the women, but he was right about your poor decision to throw a chaos-bolt at a single rider. Especially in the middle of all that dry grass. Now . . . don't interrupt again." He looked back at Beltur. "What happened after that?"

"They all rode away. I hoped that they thought the chaos-bolt was just a warning."

"So do I," replied Kaerylt dryly. "Did the chaos start a fire?"

"No, ser. I checked on that. After that we rode another kay or so, and then took another path that headed south and led back to town. We only saw one grass antelope and that group of herders the whole time. There was no sense of excessive order anywhere."

"Do you have anything to add?" Kaerylt asked Sydon.

"I still think they were dangerous and that warning them was a good idea."

Beltur decided against pointing out that warning hadn't been Sydon's intention. If his uncle hadn't understood that already, nothing Beltur said would change that.

"Let us hope they thought it was just a warning." Kaerylt coughed. "As I told you, I went south, more to the southwest, actually. Unlike you, I saw no riders, but I did see quite a few hoofprints, enough that there must be several bands of herders around. We also spooked a large grass cat. It thought about attacking, but decided seven men and mounts weren't good odds and vanished into the grass." He stood. "I'm hungry, and we might as well eat."

"What are we going to do tomorrow?" asked Sydon.

"What we did today. After your . . . encounter, I'd like to see how the herders react."

"I just—"

"Not another word about it, either of you." Kaerylt opened the door. "If you want dinner, I suggest you two accompany me."

Beltur let Sydon leave before him, then closed the door and followed the other two.

XI

On fiveday, Kaerylt decided that all three mages and all the troopers should ride out together. That might have been because Kaerylt had decided he couldn't trust Sydon and Beltur to scout on their own, but he didn't explain. They spent the entire day riding through the grasslands largely to the southeast of Kasiera, and although they glimpsed several bands of herders, not a one of them was accompanying the grassland sheep for which they were known. More important, while one group of riders shadowed the mages and troopers for several glasses, they never even came within a kay of the fourteen, although by the time those riders turned away, Beltur had been able to sense them clearly, and one was definitely a woman, but Beltur saw no point in saying so.

On sixday morning, after breakfast, as the three mages were getting ready to leave for the stable, Kaerylt said, "Pack all your gear and bring it with you."

"Ser?"

"We might not be returning here if the herders invite us to Wulkyn."

"Why would they do that?" asked Sydon.

"You never know, and if the opportunity affords itself, the last thing I want to do is defer and return here. We might not get a second chance."

Beltur didn't pretend to understand. He just packed his gear and carried it to the stable, where he fastened it behind his saddle, arranging it so that he could easily get into his saddlebags for the leftover bread he'd brought from breakfast.

Once all the troopers were also there, Kaerylt gathered everyone around him in the stable yard, rather than simply telling everyone to mount up and giving directions from the saddle. "Yesterday, you all may have noticed that the herders followed us for a time. This may happen again. Or it may not. I've put out word that I'd like to talk with them. I don't know how that will be taken. They may approach peacefully, but if . . . if they decide to attack, we won't have much warning. For that reason, I'd like all of you to stay fairly close to me once it's clear that there are herders—or raiders— nearby."

"You heard the mage," added Pacek firmly.

Beltur kept his frown to himself. His uncle had made no mention of putting word out to the herders. How had he done that? Through the town elder? And when? Beltur didn't recall Kaerylt being that far away . . . and certainly not long enough for a lengthy conversation.

"It's time to mount up," said Kaerylt evenly.

Beltur did so, and he and Sydon took their position in the column behind Kaerylt and Pacek as the fourteen rode out of Kasiera, this time heading to the southwest over the narrow brick and stone bridge across the stream and definitely in the direction of Wulkyn.

Less than a glass later, Kaerylt reined up and turned in the saddle. "There are raiders beyond the next rise. Sydon, you and Beltur need to ride ahead of the under-captain and me, a good twenty yards. Don't worry. The raiders are a good kay beyond the rise."

"You want them to see us first and think we're alone?"

"That's the idea. Then we'll see how friendly they really are."

"They won't be," declared Sydon.

"That may be, but you're not to use chaos until you and Beltur both agree that it's necessary. Both of you. Is that clear?"

"Yes, ser." Sydon's voice was not quite sullen.

"Now . . . you two ride around us and lead the way."

Beltur let Sydon take the lead, then moved up beside him.

"If they attack," said Sydon sardonically, "I'd appreciate your agreement before the arrows strike us."

"If there's a real attack, I'm no more interested than you in being a target."

"Good."

As he neared the top of the low rise, even before he could see beyond the crest, Beltur could definitely sense the herders or raiders, and they seemed to be more like a kay and a half away. Yet when he reached the top of the dirt path and looked to the southwest, it appeared to him that the mounted riders were indeed more than a kay away, possibly even closer to two kays. He immediately studied the grassy expanse closer to him and Sydon, but could not see or sense anyone or anything large hidden any closer.

At the same time, he could feel a line of chaos not

that far behind him and Sydon. He frowned as he realized that Kaerylt had created a partial concealment over the Gallosian troopers and himself, one that only concealed them from anyone looking at them from the southwest, but one that left Beltur and Sydon fully exposed to the view of the raiders. For a moment, Beltur wondered why, then realized that the line concealment allowed the troopers to see where they were going, unlike a full concealment. But that raised another question—why a concealment at all? *To see if they'll attack two men riding alone?* That would certainly determine how peaceful the herders—or raiders— might be.

Beltur was still puzzled as to why he could sense the grasslands riders from as far as he could, almost half a kay farther than on fiveday, and a good kay farther than he'd been able to do before he had left Fenard. It couldn't be just practice, because he'd practiced glass upon glass for years before trying to use order as a structuring method. The only conclusion he could come to was that, at least for him, Jessyla had been right . . . or that his interpretation of what she had suggested worked better for him than what Kaerylt had taught him.

He pushed that conclusion to the back of his mind as he realized that even more raiders were appearing, seemingly from everywhere, and all of them were headed toward him and Sydon. *Why now?* Just because there were only two Gallosians visible?

"This looks like an attack to me," declared Sydon.

"It looks that way, but we don't know yet, and there's no point in using chaos until they're close enough for you to be effective."

"Just keep riding!" called out Kaerylt. "We'll move up as necessary."

Beltur thought about trying to count the oncoming

raiders, who were now moving at a fast trot and less than a kay away, turning closer to due north as they neared. There were certainly more than a score, possibly two score, if not more, and he could sense others farther away, some of whom were riding toward the northwest to flank Beltur and Sydon, at least if the two kept riding along the dirt road. Beltur glanced back, but he saw nothing but grasslands because of his uncle's concealment.

"Stop when they're about two hundred yards away!" called Kaerylt. "Then see what they do."

The first riders kept coming, and by the time they were some three hundred yards away, Beltur could tell that all of them held bows.

"They're all carrying bows," he called back.

"Don't use chaos until they loose shafts. Then take down as many as you can as quickly as you can."

As if we could really do anything else once they attack . . . if they attack. Beltur turned back to Sydon. "I'll shield so that you can use all your chaos on the attackers. I'll add what I can beyond shielding."

"That makes sense. Let's rein up a good bit before they reach two hundred yards."

"Fine." Beltur doubted that either of them could determine two hundred yards to the digit, or even to the cubit. He kept watching the raiders, who still approached through the high grass at a fast trot. He thought, but wasn't certain, that some of the attackers were women. They might have been youths, but he didn't think so. "They're at about two hundred fifty yards, but they haven't nocked shafts yet."

As the distance closed, Beltur watched the lead riders even more intently, even while he edged his mount closer to that of Sydon and prepared to lift his order-linked shield. The smaller he could keep the shield the stronger it would be and the longer he could hold it.

"Rein up!" said Sydon.

Beltur didn't argue. He reined up alongside Sydon. The raiders looked to him to be considerably farther away than two hundred yards, but they would cover the extra yards in no more than a few moments.

Nearly instantly, even though Beltur heard not a word, all the attackers urged their mounts into a gallop, raised their bows, nocked arrows, and loosed shafts so quickly that their hands seemed almost to blur, and a second volley was off just as Beltur locked the shield in place. Arrows shattered against the shield, spraying away from the two mages. Beltur's mouth dropped open. While he could feel pressure as the arrows struck the shield, he could bear that impact.

Chaos-bolts flared from Sydon, and three, then four of the lead riders went down, little more than a hundred yards away.

Beltur tried one of his order-latticed chaos shafts, and it went through the chest of a rider, but as it did, and the rider flew out of the saddle, Beltur was rocked back, and he had to grab the horse's mane to stay mounted. For a moment, he felt like he was losing control of the shield, and he just concentrated on holding it as a handful of riders bore down on them, curved blades in their hands instead of bows, although Beltur had not seen them change weapons.

Sydon took out two more, their riderless mounts shying to the side. Then one of the mounts crashed into the unseen order-linked shield, and the other two riders tried to turn their mounts from the fallen rider and horse. One succeeded. The other went down, as did yet another following rider.

Belatedly, Beltur realized that other chaos-bolts were slamming into what remained of the attacking raiders, before, almost as quickly as the raiders had come, those who had survived had turned and ridden off into the grasslands, swiftly leaving the Gallosians alone on the dirt road . . . except for the fallen attackers.

Beltur lowered the shield. His legs were shaking, and he was a little light-headed, but his new shield had held. *It really held*.

Kaerylt reined up beside Sydon. "You did a good job of dealing with them." His eyes then went to Beltur. "All that work with shields paid off, didn't it?"

"Yes, ser."

Kaerylt glanced toward the two mounts that had fallen when they contacted the shield. One of the riders was clearly dead, his body limp and his head at a strange angle. The other one was trapped under the body of her mount. Kaerylt immediately launched a chaos-bolt, one with enough force to turn the fallen raider woman into a charred and unrecognizable heap. "Too bad about that." He looked at Beltur. "Not a word. Ever."

"But . . ."

"You were right, and I don't want you ever to mention it. Is that clear?" Kaerylt's words were colder than ice. He turned to Sydon. "You either."

After a moment of clear surprise, Sydon replied, "Yes, ser."

Kaerylt turned in the saddle. "Undercaptain! We're done here. We'll head back to Kasiera, but we won't be stopping there."

"Yes, ser mage." Unlike Sydon or Beltur, Pacek didn't seem in the slightest bit surprised. "Spoils, ser?"

"If you make it quick. Once your men are spread out . . ."

"Yes, ser. They know."

Kaerylt looked back to Sydon. "Once they return, you need to ride rearguard now . . . just in case there's some raider sneaking through the grass. Beltur will switch places with you later."

"Yes, ser." Sydon didn't sound all that pleased.

Kaerylt ignored that displeasure.

Beltur took out his water bottle, drank, and waited.

When the troopers returned, Pacek rode over to Kaerylt and extended a leather pouch.

"The share for you mages. Not that much in coppers. No jewelry. I'll see about selling the blades when we can."

"Thank you. I'll leave the details to you."

"Our pleasure, ser." Pacek sounded as though it was indeed a pleasure.

Beltur did notice more than a half score of scabbards and blades fastened behind the saddle of one trooper. No wonder the undercaptain was pleased.

Once the troopers began to re-form, Kaerylt then turned his mount and motioned for Beltur to ride beside him as they began to retrace the route they had taken.

"If you wanted them to attack," Beltur asked his uncle, now that they were well away from Sydon's earshot, "why were you so upset that Sydon tried to use chaos on those herders the other day?"

"Because I needed them to actually attack you two—or me. You half rescued the situation by turning his chaos-blast into a warning. That also meant that we've had to stay here days longer than I would have preferred."

"Why did you want them to attack?"

"Because I tried to make it attractive to them. Let's leave it at that for now. You'll see as matters develop."

Beltur certainly hoped so, because nothing seemed very clear at the moment, and much as he wanted to ask just how his uncle had made the attack "attractive" he knew that asking when Kaerylt had said not to would only anger his uncle without Beltur learning anything.

"You're pale," added the older mage. "Drink some

water and eat that chunk of bread you took from the table."

While he rode the next kay, Beltur did just that. When he finished the last crumbs, he still felt tired, but the light-headedness had vanished.

Little more than a glass later, as they neared Kasiera, Beltur could see smoke rising from several places in the town, as well as from spots in the grasslands adjoining the tilled plots along the stream.

"They attacked Kasiera," said Beltur. "Why? Everyone here thought that wouldn't happen."

"Apparently, they were mistaken," replied Kaerylt calmly, as if he considered the attack a matter of course.

"You *knew* this would happen, didn't you?"

"It would have happened sooner or later. After what we've done, I considered it likely. Obviously, we won't be stopping here tonight."

"You knew that as well, didn't you?"

"You'll learn that some things become obvious in certain circumstances."

That was another of his uncle's cryptic utterances that Beltur let pass. As he studied the town, he saw a rider heading toward them. "Here comes someone."

"Most likely the elder. This won't take long." Kaerylt didn't rein up until he was within a few yards of the single rider, who waited in the middle of the dirt road.

"Why didn't you leave us alone?" demanded the gray-haired and green-eyed man in a voice tightly controlled, but still bearing ill-concealed anger.

"We did. You offered nothing in the way of information, and we offered nothing in the way of protection," replied Kaerylt.

"They fired the grasslands to threaten the harvest. Then they attacked." The elder's voice was bitter. "We lost men, and we lost daughters. This was your doing, ser mage, and may you reap the rewards you deserve for this evil."

"We have done nothing but ride and inspect the grasslands. We've been attacked by the raiders, as you have. In no case did we begin hostilities."

"It was still your doing. By your very presence you have led them to attack us. We had reached a hard-earned agreement with them."

"Your agreement meant that you supplied the raiders with enough food and other goods to enable them to raid other towns farther inside Gallos. You let others pay the cost for your agreement."

"What choice did we have? Your prefect never protected us."

"You've failed to pay tariffs for years. Why should he risk troopers for you?"

"He offers nothing but words."

Kaerylt shrugged. "You had a choice. You made it, and you paid for it."

"You will pay as well. You are not welcome in Kasiera. Ever."

"We will be welcome when we choose. We choose not to be welcome today." Kaerylt's words were not cold, merely dismissive. "Now . . . I suggest you let us pass."

The gray-haired man turned his swaybacked mount and rode into the slightly lower grass, then watched as the Gallosians rode past and toward the narrow bridge.

Beltur did not speak again until they were a good kay northeast of Kasiera. "How did you know all that?"

"From what you reported, from what I saw, and from what the elder said the one time that I met him. It couldn't have been any other way."

Beltur had his doubts, and his expression must have revealed them.

"You saw Kasiera, and you saw almost a hundred well-armed raiders in one place or another. They are but a fraction of those on the grasslands. Kasiera did not choose to defend itself the way those in Arrat did. How else could they have avoided raids?"

How else indeed?

"Where are we headed now?"

"Back to visit some of the towns east of the great wash to see how much they have suffered from the raids. I'll need to report that to the Prefect when we return."

Beltur nodded. That, at least, made sense.

XII

Midday on threeday found the fourteen Gallosians on the road from Arrat to Paalsyra, the nearest hamlet south and east of Arrat and east of the great dry wash, a town Pacek described as smaller but slightly more welcoming than Kasiera, perhaps because it had a larger inn and a better public room. The road was still packed clay and dirt, but wider than the one from Desanyt to Kasiera, and clearly more traveled, although they encountered only a few wagons and a single Gallosian dispatch rider after leaving Arrat.

Beltur, quietly elated by the success of his new shields, kept working on their structure as he rode, trying to hold larger and stronger shields longer. He would have preferred to work more on developing better ways of using chaos as a weapon, given that his single use of an ordered chaos-bolt, while effective, had resulted in a definite backlash. That was something he hadn't anticipated, but, for obvious reasons, also something he couldn't discuss with Kaerylt.

His uncle was clearly lost in his own thoughts, or practicing some strange manipulation of chaos, apparently as an exercise, for much of the time.

Sydon didn't speak all that much, but again, while Beltur was resting from working on shields, he offered what he thought was a pleasant question. "Didn't you think the ale in Desanyt and Kasiera was a bit different?"

"Different? How about terrible? They must have fermented moldy grain, or worse. They couldn't have made it less drinkable."

"Wildgrass seeds, one of the servers told me.'

"Ugh . . . that's disgusting. Grass ale? I hope what they serve in Paalsyra is better."

"We'll have to see." Beltur decided not to tell Sydon that wheat and barley were also grasses. He had the feeling that Sydon apparently wasn't thinking all that much, but then, maybe he was doing the older mage a disservice, although with all the years he'd spent in his uncle's household, he had his doubts. *Except you keep a lot to yourself. Who wouldn't with Uncle's sharp words?*

Beltur was jolted out of his musing by Pacek's words.

"Ser! There are riders below that rise to the southeast. They look like raiders."

Beltur immediately looked to where Pacek pointed, trying to sense as well as see the raiders . . . and succeeding, with a clear feel for at least a score of riders—only a little more than a kay away. He should have sensed them earlier, he realized, but that was because he'd been thinking about other things, as had his uncle, apparently.

The raiders were still riding toward the Gallosians, obviously doubting that fourteen riders would prove a problem.

"Ser?" Pacek asked.

"We'll let them get a little closer," said Kaerylt. "They need to understand that the Prefect has long arms and a longer memory." He turned in the saddle. "Sydon, when I give the word, I'll take out one of the lead riders. Then you take the next. We'll alternate until they break off the attack. If they don't, once they start to loose arrows, Beltur can shield us all—he's proved he can do that—while we take down the rest."

"Yes, ser."

Beltur could see that not all the raiders were moving toward the Gallosians. Several of the horses being held back bore two riders, and one rider in each case was a woman dressed in cloth garments, rather than the leathers of the raiders. He called out to Kaerylt, "Those who are riding double—"

"They've likely captives, but they're staying back. So we don't have to worry about that. Just concentrate on holding your shield."

That really wasn't an answer, but Beltur understood that the immediate problem was dealing with the oncoming attack.

"Rein up," said Kaerylt. "We'll let them come to us. That way, it will be clear that they're attacking."

Beltur reined up and watched as the raiders continued to approach, carrying bows and moving at a fast trot, just as the other raiders had.

This time, when the raiders raised their bows and let fly the first volley of arrows, Beltur raised his shield, recalling just how soon those shafts arrived. At the same time, Kaerylt let fly with a chaos-bolt that took down one of the lead riders. Sydon followed with a second, and Kaerylt incinerated a third rider before the first arrows clattered off Beltur's order-linked shields.

Sydon's second chaos-bolt dropped another rider, and when Kaerylt struck a fifth, all the raiders turned and raced away from the Gallosians. Several more arrows rebounded from Beltur's shield, which he continued holding until he was certain that all the raiders were well away.

"They got that message quick," declared Pacek.

". . . be a lot easier . . . had mages all the time," came a low-voiced comment from somewhere behind Beltur and Sydon.

"Be glad you got 'em now . . ."

That brought a quick and wry smile from Beltur before he thought about the riders who had not been part of the attack and asked, "What about their captives?"

"There are still close to a score of raiders left, if not more," replied Kaerylt, "and they know the land. We don't, and trying to track them down wouldn't be the best idea . . ."

"No, ser, it wouldn't," interjected Pacek quickly. "They set traps and ambushes in the high grass."

Traps might be a problem, reflected Beltur, but since he and Kaerylt could sense where raiders were hiding . . .

"That's good to know," Kaerylt said quickly. "It seems it would be best if we just proceeded to Paalsyra."

"I'd suggest it, ser," replied Pacek.

Outnumbered and in no real position to object, Beltur closed his mouth.

"Beltur . . . see if you can sense any concentrated chaos that may have caught fire."

"Yes, ser."

"Ser mage, since the raiders are all out of sight, I'd like to have the men search the dead."

"If they can make it quick. The raiders could return, and we can't protect the troopers if they're scattered."

"Yes, ser. We understand."

After carefully sensing the surrounding grasslands, Beltur could only find two places where the free chaos of the firebolts remained, and it didn't take him that long, or that much effort to quell the small patches with order-lattices, something he wouldn't have considered eightdays before. After that, he watched as the troopers quickly looted the bodies of the dead raiders, then returned to the road and reported to Pacek, who collected all the coins and valuables, while the men strapped blades behind their saddles. Beltur wouldn't have been surprised if a few small items, such as rings, never made it into the spoils pouch.

When all the troopers were back in formation, Pacek rode to Kaerylt. "I'll provide your shares once we're in Paalsyra, ser. We likely won't be able to sell the blades anywhere but in either Fenard or Kyphrien, but you'll get your shares. You mages more than earned them."

Beltur had no doubts that Kaerylt would be paid. What Beltur's and Sydon's shares would be was another question. Then again, any share of the loot would be welcome, and it was far more likely that Pacek could obtain a decent price for the blades than could any of the mages.

Kaerylt nodded. "While the shares will be welcome, you and your men have also earned them. I do hope we don't have to earn any more, not because the shares wouldn't be appreciated, but because that would indicate far more unrest in the grasslands than the Prefect would prefer, and he might even think that we created that unrest to personally profit."

"Yes, ser." Pacek nodded.

"Carry on, Undercaptain."

Sydon and Beltur again fell in on their mounts behind Pacek and Kaerylt.

Beltur realized that he'd never really considered battles or skirmishes as a way to better oneself. "How much do you think a trooper's share is worth?" he asked Sydon quietly.

"There's likely not more than a few silvers' worth of coppers so far. The blades are another matter. A good blade costs as much as a gold. Even a poor but serviceable one will run three or four silvers."

"But used blades . . ."

"I'm talking used blades, Beltur. A blade forged custom will cost three times that."

"Oh . . ." Beltur swallowed. "I knew they were costly."

"And then some," replied Sydon.

"Thank you." Beltur had seen the looted blades fastened behind saddles, possibly as many as thirty after the two attacks where the troopers had gathered spoils, not surprisingly, given that the raiders each seemed to carry two. Thirty blades at an average of even seven silvers . . . that was twenty-one golds. Beltur was lucky to see a silver now and again. It brought a whole new meaning to the words "spoils of war." It also suggested why the raiders were so willing to attack armed men.

Almost another glass passed before Beltur realized that he was a little tired, but not nearly so worn out as he had been after using order and chaos at the beginning of the journey. His uncle was certainly doing better, but then, Kaerylt had been practicing almost as much as Beltur, which was likely the reason he hadn't noticed how Beltur was using order. Then again, Kaerylt had always been interested in results . . . so long as Beltur didn't overtly flout his orders.

Another two glasses passed with no sign of other travelers, or of more raiders. Shortly after that, when the Gallosians crossed another of the gentle rises that also seemed unending, Beltur saw a considerable change in the terrain ahead. Instead of apparently endless grasslands, there were only patches of grass, and far more of what looked to be forests, if set on lower ground, and squares of fields with varying crops. There were,

Beltur noted, no dwellings near those fields, although
he could see a village perhaps five kays to the southeast.
He could also see lines of smoke rising into the sky and
a haze blanketing the village.

"That's Paalsyra," announced Pacek. "Looks like
that's where those raiders were before they ran into us."

The haze turned out to be smoke that became ever
more acrid as Beltur and the others neared Paalsyra.
While smoke continued to rise from a number of burned
houses, he did not see any actual flames as they rode
past the small cots beyond the edge of the hamlet proper,
three of which were little more than heaps of charred
wood.

When they reached the main square and reined up
in front of the inn, two solidly built men stepped forward.

"You arrived too late, great undercaptain," declared
the taller of the two men, addressing Pacek and then
gesturing to his right in the general direction of the
smoldering ruins of what had been a small dwelling.

Beltur could tell that the speaker would like to have
said more, likely along the lines of the Prefect's troopers should have arrived far earlier, when they could have
been of some assistance.

Pacek gestured to Kaerylt. "He'll explain."

"We arrived when we did because we had to deal
with a raider attack in Kasiera," replied Kaerylt evenly.
"We've been riding for four days. We encountered your
raiders earlier today. We killed a good half score, but
most were too far away for us to get to them before
they were where we could not reach them."

Beltur managed not to react to his uncle's overstate-
ment and kept his eyes on the two men.

"A few raiders. What will that do? They breed like
coneys."

"We killed far more than a few outside of Kasiera.

We also learned the reason why towns away from the grasslands have been raided more often." Kaerylt paused, enough that both men leaned forward slightly, waiting. "Kasiera made an agreement with the raiders to trade with them, more favorably I would judge, in return for the raiders not attacking them."

"Sounds about right for them." The calmly bitter words came from the slightly shorter and grayer man. "What did you do about that?"

"Left the town to the mercy of the raiders," replied Kaerylt. "They've never paid tariffs to the Prefect."

"Then what were you doing there?"

"Tracking the raiders who were shadowing us and who tried an earlier ambush," continued Kaerylt.

"What good did that do? Didn't help us much, and we pay tariffs."

"The raiders are much more likely to return to raiding places like Kasiera," Kaerylt pointed out, "especially since they know we're here."

"Just fourteen of you?" asked the taller and younger man.

"Eskar . . . three of them . . . they're mages . . . the white tunics . . ."

The younger man swallowed. "I'm not seeing so well as I should. The fire and smoke . . ."

"We've been dealing with fires all day," added the older man. "It's hard on the eyes."

Although Beltur could see the redness of Eskar's face, and the smudges of charcoal and soot, he wondered if the smoke had really been that bad. Or was the man just so upset for some other reason that he hadn't even noticed the mages when he'd addressed Pacek?

"We regret that we could not arrive sooner, or that we are not more numerous, but the Prefect sent us as a first step to determine what might be done to deal with the problems caused by the raiders and how best to stop their acts . . . and the loss of your women to both the raiders and the dark ones of Westwind."

"One's as bad as the other," replied the older man, adding quickly, "Right now the raiders are worse."

"Always be worse," countered Eskar.

"Is the inn open?" asked Kaerylt.

"I imagine so," said the older man, "but you'd have to ask Jarath. He's the owner."

From that point on, matters settled into the routine that wasn't entirely to Beltur's liking, with him handling the three mounts while his uncle dealt with the inn-keeper and Sydon carried gear and did whatever else Kaerylt asked of him. All told, almost two glasses passed before the three entered the public room, which held only a handful of patrons, and took a corner table.

The first things Beltur noticed after sitting down were that the very first serving girl he saw was younger than any he'd seen since leaving Fenard, possibly even his own age, that she was blond and moderately attractive, that her blouse had a modest scoop neck and three-quarter-length sleeves, and that she was not wearing a dirk.

"Much better scenery here," observed Sydon, following Beltur's glance.

Beltur couldn't help but notice that the server's eyes lingered on Sydon, not that such surprised him, not with Sydon's height, jet-black hair, solid features, and blue eyes so intense that every woman or girl seemed to fixate on them, at least until they got to know Sydon better.

"Just leave the scenery alone," said Kaerylt.

Within moments, the blond server was beside their table. "What might you mages like?"

"Dark ale," offered Kaerylt. "What's the fare?"

"We have seasoned mutton stew or a beef pie."

"Seasoned meaning lots of chilies?" asked Sydon with a winning smile.

"Yes, ser." The server's smile was definitely warm.

"The beef pie with the dark ale," said Kaerylt.

"The same," added Sydon.

"I'll try amber ale, if you have it, with the stew." Beltur couldn't honestly have said what prompted him to try the stew, except that he didn't want to be seen as merely going along.

"Thank you. That will be nine coppers."

As she walked toward the kitchen, Beltur glanced at the other server, who had just appeared, perhaps ten years older than the first, but attired in a similar fashion, and also not wearing a dirk. He also noticed an older graying woman sitting at a table with two older men, the first time he'd seen a woman patron in a public room since leaving Fenard. "No dirks," he offered in a low voice.

"These aren't really the grasslands," replied Kaerylt.

"Then why are we here?" asked Sydon.

"We've seen enough of the grasslands for our purposes. All the hamlets will be like Kasiera, or worse, and we'd simply end up killing more raiders."

"Is there anything wrong with that?" Sydon's words were somewhere between matter-of-fact and sardonic.

"If we kill too many, that won't help the weavers, and the price of wool will go up, and when prices go up, people get unhappy, and that makes the Prefect unhappy."

"Seems like everything makes him unhappy," observed Sydon.

"A great deal does," replied Kaerylt equitably. "That's why I'd prefer we not do things to increase his unhappiness."

Beltur didn't nod, but his uncle's words about the

Prefect made sense to him. What didn't make sense was
the way his uncle had handled the raiders, given what
he had told Beltur their task was. There had been no
attempt, from what Beltur could tell, to use magery to
persuade women not to go to the Westhorns, and from
what Beltur had seen and heard, most women didn't
seem all that inclined to do so.

Kaerylt looked as though he might say something
to Beltur, but Beltur was immediately spared that attention by the return of the young server with three
heavy mugs.

"Two dark and one amber. I'll collect when I bring
your food." After another almost inviting smile at Sydon, she turned and headed back toward the kitchen.

"Don't leer, Sydon. It's unbecoming, especially for a
mage."

"I wasn't leering, ser, just appreciating."

"You don't seem to know the difference."

Rather than reply, Sydon lifted his mug and took a
small swallow. "Better than Kasiera. Still not great."

No one spoke for a moment, and by the time that
Kaerylt had sampled his ale, the server returned with
their food.

While Kaerylt paid her, Beltur looked first at the
browned crust on the top of the sections of beef pie
served to both his uncle and Sydon and then at the
reddish gray liquid inundating the meat, potatoes, and
other root vegetables comprising his bowl of stew, wondering if he'd made a very bad mistake. He glanced at
the small and warm loaf of bread that accompanied the
stew. At least that would be edible. Gingerly, he took
the large spoon and dipped it into the stew, bringing up
a chunk of meat and a fragment of something else, then
eased them into his mouth.

He would have laughed if he hadn't had a mouthful.
The stew was but mildly spiced, at least compared to

what he had been eating much of the time, and quite tasty. He took another mouthful, and yet another, interspersed occasionally with bites of bread, until the bowl was almost empty. Then he used what was left of the bread to sop up the remainder of the stew.

Managing not to grin, he sipped the remainder of his ale—still a form of grass ale, he thought—as he watched Kaerylt and Sydon struggle through the apparently tough and greasy beef pie and a thick crust that was almost inedible.

For once you made the better choice. He contented himself with that thought as he sipped the last of the amber ale.

XIII

Beltur woke up with a start, immediately sensing that Sydon was not in the tiny chamber that they shared. Disoriented as Beltur was, he had no idea exactly what glass it might be, except that it was likely well before midnight, since he was feeling groggy. But where was Sydon, and what was he doing?

The serving girl! Sydon must have slipped away after Beltur had drifted off to sleep.

At that moment, the door opened, remained open for a moment, then closed. Even in the darkness, Beltur could sense the other mage. Then Sydon's shadowy form appeared as he released a concealment and immediately slid the latch bolt.

"What . . ." mumbled Beltur.

"I've been here all along," hissed Sydon. "Just remember that."

Beltur didn't reply, being more concerned with the heavy footsteps outside on the wooden floor of the hall, footsteps that halted outside their door, then, after several moments, retreated.

"I didn't think he'd dare," murmured Sydon.

"Who?"

"The innkeeper. How was I to know that the girl was his daughter?"

"Now what have you done?" hissed Beltur.

"Not enough to get us in trouble . . . or much trouble."

"Us? I didn't exactly have anything to do with this."

"No, you didn't. You're too orderly to enjoy life."

"What does making trouble have to do with enjoying life?"

"I enjoy life. So should you. Let other people make the trouble," replied Sydon complacently, sitting on the narrow bed and pulling off his boots, then his tunic. In moments, he was stretched out. "Get some sleep."

For a time, long after Sydon had dropped into slumber, Beltur just lay there, wondering how Sydon could do what he'd done so casually and then immediately fall asleep. He shook his head, still thinking. Finally, he also felt his eyes growing heavy and closed them.

The second time Beltur awoke, it was out of an uneasy dream in which he was trying to untie an elaborate knot made out of an iron chain in order to get into a room where he would be safe from some threat he could not identify. What awakened him—and Sydon—was the pounding on the door and Kaerylt's voice. "Wake up, and open this door!"

Beltur got to the door first and let his uncle in.

Kaerylt strode past Beltur and glared down at Sydon, who was struggling to sit up. "I told you to stay away from the women." Kaerylt's voice was as cold as Beltur had ever heard it. "What do you have to say for your-self?"

"I stayed away from her, but she didn't want to stay away from me."

I didn't hear her slipping in here last night, thought Beltur.

"That excuse grew old more than a year ago. We're trying to find out about why women are leaving their families and consorts to go to Westwind, and you're giving them yet another reason? How do you think the Prefect would feel if he found out?"

"Ser . . . I didn't do more than kiss and embrace her."

"Only because her father arrived. Didn't you think about why such an attractive young woman was serv-ing at an inn? Did it not even cross your mind that most who work in the inns are related to the owner?" Kaerylt delivered each word in a witheringly scathing tone.

"I thought that if she was interested—"

"What she felt should never interfere with what I told you. Ever!"

Beltur winced as he felt the chaos gathering around his uncle.

Even Sydon paled. "I'm sorry, ser. I didn't mean any harm."

"What you *meant* and what you almost did are two entirely different matters. If you disobey my instruc-tions one more time, you will find yourself on your own and walking back to Fenard . . . or to any other place you deem more satisfactory."

Sydon actually gulped, Beltur saw.

"Now, both of you get dressed. We have a great deal to do, and little time in which to accomplish it."

Beltur managed to conceal his puzzlement. His uncle had not even hinted that they were limited by time.

"After we eat, we'll be leaving and riding to Buoranyt. That's a slightly larger town a day's ride south. It's the closest town to the great dry wash." Kaerylt turned. "I'll wait in the hall."

In less than a quarter glass, Beltur and Sydon were again sitting in the public room, being attended to by the older server. The younger blonde was nowhere in sight. Beltur had the amber lager and the egged ham-cakes. Kaerylt and Sydon opted for fried egg toast and dark ale.

Once Kaerylt had finished his breakfast, except for what remained of his ale, he cleared his throat. "A dispatch rider arrived late last night. We only have three days to do what we can before we begin our return to Fenard."

"From the Prefect?" asked Beltur.

"From Arms-Mage Wyath on behalf of the Prefect."

"Did he say why?" asked Sydon.

"Neither the Prefect nor Wyath is in the habit of explaining," said Kaerylt dryly. "I suspect that events have preempted our task."

"Do you think the Viscount has done something?" asked Beltur.

"That's possible. Other things are possible. I'm not inclined to speculate, especially where the Prefect is concerned."

What his uncle left unsaid implied that the summons to return to Fenard was the result of something unforeseen, and that the unforeseen was seldom good, especially where the Prefect was concerned.

XIV

When everyone was mounted up in the inn yard early on fiveday, Kaerylt addressed the riders. "Buoranyt's not a full day's ride from here. Not by the direct road. We're going the longer way on a back road so that I can report on the great dry wash. The Prefect wants to know if it's as impassable as the locals claim . . . and also whether the raiders have a camp within it."

"It's rather long, I thought," offered Beltur.

"Something over twenty kays," replied Kaerylt. "We'll do the best we can with the time we have." He gestured to Pacek, and the two began to ride out into the square.

Beltur and Sydon followed, as did the troopers behind them. Pacek and Kaerylt took the main road southeast for slightly more than a kay before turning onto a much narrower way, a dusty track barely wide enough for a single wagon or two riders abreast that led west-southwest. Beltur could immediately see hoofprints on the road, much more than he would have expected on a side road. Although they were heading in the same direction as the Gallosians, they were blurred, suggesting that the riders had not passed that way in the past day or so.

After studying the tracks for several hundred yards as he rode, Pacek announced, "Those are raider tracks . . . some of them came this way when they left Paalsyra."

"On their way to the wash?" Kaerylt's words were barely a question.

"It seems more likely than going this way to reach Buoranyt."

Beltur almost asked why the raiders had split their forces after attacking Paalsyra, but did not when he considered the captive women. Even if the local people were unable to attack whatever outpost the raiders might have in the wash, it wasn't likely to be a place where they'd want to bring women, for a number of reasons, including the fact that it would be easier for them to escape and make their way back to Paalsyra.

The surroundings of the back road didn't seem all that different from those around Paalsyra, with a mixture of fields and woodlots, even small forests, with some sections of grasslands, which became more prevalent by the time they had ridden some two glasses. A short while later they rode over the crest of a low rise and all that lay before them was grass, except that perhaps a kay farther ahead the grass became sparse, and what there was grew in the fissures of an expanse of crumbling and cracked red sandstone that stretched to each side both north and south as far as Beltur could see. Directly ahead, beyond the sandstone, there was . . . nothing . . . a wide gap of emptiness that extended more than a kay before it was bounded by the same red sandstone that bordered the west side of the great wash. Some fifty yards short of the edge, the road turned to the south, roughly parallel to the wash, although there looked to be a less traveled path heading north from where the road turned.

When Kaerylt reached the turn, he and Pacek reined up. Beltur and the others waited while the undercaptain studied the tracks in the road.

Finally, Pacek straightened in the saddle. "Most of the riders headed back north."

"Then we'd better take a look at the wash from here first," said Kaerylt, easing his mount forward toward the edge, reining up a good five yards back from where the ground dropped away.

Beltur followed, but stopped short of his uncle. While he could make out the far rim clearly, he couldn't see the bottom.

Kaerylt dismounted and handed his mount's reins to Sydon, then turned to Beltur. "Dismount and come with me."

Beltur did so, following his uncle toward the edge of the wash with a certain amount of trepidation, but grateful that Kaerylt angled his steps onto the middle of a solid-looking chunk of the red sandstone and stopped a yard back from the crumbled edge. From there, Beltur could see most of the bottom of the wash, some two hundred yards down, in his estimation. The side of the wash wasn't a sheer drop, but close to it, with the parts that were not sheer covered with reddish sand. In those places, red sandstone pillars jutted up from the steep slopes, as well as along the bottom of the wash near the sides. A dry streambed wound down the middle of the wash, and the only vegetation seemed to be sparse bushes here and there rising from the reddish sand and red stone boulders that seemed to cover the entire bottom of the canyon-like wash.

"There's no sign of a path or a road along the bottom," observed Kaerylt. "Not here, anyway. Can you sense anyone or any large animals?"

Beltur hadn't thought about that, and it was several moments before he replied. "Only some vulcrows, I think."

"That's all I could find, either." Kaerylt turned. "We'll keep heading south and see if we can find any traces of raiders along the way."

For the next three glasses, covering more than ten kays, Kaerylt and Beltur checked the wash, and found no sign of any large living creatures except vulcrows. Beltur was more than happy when Pacek announced they were less than a kay from the road back east to Buoranyt.

"It's clear that they don't have a camp or a hamlet in the middle of the wash," Kaerylt said as they turned onto the road away from the wash. "There's no sign of anything there, and no water." He shrugged. "There might be springs near the south end, but if there's a camp there, it wouldn't seem that hard for troopers to get to it. The north end is dry, according to you."

"Yes, ser. There is a problem with the sand, though," replied Pacek. "It's so fine that it would be hard on the horses to go far."

"Then it would be hard on the raiders' mounts, too, unless they have a path they take, and there should be traces of that."

"There might be." Pacek's tone was just short of grudging.

"We'll see what the next kay brings," said Kaerylt.

Over the next kay the bottom of the wash changed little from what they had seen before, except that the walls became slightly steeper.

Two glasses later, the riders neared Buoranyt, a town set in a low and wide valley largely surrounded by fields and orchards, a setting Beltur found so much of a change from the grasslands and the wash that it seemed most unlikely . . . except, from what he could see, it appeared that the same kind of terrain would have continued if he and the others had kept riding eastward. The other thing he noticed was that all the dwellings he saw were of fired brick, not mud brick, and the roofs of the dwellings were of a reddish tile.

Pacek led the way to the small main square, which was brick-paved. The inn located on its east side actually had a signboard with a green-leaved tree and the name Olive Inn, suggesting what the trees of the orchards might be. From there, the riders rode into the rear inn yard.

There, Kaerylt turned to the younger mages. "Sydon, you come with me. We'll settle matters with the innkeeper. Then you will deal with the gear and Beltur with the horses. It's early enough, not even fourth glass, for me to find the village elder or someone else who can tell me what I need to find out."

Beltur wasn't exactly surprised to find himself dealing with the horses once more. He was pleasantly surprised when Sydon returned to help him. Then they both carried the gear to the inn, putting Kaerylt's in one small chamber and their own in the adjoining room. They even had more than enough time to wash up and attend to other matters . . . and still wait for almost half a glass after that before Kaerylt returned and the three made their way to the inn's public room.

Both serving women in the public room were neither young nor old, and both were not unpleasant to the eye and dressed in a similar fashion to those in Paalsyra— and without obvious weapons. There were also several women sitting at tables with men.

Kaerylt made for the single corner table remaining and seated himself with his back to the wall. The shorter of the two servers was at their table within moments.

"Good evening, sers." Her eyes took in the three white tunics and widened slightly. "We don't see white mages here often."

"We don't get here often," replied Kaerylt pleasantly. "What is the fare? Is there anything you'd suggest?"

"There's a shepherd's pie tonight, mutton cutlets with boiled potatoes and milk gravy, or boiled cabbage and ham. I like the shepherd's pie. The pie and cutlets are two coppers, three with ale, and the cabbage is one, two with ale."

All three of them decided on the shepherd's pie. As they sat with their respective ales, waiting for their food, Kaerylt took a small swallow from his mug, then said, "We'll be starting back to Fenard in the morning."

"Don't we have another day?" asked Sydon.

"There's no point in taking it. You can see that Buoranyt's not like the other towns."

"Neither was Paalsyra," Sydon pointed out.

"True. I talked to one of the town councilors, and they've not had problems with raiders here. According to him, the towns south of the great wash continue to have difficulties, but it would take us three days more to get there."

"Why don't they have a problem here?" asked Beltur.

"They have a town militia, and they deploy scouts any time they get word that raiders are anywhere near."

"Why would that make a difference?" asked Sydon.

"They're ready to fight back at any time. Their houses are also sturdy, with brick walls and tile roofs. It's hard to set tile on fire. Over time, the raiders have learned that they'll lose more than they can gain."

Beltur frowned. "Why doesn't Paalsyra do something like that?"

"They can't afford it. Buoranyt makes enough in coin from all the olive groves to afford brick and mortar. There's not only sand around here, but lots of wood and limestone."

Beltur was having problems with what Kaerylt had said. He could certainly see that the growers could afford brick and tile, but even the small houses had been built of brick and tile.

"Beltur? You're looking puzzled." Kaerylt appeared amused.

"How do the poorer families afford brick and tile?"

"The growers pay for them."

"But why?" asked Sydon.

"I asked the councilor the same question. He's a grower, by the way. He said it was cheaper that way."

This time, Sydon was the one who looked puzzled.

"I don't claim to understand," said Kaerylt, "but he insisted that solid housing for everyone who worked made sense. They don't build houses like that for people who don't work for them, or for those who can afford them without help. He said that over ten years, everything worked out. Who am I to question their success?"

Beltur was still pondering that when the server returned with their food.

The shepherd's pie was tasty enough, with a heavy brown crust, tough, if edible, but Beltur had the feeling that the spiced mutton stew he'd had the night before had been slightly better. On the other hand, from the way Kaerylt and Sydon ate, it was clear the shepherd's pie was a great improvement from what they had eaten.

Just about the time the three finished eating, a pleasant-faced woman with a guitar took a seat on a high stool set between two stools on the east side of the public room and began to play and sing. Beltur turned slightly to look as well as listen.

"*Oh, black was the color of the night,*
as deep and dark as blinded sight
and false was he, as gray as sky,
Whose lightning bared his lie . . ."

While the singer strummed the guitar for a moment, Kaerylt said abruptly, "We need to leave early tomorrow. I'll see you then. Stay away from the women, any of them, Sydon." With that, he slipped away, visibly uncomfortable, it seemed to Beltur.

Was it the song . . . or the singer? Beltur concentrated on the singer and the words as she continued, and especially on the concluding stanza.

"Ask not the song to be sung,
or the bell to be rung,
or if my tale is done.
The answer is all—and none."

From what Beltur could tell, there was nothing especially unnatural about the words, except that he felt that there was the faintest hint, almost of order, a silvery black order, carried with each sung word, not that it bothered him in the slightest. The fact that the singer could carry it off rather intrigued him.

Moments after the singer finished, several men called out, "Another one."

Sydon looked to Beltur and said in a low voice, "One a bit more cheerful."

"You don't like reminders, do you?"

"You know . . . that was a bit harsh, Beltur. I've never done anything that a girl or woman didn't want."

At the moment you were seducing them, anyway.
"I'm sure you didn't."

"Aren't you the high-minded one."

"Hardly. I'm just not quite as low-minded as some others."

"You can't have it both ways. That means everyone will dislike and distrust you."

"You're saying that looking at both sides is dangerous and makes people distrust you?"

"Not looking," replied Sydon. "Talking about it and letting people know you don't like either side."

"That's a good thing to think about." While Beltur had his doubts, Sydon might be right, and there wasn't much point in continuing that discussion. Besides, he'd already missed the opening of the next song.

"When rich men find their golds a curse,
And Westwind's marshal fills your purse,

When traders try to spend each gold
To buy the songs that I've been told,
Then sea-hags will dance upon their hands
And dolphins swim through silver sands.
Hollicum-hoarem, billicum-borem . . ."

At the end of the song, Sydon nodded. "Much better." He pushed back his stool. "We'd better go if we're to be up as early as your uncle wants."

Although there was a definite truth in what Sydon said, Beltur had the feeling that avoiding his uncle's displeasure was not the only reason for Sydon's desire to leave. He said nothing until the two were back in their room. "What didn't you like about the singer? That she wasn't young and beautiful? She had a good voice."

"There was . . . just . . . just something that bothered me. I couldn't tell you what."

"About a singer? I've never seen you avoid a woman."

"Not her. The songs. Maybe the way she sang them. I don't know." Sydon shook his head, clearly unable to explain his discomfort.

As he undressed, Beltur couldn't help but wonder if that hint of silvery order behind the words had been what had discomfited both Sydon and his uncle. *Such a small amount of order?* He frowned, thinking it over. Then again, the structure of music had to be ordered, and if somehow the singer added more order . . . ?

He didn't have an answer, but it was something to think about, among many other things that had come up over the past eightdays.

XV

By second glass on twoday afternoon, Beltur could see
the great walls of Fenard, at least immediately after he
used his kerchief to blot away the dust and sweat from
his eyes. Although they were now more than two eightdays into harvest, if anything, the day felt hotter than
those of summer, and Beltur was too hot even to work
on his shields. Tellingly, Kaerylt hadn't mentioned the
need to practice, either, and he wasn't doing the intri-
cate chaos exercises he often ran through. Thinking
about their journey, Beltur shook his head. He really
couldn't see that they'd accomplished much except killing more than a score of raiders.

"Why are you looking so glum?" asked Sydon.
"We're almost home."

"I'm still trying to figure out what it was all about."
Beltur kept his voice low. "We've traveled for nearly
four eightdays—"

"Just barely three," countered Sydon.

". . . none of the elders or the locals seem to think
that any more women are leaving. Even Kasiera and
Paalsyra didn't have a problem until we showed up and
got the herders mad enough to attack us," finished Beltur quietly. "I don't see why Uncle agreed to undertake
this task."

"You still haven't figured that out?" Sydon's voice
was low but sarcastic. "You're the bright one, and you
haven't the faintest idea? Just who has the silvers? Who
is the only one who really needs white mages for anything important? Haven't you noticed how little lamb
or fowl we were eating in Fenard?"

"I did notice. But Uncle never said anything, and he won't let anyone see his ledgers."

"Do you think he wants to admit that he's short of silvers? Or that he was practically forced to do the Prefect's bidding?"

"But that doesn't make any sense, either. Why would the Prefect spend coins to send a mage to the grasslands to find out what the undercaptain and other troopers already knew?"

"Do you honestly think that the Prefect trusts anyone?"

"So he paid Uncle to confirm what he already knew?"

"What he *thought* he already knew."

Was that why Uncle didn't bother with spending another day in Analeria? Because he realized that spending more time would reveal nothing new? "I'm just glad we aren't the ones who have to deal with the Prefect."

"Sooner or later, every mage in Fenard has to deal with the Prefect, or with Arms-Mage Wyath." After the slightest hesitation, Sydon added, "That's what they say anyway."

"I'm in no hurry," replied Beltur dryly. He blotted his face again, particularly around his eyes.

The air was even hotter, as well as damp and sticky as the fourteen riders made their way along the road through the fields south of the outer gates. Beltur eased his mount forward, closer to his uncle, and finally asked, "What happens when we reach Fenard?"

"I'm to report immediately to the palace with the undercaptain. It's likely I'll have to tell the Prefect what we discovered. If we're fortunate, he won't be dissatisfied, and I'll get the rest of what he promised. If he's pleased, there might be more. If he's displeased, I'll be dismissed and likely won't get another commission . . . or not one I could afford to take."

"Such as?"

"Being a battle mage against the Certans. Or being sent to Sarronnyn to assist the Prefect's envoy there." Kaerylt shook his head. "That wouldn't be so bad if the land weren't ruled by women."

Beltur understood very well that his uncle didn't think women should rule or have any authority in anything, but he'd never been able to get a satisfactory answer as to why, other than a few words about how the most a woman should ever be in charge of was a household, and perhaps not even that, and so far as Beltur could determine, Kaerylt had never considered consorting. At the same time, he had no close male friends, either. After a long moment, he ventured, "You've certainly done what the Prefect asked, haven't you?"

"Doing what's asked is usually the easiest part. What leads to success is determining what else needs to be done and doing it without being asked and without it costing any more."

"You're worried about that, aren't you?"

"With the Prefect, a man would be foolish not to worry. That's all that I can say."

Beltur let his mount slow until he was again riding with Sydon. "He's really worried."

"Wise man."

Beltur was still thinking over what his uncle had said when they reached the outer south gates. The guards there looked at Pacek and then Kaerylt and waved the returning travelers through. Those at the inner gate barely looked at the fourteen riders after seeing Pacek and the white tunics. From the inner gate, Pacek led the way along the Avenue of Fenardre toward the Great Square. As always, at the sight of mounted troopers, the avenue cleared in front of the riders, if not without some resentful glances from teamsters. Beltur kept blotting his face. Inside the walls, the heat of the sun made the air even hotter than outside in the fields.

"It'll be good to get home," said Sydon.

"Didn't you hear? We're headed to the palace."

"We are?"

"That's what Uncle said." Beltur sometimes wondered how much Sydon listened to anything that didn't seem to deal directly with him.

"Then we're going to the palace. We'll still be home before sunset."

When the column reached the Great Square, Pacek guided the way around the square and onto the Boulevard of the Prefect toward the gates of the palace ten long blocks away.

As they neared the palace, Kaerylt turned in the saddle and said, "We're headed to the stables. Once we're there, Beltur, Sydon, you two unload our gear while I report to the Prefect's arms-mage. You can leave the horses for the palace ostlers to groom. Just wait at the front of the stables for me."

Rather than entering by the main gates, Pacek turned north on the Avenue of the First and continued to a much smaller and far less ornate iron gate a block away, where the riders entered the paved stable yard. Kaerylt immediately dismounted, and Pacek escorted him in the direction of a door on the north side of the massive building that was the Palace of the Prefect.

Dismounting and unloading the gear took the two only a fraction of a glass. Then Beltur and Sydon stood in the shade just inside the stable doors with all three duffels stacked against the wall beside them. The troopers soon vanished, carrying their gear and leaving Beltur and Sydon. Every so often one of the gate guards looked in their direction, as if to see if they were still there.

"It's taking an awfully long time," observed Beltur when close to half a glass had passed.

"Everything dealing with the Prefect takes time. That's what I've heard from Kaerylt more than once."

"But he ordered us to return quickly."

"That doesn't mean he'll see Kaerylt quickly."

Beltur had to admit that Sydon had a point, but as the glass stretched out, he couldn't help but worry. More than another half glass passed before Beltur caught sight of his uncle walking toward them through the late afternoon shadows cast by the palace walls. No one was with him.

When Kaerylt reached them, he looked to the stacked duffels and said, "I see you're ready to go."

"What happened, ser?" asked Beltur.

"Nothing. I had to wait to see Wyath. We are to attend the Prefect at ninth glass tomorrow morning. At that time, we are to report on what we discovered about the herders and raiders and the towns bordering the grasslands."

"We? All of us?" asked Sydon, clearly surprised.

"All three of us. Undercaptain Pacek is already reporting to the Prefect's arms-commander." Kaerylt's voice carried tiredness, or resignation, as he lifted his duffel and started toward the iron gate. "We might as well head home. We can eat at the yellow bucket after we stow our gear."

Not even a wagon to cart us back? Over something like fifteen blocks? "That's all the Prefect said?"

"I didn't see the Prefect. Arms-Mage Wyath was quick to point out that we were not expected until threeday or fourday, and ninth glass tomorrow was the first time the Prefect could see us . . . and that meant another meeting would be delayed."

Beltur took a deep breath and slung his duffel over his shoulder, as did Sydon, and the two followed Kaerylt along the Avenue of the First north toward Middle Street. That way was slightly longer than going through the Great Square, but Beltur could see why his uncle didn't wish to go that way. A white mage, even more so three white mages, walking and carrying duffels through the Great Square suggested a certain lack of dignity, possibly even disgrace. Fewer people would notice on the avenue.

XVI

The three mages left the dwelling on Nothing Lane at eighth glass, not wanting to hurry, especially since three-day morning was every bit as hot as twoday morning had been. Beltur had been up earlier than the others, not only shaving and washing himself thoroughly, but managing to make a simple porridge breakfast from what was left in the comparative cool of the storage cellar. Even so, both Kaerylt and Sydon had grumbled.

Walking the fifteen blocks was easier without carrying gear, but Beltur was soon blotting his face, and that became almost continuous by the time they neared the palace, slightly after half before the glass. The guards merely nodded to the three white mages as Kaerylt led the way through the same iron gate through which they had entered the day before. Beltur and Sydon followed him to the side door where two guards in their black uniforms and leathers were posted.

"The Prefect requested our appearance at ninth glass."

The outside guards allowed them inside, into a stone-walled hallway that was far cooler than the courtyard, and Kaerylt walked to the grizzled squad leader sitting behind a table desk some four yards down the corridor.

"Ser mage, you're early."

"The last thing I'd wish to do is to displease the Prefect by being late," replied Kaerylt.

"Something to be said for that." The older trooper nodded. "You'll have to wait here until a page comes to escort you to the audience chamber."

"We can do that." Kaerylt stepped back and turned to the other two. "At least it's cooler here. The good thing about having a meeting early is that there's less chance that the Prefect will be delayed."

Almost a quarter of a glass passed in the gloomy hallway before an angular and graying white mage walked toward the squad leader and then past the table desk.

"Arms-Mage Wyath would like to see Mage Sydon." The older mage inclined his head, if slightly, to Kaerylt.

"I thought the three of us were to have an audience with the Prefect," said Kaerylt.

"The Prefect has determined that is not necessary. One of your assistants should provide enough details for his purposes. The Arms-Mage has certain . . . concerns . . . about Mage Sydon. He would like to discuss them with him."

Sydon swallowed.

Beltur covertly sensed the mage, trying to see if there was any hint of deception behind the words. He had the feeling that the mage was not telling the entire truth.

Kaerylt looked to Sydon. "Go on. We'll meet here afterward." After speaking, he returned his attention to the older mage. "Unless Arms-Mage Wyath plans a lengthy conversation with Sydon."

"He did not inform me about what he has in mind."

"It would have been helpful," said Kaerylt almost mildly.

"I'm sorry I can't oblige you, Kaerylt."

"You never have, as I recall, Naeron."

Naeron gestured to Sydon, who shrugged as if to indicate there was nothing else he could do, and then left with the angular mage.

"That's not good for Sydon, is it?" murmured Beltur.

"It's either not good for him, or worse for us," replied Kaerylt in an even lower voice. "We'll just have to see."

"Why do you think that?"

"Now's not the time or place to discuss it."

Beltur considered that Naeron had not offered anything that seemed to be an outright lie, and was about to say that when a thin page appeared, a youth almost as tall as Beltur and clad in a gray tunic and trousers with black piping.

"Honored mages, the Prefect will see you."

The two followed the page past the table desk for another twenty yards or so to a circular chamber, then took a stone staircase up two flights and through a heavy oak door out into a wide corridor, lit by high clerestory windows. Hung on each side of the corridor were paintings, life-sized images of men that Beltur supposed were portraits of past prefects. Polished gold marble tiles comprised the floor of the empty corridor, in which every bootstep echoed as they walked toward the shining brass-bound doors of the audience chamber. Two tall and muscular guards in the same gray and black as the page flanked the doors. Neither seemed to look at the page and the two mages when the page stopped two yards back from the doors.

"You are to wait here. When the doors open, walk to the foot of the dais and bow. Then wait for His Mightiness to speak." After those words, the page turned and disappeared through a side door, one that Beltur had not even noticed.

After a time, a single chime echoed along the corridor, and the double doors opened inward, revealing a high-ceilinged chamber beyond that stretched some twenty yards from the doors to the foot of the dais. Unlike the corridor, the floor tiles were of a polished reddish marble, through which ran faint golden lines.

Beltur was so stunned that he had to take three quick steps to catch up with his uncle. Then he matched steps as they walked to the foot of the dais and bowed.

"You are prompt. I grant you that, Kaerylt," boomed out the voice of Denardre the Great, for like all prefects of Gallos since his ancestor, Fenardre the Great, he retained the suffix of past grandeur, not that Gallos had declined into insignificance in the ensuing years. His glare was scarcely lessened by the good five yards from where Kaerylt and Beltur stood below the dais to the Great Chair that might as well have been called a throne, had custom not forbidden that appellation. The Prefect wore no crown, nor any jewelry except a massive gold band on the ring finger of his right hand. His formal tunic was of black velvet, with gold piping, and his trousers and shimmering boots were black.

From what Beltur could see and sense, Denardre was older than Beltur and younger than Kaerylt, with pale blond hair above a fair-skinned face that was wide and square-jawed. His eyes were watery green, and they fixed on Kaerylt. Standing on each side of the Prefect, if on the dais with their heads barely level with the Prefect's knees, were two white mages, neither of whom Beltur had ever seen.

"You summoned us." Kaerylt's voice was matter-of-fact. "We are here."

"So you are. Tell me what, if anything, of import that you discovered while you lived off my silvers."

"We traveled, as you requested, from Arrat to Desanyt to Kasiera . . ." Kaerylt quickly summarized their travels and the attacks by the raiding herders, then went on, "You told me you received word that the Marshal of Westwind was acting to entice women to leave the herders and that the loss of women caused them to attack the towns east of the great wash to raid for other women. What we discovered was that Arrat has developed a system that makes it near-impossible for such raids to be successful, as has Buoranyt. Kasiera came to an agreement with the raiders to supply them with goods in return for not being attacked. I can only surmise that, when the raiders became aware of our presence, they believed that we had discovered that agreement, and they attacked us and the town, believing the town had betrayed them. Then they went on to attack and raid women from Paalsyra. No one knows anything about the Marshal of Westwind enticing women."

"You mean they did not tell you anything."

"No, Your Mightiness. They know nothing. I can tell, as can most mages, when I am being lied to or when people do not tell me everything."

"Then why would I receive such reports?"

"I cannot speak to that, Your Mightiness. I can only report what we did and what we observed."

"Then it was because of your actions that the raiders attacked both Kasiera and Paalsyra, was it not?"

"That is far from certain. We took no action. We only observed and asked a few questions."

"If you were so circumspect, Mage, tell me how else these attacks occurred," demanded Denardre.

The blond-and-silver-haired Kaerylt inclined his head. "The raiders saw Gallosian troopers and Gallosian mages. They feared that their extortion of goods from the local people would be revealed. They attacked."

"A simple explanation for a simple people. Yes, that must be it." Denardre nodded, then added cheerfully, "You may go, Kaerylt, and you as well, young Beltur.

You've told me all that I need to know. Arms-Mage Wyath awaits you in the adjoining chamber." Denardre gestured to his right.

Beltur didn't trust either the Prefect's warm tone of voice or his smiling green eyes, not that he could have said why. *And he never asked you anything, yet you were required to be here.* That bothered Beltur, more than a little, although he couldn't say why. So did the fact that he hadn't detected any lies in the Prefect's words, although he had the feeling that Denardre had not said all he might have . . . as if something were being withheld.

"As you command, Your Mightiness." Kaerylt bowed, took two steps back from where he stood at the base of the dais, then motioned to Beltur to accompany him as he turned toward the left and walked toward the modest door set in the wall.

Without looking, Beltur could sense that the two white mages took the steps down from the dais and were beginning to follow them.

Without so much as looking at Beltur, Kaerylt said in a very low voice, "When we step through that door leaving the audience chamber, raise the closest, but strongest shields you can manage, and be ready with an immediate concealment. We may find the Prefect's archers waiting with iron shafts, as well as Wyath and his strongest subordinates. They may underestimate your strength and abilities, as I did."

"But . . . why . . ."

"Explanations can wait. Promise me one thing. If we are attacked, do not think about me. I can hold my own. I can't do it if I'm worrying about you, or trying to shield you as well. Use your shields and escape any way that you can while they are concentrating on me. Do you understand?"

"Yes, ser," murmured Beltur, seeing that they were within yards of the side door.

"Do not hesitate. You must escape and tell others what happened. Your mother would never forgive me if you didn't."

Beltur couldn't help wincing at those words.

As he stepped through the door pushed open by a footman just before they reached it, he saw that they were entering a small passageway with another closed door just ahead, and he immediately created an order-linked diamond shield that was mere digits from his body. Then the door in front of them opened. For a moment, because he was also sensing the two mages behind them, blocking any retreat, all Beltur could see was another high-ceilinged chamber with a black marble floor—a totally empty chamber . . . to the eye. At that instant, he sensed a line of archers behind a concealment less than fifteen yards away, and possibly six other mages. Then the concealment vanished, and arrows flew toward Beltur and his uncle.

Kaerylt flung himself sideways while shielding himself and throwing a line of chaos-fire across the front of the archers, fire that didn't reach them, doubtless because the handful of mages to one side were shielding them.

Beltur raised a concealment in addition to his shields and darted toward the side of the room away from Kaerylt. Even so he could feel the impact of several chaos-bolts on his shield. Seeing the mages before them focus on Kaerylt, Beltur looked back to discover that the second door was ajar. He immediately dropped to his hands and knees and scuttled toward that door. As he did, he saw one of Kaerylt's chaos-bolts strike an overhead beam, in two widely separated places, once and then again. The heavy beam shivered, and a large section broke free and fell toward the mages and one end of the line of archers.

"Overhead shields!" ordered someone.

A chaos-bolt from Kaerylt seared through one mage, and a second took down another.

Beltur forced himself to use that confusion to scurry into the small hallway, closing the door behind him, although he could sense the chaos-bolts going everywhere beyond the closed door.

Now what? The only place he could go was back into the audience chamber, but if he didn't move . . . in moments someone would be after him.

Still holding the concealment, Beltur eased the door open a crack, then pushed it gently, hoping to create the impression that the latch had not caught. As soon as it was wide enough for him to slip out, he did, flattening himself against the wall, just before Denardre's voice boomed out, "Close that door!"

Beltur darted around the footman and began to ease his way along the side wall of the large chamber, and then along the front wall toward the main doors, trying to make each step as silent as possible. He wondered where the other mages had gone—or had they taken another way to join those attacking his uncle?

He was within a few yards of the main doors when they opened, and two men, not mages, but men whose very beings were surrounded with chaos, entered. Beltur hurried to the doors, slipping through and brushing one of the guards.

"I told you to keep clear of me," hissed the one Beltur had brushed. "Won't have the squad leader dressing me down for smudges and soil."

"Didn't touch you," hissed back the second.

Beltur kept moving, as swiftly as he could, knowing that if any strong mage appeared, he could easily sense Beltur. It seemed like he spent glasses worming his way out of the palace and then across the courtyard and through the gates. By then he was drenched in sweat. His smallclothes were soaked; and he was shaking.

Where can you go that they won't find you? Beltur knew that there was no way for him to return to the dwelling on Nothing Lane. Wyath's stronger mages would certainly be there before he could get there . . . and even if he did get there before them, he risked being trapped there.

The black quarter! If he could keep free chaos away from himself and only use order, then Wyath's minions wouldn't recognize him anywhere—because few had ever seen him, simply because his uncle had never brought him to see the Arms-Mage. Even his examiners had been white mages who were not beholden to the Arms-Mage and the Prefect.

As he slowly walked toward the Great Square, because the number of bodies there would certainly make it hard for anyone to pick him out just through sensing, one stark thought struck Beltur. His uncle had sacrificed himself. He had known that he would not survive, and he had flung chaos everywhere to cover Beltur's escape . . . hoping that Wyath's minions would believe that they had turned both Beltur and Kaerylt to ashes with all the power that had filled the side hall.

Beltur kept walking. *He sacrificed himself.* That thought kept pounding at him.

After a time came another question. Why had Fenardre—or Wyath, or both—wanted them dead? And was Sydon dead as well . . . or had he somehow been a tool of Wyath and the Prefect? How could Beltur find out without revealing that he was still alive?

First, though, he had to find somewhere safe and then get out of Fenard and eventually out of Gallos. He had to escape, or his uncle's death would have been for

nothing. That meant someone he could trust . . . and
that left out the handful of white mages he knew, because none of those Beltur knew could stand against the
power Wyath's mages had unleashed against Beltur and
Kaerylt. Although black mages wouldn't be as likely to
support Wyath, that didn't mean some wouldn't, and
more to the point, Beltur didn't know any. Healers were
blacks of a sort, and they couldn't stay healers if they
used chaos, but how much could he trust Margrena and
Jessyla? That is, if he could even find them. He only
had a general description of where they lived.

But they were the only ones he could think of. Jessyla
had seemed very honest and very orderly, and with a
mother as a healer, it was doubtful that they'd turn on
him. Whether they would be much help was another
question.

The Great Square was crowded, as it always was
during harvest, and he threaded his way amid the
people, finally dropping the concealment and just trying to sense either white mages or ordermages amid
the throng. But he could find no trace of either, although there was a fair amount of natural chaos swirling about. That gave him another thought. *Could you
push away the chaos? Or leave it on the outside of a
shell of mostly order?*

That was harder than it sounded. In fact, for all of
his efforts, he wasn't sure anything had changed by the
time he turned down Joiners Lane, the first way past
Nothing Lane, because he wasn't about to go past his
uncle's dwelling, not where a mage might be waiting
and able to sense him. As he walked by the shops of the
various cabinet and furniture makers, his eyes took in
several of the display pieces, in particular a simple chair,
crafted out of black wood, that seemed to embody
graceful strength . . . even order, but that order wasn't

raw free order with its somehow almost cold edges, but something integral to the chair.

He kept walking, thinking while still trying to be alert for anyone seeking him. Since his uncle's dwelling was four blocks west of the Great Square, and Jessyla had said that she lived eleven blocks away in the northeast, that meant the farthest she and her mother lived was fifteen blocks north from the square, but they could live eleven blocks east of his uncle's dwelling. He shook his head. He'd watched them walk at least two blocks farther north, and that meant the farthest east would be around nine blocks.

So far, no one had given him much more than a passing glance, and that was fine with him. While he hoped that Wyath thought he was dead, he doubted that he could count himself that fortunate.

Most of the houses and buildings in the black quarter were of old brick, likely salvaged from far older structures that had burned or been razed, yet the streets were well-swept and clean, certainly as well-swept as Nothing Lane, but then Beltur had been charged with keeping the sidewalk and street at the corner clean.

When he reached the corner ten blocks north of the square, he glanced around. There was nothing significantly different from any other block, but he had to start somewhere, and he didn't want to knock on doors or accost people on the streets. So he entered a small café that seemed almost empty, not surprisingly, given that it was late midmorning. As an older woman appeared, he said politely, "I'm trying to find a healer named Margrena . . ."

"Never heard of her, ser mage."

"Do you know anyone who might know?"

The woman shook her head.

Beltur walked north to the next corner, where he saw

a woman weaving straw hats for sale on her doorstep and asked the same question.

"I know of no healers near here. You might ask at the felter's shop a block east of here. If anyone might need a healer, he would."

Beltur followed that advice, although the felter was not in the shop, and the boy who was sweeping offered little assistance.

More than a glass later, some blocks east and north, he found a runner coming out of a shop that displayed bolts of all types of cloth. "You run this area a lot, I hope?"

"More than most, I'd say." The wiry young man looked at Beltur warily.

"I'm looking for a healer named Margrena who lives somewhere around here."

"Don't know her name, but there is a blond woman they say is a healer. Two blocks over on Coopersgate."

"Thank you." Beltur parted with one of the few coppers he had. Runners expected to be paid for information.

He headed in the direction the runner had pointed. It took almost another glass before he knocked on the plain brown oak door. The only suggestion that a healer might live there was the green paint that edged the brown first-floor shutters. He waited, glancing around and hoping that no white mages would appear.

No one answered.

He knocked again, harder and more insistently . . . and waited, wondering what he should do next if Margrena or Jessyla didn't answer. The only thing he could think of was to hide somewhere and wait. Surely, they'd have to come home at *some time*.

If you even have the right dwelling.

At that moment, the door opened slightly, then wider. Jessyla's mouth opened as she saw Beltur.

"Might I come in?"

"Why are you here? I thought you'd gone to Analeria."

"We did. We came back last night. The Prefect was less than pleased. Might I please come in?"

"I suppose so. Mother and Athaal will be back shortly."

"Good." When he said the words, Beltur wondered if it would be, but he was glad to get out of the sun . . . and off the streets where he could be more easily seen. He was so tired that he doubted he could hold a concealment for very long in any case.

As she closed the door, Jessyla frowned. "Are you all right? You look awful, and there's chaos dust all around you."

"I'm in trouble. We went to see the Prefect this morning at his request. When we left the audience chamber, Arms-Mage Wyath and the senior white mages attacked Uncle and me. They had archers with iron arrows, too. He told me to use my shield and escape and that . . . and that he couldn't fight them if he had to protect me, too. I didn't question him . . . but . . . it was . . . his way . . ." Beltur couldn't say any more. He just stood there mute, ashamed of the tears oozing from his eyes.

For a moment, Jessyla said nothing.

Neither did Beltur.

Then she said, "You're pale, and your eyes are pinkish. They're also twitching. Have you eaten lately?"

"Just some porridge early this morning."

"Come into the kitchen. You need something to eat and drink. When Mother and Athaal get back you can tell them the whole story."

The slightly stale bread and the hard cheese that Jessyla offered him were more than welcome, as was the mild ale.

As he sat on the stool and took a last sip of the small mug of ale, she said, "You look better. Much better."

"I feel better. Thank you so much for taking me in."

"You're not exactly a stray dog."

"At the moment, I might as well be. Uncle is dead, and Wyath might still be looking for me. There's no way I can go home. I can't risk the fact that someone might be watching."

"Can't whites do concealments?"

"Of course, but I can sense a concealment, and so can they."

At that moment, there was a rap on the front door.

"That should be Mother and Athaal." Jessyla rose from her stool.

"I thought he was from Elparta."

"He is. He'll be leaving next eightday. We won't see him for another year, most likely. You just stay here." Jessyla walked quickly from the kitchen.

Beltur just hoped that the knock was that of the healer and not a white mage, but as soon as the door opened, he could sense the solid blackness of two people.

After a short time, and a quick conversation Beltur could not hear, the two entered the kitchen, followed by Jessyla.

"Beltur, Jessyla tells us that Arms-Mage Wyath killed your uncle and that you escaped." Margrena paused, then gestured to the stocky man at her side. "Oh . . . this is Athaal."

Athaal wasn't at all what Beltur expected. Despite the fact that he was clearly less than ten years older than Beltur, he was already balding on the top of his head, although his black hair was thick at the sides, and he had a full black beard, if well-trimmed. He offered a concerned look, one not in conflict with the basic blackness of order that suffused him. "How did this all come to be?"

"I know what happened, but I still haven't the faintest idea why it happened. It certainly wasn't something unplanned, not with all those white mages and archers with iron shafts waiting for us when we left the audience with the Prefect—"

"Stop there." Athaal smiled ruefully. "It might make more sense if you gave a quick history of what happened after you left Fenard. Margrena said that you and your uncle and his assistant Sydon were going to Analeria to do something for the Prefect."

"Yes, ser." The "ser" was unplanned, but it felt right.

"I'm no more a 'ser' than you are." Athaal looked to Margrena. "This will take some time. Would it be acceptable if we went into the parlor where we could all sit down?"

"Of course," replied the healer.

When Beltur stood to follow the others, he realized that he was still a little shaky, but the feeling seemed to pass after several steps.

The parlor wasn't all that large, perhaps four yards square, but there were a long backed bench with a pad on it and three straight-backed chairs, as well as several side tables. A braided rug with a design of green and brown was on the floor. There was a single wall lamp. Margrena and Athaal sat on opposite ends of the bench with perhaps a yard between them. Beltur took one of the chairs that faced the bench, and Jessyla took the chair to his right.

"Now," said the black mage, "go ahead and give us an idea of what led to what happened at the palace."

Beltur cleared his throat slightly and began. "Uncle said that we were to look into the reasons why women were leaving the raiders to go to Westwind and why that was causing more raids—except it wasn't like that at all." He shook his head and went on, "We left Fenard on the last threeday of summer . . ." From there he gave a quick recounting of what had happened on the journey until they returned to Fenard three eight-days later. ". . . when we got to the palace, Uncle went to see Wyath, and then he came back and told us we had to meet with the Prefect the next morning at ninth glass because we'd returned two days earlier than the Prefect had anticipated. We didn't even get to use the horses to carry our gear home. We had to lug it back on foot."

Both Margrena and Athaal frowned.

"What happened at the palace the next morning? Tell us everything, no matter how unimportant it seems."

Beltur did just that, finishing with, ". . . and once I got out of the palace I used a concealment until I reached the Great Square. I knew about where you lived"—he nodded to Margrena—"and I walked to the black quarter and kept asking until I found your house."

"It would have been better if you hadn't asked, but that can't be helped," said Athaal. "At least, no one saw you go from the palace to the Great Square. Now let me get several things clear. You don't know what happened to Sydon."

"No . . . I don't." Beltur almost said "ser" again.

"And you don't know if Wyath actually knows that you escaped? And you didn't sense anyone following or looking for you?"

"I didn't."

"That's good." Athaal nodded, then turned to Margrena. "They might have been trying to sense him, but he doesn't carry that much free chaos, and most whites have trouble sensing anything but chaos at any distance."

Beltur almost winced at Athaal's almost casual appraisal of his minimal ability in holding chaos, but simply asked, "Have you heard anything that might explain what happened to Uncle and me?"

Margrena and Athaal exchanged glances. Beltur noticed that Jessyla was watching them both intently.

Finally, Athaal spoke. "We've been hearing that the Prefect wants all the white mages under the control of his Arms-Mage. Until the last eightday, we had thought this was just a suggestion or a plan. One the healers and the blacks didn't like at all."

"Then in the last few days, after two white mages vanished," added the stocky blond healer, "several lesser white mages left Fenard hurriedly. Your uncle was the strongest of those who had opposed the idea of all the white mages obeying Wyath." She frowned. "Didn't he say anything about that to you?"

Beltur had to think a moment before he recalled what his uncle had said. "He said it would be good to get out of Fenard for a little while. He also said that Wyath was trying to persuade the Prefect to have more mages in the palace . . . and that he didn't want to be one of them because he'd have to bow all the time to Wyath. But he never said anything about opposing the Arms-Mage. He just didn't want to see him very often."

"Apparently, Wyath decided to make an example out of your uncle," said Athaal. "He might not even want to pursue you . . . so long as you don't say anything and don't remain in Fenard . . . although I wouldn't take that for granted, were I you."

"What good would saying anything do?" Both anger and despair colored Beltur's words . . . and probably his chaos-order balance as well. "But where could I go?"

Athaal offered a sympathetic smile. "You could come to Elparta with me. That's assuming you'd be interested in learning how to better handle order."

Go to Elparta with a black mage he didn't even know? Even one that his uncle had grudgingly approved of . . . at least in a backhanded way. Beltur wasn't sure what to say . . . or do. *But Uncle is dead . . . just like that.*

"Better handle?" questioned Margrena.

"He's already been using far more order than any white I've run across." Athaal looked to Beltur. "Haven't you?"

"It was the only way I could come up with strong enough shields when we were being attacked by raiders. I got the idea from Jessyla. She said something about order being better to handle chaos."

"I don't know about 'better,'" replied Athaal. "Using order to manipulate chaos is certainly better for the health of the mage, but usually a strong chaos-mage can create more unfocused destruction with minimal use of order."

"More order is always better," declared Jessyla firmly.

"From our point of view," said Athaal. "Wyath doesn't agree. He's killing or driving out any white mages who question him or dispute his authority. Once he does that, he'll start on black mages."

"Why didn't he start by going after black mages first?" asked Margrena.

"Because he's cunning. Most black mages don't and can't use power in destructive ways, but they often have better shields. There are also fewer of them because it takes more time and effort to master order, and the benefits aren't as obvious. If he starts by consolidating his power over the whites, then many blacks will leave of their own accord. Several already have, you've told me."

Thinking about his efforts to use order to project chaos, Beltur found himself nodding.

"Is that nod because you agree with what I said?" asked Athaal. "Or because you're considering accompanying me to Elparta?"

"Ah . . . both, I think. Uncle did say you were one of the better blacks . . ."

Athaal laughed. "Only in having a more tolerant attitude, I fear. There are quite a few others who are more powerful. That's one reason why Elparta suits me." He paused. "Before I agree to take you with me, and you make a final decision to accompany me, we need to go over a few things."

"I don't know that I'm suited to being a black mage," Beltur said.

"You may not be. But if you learn more about handling order you can't help but become a more effective mage."

"You wouldn't try to make me black . . ."

Athaal shook his head. "We have to be what we can be. The only question is whether we'll work to be the best at what we are, rather than trying to be something we aren't."

Beltur was still thinking that over when Athaal spoke again.

"I will insist that you try certain techniques just to see if they might prove useful. I also want your personal word that you will not use chaos against anyone or any living thing except in self-defense or in defense of others."

As he thought about what Athaal had requested, Beltur realized the second condition wasn't even difficult. "In fact, the only time I've used chaos that way was when we were attacked. Even Uncle . . . so far as I know . . . he didn't either." Beltur swallowed.

"That doesn't surprise me," said Margrena. "Your uncle was a good man."

"Even if he looked down on women," added Jessyla.

Margrena gave her daughter a hard glance.

"I'm sorry."

Beltur could tell what Jessyla wanted to say but

didn't. "What she said was true. I don't know why. He never talked about it." *And I never asked.*

"Sometimes, there's a time for truth, and sometimes it can be saved for later," said Margrena, her eyes and words aimed directly at her daughter.

Athaal nodded, but did not comment.

"Do you really want to go with Athaal?" asked Margrena.

"I think staying in Fenard would be dangerous and stupid," replied Beltur. "Also . . ." He swallowed again. "Uncle's last words were . . . he wanted me to escape. Staying here . . ." He shook his head because, for a moment, words wouldn't come.

Athaal looked at Margrena. "I think we should leave tomorrow. I know . . ."

"You'd planned to stay longer, but it would be better for both of you to leave Fenard as soon as you can."

"What about you and Jessyla?" asked the black mage. "After what happened to Beltur's uncle . . ."

"I've been making plans. I was thinking that . . . Kleth is a pleasant place, isn't it? Grenara wrote me that it is."

After a slight pause, Athaal asked, "How soon?"

"We were going to wait until you left anyway, and there are a few things I need to finish. We could leave by next fiveday or sixday, not this one. Hogarth has said we could accompany one of his wagons to the river at Maeryl. They leave every sixday, and most people go to Portalya because it's closer."

"The Prefect may not wish to lose healers," cautioned Athaal.

"We'll go to the herbalist and meet the wagons well beyond the outer gates. What about you?"

"I'm an assistant mage in Elparta for the Spidlarian Council. I have a safe-conduct. For now, anyway. Beltur looks young enough to be my apprentice." Athaal grinned. "You will have to wear dark gray, though."

"I can manage that." In truth, Beltur wasn't certain he really ever wanted to wear a white tunic again, not after what had happened in the Prefect's palace.

"Good." Athaal stood. "If we're to leave tomorrow, I need to change the arrangements, and that will take the rest of the day. I might not be back until sixth or seventh glass." He looked to Margrena. "If you could see about a gray tunic and trousers for Beltur . . . and staining those boots gray or anything but white."

"We'll come up with something," affirmed Margrena.

As he sat there, Beltur almost couldn't believe what he was hearing—two healers and a black mage working to get him safely out of Fenard, and, if it worked, to change his entire life.

He still couldn't quite believe that Wyath and his mages had killed his uncle. *Or that he's dead.*

XVII

Beltur woke up with a start, and for a moment everything ached, and he had no idea where he might be. Then he realized that he had been sleeping on the floor in Margrena's parlor, lying on the bench pad that the healer had placed there. She had insisted that he stretch out, that he needed to rest. The fact that he'd dropped off to sleep so quickly suggested she had been right. He also realized, again, that his uncle was really dead.

For a moment, he felt like he couldn't breathe. Then he sat up slowly.

Almost immediately Jessyla appeared, coming through the archway from the tiny front hall, presumably from the room on the other side. "How are you feeling?"

"A little stiff and sore." Beltur stood, then lifted the bench pad and replaced it on the bench before sitting there.

"It's been a day for you."

That was so much of an understatement that Beltur was silent for several moments. He'd lost his uncle, his only living relative, as well as the place that he'd called home for over ten years. The Prefect of Gallos and the Arms-Mage wanted him dead, and to survive he was going to have to go to a strange city with a black mage he'd just met. Finally, he managed a rueful smile. "That's one way of putting it."

"You're really not that calm."

How did she expect him to act? He managed a shrug.

"I understand, Beltur. You don't have to say anything."

Margrena appeared in the archway that led to the kitchen. "Athaal should be back before long. I have some clothes here. We'll see what we can do to make you look like a black apprentice." She extended a dark gray tunic. "Try this on."

As Beltur pulled off the white tunic he became well aware of just how rancid it smelled, and probably himself as well. "I really should wash up before trying on things."

"Already spoken like a black," murmured Jessyla.

Margrena darted a sharp look at her daughter. "There's a fresh pitcher of wash water at the corner table in the kitchen. You can use the towel and cloth there. We don't have a razor, though. Jessyla and I will be in the bedroom going over a few matters. Just leave the white tunic on one of the wall pegs."

"Thank you." Beltur carried his tunic into the kitchen

and hung it on the peg closest to the wash table, then proceeded to wash up as thoroughly as he could, at least from the waist up, before drying himself.

The parlor was empty when he returned, but he immediately tried on the dark gray tunic, which fit well enough, although it was a shade looser than his own had been.

"That fits well enough," observed Margrena when she returned. "Try on the trousers as well." With that she turned and left.

The trousers were a bit larger in the waist, but not enough to worry about, especially after Beltur tightened his belt.

Jessyla reappeared first. "You look better in darker colors."

"I'm glad you think so. It might take some getting used to. I've worn white for the past several years."

"You'll find it suits you, I think."

"Anything that keeps a person healthy suits one," said Margrena wryly from behind her daughter. "You do look better in the gray. We'll need to do something about those white boots, though. I'd like to try something. I've got some oak gall ink, but it won't stick well to tanned leather. I was wondering if you might try doing something with order and seeing if you can put the ink into the leather if I spread it on top."

"I've never done anything like that. I can try."

"Maybe if I put a dab on the top edge . . . You'd better take your boots off, though, and we'd best go to the worktable in the kitchen."

Beltur pulled off his boots and followed the healer.

Once they were at the table, Margrena poured a small amount of the black ink into a bowl, then took a smooth and narrow wooden rod tipped with a bit of wool and touched it to the ink, transferring the ink to the top edge of Beltur's left boot where he had put it on the table. Even that small amount just sat on top of the oiled leather that was really, if Beltur had to admit it, a slightly yellowed white.

The first thing he tried was to sense the leather, something he'd never attempted. That really didn't tell him much except that the oil had formed almost a fine net over the order of the leather itself. Still . . . what if he tried to open or widen the net? But how? He couldn't use chaos. That would just destroy the net. And he'd never tried to use order to move anything.

No matter what he tried, that didn't seem to work.

What about lifting the whole oil net just a bit and letting the ink spread under it?

After three or four, perhaps even five attempts, abruptly the ink droplet seemed to flatten and then spread, covering an irregular space roughly three digits by three.

"I think you've done it," said Margrena. "I hope we have enough ink."

"You could dilute it a bit," said Beltur. "Where I spread it is still black."

Margrena did so, and, bit by bit, they dyed Beltur's boots a shade of gray slightly lighter than the tunic and trousers . . . except for the first black spot that Beltur had created. It also took more than a glass, and when they finished, Beltur was surprised to see Athaal standing just inside the kitchen. He also had a slight headache.

"You were just using order," said the black mage.

"Chaos would have weakened the leather."

"You actually strengthened it a little, it seems."

"Why don't you two go into the parlor," suggested Margrena. "We need to prepare some things to go with the ham that Athaal kindly brought for dinner. That is, if you don't want to wait until ninth glass to eat."

Beltur hadn't actually thought about food, but he immediately followed Athaal through the archway and into the parlor.

"The grays make you look younger, and that's for the best." Athaal took one of the chairs.

Beltur took one of the other chairs and turned it to face Athaal before sitting down.

"When you arrived earlier today, it looked like you'd tried to discard the chaos around you. Did you?"

"Did it show that much?"

"Only because I know you practiced chaos magery."

"You think I'm as much a black as a white, don't you?"

"I don't know what you are. Not yet. I do know that you're really not a white. You were handling small bits of order in the kitchen without any trouble. You could be a black, or you might be a gray."

"It left me with a bit of a headache," pointed out Beltur.

"That's more likely because you haven't had much to eat and you're not used to working with just order alone. Initially, it takes more concentration."

"I'm not a white? A gray mage? The worst of both?"

"Is that what your uncle said?"

"A few times."

Athaal sighed. "Most whites and, indeed, most blacks worry about and fear gray mages. They both have reasons. Some are good reasons. Most are not."

"Should I avoid being a gray mage?"

"I cannot say whether you will be black or gray. Not yet. What I can say is that you will never be a powerful white mage and that if you continue on the white path, you will die young. You already suspect that."

"Why do you say that?"

"Raise a shield first, the strongest that you can."

Beltur felt apprehensive about doing so, but Athaal

certainly didn't seem as though he wished Beltur harm . . . and what harm could come from a shield?

Athaal did something—it felt as though a shaft of order touched the shield—and asked, "What do you feel?"

"That you're using order to probe my shield."

"I'm going to use a bit more force."

Again, Beltur could feel an impact, but certainly not with the force with which all the raider arrows had struck his last shield in Analeria.

"You can drop the shield."

Beltur waited to see what the black mage would say.

"Your shield is one of the stronger ones, and it's almost all order. Can you put one shield around yourself and hold a totally separate one around something else?"

"I'll have to see. I've never tried that."

"It can come in useful for restraining cutpurses or dealing with malefactors without causing them harm. But you have to be careful. So you want to try? Put a shield around that empty chair and hold one around yourself."

Why not? "I'll see what I can do." Beltur concentrated. The shield around himself came even more easily, and, after several moments, he found that he had managed a circular shield around the chair.

He could feel Athaal's probes were equally strong against both shields, and he had the feeling that a really strong blow against the second shield would hurt just as much as one against his own personal shield.

"You can drop them." Athaal frowned momentarily. "That's not bad, but you need to practice that more. It took you too long to get the second shield in place."

For a moment, Beltur wondered why Athaal was so concerned. Then he realized that, since blacks didn't use chaos-bolts, not that he knew, being able to use shields that way against people who might be a danger would be even more important to blacks.

"You mentioned concealments. Would you raise one?"

Beltur did so.

"Good. You can drop it."

"That was almost like yours, Athaal," said Jessyla from the archway. "In terms of order." She looked to Beltur and added quietly, "I did say you were more of a black than you thought."

"You could sense that?" asked Athaal.

"Mostly. I can feel order even more than Mother can. Chaos, too." She shuddered slightly.

"Chaos isn't evil," said Athaal. "Often destructive, but not evil."

"You don't think Wyath is evil?" asked Jessyla.

"You're confusing the tool with the user. You and your mother never thought Kaerylt was evil, but both Kaerylt and Wyath were whites."

"Wyath still is," corrected Jessyla, "and he's evil."

"That he is. Now . . . I need to keep working with Beltur. We don't have that much time, and I need to know more."

Jessyla retreated to the kitchen.

Athaal returned his gaze to Beltur. "In some ways, it will be easier for you to be considered black than I'd thought, but you're too accomplished to pass as the usual apprentice. I think I'll be saying that somehow you essentially trained yourself, and I've taken you on as an apprentice in order to help you improve your order skills." He smiled humorously. "That's even truer than saying you're just an apprentice so that I won't be lying or misstating. That will also help with the black council of Spidlar, should it come to that, although it probably won't."

"Do blacks have the same kind of examinations whites do before one can be truly called a black mage?"

"Not in the same formal way. Not in Spidlar. Two

black mages have to agree, but if another black objects, at least two more blacks have to support the determination of the first two. I think it's the same in Gallos, but there are so few blacks here that I'm not sure you could find four or five."

"I don't know any. Uncle said there weren't many here, and most were in Sarronnyn. He also mentioned you." Beltur paused. "Won't they notice the chaos around me?"

"We all have chaos and order around us. If you keep working with order, by the time we get to Elparta, you may not be showing that much more chaos than some blacks. You'll likely never be called the blackest of blacks, but I wouldn't wish that on anyone."

"You wouldn't?"

Athaal laughed softly. "Too much order can make a mage rigid in thought and act, just as you've seen how too much chaos can make a white mage far too destructive."

Beltur hadn't thought of it in that way.

"Now . . . while we're waiting for dinner, you need to tell me about yourself. If you're to pass as my apprentice, and for other reasons, I need to know more than you lived with your uncle. I'm not talking about magery, just what you remember about your family, where you grew up, who taught you your letters and numbers and the like."

That also made sense, even as the request made Beltur a little uneasy.

"I'm not asking for deep personal secrets, just what any good acquaintance ought to know."

Somehow that helped, and Beltur began, "I've spent my whole life in Fenard. I don't remember much about my mother except she had long blond hair, the same color as Uncle Kaerylt did, well . . . until his began to turn silver. I must have been six when she died. I don't know how, except I got the impression it was some kind of flux. Neither Father nor my uncle would ever talk about it. I was only nine when my father died of a flux. My uncle said it was so bad that even the healer couldn't save him. I don't think the healer was Margrena, but I don't recall . . ."

Athaal just listened as Beltur talked.

XVIII

Beltur did not sleep well. When he woke, lying on the bench pad on the floor in Margrena's small dwelling in the gray before dawn on fourday morning, he was again stiff . . . and worried. Was going to Elparta with an unknown black really a good idea? Yet with Wyath after him, what else could he do? If he went to Elparta, he would know someone, and he wouldn't know anyone anywhere else. His uncle . . .

Beltur swallowed at the thought of his uncle, even as he recalled how Kaerylt had said that Athaal was one of the better blacks, at least in terms of character.

He dressed quickly and made his way to the kitchen, where he found Margrena already with pots suspended over the coals in the hearth. The fact that the healer had no stove was another indication that she was not all that well off.

"Can I help?"

"Just sit down at the table. Jessyla's still sleeping. Or she was. Athaal went out to make sure that the wagon would be here at seventh glass."

"Wagon?" Beltur took a seat on one of the stools at the table.

"Much as we like to see Athaal, he came to buy certain goods that are hard to get in Elparta or much, much less expensive here. The wagon will carry them, and the two of you, to the River Gallos, where you'll get on a flatboat that will carry you downstream to Elparta."

"He mentioned the flatboat, but not the wagon, last night. I thought we might be riding to the river."

"Hiring horses costs almost as much as buying them, and you know how much use a mage has for horses in a city. There are always wagons for hire to go to the river and back."

"What sort of goods?"

"You'd have to ask him. Some things are for magery. Some he buys for others and makes a few coins on. The rest . . ." The healer shrugged.

"Can I ask why you and Athaal are being so good to me?"

"Because you have no one else, and it's the right thing to do. Also, your uncle, in his gruff and sardonic way, was often helpful and kind to us. You also have great promise, and it would be a shame to see it wasted. You also have been appreciative and undemanding."

"Also," added Athaal from the archway, "the loss of someone so talented would be a terrible waste."

"So talented? Me? A third-rate white?" *If that.*

"That's because you're not really a white. Trying to be something you're not always makes one weaker. As I told you last night, I don't know what you'll turn out to be, but you're definitely not a pure white, or really any sort of strong white. Your shields are very strong, as strong as any I've seen, but they're a dark gray that's almost black."

Beltur wondered why Athaal hadn't said that the day before. *Because he was still deciding whether to help?* "And you'd like it black?"

Athaal shook his head. "It would be weaker, not stronger, if you tried to make it all black."

"Even Athaal's shields aren't pure black," added Jessyla as she followed the black mage into the kitchen.

"For someone who's going to be a healer," said Beltur in an amused tone, "you seem to know a lot about black magery."

As Athaal seated himself across the kitchen table from Beltur, Jessyla started to say something, then closed her mouth. Finally, she said, "I'm not strong enough to be a good mage. In handling order, I mean. I can see it as well as Athaal does, but I can't make it do things, except little things."

"Oh . . ." Beltur immediately felt sorry for her. *To be able to sense and understand order and chaos . . . and to able to do very little with it . . .*

"Don't give me that look!" Jessyla snapped.

"I'm sorry. It's just that . . . I do understand. I really do."

Abruptly, Jessyla turned and strode from the kitchen.

"I didn't mean . . ." stammered Beltur.

"No," said Margrena gently, "it's obvious that you understood immediately . . . and completely. But she took that for pity, and she hates being pitied."

"That's another reason why she has to be a healer, isn't it?"

From where she worked at the hearth Margrena nodded. "She is already more accomplished than I am in some ways. Healing is all about the mastery of small bits of order and chaos within a person. There are few mages who are also healers, and few healers ever become mages." She set a pitcher on the table, then raised her voice. "Jessyla, we're ready to eat."

Several moments later, the younger healer eased back into the kitchen, and seated herself, then looked at Beltur. "I'm sorry. I didn't mean to be rude."

"I'm sorry also. I didn't mean to upset you."

"Now that we have that out of the way," interjected Margrena cheerfully, "could we get on with breakfast so that Athaal and Beltur can eat before the wagon gets here?"

Breakfast was hot porridge and hot bread, along with warm ham strips, left over from what Athaal had provided for dinner the evening before, along with a golden ale that was somewhat heavier than the amber Beltur usually preferred but far better than the dark brew of his uncle's preference.

Before all that long, Athaal led Beltur out toward a two-horse wagon that had pulled up outside, driven by a bearded man who looked to be about the same age as the mage. "Carmanos, this is my apprentice, Beltur. Beltur, Carmanos is one of the best teamsters in Gallos, and he actually prefers to work for a black mage."

Carmanos grinned. "Black mages pay fair. I never have to worry about being cheated. Also, don't need to hire a guard or two."

After that brief introduction, Athaal and Beltur went to a small storeroom at the back of the house, one seemingly filled from floor to ceiling with items. From there they carried bundles wrapped in rags and other forms of well-worn cloth out to the waiting wagon. There were also baskets and small bales. Beltur carried one particularly heavy long roll, long enough almost to extend from one end of the wagon bed to the other. "What is this?"

"That's a carpet. It's a design out of fashion here. I got it very cheaply. I know a trader who can sell it for a great deal more in Spidlaria."

"You trade as well as are a black mage?"

"Just like your uncle, I need to make a living. Helping healers doesn't pay well unless it's for someone wealthy, and there aren't that many people that well off in any town or city. So I do lots of things. We can talk about those on the way."

When the wagon was loaded, Athaal walked back to the stoop where Margrena and Jessyla stood.

Beltur hurried after him, but didn't hear Athaal's first words to the healer.

". . . a good four days to the river. If I hear anything, I'll send a message back with Carmanos. Promise me you won't stay here much longer."

"We'll do what we must, Athaal, just as you do."

"I know." The black mage offered a rueful chuckle. "That's what worries me."

"Just get the two of you to Elparta."

Athaal nodded.

Beltur stepped up and said, "I can't thank you enough for everything. I just wish I could give you something or do something in return."

"You can," replied Margrena. "Just help Athaal and help others when you can."

"I'll do my best."

"Good. Both of you take care," said Margrena warmly.

"Beltur," added Jessyla, "listen to Athaal. Don't be stubborn."

Beltur grinned at her. "With you telling me that, I wouldn't dare."

Athaal gave a cough that Beltur suspected was a muffled laugh, then said, "We need to be on our way."

As the two walked from the doorway of the small dwelling out to the wagon, Beltur offered, "If it would be better, I could just sit in the back of the wagon under a concealment."

"What if Wyath posts white mages at all the gates?" countered Athaal, stopping immediately, as if he didn't wish Carmanos to hear. "Last night you told me that only one would likely recognize you, if he is still alive.

Any white mage would sense a concealment. That concealment would identify you immediately. If it looks like there is a white mage at the north gate, I'll shift some free order over you. It won't last long, but it should hold up enough. Any white mage strong enough to pose a problem is going to have difficulty probing beneath an order cover. That's if he even thinks it's necessary. Also, most whites would think you a black, possibly what they would call a corrupt black, because your inner being is largely black."

"It is? Uncle never said anything about that."

"How could he? He wanted you to be white."

"But how did he believe I was a white if there's so much order there?"

"We all must have both order and chaos within us to survive. Surely, you have sensed that."

Ashamed as Beltur was to admit that he'd never probed or observed other mages that closely, he said nothing, just listened as Athaal went on. "Whites are not all chaos, and blacks are not all order. Also, it's harder for whites to delve into order, just as it is harder for blacks to delve into chaos." After an instant of silence, he said, "We do need to go. We can talk about this later." He motioned to the wagon bed. "There's a space there for you behind the seat. Once we're on the road outside of Fenard, we'll be doing a fair amount of walking. That makes it easier on the horses."

Beltur climbed up and sat on a narrow board seat, against the side of the wagon roughly behind Athaal. He had the feeling that walking might be more comfortable. He could only hope that if there happened to be a white mage at the north gate, it wasn't Sydon. He couldn't explain why, but he had the feeling that Sydon was alive and that Wyath had "summoned" him to keep him safe.

Yet Sydon had clearly been surprised. Or did Wyath

think he could bring Sydon to support him? There was so much Beltur didn't know. *And so much you may never know.*

Carmanos flicked the leads lightly, and the wagon began to move. He turned to Athaal. "What will the weather be like?"

"What is the weather always like in harvest? There are no clouds. So we will not see rain today, and not tomorrow. What I can tell you is what you can see."

"I see today. You see tomorrow," replied the teamster with a laugh.

Beltur had heard that some black mages could predict the weather and that some could even change it. Was Athaal one of those? He decided not to ask, not for the moment.

Not quite a half glass later, they neared the inner gate on the north side of Fenard. Despite the difficulty of sensing with all the buildings and structures, Beltur could sense that there was a white mage posted there, something he had never seen before in the city. That alone was enough to worry him, but as they neared the gate, he could tell that the mage was only moderately powerful—and not Sydon.

Carmanos followed another cart that the pair of guards waved through. Behind them, on a seat mounted on a tall framework shaded by a small awning, sat a black-haired white mage whom Beltur had never seen before.

"Stop the wagon!" called out the white.

"They do this all the time with me," murmured Athaal.

From what Beltur could sense, Athaal was telling the truth, and Beltur knew that lies disturbed blacks more than they did most whites.

"Are you from Fenard, ser mage?" asked the shorter guard, approaching Athaal.

"I'm from Elparta on business for the Council of Spidlar."

"Bring me his pass," called out the mage.

Athaal handed over the pass.

As Beltur waited for the mage to look at the documents, he forced himself not to raise a shield or do anything resembling magery.

"What is your business?" asked the white mage, his tone somewhere between scornful and dismissive.

"To obtain goods that are not readily available in Spidlar, such as the green glazes and the wool for the official tunics of the council."

Again, Athaal's statement was totally truthful, according to what Beltur could sense.

The mage handed the documents back to the guard, who walked them back to Athaal.

"Thank you," Athaal said politely.

The guard nodded and gestured for Carmanos to move on and clear the gate.

Even before the wagon began to move, the white mage called out, "When your council must send a black mage and an apprentice for supplies, that shows how little they trust their traders."

"I cannot speak for the Council," returned Athaal. "Each of us does what he must."

The white mage did not respond, and Beltur was careful not to look back, although he remained ready to lift his shield at the slightest hint of weapons or chaos.

The guards at the outer gates waved them through, but Beltur did not breathe easily until the wagon was several kays beyond them, just before Carmanos brought the team to a halt and Athaal vaulted off the wagon seat.

"Time for us to walk. We'll let Carmanos set the pace." Athaal smiled, as he gestured for the teamster to continue, then waited slightly for the wagon to pull ahead before beginning to walk. "That will also let you ask all those questions that must be swirling through your head. After that, it wouldn't hurt for you to practice multiple shields some more."

"I'm not the first you've gotten out of Fenard, am I?"

"No, and yes. You're not the first, but you are the first white-tinged mage. I wouldn't have done it, even with all the order potential you have, if Margrena hadn't told me it was a good idea."

"I scarcely know her, really, and I only met Jessyla once." Beltur hesitated, but kept walking. "I know I don't know very much, but I don't think it's going to be all that safe for either of them in Fenard before long."

"Why do you think that?"

"If Wyath doesn't want whites like Uncle . . ." Beltur shook his head. "Uncle was white. There was only what order there that had to be."

"I suspect that once he was very much like you. What one does with order and chaos in the present shapes the man he will become in the future. Still . . . your point is well-taken. Kaerylt would have most likely supported any reasonable measures suggested by the Arms-Mage. That does suggest that what Wyath has in mind is less than reasonable."

"But the Prefect is the ruler, not the Arms-Mage."

"That can often make such control easier. If Denardre does what Wyath wishes, does it matter who rules?"

Beltur could see that. "Might I ask why Margrena persuaded you to help me?"

"She didn't persuade me. She just asked me to see you and then decide."

"Why did you decide to help me?"

"I believe I answered that before," said Athaal with a slight laugh, "if not in detail. I'll just add that I have the feeling you'll do well in Elparta, and that your doing well will be anything but beneficial to Wyath and what he has in mind." Athaal held up a hand. "I can't explain the feeling, but even if that part is wrong, you certainly don't deserve what Wyath had in mind for you."

Beltur wasn't sure he knew much more, or that he'd find it out through questions. "Outside of the time in Analeria, I've never been far from Fenard. Would you tell me more about the trip and what I can expect along the way and in Elparta?"

"Well . . . if it doesn't rain, we'll walk and ride for four days, possibly five, depending on the horses, until we reach Portalya. We may be there for a day or an eightday before we load what's in the wagon on a flatboat . . ."

Beltur kept walking and listening.

XIX

By midday on sevenday, Beltur was tired of walking, talking, and even riding, and from what Athaal had said, they were only slightly more than halfway to Portalya. Fortunately, the weather had been slightly cooler than seasonal, with a few high clouds now and again, and that had meant that Beltur only had to blot his face occasionally, rather than continually, in order to keep his salty sweat out of his eyes. They encountered far more wagons heading to Fenard, all loaded, than Beltur would have thought, and only occasionally passed a heavy-laden one or one stopped to rest horses or oxen going in the same direction. Once they stopped to help a pair of teamsters replace a broken wheel. The only riders they saw were troopers carrying dispatches, always riding in pairs, and once there were three riders, but never just one.

Three or four times a day, Athaal drilled Beltur on raising two shields at once and on maintaining them, always cheerfully, but in a way that suggested that Beltur was going to need that ability. That also raised the question as to why his uncle hadn't really emphasized shields until Beltur had accompanied him to Analeria. *Because Uncle had never really wanted to expose you to danger?* Or for some other reason? Beltur knew he'd likely never know, and that bothered him, especially since he felt that there was so much he hadn't known about his uncle . . . and now . . . now he never would.

He swallowed.

As yet another pair of dispatch riders went by the two mages as they walked beside the wagon, Athaal said, "All the dispatches suggest that there may be trouble with Certis."

"Because the road to Portalya goes on to Passera, and that's the only real way to get to Jellico?"

"And because so many riders mean that some officer wants to keep the Prefect informed about a changing situation. Also, while it's also the fastest way to Hydlen or Lydiar, right now there's no trouble with them, unlike Certis."

"All Uncle said was that the Viscount was thinking about increasing tariffs coming into Certis." Beltur then added, "He also said that the Spidlarian Council was thinking about the same thing."

"They both are because Denardre already increased tariffs on goods entering Gallos."

"He didn't mention that. Or maybe I didn't hear that part."

"We often don't hear what is less pleasant, and sometimes we don't mention it, either. It has been known to happen."

Beltur nodded, and kept walking. "It does seem like this road goes on forever. I know it doesn't, but it seems that way."

"We would make better time if the road were better," announced Carmanos for at least the fourth time since they had left Fenard. "If they paved the roads the way they pave the streets of the city, everything would be so much faster."

"Who would do that?" asked Athaal with a wide grin up at Carmanos.

"Why not you mages? You can do wondrous things, they say."

"To quarry stone with magecraft requires a white mage. Black mages can make the stone last longer."

"Like so many things, it takes opposites, like a man and a woman, or a good mule takes a placid donkey and a spirited horse, or maybe a spirited donkey and a placid horse, I forget which . . ." Carmanos, who apparently never tired of talking, continued in that vein for some time before bringing the team to a halt at the top of a low ridge, below and beyond which stretched land that seemed as flat as the surface of a lake, dotted with patches of trees, tilled fields, pastures, and, not too far from the base of the ridge, a small town.

"That's Sluryn. There's a small inn there. We can stop and eat, and Carmanos can water the horses."

Beltur worried about that. All he had was the seven coppers he'd been carrying when he'd gone to the palace. Athaal had paid for both the meals they had eaten at inns so far, and Beltur hated to have to let the black mage pay for everything, but his coppers would only pay for one meal for two, if that.

"You look concerned," offered Athaal.

"You pay for everything."

"I can. You can't. I offered to help you, and you accepted. There are times when we all have to accept help, and times when we have to offer it."

"You didn't have to . . ."

"One of the old blacks said it best. 'The world would be a pretty sorry place if we only did what we had to.'"

"Who was that? One of the dark ones? Maybe Nylan?"

"No one as fearsome as that. He didn't give his name to many, and no one who knew it ever said it because the Prefect back then offered a hundred golds for his head. Centuries ago he built what he called a temple to order in Passera. The Prefect wrecked it. The ruins were still there when I was a boy. Wyath had them destroyed. It took four white mages three eightdays to get rid of the order that suffused the ground."

"I thought you said order couldn't be moved in large chunks."

"I did. It wasn't. People came to the ruins for peace and comfort. They found it, and in finding it, each added to the order already there."

"Could Wyath do something like that with chaos?"

"I have my doubts. Order likes order and tends to stay together. The more chaos there is in one place, the harder it is to keep it there. That's one reason why it seems like there's more free chaos in the world, because it tends to move around—unless it's gathered somehow."

"You mean by mages."

"That's just one way. The world itself must have a way of gathering or containing it, too, because sometimes mountains fountain lava and chaos, and geysers release boiling water, steam, and chaos."

"Geysers?" Beltur had never heard of them.

"They're places where boiling water and steam shoot up from the ground intermittently. The chaos causes it."

"That must take a great amount of chaos."

"I think I suggested that," replied Athaal humorously. Beltur offered a rueful grin in return.

XX

By the middle of oneday, Beltur was more than glad that they were nearing Portalya. Although Athaal insisted that they were within ten kays, the combination of the flat land, the hedgerows that lined the road, and the intermittent stands of tall oaks all blocked sight of anything more than a few kays away. Even when they passed the keystone simply inscribed PORTALYA—5K, and Athaal and Beltur climbed back onto the wagon, Beltur had his doubts.

A half glass later, the scattered cots and fields gave way to small dwellings, all of them wooden and roofed with something like thatch. Beltur also didn't see any walls around the rear of dwellings, or even rear terraces, just what looked like extensive gardens, some of which were neat and well-tended, and others of which looked as though whoever lived there had thrown seed or planted almost haphazardly.

"Welcome to Portalya, Mages," announced Carmanos cheerfully, "the garden town of the River Gallos. The soil is so fertile that anything grows, and seldom do even the poor go too hungry for too long." The teamster waited for a moment, then added sardonically, "They die quickly because all of Gallos and Spidlar buy the most excellent fruits and vegetables and leave little for the poor."

Beltur looked to Athaal.

"He's correct, unhappily."

After they had traveled perhaps half a kay into the town, the main road, although Beltur supposed it was a main street now, abruptly began to descend, very gradually, but definitely, and at the end of the street, possibly a kay away, Beltur caught sight of block-like structures.

"You can see the warehouses beside the inns on the riverfront square," said Athaal. "That's where merchanters or teamsters store goods when the river runs wild or when there are no flatboats available."

"Or when the prices are too low and the greedy ones wait for them to rise," added Carmanos.

"You're always so cheerful," said Athaal with a laugh.

"Calling a cactus a pearapple will only leave you with spines in your mouth."

"And calling a pearapple a cactus will leave you hungry," replied Athaal, still smiling.

As the wagon neared the warehouses, Beltur asked, "Do you have any idea whether there will be a flatboat leaving soon for Elparta?"

"At this time of year, there are always boats leaving. The question is whether they have space and how much it will cost."

"I thought you were on Council business."

"The Council is not like the Prefect. They pay for what they require. That means we have to pay. Since the Council doesn't like unnecessary spending, I'll be bargaining, and we may have to wait." Athaal turned on the wagon seat to Carmanos. "Just stop at the portmaster's post."

At the end of the street was a small brick-paved

square, its east side parallel to the river, with two inns situated on the north side, and a larger and more imposing one on the south side. Stretching out along the river behind the inns were the warehouses, rough-timbered two-story buildings with a simple grace but devoid of any ornamentation. A wide brick walkway extended from the square to the foot of a large pier, but some ten yards short of the pier was a rectangular timber building.

As Carmanos turned the wagon to bring it to a halt opposite the building, Athaal pointed to the south. "Over there past the warehouses is the slip for the ferry that carries wagons and goods."

Beltur studied the river. At most it was perhaps a hundred yards wide. "There's no bridge?"

"People say the river is too wide and too deep," offered Carmanos.

"Too wide and too deep to build a bridge easily," added Athaal. "There are bridges in Spidlar, where the river is wider and deeper. Good stone bridges. No Prefect has wanted to build one, but there are signs that there once was one a kay south of here in the oldest part of Portalya."

"Why don't they want to build another one?"

"It might be that the ferry is owned by a cousin of the Prefect. Or that the Prefect's tariff enumerators have their inspection post next to the ferry slip. You can't see the red brick building from here. Or it might be that the Prefect would prefer to use his golds for something else."

Once the wagon stopped, Athaal vaulted down from the seat. "I shouldn't be that long."

"I have heard that before, ser mage," declared Carmanos, the seriousness of his tone belied by the grin that followed.

"But I pay you if Whaaryl keeps me and you have to

wait." Athaal returned the grin with one of his own before turning and striding toward the timber building.

Beltur slowly looked around the square. It certainly wasn't a market square, because there were no vendors or peddlers in sight, but he did see men standing and talking on the covered front porches of the two smaller inns, if not before the more impressive one, with its white-painted siding and green shutters. From the square his eyes went to the long pier behind the portmaster's building, where two long flatboats were tied up, as well as some sort of sailing craft. Two men armed with blades stood on the pier above the flatboats.

Before long, Athaal returned and announced, "There's no one leaving in the next few glasses. That means no one will leave until tomorrow. There are three flatboats that *might* have space. Carmanos, if you would wait here while I see about that? Beltur, you stay here to protect the goods. If anyone tries to snatch anything, put a shield around them." Athaal paused. "You can do that, I hope."

Beltur understood what the black mage wasn't saying—that he wasn't to use chaos. "I can do a complete shield, but I've never done a small one around just one person."

"Just make it smaller."

"I can do that."

"Do what you can. You probably won't need to here in midafternoon, but as soon as I say that you will."

"By saying that," said Carmanos, "you undo what you have done."

"I hope so." Athaal surveyed the empty square and the three inns quickly before heading south on the brick-paved lane along the riverbank that joined the warehouses and the piers.

"Ser mage," said the teamster, "you are just one person. Have you not shielded yourself?"

"It's easier when you're inside the shield," Beltur replied. "I've never had the occasion to use a shield to
imprison someone." He glanced around the square, but
no one was within twenty yards of the wagon, and he
couldn't sense any concentrations of order or chaos
nearby, and only one pattern of order anywhere near,
which was to the south and had to be Athaal.

"You have never used this shield?" Carmanos looked
unbelieving. "A black mage?"

"Just for self-protection and protection of others." As
Beltur spoke, he could see the mischievous smile appearing on the teamster's face, and he realized that
Carmanos had played on his gullibility. He just shook
his head and smiled ruefully, immediately asking, "What
should I know about Portalya?"

"What is there to know? It is a town like many other
towns. It has good people, and it has those who are not
so good. You are a mage. You can tell."

Beltur shook his head. "I can tell if someone lies, or
isn't telling the whole truth. But telling the truth doesn't
mean that a man is good." He could recall Naeron, the
white mage who had summoned Sydon. The man had
not uttered anything untrue. For that matter, neither
had the Prefect, although, in hindsight, Beltur realized
that some of the Prefect's words could have been meant
in a different way than in which he had taken them. He
glanced around again, and his eyes lighted on a youth
in patched clothes moving along the side of the larger
of the two small inns . . . seemingly in the general direction of the wagon.

The youth looked up, saw Beltur studying him, and
immediately retreated. *Portalya might not be quite as
safe as Athaal suggested.*

"You looked at him, and he fled," Carmanos said. "It
is much better that way."

Not wanting to follow up on those words, Beltur asked, "What will you do after we unload?"

"I will drive the wagon home and get a good dinner and a good night's sleep."

"You live here in Portalya?"

"We are all growers in my family. We live two kays south of here. We are teamsters, too. When the crops are bad, or in the winter, some of us work more as teamsters."

"Besides trusting black mages, how do you know when to work and for whom?"

Carmanos smiled. "Whaaryl is my consort's cousin."

"Whaaryl? Is he the portmaster?"

"He is the portmaster's assistant. He is the one who does all the work. The portmaster is chosen by the Prefect. Surely, you do not expect a man of his stature to work." There was only a gentle hint of the sardonic in the teamster's last words, soft enough that no one besides Beltur could have seen or heard it.

"There are many of stature in Gallos these days," replied Beltur mildly, keeping a smile from his face and a certain bitterness from his words.

"I think I would rather be a grower and a teamster . . ." Carmanos broke off as he saw Athaal striding toward them.

"You've had no trouble, I see."

"One cutpurse looked at the wagon," said Carmanos. "Mage Beltur looked at him, and he decided to go elsewhere."

"Good for us, but perhaps not so good for someone else. We'll need you to move the wagon down to the second warehouse to the south. We have a flatboat for tomorrow, with space for our cargo, but there's other cargo that has to be loaded first. So we'll have to unload into a storage room and then reload in the morning."

Because the wagon was facing north, Beltur hopped out and joined Athaal while Carmanos turned the wagon. Then they walked beside it as he drove down the lane to the second warehouse, where Athaal guided Carmanos to the second doorway.

After pulling out a large iron key, Athaal opened the heavy lock and then the door, before returning to the wagon and taking a cloth-wrapped bundle handed to him by Carmanos.

Beltur took the next bundle, fabric of some sort, and followed Athaal into the warehouse chamber, setting the bundle down beside the one Athaal had unloaded. "Will everything be safe here?"

"The warehouse is bonded, and there are guards." Athaal smiled. "There are a few small protections I can add."

"Wards?"

"I'm not the best at that, but you'll see." He pointed to a stack of heavy-looking bales of wool. "We'll need to move those forward after we finish."

"How far away is the flatboat?" asked Beltur, thinking that they wouldn't have a wagon on twoday.

"It's at the pier just across the access lane from the warehouse. It's not that far, but Boraad has a hand-cart we can use." Athaal turned and headed back to the wagon.

Half a glass later, everything that had been in the wagon was in the warehouse, and the two mages started to move the bales of wool.

By the time Beltur and Athaal had carried and pushed the bales of wool into a wall that was a little taller than Beltur himself, Beltur was definitely feeling hungry and tired. Still, he couldn't complain. Unlike his uncle, Athaal worked even harder than Beltur, a comparison Beltur was reluctant to make. After all, his uncle was— had been—older than Athaal.

Athaal stood at the open door.

Beltur could sense a positioning of order, and a curtain-like shield just inside the heavy door. "What did you do?"

"It's a variation on a concealment. If someone enters the storage room, it's like they're inside the concealment."

"They can't see anything?"

Athaal nodded. "It's hard to take much when you can't see what you're looking for or where to find it, especially when all you can feel is a wall of wool." He closed the door, replaced the lock through the heavy iron hoops, and forced it closed. "That should do it." He turned and walked out to the wagon. There he pulled out a cloth bag from his tunic and extended it to Carmanos. "As agreed and promised."

The teamster inclined his head. "I thank you. You'll let Whaaryl know when you need me again?"

"I will."

"I can take you back to the square," offered Carmanos.

"It's in the wrong direction for you, and it's a short walk. Give my best to your family."

"I can do that."

Athaal lifted a small duffel from the wagon bed and stepped back as the teamster flicked the leads and the wagon moved away. Then he turned and said, "We need to get a room and some food."

"At one of the inns?"

"The Ferry House. That's the smallest. The rooms are small, but they're cleaner." Athaal began to walk.

Beltur matched steps with him. His feet hurt, not so much as they had on some days of the journey from Fenard, but he was glad that the square was only a few hundred yards away.

When Athaal stepped onto the inn porch, there was

the slightest pause in the conversation of the three men standing on one side of the door, and all three inclined their heads to the mage. Athaal nodded in return, as did Beltur. As the two stepped inside, Beltur caught a few words passing between the three.

". . . comes here, regular-like . . ."

". . . works for . . . Spidlarian Council . . ."

". . . might not be seeing him for a while then . . ."

The black mage walked several steps to the far side of the entry foyer.

"Mage Athaal. How long will you be staying this time?" asked the round-faced woman behind the counter barely a yard wide. Wisps of gray hair escaped from an otherwise tidy bun.

"Just tonight. For my apprentice as well."

The woman's eyes flicked to Beltur, then back to Athaal. "There's a double on the second floor. I can give it to you for four, the same as your usual."

"That will be fine." Athaal handed over the coppers. "What's the best fare tonight?"

"The river trout with pearapples and new potatoes."

"Thank you." Athaal's smile was warm, and the woman smiled in return.

Beltur just followed him up the narrow steps to the second level.

Once they were in the room—less than four yards by a little more than three—with two narrow beds, Athaal set the duffel on the foot of one and said, "Once we get to Elparta, we'll need to find you a razor. Bronze or cupridium, if we can find it."

Beltur couldn't help looking surprised.

"Some people look good with beards. You're already looking scruffy and sinister, not at all like a mage, and you don't need that."

Not at all like a mage? Had he ever really looked like a mage? Beltur wondered. His uncle, tall and blond, had

looked like a white mage. Athaal certainly looked like
a black mage. Beltur wasn't sure that he looked like any
kind of mage, or even a mage's apprentice. "That's fine
with me. I get a rash if I don't shave. Too much salty
sweat. I just didn't dare to go back to the house."

"Not going there was a very good idea. If you'd taken
anything, Wyath and his mages would know for certain
you're still alive."

"Carmanos is probably the only one I've met who
knows my name—except you, Margrena, and Jessyla."

"It's unlikely that Wyath or any of his mages will
be asking a grower teamster in Portalya about a white
mage in Fenard."

"I worry more about Margrena and Jessyla."

"If they leave when they plan they should be safe.
Right now, white mages who don't agree with Wyath are
in more danger."

"If there are any left by now," replied Beltur.

"There is that." Athaal paused. "We need to wash up
and eat. The river trout sounds good."

Beltur hoped it was. He'd almost never eaten fish.

XXI

Although Athaal snored, he snored lightly enough—or
Beltur was tired enough—that Beltur slept soundly and
woke comparatively refreshed on twoday, despite the
grayness of the morning, a gray created by the low-
hanging clouds and the fine misty rain that fell from
them. When he saw the rain, Beltur wondered if that
would delay their departure and asked just that after
they had what passed for breakfast—cider, hard cheese,

and a half a loaf of day-old bread—and walked toward the warehouse.

"The rain's coming in from the south," replied Athaal. "That's why it's so warm. The river will carry us ahead of it, and the cargo has to be covered with oilcloth anyway."

Athaal and Beltur did not go to the warehouse, but to the flatboat, since he had returned the key to Boraad before breakfast at the inn . . . and also removed the concealment protection, Beltur had to assume. When they reached the pier, the wiry and black-haired Boraad was supervising the placement of the heavy bales of wool, and the two mages waited.

Beltur studied the boat, an oblong about twenty-five yards long and six wide, with a flat deck over the rear twenty yards. The upper deck was not quite two yards above the lower deck, which was in fact the bottom of the hull. There was a small pilothouse at the front of the upper deck, with two long sweeps laid out on each side of the upper deck and a fifth one at the stern.

Abruptly, Boraad turned from where he stood on the pier. "Be another half glass before we're ready for your small lot. Go wait in the warehouse. It'll keep you dry for a while."

"Just let us know," said Athaal.

"You'll know when my crew shows up and asks about what to cart and stow." The boatman turned back and shouted, "Keep that bale even with the forward edge. Make sure the oilcloth's under the bottom pallet. On the starboard side, make sure those barrels are lashed tight."

Beltur noticed that the barrels being stowed were lowered with a sling, and then slid along a plank into place, rather than being rolled the way flour barrels were. "What's in those barrels?"

"Wine, I imagine. It's a favorite of the rich traders in Lydiar and much cheaper than vintages from Hamor."

Beltur hadn't thought of wine going down the river and then being shipped all the way from Spidlaria to Lydiar. As he walked with Athaal toward the warehouse, Beltur supposed that the pallets were under the bales and barrels to keep them above whatever water seeped or splashed into the boat.

About half a glass later, Beltur, Athaal, and two crewmen started moving Athaal's goods. Less than a quarter glass passed before it was all stowed under the upper deck. Even so, when they finished loading and boarded the flatboat, Beltur felt he couldn't have been wetter than if they'd stood in the fine rain the entire time.

Then Athaal motioned for Beltur to join him on the upper deck next to the pilothouse. "You should see how they maneuver the boat. We might be called on to man one of the sweeps. Boraad has always had small crews."

As the crew prepared to cast off, Beltur noted a long pier downstream and to the north with what looked to be a river galley with furled sails tied there. "Is that an actual galley there?"

"It is. There are two there, and one farther downstream. They're to catch anyone who fails to pay their tariffs. The one downstream can drag cables across the river. The Prefect doesn't care for merchants who don't pay their tariffs."

"Tariffs on goods *leaving* Gallos?"

"Entering, passing through, or leaving. The Prefect doesn't make fine distinctions." Athaal's tone was sardonic.

"Did you have to pay tariffs?"

"Just a silver, because I bought the goods in Gallos and what I have is considered a small and mixed cargo. You can pay to the portmaster or to the Prefect's man at the ferry. I much prefer dealing with Whaaryl."

Beltur nodded, although a silver didn't seem small to him. After a moment, he studied the flatboat more carefully. Not including Boraad, who stood beside the pilothouse, Beltur counted six men, five at the sweeps, and one with a long pole that he used to push the flatboat away from the pier and toward the center of the river.

Between the man poling and the sweepmen, in little more than a few moments the flatboat was clear of the pier and shore and beginning to move downstream, in the grip of the current. Despite the rain, there were no waves to speak of, and the flatboat seemed almost to glide through the dark water.

By midmorning Beltur was feeling happier . . . and beginning to dry out. As Athaal had predicted, the river had carried the flatboat away from the low-hanging clouds and the fine drizzle, and the sun shone down brightly. That meant Beltur was again mopping away sweat from his face and eyes.

As much to keep his thoughts from dwelling on how itchy the combination of sweat and nearly an eightday's worth of beard made his face feel as from curiosity, although he was interested, he asked Athaal, "Can you tell what the weather is going to do?"

"That depends on what you mean," replied the black mage, turning from looking at the west bank of the river, no more than ten yards away. "When it's raining and the clouds are almost black, anyone can tell that it's going to keep raining for at least a while. And when the wind's blowing toward you and you can see rain in the distance . . ." Athaal grinned. "That's not what you meant to ask, though."

"No. Uncle always claimed that good black mages could tell what the weather would be before it was obvious."

"If you know what to look for, any mage can figure out some things about the weather. I've heard there are mages who can actually change the weather. I'm certainly not one of those."

"What should I look for, then?"

"The patterns of order and chaos in the sky. Just try to sense patterns directly above you."

Beltur concentrated for a time, but all he could sense were what he might have called a diffuse mist of order and isolated small clumps of free chaos.

"What are you sensing?"

Beltur told him.

"That's what you should be sensing," replied Athaal. "When clouds form you should be able to sense clumps of chaos being confined by a shroud of fine order. The greater the chaos, and the more violent the flows or swirls in the cloud, the more likely there will be lightning. Now . . . if both order and chaos remain scattered, you're more likely to get the kind of rain we saw this morning in Portalya."

"That explains it when it's close," said Beltur, "but how can you tell what's going to happen a lot longer before it does?"

"I can't tell you. I'm not a weather mage. That's what I know."

"Part of it must be that they can sense those patterns from farther away." Beltur paused. "Or they've studied them long enough to know what patterns happen before a cloud forms."

"That might be. I couldn't say." Athaal looked back to the shore. "There's always a chance we'll see river brigands. That's why it doesn't hurt to keep an eye on the shore. They like to hide where we can't see them until we're almost past them. More flatboats get plundered because they didn't look back."

"What's the best way of dealing with them?"

"Anything that keeps them from getting close. White wizards have problems with using chaos on the river.

Water has a lot of order in it, despite the chaos that turns up in some of the currents and eddies." Athaal looked back at Beltur. "Don't white mages have trouble using chaos in the rain?"

"The stronger ones say that using chaos in the rain gives them a bad headache. Those who aren't that strong have trouble using it at all in a downpour. Do the river brigands attack in the rain?"

"It might have happened, but I've never heard of it. In their boots I wouldn't want to. Too easy to get swamped. Or get struck by lightning."

"That's something else I've wondered about. Rain hampers white mages, but I've never heard of a black mage using lightning. Could a weather mage do that?"

"I don't know. That doesn't say much," added Athaal with a grin, "but I've never known a weather mage. There is an old song about Nylan, the smith of the angels, that mentions a hammer of lightning and an anvil of night. Everyone thinks he was a black of some sort. I'm inclined to believe he was the first of the grays, either him or Saryn."

"The first Tyrant was a mage?"

"Very much so, if there's even a grain of truth in the stories and legends. She threw black blades through armor and even through solid doors. She conquered Lornth with little more than a company of troopers, and they were all women."

"That's just a story."

"Is it?" asked Athaal gently. "To this day, the Sarronnese women hold their own, and Westwind certainly does."

"I didn't mean about the women, but about throwing blades through armor and doors."

The black mage shrugged. "Every land that endures has a great story behind it. Some are even true. Nylan, Ryba, Saryn, Ayrlyn . . . they all were real. There's too much written about them that it couldn't be otherwise. That means there's at least a grain of truth in the stories. There must have been great stories about Cyad, too, but they perished with its destruction." He laughed. "I suppose the point is that, to be remembered, you need to do something remarkable and have a great story."

Doing something great was the last thing on Beltur's mind. Getting out of Gallos and away from Denardre and Wyath was a far more immediate concern . . . and perhaps getting ahold of a razor before too long, given how his beard and the skin under it itched.

XXII

By fourday afternoon Beltur was getting more than a little tired of looking at the river and its banks, which, after a time, tended to look much the same—woods and fields and small hamlets perched on the bank, with an occasional isle somewhere in the river, and faster stretches of water alternating with wide and lazy patches, not to mention marshes and reeds, and cattle and sheep drinking. While there were quite a number of hamlets along the river, the only real town was Maeryl, which the flatboat passed early on threeday, and which boasted only two piers, one of which was for the Prefect's tariff-enforcing galleys. The river water was clean enough, if touched with a bit of order, which he had to work out at first, but found it more effective than using chaos had been, and that the order-tinged water was not only useful in washing his face and beard, but drinkable.

As he stood on the upper deck, where at least there was a light breeze that kept flies and other insects mostly at bay, Beltur kept looking around, because he was trying to space out his questions and didn't wish to annoy Athaal by peppering him with inquiries, although he'd asked more than a few questions about Elparta already. And so, after a decent interval, he asked, "How do you use free order to heal, or to strengthen something?"

"If you're trying to strengthen something in order for it to last, it can be a very good idea or a very bad idea, depending on the material and the circumstances. It's a very bad idea for healing unless someone will die otherwise."

Beltur couldn't help but frown.

"Find me a dry twig or stick, and I'll show you a few things." Athaal returned to studying the western shore, which was largely wooded, perhaps because the ground between the trees appeared rocky and uneven, while the eastern shore was more like pasture.

Searching for a dry stick in a flatboat that had a tendency to ooze water, despite the caulking and the intermittent bailing of the crew, took Beltur what seemed like a glass before he found several stuck to the bales of wool, but it was doubtless more like a fifth of that when he returned with two and presented them to Athaal. "Here you are."

"Good." Athaal tucked the slightly larger and longer stick in his belt and held up the smaller, perhaps the length of spread fingers. "When this was growing and green could you have snapped it easily?"

"No."

"That was in part because of the combination of order and chaos that infuses all living things. When they depart, the stick slowly dries and loses its strength. That leaves space, if you will, for order, or chaos, to be infused. If you infuse enough chaos, the stick will burn. If you infuse order . . ."

Beltur could sense order flowing from around Athaal into the stick.

The mage handed the stick to Beltur. "See if you can break it."

Beltur took the short stick in both hands, tried . . . and failed, partly because of the order, and partly because the stick was so short.

"Wood is one substance that can be safely strengthened." Athaal produced a copper from his wallet and handed it to Beltur. "Try to infuse some order into the coin."

"I . . . don't know . . ."

"Go ahead. You can put a little in."

Beltur found gathering the order easier than gathering chaos, which disturbed him. *Are you really a black?* But after easing the first few bits of order into the copper, it was as if the coin had developed a wall against more order.

"You can stop trying," said Athaal. "It's not you. I might have been able to put a little more in than you, but not much more. That's because metals, especially iron, are already highly ordered. There's not much room for more order. Wood isn't as ordered, but woods vary by the tree they come from. Lorken is the heaviest and most ordered, followed by black oak, but lorken is so ordered that it's hard to work. That's why staves and ax handles and the like are usually made from oak."

"But . . . black iron . . . ?" Beltur returned the copper.

"It's made when a smith and a mage work together. The order has to be infused when the iron is red-hot and in just the right way. Don't ask me exactly how. I don't know. I do know that once it's forged, it can't be reworked, except by a mage and a smith."

"What about healing?"

"You know that chaos takes different forms—the chaos of a fire, free chaos, the chaos of illness . . . ?"

Beltur nodded.

"So does order. The order that is within living things is different from free order, or the order of the clouds or of metals. Only that order of the living type can truly heal, and it comes from the healer. A very experienced healer can mix free order and the healer's personal order, but it still requires some order from the healer. That limits healing. Also, order that is infused from outside one's body tends to seep away, unless it's used to destroy wound chaos or flux chaos. Now, outside order can be useful in combating wound chaos and keeping someone alive while their body recovers, but knowing how much order is enough and how much the healer can afford to give takes years of training and experience. Healing can be very dangerous to a healer, especially one without much experience."

"No one ever explained that to me."

"I'm not surprised," replied Athaal dryly.

"You don't have a very high opinion of white mages, do you?"

"Of most of them, I fear not. Your uncle was one of the few I actually liked and respected, not that I knew him all that well."

"He felt the same way about you," Beltur admitted.

"I wonder if he knew you weren't a pure white, or possibly even a white at all."

"He might have suspected it after we left Analeria. I'd changed my shields to use more order, mostly order, in fact, and he said that my shields were much stronger. So he had to have noticed something. But he never said anything about it." *Because he really never had that much time to before . . . Wyath . . .* Beltur shook his head. Even after an eightday, it was so hard to believe that his uncle was gone.

"It could be he felt he couldn't help you as much if he acknowledged that you weren't really a white mage."

"Because Wyath and his white mages were beginning to drive the blacks out of the city?"

"They hadn't done that yet, but it's coming. Your uncle was wise enough to see the possibility." Athaal turned his head abruptly, looking toward the west bank of the river.

Beltur did as well, in time to see a narrow boat, perhaps five yards in length, paddled by eight men, with a single sail, appear out of the reedy marsh, swiftly moving toward the flatboat that lay less than twenty yards away.

"Brigands!" shouted Boraad. "Sweeps in! Blades out!"

"Look to the east!" Athaal told Beltur.

Beltur saw a second boat of the same kind as the first pull away from behind a point in the still waters close to the eastern shore of the river. There were seven men, also paddling furiously.

"Here's where we prove our worth," said Athaal. "Not to mention staying alive and saving my cargo along with the others."

"River pirates?" Beltur's rhetorical question had definitely been unnecessary, but while Athaal had mentioned pirates, he hadn't really believed he'd be in the middle of an attack.

"Do what you can to those on the east side. Do it quickly."

Beltur hurried across the upper deck and stood about two yards outboard from the pilothouse, just trying to think what he could do. Shields were all that he could think of, and he immediately clamped one around the approaching craft, then began to contract it so that the men couldn't paddle.

While he could maintain the shield, he wasn't strong enough or skilled enough to be able to use it to crush the sides of the boat. That left him with a problem. Although the brigands couldn't row, the current was carrying them at about the same speed as the flatboat, and their shielded craft was drifting closer and closer to Beltur.

Beltur began to compress the shield downward so that the men were forced to bend down. When he saw them flailing, he abruptly released the shield and blanketed the boat with a concealment. One rower jumped out of the boat, and then another, followed by a third and a fourth. Finally one man was left huddled in the back of the boat, grasping the gunwales frantically. Beltur used a small shield to push him out of the boat, then released the concealment, leaving the boat floating free and seven men struggling, with various degrees of success, to swim toward the shore, while their boat continued to drift closer to the flatboat. In just a few moments, it was clear to Beltur that none of the brigands were going to end up anywhere close to the flatboat.

He scanned the eastern shore, but didn't see any more brigands or boats. So he turned to move across the deck to see what Athaal might have done, only to see the black mage standing behind him and smiling.

"Rather drastic, but effective," observed Athaal.

"I couldn't think of what else to do. Not in a hurry." *Not that wouldn't have killed them outright.* And Beltur hadn't wanted to do that, since he had the feeling that Athaal would have felt that excessive. "What did you do?"

"I just created a shield that angled across the water,

and moved the order away from part of the bow. The current and the shield forced them onto a mud bar, and the bow split."

Beltur wished he could have thought of something that simple and elegant.

"Sweeps! Gather in that boat!" ordered Boraad. "Be a shame to see it go to waste."

"If Boraad takes the boat," added Athaal, "it will also be a while before that crew can attack anyone else. He'll be pleased to have the boat. It looks to be a nice craft. He can sell it in Elparta."

Beltur watched as two of the men used their sweeps to bring the empty boat alongside the flatboat, but it took almost half a glass before they were able to hoist it aboard.

Once that was accomplished, Boraad moved from the pilothouse to stand beside Athaal. "I like your apprentice's sense of justice, but why did their boat vanish for a time."

"It just seemed to vanish," replied Athaal. "He was making the brigands think they had been blinded. That's why they all jumped into the water. They realized that they wouldn't be able to see if they stayed with the boat."

Beltur could see that Athaal didn't want to talk about concealments, and yet everything the black mage had said was perfectly true.

"I wouldn't want to be out in the water and blind," agreed Boraad with a nod. "Neatly done, and the Prefect can't complain that an Elpartan trader killed innocent Gallosians." The trader snorted. "He'll find some other excuse to increase tariffs."

"Is everything tariffed?" asked Beltur.

"No," replied the trader, "just everything of value."

"Are there brigands all along the river?"

"No, but there's no telling where they might be," said

Boraad. "They move a lot so that the Prefect's men have a hard time finding them."

"The Prefect's efforts aren't out of kindness," added Athaal. "If the river gets too unsafe, traders will send goods other ways, and he'll lose tariffs."

Beltur almost asked whether Denardre cared about those killed by brigands, but he already knew the answer to that question. Instead, he just nodded.

The flatboat continued downstream as if nothing had happened.

XXIII

Well before midmorning on oneday, another warm and clear day, but one cooler than had been the case previously, Boraad called out, "Junction Rapids ahead! All sweeps out!"

Beltur immediately looked around. The west shore of the River Gallos gave no indication of anything unusual, and the only thing different on the east side was that the riverbank sloped upward and kept climbing up a tree-covered slope to a ridge a good hundred yards above the river and possibly almost a kay to the east. He looked ahead, but all he could see was that the river curved eastward around a point about two kays ahead that looked to be where the long ridge ended. "I don't see any sign of rapids."

"You will," said Athaal with an amused expression. "Just beyond that point is where the Passa River joins the River Gallos, and the river shoots down the Junction Rapids into the Border Gorge."

"Between Gallos and Spidlar?"

"That's why it's called the Border Gorge."

Not again. Beltur wanted to hit his own head. The last thing he needed to do was ask stupid questions. Instead, he just nodded and looked forward as the flatboat neared the curve in the river.

"The name isn't quite accurate. Maybe it was once. The gorge is entirely in Gallos, and several miles of river beyond the gorge are also Gallosian."

Beltur still didn't feel that much better after the explanation.

"We'll need to clear the upper deck before long," said Athaal after a time. "It'll be a bit rougher than the Rushing Gorge."

Beltur nodded again. The Junction Rapids would be the second rapids since they had passed Maeryl, the first being the Rushing Gorge, where the water had seemed to tumble over itself and wind through some tight curves before settling into a more placid section. Outside of the flatboat's bouncing some in the rough water and occasional spray, the Rushing Gorge hadn't been particularly uncomfortable, although the boat had rolled and pitched a little, but not enough that he and Athaal had been discommoded as they had remained on the upper deck and watched Boraad and the sweepmen guide the boat through the gorge.

Beltur looked forward again, but the water seemed calm, almost placid, although it seemed as though the flatboat was moving faster than it had a short time before.

As they neared a point near where the ridge on the east side of the river ended, Athaal said, "Time to go below." He made his way to the side of the upper deck and then climbed down the wooden slats affixed to the inside of the hull that doubled as a ladder, then along the half bulkhead that restrained the cargo until he stood at the back of the open section of the lower, roughly near the middle. Beltur followed.

"When it gets rough, you might want to grab a timber or the top of the bulkhead."

"You know all the sailor's terms," said Beltur cautiously.

"When I was younger, I accompanied my father on a few trading voyages." Athaal shook his head. "River trips once or twice a year are more than enough for me."

If he accompanied his father . . . That meant his father had to be a wealthy trader himself or likely a ship's captain . . . possibly a ship's officer, but nothing less.

Beltur was still thinking about that when he became aware that, from somewhere ahead, he could hear an unfamiliar sound, one that combined a roaring and a rushing. Then, suddenly, the flatboat lurched, and Beltur had to grab one of the timbers behind him that braced the upper deck just to keep his feet. When he looked up, he saw that the bow had dropped enough that all he could see above the double timbers was river, and mostly spray and foam.

The flatboat rolled side to side, then pitched, and a line of spray sheeted over the bow, a fraction of which struck Beltur across the face and neck. The water felt like ice, far colder than anything he'd felt from the river water so far.

"Ohh!"

"Cold, isn't it?" asked Athaal, raising his voice above the roaring of the water through which the flatboat seemed to alternately bounce, skid, or drop.

More cold spray flared across Beltur.

The flatboat seemingly jerked to one side, moving quickly enough that Beltur felt as though his arm would be pulled from his shoulder. Then a wave, or part of one, came over the side and drenched Beltur in ice-cold water, just before the bow rose, and then plunged, with the result that more spray and water cascaded into the open section of the lower deck, sloshing back and forth as the flatboat rolled back and forth as the bow rose and fell, rose and fell.

When the bouncing, rolling, and pitching finally subsided into a slight rocking, Beltur was shivering from the cold water that had soaked him through and through, and was ankle deep.

"Time to bail," announced Athaal, untying a pair of buckets that had been lashed to one of the bracing crossbeams. "The sooner we get the water out, the less damage to the cargo. Only fill the bucket half full. Then lift it and pour it over the side." He handed Beltur a bucket, keeping one for himself.

As he bailed, Beltur realized that the rapids had answered another question he'd had but not asked, and that was why Boraad's flatboat was among the largest he'd seen on the river or at the few piers they had passed, but after going through the Junction Rapids, he definitely understood. He doubted a much larger craft would have been able to survive, not without even more flooding or damage.

For the first quarter glass, bailing wasn't that hard— just set the bucket sideways, let it fill with the slight rolling of the boat, then lift it overhead and tilt it so that the bilgewater went into the river. Bailing for the second quarter glass was uncomfortable, but because two crewmen joined them, the four removed more water. After that, bailing became painful and tedious, because even with the sloshing it was impossible to get more than a few digits of water into a bucket.

When Boraad called down, "That's enough," Beltur's shoulders and arms both ached and twinged. His hands were wrinkled and cramped from the cold water, and his clothes were still soaked.

Once they climbed back to the upper deck, Beltur glanced around, taking in the river, now almost twice as wide as it had been before the rapids, and the straight but rocky cliffs of the Border Gorge before asking, "Why is the water from the other river so cold?"

"The Passa River comes out of the Easthorns. It's mostly meltwater from the snow. The Easthorns aren't as high as the Westhorns, but they still have snow at the top all year around."

No wonder it's so frigging cold. Beltur just nodded.

The air was also definitely cooler, but then, they'd been traveling north for almost an eightday, and they were floating down a much colder river through a high-walled gorge that had to be shaded about half the day. The sky was clear, however, and after two glasses or so, Beltur's garments were mostly dry. While the walls of the gorge were not nearly so high as they had been farther upstream, the ground on each side of the river sloped up fairly steeply and consisted mostly of rocks and large boulders. From time to time, to the west of the river, Beltur caught glimpses of a narrow road that ran through the seemingly inhospitable land. Then the land bordering the river began to flatten.

Slightly after midafternoon, as the flatboat began to leave the rocky terrain behind, except for a long red-stone bluff several hundred yards to the east of the river, Athaal pointed ahead. "There. You can see the great south wall of Elparta."

When Beltur looked, he realized that Athaal meant exactly what he said. Even from what had to be a distance of more than two kays, the walls were impressive. As the flatboat drew nearer, and the sweeps guided it toward the east side of the river, Beltur could see that the piers were outside the walls and that a tower stood at the southwest corner of the city walls, just at the edge of the water, with another tower directly across the river from it, with roughly a hundred yards between them. The walls were a good twenty yards high, and the towers overtopped them by another ten yards. Perhaps a hundred yards upstream of the first pier, on both sides of the river, was another kind of wall, a crude line of heaped rocks and boulders almost twenty yards high that ran to the river's edge.

Beltur looked back to the towers. "Does Elparta have a net or something to stop those who don't wish to pay tariffs?"

"Cables. They're seldom used. Anyone who is stopped by the cables forfeits his craft and all his cargo."

"What about at night or in bad weather?"

"The towers are manned at all glasses, except for the few times in winter that the river freezes over. What is gained from one or two seizures will cover a year or more of pay for the trade guards."

Boraad and his men guided the flatboat toward the second pier, because two other flatboats were already tied at the first pier, and Beltur watched closely as they eased the unwieldy craft alongside the pier. One of the crewmen threw a cable to a dockhand, who quickly secured it to a bollard.

Almost as soon as the flatboat was secured to the pier, Beltur could see several figures walking toward them.

"Here comes the tariff inspector," said Athaal.

A man in a solid blue tunic stepped onto the flatboat. He was shorter than Beltur with a small paunch that did not quite ooze over his wide black belt, and he carried a flat leather case. Two troopers in uniforms of a slightly lighter blue remained on the pier. The inspector nodded to Boraad, but walked first straight to the black mage. "Mage Athaal, I presume your goods are for the Council?"

"Not all of them." Athaal handed two sheets of paper to the man. "The longer one lists the Council goods, the shorter one my personal purchases."

The inspector took the two sheets, but barely glanced at them. "Are the Council goods staying with the flatboat and going on to Spidlaria?"

"They are."

"Will you be accompanying them?" After a moment, the inspector offered an embarrassed smile. "I know, Athaal. You never do, but I still must ask. Procedures, you understand."

"I know, Paartyl. I will not accompany them. The second list is the one with the goods for the Council."

Paartyl shuffled the sheets and looked back at the first and shorter list. "This looks like two coppers for your personal goods." He took out a grease stick and wrote the number on the sheet before folding it in half and placing it in the leather case.

Athaal extracted two coins from his belt wallet and handed them to the inspector. "Here you are."

The inspector scrawled something Beltur couldn't read on the other sheet, folding it as well and also slipping it into the case. Then he jotted a few letters on a pasteboard square and handed it to Athaal, before turning to Beltur. "Mage, do you have anything to declare?"

Beltur might have laughed at the words, since he had nothing at all but what he wore, but that clearly wasn't appropriate. "No, inspector, I don't."

"Beltur will be my apprentice for a while," added Athaal. "Fenard is not the best place for any mage who does not worship the Prefect's current arms-mage."

"That explains it." Paartyl nodded. "There have been several mages arriving recently. More than I've seen in years." He offered another apologetic smile to Athaal. "Except, until the last few eightdays, you're the only mage I've ever seen on the river. A healer or two, but no mages."

That surprised Beltur, although he couldn't have said why. But then, he realized, he never would have left Fenard if his life hadn't been forfeit if he had stayed.

"You may see more," said Athaal. "Either healers or mages, if not both."

"Does the Prefect plan to attack Elparta?"

"I know of no plans. Nor is he gathering an army. But he is gathering white mages, and that is worrisome."

"Thank you. I will pass that on." With a nod, Paartyl turned and walked toward Boraad.

"We can gather our things and get ready to disembark," said Athaal quietly.

"How will we get your goods to where they must go?" Beltur phrased the question that way because Athaal had never indicated anything about his dwelling or how far it might be.

"We'll carry them. It's a good walk, but what's mine isn't that much. If you would carry a satchel, I'd be most appreciative."

"Of course." How could Beltur not agree with all that Athaal had done for him? Besides, a satchel couldn't be that heavy.

Gathering Athaal's gear and goods didn't take long at all. In addition to his bulging pack, into which Athaal had placed a number of smaller items, the black mage carried two bolts of black cloth, cloth woven from the black sheep of Montgren. The large satchel that Beltur carried held several books, one of which bore the title *Historie of Spices* and another entitled *Halmaar's Geography of Candar,* a large bag of peppercorns, another of cloves, and a third of nutmeg. There were also ten beeswax tapers, which Athaal had noted were far less expensive in Gallos than anywhere else.

Once he stood on the pier, Beltur had a slightly better

view, not of the city, because of the towering walls, but
of where Elparta was situated—near one end of a narrow river valley into which the River Gallos flowed.
Although he couldn't tell for certain, it appeared that
there were no rocky hills or mountains farther to the
north, as if the valley widened considerably once north
of Elparta, although the high hills or low mountains
through which they had passed looked to extend eastward as far as he could see.

"The trade gate is over there, just beyond the end of
the third pier." Athaal nodded his head in that direction
and began to walk.

Beltur matched steps with the slightly shorter black
mage, noticing almost immediately that a miasma of
fish, mustiness, rotten wood, tar, and, strangely, roasting fowl enveloped the shore end of the pier. "The fowl
smells good."

"I think any hot food would smell good right now,"
replied Athaal humorously.

"Ah . . . where are we headed?"

"Home, of course. My home and Meldryn's, that
is. We live in the southeast quarter about halfway
from here to the eastern wall. It's not quite a kay. The
wealthier traders live on the higher hills, either those
immediately to the east of the river or those farther to
the northeast. We live halfway up a low rise between
them. That's where many successful crafters have their
homes and workshops. Not the metalworkers. They're
required to live outside the walls. Some have homes
and shops to display their work in the far northeast
quarter."

"What do you do—I mean to bring in coppers—
besides what you just did for the Council?" That was a
question Beltur had debated asking for well over an
eightday because it seemed almost crass after all Athaal
had already done—and paid for—for him.

"Whatever I can. I offer my services to the mills and to the herders and the large growers."

Beltur hadn't the faintest idea what Athaal meant by services.

"You haven't ever talked to many blacks, have you?"

"No, ser."

"I'm not . . ." Athaal shook his head. "After we get through the gates, I'll explain what I thought you knew."

The blue-clad guards at the gates looked at Athaal then Beltur and then turned their attention to a man with a handcart piled high. Once the two were through the gate in the great wall, Beltur found himself in a small square or open space, but one without peddlers or hucksters.

Athaal pointed to the northeast corner of the square. "We take the winding street up some three blocks and then turn north again on Bakers Lane."

Beltur couldn't help but sense the mixture of order and chaos from the scattered handfuls of people crossing the square, a few heading for the gates, but most just crossing it, heading toward the river or away from it. The city didn't really feel that much different from Fenard, except it was cooler, if still slightly more than pleasantly warm, but he found that much more to his liking.

"Now . . . I assume your uncle was paid for doing other things than what the Prefect requested. It's no different for blacks, either here or in Gallos."

"I understood that, ser, but what I don't know is what kind of services a black provides to mills, herders, and growers."

"Let's take the millers. Sawmills, for example. If a blade cracks or breaks while it's cutting a log, it's moving very fast, and fragments of the blade could break off and do more damage than a volley of arrows."

"Oh . . . and you can detect the chaos that forms be-fore it's bad enough that the blade breaks."

"Exactly. With growers, I can check their root cel-lars and find traces of rot long before it becomes ap-parent to the eye. I can also show them lots of bad seed, or seed that won't grow. I don't get that much from any of them, but a few coppers from scores of growers does turn into silvers."

"You get more from the millers, though, don't you?"

Athaal nodded. "They have more to lose if something goes wrong."

"Couldn't a healer do the same thing?"

"Most healers can't sense as deeply into plants and solid materials. Those that can are usually the best heal-ers and don't need to travel from grower to grower to grower."

"Do blacks do other things as well?"

"Most do. I once knew a cabinet maker. He could sense the wood, and he was good with his hands. I can sense the woods, but I'm not that good with my hands. Meldryn is an excellent baker as well as a black, and his sense of order is part of what makes his breads and pastries good enough that people will pay a bit more for what he bakes. That's why he runs a small bakery next to our dwelling. Well, it's really part of it, and it's not so small anymore." Athaal stopped to let an older woman leading a donkey cart pass, then turned toward the narrow street to which he had earlier pointed.

The cobblestone pavement of the street was rough and uneven with even occasional small potholes and ran from building wall to building wall with nothing resembling a sidewalk. It was also fairly steep, which had Beltur wondering just what the streets or avenues going up the taller hills were like. The next three blocks felt like six. When Athaal turned left onto Bakers Lane, marked as such by a crude picture of a loaf of bread painted on the wall of a building that had no marking and could have been used for anything, Beltur took a long slow breath, relieved that the incline of the lane was much gentler. As he exhaled, he realized that Elparta wasn't as "fragrant" as Fenard, with a much greater share of less unpleasant odors.

Almost a kay later, Athaal declared, "There's our place," pointing ahead to a corner dwelling, one with two doors. Over the left doorway, the one stained a warm golden brown, was a signboard on which was the painted image of two long loaves of bread, crossed. The right doorway was more somber, a very dark brown. Athaal walked more quickly toward the darker doorway, where he stopped.

Beltur sensed how the black mage used order to manipulate the order block on the inside of the door to release the latch bolt. Then he opened the door and stepped inside. "Meldryn! I'm home!" He wiped his boots carefully on the heavy cloth mat.

Beltur followed gingerly, closing the door behind himself, and also wiping his boots. The odor of baked bread and other goods immediately surrounded him, although the strong scent was different. It took him a moment to realize that there was not even a hint of a burned crust or the like, and that the entire dwelling had a peaceful feeling.

"I'll be there in a moment. After I get the pies out." The speaker's voice was mellow, but powerful.

Beltur took a longer survey of where he stood, a small entry area perhaps two yards wide and not quite that deep. A single heavy black cloak hung from one of the long and sturdy wooden pegs set in a hanging board on the wall that would be behind the door when it opened. The entry hall floor was not wood or stone, but a dark gray tile, mortared in place. Beyond the archway leading from the entry was a narrow oak-floored hallway heading straight back, off which were archways on both left and right. From what Beltur could see and sense, the archway on the right opened onto a larger room, perhaps a parlor, while the one to the left fronted another narrow hall—most likely to the bakery, surmised Beltur.

"Just put the satchel against the wall there for now. Under the cloak." Athaal walked into the parlor and set the bolts of cloth across an armchair, then eased off his heavy pack and set it on the floor beside the chair.

After putting down the satchel, Beltur remained in the hall, uncertain of where to go. He was still considering what he should do when he heard footsteps coming down the hall from the direction of the bakery. He also sensed a presence filled with order—definitely a black mage.

The gray-haired man in black who emerged from the narrow side hall wrapped Athaal in a full-body embrace that was clearly warm and more than just casually affectionate, if but for a moment, before stepping back and saying, "And your friend here?"

"Meldryn, this is Beltur. You might recall my mentioning the white mage Kaerylt? Beltur is his nephew. They both ran afoul of Wyath and his crew. Beltur managed to escape to Margrena's, but his life would be forfeit if he remained in Gallos. Oh . . . we might be seeing Margrena and her daughter in a few eightdays. She's planning to go to Kleth, I think."

Meldryn offered a puzzled expression. "Not here? Is her sister going to Kleth, too?"

"Margrena's sister Grenara? I doubt it."

"Then why . . ." Meldryn shook his head. "Sisters. They're either inseparable or can only tolerate each other for a short time."

"Some brothers are like that as well."

The older mage nodded knowingly, then said, "I hadn't expected you for another few days at the most."

"With Beltur's need to leave Fenard and the unpredictability of Wyath, I thought remaining would be less than perfectly wise."

"Then it's good you're both here now. I do happen to have some meat pies I didn't sell and a few other things. It might take a little bit before I'm finished in the bakery."

"I did get the cloth, two full bolts . . . and some of the spices, and some good beeswax tapers, at a very good price."

"Excellent! Excellent!"

"While you're finishing up," said Athaal, "we'll put things away. The small bedroom?"

"It's ready. I had a feeling you might bring someone, but I thought it might be Waensyn."

Athaal shook his head. "He thinks I worry too much. He says Wyath doesn't want problems with the blacks. I couldn't persuade him." There was a pause. "I can't say I tried very hard after talking to him a while."

"And you could Margrena?"

"Beltur and his uncle were friends of hers, and Kaerylt was one of the more powerful whites who wasn't a favorite of Wyath. I think seeing how Wyath turned on even whites who weren't slavish in their devotion . . . I told Margrena to make sure Waensyn understood that. Maybe he'll listen to her. He just dismissed my concerns." Athaal smiled ruefully. "You'd better get back to your pies. We'll be fine. Laranya's left for the day, I take it."

"There wasn't any reason for her to stay. I didn't think you'd be back today, and everything's clean. Her son . . ." Meldryn shook his head. "I keep doing what I can." After a warm smile at Athaal, he turned and headed back toward the bakery.

"He's not open this late, is he?" asked Beltur, when he really wanted to ask something about Laranya, although he hoped her position with the two would become clear if he just listened.

"No, but the space in the bakery is limited, and his fruit pies will keep for days. So he makes them the afternoon before so that he can work on the bread in the morning. Bring the satchel into the kitchen, if you would." Athaal picked up his pack.

Beltur recovered the satchel and followed Athaal past the narrow staircase leading to the upper level. Past the staircase and just before the archway into the kitchen was a half-open door to the left. The long narrow room held very little except two sideboards and a long trestle table of oiled dark oak and two backed benches on each side.

Athaal gestured. "That's the dining room. We don't use it much, except when some of the blacks come over here for a dinner gathering . . . or when we host some of the healers. We usually eat in the kitchen. It's easier."

"Do you do healing?"

"Not if we can help it. Laranya's son . . . he just doesn't have enough natural order in his system. The healers can't do anything about that, except add a little order. We can do that . . . for now, but he'll need more as he grows, and . . ." This time Athaal shook his head and set his pack on the kitchen worktable. "If you'd hand me the spices from the satchel . . ."

In only a few moments, Beltur had handed Athaal all the items he wanted, and he was again following the black mage, this time up the narrow staircase that climbed halfway to the upper level before reaching a landing and then going to the right.

Just to the left at the top of the staircase was a short and very narrow hallway that Athaal took, opening the door to a small chamber with a narrow bed, a writing table, and a chest, and a wall board with pegs for garments. The single narrow window looked out on Bakers Lane.

"This is where you'll stay for now. It might take you a while to learn what else you need in the way of order and to get settled into Elparta, but you can stay here as long as you need to."

Beltur understood. So long as he was learning, progressing, and working, he was welcome. "I can cook. I've been doing that for years for Uncle and Sydon." *And other domestic chores as well.*

"There are times when that would be most helpful. In the next day or so we'll need to get you another set of blacks. Otherwise you'll wear those out in eight-days. The washroom's at the other end of the hall. There's a chamber pot under the table. I'll show you where you'll need to dump it into the sewer. The nearest clean fountain is only a block away, farther north on the lane . . ."

After Athaal's explanations and while he was putting away his gear, Beltur washed up and then went down to the kitchen to wait. Almost a glass later, the three sat around the kitchen table, finishing off one of Meldryn's large meat pies, accompanied by a moderately dark ale that thankfully wasn't bitter.

"This is the best meat pie I've ever eaten." Beltur wasn't shading the truth in the slightest.

"That's one reason why we could afford this place," said Athaal. "People come from all over Elparta to buy what Meldryn bakes."

"It's not just that," the older mage added. "Being able to sense how good the ingredients are and what to buy means we waste less."

That was something Beltur hadn't even thought about. "You still have to be a very good baker."

"Well put," said Athaal with a laugh. "Meldryn doesn't like to admit that he's the best."

"I'm good. So are others."

"See what I mean?" Athaal grinned.

"Enough," replied Meldryn genially. "Do you have any particular skills, Beltur?"

"Such as crafting, or the like? I fear not, ser. I'm good with shields and concealments. I can cook some, and I can clean fairly well."

"Hmmmm." The older mage frowned for a moment. "How far can you sense order and chaos?"

"In open spaces, perhaps two kays. In a town or city, it's much less."

"A block?"

"Three or four, depending on how many people are around."

"It sounds like your uncle really didn't know what to do with you. What exactly did he do?"

"Whatever brought in coins. Sometimes he worked for the Prefect. That paid the best. The last thing he did was go to Analeria to find out why so many women were leaving the herders and going to Westwind or elsewhere."

"Did he find out?"

"Not exactly. He found out that several towns had made agreements with the grassland herders. That meant the herders could trade with them and not raid them, but then the herders raided other towns farther inside Analeria. He didn't find any sign that women were leaving. The Prefect wasn't pleased. That may have been one reason why Wyath and the other mages attacked us."

"Sounds like an honest man, if not terribly wise in reporting what a ruler doesn't want to hear."

"He didn't have much choice. The Prefect wanted to see him before he paid him."

"He could have left Fenard."

"I don't think he had any idea that our lives were in danger. Not until we were in the palace and on the way to the audience chamber."

"There's more to that, isn't there?"

"There is, ser. Uncle, his assistant Sydon, and I were all summoned, but while we were waiting, the Arms-Mage summoned Sydon . . ." Beltur went on to explain what happened after that.

When Beltur finished, Meldryn nodded. "It sounds like treachery to me. Was Sydon surprised? Was there any deception on his part?"

"No, ser. He was honestly afraid he'd done something wrong. I could sense that."

"What do you sense with me? Right now?

The question took Beltur totally off-guard. For a moment, he could say nothing. Then he just tried to sort out what he sensed. Finally, he said, "Outside of the inside, you're almost all black, but there's a fuzzy patch, and that usually means someone's confused or puzzled. Maybe skeptical. You've also got tiny chaos flecks in your hands and fingers, not quite like wound flux and not like the red flux—"

"That's enough." Meldryn laughed, not quite humorously. "That's more than many healers can sense, yet . . ." He shook his head. "How did your uncle take to your trending toward the black?"

Beltur could sense a greater concern. "He kept trying to insist that I could be the perfect white. I never had that talent. It was only when I really started to use order that I developed strong shields."

"You still have strong traces of white."

"That's not surprising," said Athaal. "He was his uncle's ward from the time he was nine or so, as I understand."

"You had no other family?"

"My mother died when I was six. All her family except Uncle Kaerylt died from the red flux years before. My father was an only child." Beltur didn't really want to get into the fact that his father and his uncle had barely been on speaking terms . . . or that his father had been an orphan fostered by a childless scrivener and his wife. Beltur could barely remember them, except that they had both been white-haired and old.

"Was your father a mage?"

"No, ser. He was a scrivener. That's how Uncle got some of his books, like *The Book of Ayrlyn*."

"Your uncle has a copy of *The Book of Ayrlyn*?" Meldryn's voice bore a tone of astonishment.

"He did. I imagine Arms-Mage Wyath or one of his mages has it now."

Meldryn sighed. "Such a loss. They'll likely destroy it." He paused. "Did you read it?"

"Yes, ser. Several times."

The two black mages exchanged glances, but Beltur couldn't sense what that meant.

"Can you handle chaos without it hurting?" asked the older black mage.

"In small amounts, more if I use order." That was certainly true, because Beltur had never been able to handle the quantities of chaos either his uncle or Sydon had.

"Maybe with some of the smiths," ventured Meldryn.

"It's possible. He'd likely be helpful to any metalworker. We'll have to see," said Athaal, looking to Beltur and adding, "We're trying to see what magely skills you have that can be used here in Elparta."

"I appreciate everything you've done already . . . and how you're trying to help me become useful and not a burden." Beltur definitely meant those words. He looked to Athaal and added, "I've told Athaal already, but I'm more than willing to do anything around here, from

cleaning to helping with cooking, or cooking if you
don't feel up to it."

"You did that for your uncle?"

"I did. I'm obviously not the cook you are, but . . ."

"There are times when that would help." Meldryn
smiled. "I did make a small berry pie that isn't quite
what I'd like to sell. It's somehow got lopsided, but I'm
certain it will taste good."

Beltur had no doubts that it would, and for the next
little while he would enjoy himself.

XXIV

"I thought that the best way for you to get used to Elparta would be to accompany me for a while, perhaps
an eightday or so." Those had almost been Athaal's first
words to Beltur on twoday morning at breakfast, another solid meal of egg toast, sliced pearapples, bread,
and mixed berry conserve, prepared by Athaal, since
Meldryn had been up for glasses and the pleasant scents
of baked goods already suffused the entire dwelling.

Less than a glass later, well before seventh glass,
Athaal and Beltur were walking north on Bakers Lane,
which already had more people and carts on it than
Beltur had ever seen on Nothing Lane. But then, again,
there had been a reason everyone called it Nothing
Lane.

"We'll be going to a number of growers today."

"How many is a number?" asked Beltur lightly.

"As many as we can before we're too tired to do what
has to be done." Athaal gestured to yet another bakery.
"That belongs to Ghramont. He bakes in the style of

Axalt, and the one on the far side, that's Chezryk. He does Suthyan breads and cakes mostly. Up ahead, the place with the maroon shutters, that's Moonal, and he does Sligan cream cakes and all kinds of sweets, too rich for me most of the time, but folks love them . . ."

As they walked Athaal gave a little background on each of the bakers or bakeries, as well as for the few shops that sold other goods, but paused two blocks later, saying, "Here's where the bakers end. After this, it's mostly just dwellings. I know some of them, and I'll tell you what I know."

Beltur lost count of the blocks they traveled, because he was trying to take in everything that Athaal was telling him, but they had walked close to a score when they turned west for two blocks before reaching the River Boulevard where, two blocks to the north, Beltur could see another gate in the tall city wall. Less than a hundred yards beyond the northern wall and the city gates, where a single blue-clad trooper stood guard, looking slightly bored, Athaal immediately turned east on a well-packed clay road.

"Just another kay or so."

"Do you walk this much every day?" asked Beltur.

"We've scarcely started," replied Athaal with a smile. "You haven't thought about having a horse?"

"Horses are costly. We'd also have to pay to stable a horse and feed it, and buy the tack, and pay for a farrier. Those are coins we really don't have, and it wouldn't save that much time."

Beltur was sorry he'd asked.

By the time they walked up to a modest one-story stone dwelling set before fields with rows of dark green-leaved low plants, Beltur was beginning to see why the stocky but muscular Athaal didn't have any weight on his frame except muscle and bone.

An angular man with rust-red hair and beard, looking to be ten years older than Beltur, walked from a shed beside the house toward the two, smiling warmly and carrying a large empty sack. "I see you're back, Mage. I'm glad to see you. We had a heavy rain the other day."

"Have you seen any sign of blight?"

"Not yet, but I've got a feeling it might be lurking in places."

"We'll have to see. Haestyl, this is Beltur. He'll be working with me for a while. He's a mage, but he hasn't worked much with plants and would like to learn more."

Haestyl looked from Beltur to Athaal and grinned broadly. "That's fine with me just so long as you don't charge double."

"While he's learning you get two for one. When he's learned enough, he'll be on his own. Just the potato fields?"

The grower nodded, then turned and walked toward the edge of the field east of the house. Athaal and Beltur followed Haestyl to the southeast corner, less than five yards from the low stone wall that lay an equal distance from the road.

There Athaal turned to Beltur. "We're looking for the early signs of potato blight. The blight creates a kind of plant wound chaos. If I find any, I'll point it out. Once you're familiar with what to look for, it's not that hard to sense."

Beltur certainly hoped so, but he still wondered if he'd be able to do what Athaal seemed to think that he could.

Athaal began to walk along the easternmost row of plants, taking a step and pausing, then another one and pausing. Although Beltur had no idea exactly what he was trying to sense, he followed Athaal's example, while trying to sense any unusual patterns of chaos in or near the plants. He could easily sense specks of free chaos and order, as well as the faint pattern of order and chaos in each plant. The three had gone almost fifty yards down the first row when, ahead, Beltur *thought* there was the slightest difference in one plant, almost the tiniest shading of the "cool" red of living chaos toward the orange, but he wasn't sure.

Except that Athaal stopped and bent down to examine that very plant. The black mage nodded. "The first hints of blight." He pointed. "You see those tiny brown spots on the leaf. There's even a hint of yellow around that one." Athaal turned over the leaf, squinting at the underside. "Good. There's none of that white fuzz there." He looked to Beltur.

"There's a hint of orange to the regular cool red of living chaos," Beltur said. "At least, that's the way it feels to me."

"Do you sense it anywhere else?"

"There's a tiny point of it on the next leaf." Beltur started to touch the leaf.

"Don't touch the spots. You can spread it." Athaal stepped back, as did Beltur.

"Which two?" asked Haestyl.

Athaal pointed with his belt knife, which was almost a silvery copper in color, actually touching each leaf.

Beltur frowned. If he couldn't touch them . . .

"The blight doesn't like copper or cupridium," explained the black mage, who then looked to the grower.

Cupridium? Athaal actually had a cupridium knife?

". . . That's the only plant that shows signs here," continued Athaal. "The ones nearest in the next row don't either. We got this one early."

"What about the tubers in the ground?"

"There's no trace of the potato chaos there."

The grower nodded, then bent and cut off all the foliage, which he carefully placed in the large cloth bag he carried.

"He'll burn all the chaos-tinged plants," explained Athaal. "Otherwise, little flakes of that chaos will get on the other plants and spread. There might be some too small to sense."

"It's like a flux with people?"

Athaal nodded. "Very much like it, except it spreads even faster. We can talk about it on the walk to the next grower. Right now, we just need to concentrate on finding any blight chaos."

Beltur could also sense that Athaal wasn't exactly comfortable with what he'd said, although the other mage also wasn't lying, which meant there were things he didn't want to reveal in front of the grower.

Almost a glass later, the two mages stood with Haestyl in front of his dwelling. In the entire field they'd only found three plants with signs of the blight, one plant in the first row, and two, side by side in the last row.

"I thank you, Mages." Haestyl extended several coins.

Athaal took them and nodded. "We thank you."

Once they left Haestyl, Beltur couldn't resist asking, "That's actually a cupridium knife? I didn't know . . . I mean, I thought no one forged cupridium anymore, not since Cyador fell."

"It is. My father gave it to me when he learned I was a mage. He picked it up somewhere on one of his voyages."

"Was he a trader or a ship's officer?"

"He was a captain." Beltur paused. "His ship vanished on a voyage back from Hamor eight years ago."

"I'm sorry. I didn't know."

"There was no reason you should." Athaal smiled. "Meldryn says the knife's the most valuable thing in the house. It might date back to Cyad, but there's no way of telling." He paused. "It's also useful in dealing with the blight and other chaos-fluxes . . . as you saw."

Beltur nodded.

Athaal continued eastward, past the woodlot adjoining the potato field. "This year hasn't been too bad. The rain he got last eightday couldn't have been that heavy, and it wasn't too damp or too warm. I wouldn't have wanted to go to Fenard if it had been truly hot and wet."

"But you were worried that the way the Prefect was dealing with mages you might not have been able to go later?" That was a guess on Beltur's part.

"That's right."

"You were going to tell me something . . ."

"Oh . . . yes. I was afraid you'd ask about using order on the plants. That's not a good idea."

"Because it's like using free order for healing?"

Athaal nodded. "Also, a mage's order isn't quite so strange to a plant as free order, but it doesn't always work, and there's the problem that if the blight's bad, there might be ten or fifteen plants in a field that have it, and you may have to do ten fields in a day, sometimes more. It may not seem like much, but after a few days you'd need a healer or a good long rest. Sensing for blight once or twice isn't that hard, but making sure you sense every cubit of ground for it—that's hard. It's also important, because the blight can spread quickly once it's easy to see. Then it's hard to keep it from destroying a good portion of the field. Our job is to catch it before it can spread. Once there's fuzz on the undersides of the leaves, the grower will likely lose a lot of plants and potatoes. Now, the next stop is an orchard. Well . . . two orchards owned by the same grower. One's apples, and the other is pearapples."

"What are we looking for there?"

"At this time of year, cankers, mainly. Doraal takes good care of his trees so we'll not see fire blight and scabbing usually only happens in the spring or late fall. We're really just going to sense if there are bark cankers that were so small earlier that they didn't show chaos then. Most growers won't bother with having me look this time of year, but Doraal is more careful."

Past the woodlot was hedgerow that not only fronted the road for perhaps four hundred yards, but apparently also ran back at least several hundred yards. "You couldn't tell it, but there's a fine pasture within that hedgerow. Doraal owns that as well. He has some fine dairy cows, but they're for the cheeses he and his family make."

Past the hedgerow was an orchard, bounded in front by a well-kept stone wall.

"All the stone walls . . . ?" Beltur offered.

"Most of the land here grows stones as well as crops. The winters are cold and snowy, and when the snow melts and the mud dries, well, there are always more rocks in the fields and pastures. They do make good fences, though."

Beltur had to look several times at the orchard before he realized that the trees were pearapples, but only because he recognized the fruit. He'd actually never seen a pearapple tree, but then he'd never been far from Fenard before the journey to Analeria, and most of Gallos was too hot for growing pearapples. He'd only seen a few in his life. Past where the orchard wall ended was a long lane paved with flat stones of various shapes, leading back to a thatched stone cottage some fifty yards back from the road.

Athaal stepped onto the lane and walked perhaps ten yards toward the cottage before stopping. "We'll wait here. It won't be long."

Beltur was about to ask how Athaal knew that when

the door to the cottage opened and a short and wiry white-haired man strode toward the mages, his steps light, almost as if he had once been a dancer or the like. The grower carried a short saw, the like of which Beltur had never seen, with fine teeth and a very narrow blade. "Athaal, an apprentice after all these years?"

"I'm afraid not, Doraal. Beltur's a mage in his own right, but he's never dealt with growing things in a magely way. He's a city mage from Fenard."

"You'll find things a mite bit different here," the grower said to Beltur.

"Much more pleasant so far." Beltur smiled.

"It's good to hear that." Doraal looked to Athaal. "We might as well start with the pearapples. I've noticed some lumps in the bark on a few of the trees, but you ought to look at them all."

The three walked west to the far side of the pearapple orchard, where Athaal studied the first tree for a time, as did Beltur, before he moved to the second, then the third. At the fourth, the black mage stopped and circled the tree. Beltur thought he sensed what Athaal did, an off-chaos patch under the bark of a small branch.

"There's some rot or something under the bark here." Athaal used the narrow cupridium knife once more to point.

"How big is it?" asked Doraal.

"About thumb-tip size."

"Can you do anything so I don't have to prune the whole branch?"

"A bit of free chaos surrounded by order *might* work. Beltur could do that. It also might create a canker in a few weeks."

Doraal looked to Beltur. "Try it. I can always prune it."

Beltur spent several moments sensing what he sensed as a twisted chaos within the branch, then eased a tiny bit of free chaos down an order-tube into the rot, which he immediately surrounded with order, holding the containment until he could feel no twisted chaos. Then he eased the free chaos out and let it disperse to the air.

He took a deep breath. "It's done."

Doraal looked to Athaal.

"The rot is gone. The question is whether the tree heals normally or with a canker. The rot hadn't touched the underside of the bark."

"You don't much like using chaos, either, do you?" Doraal asked Beltur.

"I can handle small amounts surrounded with order. I really wouldn't want to try using large amounts, even using order."

The grower nodded.

After the mages stepped back, Doraal reached up and tied a length of brownish wool yarn loosely around the branch, over the spot that Athaal had marked.

After inspecting another half-score trees, Athaal stopped again. "Is this one of the ones you worried about?"

"No. Why?"

"There's a pretty large canker on the shielded side of that branch up there, and if it gets much larger it could affect the trunk underneath."

"Let me see." Saw in hand, the wiry grower climbed up and studied the branch. "Right as rain you are. I'll prune it. You can do what you can after that."

In what seemed like moments, the grower had finished sawing through the branch and was lowering it. Athaal took it and eased it onto the ground, then waited for Doraal to descend before concentrating and applying just a small amount of free order to the cut stump of the branch.

"I'll coat that with pitch after we finish," said Doraal.

Although there were far fewer trees than potato

plants, it took much longer to deal with each of the remaining trees, in both orchards, another three of which
required some pruning, with the result that close to two
glasses had passed by the time the three once more
stood on the stone-paved lane in front of the cottage.

There Doraal handed two coins to Athaal, both
silvers, Beltur sensed, and said, "I'll start picking the
pearapples in two eightdays. Sometime a few days after that?"

"That would be fine."

"I'll see you then." After a friendly smile, the grower
turned and headed for the pearapple orchard, presumably to collect the pruned branches.

Athaal stretched and took a deep breath, then began
to walk toward the road.

Beltur scrambled to follow, asking as he drew abreast
of the black mage, "There won't be more cankers in just
two weeks, will there?"

"No. There shouldn't be. He wants me—or us—to
make sure there's no chaos inside the pearapples. He
charges more for them, and he doesn't want complaints
that they spoil too soon."

"How did that canker, the one you found, get so large
without your sensing it earlier?"

"Sometimes, the cankers grow for a time without
chaos. If they're in a place like that one was, you can't
always see them. Even Doraal didn't know about it, and
I can't physically climb every tree and inspect every
branch. Then, over just a week or two, there's a lot of
chaos."

"So that's why he has you come regularly."

"It is. It's also why everyone wants his apples and
will pay more for them."

"Why did you have me use the chaos? It only took a
tiny bit."

"Even tiny bits of chaos make me uneasy. That's why

I'll never be a great mage. Doraal knows I won't use chaos, but he wouldn't have let you do it without my suggesting it."

That made sense to Beltur. "Where are we going next?"

"To look at some bean fields. Green beans, not dry beans. Bush beans."

Bush beans? Is there any other kind? Once more Beltur followed.

By the time Beltur had trudged back to Bakers Lane at close to fifth glass of the afternoon, his calves ached, he was once more sweaty, despite the fact that Elparta was considerably cooler than Fenard, and he'd learned more about growing in one afternoon than he'd known in his entire life. He'd also learned to sense three kinds of blight, apple and pearapple canker and rot, and the signs of plants that had received too much water, among other things that he couldn't immediately remember.

From five growers, in addition to Doraal, Athaal had received, from what Beltur had glimpsed, slightly more than four silvers, certainly a more than respectable amount for a day's work. *But a very hard day's work.*

After washing up, Beltur sank onto, as much as sat down on, one of the kitchen stools across the table from the seemingly always cheerful Athaal.

"What do you think now, Beltur?"

"Besides the fact that you work hard? I don't know what else to say. So far, it looks to me that I can learn to do most of what you're doing." That was true, but a slight understatement. Beltur suspected he could do everything he'd been shown, but he had to admit that he wouldn't have been able to do any of it without either being instructed or having watched Athaal first. "But that's because I got to watch you first. Without that . . ." Beltur shook his head.

"Magery has two basic parts. One is the ability to

handle the requisite amounts of order and chaos in the proper fashion. The second is knowing what to do, when to do it, and when not to. You have the ability to do anything I do. Right now, you don't have the knowledge. That will come." Athaal smiled. "You're already more black, but whether you'll change more . . . only time will tell."

"Am I black enough that other blacks won't consider me a white?"

"You were that before you got to Elparta. People might question whether you're a black or a gray mage, but I don't think anyone would consider you a white." Athaal added sardonically, "I still wouldn't recommend going back to Fenard or anywhere in Gallos."

Beltur laughed, if ruefully. "I'm afraid you're right about that. Has Meldryn heard anything about what's happening there?"

"He hears more than you or I do, but nothing about that."

"Nothing about what?" asked Meldryn as he entered the kitchen carrying some meat pies on a tray.

"About Arms-Mage Wyath and the troubles in Fenard and Gallos."

"Do you think the Prefect would send an army to attack Spidlar?" asked Beltur.

"Not Spidlar—Elparta. And not just an army. A force backed with the Arms-Mage and the most powerful white mages."

Beltur frowned. "I thought he was more worried about the Viscount of Certis."

"What better way to deal with him than to propose a joint attack? The Viscount can't really attack Spidlar unless he can destroy Axalt or conquer Sligo, and attacking either one would cost him far too many men and gain him little in the way of golds or goods."

"So Denardre offers a token force with a lot of mages," suggested Athaal, "and has the Viscount use his troopers. They come down the Passa River . . ."

Meldryn nodded. "That way they don't come far into Gallos, and there's not much to plunder where they do."

"What about Passera?" asked Beltur.

"It's not much of a place, anymore, sad to say," replied Meldryn. "It never really recovered after Denardre's ancestor sacked the place because Relyn built his temple there."

"Relyn?" Beltur turned to Athaal. "Was he the one who started the worship of the black temples, the one you said never gave his name to many?"

"That was the name he used . . . when he used one. No one really knows if that was his name. He ended up in Axalt, and no one wanted to attack a mountain fortress to get just one man."

"If he left Gallos so long ago, why did Wyath need to destroy the ruins of the temple?"

"Because they were so ordered that blacks came from all over Candar to see them and learn from them," replied Meldryn. "I suspect that was an excuse. I'd wager that Wyath used the destruction to learn how to use chaos to fragment order. That would enable his white mages to break through any shields black mages might raise against them."

"Do you think they did?"

"I'd be doubtful," said Meldryn, "but you never know."

"Do you think the blacks in Gallos will come here or go somewhere else?" asked Beltur.

"As in all things, that depends on the individual," replied Meldryn. "Some wouldn't come here because it gets too cold in winter. On the other hand, neither the Viscount of Certis nor the Duke of Hydlen is particularly trustworthy. Montgren and Lydiar are hard to reach from Fenard, as is Suthya, and it takes a particular . . . temperament . . . to feel comfortable in Sarronnyn."

"How gently you put that," commented Athaal, grinning.

"It's true enough. How about some dinner?"

"That's an excellent idea." Athaal rose and moved toward the cupboard that held the platters, plates, and mugs.

"How did the day go?" asked Meldryn, following him.

"Well. We brought in four silvers and two coppers, but two of the silvers were from Doraal, and he won't need us for another two eightdays, and there are only four other orchards that we'll need to visit over the next eightday or so."

"Was it useful for you, Beltur?" asked Meldryn.

"Very useful. It's also clear that I have a great deal to learn." Beltur followed the two and got three mugs.

"That's true of all of us, all the time. The only question is whether we realize it." Meldryn set a small meat pie on each of the plates that Athaal had set on the worktable. "If you'd pour the ale, Beltur, since you have the mugs."

Beltur did, carefully, then set the mugs on the table, thinking how good the meat pies looked. He seated himself with the others, and just hoped that the crust wasn't as tough as most, but even if it happened to be, he was still eating well, and far better than he had in Fenard.

XXV

Over the next eightday, Beltur followed largely the same
pattern each day—rise, wash, dress, eat, and then accompany Athaal as he made his rounds through the
fields and orchards and small hamlets to the north of
Elparta. Amid all the various chores along the way, he
did find a copper razor in a small hamlet to the northwest of Elparta and, with his remaining coins and a
silver that he borrowed from Athaal, he purchased it.
Getting rid of the scraggly reddish-brown beard made
him feel much better. Athaal also presented him with
some garments, slightly worn, but not obviously, which
were a faded black and were only a trace roomier than
what might have been ideal.

On fourday morning, as Beltur and Athaal once more
set out, this time to inspect some gristmills set along a
stream that flowed into the River Gallos a kay or so
north of Elparta, Beltur realized, if belatedly, that already more than half of harvest season had passed. He
didn't recall time passing that quickly in Fenard.

*You weren't working that hard in Fenard . . . or at
least not until the journey to Analeria.*

This time, they left the city by the north river gate and
walked along the river road, first past the piers on the
north side of the wall, and then past shorter piers with
warehouses at their shore ends.

"Have you ever been inside a mill?" asked Athaal.

"No," admitted Beltur.

"Then just observe, and don't touch anything or get
close to the wheels and gears. Men have been killed
when their clothing or hair got caught in the gears."

The first mill was set in a small square timbered building that had seen far too many winters without proper oiling of its plank walls. The waterwheel at the side of the building was not all that large, looking to be some three yards across, and was fed by a narrow millrace.

"That's Fhawal's. It used to be a gristmill, but it wasn't that good, not with a small undershot wheel and a narrow millrace. So Fhawal turned it into a fulling mill. He's not the best fuller, but he's the cheapest."

"We're not going there, then?"

"No. If he can't do it himself, it doesn't get done."

The two crossed the bridge over the millrace and then turned east and began to walk up a slight rise toward a much larger stone building, one that looked to have been partly dug into the hillside. Beltur didn't see a waterwheel, although a millrace entered the east side of the building, and what looked to be a tailrace flowed from the bottom of the west side that angled into the stream ahead.

"That's Hohdol's gristmill, and we will stop there."

"Is the waterwheel inside?" Beltur had always assumed waterwheels were on the outside of buildings, but if water entered the building and then left it, where else could the wheel be?

"It is. That way he can use the mill except in the very depths of winter. That's when the snows are yards deep and the river freezes over. He claims the wheel will last longer between repairs." Athaal laughed quietly. "Waterwheels are solid. Only his sons may know if he's right."

After they walked over the road bridge that crossed the tailrace, Athaal and Beltur took the uphill lane to an entrance on the mill's upper level. Just beyond the entrance was a loading dock, although no wagon was there. The mill door was closed, but a roaring sound still came through the heavy oak door. Athaal pounded on the door, then opened it and stepped inside.

A youth looked at Athaal, then Beltur, before saying in a loud voice, "Honored mages, I'll tell Father you are here." He turned and hurried around the curved wood enclosure above which was what looked to be an inverted pyramid with a sloped chute leading from it in the direction of the loading dock. On the far side of the enclosure and pyramid stood a bearded man whose faded shirt and trousers were liberally coated with white powder.

Flour, thought Beltur.

The youth was telling his father something, but Beltur couldn't hear a single word. The miller spoke to his son.

After that, the youth hurried back to Athaal. "You'll have to wait until he finishes this run, sers."

"We'll wait." Athaal turned to Beltur. "I might as well tell you how this works before we start trying to sense anything that might be about to go wrong. The millstones are inside the wooden box. The upper stone is the one that moves. It's the runner stone. Both stones have a pattern of grooves—they're called furrows. The grain goes from the hopper there into an eye in the middle of the runner stone . . ."

Beltur listened intently, watching where Athaal pointed as he described how the mill worked, ending up with, "That's just a brief description, but you should get the idea."

"What are you looking for?"

"Any weaknesses in the gears, belts, or the wheel."

"What about the millstones?"

"They're stone. They should last a long time. Now . . . I'm going to see what I can find. It wouldn't hurt for you to try as well."

Not knowing where might be the best place to begin, Beltur let his senses follow the grain from the chute to the hopper and into the millstones . . . except there was something there, something with the upper stone. It wasn't chaos, but more like something that wasn't as ordered as it should be. Yet how could he tell where it was with the millstone turning as fast as it did?

For the moment, he couldn't do anything.

Next he began to trace things back from the rapidly spinning shaft that turned the runner stone, and the gears beneath that that changed the modest speed of the waterwheel into the rapid turning of the millstones, and the belts that did various other things. He didn't sense any destructive chaos, although there were certainly places of heat chaos. There was one place where he thought that heat chaos on one of the belts was possibly too high, but only because it was higher than anywhere else, and he'd have to ask Athaal about that.

He also marveled at the complexity of the mill. Even after Athaal's explanation he doubted he understood more than the basic idea, if that. Slowly, he drew his senses back to himself, only to find Athaal looking at him.

"Did you sense anything?"

"I did, but I don't know how much of the heat chaos is normal and what might not be . . ." Beltur offered a shrug that he hoped conveyed ignorance.

"Where was there the most heat chaos?"

"The belt—it must be leather—that turns the wheel that shakes the flour in the flour hopper. It seemed too hot to me."

Athaal nodded. "I felt that, too. Anything else?"

"There's something about the top millstone, the one that spins. It's not chaos, but it bothers me. It moves so fast that I can't really tell more."

"When he shuts the water gate and the mill stops, we can look at that more closely."

Beltur wasn't certain, but he thought that a good half glass must have passed before the mill began to slow. Then, the only sound was water flowing down the back of the waterwheel to the tail and out to the tailrace.

The miller walked around the millstone apparatus. "What brings you here, Mage? And your friend?"

"It's been a while, Hohdol, but you did tell me to stop by in mid-harvest. Beltur's a city mage who decided that Fenard wasn't the safest place for him."

"What I hear, it's not safe for many anymore. I did tell you to come mid-harvest. That I did." The miller was almost shouting, perhaps out of habit to be heard above the roaring of the mill, or perhaps because years of milling had dulled his hearing. "You looked to be maging or whatever you call it. What did you find? Shouldn't be finding much. She's running sweet."

"You might check the belt running the flour-collection-bin sifter. It's running hotter than I recall."

"Aye. I wondered about that myself. Didn't smell quite right."

Beltur abruptly forced himself to concentrate on the runner stone, now stationary. There was definitely an odd-shaped section of the stone that felt . . . all he could think was that it lacked the order that the rest of that millstone had, or that the bed stone had.

"What is it, Beltur?" asked Athaal.

"There's something not quite the way it should be with a part of the runner stone. It doesn't have the same order that the rest of the stone has, or that the bed stone does. It's different, not as strong. It might . . . break?"

"The runner stone is iron-bound, and that's inside a wooden collar," declared Hohdol.

"I don't think the stone is going to break apart," said

Beltur. "There's a chunk that might come loose. Or flake off. Something."

"There's no way that can happen," declared the miller. "Stones wear out. They can break if they're dropped, but they don't break from just milling. These are special stones. They were mined in Hrisbarg and shipped from Lydiar."

"Beltur . . ." offered Athaal. "Can you go over there and point to where this might be?"

Beltur nodded and walked over to the millstones, going a third of the way around. "Under here. An area bigger than a spread hand. There's no chaos, but there's a lot less order there. I don't know what that means. I just know that it's not the same."

Athaal was clearly concentrating. Then he frowned. "There is something there." He looked to Hohdol. "It might not be anything, but there's a section of the runner stone that's weaker."

"Two mages telling me something that can't be." Hohdol shook his head. "But you caught the belt. Now, you'll have me worrying, wondering what might go wrong." He shook his head again. "Might as well look."

Hohdol first pulled out two pegs from the chute, then swung the hopper to the side. Next he pulled on a long rope that ran up to a pulley attached to a lever, and then back down. Each pull ratcheted the lever, which in turn raised the runner stone.

Seeing how much effort it took to raise the runner stone, Beltur hoped he hadn't put the miller to so much work for nothing. *But there is something there . . . or rather something isn't there.*

After much effort, Hohdol peered at the underside of the runner stone. "I don't see anything." He used a dressing pick to tap the underside of the stone.

"Farther to the right," suggested Beltur.

The miller handed the pick to Beltur. "Show me."

Beltur used his senses to guide the pick to the edge of what appeared to be a break, then tapped it once, then twice, then moved to the other side, and tapped again.

Abruptly, an irregular section of gray stone dropped onto the bed stone—a piece no larger than a man's hand and spread fingers and no thicker than the width of his little finger.

Hohdol just gaped.

"I didn't know if that would be a problem," said Beltur, apologetically as he handed the dressing pick back to the miller, "but Athaal said to let you know if I sensed anything that seemed wrong."

"You just tapped it a little . . ."

"I knew where to tap. It would have lasted a little longer. I don't know how much longer."

Hohdol looked at the runner stone again. "That bastard Murdyth. That bastard. He must have cracked it when he dressed the stone. But how? That quartz is mortised in there."

"Was anyone with him?" asked Athaal.

"An older-looking fellow. Said he was his cousin. Why?"

"Someone removed the order from that section, just that section. What would have happened if that piece had dropped while the mill was running?"

"Wouldn't have dropped far, less than a grain's worth, but it might have ruined the bed stone as well, gotten stone and quartz dust into an entire bin of flour. Demon spawn . . . doesn't matter. Either way, I've got to replace both."

"I'm sorry," Beltur offered. "I didn't . . ."

Hohdol shook his head. "Better that you found out. If that had happened when we were milling, no telling what else might have busted." He looked to Athaal. "You think Murdyth had a renegade white?"

"That's possible, but why would he do something like that? You told me you've kept a spare set of stones."

"Most folks don't know that. Blacks don't tell. Didn't worry about telling you." The miller took a deep breath. "No sense jawing more. Nadol and I got a long day ahead of us. Wait here for a bit."

"He's not happy," said Beltur quietly after Hohdol walked toward the loading dock.

"Would you be? A pair of stones like that costs ten golds, maybe more. And another gold to ship them here."

Beltur winced. "I really didn't think it was that weak." He paused. "Someone had to have removed that order. That wasn't natural."

"No, it wasn't. I'm going to have to have Meldryn ask around, to see if anything else like this has happened. It's likely worse than Hohdol thinks."

"What do you mean?"

"A millwright or dresser wouldn't do that. Not unless he was forced to. Or compelled."

"That would take a very strong white," Beltur pointed out. "I don't think Uncle even ever tried anything like that."

Shortly, Hohdol returned with a cloth bag that he handed to Athaal. "There's what's usual for going over things, and a few coppers extra for finding that weakness. And if Murdyth ever comes back . . ."

"After that, he may not," said Athaal. "Thank you. We wish it hadn't turned out this way."

"You and me both. Well . . . we need to replace some stones."

Athaal and Beltur both inclined their heads before departing.

Once they were well away from the mill, Athaal stopped. "You get two coppers for what you did. You found what was important. I could barely sense that even when the millstone wasn't moving."

Beltur thought for a moment. "Just one. I wouldn't have been able to do it without you and Meldryn taking me in and helping me. I owe you more than I can repay at the moment, but once I start earning coins, I'll start repaying you . . . if that's acceptable."

Athaal grinned. "That's more black than many blacks."

Beltur wasn't certain about that, but he was pleased that Athaal thought so.

XXVI

"Where to today?" asked Beltur as he finished the last morsels of his breakfast on sixday morning, then stood to begin cleaning up the kitchen, a task he'd taken over within days of arriving in Elparta. Cleaning up after breakfast and the evening meal was about all he could do, because Athaal and Meldryn insisted that Laranya do the rest of the house cleaning.

"We're doing sheep-checking," replied Athaal. "Ewes. Kassmyn has me do this every harvest, usually just before fall, and again in the spring. He likes to know which ewes are strong enough to breed, and if any are diseased or carry some form of chaos."

"Do sheep show illness and weakness with order and chaos in the same way as people and horses?" Beltur carried the plates to the tin washtub.

"All larger animals do. So do even the smallest ones, I understand. I'm going to check with Meldryn to see if he needs anything from Kassmyn."

As Beltur began to wash the plates and mugs, his mind went back over what Athaal had just said. . . .

even the smallest ones, I understand. That suggested that it was harder to sense order-chaos patterns in smaller animals. Beltur didn't know. He'd just assumed that was the case, but he'd never tried, except with people and horses, perhaps because he'd grown up in the city and never been near many animals, even dogs or cats. He'd simply never thought about sensing them for order and chaos.

By the time Beltur had finished in the kitchen and washed himself up again, Athaal was ready to leave the house.

They hadn't walked two blocks when Beltur saw a sooty and scrawny gray cat at the edge of an alley. The moment he looked at the feline, it dashed back into the shadows, gone too quickly for Beltur to get more than a quick sense of the animal's order-chaos balance, although it seemed to him that the order and chaos were more spread through the body, while in people order and chaos were more concentrated in the upper body and head.

While he was trying to be more aware of small animals, it seemed that his very interest in them resulted in his seeing none, and it appeared that he had difficulty sensing animals he had not seen first. *Could it be lack of experience?*

As seemed normal, the city gate guards scarcely looked at the pair of mages, and the two were well beyond the northeast city gate and headed east along the road that Beltur recalled taking the first day he had accompanied Athaal when the bells rang out seventh glass.

"How far is this herder?"

"A good three kays. Uphill."

Beltur just nodded. After almost two solid eightdays of brisk walks that totaled well over ten kays a day, three kays no longer seemed unnatural . . . even uphill,

"We're going to that part of his lands that's closest to Elparta," added Athaal.

"He owns the lands he grazes?"

"Most of them. Some he pays to graze."

"He must be well-off."

"You sound surprised."

"The only herders I've encountered were in the grass-lands of Analeria, and they definitely were anything but well-off."

"They probably lose too many animals to the grass cats." Athaal's words were almost dismissive.

Somehow that bothered Beltur, even though he certainly didn't have any reasons to defend the grassland herders, not when they had attacked him and the others. "They also hunted antelope."

"Most likely to eat and also to keep them from eating too much of the grass, except that would make the grass cats more likely to prey on their herds."

Although Athaal's words made sense, Beltur had his doubts, but he wondered whether he should be doubting when he knew so little about herds, sheep, and the nomad herders.

Somewhat less than a glass after leaving Elparta, Beltur turned and looked back. Although the slope had seemed gentle, they were at least several hundred yards higher than the River Gallos. He continued walking.

Before long, Athaal pointed ahead toward an ancient hedgerow paralleling the road and also running north. "That's the southwest corner of Kassmyn's lands."

"Are they all surrounded by hedgerows?"

"The lands here are. I don't know about the others. The main gate's another half kay ahead."

The main gate could have graced the country grounds of a wealthy trader. Two square stone gateposts, half a yard on a side, anchored the double iron-bound gates, each of heavy well-oiled oak planks, standing two yards wide and two and a half high. A stone wall ran a yard or so from each gatepost into the hedgerow, which was so thick that Beltur couldn't tell how much farther the wall actually extended, although he doubted it was much more than a few yards. The east gate was partly open, with the end resting on a circular gate rest sawed from a tree trunk. Beyond the gate was a narrow stone-paved lane.

"He's expecting us." Athaal stepped through the opening in the gate.

Beltur followed. Once past the gate, he could see that the lane ran north for a good two hundred yards to a circular paved area in front of a two-story stone dwelling, some twenty-odd yards across the front, with a split slate roof. The house was not small by any means, but certainly not anything like homes of the larger merchants and traders in Fenard. On both sides of the lane was just pasture, or meadow.

As they walked closer, Beltur made out several pens behind and to the north of the house, in which were sheep. The lane circled around the house to the north, toward a large barn. On the south side of the house was a garden, enclosed by a stone wall no more than a yard and a half high. For a moment, Beltur wondered at the odd height of the wall, then smiled. The last thing Kassmyn wanted was his sheep grazing in the garden, but the low wall allowed a better view. A red-haired girl stood waiting on the small stone terrace before the brass-bound main door.

"It's good to see you again, Mistress Mynya. You've grown since the spring."

"You always say that, Mage Athaal. Is he your apprentice?"

"No. He's a city mage who's learning what I do." Athaal half turned. "Beltur, this is Mynya, Herder Kassmyn's youngest daughter. Mynya, this is Beltur."

Mynya inclined her head. "I am very pleased to meet you."

"And I you," returned Beltur warmly.

"Father is out in the back. He's expecting you."

"Will you be joining us?"

"No. I have to do my lessons."

After Mynya entered the house and closed the door, Beltur studied the dwelling more closely. All the windows were glazed. Those on the lower level were narrow, and all of them had heavy shutters. Those on the upper level were much wider, but were also shuttered. Beltur counted the chimneys—eight.

"I take it that it's cold here in winter, and the snow can be deep."

"Deeper some years than others, but there's usually never less than a yard on the ground after the beginning of winter. That's because it's higher here. It's warmer near the river."

Once they were on the north side of the house, Beltur could see a small forest or a large woodlot farther to the northeast, another hundred yards beyond the farthest sheep pen.

Standing in front of the nearest pen, which was empty, stood a sandy-haired man wearing light gray trousers and shirt. He raised an arm and called, "You're just about when I expected you, Athaal."

As they walked toward the herder and the two dogs who flanked him, both sitting alertly on their haunches, Beltur looked at the mass of black-faced sheep in the large fenced pen to the north of the empty pen. There had to be hundreds there. He paused, seeing a temporary double fence between the two pens. His eyes went to a much smaller and empty pen, and then to the dogs. The two looked almost identical, with the same glossy black coats and patches of white between their eyes and on their chests. They studied Beltur, and he reached out with his senses to them, nodding to himself as he saw the patterns of order and chaos, much the same as in people, if not quite so much of either order or chaos around their heads.

"You brought help this time, I see," offered the herder.

Beltur jerked his attention back to Kassmyn.

"Beltur, this is Herder Kassmyn. Kassmyn, Beltur is a city mage from Fenard who decided to come to Elparta for his health."

"Wise man, from what I've heard about the present prefect. Welcome to Mynholm."

"Thank you."

Kassmyn turned to Athaal. "They're all ready."

"The same as always? You and the dogs will herd the weaker ones to the small pen?"

The herder nodded.

"Make the first few farther apart so that Beltur can see what I do."

"We can do that."

In moments Athaal and Beltur were standing on one side of the chute formed by the temporary pole fences. Beltur took a closer look at the sheep. Each one was black-faced, with grayish white wool everywhere else. A faint but definitely oily odor drifted toward him on the light breeze.

Then the first sheep headed down the fenced chute.

"Just try to sense any off-chaos."

"Like wound chaos?"

"It's pretty much the same for sheep as people."

The first sheep seemed healthy enough to Beltur, and obviously, to Athaal as well, as did the next six or seven. Then another ewe appeared, and Beltur could sense something wrong with her even from several yards away. "There's something wrong with the next one— orangish chaos in the chest and in the middle between the hindquarters."

Athaal frowned, but then nodded as the ewe reached him. "This one!"

Behind them Kassmyn moved a section of the fence so that the ewe left the temporary chute, where the two dogs, following gestures from Kassmyn, herded her into the small pen where another youth, older than Mynya, but looking similar to the herder, opened the gate, and then closed it behind the ewe. Beltur didn't have time to see exactly what gestures the herder made, but the two dogs clearly understood and acted on those gestures.

The sheep kept coming, faster and faster, or so it seemed to Beltur, and his nose began to run, and he found himself sneezing more and more often. He didn't keep track of the unhealthy ones, either with internal wounds or disease or with such a low level of order and chaos that he wondered how they could even trot along the chute.

Then, after what felt like glasses, the pen at the head of the chute was empty, as was the chute.

Beltur glanced toward the smaller pen, where there were almost ten ewes, and then up at the green-blue sky, not quite looking at the blazing white sun, but noting that it was definitely past noon, and close to first glass. They had been working as long as it had felt.

"Time for a break," Kassmyn called out. "You two look worn out."

"That's hard work," murmured Beltur as he stepped back from the fence.

"Most of what people pay mages to do is," replied Athaal quietly, turning and heading toward Kassmyn.

Accompanied by the two children, the herder led the way back to the house and through a rear door to the kitchen, where two women were serving from a large pot set on a woodstove, and then to a room off it. "The breakfast room. It's where we eat most of the time." He gestured to the youth. "By the way, this is Dormyn.

Dormyn, you should remember Mage Athaal. The other mage is Beltur. Just sit down. Ekatrina will be joining us in a moment."

Beltur had barely seated himself when a woman almost as tall as Kassmyn appeared, wearing an apron over a tunic and trousers the same shade of gray as worn by Kassmyn and his children.

She smiled as she slipped into the chair at the far end of the table from Kassmyn. "The food will be here in a moment or two."

"My consort, Ekatrina. My dear, you might remember Mage Athaal, and this is Mage Beltur."

"I'm pleased to see you both." She looked back to Kassmyn.

The grower cleared his throat, then spoke. "For order in life, in all things, and with gratitude for its bounties."

"For order," repeated everyone but Beltur.

"There!" declared Kassmyn. "Now for some ale."

Immediately, the serving woman appeared. All the adults received a full mug's worth, while the children got perhaps a third of a mug. Then came the platters.

Beltur looked down at what was on his plate, the same as on each plate—a heap of thick noodles, almost dumpling-like, covered with a dark brown sauce in which were mushrooms, carrots, and plenty of thin slices of meat. He waited until Kassmyn began to eat before he took a mouthful. While the meat was lamb or mutton, it was tender, and had a rich flavor that he couldn't place.

"Ekatrina makes the best pearapple mutton," declared Kassmyn with a broad smile toward his consort.

"And you brew the best ale," she replied.

Beltur realized that, preoccupied as he'd been with the meal proper and observing the family, he'd never even tasted the ale. He did so, noting as he raised his mug that the brew looked almost black. He was ready to wince at the taste, recalling just how bitter the dark ale his uncle preferred had been, only to find that the brew was smooth and rich without being either bitter or sweet. *If only Uncle could have tasted this . . .* Beltur just held the mug for a moment without speaking.

"What do you think of the Prefect?" Kassmyn asked, looking at Beltur.

"I wouldn't trust him. He can hide what he feels even from accomplished mages, and Arms-Mage Wyath has been removing any white mages who won't offer Wyath unconditional support. I heard that he was considering raising tariffs on any goods that enter or leave Gallos."

Kassmyn turned to Athaal. "And you?"

"I've heard similar stories. We know of at least one white mage who was killed by Wyath, and I know of another who left Gallos in fear for his life."

The herder nodded. "That's the problem when one man rules. There's nothing to stop him when he starts making trouble." He offered a mischievous smile and added, "Might say the same about one woman ruling."

"Except neither the Marshal nor the Tyrant ever start anything," replied Ekatrina. "They just put an end to men's foolishness." She smiled back at her consort.

Mynya smiled as well.

"You can see that my ladies have minds of their own."

"As well we should," replied Ekatrina. "How are the sheep?"

"Looks like a few more might be chaos-tinged this year. We'll have to see. It might also be because last winter was so hard."

The rest of the mealtime conversation centered on the weather.

When everyone had finished eating and stood to leave the table, Beltur looked to Kassmyn, and then to Ekatrina. "Thank you. That was one of the best meals I've ever tasted."

"You see," said Athaal with a grin, "Elparta has many advantages over Fenard."

"Every day I'm discovering that."

The afternoon was much like the morning, except longer, with another two full pens of sheep that required studying.

Then, after that, Athaal and Beltur went back over each of the ewes that had been separated out, explaining to Kassmyn what they had found and where.

In some cases, the herder just nodded, saying, "I've been watching this one. Knew she was getting along," or words to that effect. In other cases, where there did not seem to be any immediate physical symptom, the grower notched an ear.

As the three left the last small pen that had held separated ewes, Kassmyn mused, "There were close to thirty ewes that shouldn't be bred. Last year it was more like twenty. That's worrisome."

"Some were just getting old," Athaal pointed out. "That just happens."

"Happens to all of us, Mage."

"Some of them might get better."

"Not many that you've found got better, I have to say."

"A few got stronger and recovered."

"True. I wish it had been more."

As the three walked back toward the main dwelling, past the sheep sheds, Beltur saw a large gray dog sitting alertly beside the door to the shed nearest to the pen that held the healthy sheep from the first sorting, in fact, a dog so large that he'd first thought it might have been a sheep. "That's a large dog. Is it something special?"

"He's just a mongrel," offered Kassmyn. "He showed up one day, barely more than a pup. I tried teaching him to work the sheep. He was hopeless. Good watchdog, though. Nothing gets close to the sheep without him letting me know. He gets along with the sheepdogs. He's touchy with strangers, and he's even chased off a mountain cat when I took him to the back highlands. That's why I feed him and keep him."

Beltur felt that wasn't the only reason, but he just nodded.

Then the two waited outside the front entry while Kassmyn entered the house, only to return shortly with a small leather pouch that he handed to Athaal. "Thank you both. If I need you before mid-spring, I'll send a messenger."

"We appreciate it," replied Athaal.

When the two mages walked away from the holding, the sun was low over the hills to the northwest, and Beltur knew it would be deep twilight by the time they reached the dwelling on Bakers Lane.

"Is it always like this? When you do sheep, I mean?"

"It always has been." Athaal paused. "I think Kassmyn's right, though. It seems to me that we're seeing more chaos this year."

"Could it be because of the winter?"

"We've had harder winters before."

"What else could be causing it?"

"Nylan claimed that when chaos increased, order also increased. It seems to me that the other way might hold as well."

Beltur recalled something along those lines from *The Book of Ayrlyn*. Still . . . "But where is order increasing?"

"It's increasing here. We have more black mages than we've ever had. It might be increasing somewhere else in Candar or maybe in Austra or Nordla or even Hamor. Something has to be causing it."

"But wouldn't Wyath's killing of mages decrease the chaos?"

"It's not just the number of mages, but also how much order or chaos they've gathered and continue to hold."

"I thought holding too much of either wasn't a good idea."

"Holding too much chaos is never a good idea if you want to live for long, but it will give you greater power over others."

"Which is what Wyath wants."

"So it would seem."

"What about order?"

Athaal did not reply immediately, but Beltur kept walking without saying a word.

Finally, Athaal said, "I don't know. Meldryn and I have talked about it. Too much order without some chaos will kill anyone, even a mage."

Beltur thought about that for a time. "Then . . . would handling a great deal of order require some additional chaos?"

Athaal again hesitated before replying. "No one seems to know."

"Has anyone tried?"

"Gathering chaos in order to gather more order?" Athaal actually shuddered.

"That suggests it's dangerous." Beltur wasn't so sure of that, but, given his own limited experience, he wasn't about to say so.

"Very dangerous. I wouldn't want to try it. Neither would Meldryn."

"Do you think that any mage who tried that would show a different pattern of order and chaos? I mean one that we could easily sense?"

"I'd think they'd have to. Animals have a different pattern, and people do, depending on how attuned they are to order or chaos. We can certainly sense concentrations of order or chaos."

Beltur immediately wondered what the differences would be between a truly powerful white mage and a black mage of equal power, besides the fact that one would concentrate chaos and the other order. *Would they be mirror images of each other, or would they come to resemble each other?*

"Anyway," said Athaal, "I don't think that's something we'll need to worry about. What did you learn today?"

"I've got a much better feel for the patterns of order and chaos in animals, larger ones, anyway." *Thanks to both the sheep and the dogs.* There were also a few other things he needed to think over as well, such as the fact that he seemed able to discern "unnatural" chaos, at least in small bits, from a greater distance than Athaal. Was that just because he had been trained as a white? Or for some other reason?

"That's good. That might be useful in the next few days."

"Oh?"

"You'll see. I'd rather have you encounter what I have in mind without your getting the wrong impression from me. On the way back, you can practice throwing a few shield confinements around me. You'll get stronger if you practice when you're tired."

Although Beltur couldn't sense any deception or untruth behind Athaal's words, the other mage's statements worried him, as if Athaal had plans for him, or was preparing him for some trial. *A trial to be accepted as a black mage?* Since there wasn't much he could do about it, and since it appeared that such a possibility might just be necessary, he kept walking.

XXVII

When Beltur woke on sevenday in the dark, his head ached, and he could hear rain pelting down outside the single small window of his room. He found he was chill under the single blanket, and there was little point in remaining in bed and shivering. He got up and made his way to the washroom, thinking that he was likely the first one up, only to hear voices from downstairs. He washed, shaved, and dressed, heading downstairs as quickly as he could.

"Yesterday must have worn you out," said Athaal from where he sat at the table.

"I'll see you both later," added Meldryn as he headed toward the bakery.

"What time is it?" asked a confused Beltur.

"Not quite sixth glass."

"That late? It's almost pitch dark outside."

Athaal laughed. "I forgot. You've never seen a real northeaster. We usually don't get them until fall. The clouds are always so thick it's like twilight in midday. Those days, like this morning, we have hot cider."

"And the rain must be like ice," said Beltur as he filled his mug and then sat down, hoping the cider was indeed hot. He sipped. It was only warm, but he could hope it would ease his headache.

"The rain outside is mixed ice and rain. When a northeaster comes in late fall, it's either all ice or snow. In winter, a yard of snow can fall in a day."

"We're not going out in this, I hope?"

Athaal shook his head. "There's no point in it. That's why I didn't wake you. We'll help Meldryn in the bakery. If we finish early, then I'll go over some order exercises that might help you." He smiled. "I'm not sure you need that much help, but we'll see. Finish your breakfast, and clean up here. Then meet me in the bakery. By then, I'll know what Meldryn needs us to do."

Beltur didn't exactly hurry to eat the egg toast, also barely warm, or the small piece of leftover shepherd's pie, but he also didn't dawdle. He did clean up the kitchen before leaving.

The first thing Beltur noticed when he entered the bakery was that he no longer felt chilled. In fact, in moments he was uncomfortable. Then he saw that Meldryn wore a shirt that looked to be linen, very thin, worn, and patched linen, and there were damp patches of sweat on it. Athaal had hung his tunic on a wall peg and stood there in a sleeveless smallshirt. Beltur immediate doffed his own tunic and hung it on the peg next to Athaal's.

Athaal turned from inspecting what looked to be an iron scraper with a long wooden handle. "Good. You're here. We need to clean out some of the pie ovens."

Clean the pie ovens? In Fenard, the only ovens Beltur had ever seen in houses were small iron containers with iron legs to be used in a hearth. He glanced around to see if he had missed something. In the far corner of the bakery—the corner formed by the outside walls—was a large stove that stood over two yards high. The entire outside was composed of ceramic tiles, but Beltur couldn't tell if they were set in mortar or mortared together like bricks to form the oven. In addition to the wood-loading door, the stove had seven other iron doors, three large ones about a yard above the stone floor, and four smaller ones whose base was about half a yard above the top of the lower doors—except the four smaller doors were spaced so that they were actually placed between and above the lower doors. All of the doors were open, and that well might have been where the heat came from.

"The scrapers are here on the worktable in the back. We need to scrape all the char off the inside and outside. Meldryn's finished with baking the bread. He didn't load the stove full once he saw the northeaster because he won't be selling nearly as many pies, not early in the day, anyway. So now is a good time to clean them."

Beltur walked over to where Athaal stood beside the worktable. There were several of the long-handled devices. Two had blades, and two had awl-like points.

"The ovens and the doors are still hot. Put these on." Athaal handed Beltur two oversized mittens that looked to have been made of rags. "They'll protect your hands. You need to scrape away the char, just enough to get down to the brick."

Beltur didn't think he'd ever heard of scraping out ovens.

His expression or his feelings must have been obvious, because Athaal then said, "Most people don't really taste it, but things that are baked in ovens with too much char actually are more bitter. It's just one of the things we do that makes more people prefer what Meldryn bakes. The long awl points are for the edges and corners, and the small tin pail is where all the char and soot goes. Try not to get it on the floor."

Beltur nodded. How hard could cleaning the ovens of a bread and pastry stove be?

"You start with the top oven on the left. It will be easier if you pull the bench over and stand on it. That way you can see all the corners. And don't brush against the doors or the iron frame. They're cooling, but it takes a while before you want to touch them. And why are we doing this while the ovens are warm? Because it's easier."

Doing as he'd been told, Beltur carried one of the two

small benches over to the stove and positioned it in the same way Athaal had. Then, long-handled scraper in hand, he stepped up onto the bench and looked into the oven, blinking and jerking his head back as he felt the hot air across his face. He frowned and let his senses study the heat chaos in the oven. From what he could tell, the hot air from the wood burning—or perhaps just coals at the moment—flowed up through openings at the bottom of each side of the oven and then vented or returned through even narrower openings at the back of the oven, which was a heavy iron plate that still radiated heat.

He ran the scraper blade over the bricks that floored the oven. The black residue remained.

"You need to scrape at more of an angle," suggested Athaal.

Beltur tried that, and some of the residue appeared on the flat surface above the blade. Another scrape, and more came up . . . but not a lot more. After another series of scrapes, Beltur was sweating heavily, and it didn't look as though he'd gotten that much of the blackened residue removed from the bricks.

"Some bakers say that the tiny ash from the fire and the fine soot doesn't settle on what you're baking," added Meldryn as he slid a long-handled wooden peel into the middle oven, "but it does. Everything affects what you bake." Using the peel, he removed a long cylindrical loaf of bread, carrying it to the counter at the front of the bakery.

Beltur nodded, blotted his forehead with the back of his forearm, and then made another effort at scraping the thin black layer that seemed glued to the bricks. If it happened to be easier when the ovens were warm, he definitely didn't want to be scraping when they were stone cold. *But why would it be easier when they're warm?*

He did his best to sense the order-chaos balance of just the residue. From what he could tell, the black residue had tiny little sticky parts that clung to tiny holes in the brick. He then attempted to place the tiniest bits of chaos in the little holes. Then he scraped, and the black came off easily, leaving the small bit of brick almost as clean as new. He did that again, and it worked.

He kept at it, but after almost a glass of scraping the black stuff and easing it into the small tin pail, he realized that he was just as tired, if not more so, than if he'd just scraped. But he'd finished the first oven, and he doubted that he could have just with sheer physical effort. He sat down on the bench and blotted his forehead.

"It's hot work." Athaal paused and looked at Beltur. "You're pale. Go back to the kitchen. Have a mug of ale and cool off. Then, when you feel better, come on back."

"Thank you." Beltur stood. His legs felt a little shaky, but he made it to the kitchen, where he followed Athaal's instructions. The ale made him feel better, but he was still shaky, until he ate some of the stale leftover bread.

He sat in the kitchen for a bit longer, then returned to the bakery.

Athaal looked at him closely, then nodded and returned to working on his second oven.

Beltur continued to use the tiny bits of chaos, if slightly more sparingly, and it took him perhaps a quarter glass longer to finish his second oven than it took Athaal. That was hardly surprising, even with Beltur's use of chaos-bits, because Athaal had certainly more experience.

As soon as Beltur stepped off the bench and away from the oven, Meldryn looked at the first oven that Beltur had cleaned, then the second one. He was frowning when he turned to Beltur. "You didn't use order on your scraper, did you?"

"No, ser. Why?"

"There's usually a little chaos residue after scraping, unless you actually scrape off a bit of the bricks, but you didn't do that."

"I just did the best I could." Beltur wasn't about to mention his tiny, tiny bits of chaos, especially since he didn't know why his using them would have left the oven more orderly, rather than more chaotic. It had just felt as though it might work . . . and it had. But he was surprised that neither black mage had noticed. Was that because his use had been so small compared to the large amount of chaos and order freed by the burning wood and coals? He blotted his forehead again.

"That was a good morning's work," said Meldryn approvingly. "It's still raining hard, but there's nothing else I need."

"Then we'll leave you," replied Athaal.

Meldryn was already firing up the stove again before Athaal and Beltur left the bakery. Beltur washed up thoroughly and changed into his other smallshirt before meeting with Athaal in the parlor.

"Did you have a headache this morning?" asked Athaal.

"A bit of one, but after I ate it went away."

"What about now?"

"My shoulders and hands hurt, but not my head." Beltur grinned ruefully. "Cleaning those ovens is hard."

"You did well. Better than I'd expected. You're sure your head doesn't ache?"

"I'm sure. It doesn't hurt or ache. Why?"

"That's very good. Most white mages get a splitting headache when northeasters strike Elparta. That's another reason why white mages generally don't find Spidlar, and particularly Elparta, to their liking."

"Another?" asked Beltur. "That's the first I've heard."

A momentary frown appeared, then vanished before Athaal replied. "The first is similar to why few blacks remain in Gallos. It appears as though where there are many blacks, the whites feel uncomfortable, and where there are many whites, blacks generally feel less comfortable."

Beltur thought about that for a moment. "That seems to be true in Spidlar and in Gallos. What about Westwind, Sarronnyn, Suthya, and other lands?"

"I can only speak to those lands in Candar. Westwind prefers to do without mages, although blacks and druids are welcome to travel there. Sarronnyn has some blacks, and few whites, although there have been those in the Tyrant's bloodline who have been both black and white. The Viscount of Certis is much like the Prefect. Both prefer only mages at their beck and call. Montgren is mostly herders and has little need of powerful mages and even less with which to pay them. As for Lydiar," Athaal shrugged, "who can tell? The dukes' wishes have changed with each succession, at least since Heldry the Mad, and that was centuries ago."

Heldry the Mad? "I've never heard of that duke. If he was a duke."

"He was. He's said to have challenged his flatterers to stand in the middle of a storm with him. All the sycophants who insisted he was powerful enough to turn back the storm were struck dead by the lightning."

"And he wasn't?"

"He survived. It's a cautionary tale about flattery. Probably greatly exaggerated. It might not even be true, but it's a good story. Sometimes, the best ones are true, and sometimes they're not. Anyway, there don't tend to be many whites here or in Sarronnyn, or many blacks in Gallos, Certis, or Hydlen. There aren't any whites at all in the Great Forest of Naclos. The druids and the forest see to that."

That was no surprise to Beltur, but Athaal's questions about headaches and rain raised another question. "Heavy rains always made magery difficult for my uncle, but I haven't had those kinds of problems . . ." At least, he hadn't in the bakery.

"Are you asking if the rain can cause problems for blacks and grays?"

"I suppose I am."

"Water tends to make it harder to do any sort of magery, black or white. Oceans and lakes attract order. Rivers and rain create . . . well . . . a tension between chaos and order. For some reason, it usually affects whites more. I don't know why. Neither does Meldryn."

"What would you suggest that I do to improve my ability to handle order?" asked Beltur.

"Just keep doing what you're doing. No one even here would think you were ever a white. I'm honestly not sure you ever were. Meldryn thinks that there aren't any mages that are naturally black or white. He believes that some people have an ability to sense order and chaos. A smaller group of those people can manipulate those forces. Whether someone is white or black depends on how they learn to do it. That's what he thinks."

"You think that people have an attraction to one or the other, don't you?"

Athaal paused before replying. "That's the way it seems to me. I think you weren't a very good white because you are more attracted to order."

"Couldn't you both be right?"

Athaal laughed good-naturedly. "We could. We could also both be wrong." He stood and took a deep breath. "Enjoy having a little time to yourself. I'm going to see if there's anything I can do for Meldryn. After that, if the rain lets up, I may visit Lhadoraak and Taelya."

"You haven't mentioned them," said Beltur cautiously.

"Lhadoraak's a black about ten years older than you. Taelya's his daughter. She does call me 'Uncle Athaal,' and she's likely the closest to a niece that I'll ever have." He smiled.

After Athaal left, Beltur walked to the window and looked out. The heavy raindrops continued to pelt down so quickly that he could barely see across the small courtyard garden to the rear wall. Athaal had mentioned a tension between order and chaos in rain. Beltur had sensed something like that when he'd created a lightning bolt . . . or something close enough to it that his uncle had thought it might have been one— or something created by an ordermage. *And Uncle wouldn't have said it that way if he hadn't known something.*

Standing behind the glass panes of the window, he just tried to gain a feeling for the flow of either order or chaos in the rain and the low-hanging and dark clouds from which the heavy droplets fell, although he had the impression that the storm hurled them, rather than just let them fall. The more he concentrated on the rain, the more he got the impression, not of falling raindrops, but of falling bits composed of order and chaos, and that the larger droplets tended to have either more order or more chaos, and that there were continual flows of order and chaos.

After a time, his head began to ache, and he turned from the window, thinking. *Why would those patterns create a headache for a chaos-mage but not an ordermage?*

Abruptly, another thought came to him—*because the*

flows are chaotic and that chaos disrupts the white mage's ability to deal with chaos. That made a strange sort of sense because ordermages used order, and when they did deal with chaos, it was usually with order as a buffer. Even so, if he were correct, the chaotic nature of the order and chaos flows in the rain would reduce the effectiveness of any attempt to use magery. And that certainly agreed with what Athaal had said.

Beltur smiled, if ruefully. While he was pleased with what he had learned, or thought he had learned, he hadn't the faintest idea of what use that knowledge or understanding might be.

XXVIII

The heavy rain of the northeaster continued well into eightday, but on oneday morning, the skies were bright, and the air clear. Beltur had just finished cleaning up the kitchen when Athaal and Meldryn returned, both looking somber. Athaal held several sheets of paper.

"We just received this at the bakery a few moments ago," announced Athaal. "Margrena and her daughter won't be here for at least another eightday."

"They won't? What's happened?" asked Beltur.

"Margrena got some sort of flux. She's on the mend, but she didn't want to travel until she feels better."

"Likely because she overdid it in healing," added the older black mage.

"She's always had a hard time not helping people," said Athaal with a smile that quickly vanished.

"For which I am very grateful," admitted Beltur,

knowing full well that Athaal likely wouldn't have considered helping him if Margrena hadn't put in a good word.

"There's more. They had to leave Fenard quickly. All the healers in the city and nearby are being required to serve as healers to the Prefect's armsmen. She wrote that they would be on their way before we received the letter. She didn't say where they were, just in case the letter was intercepted and read . . ."

Intercepted and read? That bothered Beltur.

". . . that's why she said that her acquaintance from the vineyards had left hurriedly—that's Waensyn, you might recall," Athaal said to Meldryn. "The Prefect is marshaling an army, but no one seems to know why." Athaal paused. "I'll need to tell Jhaldrak about that immediately. He might know, but . . ."

Meldryn nodded.

"Jhaldrak is the councilor for Elparta. He can get word to Kleth and Spidlaria," explained Athaal. "He can also alert the river guards and others."

"You might as well get that over," suggested Meldryn.

"I'll take care of that immediately. It shouldn't take long."

Beltur was still thinking over what Athaal had related when the black-bearded mage said, "You're looking worried, Beltur."

"I just wondered if she said anything about Jessyla."

Athaal grinned. "You like her, don't you?"

"I probably wouldn't be alive without her."

Athaal frowned. "Oh?"

"I thought I told you that she was the one who said I wasn't really a white and that the strongest mages used order to handle chaos. I wouldn't have known how to change my shields without her saying that, and they wouldn't have been strong enough to escape Wyath's mages."

"And, most likely," added Meldryn, "the order in your shields helped conceal you when you escaped."

Beltur hadn't thought of that, but only nodded.

"I'm sure Jessyla is fine. Margrena wrote that they would be here as soon as they could be, and I can't imagine she'd be coming without Jessyla." Athaal cleared his throat. "I shouldn't be too long. When I get back, we'll head out. Today, I thought we'd inspect the piers." With a nod, Athaal folded the letter, then turned and hurried toward the front door.

Meldryn headed back toward the bakery, and Beltur once more stood alone in the kitchen, thinking about what he had just learned . . . and that it all pointed to a Gallosian attack of some sort on Spidlar.

He'd washed up and was sitting in the parlor reading a small old leather-bound volume entitled *On Healing* when Athaal returned. Beltur immediately closed the book and stood, replacing it in the small bookcase.

"Leantor's a good place to start," said Athaal. "Especially about anatomy. He relies too much on order for healing, though."

"Did you ever think about being a healer?"

Athaal shook his head. "It doesn't suit me. I've had to do some, enough that I'd prefer to leave it to true healers. We should be going."

Beltur had the definite impression Athaal didn't want to talk about why healing didn't suit him, and he didn't want to press the older mage.

In moments the two were walking south along Bakers Lane. Although the lanes and streets in Elparta had seemed clean to Beltur, perhaps because of the sewers, the lane seemed especially clean at that moment, and the air was cooler almost without the myriad of odors that usually filled the air, both possibly the result of the heavy rains of the previous two days.

After the two had walked a block or so, Beltur spoke. "Margrena's letter means Denardre is planning to attack Spidlar, doesn't it? Or at least Elparta."

"Why do you think that?"

Athaal's voice had an amused tone that disturbed Beltur, but he replied, "No other attack makes sense. He'd have to go through Westwind and cross the Westhorns to get to Sarronnyn or Suthya. He'd have to cross the Easthorns to attack Certis, and even if he conquered Certis, trading goods would still have to go through Sligo to be shipped from Tyrhavven. If he controls the River Gallos from beginning to end . . ." It seemed obvious to Beltur.

"Your reasoning is correct, but attempting something doesn't mean he'll succeed."

"Even if he has close to a score of white mages?"

"You think he has that many?" The amused tone vanished from Athaal's voice.

"Well . . ." Beltur paused. "When Wyath attacked us in the palace, there were two in the audience chamber. There were five others, and that didn't include the older white Uncle knew . . ." Beltur struggled to recall the name. "Naeron, that was his name. And Sydon. I don't know if any of the other whites I knew would be with Wyath, but there are three others who were friendly with Uncle, and they didn't worry as much about Wyath as Uncle did."

"That's just thirteen."

"I don't claim to know all the white mages in Gallos." After Athaal's faintly superior tone, Beltur didn't feel like mentioning that his uncle had likely killed two of his attackers.

The two walked along Bakers Lane for several moments more before Athaal spoke again. "I hadn't realized there were so many." Another pause followed. "Your uncle must have been very powerful."

"He was. I didn't want to leave him. He insisted. He said my mother would never forgive him."

"He must have cared for her a lot."

"He never said, but I think he did." For a time, Beltur hadn't realized it, perhaps because his father's grief had been far more obvious.

"I know you don't know all the white mages, but did your uncle ever mention any others you haven't counted?"

"He might have, in passing, but he was very private. Outside of Mhortan, Kassyl, and Zeonyt—those were the three he was close to—he seldom saw any others, and there weren't any others that ever came to the house. Except Sydon, of course."

"You don't think Sydon was killed?"

Beltur shook his head. "I can't say why, but I don't think so."

"Were you close to him?"

"No. He was condescending, and he always left the dirty work to me."

"Your uncle let him do that?"

"He never did it when Uncle was around. Also, he was a terrible cook, and when he tried to clean there was more chaos around than before he did."

"It sounds more and more like you never really were a white." Athaal turned onto the winding street that, as Beltur recalled, led down to the square where they'd entered Elparta through the trade gate. "We'll inspect the piers there first, and then come back through the gate and walk the riverfront and check those inside the city."

"Can the flatboats move to other piers after they're inspected and tariffed?"

"Most do."

"How do the tower guards know . . ."

"The boats are given an ensign to fly. The patterns are coded. Flying a false ensign means the entire cargo is confiscated."

"Most traders wouldn't want to risk losing everything."

"There are one or two a year. They're probably the ones who have helped persuade the Prefect that Elparta is a rich and willful city whose streets are paved with gold, instead of cobblestones. Sometimes, very rough cobblestones."

Before long, Beltur and Athaal were crossing the small square toward the trade gate. One of the gate guards nodded to Athaal, but said nothing as the mages passed through the walled gate. Once outside the tall and massive stone wall, Beltur only saw three boats tied up, one at each pier. Two of them were flatboats. The third was a small sail galley.

Athaal strode to the southernmost pier and turned to Beltur. "We'll walk out to the end, and then back. Slowly. See if you can sense any chaos or breaks in the timbers."

Beltur started on the north side of the pier, the one closest to the wall, and tried to follow Athaal's instructions. When he passed the flatboat, he stopped and studied it, but it appeared largely empty except for a score of barrels and two men with blades standing beside the barrels, which contained wine, Beltur suspected.

He nodded to the guards and continued on. There were certainly tiny bits of chaos everywhere, especially on the outside of the massive iron bolts that anchored the timbers of the piers to the round posts sunk deep into the riverbed, but when Beltur looked at several with his eyes, it was clear that those were merely superficial patches of rust. Still . . .

"You don't mean little patches of rust, I take it?"

"No. Not unless it's gone deep into the iron."

Beltur was almost to the river end of the pier before he sensed anything other than the tiny bits of chaos. The lower bolt on the post that was the next to last one had more than just a touch of chaos on the iron just inboard of the huge turnbuckle, although the surface rust wasn't all that obvious—no more than a thumbnail across. But beneath that surface patch, the chaos ran more than halfway through the iron. Beltur straightened. "This bolt . . . the chaos goes deeper than it looks." When Athaal arrived, he pointed. "Right there."

Athaal knelt, clearly concentrating before he finally stood. He took out a folded sheet of paper and jotted down "Pier 1" and some numbers. "They'll need to replace that before long."

The two found no other signs of potential failure on the first pier, or on either of the other two. Beltur studied the sail galley as he passed it, noting the blue-uniformed armsmen, and deciding the vessel likely belonged to the Spidlarian Council.

Before they headed back through the gate, Athaal stopped and entered the small building at the foot of the third pier, returning shortly. "I left word with the portmaster about that weakened anchor bolt. He wasn't pleased about it, but he'd be even less happy if it actually failed."

"How do you get paid for this work?"

"I get paid the same amount every season by the Council for regular inspections. It's extra if I do inspections after floods or severe storms."

"Yesterday wasn't a severe storm?"

Athaal laughed. "No. Just a hard rain. Those are good because they clean the streets and alleys. The river's up little more than half a yard." He turned toward the wall gate. "Now we'll look at the commercial piers on the riverfront inside the wall."

Once they were back through the gate, Athaal walked back toward the river along the lane at the base of the wall until they reached a wide street, paved in smooth stone, that stretched from one city wall to the other. At the river side of the street was an expanse of stone some three yards wide which ended in a shorter wall about a yard and a half high. The stone bordering the river wall also extended from one city wall to the other. Athaal moved close to the river wall, looking out and down as he proceeded northward.

Beltur looked down, but all he saw was the brownish-blue water of the river. "Is the river wall high enough when the river floods?"

"Look across the river."

Beltur looked. All he saw were grasslands and marshes.

"The other side is lower. The river goes there when it climbs its banks. The Council doesn't allow any buildings there—except for the guard tower, of course. You can see that there's a floodgate at every opening in the river wall. The only openings are those permitted for piers. They can't be more than three yards wide, and the floodgates have to be kept in openings in the walls so that they can be moved into place immediately."

The first pier they came to was comparatively small, extending no more than ten yards into the river, with a small building on the shore side. The door was closed, as were the shutters on the two windows. Beltur wrinkled his nose at the definite odor of fish.

"This is the pier for the fish market. They have to be inspected if they fish south of Elparta, but the Council doesn't want them to unload at the main piers. You can smell why."

"I can."

The two walked out onto the pier, but neither sensed any untoward chaos, although Beltur was definitely becoming more aware of smaller bits of either chaos or order.

Three glasses and five piers later, the two stepped away from the river wall just south of the northern city wall and began to walk toward the nearest city gate.

"We're almost done," announced Athaal. "There's one more Council pier downstream at Tuurval. It's one used by most of the herders to ship wool to Kleth or Spidlaria. That's about a two-kay walk, but it's fairly level, and it's cool today."

Beltur would have called the midday air pleasant, rather than cool. "You don't have to report any of the piers inside the walls? The way you did at the south piers?"

"Oh, I do. Just not the same way. I'll write up a report tonight and hand it to Veroyt at the Council here in Elparta tomorrow. He'll notify the owners of the piers needing work and send a copy to the Council in Spidlaria. How soon it's fixed or if it is, that's up to the owner. If they don't repair a pier and it fails, there are additional charges and penalties. They might even lose the pier to someone else. That's because the Council limits the number of piers along the city river wall."

Athaal nodded to the nearest gate guard as he and Beltur passed and then continued north on the river road, whose paving shifted from smooth-fitted stones to cobblestones less than a hundred yards from the gate.

"There aren't any piers until Tuurval?"

"They're not permitted. Small docks are allowed for crafters, fishermen, and others who own the land next to the river."

"What if someone builds one?"

"The River Patrol tears it down and fines whoever built it. If they can't pay, they have to work out the fine in service to the Patrol."

Less than a half kay north of the city wall, the road

swung eastward for a good fifty yards before again paralleling the river. Beltur could see why, given the low and marshy ground between the road and the water, but for the next kay, the road maintained that separation, although in places, there were low hills between the road and the river's edge and even a few dwellings, if raised and set on pilings. As they walked along the edge of the road, they encountered a continual procession of wagons and carts heading toward Elparta, most heaped with produce of various sorts.

Then the river began to curve westward, as did the road, and just ahead, Beltur could see small cots, half hidden by bushes and trees, a scene conveying a hamlet rather than a town, at least to Beltur. "That's Tuurval?"

"At its very best. It's quiet now. In the spring, there are wagons and wool everywhere. This time of year, there are only a few boats a week. Mostly lumber and heavy timbers."

The pier at Tuurval was at least as long as the main south piers of Elparta and several yards wider, with several flatbed wagons being unloaded into a large flatboat. As Athaal had suggested, four men were transferring timbers from the second wagon into the flatboat using a windlass hoist.

"Walking the piers again, Athaal?" called out a portly figure in the blue uniform that Beltur had come to recognize signified someone who worked for the Council of Spidlar.

"That's what you pay me for. After the rain, I thought it might be a good time." Athaal motioned for Beltur to accompany him toward the man who stood well back of the hoist.

"Who's your friend?"

"Beltur, this is Claudyt. He's the piermaster for Tuurval. Claudyt, this is Beltur. He's a city mage from Fenard who discovered that being either black or not slavishly beholden to the Prefect's arms-mage, let alone both, wasn't terribly promising in terms of his health. He's been accompanying me to learn more about Elparta and Spidlar."

Claudyt nodded. "Two of you. That'd be good."

Athaal frowned. "For what?"

"You know Cadelya, the old healer?"

"Yes."

"She's looking after Bethana's boy. He's not doing well."

"You know . . ."

"I know, but she asked if I saw you or Meldryn or Cohndar—or even old Felsyn—if you'd come take a look. She's sent word to Cohndar and Felsyn, but Cohndar's in Kleth, and no one seems to know where Felsyn is."

"Is it urgent?"

"I imagine you could inspect the pier first. A glass or two won't make any difference. A day might."

"She's at your place, then. The small house?"

"Cadelya stays there at night when she's here," replied Claudyt. "Ethanyt'll be in the main house. His own room."

"We'll go there right after we take a quick look at the pier." Athaal nodded to Beltur. "You take that side. Work out from the riverbank."

Beltur nodded and walked back toward the shore, where he turned and began to sense what he could. Again, there were minute bits of order and chaos on the surface of all the timbers, but as he moved out along the north side of the wide pier, he didn't sense anything that could correspond to a structural or support weakness. When he reached the end of the pier, well past what he thought was the stern of the big flatboat, he stopped. Deep in the water, there was *something* . . . but there wasn't, not exactly. The order and chaos particles right above the river bottom, farther down than he could see, were moving faster than the rest of the river . . . and they were deeper.

He tried to get a better feel of what he sensed. Finally, he straightened and realized that Athaal stood almost beside him.

"What is it? I saw you concentrating, but I can't find any problems with the pier or the supports."

Beltur debated whether to say anything, but realized that Athaal would sense it if he dissembled or lied outright. "It's not the pier. Not exactly. There's a deep trench that starts a yard out from the base of the last supports at the end of the pier, and there's a deep current there. I can't be sure, but I think it might be eating away at the riverbed there. If it keeps up, it might undercut the supports. It might not. I can't sense far enough under the riverbed to know how deep the supports go."

"We're not responsible for the river, but . . ." Athaal frowned.

"Could you just say that the storm or something might have changed the deeper river currents, and if they continue the way they are right now, they might eat away the riverbed under the supports farthest out into the current?"

Athaal nodded. "I can do that. We'd better get going."

The two walked swiftly back along the pier, past the hoist and the men unloading timber from the wagon.

"What did you find?" asked Claudyt as they neared.

Athaal stopped, as did Beltur, and the older mage said, "The pier's fine. It looks like the current's shifted. You'd better watch it. It might start eating into the riverbed under the end posts. I'll write that up, though."

"Good. Told Veroyt that might be a problem. He might listen if he hears it from you."

"We'll be on our way to your place, now."

"Much appreciated."

Even though Claudyt spoke pleasantly enough, Beltur felt that the functionary's eyes lingered on him unduly, and that worried him. He just hoped it had been because Claudyt was curious about a new mage in Spidlar.

Athaal didn't say more until they were well away from the pier and walking up a dirt lane off the river road toward a dwelling on a low rise. "Bethana was his only child. She died in childbirth. Cadelya was up in the hills tending to another woman. From what she told me later, I don't know that anyone could have helped, except one of the great healers—"

"Like Margrena?"

"She *might* have been able to save Bethana. She's good, but not one of the great ones."

Beltur wondered if Jessyla had that potential, but kept that thought to himself. His eyes went to the stone dwelling with the split-slate roof on the rise, a small flower garden on the north side, and a larger garden on the south that seemed to have a variety of what were likely vegetables. Behind the flower garden was a small cottage, and behind the vegetable garden was a stable large enough to hold a carriage or coach, Beltur thought. The house faced the river, and a drive led from the main lane directly to the stable. The front terrace was not covered, except for the overhang of the roof that shielded the front entry, and a stone walk went from the stone steps at the front of the terrace around the vegetable garden and to the stable. The grounds around the house looked like pasture, and Beltur wondered if Claudyt had sheep as well, since the grass was not that long.

Athaal cut across the grass toward the stone walk. Beltur hurried to keep pace with him, and the two reached the front door at the same time. Athaal rapped on the door firmly. The two waited several moments.

Finally, the door opened, and a young woman, barely more than a girl, stood there. "The master's not here, sers."

"We know," replied Athaal. "He sent us to see if we might be of assistance to Healer Cadelya. If you wish, you can tell her that Athaal and another mage are here."

"Just one moment, sers." The door closed.

"Years ago, Claudyt was first mate on a merchanter," said Athaal. "He still runs a tight ship."

"I can see."

When the door opened again, a tall white-haired woman in healer greens stood there.

"It is you. I'm so glad to see you. Come in. He's sleeping now." Shaking her head, she stepped back and opened the heavy oak door wide. "I don't know you." She looked at Beltur levelly.

"I'm Beltur. I left Fenard in rather a hurry, and Healer Margrena introduced me to Athaal, who has been kind enough to help me get adjusted to Elparta."

"Any black with any sense would have left a long time ago." She closed the door and turned to Athaal. "The boy's not well. You can see for yourself." She led the way from the small entry foyer straight back along a modest hall, past an archway on the left into a parlor and one on the right into a dining room, then turned left down another hallway, stopping outside the open door to a chamber on the right. "He's still sleeping."

Athaal and Beltur followed her into the bedroom where Ethanyt lay on his back in a narrow bed. Beltur judged the boy to be perhaps six or seven. His dark hair was damp, and his breathing seemed uneven. He was definitely pale. Beltur could see that immediately.

"How did he get this way?" asked Athaal in a low voice.

The white-haired healer moistened her lips. "I don't know when it started. Claudyt summoned me on sevenday evening. He said that Ethanyt began to wobble when he walked an eightday ago. By sevenday morning, he said his head hurt a lot. He told me it had been hurting a lot, but he didn't want to upset his grandfather. By yesterday, he was having trouble keeping broth down . . ." Cadelya moistened her lips again. "There's chaos somewhere. I know there is . . . but . . . I'm not as good as I used to be. Felsyn and Cohndar aren't around, and there's no one else. Lhadoraak . . . he's not that good with living things."

"You know I'm not close to being a healer . . ."

"Anything you can do . . . anything . . ."

"We'll see." Athaal looked to Beltur, but said nothing.

Beltur nodded and extended his senses, trying to see if he could find any chaos in the child's frame. The boy was neither fat nor excessively thin, but Beltur immediately sensed a knot of dirty orangish-red chaos within his head at the back not too far above his neck. He could also sense that the chaos-knot, somehow, was pressing outward. There was no other mass of unhealthy chaos, but the amount of order in his body seemed lower than it should be. He watched as Athaal also studied the restlessly sleeping child.

Abruptly, Athaal straightened and said to Beltur, "We need to talk." Then he looked to Cadelya. "We'll be in the hall for a moment."

The way Athaal spoke wasn't quite a command, but Beltur could sense something like desperation hidden behind the calm voice of the older mage.

Once the two stood in the hallway, Athaal said quietly, "I don't sense anything wrong with him except that spot that feels like chaos inside his skull in the back. Do you?"

Beltur couldn't help frowning. "That chaos is strange,

orangish-red, and his order levels are down. They're like an old person or like some of those old sick ewes. That's not right for a boy."

"But there's no other unnatural chaos in his body."

"He's very sick. Sicker than his grandfather thinks. Cadelya knows that, too."

"There's not anything I can do," murmured Athaal, again looking at the younger mage.

Beltur thought. He'd been able to put tiny bits of chaos into the ovens. Could he do it with order? He thought of the boy lying there. He swallowed. "I can try something. If it doesn't work, I don't think it will hurt him."

"With order?"

"With order," replied Beltur.

The two reentered the bedroom, and the healer rose from the stool beside the bed.

"He's very sick," Beltur said softly.

"I know. I just . . ." The healer shook her head.

"I'm going to try something," Beltur said. "I don't know if it will help, but it shouldn't hurt." He didn't say that the boy would likely die, sooner or later, if something didn't change for the better.

"Anything you can do . . ."

Beltur eased onto the stool, and once again let himself sense everything. Nothing had changed. Then he extended his arm and positioned his fingertips just above Ethanyt's head, right over the chaos-spot, and eased the tiniest bit of order into the chaos, sensing what happened. After a moment, he could tell that both the order and correspondingly small bit of chaos had vanished. He did the same thing again, if with a slightly larger bit of order. Bit by bit, he kept using order on the chaos, until there was only a tiny bit left.

By then, Beltur's arm was aching, and his vision was

blurring, but he had the feeling that if it didn't eliminate all of the strange chaos, it would rebuild itself. When the last bit of the orangish red was gone, he added two more tiny bits of order, hoping they would help with the healing.

By then the entire world was beginning to spin around Beltur. He started to turn on the stool so that he wouldn't fall on the boy, but his body didn't respond. As he began to topple over, he could feel Athaal's arms steadying him.

Then everything went black.

When he woke, he was lying on the floor on his back. His head definitely hurt.

"Can you sit up?" The voice was Athaal's.

"I think so." Beltur could hear the shakiness in his own voice, and he still felt dizzy. Even so, he managed to slowly ease himself into a sitting position. Finding he was out in the hallway, he leaned against the wall.

Cadelya immediately handed him a mug.

"It's ale," said Athaal.

Beltur took the mug in both hands and tried a slow small swallow, then, after a moment, another. He suspected at least half a glass passed before he began to feel close to steady.

"I think I'm better now."

"You didn't say you were a healer," said Cadelya.

"I'm not. I wouldn't have tried what I did, if he weren't so sick." Beltur stiffened. He didn't even know . . .

"He's improving," said Athaal. "His breathing is better, and there's still no sign of that chaos."

Beltur found he was also breathing more easily. He handed the mug to Cadelya, who was sitting beside him on the stool she must have brought from the bedroom. "Thank you." Then he slowly stood. He didn't feel dizzy, and his surroundings remained firmly in place.

"Are you sure you're all right?" asked Athaal.

"So long as we don't have to run back to Elparta."

"I think we can walk." Athaal turned to the healer. "We only promised Claudyt that we'd do what we could."

"It looks like you did that," she replied dryly. "I'll send word to you on how Ethanyt's doing. Claudyt won't."

"Thank you."

After they left the house, Beltur was well aware that Athaal had slowed his pace, for which Beltur was grateful. He was tired.

When they were halfway down the lane toward the river road, Athaal looked at Beltur and asked, "What did you do?" His tone was more than merely curious and less than, but not entirely lacking, a hint of the accusatory.

"What I could. I took a tiny, tiny bit of order and combined it with a tiny bit of the chaos inside his head. That destroyed both. I kept doing it until there wasn't any chaos left. Then I added two more tiny bits of order, just in case. That was all." He paused. "Why did you want me to handle that?"

"You can sense smaller bits of chaos or even order than I can . . ."

Beltur had been getting that impression, but hadn't wanted to make the comparison, especially after all that Meldryn and Athaal had done for him.

". . . I knew a large infusion of order would have been too much for him, and . . . I'm not too precise in moving small bits of order. I'm glad you are. I've been told that's often a gray trait, but some blacks have it as well. I don't." After another pause, he added, "You still might make a good healer."

"I'm not sure I know enough about anything right now." And that was certainly true, Beltur felt. He was also looking forward to dinner and to getting a good night's sleep.

XXIX

On twoday, Athaal and Beltur went to a herder's spread almost four kays east of Elparta, and Beltur was more than glad he had slept well on oneday night. Threeday was spent visiting various crafters and inspecting tools. All were in good shape except for a bow saw used by a cabinet maker whose blade was beginning to crack, an incipient crack discovered by Beltur. On fourday morning, it rained, not so hard as it had with the northeaster, but hard enough that Beltur scrubbed the kitchen, since Laranya never came or cleaned if it rained, or in the afternoon. Later, Athaal gave Beltur a tour of the important places in Elparta, from the City Patrol headquarters to the building into which river water was diverted from where it was piped to the town fountains.

By fourth glass, as Athaal stopped at the edge of a square perhaps only a third filled with vendors and carts, Beltur's feet were more than a little tired, since walking up and down the hills of the city over cobblestone streets and lanes was far harder on them than walking the roads and lanes outside of the city.

"This is the main market square. The square to the northeast of Bakers Lane is the only other square where peddlers and others may sell. Selling on the streets is forbidden."

That didn't surprise Beltur. He stood and surveyed

the square, where the peddlers and sellers looked little different from those in Fenard, although the square itself was equally large, if not slightly more expansive and far cleaner, and the vendors were clearly more separated. "The stalls and carts are spaced apart."

"That's a Council rule. It cuts down on snatch thieves and cutpurses. Cohndar had something to do with that."

Cohndar? The black mage whom Cadelya hadn't been able to find? "Oh?"

"That was back when he worked with the City Patrol. A long time ago."

"Do many blacks work with the Patrol?"

"There's always one working full-time. Right now, it's Osarus. You'll likely meet him sometime. That doesn't include those summoned for periodic duty. Ask me about that later."

While Beltur would have liked to have asked then, he resumed studying the square, sensing, unsurprisingly, less chaos and no signs of white magery. Finally, he turned and nodded to Athaal.

"The last building I'm going to show you is the Elparta Council building," announced Athaal as they walked away from the main market square and up yet another cobblestoned street, if one almost twice as wide as most—and straight, unlike so many in the southern part of Elparta. "I didn't want to give you a formal tour of Elparta until you'd been here awhile, so that you had a better feel for the city."

When the two reached the top of the hill that provided a view of the city walls, the river, and the main market square, Athaal stopped at the edge of the paved area and gestured toward the Council building—a simple rectangular white marble building with a slate roof standing alone atop the hill. A set of wide marble steps, four in all, led up to the west-facing entrance, over which was a simple frieze sculpted into the stone that depicted a sailing vessel resting on a sheaf of grain crossed with a hammer.

From what Beltur had seen and heard so far, that emblem seemed entirely in keeping with Spidlar, as did the size of the structure, no more than forty yards by twenty. "It's impressive in a modest way."

Athaal laughed. "That would please Veroyt. There's a similar building in Kleth, and a much larger one in Spidlaria, but he claims the design of ours is the most beautiful."

"What do they do here?"

"It's where they keep all the tariff and trade records, and there's a massive strongroom where they keep the tariffs the inspectors collect until they're sent to the Council in Spidlaria . . . and the coins to pay the Council armsmen who are posted here. It's also where city patrollers collect their pay. They also have the plans for all the sewers and water pipes to the fountains, that sort of thing. There's a large meeting room for when the Council comes to Elparta."

"How often is that?"

"The Council must meet here at least once in every season, except winter. Sometimes, it's more often, especially if there's a problem in Elparta or nearby." Athaal paused. "Are you hungry? Thirsty?"

"Just a little." Actually, more than a little, but Beltur wasn't going to say that.

"Good. We're going to meet Meldryn at the Traders' Rest at half past fourth glass. The fare's not bad, and the ale and wine are excellent. And don't say anything about your lack of coins. You've more than earned a good dinner and ale."

Beltur thought so, too. "Thank you." He paused. "Where is the Traders' Rest?"

"Just down the street on the other side. The owners'

father gave the place that name because he said the outland traders needed a rest after dealing with the tariff
inspectors. That's what Comartyl says, anyway. You
ready to go?"

Beltur nodded.

The Traders' Rest was indeed only a little over a hundred yards away, mostly downhill. The two-story inn
and its stable took up almost half a block. From the
heavy square timbers, the slightly sooty reddish brick
walls, and the narrow windows with their small leaded
panes, Beltur would have thought the inn was older
than just two generations. *Maybe the father just changed
the name.*

The main public room was slightly more than half
filled, and Beltur immediately noticed that all the tables
had wooden armchairs, rather than straight-backed
chairs or stools and benches. Meldryn was seated at a
corner table away from the cold hearth and motioned
for them to join him. There was a large mug set before
him. As they sat down, he said, "There's even a singer
tonight, Comartyl told me." The older black mage
looked at Athaal and added, "He liked the special berry
pies I did for him. This time and last."

"For another special dinner?"

"Trader from Jellico who's buying black wool."

"Good fortune, no matter how you count it." Meldryn then said to Beltur, "They've got good amber ale
here. I remember you mentioning you liked it."

"I also like your dark ale," replied Beltur. "Uncle's
was bitterer than I really preferred. I thought it was
almost chewy."

Meldryn grinned. "Someone once told me that was
the way I liked ale."

Athaal actually flushed momentarily, then quickly
asked, "Is Cohndar coming?"

"He said he might join us, but not to wait on him."

"He likes a drink, but not to eat." Athaal shook his head.

"He claims that eating late upsets him. I've never sensed anything wrong, though."

Beltur wondered why Meldryn had asked the other black mage. *So that you can meet him . . . or so that he can meet you?* He wouldn't have thought that much of it . . . except for Athaal's earlier mention of Cohndar once working with the City Patrol.

A dark-haired serving woman appeared. "Something to drink, sers?"

"Amber ale," said Athaal.

"I'd like that as well," added Beltur.

"The choice of fare tonight is roasted pork cutlets with apples and dumplings, fowl slices in a cherry conserve with lace potatoes, or ham and noodles with heavy cheese."

"The cutlets for me," said Athaal.

"The fowl slices," added Meldryn.

"The fowl slices as well," added Beltur.

With a nod, the server turned and left.

"Is it all the same?" asked Beltur. "She didn't say."

"For us, it is," replied Athaal. "Part of Comartyl's payment to Meldryn is a dinner for three or four each season."

"And after what happened the other day at Claudyt's," added Meldryn, "it seemed fitting that you should enjoy a good dinner."

Abruptly, Meldryn raised a hand and gestured. Beltur turned and saw a white-haired man in black standing just inside the archway, who, as he glimpsed Meldryn, smiled and began to make his way toward the corner. When Cohndar neared the table, Beltur could definitely sense the order embodied in the older man.

"Have a seat," said Meldryn warmly, "I wasn't sure you'd join us."

"I'll always join you. I'll always drink with you, but not eat this late." Cohndar eased into the empty chair, with an inquiring look at Beltur.

"Cohndar," offered Athaal, "this is Beltur. He's the one who helped Cadelya with Ethanyt."

The white-haired mage continued to study Beltur as he said, "I heard what you did with Claudyt's grandson. Cadelya told me more than once it was a good thing for me that you were there." He smiled wryly.

"How is he now?" asked Beltur. "I did what I could. I'm not a healer."

"I looked at him yesterday. He limps, likely always will, but he's not unsteady, and he's back to eating. So, for someone who's not a healer, you did just fine." Cohndar frowned. "Cadelya said you're from Fenard. I don't recall hearing your name."

"You probably wouldn't," said Athaal. "There aren't many blacks raised by a white mage. His uncle was Kaerylt. He was one of the whites who defied Wyath."

"He died because he insisted on holding them off so that I could escape," added Beltur.

"Rather noble of him."

"He swore to my mother when she was dying that he'd protect me," explained Beltur, knowing that was true, if not precisely factually accurate.

"He was your mother's brother then?"

Beltur nodded.

"Goes to show that there are some honorable whites. Wish I'd known him." Cohndar gestured to the serving woman, then waited for her. "Some of the black ale."

"Yes, ser."

Cohndar smiled briefly. "I do like Comartyl's black ale, and I thank you for inviting me to join you, Meldryn." He looked back to Beltur. "What do you make of Prefect Denardre?"

"He's not trustworthy, and he wants all the mages in Gallos to be under his control, or Arms-Mage Wyath's."

"That's what everyone says. Do you think he'll actually attack Spidlar?"

"I don't know, ser. I don't know him personally, and I never met Arms-Mage Wyath. All I know is that Uncle Kaerylt didn't trust Wyath and had as little to do with him as possible."

"Why did Wyath try to kill you and your uncle?"

"I don't know. Uncle worried about Wyath, but he never said anything about Wyath being an enemy or trying to kill him or me."

All of that was absolutely true, as it had to be, facing a fairly strong black mage.

"Here comes your ale," said Athaal cheerfully. "And in the large mug!"

"So is yours," pointed out the white-haired mage.

"But I could tell yours because of the mug size."

"Here you are, sers." The server quickly set the mugs before each, then looked to Cohndar. "Would you like supper as well, ser?"

"No, thank you. Now . . . where was I?"

"You were speculating on whether Denardre would attack us," said Meldryn. "What do you think?"

"If he attacks anywhere, it will be Spidlar. We all know that. The question is whether he's that mad." Cohndar again turned to Beltur.

"I have no idea, ser. My uncle said that the Prefect was worried about both the Viscount and the Council of Spidlar, and that they were likely to raise tariffs."

"Did he mention the blacks of Spidlar? Or traders?"

Beltur had to think for a moment. "No, ser. He said that the Viscount was short of golds, and that the Council wouldn't raise their tariffs as much as the Viscount likely would."

"That sounds as though he knew more than he told you."

"He was closemouthed about most everything, ser. Especially with me."

"Didn't he like you?"

"I think he cared for me as much as he could. I had my own room, and we all ate the same fare. He didn't dress better than he provided for me. I don't think he knew what to make of me." That was really another guess on Beltur's part.

"Hmmm . . ." Cohndar tilted his head. "You never said exactly how he was killed."

"Uncle said we were summoned to the palace . . ." From there Beltur went through the entire sequence of events . . . including his uncle's insistence that Beltur escape.

"Had you ever been to the palace before?"

"No, ser."

"And yet you escaped?"

"I have very strong shields, ser, but not much else. There was chaos everywhere."

"What happened then?"

Beltur dutifully recounted exactly what had happened from that point until he reached Margrena's house.

"Interesting." Cohndar nodded to Meldryn. "He's telling the truth, at least as he saw it, and that means we have a very large problem. Obviously, Kaerylt—that was his name?"

"Yes, ser."

"Kaerylt was almost as powerful, possibly more powerful, than Wyath. That suggests that there are no whites left in Gallos capable of standing against those Wyath has gathered. The fact that they didn't pursue immediately a known black—"

"They might have," interjected Beltur, "but I stayed

in crowds as much as I could, and I never went back home. Also, the chamber was totally filled with chaos. I think that was how they couldn't find me immediately. I couldn't sense anyone after the first few moments."

"You didn't mention that."

"I hadn't thought about it in that way."

"That doesn't change matters much. It might make them worse, especially if they believe they destroyed Beltur with his uncle."

"Because it would give them the idea that they could destroy shielded blacks?" asked Meldryn.

Cohndar nodded. "I'd still like—" He stopped as the server appeared with three platters.

In moments, the three having dinner had been served, and another server added a basket with three modest loaves of bread.

"It all looks good," said Cohndar, pausing for a moment before adding, "for a midday meal. Or for you young fellows."

Beltur managed to refrain from immediately eating until he saw that Meldryn and Athaal had started. The first bite of the fowl in the cherry conserve convinced him that it had been a good choice, although, when he looked at Athaal's platter, he had the feeling he would have liked the pork as well. The lace potatoes were light and crispy, but the bread wasn't nearly as good as Meldryn's.

". . . still like to have a better idea of what Denardre thinks he can gain by attacking us," Cohndar went on as if he had not even paused. "Even if he took Elparta, he can't conquer all of Spidlar."

"He doesn't have to," pointed out Meldryn. "If he and his white mages level Elparta, Kleth, and Spidlaria, what would be left capable of standing against him?"

"I hate to think that much destruction is just about golds."

"Are wars ever about anything else, even when proud slogans are shouted?" replied Meldryn dryly.

"Seldom," admitted the eldest mage. "Much as I'd like to hope otherwise."

As Beltur took a swallow of the amber ale, he saw a woman step up onto the cold hearth. She was older, almost the age his mother might have been, and she was tuning a guitar, just in the way he remembered her doing it. He swallowed, thinking of the few lullabies he recalled.

"Comartyl's got a singer tonight," said Cohndar.

"He has one on fourday nights and sevenday nights. You should remember that," chided Meldryn humorously.

"I've got enough to remember, thank you."

From the first note plucked on the guitar, Beltur found himself listening intently.

> *"The wind has its wings,*
> *The night has its light . . ."*

After just the first words, Beltur forgot the singer's age, caught by the beauty of her voice and the accuracy of her fingers on the strings.

> *"Wherever she falls,*
> *The blind find their sight . . ."*

As she sang, he wondered why he'd never heard anyone sing besides his mother, so long ago, except, of course, for the fragments of song he'd overheard in scouting in Analeria . . . and at the inn in Buoranyt. *When Uncle left the moment the singer began.* Had singing reminded him of too much, or did the hint of order in it bother whites? Might it have been both?

"... White is black and black is white,
   Neither matters in the heat of night.
   Sing me false or sing me true,
   Either way, your love I'll rue.
   For love is not to have or hold
   Love is not for fair or bold,
   Nor is my love just for you."

The ironic tone of her voice matched the ending,
and more than a few in the public room, especially
several women two tables over, laughed. The singer
smiled, strummed a few chords, and then began another song.

"A fire blazes on the ice of time
   Flickered flames unmelt not the old year's rime.
   Don't sing of lightning smiths or rational stars
   Or wail about your love's uncaring bars
   My love is to the man of heart and heat
   Not chaos wild or order's duller beat ..."

The more Beltur listened and watched, the more he
could discern, somehow, that there was much more
than words, more than melody, something ...
   In the lull after the second song, Athaal looked to
Beltur and asked, "What do you think? You're looking
very interested."
   Caught off-guard, all Beltur could come up with was,
"The way she plays, some of it is ... like sung silver."
   Beltur's words seemed to surprise Cohndar, and es-
pecially Meldryn, who looked to Athaal. Athaal just
smiled and nodded.
   Beltur turned back to the singer.

"... down by the river so smooth and so fair ...
   I found a turtle whose shell was so square,

> *And he said to me, as clear as a bell.*
> *That he had a fine story to tell . . ."*

When the singer finished, Athaal looked to Meldryn. "We ought to be heading home."

"You're right." Meldryn turned. "Cohndar, we're calling it an evening."

"That's fine with me. You know I'm not much of an acquaintance with night, not like that singer." Cohndar stood.

So did Athaal and Meldryn, then Beltur.

"A pleasure to spend the evening with you all," said Cohndar, who then looked to Beltur. "I'm glad to have met you."

Although Beltur had the feeling that Cohndar was less pleased than his words and tone indicated, he replied, "It was good to meet you, too, ser."

None of the three said much on the walk through the late twilight back to Bakers Lane. Beltur did notice that there weren't many people on the streets, but then, he'd already gotten the impression that most Spidlarians rose early, worked hard, and went to bed early.

For some reason, perhaps because he kept thinking of the singer, and how she had reminded him of his mother, he did not fall asleep early, but lay there, thinking about the songs and the sense of silver order that they had embodied. He also wondered why he had not seen how his uncle had avoided songs and singers. *You can't see what isn't there to see.*

The house was so quiet he could even make out that Meldryn and Athaal were talking. He strained to hear, but couldn't make out the words, not at first, but slowly he could understand some of what passed between the two. There were words about dinner, and the cherry conserve, and whether apples were better than that. Then, after a while . . .

"... has some doubts ... Beltur ..."

"... doubts ... no white could have seen ... order ... the words and notes in silver ..."

"... may be, but ... ever be a true black?"

"Does it matter?"

"We may not have any choice. He may not, either ..." Meldryn's words sent a shiver through Beltur.

With almost no coins and no way to support himself except through what work he'd been able to do with Athaal, Beltur was all too aware that he was still dependent on the goodwill of the two black mages. While he was learning about Elparta and the way things worked, he was a long way from being able to support himself.

Should you talk to Athaal about how to rely less on them?

He kept listening, but he was getting tired, and their talk shifted to names he had never heard. Although he hadn't been sleepy, he could feel his eyes closing.

XXX

"Today is market day," Athaal announced when Beltur had finished cleaning up after breakfast.

"What do we need?"

"Not much, really, but it's been over an eightday since I actually went through the market square. You can get a feel for things by browsing and talking, as well as shopping for what you need. I can, anyway. Meldryn doesn't like to go to the square. So I do it. He needs some spices, too." Athaal lifted a worn and empty leather bag. "Bring some coins in case you see something you need."

Beltur nodded. Over the past eightday, he'd actually earned some eleven coppers. Or at least that was what Meldryn and Athaal had insisted he'd earned, a silver and a copper. He couldn't help but think about all the silvers that he should have received as his share of the spoils from the fallen raiders. *That's water well downstream.*

In a fraction of a glass, Beltur was ready, with his coppers, although he had little inclination to spend them. He'd just reached the bottom of the stairs when Laranya appeared in the main floor hallway.

"You don't have to clean the kitchen," said the dark-haired woman.

"But I should," replied Beltur. "Before I came, you didn't have to clean my room." He grinned at her. "And you can always clean up whatever I missed, if that makes you feel better."

Laranya shook her head, but couldn't conceal her smile.

"How is your son?" Beltur only knew that the boy was ill and that Meldryn thought he was unlikely ever to be other than sickly.

"He is much better, thank you. He spends the day with my mother. That makes them both happy."

"I'm glad to hear it." With those words, Beltur smiled again, and then slipped past her to join Athaal in the front foyer.

Once they were outside and walking south on Bakers Lane toward the main market square, Beltur said, "I didn't want to ask her, but what sort of sickness does her son have?"

"He is deficient in order, and neither Meldryn nor Cohndar nor Felsyn has been able to find the cause. There's no unnatural chaos in his body, either. Sometimes, that happens with children. They either get stronger as they get older, or they get weaker and die. I might have mentioned that was a problem with Lhadoraak's daughter Taelya. Thankfully, I could do a little, guided by Grenara, and that was enough to get her through the hard times. She's fine now."

"You and Meldryn worry that Laranya's son will get weaker."

Athaal nodded. "We don't talk about it."

"I'm sorry."

"You didn't know, and you've waited two eightdays before asking. I should have told you. It could have been awkward if you weren't so polite. There are some illnesses that even the best healers can't do much about."

Athaal's words tended to confirm Beltur's suspicion that neither Athaal nor Meldryn was comfortable in discussing things they didn't do well. *But are you any better?* "That must be hard."

"You understand that. You would." After the slightest hesitation, Athaal immediately went on. "Once we get to the market square, there's no point in your following me around. You can discover more on your own. We'll meet at ninth glass on the middle of the north side of the square where Hill Street leads up to the Council building."

Beltur hadn't seen any sign naming the street, but he recalled it. "Are there any goods you'd suggest I look at, just because they're unique to Elparta?"

"We have good cabinet and furniture crafters here, but the best won't have works on the square. Some of the lacework is good, I'm told."

"Any produce that is particularly special?"

"Sometimes there are mountain peaches. They bloom late, but even so, many years the growers get late frosts. Nothing better than a good mountain peach, though."

And likely very costly. "I'm certain that there's plenty to look at."

"Just don't overdo it in looking at the women. You'd

find some of them worth looking at. That's one reason
why Felsyn enjoyed touring the square." After a moment, Athaal cleared his throat. "One other thing . . .
you might want to carry light shields around you all the
time in the square. Some of the cutpurses are so light
you wouldn't feel a thing.".

"Are there that many?"

"No, and there are patrollers." Athaal offered a
crooked smile. "But it only takes one. Besides, it's good
practice."

That was another thing Beltur really couldn't argue
against. Before long, the two reached the square. While
Athaal headed off, his empty leather bag in hand, Beltur just stood at the edge for several moments, raising
a shield close to his body and looking around. He definitely saw what Athaal had meant about it being more
crowded earlier in the day. "Crowded" might have been
an understatement, since there were people everywhere,
although the buyers and sellers weren't nearly as bois-
terous as those in Fenard.

He looked at the nearest line of carts and stalls,
most of which seemed to be hawking melons or root
vegetables, although he did see baskets of apples and
pearapples. Finally, he shrugged and headed for those
carts. *You might as well see everything you can.*

The fruits and vegetables for sale looked good, but
unremarkable, and Beltur moved toward carts, tables,
and stalls that held what looked to be various items for
sale. The first stall held some wooden boxes, some lacquered, but mostly wooden candlesticks, ranging from
the plain to the highly ornamented. There was one pair
that featured the figure of a heroic smith, using a lightning bolt as a hammer, with a circular depression in the
anvil for the candle, with the second candlestick that
of a woman wielding twin blades standing beside a
fallen figure curled around a fountain that provided the

circular depression for the candle. The work was good, but not outstanding, Beltur judged. "Are those meant to be Nylan and Ryba?"

"None else," replied the almost wizened woman seated on a stool behind the stall. "Two silvers for the pair."

Beltur nodded and moved on, thinking that the matched pair really should have been Ayrlyn and Nylan, at least according to what he'd read in his uncle's library. *But then, most people don't read . . . especially old books and history.*

The next few tables clearly belonged to various apprentices, from the ages of the youths behind the small tables, one displaying an assortment of tin boxes, another of breadboards and wooden canisters, and a third clay pitchers and mugs. Some of the mugs didn't look that bad, but when Beltur let his senses range over them, he detected signs of weakness, especially hairline cracks, and he continued on.

After some time, he found himself standing before a narrow stall that displayed lace collars. The collars looked good, but Beltur was momentarily impressed by the young woman standing beside the stall. With her mahogany hair and stature, for a moment, she reminded him of Jessyla, until he saw that her face was rounder and her eyes were blue, rather than green. She also wore a shirt and jacket of blue, rather than green.

"The collars are what's for sale, ser," she offered gently.

"I'm sorry. For a moment, you reminded me of someone."

"If I were her, I'd be complimented. Would you like to buy a collar for her?"

"I'd think about it, but she likely wouldn't wear it."

"She's a healer, then."

That stopped Beltur for a moment. "How . . . ?"

"You're a black mage. She wouldn't wear lace. Healers don't. Most healers prefer blacks, or at least men who are very orderly."

Beltur studied the woman for a moment, then asked, "Who made the lace?"

She smiled. "My aunt."

"I imagine the collars look very good on you."

"That's why I'm here. We both profit."

Beltur laughed softly. "I can see that."

"Wouldn't you even consider—"

"Thief! Stop him!"

Beltur immediately whirled in the direction of the shout. He saw someone sprinting past the stall one over from where he stood. Almost without thinking, just in the fashion that Athaal had drilled him, he extended a shield around the slender figure, freezing the thief in place. As he moved toward the thief, he could see that his shields held a young woman, or girl, and that she wore the clothes more suited to a young man.

For a moment, it seemed as though everyone halted. Then the woman at the adjoining table, on whose table was a series of embroidered aprons, quickly stepped back as Beltur stopped short of the girl who had stopped her brief pounding at the shields.

Around them voices began to break the momentary silence.

". . . young mage . . . stopped her . . ."

". . . never seen him before . . ."

". . . new one working with the City Patrol, you think?"

Another sharper voice called out. "Don't let him go! Cut away my wallet, he did . . ."

Beltur wasn't about to release the thief, not yet, anyway, but he really didn't have any idea of what he should do next. So he found himself standing there, just looking at the girl.

"That's it. Just stare at me. Let everyone see. Ruin me." The girl's voice held an edge, but whether it was anger or fear—or both—Beltur couldn't tell.

"You didn't have to steal."

"That's what you think. That's what they all think."

Then, at the end of the row, Beltur could see a man who had to be a city patroller, from the blue uniform and the truncheon in his hand. The patroller hurried, not quite running, until he saw Beltur, when a puzzled expression appeared on his face.

"You're not Chamyt or even Athaal."

"No, I'm Beltur. Someone yelled out, 'Thief!' and I put shields around her. I wasn't quite certain what to do next."

"That's my wallet!" declared a graying woman whose stall Beltur had passed earlier.

"It is," said an older man.

"You're not even working for the Patrol, and you did this?" The girl's voice was almost a screech.

"What else was he supposed to do?" asked a third voice, one that Beltur recognized. "Let you steal whatever you wanted, Lizabi?"

Beltur glanced at Athaal. "You know her?"

"Unhappily. I caught her several years ago, when she was a child. I hoped she'd have learned."

"The only thing I learned was that the only thing a poor woman is allowed to do is to sell her body. Stealing's more honest."

"There are scores of women here who haven't done that," snapped Athaal.

"And a few men who have," replied Lizabi in a cutting tone.

"Ah, ser . . ." began the patroller. "If you'd release the confinement."

"And don't try anything," added Athaal to Lizabi. "I won't be as gentle as Beltur was."

Beltur released the shields, and the patroller immediately wrapped leather straps around the girl's wrists.
Then he extracted the leather belt wallet from inside her
loose-fitting jacket and looked at the woman who had
claimed it. "Is this really yours?"

"Demon-straight, it is."

Beltur could sense both anger and truth.

The patroller looked to Athaal, who nodded. Then
he handed the wallet back to the woman, and took
something from his belt and handed it to Beltur. "Your
token, ser."

Beltur took the stamped leather disk, understanding
that he was supposed to, but not knowing why. "Thank
you."

"My pleasure." The patroller smiled warmly, and
nodded to Athaal. Then he returned his attention to his
captive, before pulling on the leather straps. "This way,
girl."

Lizabi glared at Beltur and hissed, "Bastard!"

"None of that!" snapped the patroller.

The stallkeepers faded away, except for the woman
whose wallet had been stolen, who looked to Beltur.
"Thank you. Would have been an awful day without
you, ser."

"I just did what I could. I'm glad I could help."

The woman inclined her head respectfully and turned,
heading back to her stall.

"The patroller didn't even ask anything about me,"
Beltur said.

"That's because I saw Trakyll earlier and told him
you were a mage new to Elparta. I didn't expect anything like this today, but I thought it wouldn't hurt."

Beltur frowned. "Was that one of the reasons why
you drilled me so hard on shields that I could use to
restrain someone?"

"One of the reasons. They're also useful for self-defense when you don't want to hurt someone. Almost all black mages spend some time working with the City Patrol, doing pretty much what you just did. Once you've lived here awhile, it's required twice an eightday for a season, about every three to four years. Usually, mages discover thieves when they're under a concealment, since the thieves wouldn't try anything if they saw a mage. By the way, you can turn that disk in at the Council building for two silvers."

"Two?"

"That's the fee for restraining a thief. If you catch someone who's assaulted and hurt someone, it's four. But it has to be witnessed by a patroller, or reported to one by credible witnesses and in a public space. You can't get much more public than in the market square. You'll have to give your name and address, but that's all. We should do that after we finish here. I'm still looking for some cardamom. That's hard to come by, even here."

"Cardamom?" Beltur had never heard of it.

"It only grows where it's hot, places like Naclos and Hamor. Meldryn uses it in some hot drinks and pastries. Sometimes traders from Sarron bring it here. It's not cheap, either." Athaal smiled. "Go look around some more. I'll see you at the bottom of Hill Street at ninth glass."

"Until then." Beltur moved to the next line of carts and tables, most of which seemed to be selling small tools, knives, and a few blades. None of them appealed to him.

Some little time later, he found an older woman selling shimmersilk scarves. One in particular caught his eye, in the way the colors shifted from pale seafoam green to a deep and rich sylvan green. He couldn't help but think just how good it would look on Jessyla.

"That one is four silvers, three for you," said the vendor quietly.

Beltur had known shimmersilk was costly—just not how expensive it was for a modest scarf. "Thank you, but I wouldn't buy it without her to see it."

"You're a wise man, even if it means that I won't be able to sell it now."

Beltur smiled and moved on.

When the chimes rang out ninth glass, he was standing on the half corner opposite the square, waiting for Athaal. He still wished he'd been able to buy the scarf, but that would have been a foolish gesture, even if he'd had the coins. *You do owe her. You wouldn't have survived without her observations.* He smiled wryly, wondering if his thoughts were just a rationalization of the fact that he found Jessyla attractive.

Carrying the leather bag that appeared half full, Athaal joined Beltur not long after.

"Did you find the cardamom?"

"No. There was none to be had." Athaal gestured. "Let's go."

Beltur and Athaal climbed Hill Street to the Council building. Halfway up, Beltur released the shield. Holding it for glasses had been tiring.

When they reached the top, Athaal led the way past the west-facing main entrance. "The small door at the north end is where we're going. That's where people pay what they owe the Council and where mages who do work for the Patrol or the council get paid."

"Did you get paid for getting the supplies for the Council?"

"Quite nicely. I wouldn't have gone to Gallos, otherwise." Athaal opened the single door at the north end and gestured for Beltur to enter.

A round-faced clerk in blue seated behind a table desk looked up, then smiled at Athaal. "I thought I'd seen the last of you for a while."

"You might have, but you'll likely be seeing some of

Beltur now and again. He's likely the first from Fenard now that the Prefect is driving out blacks and even whites who won't grovel to his arms-mage. Beltur was in the square earlier this morning and restrained a cut-purse." Athaal motioned for Beltur to join him before the desk.

"Anyone I've heard of?"

"I doubt it. Lizabi. She was in trouble a few years back. She supposedly went to Kleth. I was surprised to see her back. She won't like the women's house."

"Most of them never do." The clerk looked to Beltur.

"Beltur, this is Raymandyl. He handles tokens and quite a few other tasks for the Council."

"I'm pleased to meet you."

"You have the token?"

Beltur handed it over.

"One of Trakyll's. Don't see many of his. Most of the light-fingered types avoid the square when he's there." Raymandyl took out a thin black leather-bound ledger and opened it. "Your name here. Your profession here. That's black mage. Don't know why the Council insists on that. No one gets tokens besides blacks or grays, but I haven't seen a true gray since Sarmean died, must have been ten years back now. Oh . . . and your address here."

Beltur signed his name and looked to Athaal quizzically.

"Black enough," said the other mage, adding to the clerk, "Beltur has a few wisps of white because he was raised by his late uncle, but he's blacker than many who've never questioned what they were."

Even with that explanation, writing "black mage" felt strange to Beltur, although he certainly wasn't white any longer, and he was getting to wonder if he really ever had been, as Jessyla had suggested. "Bakers Lane at . . . ? I've never seen a sign."

"Crossed Lane."

"Staying with you?" asked Raymandyl.

"Until he gets his feet on the ground here. He left Fenard barely with even his life."

The clerk shook his head. "I daresay I don't know what this world is coming to, between the Prefect and the Viscount." He took out a small seal brazier, struck a lighter, and waited for a time before putting a tiny dollop of blue wax in the pan, letting it melt, then deftly transferring a small drop to the ledger in the empty space beside Beltur's signature before pressing his seal into the wax. "There." He took a key from somewhere and unlocked a cabinet beside his desk, reaching in and extracting two coins, and then relocking the cabinet door. "Here you are, ser."

"Thank you." Beltur offered a nod with his words.

"Always my pleasure." Raymandyl turned to Athaal. "You going to do any patrol duty soon?"

"I've done my share for a time, and with what else I've done for the Council . . ." The black-bearded mage shook his head.

Once Beltur and Athaal were outside the Council building, the bearded mage said, "Now that you're on the books, you might get a call to duty in the next season. You get paid a silver a day, and you only have to work two days out of every eight, and that's just walking either of the market squares, not every day, but the days are changed every few eightdays so that the thieves don't know when a mage is likely to be there. Duty lasts for ten eightdays, equivalent to one season, and not more often than once every three years."

"Is that what you meant by a summons to duty?"

Athaal nodded.

Beltur considered the possibilities. Given his considerable lack of coins, a silver a day didn't sound all that bad. "Why are the disks redeemed here, rather than at Patrol headquarters?"

"The Council prefers not to have any sizable amount of coin at the Patrol building. It's better to avoid temptation. Also, it gives the Council a better idea of where to locate mages, in case they need one."

"Where are we headed now?"

"Back to the house, first, so that I can give all this to Meldryn. Then we'll head north to check a pair of windmills that pump water. After that, we'll see."

XXXI

Whether it was the howling of the wind or the fact that Beltur couldn't help but worry over the fact that he didn't seem much closer to being able to support himself, he woke up early on sixday, and immediately had another disturbing thought, one that was scarcely new. *You never really supported yourself in Fenard, either.* But then, did anyone who worked for someone else truly support himself?

Those questions still half preoccupied Beltur when he reached the kitchen and sat down at the table. He sipped the dark ale.

"You're looking thoughtful this morning," said Athaal cheerfully.

"I've had a lot to think over."

The other two exchanged worried glances.

"It's not bad," said Beltur hurriedly. "I don't think it is. It's just . . . well . . . You and Meldryn have been very good to me." Beltur wasn't sure what he could say next that wouldn't come out as either ungrateful or self-serving.

Athaal hesitated, then went on. "This sounds like you're concerned you are a burden."

"I am concerned. I still know so little about what I could do that wouldn't . . . well . . . wouldn't take from you."

"You're learning," said Athaal. "You're beginning to earn coins on your own."

"But not nearly enough."

"Others helped us get started," said Meldryn, "and we're helping you, and you'll help others. That's how it should be." He glanced to his partner. "Jorhan?"

"Oh . . . I hadn't thought about him," said Athaal. "There's a smith you might be able to help . . . if you're interested. Jorhan works both iron and bronze, but he thinks there might be a market for things made of cupridium. He's been asking if we knew someone who could help with that for well over a year."

Beltur offered a puzzled expression.

"As I understand it, forging cupridium requires a slight influx of chaos bound in order. I get very uncomfortable dealing with chaos, even through order. You probably noticed that already. You'd be better at that than either Meldryn or me."

"It's not something I'd feel comfortable with, either," added Meldryn.

Beltur hadn't noticed Athaal's reluctance about chaos so much as his difficulties in detecting and handling tiny bits of either order or chaos, although he couldn't have said that he was particularly surprised about either of the two not wanting to handle chaos.

"What he'd pay," Athaal shrugged, "I don't know, but you'd keep it all."

That would be a start. "I'd like to talk to him."

"Good. We'll go out there after breakfast. I'd thought

to head that way sometime in the next few days, anyway."

Beltur wondered about that as well, but wasn't about
to say anything, especially since he sensed no deception.
It was just that everything seemed so . . . convenient for
Athaal. Then maybe the black mage was just so attuned
to order that matters were that convenient. He took
another swallow of the dark ale, then helped himself to
some of the half-warm cheesed eggs and the small loaf
of bread that Meldryn often made for each of them for
breakfast. The eggs were good, and filling, but the bread
was warm and fresh, and Beltur savored every bite from
the crusty loaf.

Before all that long, he had finished breakfast, cleaned
up the kitchen, and rejoined Athaal in the parlor. The
older mage replaced the book he had been reading in
the bookcase and stood. The two stepped out into another warm harvest morning, if one with more wind
than Beltur could recall since he'd been in Elparta—
except for the northeaster. Athaal immediately turned
east on Crossed Lane, which surprised Beltur, because
any time before that they had left the city, they had
headed north first.

"Where is this smithy?"

"He's got a place in the hills, alongside a stream,
not more than a kay from the southeast corner of the
wall."

"That seems like a strange place for a smithy."

"Oh?" This time, Athaal looked surprised.

"All the smithies I've ever seen are in towns or cities
or really close."

"The Council doesn't allow smelting and heavy forging inside the walls. Didn't I mention that?"

Belatedly, Beltur recalled that Athaal had. "You did.
I forgot. You did say some had shops to display their
work in the northeast quarter."

"Jorhan's a little different. You'll see. He's a good man, though." ·

"What can you tell me about him?"

"There isn't much to tell. His family's been in these parts forever. His great-grandfather came from a town on the other side of the southern hills, just barely in Gallos. Back then it didn't matter, of course."

Beltur frowned.

"There weren't any tariffs on the river then. Denardre's father imposed the first ones. Before that, Gallos and Spidlar were on better terms. Supposedly, the Council just looked the other way when bounty hunters chased Relyn all the way to Axalt. They didn't catch him. Some of them vanished, according to Jorhan."

"Relyn? The same Relyn that built the temple whose ruins Wyath destroyed?"

"There hasn't been another one that I know of," replied Athaal. "Anyway, Jorhan's a childless widower, and the last in his line, except for his sister, and she consorted a merchant from Axalt. I suppose she'll get the lands, or her children will. Jorhan's never said much. I learned what I know from others." He smiled. "You can learn a lot over time, if you just listen. Meldryn taught me that. It's amazing what he's heard over the years in the bakery. And you really ought to carry light shields all the time . . . or as much as you can."

Beltur refrained from sighing, and raised his shields.

Before long, Beltur and Athaal had left Elparta through the southeast gate, where yet another guard had nodded knowingly to the bearded mage.

"Do you know all the gate guards?"

"I only know a handful by name, but they know me because most of the people I do work for live outside the city, and I've been going out through the gates for close to fifteen years."

Athaal's estimate of the distance between the city gate

and Jorhan's smithy was a little suspect, Beltur thought, since he was certain they'd walked well over a kay, if not farther, past plots with small cots, one woodlot, and several stretches of rocky pastures before the older mage turned up a short stone lane leading up a very gentle slope, at the end of which stood a graystone house with a weathered split-slate roof and a small out-building with a single chimney from which a thin line of smoke rose. The morning was hotter than most had been lately, and Beltur had been blotting sweat from his brow and face for a good half glass.

They were less than ten yards from the house when the door opened, and a man stepped out onto the stone stoop, shouting, "So you've finally decided to pay me another visit!"

Beltur was relieved to see that the broad-shouldered figure was grinning broadly.

Athaal was also smiling, but he didn't speak until he and Beltur reached the bottom of the steps leading up to the entry. "I never said I wouldn't visit. I brought someone I thought you should meet. Beltur, this is Jorhan."

"You two might as well come in and get out of the sun." Jorhan stepped back and into the house, leaving the door open.

Athaal led the way up the steps and into the house. The door just opened into a room that was furnished in largely unupholstered wooden furniture—two mis-matched armchairs, three straight chairs, and a backed bench with two side tables against the wall. One of the armchairs had a worn blue cushion on it, and the bench seat was covered with a matching pad.

Beltur studied Jorhan. The first thing he sensed was a faint black mist of order surrounding the muscular and stocky smith, not enough for him to be a healer or mage, but more than most people harbored. The second

thing was the penetrating gray eyes that were studying Beltur and looking up slightly, since the top of
Jorhan's balding head was level with Beltur's eyes.

"Beltur's a mage who had to leave Gallos with little
more than his life," Athaal said evenly.

"You don't look much like a mage."

"Why don't you shield yourself fully," suggested
Athaal. "As strong as you can."

Beltur did so.

"Try to hit him," said Athaal. "Be careful, though."

Jorhan shook his head, then walked to the wood
stack beside the cold hearth and picked up a chunk of
wood, then walked back toward Beltur. Remembering
how he'd almost been unhorsed in Analeria, Beltur
spread his feet.

"You ready, Mage?"

"Go ahead," replied Beltur.

The first blow was light, as if Jorhan wanted to make
certain that Beltur did indeed have shields. The second
one was not. While Beltur could feel the pressure of the
blow, it didn't hurt.

Jorhan dropped the chunk of wood and shook his
hand. He grinned ruefully. "You know, Athaal, you
can be an evil bastard. You bring in a mage who scarcely
looks like he could stand up in a northeaster, and I'm
going to have a sore hand for a glass." The smith gestured toward the chairs. "Sit where you please."

Beltur let his shields drop to a lighter level, watching
as the smith picked up the billet of wood and then put
it back on the stack on the hearth.

"You never come without a reason." Jorhan sat down
in the middle of the bench.

"I don't. You asked if I knew of a mage who might
be able to help you make cupridium. Beltur might be
able to."

The smith looked at Beltur.

"I haven't worked with smiths before," Beltur said, "but I can handle very small amounts of both order and chaos."

Jorhan looked quizzically at Athaal.

"He was raised by his uncle, who was a white mage."

"Hah! Finally found a mage who might help."

"I've never even tried to make cupridium," Beltur said.

"We'll have to work that out. I've got an old book that describes how the Cyadorans did it. Well . . . it's a copy of an old book. Seems to make sense. I'll pay you for the day, and if we work it out, you get a bonus, and more pay any day you work."

"No less than a silver a day," said Athaal.

Jorhan raised his eyebrows.

"Beltur doesn't know the going rates here, and for this, he's better than most."

"Most? Seems like he's the only one."

Athaal grinned. "In that case . . ."

"Off with you, you mercenary son of a sow." Jorhan's deep voice held wry humor.

The bearded mage stood and looked at Beltur. "I'm heading up the road. I'll stop by here on my way back to the city. If you finish earlier, you know the way back."

"I'll either be here, on my way back, or there."

"Then I'll see you later. I'm sure you can do what Jorhan needs." Athaal smiled warmly, then turned and made his way from the workshop.

Jorhan stood and shook his head. "That man doesn't even like talking about chaos. Do you know why?"

Beltur eased himself out of the chair, then said, "He's never said anything about it except that he's not comfortable trying to work with it."

"What about you?"

"I can use order to move or handle chaos, and but it doesn't bother me the way it does Athaal. I wouldn't

want to handle chaos without using order." *Not necessarily for the obvious reasons.*

"Fair enough. Let me show you what the old book
says. You can read it, and then we'll go out to the forge
and see what we can do."

"Might I ask why you want to make cupridium?"

"Cupridium's stronger than bronze. Cast and forged
right, it's stronger than all but black iron. For all practical purposes, a cupridium blade'll even hold against
one of black iron, and it's only a shade heavier."

"Heavier? I thought . . ."

"People got it all backward. They think bronze is
lighter than iron. It's not. It's heavier."

"Then what's the advantage to making cupridium?
Isn't it a lot of work to make a cupridium blade. Who
but a white mage or someone filled with chaos would
even need one?"

"Someone who wanted the blade to last. A cupridium blade lasts forever. It doesn't rust or corrode like
iron or even the best steel. So does anything else made
out of cupridium. And it looks beautiful forever. I could
sell a pair of cupridium candlesticks for two golds or
more." Jorhan smiled. "There's one other thing. A really
good worked iron blade can take an eightday's worth
of work. A bronze blade takes less than half that, even
with work-hardening the edge and normalizing it . . ."

"And if I can insert the right amount of order-bound
chaos into it . . ."

"Then it's cupridium, and we both benefit. There's
even more profit in creating decorative objects."

Somehow, those words, and the honest greed behind
them, reassured Beltur. Still . . . "It can't be that easy,
even for a mage who knows how to do it. I haven't the
faintest idea of how to make this work."

"If you're willing to try, so am I."

"I'm certainly willing, but I know nothing about working iron or bronze."

"I can do that. Let me get the book."

Jorhan went into the dark and narrow hallway leading back from the front room, only to reappear almost instantly with a small leather-bound book, which he handed to Beltur. "The leather strip marks the page."

Beltur took the book. With a cover that was scratched and worn, even stained in places, the book looked ancient, and it felt that way as well. Yet Jorhan had said it was a copy of an even older volume. Rather than turn immediately to the marked page, he opened the book to the frontispiece, showing a line drawing of a smith at a forge. The title page opposite held only the title, *The Compleat Guide to Working Metals,* and beneath it the words, "A Fair Copy of a Volume from Cyad."

Frowning momentarily at the fact that neither the original author nor the scrivener nor copyist was listed, he then opened the bookmarked page and read over the words slowly, before going back over the parts that seemed important.

. . . for a cupridium blade, one must begin with one part tin to twelve parts copper . . . not the one part in eight used for a bronze blade . . . once the melt is seething and the color is all the same, then the magus must infuse the melt with chaos sealed in order, as in a net woven of order, so that no part of chaos touches another except as bound with order . . . That net must be held for a tenth part . . .

Beltur frowned. *A tenth part? Of a glass?* The book suggested what seemed similar to his shields, except he hadn't the faintest idea what the spacing of the net "knots" should be.

Finally, he handed the book back to Jorhan. "It may take a while to get the spacing of the order-chaos net right."

"Figured it might. I thought we could try it on small pours of that kind of bronze. We can pour a thickness into an open greensand mold, and you can do whatever you do with the order and the chaos. Wouldn't do that for a finished piece, but there's no point in a fancy mold when we're working out just how to make the cupridium. Once we work out your side of the casting, we'll start using regular molds that have been fired so that the bronze doesn't cool so fast." The smith shrugged. "Might as well get out to the smithy and see how we can make this work."

Beltur wondered at Jorhan's optimism. Even though cupridium had been forged for hundreds of years, it was clear few smiths had ever done it, and he knew nothing of the process, and neither did the smith, really, except for the proportions of copper and tin.

Once the two were in the stone-walled smithy, Beltur watched as the smith added small chunks of coal to the recessed hearth, then began to pump the bellows. He could sense the hot natural chaos released from the coal as it began to catch fire, and he realized that all forging resulted in the release of chaos. It had to. He'd just never thought of it that way.

"Always liked coal for working with copper," said Jorhan. "Coal runs in the family."

Beltur was surprised at how small the actual furnace was as well as the stoneware crucible within it that held the melting metal.

"This is some of the base bronze I've already made, just like the book said. It's not bad, but it bends too much. Even work-hardening doesn't solve that."

About a fifth of a glass later, the smith lifted the stoneware crucible with wood-handled iron tongs and poured the orange-golden metal into the mold. "Now . . . it's up to you."

Beltur immediately created what amounted to a small shield with spacing that felt like that of a fine fishnet. Except he realized that one layer of shields wouldn't be enough. Quickly, he added two more layers, which he thought, given the comparative thinness of the melted metal, would be enough. *You hope.* Concentrating as carefully as he could, he worked at getting the order and chaos nodes where he wanted them, and then held them, waiting . . . and holding . . . and waiting. Just holding didn't take that much effort.

Finally, he slowly released his hold, then took a deep breath. For better or worse, the order-chaos pattern was embedded in the metal. Still, he kept sensing, but the pattern held.

"It's set in the metal."

"It's still too hot to work."

In time Jorhan finally lifted the small rectangle in his tongs from the mold and then brought it to the anvil, where he struck it with his hammer. The rectangle immediately split into three thick sheets. "What the sow-shit? I never saw that before."

Beltur knew immediately what had happened. He hadn't connected the three layers of shields. "I can fix that. Try to forge any one of the sheets."

The smith took one of the sheets and began to tap it with the hammer. He smiled, but only for a moment, when cracks appeared along the lines of the shield links.

Beltur sighed. He'd been afraid that learning how to forge cupridium would be anything but simple.

"You did something all right, Mage, but what we've got is too hard to work-harden. It doesn't work out under the hammer, or it splits."

"I can do better, but I think it's going to take some work."

"Smithing always takes work."

More than half a glass later, when Jorhan tried to work the second metal rectangle, the smith's hammer just rebounded from the metal. He struck harder, but the metal didn't deform at all. Jorhan looked up and shook his head. "Something that can't be worked . . ."

"Couldn't you just cast it?"

"Making a mold that precise, where any imperfection shows up and can't be ground out, where you can't remove risers or sprues . . . that's not going to be useful."

Beltur was getting hot, and he stripped off his tunic and hung it on a peg by the smithy door. Then he returned and waited while Jorhan heated more of his basic bronze. This time, as soon as the metal was in the mold, he imposed a linked pattern of three levels of modified shields, with even smaller amounts of order and chaos in a finer net.

When Jorhan began to hammer that piece of bronze, it neither split nor cracked, but the hammering revealed a slightly raised pattern on the surface of the metal.

"I think I need an even finer order-chaos pattern," said Beltur. "At least, if you want to work-harden it."

"We're getting somewhere," said the smith.

But not all that quickly.

The fourth casting, with an even finer shield netting imposed by Beltur, turned out to be workable, but softer than ordinary bronze, according to Jorhan. The fifth, with more of the thinner links, but spaced more closely, was again unworkable.

Before Jorhan could begin to heat another batch, Beltur held up a hand. "Do you have some ale or something? I'm getting dizzy."

The smith looked annoyed.

"I know it doesn't seem like it to you," Beltur said, "but trying to place order and chaos inside hot metal takes a lot of effort, and I need a little something to eat or drink. Ale works better and faster."

Jorhan looked closely at Beltur, then laughed. "Hadn't thought of it that way. Be the same for an apprentice smith first off." He added some coal chunks to the fire, then said, "This way."

Beltur followed the smith back to the house.

After drinking a mug of ale even more bitter than the brew his uncle had preferred, and part of a stale loaf of bread, Beltur felt much better, and the two returned to the smithy.

Another glass passed—with two more attempts—before Jorhan declared, "This one is workable. Not quite as strong as I'd think might be possible."

Three more brass rectangles later, the smith smiled. "That one! Can you do it again? With a real mold? We'll try a dagger this time."

Beltur nodded and blotted his forehead. He was stripped down to his smallshirt and dripping wet.

A glass later, the two waited as the mold cooled, and Beltur had finally stopped having to blot his forehead and stood in the smithy doorway, letting the wind dry him and his damp smallshirt.

"Can you remember what you did on the last one?" asked the smith, a hint of apprehension in his voice.

"I can." That wasn't exactly true. What Beltur had finally worked out, through all the efforts, was more a sense of feel as to how the net-like spread of order and chaos had to mesh with the metal.

Before that long, the brisk wind had mostly dried Beltur, and he watched closely, both with eyes and senses, when Jorhan opened the mold and eased out the blade. He kept watching as the smith brought the cupridium to the anvil and lifted the hammer.

"Tough to work. That's as it should be."

Beltur kept sensing the metal as Jorhan worked, but the pattern held.

"Demon-shame," muttered the smith, finally holding the blade up.

Beltur tensed, as he had just about been ready to don his tunic.

"Not you," replied Jorhan to the unspoken question. "Me. The mold wasn't my best. Wasn't sure how good you'd be on a full-sized casting. It's not a loss, though. This could fetch a gold in the right hands, once I'm finished."

A gold? "Daggers are worth that much?" After pulling on his tunic, Beltur moved toward the anvil, his eyes on the dagger.

"Not daggers. A cupridium dagger. There aren't many left, and no one's forged one for years. Not in Spidlar."

"I've never seen one in Gallos." *And only Athaal's here.*

"You're better than I'd hoped," confessed the smith.

Beltur wasn't so sure how good he was. *More than seven glasses of work to cast one real dagger, and not a large one at that.* "It took some work."

"Smithing always does." After a pause, Jorhan asked, "You'll be here tomorrow?"

"I'll be here. Seventh glass?" *Where else would I be that I can actually earn silvers?*

"That would be good."

"What would be good?" asked Athaal from the door.

"Well," replied Jorhan. "That your friend here can actually do what's necessary to help forge cupridium." He held up the dagger. "Be worth a great deal once it's fine-finished with a proper grip."

Athaal froze where he stood, if but for an instant.

"It only took all day and close to a score of failures to figure it out," said Beltur dryly. "And two mugs of ale."

"Ale well spent," said Jorhan. "Oh . . . wait a moment. I need to pay you." Still carrying the dagger, he hurried from the smithy.

Athaal looked to Beltur. "You obviously pleased him. I've never seen him that eager to part with coins."

"It was harder work than I thought it would be."

"Most magery that pays is." Athaal's words weren't quite a reproof.

"I think you've already shown me that." Beltur half wondered why Athaal sounded the way he did, although Beltur couldn't have described exactly what that was. "This was harder."

"That's why there's not much made of cupridium anymore."

At that moment, Jorhan returned and pressed two coins into Beltur's hand. "Here you are. Two silvers. One for the day, and one for the dagger."

"Thank you." Beltur took them and made sure that the silvers were secure in his belt wallet.

The smith inclined his head to Athaal. "Thank you for introducing Beltur. I'm in your debt."

"I was glad to be of help."

Jorhan turned back to Beltur. "Tomorrow, then?"

"I'll be here." Beltur looked to Athaal. "Shall we go?"

Once the two were walking away from the smithy and down toward the road, Beltur asked, "How was your day?"

"Moderately successful. Not nearly so remunerative as yours."

"For the moment," Beltur pointed out. "You provide services to a great many. This is only the second time I've really done anything on my own." For all of the two silvers in his wallet, Beltur was well aware of how uncertain his position in Elparta remained.

For a moment, Athaal said nothing. "We should

hurry. It is later than usual, and Meldryn will be worrying. He always does, you know."

"He's very protective of you."

"He is. I feel the same way."

"Then we should hurry," replied Beltur with a smile.

XXXII

Sevenday morning found Beltur southeast of Elparta at Jorhan's smithy, working on adding order and chaos to two simple candlestick molds. For some reason that Beltur didn't understand, but Jorhan did, one of the candlesticks ended up with a bubble in the side. The second pour worked out, but it took Jorhan a great deal of effort to do the finish work on the candlesticks.

"Why do you think it happened that way?" asked the smith.

"It might be my fault," replied Beltur. "The bronze in the base of the candlesticks has more metal. It's thicker, and I probably should have used just a hint less order/chaos there. I'm still having to go by feel."

"I don't know as someone will pay as much for these."

"They won't break easily."

Jorhan grinned. "I know someone who might appreciate them."

"Oh?"

"Don't worry about that. Go to the kitchen and get yourself some ale. I need to heat the next set of molds."

The remainder of the day was largely a repetition of the first few glasses, although the last casting was another dagger, rather than a candlestick. At perhaps a

fifth past fourth glass, Jorhan called a halt, then handed
Beltur two silvers. "Oneday morning? I don't work
much on eightday. Besides, I'll need the time to get more
molds ready and finish up what we cast today."

"Then I'll see you on oneday morning."

Beltur was heading north on Bakers Lane when the
city chimes rang out fifth glass, feeling more than a little
tired after his day ... and after carrying shields all
the way back to the city. He was also almost bemused
by the fact that, after eightdays in Elparta, he had so
suddenly earned the five silvers or so in his wallet. *And
if it weren't for Jorhan and the City Patrol, you'd only
have a fraction of that ... and not much in the way of
prospects.*

When he entered the house, he could hear voices
coming from the parlor—and some of those voices belonged to women. *Jessyla and Margrena? Or someone
else?* He forced himself to walk down the hall calmly,
then entered the parlor, seeing Margrena and Jessyla sitting side by side on the padded backed bench.

Jessyla smiled, if briefly, while Margrena did not.

"I told you he wouldn't be long," said Athaal. "He's
not the kind to make you wait."

"I would have hurried if I'd known you were here,"
added Beltur, seating himself in the straight-backed
chair across from the two healers. Then he realized that
Jessyla was wearing the darker greens of a full healer,
and not the pale greens of an apprentice. "Congratula-
tions," he added warmly.

Athaal looked puzzled for a moment, while Margrena frowned momentarily. Jessyla feigned confusion.

Despite Jessyla's expression, what Beltur sensed was
that she just might have been pleased. "She's wearing
the greens of a full healer. She wasn't when I last saw
her," he explained, ostensibly to Athaal, even as he offered a smile to Jessyla.

"She passed her trials just before we left," Margrena said quickly.

"Where are you staying?" asked Beltur, assuming that they were with Margrena's sister, since he hadn't seen any bags or duffels.

"We're staying with Grenara. For now, anyway."

"Where does she live?" Beltur asked.

"Near the north market square, on Crafters Way," replied Jessyla. "I think that's right."

"It is," said Margrena. She then looked to Athaal. "I almost forgot to tell you. Waensyn came with us. He's staying with Cohndar. He'd thought to stay with Felsyn, but that didn't work out. Grenara wasn't about to host him."

"He's always seemed nice enough," offered Athaal, his voice pleasant, but neither warm nor cold.

"That wouldn't matter to Grenara."

"She does things her own way," stated Jessyla bluntly.

Margrena looked hard at her daughter.

Jessyla looked back at her mother. "She does."

"How bad is it in Fenard?" asked Beltur quickly, given that he'd asked the question that had led to Jessyla's reaction.

"There aren't any blacks left in the city, and probably not many anywhere else in Gallos," replied Margrena. "If there are, they won't be there long, one way or another."

"The only whites left are lackeys to that demon Wyath," snapped Jessyla.

Beltur couldn't help but wonder if Sydon happened to be one of those lackeys. *If he isn't, he's likely dead.*

"Some of them just might be trying to stay alive," suggested Margrena. "Beltur's uncle was one of the more powerful whites. Look what happened to him for just avoiding Wyath. He wasn't even directly opposing the Arms-Mage."

"The Council is concerned that Denardre might attack Spidlar," said Athaal.

"They should be." Jessyla stopped short after a sharp look from her mother.

"The Prefect is increasing the size of his army," Margrena said. "Wyath is also training the remaining whites in how to use chaos most effectively."

"How do you know that?" asked Athaal.

"Dhurra told me. That's why she and Pietryl went to Sarronnyn."

"I missed the reason. What was it?" asked Meldryn from the doorway.

"She wanted to go where there wouldn't be any fighting. Her nephew is a squad leader. His company was being trained to work with some of the Prefect's mages."

"That doesn't explain—" Athaal began.

"She said there was no telling whether the Prefect would attack Spidlar or Certis, and she didn't want to guess wrong and have to flee again."

"I wasn't aware Sarronnyn was that formidable," said Athaal mildly.

"It's not," replied Jessyla, "but the Westhorns are, and so is Westwind."

"Your point is well-taken," said Meldryn. "Gallos has not had the best of fortune in dealing with Westwind."

"I can't believe that Pietryl would have agreed." Athaal frowned.

Margrena smiled. "Dhurra can be quite firm. She told him that he could come with her, or stay in Gallos, or fly to the Rational Stars, but she was going to Sarronnyn."

"That sounds as though she'll fit right in there," said Athaal dryly.

"If that's the way she feels," Meldryn replied, "then would you advise her to come here?"

"Probably not."

"How many members of the Spidarian Council are women?" Jessyla asked Athaal.

"Women don't serve on the Council."

"Why not?"

"They just don't."

"Men aren't the ones who rule in Sarronnyn," said Jessyla, her voice even. "Why is that any different from women not ruling in Spidlar?"

Still standing behind Athaal, Meldryn smiled, if briefly, but said nothing.

"Women and men are different," Athaal finally replied.

"Some men are different from most men. Should such men not be allowed to be on the Council? Some women are different from most women. Shouldn't they be allowed to be on the Council, since they're different from other women?"

While Jessyla's voice remained even, Beltur could sense a certain chaotic movement in the order surrounding her, suggesting that she was struggling to remain calm.

"You do raise some very good questions, Jessyla," said Meldryn, "but I do have some doubts as to whether what we think will much affect the Council."

Jessyla looked ready to say something else, then pursed her lips for a moment, before turning to Beltur. "You haven't said much."

For a long moment, Beltur couldn't think of what he should say, or dared to say, feeling caught between wanting to agree with Jessyla and not wanting to upset Athaal. After what seemed an interminable length of time, he finally managed to say, "Maybe it's best the way it is where it is. That way, Dhurra can go to Sarronnyn, where she's more comfortable, and Athaal and Meldryn can enjoy the benefits of living in Spidlar."

"Do you really think everything's for the best?" demanded Jessyla. "When the Prefect killed your uncle and wants to destroy Spidlar and Certis?"

"That's not what I meant. I meant that it might be best to have some lands ruled by men and some by women. I don't like the idea of the Prefect ruling anything."

"You should have said that," replied the younger healer.

"I would have," replied Beltur, as ruefully as he could manage, "if I could talk and think as fast as you do."

Margrena grinned.

Jessyla laughed.

Meldryn smiled broadly.

After a moment, even Athaal smiled.

"Now . . ." offered Meldryn in a mellow voice, "might I suggest that Beltur and I get on with preparing dinner while the three of you catch up on what has happened." He gestured toward Beltur.

Beltur rose and followed the oldest mage into the kitchen.

"If you'd get out the platters and cutlery . . . put them on the worktable. I'll bring the meat pies and some bread from the bakery while you're doing that."

"Yes, ser." As he arranged plates on the worktable, Beltur mused over the fact that Meldryn had not wanted the discussion in the parlor to continue, almost as if he had wanted to separate Athaal and Beltur, even though Jessyla had been the one who had been asking the provocative questions.

He had just finished arranging the platters on the worktable and the cutlery on the main table when Meldryn returned, carrying a large tray with three meat pies, two smaller pies, most likely berry pies, and two large loaves of bread.

"That was an interesting observation you made in

the parlor," said Meldryn. "How did you come up with that?"

"I guess what I was partly thinking was that Arms-Mage Wyath had Uncle Kaerylt killed because Uncle didn't want to be like him. People are different, and maybe not all kinds of people belong together."

Meldryn nodded. "If you had lands of different kinds of people, wouldn't the lands just fight?"

"Why would they do that? No one's attacked either Westwind or Sarronnyn in years."

"In over a hundred years. That's not very long in the life of countries. Both old Lornth and Gallos attacked Westwind until the dark angels proved it was far too costly. Both lands attacked, if the stories and *The Book of Ayrlyn* are accurate, because the women on the Roof of the World wanted to change things. After all that, Nylan and Ayrlyn had to leave Westwind because they were different."

"That may be," said Beltur, "but isn't it better to let people leave than to kill them because they're different?"

"A land won't survive unless its people agree on what's good and what's not good, and who should rule and how."

"That doesn't mean that people in different lands shouldn't be able to have different ways of doing things. That was what I meant."

Meldryn shrugged. "As an idea, I'd agree with that. But what makes the idea work in the examples of Westwind and Sarronnyn is how strong they both are. Something may be right, but without the strength to protect that idea or way of doing things, it will fall to those who are stronger. A bad idea, or a terrible way of ruling or a bad ruler—like Denardre in Gallos—will triumph over those unable to stop them. That's why the Council of Spidlar is careful to make sure everyone knows the laws and customs and does what is necessary to maintain them both."

"Does the Council drive out the people who think differently, the way the Prefect is?"

Meldryn shook his head. "Not as long as they obey the laws. At the same time, life is not as easy for anyone who doesn't believe what most people do. That's why some leave. Women who think they should be able to be on the Council would be more comfortable in Sarronnyn. Relynists usually move to Axalt, or maybe to Montgren."

"Montgren?" Athaal had mentioned the Relynists in Axalt to Beltur, but no one had ever said much about Montgren.

"What's important in Montgren is sheep. They don't get upset about much of anything else as long as people don't hurt each other. The Duchess is said to be fair." The older mage gestured. "Pour two pitchers of ale, and then tell the others that supper, such as it is, is ready."

Beltur did both. Before long, all five were seated at the main kitchen table, with Meldryn and Athaal at each end, Beltur on one side, and Margrena and Jessyla on the other.

"This looks like the best fare we've had in days," said Margrena, after taking a bite of the meat pie, and sipping the ale.

"More like eightdays," added Jessyla.

"Eating here has been a real pleasure," said Beltur.

"You did most of the cooking in Fenard, didn't you?" Margrena's words were as much statement as question.

Beltur wondered how she had known that. "For the last few years, once my uncle trusted me in the kitchen. That's another reason I enjoy eating here. The food is better than my cooking."

"It makes sense," Jessyla said. "You wouldn't spoil the food the way your uncle and Sydon would have."

"He mentioned that to you?" Beltur finally asked Margrena.

"In passing. He said he appreciated your efforts."

"'Efforts' is probably as good a word as any."

"You were friendly with Beltur's uncle?" Meldryn asked.

"Cordial. Not friendly. He was an honest man, and he sent people to me for healing. He even arranged for me to get burnet when it was hard to come by."

Jessyla nodded. "That was how I met Beltur. He helped me load it."

Jessyla's words definitely surprised Beltur, because, while he had been friendly and as helpful as he could be, he hadn't actually touched the burnet, and Jessyla had definitely noticed that when she had come for the healing herb.

"Some things are getting clearer," said Meldryn dryly. "I have a much better idea why Arms-Mage Wyath was after Beltur's uncle, and why you encouraged Athaal to help Beltur."

"How could we not?" replied Margrena. "Beltur certainly did nothing wrong according to our lights, and his uncle was the only white in Fenard who was helpful to us."

"And I have to say," interjected Beltur, "although I've said it before, that Uncle had far higher respect for Athaal than he did for almost all whites." That was also true enough, especially in the end.

Meldryn offered a thoughtful nod, then said, "There are some berry pies when you finish the meat pies."

"His berry pies are outstanding," confirmed Beltur, wanting to move the conversation away from blacks and whites.

"It seems like forever since we had something like

that to look forward to," said Jessyla, offering a brief smile.

Beltur wasn't sure if she'd meant the smile for him, but he enjoyed it anyway.

XXXIII

Eightday was quiet, so quiet that Beltur slept through breakfast, which he almost never did, possibly because the work of manipulating order and chaos had turned out to be far more exhausting than he'd thought possible for something that sounded so simple. Even so, the section of cold meat pie that Meldryn had set aside for him was more than enough. Because the two had left the house, most likely to visit friends, as they had mentioned they might the night before, Beltur cleaned up everything, washed up, and settled down in the parlor to read more in *On Healing*. Although Athaal had almost dismissed the book as more of a primer on anatomy, Beltur continued to find it informative, given that he needed something fairly basic and that he still worried about what could have gone wrong when he had used the order to destroy the strange chaos in the head of Claudyt's grandson.

Athaal and Meldryn returned in the late afternoon, but did not say where they'd been. He had half expected that they had gone to see Margrena and Jessyla, but what they said in passing at dinner indicated they had been elsewhere.

On oneday and twoday Beltur worked with Jorhan at the smithy, casting two cupridium sabres, several bowls, and a fairly ornate platter. Diligent as he was in carrying light shields whenever he was out in public, between that and the efforts involved in casting the cupridium, by the time he reached the house each night, he was exhausted.

On threeday, when Beltur came down to breakfast, he found an envelope at his place. Immediately, he looked to Athaal. "What is that?"

"It arrived early this morning by a Council messenger. It's still sealed. I don't know what's in it, but I'd wager it's a summons to aid the City Patrol. They're always shorthanded, and you came to the attention of the Council last eightday."

Beltur opened the envelope gingerly and began to read.

> Greetings and salutations, Honored Mage Beltur—
>
> As a mage resident in Elparta, you are required to serve periodically in support of the City Patrol for two days out of each eightday for a season, but no more than one season every three years, or less, if so decided by the Council. This duty is required of all mages. Failure to do so can result in either extra non-remunerative duties or immediate exile from Spidlar. For each day of duty you will receive one silver for your presence, and additional stipends based on performance.
>
> Please report to Clerk Raymandyl in the Council building within two days of receiving this notice.

The signature was that of one Veroyt. Under his name were the words "under the direction of Jhaldrak, Councilor from Elparta."

Beltur looked up. "It's definitely a summons for duty. I need to report to Raymandyl either today or tomorrow."

"I'd suggest today. Putting off Council duties can only lead to trouble. Also, if you report for your duty assignment immediately, that will make Raymandyl think more highly of you, and that could be very useful."

Beltur understood what Athaal wasn't saying—*since you're a newcomer to Elparta and you're from Gallos.*

"You should go early," added Athaal. "It won't hurt for Laranya to clean the kitchen this one time."

Beltur didn't argue with the other mage.

"Take the summons with you," added Athaal.

In less than half a glass, Beltur was on his way, headed south on Bakers Lane. It took him a bit longer, because he'd only been to the Council building twice, both times coming from the main market square, and he missed Hill Street coming south and had to retrace his steps.

When he stepped inside the door on the north side of the Council building, breathing a little hard from hurrying up the hill, Beltur didn't recognize Raymandyl for several moments, because the clerk was not at his desk and was facing the other way, so that all Beltur saw was his jet-black hair until Raymandyl turned and walked back toward Beltur.

"Clerk Raymandyl . . ."

"Just Raymandyl," replied the clerk cheerfully as he gestured for Beltur to take the single straight-backed chair before it. "I see that Athaal got to you."

"He was quietly insistent that I come immediately."

"He can be rather persuasive. I hear you're working with Jorhan." At Beltur's involuntary expression of surprise, Raymandyl laughed. "Elparta may be a city, but everyone knows everyone, or at least all the merchants and crafters and mages do, and they all talk."

"I have been working with him for the last few days."

"Good man. Honest. A little abrupt at times." Raymandyl paused. "What did Athaal tell you?"

"Even before I got the summons, he'd explained that mages had duties." Beltur laid the summons on the desk. "He said to bring it."

"Good. Your duty days for now will be fourday and sevenday. In fact, you'll likely always be working on sevenday often because some people can't go to the square any other time except sevenday afternoon, or eightday, and most would like to keep eightday for themselves, especially the Chaordists."

"Chaordists? I thought most of them were in Hamor."

"There are quite a few here, along with some Relynists."

"Relynists?"

"You know, the ancient prophet of the black temple. Most of his followers live in Axalt, but we've got a few here. Now . . . do you know where the City Patrol headquarters are?"

"Athaal showed me. The square building several long blocks from the northwest corner of the main market square?"

"That's it. The street is Patrol Street. That might even be a name painted on a building or two. That's where you'll meet the patroller you'll be supporting. You're to be there no later than two fifths before seventh glass. Your duty time runs from seventh glass to fourth glass. You get paid once each eightday, right here. You can pick up the previous eightday's pay, and redeem any disks, any day after oneday." Raymandyl turned to the cabinet beside the desk and opened a drawer, pulling out what looked to be a medallion of some sort. He handed it to Beltur.

As he took the medallion, Beltur could immediately tell that it and the chain were of worked silver. He looked askance at the clerk.

"That's the chain and medallion you wear on duty— outside your tunic where it can be seen. You lose it, and you owe the Council five silvers. When your duty is over, you hand it in when you pick up your last pay. Now, you have to sign the book and affirm that you've been informed of your duties." The clerk took a ledger-like book with a blue leather binding from the cabinet and opened it. He began to write. After a time, he turned the book to face Beltur. "Please read this aloud."

Beltur scanned the words, and then read, "I affirm that the Council Clerk has informed me of my duties and responsibilities and that he has provided me with the medallion of office as the symbol of my duties in support of the City Patrol. I understand that the medallion must be returned upon completion of one season's duty."

"Good. Sign on the left side. Leave space for me to sign on the right." Raymandyl handed the pen to Beltur.

Beltur took the pen, signed his name, and returned the pen.

In turn, the clerk signed, and then melted the wax and applied his seal. "There. That takes care of the formalities. Do you have any other questions?"

"I start tomorrow?"

"That's right."

"Do you know what patroller I'll be working with?"

Raymandyl shook his head. "That's up to Patrol Captain Fhaltar, since Patrol Chief Chamyt is trying to work out how to best use the Council forces sent from Kleth to reinforce the towers and the city garrison."

"Because of the Prefect?"

"Haven't you heard? Prefect Denardre is demanding the Council lower tariffs on goods from Gallos. He sent a missive to the Council declaring, in effect, that those tariffs will be lower, one way or another. Word is that he's assembling an army and all the white mages in Gallos."

Do Athaal and Meldryn know this? "I hadn't heard that the Prefect had put that in writing. Athaal and Meldryn knew about the army, but not that he'd threatened Spidlar. They thought something like that might happen, but . . ." Beltur shook his head.

"Did they say why?"

"Only that they'd heard from healers who had left Gallos about the army and the white mages."

"I was hoping they might know more." Raymandyl sounded disappointed.

From what Beltur could tell, the clerk wasn't hiding anything. "I don't know for sure, but I don't think so." He slipped the medallion and chain over his head but inside his tunic.

"That's a good idea. Remember . . . well before seventh glass tomorrow morning."

"I'll be there. Thank you for all the explanations."

"It was my pleasure, also my duty."

Beltur inclined his head, then made his way from the Council building, slightly amazed at the definite formality required by the Spidlarian Council. *Quite a contrast from Fenard.*

He did his best to hurry, but it was still close to eighth glass by the time he stepped inside the smithy.

"You're late," said Jorhan brusquely.

Beltur thought he detected a sense of concern. *Worry that you might not show up?* "I'm sorry. I got a message to report to the Council building immediately."

"What did you do to cause that?"

"I stopped a cutpurse in the market last eightday, and the Council found out that I'm a mage and that I haven't ever served the duty with the City Patrol. So for the next season, I have to work with the market patroller on duty on fourday and sevenday. Starting tomorrow."

Although Jorhan offered a thoughtful frown, Beltur could see that he appeared almost relieved. After a moment, the smith replied, "Fourday and sevenday? That shouldn't be a problem. We've got the casting part in hand. Come to say, that might work out better. Give me more time to do the finish work."

"I would have liked to have let you know, but Athaal and Meldryn said that, because I'd come from Gallos, I shouldn't waste any time reporting to the Council clerk."

"I can see that. You ready to get to work?"

"I am." Beltur slipped off his tunic and hung it on a wooden peg by the smithy door.

The rest of threeday was very much like the other days in the smithy had been, with another and larger blade being cast, and two decorative women's mirrors, as well as smaller items, including two bud vases.

With another pair of silvers in his wallet, Beltur left the smithy just after fourth glass, raising his full shields as soon as he stepped outside, partly because he realized that he was now carrying enough silvers to make him a more tempting target for thieves.

As soon as he reached the house late that afternoon, he hurried upstairs and washed up, changing into his clean smallshirt, and thinking that he needed to get another set of garments, especially undergarments, now that he actually had some coins to pay for them.

Both Meldryn and Athaal were in the kitchen by the time Beltur felt presentable and joined them. He could smell something that reminded him of roast fowl, but the scent was somewhat different, but still very appetizing.

"How did your meeting with Raymandyl go?" asked Athaal.

"I thought it went well. They gave me a medallion, and I have duty on fourdays and sevendays, starting tomorrow."

Meldryn raised his bushy gray eyebrows. "You must have impressed someone. Those are the days when thieves are the most active."

"Remember, Mel, he already proved that he could put a cutpurse in a shield. Also, the Council wants other mages free to help the forces if the Prefect actually decides to attack."

"Raymandyl told me that Denardre has already sent a threatening missive to the Council." Beltur went on to explain what he had learned.

After Beltur finished, Athaal nodded. "That's another reason why they're giving Beltur that duty."

"I can't believe that Denardre would make that kind of threat," said Meldryn. "He has to know how serious the Council is about trade and tariffs." He turned to Beltur. "How strong do you think Wyath's mages are?"

Beltur thought for a moment. "Uncle was able to use chaos to cut through the roof beams of that chamber in the palace and drop the beam on one of Wyath's mages. And they were strong enough to kill him." Beltur swallowed as that image came into mind. He shuddered just slightly. *If you'd only known what you know now . . .* He shook his head, doubting, even with all the exercises Athaal had given him and the effort he was making in casting cupridium, that he would have been able to hold shields against that many mages.

"You still remember, don't you?" asked Athaal.

"I probably always will."

"If Kaerylt could cut a roof beam in two places, while holding shields against that many whites," mused Meldryn, "we're going to have trouble. More than a little trouble. We need to talk that over with Cohndar and Felsyn."

The two nodded.

"How are you doing with Jorhan?" asked Athaal.

"I think he's happy I won't be there every day. He's gotten behind on the finish work."

The other two exchanged glances.

Beltur had the feeling that what he said had surprised them both, although he couldn't immediately tell why.

"We've got something different for supper this evening," Meldryn said after a moment of silence. "A fowl stuffed with pearapples and roasted with a pearapple and honey glaze."

Just hearing the description made Beltur's mouth water. He couldn't help but smile.

XXXIV

Beltur woke earlier than usual on fourday morning, not because the wind blew harder, or there was rain pounding down, but because he was worried about getting to City Patrol headquarters well before seventh glass. He was actually dressed and downstairs in the kitchen before Meldryn left to return to the bakery.

"Up early, I see," observed the oldest mage.

"I worry."

"The City Patrol won't exactly turn on you with chaos."

"Or even set Osarus after you," added Athaal. "He's not that type anyway."

Beltur poured a mug of ale, helped himself to a portion of the omelet that contained an assortment of chopped vegetables, at least two cheeses, and some small bits of undefined meat, and sat down. After several bites, he took a swallow of ale, then cleared his throat, and said, "I've been thinking . . ."

"That can be dangerous," said Meldryn with a smile.

"You rescued me, and you've fed and clothed me,

even given me my own room. So far, I've contributed
very little except trying to clean up when and where I
can. Finally, I've begun to earn some coins."

"Finally?" interjected Athaal. "You've only been in
Elparta for a bit more than two eightdays."

It had seemed longer than that to Beltur, but he
wasn't about to say that. "I know, but . . . well . . . as I
said. I'm making coins now. Not enough to buy a place
or rent a nice room, but enough that I can pay something to you and Meldryn. What about two silvers an
eightday for now . . . ?" Beltur found himself trailing
off the words.

Meldryn and Athaal exchanged glances. Then Athaal
nodded to his partner.

Meldryn offered a smile. "We both appreciate your
concern. We also appreciate that as soon as you began
to earn something you didn't want to be a burden. Right
now, you can only count on two silvers an eightday—
that's from your City Patrol duties. You might make
more from Jorhan. You might not. We'd feel more comfortable if you just paid a silver an eightday, at least
until you have accumulated a few more coins . . . and
have a more stable income."

"I can't argue with your reasons, and I'll agree to that
for now. But I don't want to be a burden. I really don't."

"You aren't a burden, and if you pay a silver an eightday, you definitely won't be."

"You're sure?"

"We're sure," added Athaal.

"Thank you. Both of you. What day would you like
to be paid?"

"You won't get paid until twoday or later," said
Athaal. "So what about fiveday? Starting next fiveday.
Not tomorrow."

"I can do that." Beltur was relieved in more ways
than one. He hated being a burden, and he'd offered

what he thought was fair, and they'd been more than kind in halving that. "If you wouldn't mind . . . what should I keep in mind about this City Patrol duty?"

"Keep your shields up at all times," began Athaal. "Don't always use a concealment. It helps to walk a row of vendors without a concealment, and then appear to vanish. If you don't show yourself periodically, people forget you're there. If you're always visible, then the thieves will strike at the side of the market square where they know you aren't."

"It also helps to be in different parts of the square from the patroller you're working with," added Meldryn.

"Also, remember that often thieves work in pairs, and one will make a fuss someplace, but not steal anything, while the other is sneaking something off a nearby table. Sometimes, they'll even fight . . ."

"Don't worry too much about foodstuffs. If someone steals an apple or pearapple, or even a melon, all they can do with it is eat it, and it doesn't hurt the seller as much as hard goods, or scarves or laces, or silks. They're really interested in things they can sell in the alleys or that their scurf can pawn or sell to outland traders, the ones that don't care where something comes from."

Beltur listened as he ate, hoping that he could remember everything that the two told him.

He left the house at a fifth past sixth glass, with a small loaf of bread wrapped in cloth and tucked inside his tunic, since both Athaal and Meldryn had said that he'd want it later. While there weren't that many out on Bakers Lane that early, the streets were anything but deserted, although most of those he saw were men, like him, hurrying to get somewhere. A brisk breeze blew out of the north, slightly cooler than the lighter winds of the past few days, but there were no clouds in the sky, and only a trace of haze to the north.

The City Patrol headquarters was five long blocks west of the market square, roughly halfway between the square and the river. When Beltur neared the building, he eased the medallion out from under his tunic and let it show. Since Athaal had told him to enter by the north door, he kept walking down Patrol Street, although it was clear that the main entrance had to be elsewhere, because there was no one heading toward the narrow single door on the north side.

Beltur took a deep breath and opened the door. He expected some kind of odor, but all he could smell was the faintest bitter scent of pine. Immediately inside the door was a modest foyer, and a table desk set forward of the other door in the foyer, presumably to a hallway leading deeper into headquarters. Behind the desk sat a graying and angular patroller in blue, who looked up, his eyes on the silver medallion.

"You're the new mage . . ." He looked down at the ledger-like book open before him. "Beltar?"

"Beltur, Patroller. I was told to be here well before seventh glass."

The patroller turned the book and pointed to Beltur's name. "Sign right after your name."

Beltur dipped the pen lying on the blotter in the inkwell and signed. "Do I sign in every time?"

"Yes, you do. If you want to get paid. You'll be working with Laevoyt. He should be here any moment."

"I haven't done this before, and I haven't been in Elparta that long."

"Laevoyt can tell you all about it. You can sit on the bench over there. Might as well. You'll be on your feet for the rest of your shift."

"Thank you." Beltur sat down on one end of the bench. He wasn't about to point out that the duty time was shorter than the days he had been putting in—all on his feet.

Before long, the door behind the patroller's desk opened, and another blue-uniformed figure stepped out and glanced at the duty patroller, who gestured to Beltur. The patroller who walked toward Beltur had a long face with a thin, beakish nose under reddish blond hair. His eyes were pale blue. Given his height and muscular thinness, he immediately reminded Beltur of a river heron—except for the friendly smile. "You must be Beltur. I'm Laevoyt."

"I'm pleased to meet you."

"The same. You're the mage from Gallos who's staying with Athaal and Meldryn?"

"I am."

"What have Athaal and Meldryn told you about what's expected?"

"Everything they could think of, I think," replied Beltur. "So much that I'm afraid I won't remember it all."

The patroller laughed. "That sounds more like Athaal to me."

"He did do most of the talking."

"We should start toward the square. I'll try to fill you in on the way."

"That would be helpful."

Once they were outside headquarters, Laevoyt asked, "How did you end up in Elparta?"

"After the Arms-Mage of Gallos killed my uncle and tried to kill me, I fled to the house of a healer I knew. Athaal happened to be there, and he and the healer suggested I should come to Elparta. I did, and I arrived with the clothes on my back and little else."

"There's usually work of some sort . . ."

"I started out by helping Athaal, and now I've been working with a smith. How long have you been with the City Patrol?"

"Not quite ten years. It's not that bad here, especially

since you mages help. Trakyll said that you've already caught one cutpurse . . ."

"I was at the market with Athaal. He was shopping. I was looking. Someone yelled out, and I saw someone running. So I put shields around them—and it turned out to be a girl posing as a boy. Then the patroller and Athaal showed up. The patroller gave me a disk, and, well, that's how I ended up getting a summons to work with the City Patrol so soon after I got here."

"How long have you been here?"

"Not quite three eightdays."

Laevoyt laughed. "They did find out about you quickly. That might have been why Trakyll gave you the disk. They're supposed to go to mages who've already worked with the City Patrol. Then, maybe it was because you were with Athaal." He paused. "You can do concealments, can't you? Some mages have trouble with them."

And they still make them work with the City Patrol? "I can. I wasn't when I was there with Athaal. I was just seeing what there was at the market. Is there anything I should know that Athaal and Meldryn might not have told me?"

"Probably. I wouldn't know what it might be. The thing is to keep moving. There are just the two of us patrolling the square. With just the two of us, we'll still miss some of the thieves. Keeping on the move helps."

"If two aren't enough . . . ?"

"Why doesn't the Patrol add more patrollers? Because mages and patrollers cost silvers. The Council figured that two are enough to keep the theft down. More men than that doesn't make it much better, and it costs a lot more. They'd have to add two more patrollers, one for each market square."

"Do you patrol the square every day?"

"I don't except when there's a mage on duty. I'll be

working with you for two days every eightday. The other days, except on eightday, someone else patrols. We only have mages twice an eightday. There aren't enough mages to have one every day."

As they neared the square, Beltur saw that it was already filled with people, not nearly as crowded as it had been when he had been there the last time with Athaal, but with far more people buying and ready to buy than he would have expected so early in the morning. "It's crowded, already."

"Morning's worse," declared Laevoyt. "Midmorning, especially. You being new, might not hurt to circle the square so they can see you. After that, try to be seen some of the time, and be unseen much more. Oh . . . I almost forgot." He handed Beltur a copper whistle on a lanyard. "Put this around your neck. If you catch anyone, blow three sharp blasts on it. If I don't show up before long, do it again until I show up. Most of the time, you should try to be in a different part of the square from where I am." Laevoyt smiled. "That's up to you, because I shouldn't be able to see you very often."

After slipping the whistle lanyard around his neck, Beltur nodded. He should have thought of that, but hadn't.

"Plan to meet me here on the corner at ninth glass, and the first glass of the afternoon, and then again just before fourth glass."

"Ninth glass, first glass, and fourth glass," Beltur repeated.

"You've got it. I'll see you at ninth glass, unless you catch someone." With a smile following his words, the tall patroller turned to his right and began what looked like an initial walk around the square.

Beltur readjusted the silver medallion and headed south along the west side of the square, past the part that seemed to host more goods, such as lacework,

scarves of various fabrics, pottery, woven baskets, even
some decorative buckets. From what he recalled, more
of the produce—melons, pearapples, apples, and other
fruits and vegetables—was concentrated more along the
south side of the square.

He kept a pleasant expression on his face as he
moved, trying to take in as much as he could, as well
as listening. Most of the talk was too far away for him
to hear, or too mixed with other conversations, but he
did pick up a few fragments as he walked.

"... younger mage ..."

"... wind's picking up ... might be rain tomorrow ..."

"... told you ... not too close to the front edge of
the table ..."

"... another new mage ... where they get them ..."

"... the best in needle lace ... can't find any better
anywhere in Candar ..."

"... any cutwork lace ... Sligan style ..."

Cutwork lace ... needle lace? Beltur briefly wondered just how many types of lace there might be.

Just before he reached the midpoint of the square, so
far without seeing or hearing anything that seemed untoward, Beltur saw Laevoyt coming the other way. The
patroller caught sight of Beltur and motioned for him
to continue, then turned down a line of stalls and tables
toward the middle of the square. Recalling what both
Athaal and Laevoyt had said, Beltur walked more
quickly as he passed the row of produce carts and baskets filled with everything from potatoes to carrots, tur-
nips, and radishes ... and assorted varieties of melons
and fruits. When he neared the corner of West Street
and Patrol, he raised a concealment.

"... young mage just vanished ..."

"... all the strong mages can do that ... still see
what's happening ..."

While "seeing" wasn't exactly correct, Beltur could

sense shapes and the flow of order and chaos within and around people. He did have to move more carefully, at least at first, since perceiving people wasn't the same as seeing them.

He kept walking, and sensing, avoiding people because they couldn't see him, but he couldn't see or sense anything untoward—not during the first glass he patrolled, nor even during the second glass. Although he was careful to drop the concealment at intervals and walk openly, none of the vendors even attempted to sell him anything, although several almost did . . . until they saw the medallion.

At ninth glass, he had nothing to report to Laevoyt.

"That's fine. Our being here sometimes is enough."

Beltur resumed his efforts.

Sometime later but before first glass, Beltur could sense a slight rise in chaos some five yards away, a row of stalls to the north, and he immediately slipped between two tables, brushing by someone he sensed to be older and likely a woman.

"Who was that?"

He didn't stop to become visible or explain. Ahead of him, two women were arguing, loudly, almost screaming.

"You slut! You ripped my scarf!"

". . . did not!"

Beltur didn't sense the chaos that should have increased with those words, but a lower-level chaos at an adjoining stall.

A distraction! He immediately moved toward the chaos, but before he reached it, the figure had grabbed something and started to slip away.

Beltur dropped the concealment and clamped shields around the thief, even if he wasn't certain what the person had grabbed.

The screaming stopped. Then both young women

turned and started to run. Beltur managed to put shields around the nearest one, but realized he couldn't add another shield. He'd never tried to hold more than two at once, in addition to his own personal shields, and he didn't want to let go of the two he held.

The thief appeared to be an older woman, slightly bent, wearing a voluminous dress of nondescript gray. Held in the shield, she glared at Beltur with undisguised hatred, but said nothing. Beltur looked at his other captive, a much younger woman, dressed in loose trousers, a light tan linen blouse, and a sleeveless maroon vest embroidered in white designs. She tried to spit at Beltur, but the spittle splattered on the unseen shield.

Belatedly, Beltur grabbed the whistle and blew three sharp blasts.

"She's got three shimmersilk scarves!" the vendor to Beltur's left cried out.

"Sow-sucking mage . . ." muttered the thief.

Beltur was about to blow the whistle again when he caught sight of Laevoyt's tall figure striding along the space between the stalls, with buyers moving out of his way.

"What have we here, Mage?" asked Laevoyt loudly when he came to a stop short of the thief.

"The one in gray lifted something from that table and started to escape when I caught her. The one in the vest was arguing loudly with another young woman, and everyone was watching them. I could only catch these two."

"The granny thief has three of my silk scarves!" declared the graying woman vendor.

"You can't count," muttered the woman in gray, almost under her breath.

"With that dress," said Laevoyt, "she just might have

a lot more." A pair of leather cords appeared in his hands, and he stepped toward the thief. "Mage?"

Beltur released the shield, but was ready to throw one around both of them if the older woman attempted to flee. The thief didn't offer resistance, but she continued to glare at Beltur as Laevoyt bound her hands behind her back and then placed a leather collar around her neck attached to a chain.

Laevoyt's hands ran over the thief's clothing, and in moments, he held four silk scarves. Then he came up with a small tooled leather bag, and a lace collar. "I do believe this will send you to the women's house, granny." He returned the scarves to the vendor, then addressed Beltur. "Hold her again, if you will."

As soon as Laevoyt stepped back Beltur replaced the shield. Even so, the thief attempted to run and was brought up short.

At the patroller's gesture, Beltur dropped the shield around the younger woman. Once the decoy was bound and collared, and both collared thieves were chained, Laevoyt had them walk in front of him toward Patrol Street. Beltur walked beside him, all too conscious of a growing headache. *From holding three shields . . . or just because it's been a long morning?* He hoped what they had to do at headquarters didn't take that long.

"You might as well come all the way with me," said Laevoyt. "If you caught anyone else, you'd be waiting a long while. I'll need to return the lace and the leather bag when we return to the square, but they'll feel fortunate to get them back."

Laevoyt and Beltur and their prisoners walked back to the north door of headquarters. Beltur opened the door and held it wide for the other three, then followed them inside.

"Two of them?" asked the duty patroller.

"They were busy," replied Laevoyt. "The one in gray probably has more hidden in that dress. She took four shimmersilk scarves, and this collar, and this bag. The one in the vest was one of the decoys. The other decoy split before the mage could hold her."

"Two out of three. Not bad." The duty patroller produced another leather-bound book, then looked at the older woman. "Your name."

"Cassyndra."

"I doubt that's her real name," said Laevoyt.

"It doesn't matter," replied the other patroller, writing down the name and several more words before looking to the decoy. "Your name?"

"Shaedra."

Then the duty patroller looked up. "Beltur, right? You're the one who captured them?"

"That's right," said Laevoyt.

"Yes," answered Beltur almost simultaneously.

After writing several lines in the book, the duty patroller reached down and picked up a large bell that he rang vigorously. Several moments passed before another patroller opened the door behind the duty desk.

"Two more prisoners. Grand theft. Main market square."

"What happens now?" asked the younger woman in a thin almost squeaky voice.

"You'll go before the Council magistrate," replied the duty patroller. "She'll decide whether you keep both your hands and how long you'll work in the women's house."

The younger woman swallowed.

The third patroller took the two prisoners and gestured for them to precede him through the inner door.

Once the three were gone and the door closed, the

duty patroller handed Laevoyt two more sets of leathers, chains, and collars. "Have a good afternoon."

"We'll try," replied Laevoyt cheerfully.

Beltur just nodded.

When Beltur and Laevoyt were outside and walking back toward the market square, the patroller said, "You're one of the few mages I've seen that can handle two shields."

"It's actually three. I was holding my own at the same time."

Laevoyt raised his eyebrows. "You're pretty young for that, if I do say so."

"There are lots of other things I can't do," Beltur said. "Shields just happen to be one of the things I'm good at." *Thanks to Jessyla and Athaal.*

"You also picked up the actual thief. Many times the mage only gets the decoy."

"That's because Athaal and Meldryn . . ."

"Told you what to watch for?"

"Yes." *If not in so many words.*

"That will make your work here easier, but you'd better never let those shields down when you're on the streets. They don't care all that much about their decoys, but that false granny in there will likely lose a hand. It won't be long before word gets out that you're catching the thieves, and not just their decoys. Someone just might pay an assassin to try to put a crossbow bolt in you. Of course, if you stop that and catch the assassin, then that's worth five disks, and no assassin will try again. If you just stop the bolt they likely won't try again, either."

"I have the feeling that mages without shields are better staying away from Elparta," said Beltur dryly.

"That's generally a good idea," said Laevoyt, again cheerfully.

"Is there anywhere here that has ale?" Beltur asked.

"Ale?"

"I brought some bread, but I need something to drink. Holding three shields at once isn't easy."

"We'll go by Fosset's cart. He'll give you the first one free. A small mug."

"I can take that?"

"One per day, all day, is allowed. After that, you pay." Laevoyt led Beltur back down the west side of the square to where a man stood beside a small cart, with two kegs set upon it, with a three-level rack between them, each level containing earthenware mugs, with the smallest mugs on the top row, and the largest on the middle. "Good afternoon, Fosset. This is Beltur. You'll be seeing him for a time."

The clean-shaven and stocky Fosset had curly black hair and offered a broad smile. "Best brew on the square, ser mage." The smile turned into a grin. "Might be because it's the only brew. You get one free. Would you like it now?"

"If you please."

"My pleasure."

Beltur took the proffered small mug, let his senses range over it, and, detecting no chaos, took a sip. The brew was about as dark as Meldryn's and slightly bitterer, but not nearly so bitter as what his uncle had preferred. "Thank you." He took a longer swallow, then extracted his loaf of bread and bit off a chunk.

"I wondered if you'd thought about some provisions," said Laevoyt. "Some mages don't the first time they patrol."

Beltur swallowed what he'd taken and replied, "Athaal suggested it."

"Good advice helps."

"Where are you from, ser?" asked Fosset. "You don't talk quite like the mages from here."

"I came from Fenard. The Prefect wasn't exactly fond of mages who didn't want to do his every bidding." That was a great oversimplification, Beltur knew, but he really didn't want to explain in detail.

"That's been a problem for more than one ruler. Head gets too big for the crown." Fosset shook his head. "Always leads to trouble afore it's over."

"Mostly for everyone else, till the end, anyway," said Laevoyt.

Beltur finished half the loaf of bread, and then the remainder of the ale. "Thank you." He returned the mug to Fosset. "I do appreciate it."

"Can't have you too thirsty to do your job proper."

By the time Beltur finished a half circuit of the square, in plain sight, his headache had vanished. Nor did it return when he raised a concealment. For the next glass or so, he kept the concealment up, lowering it a few times just to let people know he was still around. Sometime before third glass, he caught a glimmer of chaos in the row of stalls and tables that ran almost across the middle of the square, but by the time he got there, he could sense nothing, and none of the remaining vendors seemed to be upset, since more than a third of them had either packed up and left or were in the process of doing so.

Beltur arrived at the corner of Patrol and West Streets just as the chimes rang out fourth glass.

Laevoyt was already there, smiling. "Some of the vendors are still talking about those two you caught. That group has been getting away with a lot. Most scurfs are men. Before I forget." He handed Beltur two of the leather disks. "You already know what to do with these."

"Thank you. Do you get anything for catching people?"

Laevoyt shook his head. "That wouldn't be right. It'd

tempt too many patrollers into making up lawbreaking. Black mages can't do that. It works out better the way it is. We need to go sign out."

The two walked for a few paces before Beltur said, "Was today the way it usually is?"

"There are always sellers and buyers. There are always thieves. Sometimes they try and get caught. Sometimes, they're successful, and we don't catch them. Sometimes they're so good we don't even see them. Sometimes more than one or two try. Sometimes, no one tries. You can't ever tell how any day will turn out."

Beltur understood that a single mage and a single patroller couldn't see everything, but he didn't like the idea that thieves could get away with stealing and never be seen, let alone not be caught.

"Just remember," Laevoyt added, "We'll never catch them all. We're here to keep the theft down and to keep people from getting hurt. Just being here does most of that."

When they reached the duty desk, Beltur discovered that signing out amounted to signing the duty book. Once he did, he followed Laevoyt out onto Patrol Street.

There, the tall patroller stopped. "I'll see you on sevenday. Until then." After another cheerful smile, he turned and walked away, heading west.

Beltur made his way past the square and eventually to Bakers Lane, absently tucking both the whistle and the medallion inside his tunic, but still maintaining his personal shields—especially after what Laevoyt had said. He couldn't help but think that, in some ways, Elparta wasn't all that different from Fenard. Both had rules, and both enforced those rules. *But it doesn't appear that the Spidlarian Council kills people just for disagreeing.* At least, he hoped it didn't, but every day he seemed to learn about some new law or requirement.

XXXV

On fiveday, Beltur returned to working with Jorhan at the smithy, casting four separate daggers, each one different enough to be described as unique, although Beltur could certainly see a basic similarity.

"They'll look very different when they're finished," Jorhan insisted at the end of the day. "You'll see."

Beltur had to admit that the finish work he had seen so far was excellent, especially on the two sabres, but that raised another question. "Who in Elparta will buy such expensive blades?"

"Men with golds and good taste, who also like good weapons. There are a few in Elparta. Once their friends in other cities see them, there will be more who want them."

"Have you sold any of the others?"

"I'm keeping one of the sabres. The other one will be picked up tonight. He'll also deliver a design for a pair of candelabra. The mold on that will likely take several days. I even sold that first dagger to someone else. He thought it was a bargain. It was. I didn't put my mark on it. Should have done a better job on the mold."

"It was a good dagger, wasn't it?"

"It was. It just wasn't one I wanted my mark on. He got a good blade for less than he could have spent, and I got paid." Jorhan handed over a pair of silvers. "Until tomorrow."

After leaving the smithy, Beltur headed back to the city. He walked swiftly because he wanted to stop at the shop of the seamstress Meldryn had recommended to

order some more smallclothes and, if he could afford
it, a better-fitting pair of trousers to wear when he
wasn't working in the smithy.

At the same time, his thoughts went back to the
previous day, when one of the thief's decoys had escaped simply because Beltur hadn't been able to hold
four small shields at once. *Why couldn't you do that?
It ought to be possible.* After all, he had held a shield
strong enough to protect a mounted squad and strong
enough to stop flights of arrows. And that had been before all of Athaal's drills and practice sessions.

As he passed a recently harvested wheat field, he saw
almost a score of crows gleaning for grains that had
dropped on the ground. Several of the crows flew from
the ground closer to the road and then settled farther
away, but the remainder kept foraging, if with quick
looks in Beltur's direction. *What if . . .* Beltur immediately put shields around the two nearest crows, then
concentrated on forming a fourth shield around a third.
Small as the shield was, he could only hold it for a few
moments. *But you could do it.*

He released the other two shields, smiling as the
outraged crows took wing. The smile vanished when he
felt the beginnings of a headache. Still . . . if he worked
at it . . .

The guards at the southeast gate still looked at Beltur as he passed, but only for a moment. Once inside
the walls, he followed the street adjoining the east wall
north for three blocks, and then turned west on Tailors
Way. He massaged his forehead with his left hand several times, but that didn't seem to help the slight headache. It didn't get any worse, though.

Meldryn had described the shop as being in the first
block on the north side in the middle and having only
a small square sign showing a needle crossed with
scissors. Beltur almost missed it and had to take two

steps back. The door was narrow, and there was but a single high window beside it.

He knocked on the door and waited.

After several moments, there was a faint scraping sound, and the back cover on the door peephole opened.

"My name is Beltur. I'm looking for Celinya. I need some shirts. Mage Meldryn sent me."

The peephole closed. After a moment, Beltur heard a latch moving, and then the door opened.

"Please come in, ser mage." The thin seamstress holding onto the door looked to be only a few years older than Beltur, but there were lines in her face, and she seemed to stand at an angle, or with one shoulder lower than the other.

After a moment, he realized that one of her legs was shorter than the other and that the foot on that leg was smaller and twisted slightly. He said quickly, "You're Celinya?"

"I am." She closed the door, and slid the latch back into place.

He glanced around the small room, no more than four yards across and perhaps slightly more than three deep. The single door on the left side of the rear wall was closed. There were only two wooden straight-backed chairs in the room, and two worktables, on one of which sections of cloth were laid out. There was also a wooden rack with what Beltur guessed were devices on which to hang garments. A single oil lamp—unlit—hung from a brass wall bracket near the larger worktable.

"I need some sturdy smallclothes," Beltur finally said. "A shirt and drawers. Two of each."

"I can do that. It will take an eightday."

"How much?"

"A silver and three for each shirt. Six coppers for each of the drawers."

Not quite four silvers. "What about a pair of black trousers?"

"Three silvers."

"The trousers will have to wait." Beltur paused. "Meldryn said that you'd require something in advance?"

"A silver and eight for the drawers and smallshirts. I will need to measure you. Over here, please."

Beltur moved to where she pointed and stood there while she used a cloth tape with embroidered marks indicating the digits.

"Hold out your arms."

Beltur did so, although he noticed that she only really measured one. Her hands were deft, and she barely touched him. When she finished, a faint smile crossed the thin lips of the brown-haired seamstress. "You should have a better tunic. For a mage . . ." She shook her head.

"I'm not a wealthy mage. In fact, until an eightday or so ago, I was almost a copperless mage."

Celinya frowned. "A mage without coins? How can that be?"

"I had to leave Gallos in a hurry. Black mages . . . well, any mages who do not absolutely serve the Prefect are not welcome there. Some have been killed."

"But who would kill a mage?"

"A powerful white mage and those who obey him and who want all mages to support the Prefect."

She shook her head. "You serve the Council, do you not? Should not the mages in Gallos serve the Prefect?"

"The Council doesn't tell mages to kill other mages or to help the armsmen attack other lands, does it?"

Celinya's eyes widened. "The Prefect does that?"

"He's gathering an army to attack either Spidlar or Gallos."

"The more fool he. Even chaos-mages cannot destroy the city walls."

Beltur hoped that was so. "That's why I have few coins."

"Then you should come back again when you do. I'll sew you a fine black tunic to go with those trousers you need."

"The trousers will have to come first." Beltur smiled. "You'll have these next sixday, you said?"

"Sevenday would be better."

"After fourth glass, then. I have patrol duty on sevenday."

"I won't be anywhere else."

Beltur extracted the silver and eight coppers and offered them to Celinya.

The coins vanished into her hand, and then somewhere into the jacket she wore, despite the comparative warmth of the small room. "Thank you."

"My thanks to you." Beltur turned toward the door, studying the seamstress. He didn't sense any chaos around her leg or foot, and in fact there was a certain orderliness about her that reminded him of the order around healers, but then, he supposed that the best seamstresses were indeed orderly.

Celinya opened the door.

Beltur stepped out onto the street, the door closing behind him almost immediately. He continued west until he reached Bakers Lane and then headed north, happy that he'd be able to have a few more clothes so that he wouldn't be washing what he had so often. He still had the slight headache, but some of Meldryn's ale and bread would likely take care of that.

XXXVI

On sixday, Beltur left the smithy, walking swiftly because a stiff wind blew out of the east-northeast, and
behind that wind was a line of dark clouds that looked
like it might be the edge of a northeaster—or at least a
heavy downpour. By the time he could see the southeast gate to Elparta, intermittent fat droplets of rain
were beginning to pelt him, and the raindrops were falling even more heavily as he hurried through the city
wall.

He slowed for an instant, only to hear one of the
guards shout, "Get a move on! No sheltering here!"

While Beltur doubted the guard was shouting at him,
he kept moving, deciding to take the wall street north,
because he could see that at least some of the rain was
being blocked, especially if he stayed on the side of the
street beside the wall. He managed to cover another
two blocks at not quite a run before the downpour
turned into a deluge.

He stopped as he saw a coach moving toward him
and flattened his back against the wall, strengthening
his shields—and getting a headache in the process, no
doubt because of the heavy rain. Then, out of the side
street ran a young woman, chased by two men, seemingly into the path of the carriage. The coachman managed to bring the horses up short, only to find one of
the young men up beside him with a blade at his throat.

The "young woman" discarded the dress, and he and
the other man approached the coach doors, blades in
hand. Beltur moved quickly toward the coach, putting
a shield around the coachman that forced the blade

away from his throat, and a second shield around the coach.

The bravo beside the coachman tried to strike with his blade, a shortsword somewhat shorter than a sabre, but the blade skidded off the shield. By then, Beltur was beside the two-horse team.

The two others attempted to reach for the coach door, but could not.

Then the bravo on the coach caught sight of Beltur. "There's a mage here!" He scrambled off the coach, and the three men disappeared into the rain.

Once Beltur was certain the three were well out of sight, he dropped the protective shields and looked up to the coachman. "Are you all right?"

"I am, thank the Rational Stars. You did something to keep that blade from my throat, didn't you?"

"I shielded you and the coach."

The coach door opened and an older woman peered out through the rain, while trying to avoid getting wet. Then she glared at Beltur. "Why didn't you catch them?"

"Because it took all I had to shield you and the coachman." Beltur could see that the woman wasn't the type who cared or understood that handling magery, especially three shields at once, was even more difficult in the rain.

"And you let them get away because of that?" asked the fresh-faced young man, who peered out from beside the woman who was likely his mother. To Beltur, he looked to be barely old enough to wear the silk jacket and fine ruffled linen shirt.

"Would you rather you or your coachman were stabbed and robbed?" asked Beltur, trying to keep his voice calm.

"You're a mage. You're supposed to take care of ruffians like that."

"I did the best I could, and it saved you from being robbed or worse."

"You should have apprehended them. Disgraceful." The woman raised her voice. "Pelhant! Drive on! If anyone else gets in front of you, run over them! Go!"

The coach door shut.

The coachman looked down at Beltur. "Thank you, ser."

"I'm glad I could help you." Beltur managed not to emphasize the word "you," although that was definitely the way he felt.

As the coach eased away from him, Beltur studied the design on the coach door—an ornate "C" surrounded by a wreath of some sort. Then he massaged his forehead and resumed walking, trudging, it felt more like. By the time he reached the house, he was soaked through and shivering. Athaal actually hurried from the kitchen to meet him.

"You need to get into dry clothes. I've got a fire in the kitchen hearth." Athaal looked at Beltur. "Is something wrong?"

"It might be. I'll tell you as soon as I get into something dry."

Both Athaal and Meldryn were waiting in the kitchen, and there was a mug of hot spiced cider waiting at Beltur's place at the table.

"You can tell us while we eat," suggested Athaal. "But drink some of the cider first."

Beltur was more than happy to follow Athaal's suggestion, since his head still ached and he was still feeling a little chilled, despite the warmth from the low fire in the hearth.

After several swallows, he began. "Everything was fine at Jorhan's. We worked on some elaborate candelabra, and a pair of small daggers—waistcoat daggers, he called them. I left a little early because there wasn't really anything I could do and because I could see the storm coming in. I was just inside the walls when the rain began to come down . . ." Beltur went on to relate exactly what happened and what he had done. ". . . and the coachman drove off, and I came home through the rain with a headache. It's better now."

"Likely the combination of your not having eaten for a time and trying to hold shields in the rain," said Meldryn. "Did you really put a shield around the whole coach?"

"I didn't know what else to do. I've been practicing on my walks to and from the smithy, but so far, I can't hold four shields for long. Well, I can hold three, but I can only hang on to the fourth one for just a very short time. And not at all in the rain." That wasn't quite true. He'd been afraid to even try. He also didn't miss the quick glance Meldryn gave Athaal.

After a moment, Athaal spoke again. "Do you know who the woman was?"

"She never said. I didn't ask. My head was almost splitting at that point. I did see the design on the coach door. It was a very elaborate 'C' surrounded by a wreath."

"I don't know who that would be." Athaal turned to his partner. "Do you have any idea?"

"It might be Caalsyn or possibly Chaeltyn. They're well-off enough for a coach. There must be others, but I wouldn't know who. People that wealthy don't come to the bakery themselves. They send their servants. Sometimes, the servants tell me who they're buying for. Most times, they don't."

"So even the wealthy who can afford their own cooks buy from you?"

"Fewer than we'd like," replied Meldryn, "but more than they'll admit."

"Are there any mages who are wealthy?" asked Beltur.

Meldryn laughed. "Not that I know of."

Beltur couldn't help wondering why that might be so. "I'd think there might be a few."

The graying mage shook his head. "Those who become wealthy deal in goods or coins. You'll never see a healer or a scrivener or a musician who's wealthy. People who only earn by the work of their body or mind seldom if ever become rich. Mages are the same."

"We would not live half as well as we do," added Athaal, "if Meldryn had not started the bakery."

"I had to," added the older partner. "I'm not half the mage Athaal is."

"But now we have a house and eat very well." Athaal smiled for a moment. "You're on duty tomorrow at the main square, aren't you?"

"I am."

"It might not hurt to tell the Patrol about the attack on the coach."

"And we ought to be getting on with supper," added Meldryn, standing and moving toward the hearth and the small warming oven there.

Outside, the rain continued to pelt down.

XXXVII

When Beltur arrived at City Patrol headquarters on sevenday, a day much cooler than those previous, although the sky was clear, and the air crisp, a different patroller manned the duty desk.

"Mage Beltur?" The patroller pushed the duty book forward. "Sign in first. You need to see the Patrol Mage."

Beltur signed, then laid the pen on the blotter. "I also need to talk to someone about an attack last night."

"You can tell Mage Osarus. He wants to see you." The patroller gestured to the door behind him. "Go on back. He's in the first study on the left."

As Beltur opened the inner door, he wondered whether Osarus had already heard about the attack . . . or if there was another problem. He stepped into the empty corridor beyond, then closed the door, and made his way to the first door, where he knocked.

"Come in."

Beltur eased the door open and entered, carefully closing it behind him.

"You're Beltur?" The man who rose from behind the table desk was of moderate height, with black hair slicked back, and pale blue eyes. He wore a black tunic and trousers, but the cuffs of the tunic were the same shade of blue as the uniforms of the patrollers, and he wore a large silver medallion similar to the one Beltur displayed. He also radiated enough order that Beltur scarcely felt like a black at all, although Beltur suspected that was more his feeling than what Osarus sensed.

At least, Beltur hoped so. "Yes, ser."

"Please sit down." Osarus seated himself and waited for Beltur to take the straight-backed chair in front of the table desk before continuing. "Laevoyt said you did an excellent job last fourday. Especially for a first patrol. It was your first, wasn't it?"

"Yes, ser."

"You're from Fenard, I hear. Were you an armsman for the Prefect or a patroller there?"

"No, ser."

"Were you a mage for the Prefect?"

"No, ser. My uncle was hired to do things for the Prefect. I went with him on his last trip to Analeria."

"What was that about?"

Beltur explained as briefly as he could.

"I heard that the Prefect ordered your uncle killed."

Beltur explained that as well, including how he had come to Elparta.

"Are you always this truthful?"

"I suppose so. I try not to offer information unless it appears that it will be necessary."

"Do Athaal and Meldryn know all you have said here?"

"They do."

Osarus nodded. "There is one other thing."

"Before that, ser . . . I'd tried to report something to the patroller at the desk, but he said to tell you. Late yesterday afternoon, just as the worst of the storm hit . . ." Beltur related the incident with the coach and the three men. "Athaal said I should report what happened as soon as I arrived here this morning."

Osarus smiled tightly. "That's interesting, because that was what I was going to ask you, whether you were the mage involved, or whether you knew anything about the matter."

"Just what I told you. That's all I know."

"The trader whose coach you encountered claims you were disrespectful to his wife and son. Were you?" Osarus's deep voice was even, neither encouraging nor accusing.

"No, ser. She yelled at me because I didn't apprehend the three who tried to rob them. I told her I'd done the best I could. She said it was disgraceful and then she ordered her driver to go on . . . and to run down anyone who got in the way of the horses."

The Patrol Mage nodded. "I thought it might be something like that. How did you manage three shields in that deluge?"

"With great difficulty. I had a headache for glasses afterward."

"Why didn't you try to attack them?"

Beltur thought he sensed a certain curiosity in the other mage's voice, but he answered the only way he could. "With what, ser? I don't know of any way to use order for an attack, except by using the shields as I did."

"Hmmmm . . . you said your uncle was a white. You didn't think of trying to use chaos?"

"He wanted me to do that, but I was never much good at it. I haven't tried anything like that since I left Fenard." Beltur paused, then added, "I don't know if any white could have used chaos effectively in that rain."

"Probably not." Osarus stood. "That's all I wanted to know. You'd better get on with your day. Laevoyt is probably waiting for you. Don't worry about Trader Chaeltyn. I'll tell him everything's taken care of. And it is. I talked to you. You did what you could. He'll be happy."

"Thank you, ser."

"Thank you. If you hadn't stopped those three, we'd have had a real problem. That sort of robbery can occur when it rains. Only those unable to get to shelter quickly or the wealthy in their coaches are on the streets."

Beltur inclined his head and then left the small study. He didn't think it was a slip that Osarus had mentioned the trader's name, almost in passing.

Laevoyt was waiting beside the duty desk, where he had apparently been talking with the patroller. He straightened and smiled. "Ready to set out?"

"I am." Beltur let Laevoyt lead the way.

"Care to tell me what the Patrol Mage wanted?"

asked Laevoyt once the two were out on Patrol Street and walking toward the main market square.

"I stopped a robbery last night, and the trader whose wife I saved complained that I was disrespectful because I couldn't catch the attackers. All I did in the middle of a downpour was save her coachman from getting his throat slit and block the attackers from the coach. They ran off when they realized I was a mage."

"Do you know who the trader is?"

"I didn't. Patrol Mage Osarus let it slip that it was someone called Chaeltyn."

"He never lets anything slip."

"I didn't think so. Do you know anything about Trader Chaeltyn?"

"He's one of the wealthiest factors in Elparta. Owns both a timber mill and a gristmill. He also has a lot of land across the river. Some of it's timberland. Some he rents to tenant growers. He also owns the rendering yards, but he won't talk about that. Rendering is where his father got started. Word is that he's never forgotten that. He doesn't like anyone to mention it."

"Is he on the Council?"

"He'd like to be, but he's not. He's got enough golds that the Council has to pretend to listen to him. Leastwise, that's what's said. Did you tell his wife your name?"

"No. I never had the chance."

"That's good. It could have been any mage."

"Why would he complain to Osarus? Because most mages have summonses to serve?"

"Who else might know who it was?"

Beltur nodded.

When they neared the corner of Patrol and West Streets, Beltur asked, "Same pattern as on fourday?"

"Make your way around so you're seen, then start weaving in and out of the stalls. A glass from now, it'll be really crowded."

To Beltur the square already looked crowded. He made sure his medallion was showing and that the whistle was where he could reach it. Then he nodded to Laevoyt and turned down West, while the patroller continued along Patrol Street.

Beltur didn't see Fosset during his first circuit of the square, and for a time after that he was slipping along the tables and stalls more to the east, because he'd sensed some slight chaos, but that had vanished before he could find anything. He suspected that it might have been a successful cutpurse, but it also could have been someone arguing with a vendor, since no one was yelling about a thief.

Sometime before ninth glass, he did notice Fosset and his cart, and he stopped for a moment. "How are you this morning?"

"Passable, Mage. Passable." Fosset grinned. "Too early to be anything else."

"You said you would be the only one with ale for sale."

"You'd like to know why?"

"I'm curious, but I'm not about to press."

"The Council only allows one, and it has to be someone who works for an established inn. My uncle owns an inn, and he'd like to keep me out of too much trouble. So he paid the fee to the Council." Fosset shrugged.

"The only inn I've seen is the Traders' Rest."

"Then you've seen his place."

"No wonder your ale is good."

"Thank you. It's not his best, but it's better than the bitter stuff that Holagryn used to peddle."

"Do you have to work at the inn after you finish here?"

"What else?"

"An ale, Fosset!" came a loud voice belonging to a short and stocky graybeard.

Beltur nodded to Fosset and moved away, heading into the middle of the square, and drawing a concealment around himself.

"... mage just disappeared ..."

"... always are doing that, dearie ..."

Abruptly, Beltur frowned, sensing a concentration of order ahead of him and to the right. He dropped his concealment for a moment, but he could see nothing where he sensed the order, which meant that the other mage was also using a concealment. There was something about that very organized pattern of order ... *Osarus! It has to be Osarus.*

Beltur let the other mage move away, then continued along the parallel line of tables until he reached the end. There he turned north, away from Osarus, and moved toward the stall with the more valuable merchandise. From what he could sense, the Patrol Mage was moving in the direction of headquarters.

At ninth glass, he met on the northwest corner of the square with Laevoyt.

"Have you seen anything?" asked the patroller.

"The Patrol Mage was here for a while."

"You saw him?" Laevoyt frowned.

"No. He was under a concealment, but he was here."

Laevoyt hesitated slightly before saying, "Likely he was just checking on the market."

"And his patrollers and mages," added Beltur.

"That, too. Too quiet for my liking."

"The quiet before trouble?"

"Could be. Might just be quiet."

After leaving Laevoyt, Beltur raised a concealment around himself and made his way back in the direction of the more expensive wares, where the silks and laces and some jewelry were laid out, along with one stall that had an array of tools of various sorts. One of the problems with a concealment was that it was often hard to tell much about what people were wearing, although newer garments tended to be more orderly, and worn ones had a misting of chaos, but clothes that had been very expensive when made and worn for years also had a chaos-mist.

Beltur lowered the concealment to look at the goods on a table that he hadn't been able to figure out from just sensing them. He discovered an array of black-lacquered boxes with lacquer images on them. "The best lacquered boxes anywhere. They come from Hydlen," explained the deeply tanned man behind the table, whose eyes never stopped moving.

"Thank you."

As he moved toward another table, one filled with elegant-looking porcelain platters, he sensed something behind him and immediately created a shield around the small figure with a tiny but sharp blade.

The boy looked up at the medallion that became visible as Beltur turned, and his eyes widened. Beltur shook his head and then blew the whistle the requisite three blasts. At the same time, he tried to sense if the boy had an accomplice.

"Ser . . . didn't mean nothing, swear I didn't . . ."

Then Beltur frowned and whirled, throwing a shield around a well-dressed woman as she sidled away from a jewelry stall.

"Aren't you being rather presumptuous, Mage." The young woman offered a scathing glance.

"I'm afraid not. Now . . . please show me what is in your hand."

"You are being very insulting." The woman drew herself up in a posture that was both arrogant and offended. "To think—"

"Open your hand, palm up." Beltur tightened the shield around her hand, preventing her from opening it and dropping whatever she had in it.

At that point, Laevoyt appeared.

"I believe that woman picked up a piece of jewelry from that table, and left something in its place. I've put a shield around her hand so she cannot drop what is in it."

The older man behind the table leaned forward, studying the items, then lifted a ring. "This one is brass! Mine was gold."

The woman whom Beltur had restrained seemed to swoon.

"She's acting," said Laevoyt dryly. "Shall we see what's in that hand?"

The young woman straightened. "You wouldn't dare. My father is Trader Eskeld."

"The Patrol captain will decide. Now about that ring . . ." Laevoyt nodded to Beltur.

Beltur released the shield.

Laevoyt's hand picked the ring out of midair. "You have good taste."

The woman offered a withering glance.

"About the ring?" said the vendor.

"That will have to wait, ser," replied the patroller.

As Beltur and Laevoyt began to escort the young woman away from the jewelry table, Beltur released the shield around the boy with the knife, murmuring, "I never want to see you again."

The child swallowed, then darted away.

Beltur feared he would see the boy again, but he had no real evidence, and no one had seen or lost anything to the boy, from what he'd been able to tell. *Yet* . . .

"I presume you are escorting me to my coach," the woman said. "It's over there, with the matched grays."

Beltur's eyes took in the black-trimmed gray coach, noting the well-groomed grays and the coachman, whose eyes were now on the three of them.

"Your coach will have to wait," replied Laevoyt cheerfully.

Beltur would have wagered that the patroller wasn't nearly as cheerful as he sounded.

The duty patroller's eyes widened as Laevoyt and Beltur escorted the woman into headquarters.

"We'll need to see Captain Fhaltar. It might be best in his study."

The patroller stood and opened the inner door.

Laevoyt escorted the woman to the third door, which he opened, and said, "This is a matter for you, ser." He ushered the other two into the study and closed the door.

The Patrol captain was already standing beside the table desk. He was almost as tall as Laevoyt, broad-shouldered with close-trimmed blond hair and blue eyes. "What seems to be the difficulty here?" His voice was warm and friendly.

"This lady," said Laevoyt firmly, "lifted this ring from a jewelry stall in the market and attempted to leave without paying for it."

"I fully intended—"

"And," continued the patroller, "she left a brass ring in its place. The mage caught the deception and contained her. She attempted to drop the ring, but I was fortunate to be able to catch it. She then declared that she was the daughter of Trader Eskeld and demanded that we escort her to her coach and release her. We felt that, under the circumstances, you would wish to see her."

Fhaltar nodded. "I would indeed." He looked to Laevoyt. "Do you still have the ring?"

Laevoyt extended it.

The captain took it. "Good workmanship." He turned to the woman. "You do have good taste, Lady." Then he looked back at Laevoyt and Beltur. "Thank you for bringing her to me. I'll handle the matter from here on. You can return to your duties."

Laevoyt inclined his head. "Yes, ser. By your leave, ser?"

Belatedly, Beltur added, "Yes, ser," and also inclined his head. Then he followed Laevoyt from the study and back out to the north chamber.

"The captain sent us back to duty," Laevoyt said as he passed the duty desk.

Once the two were outside headquarters, Beltur said quietly, "How was I to know?"

"How was either of us to know?" replied Laevoyt. "The captain will handle it. That's what we have to do if it involves someone of wealth. You just can't tell by garments, but the coach was the telling point."

"What will he do?"

"Smooth it over and suggest to her father that such acts might be best avoided."

"But if someone else—"

"They'd end up in the workhouse or without a hand. I know that. So do you. The young woman will likely suffer in a different fashion."

But she'll escape most of the consequences.

"You'll notice that the captain never used either of our names. It's better this way. You'll see after a while."

Left unsaid was the implication that Beltur definitely should see. He nodded.

"You do get a disk for catching her."

"Even if she's never . . . disciplined?"

"You restrained her so that the City Patrol could determine what happened. That's what the disks are for. That goes along with the other thing. Everyone in the market saw us take her off to Patrol headquarters. We didn't just let her go."

But the captain likely will. "So people get the idea that everyone is treated the same?" *Even if they're not?*

"Can you think of a better way? Especially with the power of those with golds?"

Laevoyt had a point, a very good one. Beltur had to admit that. He just didn't have to like it. "I hope nothing too bad has happened while we were gone."

"We weren't gone all that long. Most people probably didn't notice."

Laevoyt was probably right about that as well. Beltur took a deep breath and managed a smile as he approached the square.

XXXVIII

Early on eightday afternoon, Beltur was in the parlor reading *On Healing,* which he found instructive, even beyond the anatomy that Athaal thought was the best part of Leantor's treatise. At that moment, there was a knock on the door. Beltur immediately set aside the leather-bound volume and headed for the entry, only to find that Athaal, coming from the kitchen, had reached it first and was ushering in Margrena and another black mage, whom Beltur did not recognize.

"Good afternoon," Beltur said.

"The same to you," replied Margrena, who then looked back to Athaal. "I thought I'd bring Waensyn by, since he hasn't ever met Meldryn or Beltur, and he wanted to pay his respects."

Beltur took another quick look at Waensyn, who was perhaps a few digits shorter than Beltur himself and who had black hair and black eyes, as well as a well-trimmed short black beard.

"Come on into the parlor." Athaal led the way, but

stopped by the side hallway that led to the bakery and called out, "Mel! We have company!"

"I'll be right there."

In moments, Athaal and Beltur and the two arrivals were in the parlor. There, Waensyn took the armchair where Meldryn usually sat, and Margrena sat on the padded bench. Beltur remained standing beside the armchair that Athaal usually took, but Athaal took the straight-backed chair. Beltur sat on the bench beside Margrena.

"Meldryn will be here in a few moments. He was working on the ovens." Athaal looked to Margrena. "Are you getting settled?"

"I don't know about settled." Margrena glanced at Beltur. "What about you?"

"I'm doing some work with a smith." Beltur really didn't want to say more. "And you?"

"We've been called on to do some healing."

"There aren't as many good healers here in Elparta as there should be," said Athaal, looking up as Meldryn entered the parlor, glanced around, and then took the vacant armchair.

"This is Waensyn," offered Margrena, looking at Meldryn and gesturing to the man who had accompanied her.

"We're glad to see that you arrived safely," replied Meldryn. "What can you tell us about matters in Gallos?"

"There's little good to tell. Wyath and the whites control the Prefect. Anyone with even a shade of ability with order has been killed or driven out, as have white mages who did not worship the Arms-Mage. He now styles himself the Arch-Mage, by the way."

Beltur almost nodded. *That would follow.*

"Have the blacks of Gallos managed to leave?" asked Athaal.

"I believe most have. Some have gone to Certis. That I do not understand, since the Viscount is almost as evil as the Prefect. Some have gone to Sarronnyn, for all the good that will do them. Some to Suthya, a place too cold for me, but suitable and similar in governance to Spidlar. None that I know of to Westwind, except one healer. I tried to tell her that was a great mistake. She did not listen."

The more Waensyn talked, the less Beltur liked the man, although he managed to maintain a pleasant expression on his face.

"How are you finding Elparta?" asked Meldryn.

"It has been most welcoming. I have spent some considerable time with Cohndar. He seems both helpful and knowledgeable, and I think we share many of the same thoughts."

"How soon do you think it will be before Denardre attacks someone?" Athaal leaned forward slightly in the straight-backed chair.

"He was gathering his forces even before we departed. He will attack here within a few eightdays, if not sooner. We need to ready ourselves, and to make sure there are no traitors or those who would throw in with the Prefect for their own gain."

"How would you suggest such preparations be made?" Meldryn's voice was level.

"By whatever means necessary, of course. Any reasonable man should see the necessity for that. If Gallos holds the River Gallos for its entire length, then no one in the entire midsection of Candar will be safe."

"That is obvious," Meldryn said dryly, "but what preparations might be necessary? Does he have engineers with his forces? Is he assembling siege engines or trebuchets?"

"I'm not an arms-mage," replied Waensyn, almost

stiffly. "I could not say. All arms-mages I have ever heard about were whites."

"One force was assembling piles of large logs near the river just north of the port at Maeryl," said Margrena. "They were large enough for siegeworks or catapults. There were more than a thousand armsmen there."

"That does make it seem rather likely that they'll attack here soon," observed Meldryn.

"Why aren't you two involved in helping defend Elparta?" asked Waensyn.

"Because our talents don't lie in that direction, as apparently yours do not, either," replied Meldryn. "If necessary, and we are called upon, we will do our best to shield the Council forces, but I fear that is the limit of what we can do."

"Can do? Or will do?"

"Can do." Meldryn offered a strained smile. "Is there anything else you'd care to know? That we might know about?"

"There is." Waensyn turned to face Beltur. "I am curious to know why the offspring of a disgraced white is here in Elparta." Waensyn offered the words casually, as if asking what might be for his next meal.

"For the same reason that a second-rate black might be," replied Beltur. "When one's life is threatened for no reason, it's generally a good idea to go where it isn't so dangerous."

"Wouldn't it have been so much easier just to toady up to Wyath? I mean, pretending to be a black . . . ?"

"You're twice wrong. I'm not pretending to be anything. I was most likely pretending to be a white, although I didn't realize it, and, second, toadying up to someone who's killed your uncle and tried to kill you isn't the wisest of acts."

"I'm not sure I understand. Wyath killed your uncle,

who was far more powerful than you. Yet you survived. That seems unlikely. Most unlikely."

"Uncle held off Wyath long enough for me to escape. He insisted. I didn't argue."

"How utterly noble of you. And now you're trying to be a black . . . much good that will do you."

"I do believe you've said enough," interjected Meldryn, standing. "I certainly wouldn't wish you to be uncomfortable a moment longer. Let me escort you to the door."

Waensyn looked stunned, as if he could not believe what the oldest mage had said. "You . . ."

"We do tend to judge people by their character, not merely by the amount of order in which their prejudices are sustained. Now . . ."

"I can find my own way out."

"Let me make sure," said Meldryn coldly.

"Are you coming?" Waensyn asked Margrena as he rose from the armchair almost sinuously.

"I think not. I'm certain you can find your way to wherever your den is," replied the healer.

"If that is what you wish, you'll get it." Waensyn turned and strode out of the parlor.

Meldryn followed him.

Beltur looked at Margrena, who was clearly upset. That he could tell from just the chaotic flow of the order that surrounded the healer. He wasn't quite certain what to say.

"That was quite a departure," said Athaal dryly. "It did seem to suit him. He only needed to slither."

A faint and momentary smile crossed Margrena's face.

When Meldryn returned he immediately went into the kitchen and returned with a small brush, which he used to dust off his armchair. He then went back to the kitchen, returning without the brush, and seated himself.

"I'm so sorry . . . I had no idea," said Margrena. "He was pleasant enough for the whole trip. Earlier today, he came by Grenara's. He said he wanted to meet you and to say a few words to Beltur. I never imagined . . . I couldn't believe . . ."

"Do you know why he would have been so vitriolic toward you?" Athaal asked Beltur. "Could you have offended him somehow in Fenard?"

"I don't see how. I've never meet him before." Beltur thought for a moment. "The only thing I can think of that possibly might have something to do with it was something my uncle said. Jessyla had told me that you had said that the only way to handle chaos effectively was through the use of order. I mentioned that to Uncle Kaerylt. He then said you were a very decent sort, unlike some of the blacks in Fenard who put on airs of being superior." That wasn't exactly how his uncle had phrased it, but that was definitely how he had meant it. "He wouldn't tell me who those blacks were. I had no idea . . ."

"That's strange," mused Athaal. "I never met your uncle. When you mentioned that before, I just thought you were being kind."

"No. He said that." Beltur turned to Margrena. "Did you ever mention Athaal to Uncle?"

"Once, possibly twice, in passing."

"Then he must have respected your judgment, Margrena," said Meldryn, adding, "and I'm beginning to think that your uncle had very good judgment about people."

Except for women he didn't know. "I thought so, but I'm not that experienced."

"You'll be more experienced after another few eight-days with the City Patrol," said Athaal.

"I'm curious," Beltur ventured. "Was there a particular reason Jessyla didn't accompany you?"

Margrena frowned. "She was helping Grenara. She's better about that, and Waensyn said there was no need to deprive Grenara of her assistance."

Beltur nodded. "I just wondered."

"So he planned it all along. Just because Beltur's uncle didn't care for him?" asked Athaal.

"Waensyn obviously has a very high opinion of himself. Sometimes, people who feel that way tend to dislike others who don't share that level of regard." Meldryn sighed. "This all means I'm going to have to have a talk with Cohndar about Waensyn. I think I'd like to see if he approaches me, first. If he doesn't in the next few days, then I'll find a pretext to run into him."

Margrena rose. "I think I'd better get back to Grenara's."

"Would you like me to accompany you?" asked Athaal, standing.

"That's very kind of you. I think I would." Margrena turned to Beltur, who had also stood. "I'm so sorry, Beltur. I really had no idea."

"I know."

The healer nodded. "I thought so."

Beltur understood what she wasn't saying, and he wondered if she could sense personal order-chaos flows as well, or if she'd just read his face.

After the two had left, Meldryn turned to Beltur. "You did mean what you said about Athaal? Your uncle actually said that?"

"Yes, ser. I even asked him if the Sarronnese blacks put on airs. He said he had no idea because he didn't know any."

"That would seem to indicate that he knew Waensyn and didn't much care for him. Do you think he let Waensyn know his feelings?"

"I doubt it. Uncle seldom was that direct."

"Well . . . someone must have told Waensyn . . . or your uncle's attitude must have been obvious."

"Ah . . . that is very possible. Uncle seldom said much, but it wasn't hard to know when he thought you were being stupid or arrogant."

"And Waensyn strikes me as possibly being both . . . unfortunately." Meldryn paused, then said, "It might be best if you didn't talk about this afternoon with anyone but Athaal, Margrena, or me."

"Yes, ser." *And possibly Jessyla.*

Meldryn smiled. "You can get back to your reading. I'm headed back to the bakery."

"Can I do anything to help?"

The older mage shook his head. "Your reading *On Healing* might serve us all better." Then he turned and left the parlor.

Beltur stood there for a moment, pondering Meldryn's last words; then he bent and picked up the leather-bound volume.

XXXIX

Beltur woke slightly early on oneday morning, still wondering what had caused Waensyn to attack him with so much venom the day before, especially since he'd never even met the black mage before. Although the attack didn't seem to make much sense, from everything Beltur had seen and heard, Waensyn was anything but impetuous, and the way in which he had asked the scathing questions had been calculated. Beltur was just glad that he hadn't hidden anything from Athaal and Meldryn.

Otherwise, Waensyn's questions could have proved disastrous. *Had he expected you to hide your past?*

That suggested to Beltur that Waensyn wasn't likely the most direct of individuals, and that he expected the same of others. Either that, or all the whites he had met were liars, and while Beltur thought little of Wyath, his uncle certainly hadn't been a liar. *And Wyath had him killed.*

No matter how he puzzled over it, Beltur didn't know enough to determine why Waensyn had done what he did. It was more than clear, though, that the man was anything but friendly, but Beltur didn't know what he could do about it except be careful and not to trust Waensyn or what he might do. He couldn't help but worry about what Waensyn might say, especially to Cohndar and the other Spidlarian blacks that Beltur hadn't met.

He tried not to think about it as he made ready for the day, ate his breakfast, cleaned up the kitchen area, and then headed off to help Jorhan at the smithy.

The morning was slightly warmer than it had been, and almost muggy. The still air made it seem warmer than it was, but Beltur reminded himself that it was still harvest, for almost another two eightdays, and harvest was warm. Early fall wasn't much better, but it might be colder in Elparta than it was in Fenard, given that Elparta was farther north.

Beltur was feeling better, or less worried, when he arrived at the smithy.

"We'll be working on sabres for the next two days," Jorhan announced from where he was building up the forge fire. "There's a trader from Lydiar who wants three of them. I'm giving him a good price on them— not too good, but good."

"You'd said . . ." Beltur ventured, then broke off his words.

"That's for anyone in Spidlar. There are only so many who'll want to pay for blades like that here, but ships from everywhere port in Lydiar. Far more than in Spidlaria. If he does well with them, we'll have orders for years." Jorhan shrugged. "If not, we've still made more than we would have otherwise."

"Do you really think there are that many people who would pay that much for a cupridium blade?"

"I do." Jorhan grinned. "I wasn't as straight up with you as I might have been. I've tried with a mage or two over the years. It didn't work."

"Why not?"

"One just tried to put order into the bronze. Leastwise, that was what he said. It just split into sections that I couldn't even dent. The other one created a bronze that acted like black iron, and wasn't as hard. They weren't interested in trying to work it out. Said they had better things to do. So I told your friend Athaal that if he came across a young mage, just starting out who was willing to work with me, I'd like to talk to him."

"You were willing to pay me even if it didn't work?"

"There's a risk to everything. If you couldn't do it . . . I'd be out a few silvers. If you could—and you did— we're both doing a whole lot better."

Beltur frowned. "Then there can't be that many smiths who are making cupridium."

"I don't know of any. The old cupridium blades go for more than five golds, sometimes ten, if you can even find anyone who'll sell."

"You're not asking that much?"

Jorhan shook his head. "They're paying for history and mystery. I figure I can't ask that, not yet. I took one of the blades to the Council's master armorer, and asked him about it. He couldn't believe we'd forged it. He did all sorts of tests, but he thinks it's about the same as the old blades."

"He *thinks* it is?"

"Each blade is a little different. A real master armorer can tell the slightest difference. He said it was as close as it was possible to be to those he had seen before and the one he has. I wasn't about to sell one as cupridium without his seeing and testing the blades."

"You're telling me that we're doing something that no one's done since the fall of Cyador?"

"That's what I figure. I haven't heard of anyone who's making cupridium anywhere in Candar or Nordla. I might be wrong. I don't know about Austra, and who knows what they're doing in Hamor? They say that there are descendants of the Cyadoran imperial family ruling Cigoerne. If anyone would be forging cupridium, they'd be the ones." Jorhan shrugged. "That's what I've heard. Maybe some cousin was at sea or just happened to be way to the west. Anyway, I don't see them shipping cupridium blades all the way to Candar. That's if they're even forging them." The smith grinned. "Might just be that most mages don't want to spend time sweating in a forge."

Most mages don't end up copperless and without relatives in a strange city. "That could be. Athaal wasn't sure I'd be interested."

"You keep working with me, and you'll have more silvers in a year than he's seen in ten."

Beltur eased off his tunic and hung it on one of the pegs. "I won't count any silvers I haven't earned and collected."

"Wise man. The first mold's hot enough now."

Beltur walked toward the forge and the bellows he'd learned to work the way Jorhan wanted.

By midday, he was sweating and had gone through two mugs of bitter ale, and they had only cast one sabre, largely because the melt hadn't felt right to Beltur, and he'd insisted that Jorhan add more copper. The smith hadn't protested, not beyond saying he hoped Beltur was right. The order-chaos pattern had fixed well in the metal, though, and Beltur felt much better about the result.

Between heating the molds and getting the melts right, the next two castings took most of the rest of the afternoon, but Jorhan announced himself pleased, adding, "I might do some finish work on them later."

Beltur had no doubts that the smith would be working. He seemed to work most of the time. "I'll see you in the morning?"

"Right as rain."

Beltur donned his tunic and then began the walk back toward Elparta. After he had gone several hundred yards, he began to raise multiple shields. Raising and holding two in addition to his personal shields was definitely getting easier. Then he tried for a third. He managed to walk perhaps ten paces before he lost control of the last shield. *Still . . . you had it for a little while.*

He did replicate holding a third additional shield for several moments twice more before he sensed that he'd done enough for the time being. Part of that might have been because it had been a while since he'd either eaten or drunk any ale, and part because the day was so muggy. Once inside the city walls, he took the shaded street beside the wall until he reached Crossed Lane and turned west toward Bakers Lane.

When Beltur entered the house, he heard a woman's voice, one that sounded familiar, yet one he couldn't place, and he walked straight toward the parlor, rather than washing up immediately.

"You've got a visitor, Beltur," called Athaal.

Although he had half hoped it might be Jessyla, he was still more than a little surprised to see her sitting on the bench and watching him enter the parlor. "Jessyla . . . I didn't expect to see you here."

"I didn't expect to be here."

"I was near Grenara's place," said Athaal, "and after what happened yesterday, I thought I'd stop by."

"I persuaded him to let me come to dinner here," added Jessyla.

"In that case, you're going to be here a bit. Would you mind if I washed up? Smithing isn't nearly as neat an occupation as healing."

"Not always," she replied. "We can talk about that after you clean up."

Beltur hurried upstairs, washed quickly, changed into his other clean shirt and then made his way down to the parlor, catching the last words of what Athaal was saying.

". . . be more like winter by the last two eightdays of fall."

"Does it really get that cold here that much earlier?" asked Beltur as he settled into the straight-backed chair across from Jessyla. He found himself gazing directly into her intense green eyes, then abruptly looked away.

"I don't claw, Beltur," she said gently before turning to Athaal. "You didn't answer Beltur's question."

"I didn't. Elparta is colder than Kleth, and much colder than Spidlaria. The snows are deep, and they last into spring. That's because we're higher here than in Kleth or Spidlaria, and because Spidlaria's on the ocean." Athaal stood. "If we're to have that dinner I promised, I need to do a few things." He gestured to Beltur. "You stay put and entertain Jessyla."

Beltur didn't even think about arguing. He once more looked at Jessyla. "You were going to tell me that sometimes healing is anything but neat."

"Childbirth isn't neat. The red flux certainly isn't."

"I know."

"Oh . . . I'm sorry. I forgot."

For a moment, Beltur wondered what she had forgotten, then realized what she'd been referring to. "That's all right. I don't remember much. I was only six when she died."

"I can't imagine how hard that was."

"It was harder when my father died. I was almost ten, and he was very caring." Beltur half wondered why he was even sharing that with her.

"So your uncle raised you from then on?"

"He did. He was sometimes gruff, but I knew he cared. In that way, I was fortunate. Not many people have that much care growing up." He added quickly, "I'm guessing that your mother cares for you a great deal."

"She does. That's why I'm here."

To Beltur that didn't make sense, and he wasn't quite sure what to say in response. He didn't have to, because Jessyla went on.

"She didn't even tell me how awful that bastard Waensyn was last night. He'd been pretending all along, talking about how respected your uncle was, and then to attack you . . . Mother didn't want me to know, but I heard her and Athaal talking." Abruptly, Jessyla blushed. "I was eavesdropping, really, but I got so mad that I made them both explain. Athaal and Mother, that is. So I just had to come and explain that I didn't know what that horrible little man was going to do."

Beltur refrained from smiling at her reference to Waensyn, who, while somewhat shorter than Beltur, was certainly not little. "I'm glad to see you. I'd wondered why you hadn't come with your mother."

"She wanted me to help my aunt with laundry. Aunt Grenara's not young."

"Oh?" Beltur had his doubts, but he wasn't going to raise them . . . yet.

"She's much older than Mother, something like fifteen years. That's why she doesn't do much healing anymore. Mother says I'm more like her in looks. She was a redhead. I don't recall her hair ever being anything but gray. I wanted to come, but . . . Anyway, this is better."

"How is living there? With your aunt, I mean?"

"She's not used to having other people around—just Growler."

"Growler?"

"Her cat. He doesn't care much for either Mother or me. I like dogs better."

"Why does she have a cat?" Beltur had never thought about dogs or cats as pets.

"He keeps mice and rats out of the house. He's very good at it. He also thinks the entire house is his."

"Are cats really like that?"

"So Mother says." Jessyla offered a wry smile.

Beltur was silent for a moment, then said, "I never did thank you. Not properly."

"Thank me?"

"If you hadn't told me what Athaal said about handling chaos through order, I never would have discovered that I wasn't really a white. I never would have changed my shields, and Wyath and his mages would have killed me, too. I know you said you didn't think I was really a white, but it was the suggestion that got me to change."

"You don't like to deceive people, do you?"

"No. Why do you ask?"

"Because I don't either."

"Doesn't that get hard for a healer?" Beltur asked. "I mean . . ."

She smiled, a wide and open expression. "You understand, don't you?"

"I think so. You're supposed to heal people, but what if you can't? What if all you can give them is a little comfort, and they ask you if they'll be all right?"

"You sound like you've had to try healing."

"Only once. There was this boy . . ." Beltur quickly summarized what had happened with Claudyt's grandson. ". . . and I think I saved him, but he'll always limp and stumble. If I'd known more . . . but then, maybe, it wouldn't have made any difference."

"You really did that?"

"I did. I didn't want to, but he would have died. Even the old healer felt that way. So did his grandfather. There wasn't anyone else."

"Mother says you can only do your best." Jessyla paused. "What if it's not enough? I know it's that way sometimes. I've already seen it. I hate it."

"I still worry about the boy." Beltur also worried about whether somehow he'd be faulted for trying something beyond his understanding and skill. "I've been reading this book—*On Healing* . . ."

"Do you want to be a healer?"

"I don't know that I'd be that good. But I've already had to do something, and if something like that comes up again, I want to know more. I know a book's not as good as doing, but you have to start somewhere."

"Maybe you should come with us on a day that you're free."

"I don't have many of those right now . . ."

Before Beltur knew it, Athaal and Meldryn stood in the archway to the kitchen. He looked up, surprised. "Is dinner . . . I should have helped. I'm sorry."

"It's good to see you two enjoying yourselves," said Meldryn.

Beltur stood, then motioned for Jessyla to precede him into the kitchen, where he sat across from her. A mug of ale stood beside each platter, each of which held a generous section of meat pie, with sliced pearapples on the side.

"This looks wonderful," Jessyla said.

THE MONGREL MAGE 401

"That's one of the special things about living here," Beltur said.

"Don't just look at it," said Meldryn. "Please eat before it gets cold."

"It would still be good," replied Athaal. "Mel's meat pies are good cold . . . unlike some."

Beltur wanted to dig into the pie, but waited until Meldryn and Jessyla started to eat before he did. No one said anything for a time.

Then Jessyla looked across at Beltur. "You never said what sort of work you were doing with the smith? Are you trying to make black iron?"

With his mouth full of the warm and crusty meat pie, Beltur could only shake his head. He finished swallowing and took a sip of the ale before answering. "He's mostly a coppersmith. We're casting and forging things out of cupridium."

"Real cupridium? I didn't know anyone could do that anymore."

"The smith thinks it's cupridium. It's harder than bronze and more silvery. It's taken quite a bit of effort to make it work. Some people will pay for it. Since they will, I can actually begin to make some coins. I wouldn't have been able to do it if Athaal hadn't introduced me to the smith."

"Doesn't that involve chaos?"

"Some," admitted Beltur, "but what makes it work is that the chaos has to be locked in order. In a way, it's no different than with people. We're a mixture of order and chaos, but in healthy people, the chaos is contained by the order."

"People . . . yes." Jessyla frowned momentarily. "I never thought of cupridium as ordered."

"You couldn't use it if it weren't," Beltur pointed out.

"Everything in life is a matter of balance," added

Meldryn. "That's what makes a lemon tart good, the balance between sweet, tart, and the fullness of the pastry."

After a time, of eating, talking, and listening, Beltur looked down at his totally empty platter, which held not the slightest remnant of the small berry tart that had followed the meat pie. He almost didn't recall eating.

"You'd better leave now," suggested Meldryn, turning to Jessyla. "Beltur will walk you home."

"And put a shield around Jessyla," added Athaal. "Just to be on the safe side."

"I wouldn't want . . ." she began.

"Beltur's good with shields. He can handle two of them all day," said Athaal. "You'd better be going or Margrena will worry." He looked at Beltur.

Beltur nodded and rose from the table. He understood very well what Athaal was suggesting. So did Jessyla, he suspected, because she stood immediately.

She inclined her head to the seated couple. "Thank you both so much. I've had a lovely time."

"You're more than welcome," replied Meldryn. "I hope we see both you and your mother often."

"I'll tell her that."

Beltur understood that message as well.

When the two of them were outside in the early twilight, Beltur immediately raised separate shields for each of them.

"They're nice," Jessyla said.

"They are. They certainly helped me. Otherwise, I'd practically be begging."

"I don't think you'd make a very good beggar."

"That's why I said practically, and why I'm grateful to Athaal and Meldryn . . . and your mother for persuading Athaal to help me. Did you have anything to do with that?"

Jessyla was silent.

Beltur kept walking, looking forward and then back at her.

Then, out of a side lane dashed two ragged figures, both of whom lunged at Jessyla—and both rebounded from the shield around her. One went to his knees and just looked.

The other staggered away, yelling, "Get away! He's a mage!" Then he darted into the side lane, the sound of his footsteps becoming ever fainter.

Jessyla stopped, startled.

Before she could say anything, the second man scrambled to his feet and sprinted for the side lane. Finally, she looked at Beltur. "You do have strong shields. I didn't even remember that you put them around me."

"I take Athaal and Meldryn's advice seriously. We should probably hurry. How far is Crafters Way from here?"

"Another ten blocks, I think."

They resumed walking.

After another period of silence, Beltur said gently, "You never answered my question."

"I hoped you'd forget."

"I haven't forgotten much of what you've said."

"It's embarrassing."

Beltur kept walking, and she kept pace with him.

Finally, she said, "I told Mother that I didn't see how you could possibly be a danger to anyone except yourself. You just proved that I was wrong."

"At that time," he admitted, "you were right."

"You're trying to placate me. I don't like to be placated. Mother does that."

"I am not," replied Beltur firmly. "Because of what you and your mother did, Athaal guided me here. He taught me exercises the whole way to Elparta. I'm a much, much better mage than I was when you said that."

"You really mean that, don't you?"

"I wouldn't lie to you." *I couldn't.*

"I don't think you would. Unlike some people." Her voice turned sardonic with the last words.

After another awkward silence, Beltur said, "I have the feeling that your mother might not want us to become too friendly."

"She likes you, and she respects you . . ."

"But . . . ?"

"You might be right. She said that you really haven't decided what you want to be."

"And we shouldn't be too friendly because I'm still trying to work that out?"

"You're forging cupridium . . ."

"I'm helping Jorhan to cast it. He forges it after that."

"You're the one who makes it possible. There aren't many mages who can. I know enough to understand that."

"Different mages can do different things."

"You're different, Beltur. That's one of the things I like about you. Mother and most black mages don't like different. Meldryn and Athaal are . . . different, too. That's why they're willing to help you."

"I'm not different in that way." Beltur looked directly at her. Even in the dim light, he could half see, half sense that he was blushing again.

"I'm very well aware of that." Her voice lowered. "And glad." Then she looked forward along Bakers Lane.

"Are you and your mother doing much healing?"

"Enough. Most of it doesn't pay, but we do get a small stipend from the Council for each day we spend healing those who come to the Council Healing House. It's good experience. It helps healers like us, and it helps the poor. Aunt did that for years. She only can do it occasionally now."

Before all that long, Jessyla was rapping on the door of a narrow two-story dwelling squeezed between two other similar dwellings, one with a narrow window similar to that of the seamstress Beltur had visited.

The door opened almost immediately, and Margrena stood there. "I thought Athaal would escort you home."

"He said I'd be safer with Beltur. He has stronger shields."

Margrena's stern expression softened into one of mild concern. "You didn't have . . . any trouble?"

"Athaal and Meldryn fixed a wonderful dinner, and then Beltur brought me home."

The older healer eased to the side, suggesting by her posture that Jessyla needed to come inside. Jessyla did not move.

"Would you like to come in, Beltur?" asked Margrena.

"I'd like that very much, but I think I'll have to pass. Athaal and Meldryn might worry, and I do have patrol duty early tomorrow."

"You're part of the City Patrol?" Margrena's eyebrows rose.

"You didn't say anything about that," added Jessyla.

"I'm not a full part . . . exactly. Every black mage has to spend ten eightdays every three years working with the City Patrol two days out of every eight. They pay me for it. My job is to patrol the main market square with a patroller."

"Have you caught anyone?" asked Jessyla.

"Some thieves," Beltur admitted, "and a cutpurse."

"You seem to be fitting in here."

"Only because of Athaal and Meldryn." After the slightest hesitation, Beltur added. "I do have to go, but, as Jessyla can tell you, Meldryn hopes that both of you will visit."

"Thank you," said Jessyla, slipping toward her mother.

He barely managed to release the shield around her before it knocked Margrena sideways.

She turned and smiled.

"I'd like to thank you as well," said Margrena. "Good night."

Beltur nodded and then stepped back, turning as the door closed to begin the walk back, one that would feel far longer than the walk out had been.

XL

Twoday passed uneventfully, except for the misty drizzle that Beltur had to walk through on his way to the smithy that morning, a drizzle that vanished with a cooler afternoon breeze, a welcome wind when it came through the open door of the smithy where he and Jorhan worked on the cupridium blades. Threeday dawned slightly warmer, the variation in temperature showing that harvest was drawing to an end, and that there would be more cooler days and fewer hot ones in the eightdays to come.

He and Jorhan had just cast another sabre when there was a rapping on the doorframe of the smithy. Beltur turned to see two unfamiliar men, and behind them a figure in black—whom he recognized after several moments as Cohndar.

"Smith Jorhan?" asked the first man, brown-haired and younger than the other two.

"That would be me." The smith stepped forward. "What can I do for you?"

"I'm Veroyt, chief assistant to Councilor Jhaldrak here." He nodded toward the older man who wore a dark blue jacket and trousers. "We've come to talk to you about some blades you have been forging."

As Veroyt spoke, Beltur noticed another man wearing gray-blue leathers who had entered the smithy behind Cohndar. The last man looked distinctly uneasy.

"What about them?" asked Jorhan genially, setting aside the hammer he held and moving toward Veroyt and Jhaldrak.

"There have been complaints."

"What sort of complaints?" Jorhan's voice turned from genial to polite.

"That you might be representing bronze as cupridium . . . that there might be some . . . untoward use of chaos in forging that bronze."

Jorhan squared his shoulders and faced Veroyt and Jhaldrak. "I don't tell those who buy my metalwork falsehoods. Also, cupridium is a form of bronze. It is harder and more long-lasting than other bronzes."

Beltur eased forward and asked politely, "Is there a law forbidding the forging of cupridium?"

"No. Not at all," replied Jhaldrak "There is a . . . concern." He glanced toward Cohndar. "Since the time of the fall of Cyador."

"It is frowned upon," said Cohndar.

Beltur tried to look confused, not completely a difficult task, since he was more than a little puzzled, not so much by the appearance of the men, particularly since they were accompanied by Cohndar, but by the concerns voiced. "I don't think I understand. As surely you must know, honored Mage Cohndar, any forge uses fire, and the hotter the fire the more chaos. Any form of working metal involves chaos."

Cohndar frowned. "It is not the same."

"Free chaos is the same whether it is used in metal

or for other purposes," Beltur pointed out. "Also, the amount of chaos used in making cupridium is very small, and for it to be effective, as you must know, it has to be locked in place by order."

Veroyt managed to conceal a smile.

Jhaldrak looked to Cohndar. "Is that true?"

"Ah . . . if the forging is done properly."

"And if the forging is done properly, then the result is cupridium bronze, is it not?" asked Beltur.

"If it is done properly." Cohndar's admission was grudging.

"Then perhaps we should consult with the master armorer," said Veroyt, gesturing toward the dark-haired man in the gray-blue leathers. "Have you had any experience with cupridium blades?"

"As much as anyone, ser. That's to say, not a great deal. Cupridium blades are rare. The armory is fortunate to have two of them. They're kept under lock. That's because they're good blades. They're also valuable."

"Can you tell whether a blade is cupridium and not just bronze?" asked Veroyt.

"I can give you my opinion. I can compare whatever the smith has forged to what I know of the cupridium blades in the armory."

"Then please do so," said Jhaldrak, his voice verging on impatience.

"Just a moment," said Jorhan. "I'll get you one of the finished blades. They're locked away." He moved past the armorer and Cohndar and out the smithy door toward the house.

"Locked away?" asked Jhaldrak.

"Ser . . . a plain cupridium blade can't be had for less than three golds, usually five or more," said the armorer.

Jhaldrak looked to Veroyt. "What about tariffs on such blades?"

"There's no tariff on a single blade owned for personal use. For weapons transported into Spidlar, the tariff is a copper on a silver of value. The tariffs for blades going into Certis or Gallos are higher, three coppers on two silvers. Axalt doesn't tariff blades sold in Axalt, but it does tariff those going through Axalt to other lands."

"Thank you for the most concise explanation," said Jhaldrak dryly.

Veroyt merely inclined his head.

There were only a few more long moments of silence before Jorhan returned with a shimmering sabre. "Here's the blade we've just finished. I don't have a scabbard for it yet. You can see that it's a touch more silver than regular bronze, and it's lighter than a bronze sabre of the same length because the cupridium is stronger and the blade can be a shade thinner. It's close to the weight and heft of black iron, and it's stronger than a regular steel blade." Jorhan extended it.

The armorer took it and began to examine it. "Excellent workmanship. Double-edged for the first third . . ."

Beltur just watched as the armorer handled the sabre, not really able to tell whether the man was pleased with the blade or not, although he certainly didn't seem displeased.

Finally, the armorer handed the blade back to Jorhan, who, in turn, offered it to Veroyt. After several moments, Veroyt handed it to Cohndar.

The black mage frowned and seemed to be concentrating.

"You can sense, I'm sure," said Beltur evenly, "that what chaos there is within the metal is locked in order."

"Is it?" asked Veroyt, looking at Cohndar.

"It is," the black mage finally replied, as if the admission had been dragged from him.

After another moment of silence, the master armorer

addressed the councilor. "The test would be in putting it against an iron blade, but there's no point in that. It's as close to the same as the first two blades Jorhan brought me to test . . ."

For an instant, Cohndar's mouth opened. The black mage shut it immediately.

"I see . . ." Jhaldrak said, looking to Cohndar.

"You didn't say anything about that," declared Cohndar sharply, glaring at the armorer.

"You didn't ask, ser. No one even told me where we were going. Just that the councilor needed my opinion on what someone claimed was a cupridium sword."

"Is it cupridium?"

The armorer shrugged. "Like I told Jorhan. All three are as much cupridium as the ones I have. I can't compare them to anything else. One of the ones he gave me will nick a steel blade without showing a mark on the cupridium. I don't know anything else that will."

Jhaldrak looked to Veroyt. "I think that decides the matter." He turned to Jorhan. "Thank you, Smith. I wish you well. And you, too, Mage."

Jhaldrak led the way from the smithy, followed by Veroyt, and then by Cohndar, who did not meet Beltur's eyes as he passed.

The armorer lagged behind, then said quietly, "I enjoyed coming up here, Jorhan, Mage . . . Good to see that someone has figured out how to continue making cupridium blades. Be a shame to see that lost."

"We'll do our best to see that it's not," replied the smith.

"Good."

Jorhan and Beltur watched from the door of the smithy as the councilor, his assistant, and Cohndar entered the waiting coach. The armorer climbed up beside the driver.

Once the coach was headed back toward Elparta, Jorhan said, "Gairlynt's a good man. When things have quieted down, we'll gift him with a fine belt dagger from cupridium. We'll make it in the next few days. But I'll have to wait to give it to him." The smith paused. "You know that mage, don't you?"

"I wouldn't say I know him. I met him once."

"He's got something in for you, I'd say."

"He's friendly with someone who's got it in for me. I don't know why. I hadn't thought he'd be like that."

"He's the kind who wants things to go his way. It's worse that he's a mage. I'd watch out for him."

"I'm afraid I'll have to."

Jorhan shook his head. "I expected someone would show up sooner or later asking about whether it was real cupridium. That was why I had Gairlynt look at that pair of blades early on. I didn't expect the councilor. I thought maybe his assistant."

Waensyn's doing? Except all Beltur had said was that he'd been working with a smith, not even who the smith was. That meant Waensyn and Cohndar were definitely looking into what he was doing. *Why?* Because his uncle had been a white? Or because they thought he really was a white trying to pass as a black, despite the fact that he was so much better with order than he'd ever been with chaos, and that he had only traces of chaos about him? Or for some other reason that he didn't even know?

"We need to get back to work. No sense in worrying about something we can't do much about. Not right now, anyway."

The rest of the day was largely uneventful—except for the one mold that split for no reason that either Beltur or Jorhan could ascertain. Jorhan thought it was likely that it had been heated for too long during the time that the councilor and his entourage had been at the smithy.

Beltur was almost feeling cheerful by the time he left the smithy with two more silvers in his wallet. He was feeling slightly better than that when he managed to hold four shields all at once for an actual fraction of a glass—perhaps a twentieth part. He'd only managed to hold that many shields for a few moments until then.

Both Meldryn and Athaal were in the kitchen when Beltur arrived.

"You had quite a morning, I understand." Athaal smiled, almost mischievously.

"How did you know? I didn't expect a Spidlarian councilor, his assistant, Cohndar, and a master armorer to show up at the smithy."

"Veroyt's a friend. He stopped by for a bit just a while ago."

"Jorhan expected it," said Meldryn.

"He told me that later. He'd already said that he'd had the master armorer look at the first blades. He said he didn't want to claim they were cupridium unless the master armorer agreed."

"Jorhan's nobody's fool."

"Veroyt cornered Cohndar later and said that he didn't appreciate that Cohndar had made Jhaldrak look incompetent," added Athaal.

"He told you that?"

"When he came by here. He thought we ought to know," replied Athaal.

"I didn't think this would cause trouble for you two."

Meldryn laughed. "More trouble for Cohndar, I think."

"Veroyt got him to admit that the blades were perfectly ordered," added Athaal. "And that you were definitely black, and not white or gray."

"Do you know what else he said?" Beltur couldn't help but be worried.

"He admitted you're black. He claimed that you aren't black in the right way, more like a mountain cat mimicking a mastiff, or a strong mongrel dog that couldn't be either a herding dog or a guard dog, too independent to be one and too fierce to be the other, and that you weren't the kind of black that would do credit to Spidlar. Then Jhaldrak asked how rediscovering how to forge cupridium was a bad thing for Spidlar. In the end, Jhaldrak declared that the Council wasn't about to rule on fine shadings of how black was black, that you'd done good work with the City Patrol and that the Council had to act in accord with the laws based on acts, not feelings. Cohndar sputtered something about how he was only trying to warn the Council."

"Warn them about what? That I was a total disaster as a white because I was really a black all along?"

"I don't think it's that," mused Meldryn, drawing out his words. "He didn't like the way you picked up the silver order in the songs at the Traders' Rest. Maybe because it came so easily. Or because you healed Claudyt's grandson."

"Mostly healed."

"You saved his life." Athaal shook his head. "Some people are never satisfied."

"We can't change Cohndar," said Meldryn. "We might as well enjoy dinner."

Beltur could agree with both of them . . . and he was hungry. But he still worried. And he didn't like being compared to a mongrel dog.

XLI

On fourday morning, Beltur left the house even earlier. He definitely wanted to be at Patrol headquarters well before seventh glass. After what had happened on three-day, the last thing he wanted was to be late. As he walked south on Bakers Lane, he kept thinking about Jessyla, even as he kept telling himself that he really knew so little about her, and that she might not want to be more than friends with him, especially if she came to know more about him.

Still . . . his thoughts were pleasant, at least until he reached City Patrol headquarters, and the duty patroller motioned to him even before he could reach the table desk to sign the duty book. "After you sign in, the Patrol Mage wants to see you."

"Did he say why?"

"Does he ever?"

Beltur had to smile at the ironic tone. Then he signed the book and made his way through the inner door to Osarus's study.

The older mage gestured for Beltur to sit down. "Laevoyt told me you knew I was at the market square on sevenday. How did you know? I never dropped my concealment."

"I could sense you. You have a very distinct and ordered presence. Most times, I have to meet someone several times to be able to recognize them from within a concealment."

"You did that from within a concealment?"

"Yes, ser."

"Did you sense what Trader Eskeld's daughter was doing from within a concealment?"

"No, ser. I was in plain sight. I did sense what she was doing. She was behind me a bit."

Osarus nodded. "That explains some aspects of the matter."

"I had no idea who she was. Neither did Laevoyt."

"That was probably for the best. We talked to all the jewelry vendors. This isn't the first time this has happened. No one has been caught before. There might be some reasons for that, but that's not your business. The captain had to go talk to the trader. The trader insisted it was all a misunderstanding, that she just wanted to show it to him so that he would buy it for her."

"Was he anywhere around?" asked Beltur.

"Of course not. He paid for the ring, and added a gold for the misunderstanding. The jeweler got the ring price and a gold. He's mostly happy. The captain suggested to the trader that it would be best if future misunderstandings were avoided. He explained that mages and patrollers were rotated and that, if such events occurred in the future, other patrollers and mages might not recognize his daughter. He was careful not to name either of you. I would suggest you avoid Eskeld's establishment for some time. He's a prominent mercer."

"I doubt I'll be buying any cloth anytime soon, ser."

"One other thing, Beltur. You both did a good job. It could have been very embarrassing. The captain and I told Laevoyt that, but you needed to know as well. Now . . . go find your partner."

"Yes, ser." Despite the commendation, Beltur somehow felt that he'd narrowly escaped being struck by lightning . . . or a chaos-bolt. He nodded, left the small study, and made his way out into the duty room, where Laevoyt was waiting.

"You ready to go, Beltur?"

"As ready as you are."

Once they left headquarters, Laevoyt cleared his throat, meaningfully. "The Patrol Mage or the captain?"

"The Patrol Mage. He said we did a good job in handling the trader's daughter. I have the feeling that the captain did a better job in handing the trader."

"That's what he gets all those silvers for." Laevoyt offered a sardonic laugh. "I wouldn't want to have to deal with the Council and the traders. They're harder than a cupridium copper."

"If the daughter is any indication . . ." Beltur shook his head.

"There's one other thing. One of the councilor's assistants was asking about you the other day. You want to tell me what that was about?"

That didn't exactly surprise Beltur. "I'm not exactly a typical black. I learned most of what I know and can do late. And I don't know many people here. But Athaal knew a smith, and he thought I might be able to help him. I've been working for him just a little longer than I've been on Patrol duty. We've figured out a way to make cupridium for blades and for other things. Someone complained that it wasn't real cupridium. So yesterday, Councilor Jhaldrak, his assistant, an older black mage, and the Council armorer showed up at the smithy. After going through everything, they decided that we were indeed forging cupridium. I don't think the mage was very happy about it."

"That wasn't Cohndar, was it?"

"Why do you think that?" Beltur asked warily.

"Because I've had to work with him. He's never that happy about anything, except maybe good ale."

"Anyway, the councilor decided that what we were doing was within the law and that it might even raise some tariff coins."

"He probably thought about the second thing first. For a young mage, you seem to get stuck in some tight spots."

"Lack of experience," Beltur said lightly. "I had a very sheltered childhood." As they neared the market square, he rearranged the patrol medallion so that it showed and eased the whistle at the end of the lanyard out from under his tunic. He didn't see Fosset and his ale cart, but seventh glass was too early for many customers.

By sometime after ninth glass, Beltur had caught no sight of any lawbreaking. Nor had he sensed anything, and Laevoyt, when they met at ninth glass, had also seen nothing. Yet Beltur had the vague feeling that there were cutpurses and thieves lurking around the square, possibly even successfully enough to have made off with coins or belt wallets as yet unmissed by their victims. *Aren't you just imagining that?*

He didn't think so.

Rather than continue his irregular attempts at covering the entire market square, he decided simply to go where the crowds were thickest while maintaining a concealment in hopes of sensing more than vague feelings. As he neared the tables and stalls where the crowds were heavier, he could sense an intermittent flickering of chaos but it came and went so quickly that he couldn't pinpoint it. He'd thought that the crowds would be the thickest around the stalls that offered the higher-priced goods—silks, laces, jewelry, even the rarer spices like saffron and pepper—but there were more people around the tables that held tools, such as pincers, pliers, awls, augers, saws, and, surprisingly, needles.

Still, for all of the crowding and the continuing flickers of chaos here and there, Beltur could sense neither theft nor assaults, and no one cried out. Finally, at first glass, he met with Laevoyt on the corner once more.

"It's quiet," offered the patroller.

"There are thieves and cutpurses there. I know it, but . . ."

"That's because they know you're here. Someone passed the word. The next time we patrol together, you should stay concealed from the time we leave headquarters." A smile followed Laevoyt's words. "That's not all bad, you know. Part of what we're supposed to do is to stop the stealing, not just catch people who do it."

Beltur nodded. Except he had looked forward to earning a few more silvers.

"Stay in plain sight. Go get an ale from Fosset. Let them see you. Then disappear."

Beltur took Laevoyt's advice and made his way down West Street to where the innkeeper's nephew had his cart. "I think I could stand an ale, Fosset, if you could spare one."

"I can do that, Mage, that I can."

"Thank you," said Beltur as he took the small mug. "It's warm. Not so warm as it has been, but warm enough."

"You'll be wanting it warm when you're patrolling here in winter."

"Does anyone sell anything in winter?" asked Beltur.

"More than you'd think, but only in the afternoon, and only when there's been time to clear the snow."

"It's been quiet today."

"It is when they know a mage is around. Unless they know he's not that good a mage."

Beltur nodded, deciding not to comment, and finished the ale. He handed the mug back to Fosset. "Thank you, again."

"Happy to do it."

Beltur returned to patrolling the square, largely under concealment. While he still sensed the flickers of chaos, as Laevoyt had suggested, there didn't seem to be a single instance of theft for the remaining three glasses of his duty, at least not one that he or Laevoyt found or that any vendor reported.

So much for any additional silvers, reflected Beltur as he and Laevoyt walked back west on Patrol Street toward headquarters.

When he signed the duty book at the end of his tour, the duty patroller said, "Starting after eightday, Mage, for the next two eightdays, you're to be here on threeday and sevenday."

"With Patroller Laevoyt or someone else?"

"You have the same patroller for the whole ten eight-days."

"Thank you." Beltur straightened to say something to Laevoyt, but the tall patroller had already left the headquarters building.

Beltur hurried out and strode briskly to Hill Street and up to the Council building, immediately making his way to Raymandyl's table desk.

The clerk smiled ruefully. "Mage, you're cutting it close. We close at half past fourth glass."

"I'm sorry. I had duty today. Oh . . . and there are also these." Beltur handed over the three leather token disks.

Raymandyl's eyes widened. "I don't often see that many of these at once."

"That's for three days of patrolling. We got a team of cutpurses one day and a swap thief on the other day."

"Oh . . . you came late, and this includes today?"

"No. We didn't find any thieves today."

Raymandyl brought out two ledgers. "This one is for your pay. Sign there."

Beltur signed.

"And this one you've seen."

After Beltur signed in the second ledger, the clerk added his seal and said, "You get two silvers for the last eightday, and six for the disks. Eight silvers. That's not bad for your first eightday. That doesn't even count the two you got before you went on patrol duty." Raymandyl unlocked the side cabinet and counted out the silvers, then put them on the table desk before Beltur.

Beltur took them and carefully placed them in his belt wallet. "Now I can begin to repay Athaal and Meldryn for everything." Sensing a certain puzzlement, Beltur added, "I had eight coppers to my name when I got to Elparta. They took me in until I could earn enough because a healer who knew them asked." Again, that was a great oversimplification.

"I wondered . . ."

Beltur had thought he might have. "They're good people, and I respect them both, but we are different."

"That's good to know. They're both very good people."

"They are," Beltur repeated, "and Meldryn makes eating there a pleasure." He nodded. "I'll see you in another eightday, and I'll try to be earlier."

"You could come in the mornings."

Beltur smiled. "Right now I'm fortunate to be working most days, and I have to be there early. I might be able to come in the afternoon, though."

"Working? At regular times?"

"I'm helping a smith." Before Raymandyl could question further, Beltur added, "There are a few other people I need to repay for their help and kindness."

The clerk shook his head. "Some of you blacks . . . you have to, don't you?"

Beltur nodded, although he'd never felt compelled, but what was right was right.

"Better you than me. Give my best to Athaal."

"I'll do that." Beltur easily managed a friendly smile before he turned and left the Council building.

As he made his way to Bakers Lane, he found his thoughts centering on Jessyla, wondering if and when she and her mother would be leaving Elparta, since Margrena had implied that she'd prefer any city or town in Spidlar but the one in which her older sister lived. *Or are they stuck here for the same reasons you are?* That was all too likely, he suspected.

When Beltur finally entered Athaal and Meldryn's house and reached the kitchen, Athaal rose from where he'd placed something in one of the hearth ovens. "Veroyt sent me a message. The Gallosian army is only about an eightday away. I'll be shielding the command group. It's about all I can do. I can't juggle as many containment shields as you can. He asked me what you could do, besides help forge cupridium."

Denardre's actually going to attack Spidlar? For a moment, Beltur didn't know what to say, but finally managed a few words. "Besides that, the only magery I'm good at—I mean—in terms of battles and fighting—is the same as you. That's shields."

Athaal nodded. "Good. That's what I told him."

"Do you really think they'll want me in the army?"

"They don't *want* any of us in the Council forces. They want us there to protect those forces, especially against Wyath and his chaos-mages. The Council will need every mage it can find." Athaal paused. "Are you certain you can't do anything else?"

"I wasn't much good with chaos, even with Uncle instructing me. I told you that." Beltur thought about the one time he'd managed to half create a lightning bolt. "He once said that some black mages could create lightning bolts."

"He did? Did he say anything about how they did it?"

"Only that it involved order, and that it wasn't that much different from regular lightning bolts. I think he meant that there had to be clouds and some sort of storm." His uncle hadn't so much said as implied that.

"That doesn't sound all that useful. No one's going to attack in the middle of a storm."

"I'm sorry."

"Don't be. You can't change what he said." Athaal shook his head. "Would you go tell Meldryn that dinner's almost ready?"

"I'd be happy to."

Athaal turned to the worktable.

Beltur headed for the bakery. *Could you call a lightning bolt again? Should you try?* Even as those questions crossed his mind, they made him feel uneasy, very uneasy.

XLII

Fiveday morning Beltur again rose early, this time because he wanted to catch both Meldryn and Athaal in the kitchen before Meldryn returned to the bakery.

"You're up early," offered Meldryn from where he sat at one end of the kitchen table as Beltur hurried into the kitchen. Athaal, seated at the other end, just nodded, with a bemused smile on his face.

"That's because I wanted to talk to you both."

"This must be serious." Meldryn's smile belied his deep and serious voice.

"It is. I've thought this over. I just can't do this the way you suggested." Beltur laid two silvers on the table. "Even two silvers a week won't cover what you're feeding me, but it will help more, and so long as I'm working with Jorhan and getting paid by the Council as a patrol mage, I can at least do this."

The two exchanged glances.

Then Athaal grinned. "I told Mel you'd do something like this. You can't not be fair."

"Or at least as fair as I can afford," Beltur added ruefully, although he knew he could afford a bit more. *But only for this eightday and perhaps the next.* One thing he had learned was not to count on anything promised until it was in hand.

"For now," said Meldryn. "If you make fewer coins, then pay us less . . . or nothing."

"I hope it doesn't come to that."

"We all do," replied Meldryn, "but the world doesn't respond to hope. Sometimes, it even ignores hard work and great effort."

"Sometimes," added Athaal sardonically, "those who are evil are the hardest workers, and everyone wonders why they prosper."

"Enough philosophy," said Meldryn, rising from the kitchen table. "I need to get to the bakery, and you two have work to do."

Beltur took a mug out and tapped some ale from the small keg, then took a platter and seated himself at his place at the table, noting that Athaal had not quite finished eating. There was more than enough of the ham and cheesed eggs left on the serving platter, and a small loaf of bread was beside his place as well. He smiled. "Meldryn bakes the best bread. The best everything, really."

"He does at that. I'll miss it."

"You'll have to leave here?"

Athaal shrugged. "Who knows? It's likely to be a day or so before I find out more. The command group will remain in Elparta until the marshal learns where the Gallosians are."

"They won't take the river?"

"Some of their force might, but most will take the old trading road, and that follows the west side of the river.

What the marshal does will depend on where the Gallosians form up."

"What if they just attack the west river tower?"

"So that we can't stop any trading boat that refuses to stop and pay tariffs? That's the same as attacking Elparta. In the end, it would end up as a part of Gallos."

"Wasn't it once, long ago?"

"Not in hundreds of years, and that wasn't for very long. That was why the Council back then built the walls and towers, so it couldn't happen again. If it did . . . with Wyath as the Prefect's arms-mage, we'd all have to flee."

Beltur took a mouthful of the ham and eggs, then followed it with a swallow of ale. "I'd rather not do that twice."

"We'd rather not do it once," said Athaal dryly. "It's taken years for us to become comfortable here, and to start over somewhere else . . ." He shook his head. "It would be even harder to stop the Gallosians if they took Elparta. They might end up holding all of the river."

Beltur was still mulling over what the other two had said when he left the house. Outside, the morning was cooler than previous mornings, if not much, but a reminder that fall was approaching. *Along with the Prefect and his forces.*

His concern must have carried him along, because he found himself walking faster from the southeast city gate to the smithy, and he arrived there much earlier than he usually did.

"Good thing you're here early," announced Jorhan. "Today, we're going to cast a straight-sword. I've been working on the mold, and it's being heated right now."

"A straight-sword?"

"Double-edged all the way, five digits or so longer than a sabre. Shorter than a bastard blade, but longer than a shortsword. Don't know what to call it other than a straight-sword."

"You're making it special, then?"

Jorhan nodded, then said, "Don't ask me who wants it. I don't know. Well, I do. It's for a trader from Axalt who has a commission from someone in Certis to find a straight cupridium blade of that length with both edges sharp. He's been looking for over a year."

"Whoever it was really wanted an ancient blade, then."

"The trader says not. Said it could be old or new. It just has to be cupridium. With no iron anywhere."

That sounds like a white mage or wizard. But one in Certis? Beltur managed not to frown. "I hope you're getting a good price for it."

"We have to deliver it, first. He's agreed to what I told him it would cost. I've dealt with him before." The smith paused. "It'll take more of the melt than you've seen before."

"How much more?" asked Beltur as he hung his worn tunic on the peg by the smithy door.

"A fourth part more, I've figured."

"That should be all right. Is it any thicker? Or just longer?"

"A shade thicker through the tang and the base of the blade. Just as well you weren't here yesterday. It took me all day to get it right. Well . . . to get two of them right."

"Two?"

"Just in case. Always better that way. I can save it if the first one goes right, but the first time you try something new . . ."

Beltur laughed softly, shaking his head and recalling how many attempts it had taken just to get the feel of cupridium, even before trying to cast those first sabres.

Needless to say, glasses later, when the blade came out of the mold, Beltur was shaking his head again, not humorously. "It's going to be too soft."

"We'll see."

After the blade had cooled enough for Jorhan to work it, and the hammer came down on the metal, he looked up at Beltur. "You were right. Think we can do better with the next mold?"

"I think so. I hope so. I thought I'd worked out just how much order and chaos with the extra metal . . . but it's a matter of feel."

"Aye," replied Jorhan, his voice rueful, "like all smithing. Can't say I hadn't hoped." He paused. "Can we rework this? The way you did with the others that got spoiled?"

"There's more metal there, but once you heat it, I can pull out the order and chaos, and we'll have close to the basic bronze for cupridium."

The second blade was better, but not up to what either Jorhan or Beltur wanted, and by that time, it was well past fourth glass.

"Tomorrow will be better," Jorhan said as Beltur reached for his tunic. "We'll get it right. We have before."

The only question is how long it will take. But Beltur just said, "I'll be here early."

"I'll see you then."

As he began the walk back to the city, Beltur couldn't help wondering why such a change in the amount of basic bronze had made it so much harder for him to gauge the amount and placement of the order-linked chaos nodes necessary to get the right "feel" of the alloy. He'd added more than a fourth part more, and it had felt right when the melt had been in the mold, but some of that order had "leaked" away in the cooling process.

Could it be that with more metal you'll need to hold the pattern longer because there's more chaos heat?

That was very possible. *More than possible.*

He kept walking, deciding to practice multiple shield containments, at least as long as he could . . . or until he reached the southeast gate.

XLIII

The first part of sixday at the smithy was all too much like fiveday, beginning with another unsuccessful forging, this time of a blade too hard to be worked, but by the end of the day Beltur and Jorhan finally had a straight-sword that was of the same quality cupridium as the sabres they had forged earlier. More important, Beltur had learned more about the integration of his order-chaos web-nets into the molten bronze. He also left with four more silvers.

The effort he'd put into forging on sixday had left him so tired that he went to bed earlier . . . and still overslept slightly on sevenday morning. So he had to rush to wash, get dressed, and eat . . . and then still hurry to Patrol headquarters.

He arrived there just as Laevoyt did and signed the duty book right after the patroller. The two walked outside together.

"You said I ought to disappear from sight before we neared the square," Beltur said.

"That's a good idea, even if I suggested it. We'll meet at ninth glass on the corner, then?"

"If we haven't caught anyone, I'll be there," replied

Beltur, "but you won't see me. Wait a few moments, just in case I get delayed."

"I won't see you . . ."

"You'll still be able to hear me." With those words, Beltur raised a concealment. "Just as you can now."

"I don't think another mage has done that."

Why not? "Probably because they didn't want to call attention to their being able to be near you and not seen. We can still be heard and seen . . . and have people run into us." *Or our shields.*

Laevoyt resumed walking. "It's still strange." He kept his voice low, as if he didn't want anyone to hear him talking, as if he were speaking to himself.

Belatedly, as he walked beside the tall patroller, Beltur eased out the medallion and whistle. The medallion needed to be obvious if he seemed to appear, and he needed the whistle handy. "I'll head down West Street and then into the middle of the square. We'll see what happens." *If anything.*

After splitting away from Laevoyt, Beltur moved slowly south along West Street at the edge of the square before moving into rows of vendors, listening, then stopping to catch some interesting words.

". . . goes the patroller . . ."

". . . like every threeday lately . . . no mage . . . need to keep a close watch on the stall . . ."

". . . be better if there was a mage every day . . ."

". . . Council doesn't like to spend more coins than it has to . . ."

". . . and we suffer . . ."

A brief smile crossed Beltur's unseen face as he resumed moving toward the middle of the square. While he could sense flickers of chaos, a good glass passed without incident. On his previous patrols, when there had been problems, they'd occurred around midday, and he had the feeling that was almost a pattern. He kept listening, while being careful to move so that people didn't bump against his shields.

"... tools ... good tools ... won't find any better ..."

"... fresh-squeezed cider from the north hills ..."

Two glasses later, still under a concealment, he eased back through the slowly growing crowds to the corner of West and Patrol, where an obviously impatient Laevoyt turned one way and then the other. "I'm here. So far ... I haven't run across any problems. I have the feeling that there might be some, but I had that feeling on sevenday, and nothing happened."

"That makes two of us," replied Laevoyt. "Until first glass."

Beltur continued east along the Patrol Street side of the square for about a block before turning south toward the center of the square, where he decided just to stand and wait near the stalls that featured jewelry, silks, and other small items of value, some of them likely not of the most honorable provenance, not that such would be easy to prove. Standing for very long proved tiresome, and he began to move back and forth slightly through gaps in the passersby and possible shoppers.

Gradually, he could sense that more flickers of chaos seemed to be moving toward the area where he had been moving, if slightly to the east of where he was. Beltur moved gently another two stalls that way, close to a stall that featured delicate lacquer boxes. The chaos flickers drew closer, then turned, and Beltur realized that they were likely moving toward the vendor of shimmersilk scarves.

A heavy man seemingly blundered into the side of the stall, almost upending one side and sending things sliding. Two others moved to grab scarves and rings.

Beltur clamped containments around all three, dropped his concealment, and blew three quick blasts on the whistle, while hoping he could hold all three until Laevoyt appeared.

". . . where'd he come from?"

". . . told me no mage with the patroller . . ."

The well-dressed and heavyset man said nothing. For an instant, only an instant, he glared at the two youths, one of whom, Beltur could sense, was actually a young woman dressed as a boy. Both of the younger ones were caught with goods in their hands, several silk scarves, and a necklace of polished stones that Beltur didn't recognize. Then the man donned an expression of outrage.

"This is most uncalled for. I had nothing to do with this . . . this pack of thieves."

"The patroller will decide that," Beltur replied. The perspiration began to form on his forehead as he continued to hold the three shields besides his own, waiting for Laevoyt to arrive.

". . . three of them . . . fancy that . . ."

". . . caught in the act . . ."

While it seemed to Beltur like more than half a glass passed before Laevoyt appeared, it was likely far, far less than that.

"The two in tan and gray with the silk and necklace, and the man in brown," Beltur said with a calm he didn't feel. "Use the leathers on the girl. She's the one in gray."

Laevoyt didn't question Beltur at all, but immediately bound her and removed the necklace and slipped it inside his tunic. Once the patroller finished, Beltur replaced the shield with one far lighter, while Laevoyt restrained the second light-finger and removed the silks. After that, the patroller handed both the chains to the leather collars to Beltur and moved toward the older man. Quietly, and with great relief, Beltur dropped the shields from around the two youths, but was ready to reapply them if necessary, hoping that he wouldn't have to, at least for a little while.

"I did nothing, nothing at all," declared the burly man in the matching brown jacket and trousers. "I was just standing here when those two ruffians tried to grab things and run."

Laevoyt looked to Beltur.

"He's the one who rammed into the stall and sent everything sliding. The two young ones accompanied him from two rows over. They came together."

"You weren't even here," declared the well-dressed man.

Beltur raised a concealment and said, "I was right here." Then he dropped it.

The man lunged against the shield, which held, then began to flail against his confinement.

Again, Laevoyt looked to Beltur.

Beltur concentrated on tightening the shield until the man could not move.

"I still can't put the leathers on him," Laevoyt said quietly.

"I know." Beltur was guessing, but he thought that with such tight shields, the man would have to stop breathing before long. He kept watching. The man turned red in the face, trying to gasp. His eyes began to protrude.

"Get ready," said Beltur. "Now." He dropped the shield, ready to raise it.

Laevoyt was quick with the leathers, and had the man's hands bound behind his back and the collar in place before the captive began to struggle again.

Beltur glanced at the two youths. Neither had budged. Both looked almost stunned.

"Let's go," said Laevoyt calmly. "Walk toward the edge of the square."

"Why should I—"

Beltur clamped a shield over his mouth. From just what he'd seen, he disliked the big man. After a moment, he released it. "Walk. Now."

The three began to walk, and those thronging the space before them quickly moved aside.

Laevoyt looked sideways at Beltur for just a moment, then kept his eyes on the three.

So did Beltur, ready to clamp a shield in place instantly, but the three walked slowly to Patrol Street and then west toward headquarters.

"Three at once?" said the duty patroller when Laevoyt and Beltur arrived with their prisoners.

"The big fellow might be running a ring of lightfingers," said Laevoyt. "There were only two with him today, though."

Beltur wondered if the boy he'd let go might have been one. *You'll probably never know.*

"Your names?" asked the duty patroller, pointing at the girl. "You first."

"Khassia."

Beltur watched the three as the duty patroller entered their names in the book. Then he rang the bell. In moments, another patroller stepped through the door behind the duty desk.

"Three more prisoners. Grand theft. Main market square."

None of the three spoke as the second patroller led the three away.

Then the duty patroller handed Laevoyt three more sets of leathers, collars, and chains. "You'd better get back to the square."

"We're on our way," replied Laevoyt, turning and heading for the door.

Beltur followed, wondering about the three, and hoping that the Council magistrate would be easier on the two youths.

"That was quite something," said Laevoyt once they were back outside of headquarters. "How did you manage all three?"

"I almost couldn't hold that third containment," Beltur admitted. "If you'd taken much longer . . ." He shook his head.

"But you did, and the look on those two young ones when you turned the big fellow red. I heard that some mages could do that, but I've never seen it."

"It's not something I've done much." Beltur wasn't about to admit it was the first time. "I'd rather not do it. It could really hurt someone, but I didn't see any other way."

"I'm glad you did. If you hadn't, I would have had to use my truncheon on him, and, big as he was, he'd have been hurt."

Beltur knew that Laevoyt might have been as well.

The rest of sevenday was uneventful, and there were no more flickers of chaos anywhere in the market square, even though Beltur spent most of his time under concealment, except when he visited Fosset's ale cart.

Later, after fourth glass, Beltur signed the duty book with three more tokens in his wallet, left headquarters heading south to Tailors Way, where he proceeded east until he reached Celinya's doorway. When he knocked, the seamstress opened the peephole on the door, as she had before.

"Celinya, it's Beltur. I've come for my shirts."

The latch scraped slightly, and the door opened.

Celinya stepped aside, if awkwardly, and motioned for Beltur to enter, then quickly closed the door behind him and latched it.

"You have the shirts and smallclothes ready?" He glanced around the small room, neat and well-swept. He thought he sensed someone in the adjoining room, behind the closed door, possibly a child.

She gestured toward the wooden clothes rack. "Please try one of them on."

Somehow Beltur felt almost embarrassed as he took off his tunic and shirt.

Her eyes lingered for a moment on the silver medallion and the whistle lanyard still around his neck. "You did have duty today."

Beltur managed not to frown. He'd told her that.

"Even black mages are not so forthright as they would have others believe. You are still young. If you remain as forthright as you are for another ten years, it will be remarkable. Would you like to try them both?"

"No. How about the one farthest away?"

Celinya smiled. "You should try them both."

Beltur did. When he took off the second one, he returned it to her and donned his old shirt and tunic, both of which felt shabby compared to the two shirts he had just worn. Then he eased two silvers from his wallet. "This is what I owe you, is it not?"

"It is."

"You said a pair of black trousers would cost . . . what? Three silvers?"

"Two silvers and five for gray trousers. For you, two silvers and eight for black."

"I'll do that. A silver in advance?"

"A silver and two. Black wool is more expensive." She paused. "I need to measure you."

That only took what seemed moments, and Beltur handed her the coins. "What would it cost for a black tunic?"

"Five silvers. You should have a good tunic."

Beltur winced, but then he thought about how worn his tunic was already. He did have enough silvers to pay for a new one, and the trousers, even if he made nothing more for the next two eightdays, especially with the six extra silvers he had just earned. "How much in advance?"

"Two silvers."

Beltur refrained from sighing as he handed over two more silvers. "When will they be ready?"

"Next sixday."

Beltur nodded, then watched as she swiftly folded the shirts and the smallclothes and slipped them into a cloth bag that looked to have been made out of scraps of fabric, a bag which she then presented to him. "Thank you."

Celinya moved to the door and peered out through the peephole. After several moments, she stepped back and opened the door, motioning for him to leave.

The door closed swiftly behind him.

Beltur glanced around, trying to sense any untoward chaos or order, but there was no one near him, and he began to walk west toward Bakers Lane, wondering just what had led to the seamstress being so fearfully cautious.

XLIV

Since he slept late on eightday morning, Beltur was surprised to find Meldryn and Athaal still sitting at the kitchen table when he came downstairs wearing one of his new shirts.

"I didn't think you two ever slept late," said Beltur as he took a mug and began to tap some ale.

"It happens now and again," replied Meldryn. "We got to talking last night."

"About the Prefect and the Gallosians?"

"Among other things," said Athaal. "It is troubling. Veroyt said that armsmen from Kleth were supposed to have arrived by sixday."

"Not to mention that Elparta really doesn't have that many mages compared to Gallos." Meldryn gestured to the platters in the middle of the table. "The rest is yours."

"Thank you." Beltur sat down and helped himself to the still faintly warm cheesed eggs and the ham strips. There was also a single honey roll left, obviously for him, but he decided to save that until the end. He ate several bites of the eggs before saying, "I thought Spidlar had a number of black mages. Are there any whites at all anywhere in Spidlar?"

"None that any of us know of," replied Meldryn. "Chaos is unpredictable, and it spoils things. Traders dislike unpredictability, and they hate anything that causes spoilage."

"Is that why Cohndar is skeptical of me? Because he thinks of me as an unpredictable mongrel mage?"

Meldryn chuckled. "Don't let him get to you. He's from a trader family and set in his ways. He wouldn't even accept a dinner at the inn because it upset his eating habits."

"There might be a score of blacks between Elparta and Kleth," added Athaal, "most of them here. There might be a score in Spidlaria, but the Council won't send them here."

"They wouldn't get here in time," declared Meldryn.

Beltur took a swallow of ale. "I don't know for certain, but there can't be even a score of strong whites in Gallos."

"That's more than enough to cause concern." Athaal lifted his mug, but didn't drink from it, instead setting it back on the table.

"Even strong white mages can only do so much," Beltur said. "They have limits, just like we do." He eyed the honey roll, then decided—again—to save it for last.

Athaal frowned. "What sort of limits?"

"How far they can throw chaos-bolts, and how often. From what I saw, throwing chaos-bolts was very tiring. Chaos isn't that effective against stone walls or even earthworks."

"What about earth-mages?" asked Meldryn.

"Earth-mages?" Beltur had never heard of that kind of mage.

"They can tap into the chaos deep beneath the ground. In some places, near volcanoes and steaming springs, the chaos is very strong."

"I've never seen anyone do that, and Uncle never said anything about it."

"Then we can hope the Prefect hasn't found a mage like that." Meldryn shook his head.

"Sometimes, as you always say," replied Athaal, "relying on hope is a very bad idea." He turned back to Beltur. "On a more cheerful subject, what are you planning to do today?"

"Later, I thought I'd walk to Grenara's and see Jessyla, if she's there. She didn't mention they were leaving, but her mother talked about it earlier."

"I doubt the Council would let two healers leave with a Gallosian army likely to attack shortly," said Meldryn.

"The Council can do that?"

"How long did it take for Raymandyl to have you on Patrol duty?" asked Athaal sardonically.

"Something like three days."

"And how soon was Councilor Jhaldrak at Jorhan's smithy about cupridium?"

"Three days, or so," replied Beltur with a rueful smile.

"All lands have laws," said Meldryn calmly. "Most of them are good, even in Gallos or Westwind or Certis.

Often, how they are applied and enforced—or not enforced—is what makes living in a country good or less good. The Council is far from perfect, but for the most part, it tries to be fair. Part of that fairness is looking into questionable matters early." He smiled wryly. "Sometimes, that can be annoying, but we'd rather be here than anywhere else."

"You were worrying about Jessyla?" prompted Athaal, as if he wanted to change the subject. "Is that why you have on that new shirt? To display your new-found prosperity to the young woman?"

"She likely won't even notice with it under my tunic. I didn't think wearing the new one to the smithy was a good idea."

"You could use a new tunic, for when you're not working at the smithy," suggested Meldryn.

Beltur didn't want to mention that just yet. "You think so?"

"The one we found for you in Fenard is barely dark enough," added Athaal. "Besides, a new tunic will show Margrena you're doing better." After a moment, he added, "You're worried about how she sees you. That might help."

"I am worried. I've gotten the feeling that Margrena may not want me to see Jessyla. What if she just tries to send me off after a few moments?"

Meldryn grinned. "I think I can make things much easier for you." He stood.

At those words, Athaal smiled, then added, "I think we have a large basket in the corner of the bakery."

A good half glass later, Beltur left the house carrying a large basket holding several loaves of bread, a berry pie, a fowl pie, and a bag of raisin-oat cookies, as well as a melon that Athaal had declared would spoil before they could eat it since he'd been paid with four of them.

As Beltur walked north on Bakers Lane heading for

Crafters Way, he thought about what Athaal had pointed out about the Spidlarian Council. While Beltur generally agreed with the laws and rules—*so far*—he'd seen hints, as with the trader's daughter and the cupridium incident, that Spidlar was governed as strictly as Gallos. He certainly didn't want to get on the wrong side of the Council, although it was more likely, if that happened, he'd be forced into leaving Spidlar, rather than facing chaos-bolts or the black mage equivalent.

Before he knew it, Beltur stood at the door of the narrow two-story dwelling. He glanced at the window, but the curtains blocked his view of the inside, which meant that it was likely no one saw him approach. He knocked, and then waited.

After a time the door opened a crack, and then more widely, revealing the red-haired Jessyla.

Beltur smiled.

"I'm so glad it's you. I could sense the blackness, and I worried that it was Waensyn." Her eyes went to the large basket.

"I told Meldryn and Athaal I was coming to see you, and," Beltur shrugged, "Meldryn insisted that I bring a few things."

Jessyla grinned. "You're even telling the truth."

"I am." *I wouldn't dare not to, not to you.*

"Come on in. Mother will be happy. Auntie . . . less so." Jessyla stood back and opened the door wider.

"What about Growler?" Beltur grinned.

"He's sleeping upstairs. He doesn't care for strangers, especially men. I think I told you that. You probably won't see him."

"You did." Beltur entered the front room, a parlor with two padded and backed benches, two straight-backed chairs, and a single wooden armchair with a thick but worn green cushion on the seat. A small table was set at each end of the benches. The wooden floor was largely covered by a woven or braided rush mat. Besides the front window, the only source of light was a brass lamp suspended from a wall bracket above the bench set against the side wall. At the far end of the parlor was a hearth, clearly open on two sides, the other side being the kitchen. Directly facing the door was a narrow staircase up to the second floor.

"They're in the kitchen." Jessyla hurried ahead, cheerfully announcing as she stepped into the kitchen, "Beltur stopped by to see us, and you should see what he brought."

Beltur followed her into the kitchen, immediately setting the basket on the table between the two sisters, both clad in the same healers' green that Jessyla wore. "Meldryn thought you might like these. The melon's almost ripe. Athaal sent it because someone paid him in melons, and we won't be able to eat them all before they spoil." He followed the words with a smile.

"Meldryn's fresh-baked bread," said Jessyla. "Is that a large meat pie?"

"A large fowl pie, and a small berry pie."

"You do know how to make an entrance," said Margrena with a smile, one that Beltur felt vanished all too quickly.

"I know how I felt when I arrived in Elparta, but, in all fairness, it wasn't my idea. It was Meldryn's."

"We appreciate it. Oh," said Margrena, looking to her sister, "Grenara, this is Beltur. You've heard of him, I'm certain. And, Beltur, this is my older sister Grenara."

"She makes certain everyone knows that," said Grenara. "She's never forgotten all the years I called her my younger sister." Her eyes fixed on Beltur. "You're the one whose uncle was the white mage killed by that . . . egotist . . . Wyath."

"I am."

"How did you end up a black?"

"I always was. I just didn't know it. I don't think my uncle was comfortable with it."

"Just like that, was it?"

Beltur shook his head. "It began almost a season before I left Gallos. I wasn't ever comfortable using chaos, and I tried to avoid it more and more, and use order. Then everything got much easier, and I wasn't using any chaos—except a little and that's wrapped in order. For the forging, that is."

"Beltur's working with a smith," offered Jessyla. "They're forging cupridium."

"Why? That's something that makes it easier for chaos-driven men to kill."

"It's also harder than regular iron, and it's beautiful. We've made candelabra and platters and candlesticks as well."

"Ordermages make black iron to kill chaos-driven men," said Jessyla. "Not everyone who handles chaos is evil. Beltur's uncle was a good man. That's why Wyath had him killed."

"That's true," said Margrena. "He helped us many times, and asked nothing."

A quick expression of surprise crossed Grenara's face and vanished.

"You two," Margrena said quickly, "don't need to stand around listening to us. Why don't you go into the parlor? We'll unload the basket, and I'll bring you some cider in a bit."

"That would be lovely, Mother." Jessyla gestured to the parlor.

"Thank you." Beltur inclined his head before he turned and followed the youngest healer. Once in the parlor, since Jessyla had taken the one bench, Beltur took the other one, so that they faced each other.

"It was sweet of you to bring all of that."

"I wanted to see you, but the food was Meldryn's idea. I'm glad he had it."

"So am I." After a long silence, she said, "Have you been doing any patrolling?"

"Yesterday was one of my duty days. We caught a man who was running two light-fingered youths. He tried to pretend that he had nothing to do with them. He was very well-dressed, but they were looking to him. One of them was a girl dressed like a boy."

"What will happen to them?"

"They'll go before the Council magistrate. He'll decide. Or she'll decide. I think they have a woman magistrate who deals with women."

"It seems so unfair for the two. They didn't have any choice. No one would do that if they could do anything else."

"Laevoyt said it was likely they'd get the workhouse. He hoped the man would lose a hand."

"He just hoped?"

"Patrollers and mages don't decide."

"The workhouse?" Jessyla gave a little shudder.

Margrena cleared her throat as she moved into the parlor carrying two small mugs. "Here's the cider I promised."

"Thank you." Beltur stood and took the mugs from her, then handed one to Jessyla.

"Thank you, Mother."

"You're more than welcome." Margrena returned to the kitchen.

Beltur reseated himself and took a swallow of the cider, enjoying the taste. Finally, he spoke. "You said you were doing some healing at the Council Healing House."

"It's sad. Sometimes, there's really not that much we can do. The Council just provides the basics—dressings, some ointments, usually brinn, sometimes burnet. You know, I'd never seen so much burnet in one place as when I brought it from your uncle's. We sold the ointment for almost five golds." She lowered her voice. "Without that . . ."

"It would have been hard to leave Fenard?"

She nodded, then murmured, "Mother wouldn't want to admit that. We had to leave so much." In a normal voice, she continued, "We both would have been conscripted as healers for the Prefect's armsmen. That's why all those healers who could left the city. Some are likely hiding in the towns well away from Fenard."

"You'll likely have to heal the Spidlarian forces."

"We will, but the Council pays. Not a lot, a half silver a day, but we'll get fed. It couldn't be as bad as healing for the Prefect."

Beltur wondered about that, but he just nodded. "What else are you doing?"

"Just helping Aunt." She paused. "Tell me about what else you're doing."

"It's pretty much the way I said. Five days out of the eightday, I work with Jorhan, two with the Patrol, and I get eightday for myself. The smithing . . . every time we try something different for the first time, it usually takes several tries to get the order-net in the metal right—"

"Order-net? You said you put both order and chaos into the metal."

Beltur shook his head. "It's more like little pieces— nodes—of chaos locked in order, and there has to be a balance of sorts, and it has to be spread throughout all the metal, like a fine net. Cupridium doesn't have order suffused through it like black iron, and it doesn't have chaos. It's both, evenly, and it's hard to get that balance right."

"So that's why a white mage can use a cupridium knife or sword."

"Most likely. Anyway, we've also done some platters and candlesticks and candelabra. They look almost silver-gold . . ." Beltur went on to talk about the forging and about the effort Jorhan had to put into the molds. "You can see. There's nothing that special. I'm just a smith's helper, and I'm fortunate that I can make a few silvers." He was definitely fortunate, and he was making a bit more than a few, but how long that would last he had no idea.

"You're making more than a few. I can tell that."

Beltur found himself blushing. "I can't hide anything from you. Yes, I'm being paid a silver a day, and extra when something turns out well, but there's no telling how long this work will last, and I worry about that. It could last for seasons, or it could vanish tomorrow. It's only good for as long as Jorhan can sell what we make."

Jessyla nodded. "You're cautious."

"Wouldn't you be?"

"Yes. Things change. Sometimes they change quickly. We've both discovered that."

Beltur was about to say more when Margrena entered the parlor, holding the empty basket. She looked to Beltur. "It was so good of you to stop by, and so kind to bring all of that to us. Please give Athaal and Meldryn our thanks."

Jessyla started to open her mouth.

"We still have quite a few chores to do, dear, to get ready for tomorrow," Margrena said quickly. "I'm certain we'll be seeing more of Beltur, Athaal, and Meldryn."

Jessyla stood, reluctantly, and Beltur did as well.

"I'm very glad that you liked what he sent, and I will convey your thanks." Beltur turned to Jessyla. "I very much enjoyed hearing how you and your mother are doing."

"I liked learning more about your smithing."

"We mustn't keep Beltur. I'm certain he will have a long and hard day tomorrow . . . as will you."

Beltur noticed that Grenara stood in the doorway to the kitchen, just behind Margrena, but the older woman said nothing, and her eyes were on Jessyla. He stepped forward and took the empty basket from Margrena, then turned back to Jessyla. "Thank you again. I enjoyed the conversation."

Jessyla moved to the door and opened it. As Beltur stepped past her, she murmured, "Do come back."

Just as the door closed, Beltur thought he heard a few words that he thought had to have come from Grenara.

". . . shabby-looking sort of black mage."

Were you meant to hear that? Most likely.

He shook his head. Still, he'd enjoyed the time with Jessyla, and he had the feeling that she had as well.

As he walked back along Crafters Way toward Bakers Lane, he thought over what Jessyla had said, especially that she'd felt the blackness on the other side of the front door and that she'd sensed that he'd not told the whole truth about what he earned. *Isn't that more than what most healers can sense?* But she'd told him earlier that she couldn't do what black mages could, and one thing that was certain about her was that she didn't lie. *But what exactly does that mean?*

XLV

When Beltur arrived at the smithy on oneday morning, Jorhan wasn't in the smithy itself, although coal had been added to the forge fire, and two new molds were laid out on one of the work benches. The heavy crucible stood beside the forge with chunks of copper in it, more melt material than Jorhan usually used, except for the straight-sword.

Beltur took off his tunic, hung it up, and waited.

Jorhan looked anything but happy when he appeared, perhaps a tenth of a glass later.

"What's the matter?" asked Beltur.

"We've got a bit of a problem. It's the Council."

"Are they telling you we can't forge cupridium?"

Jorhan shook his head. "They're telling me that I owe service."

"They told me I owed them time on the City Patrol. Does everyone owe some sort of service?"

"Every man does. Some women, like healers, do also."

"So you have to do something that will take you away from forging? Will you be able to forge at all?"

"It's not that. They've made me an offer we can't refuse," replied the smith almost disconsolately. "We need to forge five cupridium straight-swords. Before we can do anything else. If I don't, then I'll have to serve as a shieldman."

"They expect you to do that for nothing?"

"Might as well be. They'll give me the cost of the metal and three silvers for each blade. I can't do it without you."

Beltur didn't want to volunteer to do it for nothing. He waited.

So did Jorhan.

"What about just a silver a day, and nothing extra when we're doing the swords?" Beltur finally asked.

"You'd do that?" The relief on the smith's face was palpable.

"You've made it possible for me to make a living. I can't do it for nothing, but that seems fair to me. There is one thing, though."

Worry replaced the relieved expression.

"The City Patrol has changed my duty days to three-day and sevenday for the next two eightdays."

"Oh . . . thought they'd called you up, too."

"They've told Athaal he'll have to do something. No one's said anything to me. Why would they, when I'm already doing service with the City Patrol?"

"The Council can do almost anything it wants, it seems to me," replied Jorhan. "They say they always act within the law, but they're the ones who are making the law, and they've been known to change the laws whenever it suits them."

"Why would they want five cupridium straight-swords? Especially when they were so concerned about us forging them just days ago?"

"I asked. The Councilor's assistant said that was a Council matter. The Council doesn't have to explain, either." Jorhan snorted. "We might as well get started. I already made the molds."

"I saw them on the bench. I wondered." Beltur moved toward the forge fire.

"I'll need to get the molds heated, first, but if you'd work the bellows . . ."

Beltur nodded.

By the end of oneday, they had cast two of the straight-swords and a pair of delicate candlesticks.

When Beltur returned to the house, he didn't mention the problems with Jorhan and the Council because, somehow, he had the feeling that mentioning them would seem like he was complaining about only making a silver a day, and he feared that he'd come off as ungrateful and greedy, if not spoiled.

He was at the smithy early on twoday.

In the end, twoday ended up much the same as oneday, in that they only cast two more of the straight-swords and a small ornate platter.

At just before fourth glass, Jorhan turned to Beltur. "Thank you. I wanted to get those cast. It'll take me all of threeday, and maybe a lot longer to do the finish work on the blades. If you'd wait a moment, I need to get your silver." Jorhan immediately turned and left the smithy.

As he retrieved his worn dark gray tunic, Beltur wondered about that, since the smith usually hadn't needed to leave to get him his pay.

A silver a day is still good. In fact, Beltur suspected it was often more than what Athaal made, at least on some days.

Jorhan returned quickly. "Here's your silver for the day."

Beltur took it and slipped it into his wallet, then inclined his head. "Thank you."

The smith cleared his throat, and for a moment didn't look at Beltur, before he faced the young mage and said, "You might be wondering what happened to all the silvers I made on those other blades, seeing as they went for golds, and I gave you just a silver a day and two for each blade." Jorhan looked down. "Truth is . . . things hadn't been going all that well, and I owed almost ten golds to traders for copper and tin. With what we'd made on the blades and candelabra, I'd just paid them all off and bought more copper and tin when I got the Council summons." Jorhan offered an embarrassed smile. "I was hoping I could offer you a bit more once I'd cleared the debts . . ."

Beltur could sense the honesty behind the smith's words.

"I don't have much in the way of spare silvers because I won't get paid by the Council until after they get the blades. Oh, I have enough to pay you a silver a day, but not much extra. So . . ." Jorhan extended something to Beltur.

For a moment Beltur didn't recognize the small cupridium dagger, one of the first daggers that they had worked on, because it was in a tooled leather sheath. "Oh . . . you didn't have to."

"Aye, but I did, and more, but there's a regular bronze plaque in the grip, with your name. That's so as no one can claim it's anything but yours. Take a look."

Beltur eased the silver-gold blade out of the sheath, admiring the finish. Then he looked at the crosshatched bone grip and the inset bronze plate with the name BELTUR. "Thank you!" He meant it. He'd never owned anything as valuable as the dagger, let alone been given something with his own name forged in metal on it.

"I should be the one thanking you, seeing as you got me out of debt."

"And you kept me from going deeper into everyone's debt," returned Beltur.

"You'll be here on fourday, then?" asked Jorhan, as if he felt uncomfortable.

"I will."

"We might be able to cast that last straight-sword. I hope that the Council doesn't want more anytime soon."

So did Beltur, especially since he'd never dreamed of making a silver a day, and now, just as he was, and sometimes more . . . *But you can't tell how long you will . . . especially with the Prefect's army marching toward Elparta.* "Do you think that they will?"

"With the Council, they won't hesitate to demand anything if they think it's necessary. Especially if Elparta's threatened by the Prefect." Jorhan shook his head. "Don't know why rulers just don't tend to their own lands." He paused. "I'm just a smith, but I don't go around telling other smiths what to do or trying to take over their smithies." He offered a smile that seemed forced. "You need to go, Beltur. I could talk about this all night."

"It doesn't seem right, though."

"We can agree on that. I'll see you the day after to-morrow."

Beltur nodded, while he unfastened his belt and slipped the knife and scabbard in place, then tightened his belt and straightened. "Thank you so much for the knife. I've never had something like that. Ever."

"You deserve it. Without you, there wouldn't be any of them." Jorhan smiled happily.

The smith's expression made Beltur feel better as he walked down the lane.

As he walked westward toward the city, his fingers occasionally brushing the crosshatched bone grip of the knife, as if to assure himself that it was actually his, he was still wondering about why it was that, just as he was feeling he might be able to support himself, an attack by the very prefect who had driven him out of Gallos might snatch away his newfound self-sufficiency—*or semi-self-sufficiency*. On the one hand, he knew that the Prefect likely had long since forgotten about a former white and what might have happened to him, and even if he hadn't, he certainly wasn't starting a possible war just to make Beltur's life harder. At the same time, it was hard not to feel that it wasn't exactly fair. And yet, after seeing Grenara's small house, and recalling the appreciation and gratitude shown by the three healers for Meldryn's modest gifts, Beltur almost felt guilty for having asked for a silver a day.

He took a deep breath as he saw the city walls and the gate . . . and kept walking.

XLVI

Beltur thought he managed to keep his worries to himself, again, both on twoday night and at breakfast on threeday, at least enough so that neither Athaal nor Meldryn noticed or questioned him before he left to spend threeday on patrol with Laevoyt.

As usual, Beltur signed in at the duty desk, but the duty patroller, another man he'd not seen before, cleared his throat as Beltur laid down the pen. "Mage . . . the Patrol Mage needs a word with you before you start your patrol."

"Thank you." *Now what?* Was some trader complaining? Or had he done something else wrong and not even known it? He was still fretting when he stepped into the small study.

Osarus gestured to the chair without speaking.

Beltur sat and waited.

"So far, you've done a good job as a patrol mage, Beltur," began Osarus. "The City Patrol certainly couldn't ask for anything more. The Council, however, can."

"The Council?" Beltur didn't even pretend to understand.

"It's something the captain opposed," Osarus went on, as if he had something to say that he didn't wish to, "but he and I were overruled." The older mage lifted an envelope from the desk and handed it to Beltur. "You're being assigned to a military unit in preparation for the defense of Elparta. I've been told that you're to report on oneday."

Beltur took the envelope numbly, not certain what to think.

"Go ahead. You can open it. I'll answer any questions I can."

Beltur eased open the envelope and extracted the single sheet of paper. He read it slowly and carefully.

Beltur, Black Mage, attached to City Patrol
Residing at Crossed Lane and Bakers Lane

   Pursuant to the needs of the Council of Spidlar, you are hereby temporarily assigned, in lieu of duty in service to the City Patrol, to the Third Infantry Battalion, commanded by Majer Waeltur. You are to report to the Council Building on oneday morning, the tenth and last oneday of Harvest, on or before seventh glass, for briefing and instructions on your duties.

   This duty will require all your time until further notice. It is suggested that you make the necessary arrangements to facilitate this commitment.

          For the Council,
          Jhaldrak, Councilor from Elparta

Beltur read the short missive again. The words "require all your time" struck him with almost the force of a blow. First, there had been the Council requirement imposed on Jorhan . . . and then the one hitting him—except they both hit him. He shook his head. No . . . the two separate requirements had a double impact—and the impact would be even harder on Jorhan.

"It's not something that the City Patrol needs, or wants. We've suggested you'd benefit the city more here, but the Council doesn't see it that way."

If the City Patrol can't change this . . . He wanted to shake his head. He didn't. He finally managed to ask,

"Do you know what I'm supposed to do for this infantry battalion?"

"That's up to the commanding officer, but usually it's providing shields, or some other form of magery consistent with your abilities."

"The only really strong skill I have is with shields and containments."

Osarus nodded. "Make sure the commander knows that." He stood. "I'd much rather have had you stay here."

"Thank you." Beltur inclined his head and left the study, still clutching the envelope and the orders.

Once he reached the duty area, he read the sheet again. He was still looking at it when Laevoyt appeared.

"You're looking worried. Are you all right?" asked the patroller.

"The Council is transferring me to an infantry battalion, beginning on oneday."

"Why in the name of the Rational Stars would they do that? Black mages can't throw chaos-bolts and rip things apart. You're doing much more for Elparta as a patrol mage."

"That's what Osarus said. He said the Council overruled both him and the Patrol captain." Beltur carefully replaced the letter in the envelope and slipped it inside his tunic.

"That's not good," said Laevoyt. "It sounds like they're really worried about the Gallosians." He turned. "We'd best be on our way."

Once they were out on Patrol Street, Beltur asked, "Should I try the concealment from here?"

"It can't hurt."

Beltur raised the concealment, still thinking about all that had happened in the last eightday or so, from having the Council—and Cohndar—claim that he and Jorhan were falsely claiming to be forging cupridium to Jorhan's being tasked to produce swords for a price barely above his costs, and now his being removed from both being a patrol mage and helping Jorhan.

Could Raymandyl help? He'd just have to see. Beltur had planned to go to the Council building anyway that afternoon to collect his pay. If Raymandyl couldn't do anything, at least with the letter, Beltur could talk about the matter with Athaal and Meldryn, since now Jorhan would be the one to suffer the most if Beltur wasn't there to help him.

He pushed all of those thoughts away. In the meantime, he needed to concentrate on the task at hand and seeing if he could sense any more light-fingers or cutpurses, or even any smash-and-grab types.

By ninth glass, while he'd sensed some chaos flickers, they were intermittent and far and few between. There weren't any more by the first glass of the afternoon, and by fourth glass, when Beltur dropped the concealment as he neared the corner to meet with the patroller, he still had not found any trace of theft. At that moment, he sensed a bit of chaotic thought that quickly vanished and caught a few murmured words from somewhere behind him.

". . . see? Told you the mage was around . . ."

". . . thought most of 'em were with the armsmen . . ."

". . . not this one . . ."

Beltur smiled wryly as he walked toward Jorhan. He couldn't do anything about thoughts.

When the two were back at headquarters, Beltur signed the duty book quickly and hurried out because he definitely wanted to get paid, especially since his immediate future earnings looked to be considerably less than he'd hoped. He didn't run, but he definitely walked very fast on his way to the Council building. Just outside the north door, he took a deep breath, composed himself, and then entered. No one was there except Raymandyl.

"You're here a day sooner and almost half a glass earlier," said the clerk as Beltur hurried toward the table desk.

"That's because my duty day was switched to three-day." Beltur extracted the three tokens and handed them over. "There are these. A scurf and two light-fingers. A very well-dressed scurf."

Raymandyl took the tokens. "Those are the worst kind, I hear." He set the two ledgers on the desk, easing one forward for Beltur to sign. "That's two silvers for your pay and six for the tokens. You're doing well."

"That's about to come to an end." Beltur paused, then gathered himself together. "You recall that I've been working for Jorhan. Well, one of the projects we managed was to forge cupridium. We forged several blades. Then the Council gave Jorhan a choice. He could be a shieldman or forge cupridium blades for the Council. The problem is that, if I have to go off and protect an infantry battalion . . ."

"Jorhan can't forge those blades?"

"That's right. Osarus, the Patrol Mage, told me that he and the Patrol captain asked that I not be transferred, but they were overruled."

"Hmmmm . . ."

"I don't think it's fair to Jorhan. That might sound selfish on my part, because I'd rather forge than fight, but I do know he can't forge those blades the Council wants if I'm not there."

"I'm just a clerk, Beltur."

Beltur smiled humorously. "I doubt you're just a clerk. You might know who should know that sending me off will stop the supply of cupridium blades. If that's what the Council wants, I'm not one to stand in their way, but I worry that someone doesn't know it takes both a smith and a mage to forge cupridium. You might know who to tell. I just thought I'd ask."

"I'll pass that along. That's all I can do, Beltur."

"I don't expect you to do anything that would cause problems, but the Council wants the cupridium swords, and they can't get them if I'm spending all my time with the Third Infantry Battalion."

"That's where you're being assigned?" Raymandyl raised his eyebrows.

"That's what the missive or dispatch I got says."

The clerk shook his head. "That doesn't seem to make much sense. I can let someone know, but until you hear differently—and officially—follow the orders you've received."

"I wouldn't think of anything else."

"Good."

Beltur inclined his head. "Thank you. I do appreciate it."

"Give my best to Athaal and Meldryn."

"I certainly will." Beltur turned, hoping he'd done the right thing, but also feeling that he couldn't always rely on Athaal and Meldryn, who might well be having problems of their own if the Council was ordering all mages into some form of service to the Council.

As always, he carried personal shields on the walk back to the house, and he found himself looking at the people he passed. Nothing seemed any different from any other afternoon, and the idea that a Gallosian army was approaching Elparta seemed almost unreal.

Beltur heard Athaal's and Meldryn's voices as soon as he stepped inside the front door.

". . . could ruin us . . . set us back . . ."

". . . Council doesn't care . . ."

". . . been through this already . . ."

Given the intensity of the conversion, Beltur didn't

want to seem to be sneaking up on the couple, and he called out loudly, "I'm back from Patrol duty!" Then he walked back toward the kitchen to find Meldryn and Athaal seated at the table.

"How was your day?" asked Athaal immediately.

"I wouldn't say it was the best. Beginning on oneday, I've been relieved from City Patrol and transferred to the Third Infantry Battalion. According to Patrol Mage Osarus, both he and the captain protested and were overruled."

"They don't want to make any exceptions," said Meldryn. "They think every mage will come up with a reason not to serve with the armed forces."

"I have to report to the Council building early on oneday morning."

"Almost all mages are being required to do that," said Athaal.

"Including you?"

"Including me," replied Athaal.

"I did bring up one difficulty with my serving. If I spend all my time with the infantry, I can't help Jorhan make the cupridium blades the Council also wants. I told Raymandyl that. He said he'd pass it on."

"That might work," offered Athaal.

"It's a question of what the Council wants," said Beltur. "Me in the infantry or cupridium blades for the Council."

"They'll find a way to get both," replied Meldryn, "or something similar."

"I didn't think it was fair for Jorhan to be a shieldman because I couldn't help him with the forging."

"They threatened that?" asked Athaal.

"He told me that on oneday. That's when we started on the first of the straight-swords." Beltur paused. "You said that the Council doesn't want any mages to escape serving?"

"In some way or another," replied Meldryn. "I've been requested to supply bread—for which we'll be paid just about what it will cost to bake it."

"That means Mel will have to work even longer days to pay for anything else."

"I did get paid today." Beltur took two silvers from his wallet and put them on the table. "I know it's not a lot . . ."

Both the other two smiled.

"The thought and concern is worth as much as the coin," said Meldryn.

"You've been good to me when others haven't." At that, he thought of Cohndar and Waensyn. "Did you ever talk to Cohndar?"

Meldryn shook his head. "He's been avoiding me, and so has Waensyn. Neither has talked to Felsyn lately, either."

"Cohndar met with Councilor Rendaal yesterday, according to Veroyt," said Athaal. "I'd meant to tell you."

"Because Jhaldrak wasn't happy with Cohndar?" asked Meldryn.

"Veroyt thinks so, but he doesn't know."

"That's not good. Rendaal is very, very traditional," said Meldryn.

"I don't know that there's anything we can do. Not right now."

"No, there isn't. Except be very careful."

Beltur had the feeling that they were all going to have to be careful.

XLVII

As soon as Beltur reached Jorhan's smithy on fourday, he related what had happened, from his own orders to report for assignment to an infantry battalion to his efforts to point out the effect that would have on the Council's need for cupridium swords. He also mentioned that Athaal and Meldryn had been assigned to various duties.

"Hope you'll give us better luck with the Council than I've ever had," replied the smith sourly.

"So do I, but all I could do was to point out the situation."

"Doesn't seem like the Council knows what it's doing." Jorhan punctuated his words with a snort.

"Councilor Jhaldrak has to know that it takes both of us to forge cupridium."

"Could be that he didn't bother to tell anyone that when the Council ordered all the mages to do whatever they're supposed to do. Really bright folks forget that not everyone knows what they know. Some councilors might act the same way."

And mages like Cohndar just might forget to remind them. "We'll just have to see. They haven't asked for more blades, have they?"

"Of course. They want five sabres, too."

"Well . . . we've got three days," said Beltur. "I can work longer if that will help. At least, we should be able to finish the last straight-sword and those sabres this eightday. By then, maybe someone will decide whether they really want cupridium blades."

"They'll want them. They just don't want to pay

what they're worth. Ten blades? That won't outfit a squad. Some trader on the Council likely wants them, hoping to sell them at a profit once the fighting's over."

"Or they'll give them to a relative who is fighting, thinking it might help them?"

"And probably make them pay for the blade in the process," replied Jorhan. "I've never seen a trader who wasn't figuring a way to make more coins out of everything . . . and anything."

But don't we all? Even as he thought that, Beltur realized that wasn't quite what the smith meant. "You mean making coins at someone else's expense, rather than by honest pay for honest work or goods?"

"That's exactly what I meant." Jorhan shook his head. "Jawing about traders won't get those blades forged."

Beltur immediately stripped off his tunic and then headed toward the forge, wondering just what honest pay might be. If two silvers a day was a fair and honest wage for his helping Jorhan to make cupridium—and Beltur thought it was . . . except that was fair when Jorhan could sell a blade at five golds. He smiled wryly. A silver a day was far better than the alternatives, and those silvers weren't going to be coming in for much longer.

By the end of fourday, they had cast another straight-sword and a sabre, plus a small platter, and Beltur didn't leave the smithy until almost half past fourth glass.

Fiveday was better, because the sabres were smaller, and they managed to cast three sabres, and on sixday, they managed two more sabres and a pair of candle-sticks.

"That's an extra sabre, just in case," Jorhan said as Beltur donned his tunic. "Here's your three silvers."

"Thank you." Beltur paused as he put the coins in his wallet with the others there because he needed to pay the seamstress. "Once this . . . is over . . . do you want . . . I'm not pushing . . ."

"Of course I do! Together we've just started." Jorhan paused. "That's if . . . well, if things go right for the two of us."

"You don't think they'll really make you a shieldman, do you?"

"It might have been a threat. Then, again, it might not. Sometimes, the Council's not too smart, but it's not a good idea to say so real loud."

Beltur could definitely see that, one reason why he'd mentioned the problem with forging cupridium blades to Raymandyl rather than to even Veroyt. *But the Prefect and Arms-Mage Wyath didn't want to hear anything they didn't agree with, either. Is the Council any different?* "Maybe it's that way with anyone who rules a land?"

"That might be. I've heard that the Viscount doesn't listen too well, either. A frigging shame. What's the point of having people who can give you advice if you don't listen? Except people with golds and power always think they know better, except that there are times they don't. You're a mage. I don't tell you how to put order and chaos in the melt. You can figure that better than me."

"And I don't tell you how to make molds and forge."

"That's right. Times are that two heads can be better than one. The thing is, you've got to know when those times are . . ." Abruptly, Jorhan broke off his words and laughed. "I could talk on and on. It won't change things. I've got things to finish, and I'm sure you do as well."

"Until . . . well . . . whenever we can manage," Beltur finally said. "I've really liked working with you. I hope it won't be too long before we can get back together."

"That makes two of us, Mage. That it does."

Beltur was feeling gloomy as he walked down the lane to the road. It all seemed so stupid. Making Jorhan a shieldman wasn't going to change anything in the fighting. And the few armsmen that Beltur could shield, out of the hundreds and thousands who might be fighting, wouldn't likely change much, either. More and better blades just might.

He shook his head and kept walking.

After walking less than a hundred yards, he decided he'd definitely better work on trying to improve his shields and containments. The stronger his shields, the better his chances.

For all his resolve, he didn't have much success in trying to hold five separate shields at once. Although he could create the fifth one, he could only hold it for a moment or two, and he was feeling exhausted and had begun to sweat again by the time he neared the southeast gate. The cooler wind out of the northwest helped cool him a little once he stopped practicing and for the last hundred yards before the gate.

Once inside Elparta proper, he headed north on the wall road until he reached Tailors Way, where he turned west and proceeded to Celinya's doorway. He knocked and waited for the peephole to open.

"Celinya, it's Beltur. Are the trousers and tunic ready?"

Only the slightest click of the latch preceded the open door. Celinya stood largely behind the door and closed and latched it quickly after Beltur entered. He noticed for the first time the heavy iron of the latch and latch plate.

"Your trousers and tunic are on the rack, if you would care to look at them."

"Thank you." Beltur moved to the rack. For several long moments, he just looked at the black tunic hanging on the rack. He'd never seen a tunic that fine. At least, it didn't seem that way to him.

"You should see how it fits."

Beltur slipped off his old tunic, conscious of just how worn it was in comparison to the deep black tunic before him, and laid it on the empty worktable. The new tunic fit perfectly, and he could sense its order and harmony as he moved and walked around in it. He took it off, almost regretfully, and replaced it on the rack.

"You should also try on the trousers. I will leave."

"Shouldn't I pay you first, if . . ."

A smile crossed Celinya's face, if briefly. "I do not have to ask that of you. Try them on."

When she opened the door, Beltur caught sight of a foyer with a staircase leading upstairs. He could also sense someone else in the room beyond, possibly a child.

Beltur stripped off his trousers, also worn, and tried on the new pair, which matched exactly the tunic, a harmony that was lacking in his present attire, whose fabric and colors only generally resembled each other.

After he had taken off the new trousers and redressed himself, he knocked gently on the rear door, then stepped back and waited for the seamstress to return.

"I owe you four silvers and six. Is that right?"

Celinya nodded.

"These are very good," Beltur said, handing her five silvers. "I would give you more, but I'm not that well off."

"You are a black mage and a good man. Thank you." Celinya paused. "In time, you will come back?"

"I will. I certainly will." He watched as she carefully folded the tunic and trousers and then wrapped them in another scrap-cloth bag that she handed to him.

After he left the seamstress and walked down Tailors

Lane toward Bakers Lane, he still couldn't believe just how good the tailoring and cloth were on his new garments. *But then, for eight silvers they should be.* Still, he was pleased, very pleased. He also knew he'd look much better the next time he called on Jessyla.

While he pondered the problem of forging cupridium blades, and why the Council seemed so adamant that he shouldn't be allowed to help Jorhan, there was still a certain spring in his step when he entered the house.

"You look happy," observed Athaal from where he stood in the parlor as Beltur walked toward the staircase.

Beltur stopped, surprised to see Athaal in the parlor. "I just got a new tunic and trousers from Celinya."

"You got a tunic, too?"

"You said I needed a better one the other day."

"You must have gone to see Celinya right after that." Athaal smiled.

"Haven't I tried to take your advice?" replied Beltur. *Even if I anticipated it?*

"He just wishes a few others would," said Meldryn from behind Beltur.

"Who? The Council?"

"Among others," replied Athaal. "Veroyt listens, but Jhaldrak and the other councilors don't always listen to him."

"About what?" asked Beltur.

"How to use black mages more effectively against the Gallosians. Spreading us out among the various companies isn't going to be very effective, not when most mages can only shield a few people." Athaal shook his head.

"I was thinking about that on the way back from Jorhan's," Beltur admitted. "That forging blades might be a better use of my talents than shielding a handful of armsmen."

"If you can think of that, and I can . . ." Athaal shook his head.

"They have an exaggerated sense of our abilities," said Meldryn. "They believe that all the words of the ancient legends are true, and that we can move mountains and topple cities the way the legendary Nylan did."

"You don't think he did all that?" asked Beltur.

"He doubtless did some of it. But probably there was just a great earthquake, and he took credit for it. Or perhaps he didn't, and the scriveners who wrote the accounts gave him credit." Meldryn shrugged. "Then, possibly, he might have been that powerful. That doesn't mean that the rest of us are. I've never run across a mage that could do a fraction of what's attributed to Nylan—or even Saryn of the black blades."

"Could it be because they came from the Rational Stars?" asked Beltur.

"That might be, but we certainly don't, and the Council should recognize that, if anyone should. They aren't faulted for not having huge fireships that dominate the oceans, but we're expected to work miracles when they can't."

"Miracles or not," said Athaal with a smile, "Beltur's probably getting hungry. I know I am, and it's getting late."

"I'm sorry," replied Beltur. "I worked a little later so that we could finish casting the last blade of the second batch the Council wanted, and then I had to stop by Celinya's to pick up my tunic and trousers."

"You'll wear them the next time you visit Margrena and Jessyla?" Athaal grinned. "You're sure?"

Beltur flushed.

Both the others laughed.

"Let Beltur put away his new clothes, and then we'll eat," declared Meldryn.

XLVIII

Beltur was at City Patrol headquarters at the usual time on sevenday. He'd been careful to leave the house on time, because being late on his last day wouldn't have left the right impression, and Beltur had the feeling he'd need all the goodwill possible in the eightdays to come, especially given the animosity that Waensyn and Cohndar seemed to bear toward him.

Laevoyt was just signing the duty book when Beltur entered the building and hurried to the desk to sign in after his partner.

When the two started walking down Patrol Street, Laevoyt turned his head toward Beltur and asked, "You still headed off to be an arms-mage on oneday?"

"So far as I know. Almost all the mages in Elparta are supposed to report to the Council building then. Except Patrol Mage Osarus, I think."

"That'd be right. The Council must be summoning armsmen from everywhere. A battalion of armsmen from Kleth marched in last night. I saw them on my way off duty."

"I didn't see any on the way here."

Laevoyt shook his head. "You won't. Not during the day. I'm just glad I don't work the evening duty, especially along the riverfront. The taverns and public rooms there will be crowded." The patroller glanced skyward. "It's hazy. We might see some rain later."

"Should I raise a concealment before we get near the square?"

"There's no point on sevenday. Everyone knows there's a mage on duty on sevenday. Leastwise, any of the longtime cutpurses and light-fingers. The amateurs won't notice one way or another, and the most successful light-fingers are the ones we likely won't notice. Neither will their victims until much, much later."

Beltur smiled at Laevoyt's cheerful cynicism.

The two parted at the corner, with Beltur continuing along the edge of the square on Patrol Street and Laevoyt turning south on West Street. Beltur kept walking, not raising a concealment, but listening as carefully as he could.

". . . just saw the mage . . ."

". . . be the last time you see him for a while . . . be here anyway . . ."

Beltur concentrated on sensing chaos flickers, but there weren't many, not that he expected anything different early in the day. Partway down East Street, he raised a concealment and then turned in to the square, moving carefully along the line of tables and stalls that held all manner of baskets—grass baskets, reed baskets, wicker baskets, small baskets, and baskets large enough to hold a small woman standing. He didn't expect thieves there, but the space between the lines of vendors was less crowded, and he could move more easily into the center of the square.

After a time, he dropped the concealment and walked through other lines of vendors, especially near the silks and jewelry, but neither saw nor sensed anything. He did see a shimmersilk scarf of green and blue that would have looked striking on Jessyla, not that he could have afforded it, not after paying for his tunic and trousers . . . and the silvers he'd given Athaal and Meldryn.

At ninth glass, he returned to the corner of Patrol and West Streets, where he only had to wait a few moments before Laevoyt arrived.

The tall patroller offered an inquiring look.

"I haven't seen or heard anything. What about you?" asked Beltur.

"It's quiet. The next glass or so will tell if it's going to stay that way. I'd wager that it will. Better that way."

"We'll try and keep it that way."

With a smile, Laevoyt turned away and walked toward East Street.

Beltur raised a concealment and returned to the stalls near the jewels and silks.

Although the day was pleasant, for some reason he was thirsty, and more than ready for the small mug of ale. Just before noon, he dropped the concealment and made his way to Fosset's cart. "Could you spare a mug of that wonderful ale?"

"That I could." Fosset pulled a small mug off the rack, filled it, and handed it to Beltur.

Beltur took a swallow. The medium-dark ale tasted better than he recalled, perhaps because his throat was so dry. "Have you heard anything about the Prefect or the Gallosians?"

"I can't say as I have. My uncle told me last night that there are thousands of troopers on the old west road that comes down the far side of the river, and that there haven't been any flatboats at the south piers in the last three days."

"That might mean that the Prefect is moving men down the river."

"More likely siege machines, trebuchets, that sort of thing. Men and horses can walk."

Beltur had heard of trebuchets, but had certainly never seen one. He also wondered if Wyath's white mages would accompany the troopers or the boats. *Both probably.* "How long do you think it will be before they show up?"

"At least another three days. That's the soonest."

That made sense to Beltur. It had taken him and

Athaal almost an eightday to come down the river from Portalya.

"That was good ale," Beltur said after his last swallow when he handed the mug back to Fosset. "Thank you."

"You going to work with the armsmen, like some of the other mages?"

"That's what they tell me. I'll find out more tomorrow."

"I don't know what the Prefect thinks he'll gain by attacking Elparta. Years back, his grandsire did, and all he did was lose men."

"The Prefect wants what he wants."

"We all do, but there's a difference between wanting and getting. Sometimes, wanting what you can't have is starting down the road to ruin."

"That doesn't stop some people."

"Then they'll get what they deserve." Fosset shook his head.

Much as he hoped otherwise, Beltur wasn't so certain. So far, the Prefect was getting what he was taking, not what Beltur thought he deserved.

For all of Beltur's concealments and walking through and around the square, the remainder of the day was as unexciting as Laevoyt had hoped, and at just after fourth glass, the two of them met on the northwest corner and walked toward Patrol headquarters.

"A fine quiet day. That was good," affirmed the patroller.

"You said it would be. Do you get tomorrow off?"

"Not this eightday. Someone has to keep the peace on eightday. Tomorrow's my turn. I'll get oneday off instead."

"How many eightdays do you work?"

"Two out of every season. That's the same for all patrollers. We get off either sevenday or oneday, depending on the rotation."

Beltur nodded.

They walked the rest of the way to headquarters without talking.

After signing out, Beltur turned to Laevoyt. "Tomorrow, I report to the Council and find out what I'll be doing with the infantry battalion. I don't know when I'll see you, but it was good working with you."

"You made it very quiet, and that was good." Laevoyt's smile vanished. "Quiet's good in fighting, too. Don't let some officer make a hero out of you. Do what you do, and don't make a fuss. That's what's made you a good patrol mage. It'll serve you well with armsmen, too."

The quiet intensity in Laevoyt's voice stunned Beltur, and for a moment, he could say nothing. "Thank you. I hadn't thought of it that way."

"Wouldn't want to lose a good patrol mage. Best of fortune to you."

"The same to you. Take care."

With an almost sad smile and a nod, the tall patroller turned and headed toward the door.

Beltur followed, but, once outside, he headed north, and Laevoyt turned south.

XLIX

Eightday morning, Beltur slept late—or late for him, which was almost until seventh glass. Meldryn and Athaal were still at the kitchen table when he came down the stairs, unwashed and unshaven.

"How are you going to spend your last day of comparative freedom?" asked Athaal.

"Will it be that bad as a mage for an infantry battalion?"

Athaal laughed sardonically. "I have no idea. Nothing like this has happened before."

"Do any of the other mages know?"

"If they do, they're not saying," replied Meldryn. "Cohndar keeps avoiding me, and no one I've been able to see has even glimpsed Waensyn since he was here. Felsyn just complains about all of us being ordered into some sort of duty. Mharkyn's younger than Athaal, not all that much older than you, and he doesn't know anything. Neither does Lhadoraak. I haven't seen any other mages lately, but part of that's because it's been so busy at the bakery."

"No one seems that worried about the Prefect," said Beltur as he poured an ale and then headed to the table, where he sat down.

"Do you think they should be?" asked Athaal.

"Wyath's mages can't do much against stoneworks, but they could kill a lot of armsmen."

"That suggests that his marshal will use the mages to keep our forces away from his engineers," said Meldryn, "while they use trebuchets to batter the walls down."

"I doubt that's any secret," said Athaal. "That's why the Council wants mages. So they can get to the siege-works, but since the Gallosian armsmen are coming by road, they'll have to cross the river first, and they'll need boats before they can set up their siege engines."

"So the first fighting will be to keep them from landing on the east side of the river?" asked Beltur.

"That's a guess on my part." Meldryn shrugged. "I've never been an armsman." He paused. "Have you ever fought armsmen?"

"I've held shields to protect armsmen so that they could fight. That's what I did best. I guess you could call the Analerian raiders armsmen."

"Does the Council know that?" asked Athaal.

"I'd doubt it. No one ever asked me." Beltur scooped the remaining egg and mutton hash onto his platter and took the small loaf that had clearly been left for him.

"They just might tomorrow," said Meldryn. "Then they might not. It's been years since the Suthyans tried to take Diev. That was the last time anyone here really fought."

"That's not good," ventured Beltur after swallowing some of the hash. "Some of the Gallosian armsmen have been fighting the Analerian raiders and herders on and off for years."

"They also put down a revolt in Kyphros less than ten years ago."

"I never heard about that," replied Beltur.

"There probably wasn't any reason that you would have," said Meldryn, standing. "We'll leave the food and the kitchen to you."

"I'll take care of it," Beltur replied cheerfully.

By the time he finished eating and cleaning up the kitchen, both Meldryn and Athaal had left the house to "go visiting." Beltur didn't ask who or where.

Beltur took his time eating, cleaning the kitchen, and then heading back upstairs to wash and shave. He finally donned his new shirt and trousers and went downstairs to the parlor, where he spent a glass reading more in *On Healing*. A glass was more than enough. He looked among the other books in the small bookcase, but didn't see any histories or anything about magery.

In the end, he picked up a thin book entitled, *Considerations on the Nature of Man*, one that looked almost new, although the dust that sifted from the binding when he picked it up suggested it wasn't that new, and that it certainly hadn't been read recently. In the middle of the second page, a paragraph caught his eye, and he reread it.

Some learned scholars claim that men are orderly and well-mannered by nature, and become corrupted by the necessity to obtain the wherewithal with which to live. Others, equally learned, claim that men are born self-centered, and unless taught otherwise, will always strive for their own personal betterment, regardless of the cost inflicted upon others. I will claim neither, seeing as the world has men of both qualities, as well as those with both in assorted and not always sanguine mixtures and shadings. The question for any who would rule is not from where we came or how we arrived at the personages we have become, but how best to govern a land when it contains a myriad of people whose qualities range from the exemplary to the despicable . . .

"Very practical," murmured Beltur, turning back to the title page to see the name of the author, a name he had skipped over. The name was Heldry of Lydiar. He'd never heard of the man, or scholar, or whatever he had been. He paused. Or had he? *Heldry the Mad? Could they be the same person?* How likely was it that there were two Heldrys from Lydiar? Still . . .

He shook his head.

He read a little longer, but his eyes kept skipping over the words. He finally stood, slightly before noon, replaced the volume on the shelf, and donned his new tunic.

Moments later he was walking northward on Bakers Lane, wondering what if anything Jessyla would say about his new tunic and trousers. He had no doubt that Grenara would notice, but he doubted she'd offer a word. The day was similar to those previous, except there was a high overcast and only the slightest hint of a breeze.

He'd only walked about three blocks when he looked down a cross street toward the river, where he noticed armsmen in blue uniforms gathered outside a building, most likely a tavern or a public room. *How many will there be before it's all over?* He immediately had a second thought. *What if the fighting drags out and goes on and on?*

He pushed those thoughts out of his mind and kept walking, eventually turning east on Crafters Way and continuing to Grenara's house, where he knocked on the door.

The door opened, and Grenara looked at him. "They're not here. I don't know where they are or when they'll be back."

Beltur could tell that she was half lying, since he could sense that no one else was in the house, but the chaotic nature of the order around the older healer suggested that she very well did know where Margrena and Jessyla were and when they would be likely to return. "Oh?"

"That's all I have to say." Abruptly she stepped back and closed the door.

For a moment, Beltur just stood there. He'd known that Grenara didn't care much for him, but the suddenness and coldness of her rebuff had still stunned him.

He managed a wry smile, then turned and walked back to the nearest corner, from where he could see the door of the house, but where Grenara couldn't see him without stepping outside. Then he waited, watching as people walked by, or the occasional wagon or coach rolled by, wheels sometimes whispering, sometimes rumbling. A couple walked past, not all that much older than Beltur and Jessyla, except she was clearly expecting.

Then an older white-haired man with a cane approached. He stopped and looked at Beltur. "What are you doing here, young mage, with the Gallosians on their way?"

"I'm off-duty, and waiting for a friend."

"Hmmm." Then the oldster hobbled away, leaning heavily on his cane.

Beltur couldn't sense any chaos-infection in him, just the lower level of linked order and chaos that seemed to come with age. After a time, he walked around the corner and back. There was still no sign of the two healers.

Close to a glass later, Beltur made his way back to the house on Bakers Lane. When he stepped inside, he discovered Athaal and Meldryn sitting in the parlor talking.

Meldryn studied Beltur for a long moment. "Celinya made those, didn't she?"

"She did. You said she was good and wouldn't be as costly as some of the tailors."

"She did a very good job. You wore them to see Jessyla, I take it."

"I wore them. I hoped to see her. She wasn't there. I thought I'd wear my better tunic and trousers. That way I wouldn't look so shabby."

"Shabby?" asked Athaal

"The last time I visited, Grenara told Margrena that I was a shabby-looking black mage. I wasn't supposed to hear that. I'd already ordered these." Beltur sat in the straight-backed chair.

"I've never seen Grenara," said Meldryn. "It appears unlikely that I'll ever wish to."

"She's not quite that bad," said Athaal. "She's protective of her niece. She'll be nicer once she gets to know Beltur better."

"Perhaps." Beltur had his doubts.

"I've never met her," added Meldryn, "but I'm inclined to share Beltur's view."

"I'd like to hope," replied Athaal.

Beltur shifted his weight in the chair. He really didn't want to talk about Grenara. "Before I left I got overwhelmed by reading the healing book, so I picked up another one. *Considerations on the Nature of Man*." Beltur waited. He hesitated to ask if either had read it.

"I tried, years ago," said Meldryn. "It seemed well thought out, but . . ." He shrugged. "It seemed more about ruling, and I knew I was never going to rule anything."

"Where did it come from?"

"Oh, it was in my father's bookcase. No one else wanted the books. It seemed a shame to leave it. I did want the book on healing and some of the others."

"Was your father a healer?"

"He was. He was very good. He just couldn't heal himself."

"Most healers can't, I understand."

"That's right. Ironic, isn't it?"

"Unfair, I'd say," replied Beltur. "They do so much for others, and often risk their lives doing it, at least from what I've heard."

Athaal stood. "I'm sorry to hear that about Grenara. I'll still think hopeful thoughts." He stretched. "We were getting ready to take a nap."

"Then I'll stay down here and read, if that's all right."

"You could do worse," said Meldryn with a smile as he rose.

"I hope not," replied Beltur wryly.

"One other thing," said Meldryn. "If you do see your lady friend, there are several loaves in the cold oven. You could take two or three. They're a day old, but . . ."

"Thank you."

After the two went upstairs, Beltur debated between *On Healing* and *Considerations on the Nature of Man*, then picked up the slender volume he had started earlier in the day. As Meldryn had indicated, there was a definite emphasis on ruling. He read several more pages before another section struck him.

> ... those who praise the power of another, especially of a ruler or one placed in a position of authority over others, should be treated as flatterers seeking a favor or advantage, because power and position are obvious to the discerning. Praising one for the obvious also suggests in itself a feeling that the person praised is not intelligent enough to understand his power or is needy enough to require constant affirmation ...

Beltur nodded. *Most likely Heldry the Mad.* Except from the writing he didn't seem that mad. Beltur continued reading.

Just after the city chimes struck third glass, there was a determined set of knocks on the door. Beltur set aside *Considerations* and made his way to the front door. Even before he opened it, he could sense great order with a certain amount of superficial chaos.

Jessyla stood there.

"I went to see you—"

"I know, and I'm absolutely furious at Auntie! She could have told you."

"She would only say that she didn't know when you'd be back, and she wouldn't say where you were. Would you like to come in?"

Jessyla smiled. "I would. Would that be all right?"

"If we're quiet. They're upstairs ... napping."

Jessyla raised her eyebrows.

"I know," replied Beltur, "but that's what they said." *And if that's the way they want to put it, that's their choice, not mine.* He stepped back from the door.

Jessyla entered the house, saying, "We'll be quiet." She sat down on one end of the padded and backed bench and pointed to the other end. "Sit there. That way we won't have to talk loudly."

As he seated himself exactly where she had pointed, Beltur wondered about her real reasons for wanting him that close, but he didn't sense any chaos of confusion, and in fact, he sensed that she was already calmer than when she had arrived, but he realized something that he should have seen immediately. "You came alone? There are armsmen from Kleth and elsewhere all over the city. I saw quite a number when I walked to your aunt's."

"They won't touch a healer. Besides, I was so mad I was walking at almost a run. I knew you'd come by, but Mother said our errands wouldn't take long. When we got back, Auntie wouldn't even look at me. So I asked her if you had. She said that you couldn't stay. I could tell she was lying, and I just told her I needed to apologize to you for her rudeness, and I left."

"What did your mother say?"

"I didn't let her say anything. I did tell her that you'd walk me back."

Beltur grinned. "And if I hadn't been here?"

"I knew you would be." She smiled back at him. "If you weren't, Athaal would have done it, and that would have embarrassed Auntie even more."

"I can't say I'm not glad that you're here."

"I'd much rather be here than there. It's . . . just . . ." She shook her head.

"That you feel something's not right . . . not the way it should be?"

"Oh, no. I feel perfectly comfortable here. I meant at Auntie's."

"So did I."

Jessyla dropped her eyes for just a moment, then looked directly at Beltur.

He could feel the intense directness. He wasn't quite certain what to say before she spoke again.

"You have a new tunic and trousers. You look good in them."

"Thank you."

"Mother would be impressed. Auntie wouldn't. She doesn't think much of men. She doesn't think much of most people, in fact."

Beltur decided not to comment on that. Instead, he offered something he'd thought more than once. "You're more than just a healer."

"But I'm less than a mage, and there aren't any women who are mages anyway." A slightly disconsolate tone permeated her words.

"Saryn and Ayrlyn were mages, if not more. So was Ryba."

"That was a long time ago."

"You're every bit as black as Athaal or Waensyn."

"Please don't compare me to that little, little man. I know you were trying to be helpful, but . . ."

"Meldryn, Athaal, and Waensyn are the only . . . well, that's not true. I've met Osarus—he's the Patrol Mage—and Cohndar, but Meldryn and Athaal are the only ones I've spent any real time with."

"You really don't like being untruthful, even unintentionally."

"No. Sometimes, I just don't say things, though."

Jessyla laughed, softly and somehow warmly. "That answer says it all."

Beltur smiled wryly. "I suppose it does."

"I've met more blacks than that, and you're not like any of them."

"That could be because I'm not really a black. That's what Cohndar thinks. He compared me to a mongrel dog."

"To your face?"

"No. To the councilor's assistant, Veroyt. Veroyt told Athaal, and Athaal would have known if Veroyt lied."

Jessyla only frowned for a moment. "In a way, that's a sort of compliment."

"Being a mongrel is a compliment?"

"Well . . . it means you're not a guard dog, not a lapdog, and not a herding dog that does someone else's bidding."

"All that says what I'm not. Just what am I, then?"

"Isn't that what you have to discover?"

"The same goes for you, I think," Beltur pointed out. "How exactly do we do that?"

"Aren't you already doing that? You're the first one to forge cupridium in hundreds of years."

"It takes both Jorhan and me, and I don't know that there aren't mages and smiths doing that somewhere else in the world."

"All right," said Jessyla, with a hint of exasperation in her voice, "you're the only ones that have done it in Candar in hundreds of years. That's still something." She paused, then again looked directly at him. "Isn't it?"

"It is."

"But it's not enough. Is that what you're not saying?"

"Is being just a healer enough for you?"

"You know it's not."

Beltur shook his head. "We both want to do more, and neither one of us knows how. You at least know what you want. I just know that life has to be more than forging cupridium and earning coins."

"There's nothing wrong with having coins."

Beltur immediately wished he hadn't mentioned coins, especially after having seen Grenara's house and how little the three had . . . and how fortunate he'd been to end up living with Meldryn and Athaal. "No, there isn't. I understand how important coins are, especially when you don't have them. But I've also seen how those with the coins manipulate people. Uncle ended up walking into a trap because he needed to get paid. Athaal works long glasses doing all sorts of almost menial magery because he and Meldryn need the coins."

"Athaal said you'd started paying them for staying here."

"Almost as soon as I could. How could I not?"

"You couldn't. That's one of the things I like about you."

And there are a lot of things I like about you. Beltur felt uneasy about saying that, but only replied, "Thank you. You're being kind."

"I'm seldom kind. Mother's always chiding me for being too direct."

"I like your directness."

"For now," she said softly. "It wears on most people."

"Then we'll have to see, won't we?" After a moment, Beltur said, reluctantly, "We'd better think about walking you back to your aunt's house."

"Are you trying to get rid of me?"

"No. That's the last thing I'd want. But it's getting late, and you hurried off, and your mother will be worrying, and the . . . next to last thing I'd want is for her to be upset and angry with me."

"I'm glad you said 'next to last.'"

So was Beltur. He'd had to catch himself on that wording. "We can walk slowly. That way we can honestly say that we didn't stay long once you got here."

Jessyla smiled. "You *can* be deceptive. You just do it honestly. I'll have to watch for that."

"You're learning what few secrets I have." Beltur managed a hangdog expression.

"You don't do that well."

"Probably not. But we should go."

"I suppose so."

"You don't sound happy about that."

"Would you be? Auntie's always saying to be thankful for what we have, and that it could be so much worse. I know that. We barely escaped from what was worse. But what's wrong with wanting a little more? Or not having to worry about coins and food?"

Beltur nodded. He wasn't about to point out that he'd said almost the same thing earlier when he'd mentioned wanting to do more than forge and earn a few silvers.

"I'm sorry."

"What for?" Beltur didn't understand why she was apologizing.

"You said something like that before, and I was short with you."

"You were right to be short with me," he admitted. "You and your mother have been through some hard times."

"*We've* been through hard times? You've lost both parents and your uncle, and the Prefect and his mages tried to kill you, and you had to flee for your life—and then that insufferable little man had the nerve to attack you. Beltur, don't be too generous with me."

"But I've been fortunate in other ways. The people I lost all cared for me. Even Uncle Kaerylt cared in his own way. Athaal and Meldryn have been generous, and I've been able to make coins fairly soon after coming to a strange city."

"You make it sound easy. I doubt it was." She stood. "You are right. Mother will worry."

Beltur rose quickly, half wishing he hadn't insisted that he escort her back to Grenara's quite so soon. "She has every right to worry, especially with all the armsmen coming into the city."

"You're half right. If it were late in the evening, I'd

worry, too. In the afternoon . . . ?" Jessyla moved toward the door.

"The odds are less, but still . . ." Beltur eased past her into the foyer, then stopped. "Wait just a moment. There's one thing." He hurried to the kitchen, where he found the bread. Three loaves were wrapped together, and he smiled as he gathered them up and headed back to Jessyla.

She frowned as she saw the loaves.

"Meldryn told me to bring these if I saw you. They're a day old, but he said to bring them to you."

"If you weren't telling the truth . . ."

"Knowing you, if I couldn't tell the truth, I wouldn't have said anything." He couldn't help grinning as he opened the door.

In the time since Jessyla had arrived, the thin overcast had thickened, and Beltur could see heavier and darker clouds to the east, coming from the Easthorns. The light breeze he had felt earlier had strengthened and cooled, enough to make the walk back to Grenara's comfortable, he thought.

"We might see rain tonight," offered Jessyla.

"Later, I hope." Beltur closed the door, quietly but firmly. As he made certain he had shields in place around both of them, he swallowed, realizing what he'd never mentioned. "I need to tell you something."

"What might that be?"

"Since the last time I saw you, the Council has decided I'm not going to be a patrol mage any longer, and I can't forge any more cupridium, at least for now. I've been ordered to report for duty with an infantry battalion tomorrow."

"And you didn't tell me until now?"

"I was going to earlier, but your aunt's reaction upset me, and then I was so glad to see you. I'm sorry. It's just . . ."

"What was it you were saying about being fortunate?" Her words were dryly humorous.

"Well . . . you're here. That's fortunate. I think so, anyway."

"Why is the Council doing that? I'd think you'd be more useful helping the smith."

"We'd started to forge blades for the Council, but then I got those orders. The Council even overruled the Patrol Mage."

"Those idiots! How is the smith supposed to make cupridium blades without you?"

"I told the clerk at the Council building that, but I haven't heard anything, and I still have to report to the Council building tomorrow."

"They're all idiots. The Prefect is a bloodthirsty idiot, and the traders are greedy idiots who only know how to count coins."

Beltur didn't disagree with her feelings. He might not have said so quite so bluntly. "That was another reason . . . I mean, I wanted to see you, especially, because I wasn't sure when I might have the chance again."

"Beltur . . . did you try to wait for us?"

"I waited over a glass, on the corner where I could watch the door. Your aunt shut the door in my face."

"Good."

Good? "I don't know how good that was."

"I meant that you waited. That was good. I'm sorry. We probably didn't miss you by all that much."

Beltur figured that he could have waited almost another glass and still missed Jessyla's return, but he wasn't about to say that, not after forgetting to tell her about his orders earlier. "Without knowing how long you'd been gone or where . . . or when you'd be back . . ."

"I understand. You're quietly persistent, and sensible. I'm not always that sensible when I get upset."

"I'm not sure it's always sensible to be sensible."

Jessyla frowned. "Not sensible to be sensible?"

"Then sometimes people don't know that you're really upset or that there's a problem."

"I'm going to have to remember that."

Before all that long, the two were approaching Grenara's house.

Jessyla took a quick deep breath, without looking at Beltur, and rapped on the door.

In moments, the door was open, and Margrena stood there, looking at Jessyla. "You weren't gone too long." Her voice was level as she stepped back as if to allow them to enter.

Beltur didn't hear or sense anger.

Jessyla didn't move. "Beltur thought you'd worry."

Margrena looked at Beltur. "You're either thoughtful or calculating."

"Both, I'm afraid," he replied immediately. "I'd like to keep seeing Jessyla, and that would be difficult if you thought me untrustworthy."

The older healer's eyes went to her daughter and then back to Beltur. A trace of a smile crossed her lips as she studied Beltur. "Would you come in for a moment?"

"I would, if I wouldn't be imposing."

Jessyla glanced past her mother.

"Your aunt went to visit her friend Almaya, dear."

"How convenient," murmured Jessyla.

"Rather necessary. I told her that either Athaal or Beltur would likely escort you home. She decided that she'd have a long visit."

"Meldryn sent these," said Beltur, handing the bread to Margrena.

"Don't bring gifts too often, Beltur," replied Margrena as she took the loaves. "We might come to expect them. Please do come in."

Beltur gestured for Jessyla to go first.

"Have either of you eaten?"

"No, Mother. We only talked a few moments at Athaal's before Beltur suggested we ought to return."

"Then you should have something," said Margrena as she closed the door and latched it. "Just sit down here in the parlor. I'll join you in a bit." She paused and looked at Beltur again. "Those are new, aren't they, Beltur? Your tunic and trousers?"

"They are. I picked them up from the seamstress yesterday."

Margrena looked to her daughter.

Jessyla looked back at her mother. "I did notice them." Then she turned to Beltur. "I'm sorry. I was so upset that I didn't say more. You also look very mage-like in them."

"I'd hoped so." He smiled, waiting for her to sit down, watching as she took the backed bench farthest from the archway into the kitchen. In turn, he took the other bench and sat directly across from her. When she didn't say anything, he went on. "Working in the smithy was hard on the few garments I had. I had to get some shirts earlier, and I thought it would be good to have a really good tunic and a good pair of trousers."

"We could at least bring our clothes."

"You had to leave many things?"

"Some. We didn't own the house." She hesitated, then asked, "Did your uncle own his?"

Beltur nodded. "And all the books in the library."

"You lost much more."

"I'm alive and healthy." *And enjoying being with you.*

From the archway, moving into the parlor with two mugs in her hands, Margrena announced, "Here's some cider. I'll be right back with some bread and cheese, and some melon slices."

Beltur took the mug and set it on the side table, not wanting to drink, thirsty as he was, until both the healers could.

In moments, Margrena was back with two platters and another mug. She handed one platter to Beltur and then set the other on the bench beside Jessyla, seating herself with the platter between her and her daughter. "It's not a great deal."

"It looks very good, and I thank you." Beltur lifted his mug and took a swallow after Margrena had sipped her cider.

"The Council is making Beltur go protect an infantry battalion," Jessyla declared. "He was helping forge cupridium swords, but instead they're sending him off."

"I don't know that they're sending me anywhere," Beltur said, after taking another swallow of the cider, "but they don't seem all that interested in having me make any more of the cupridium blades that they demanded an eightday ago."

"That does sound odd," agreed Margrena. "Has anyone said why?"

"Not so far. I hope I'll find out when I go to the Council building tomorrow. Did you see all the troopers near the riverfront?"

"We stayed away from there." Margrena paused, then said, "Thank you—and Meldryn—for the bread."

"He hoped you could use it."

"I'm certain we can." There was another pause. "If you'd humor me, Beltur. I feel I know everything about you that's happened in the last season, and almost nothing of your life before that."

"It wasn't a very exciting life. My father was a scrivener. I don't really know much about my mother. I do remember her singing to me. Her voice was beautiful.

At least, I thought it was. She died when I was six. My father was kindly, well, most of the time. He didn't hold with rudeness or insolence. I got a few switchings for that . . ." Beltur went on about how his father had been the one to teach him his letters and gotten him to read a wide range of books . . . and about living with his uncle. Any time he stopped, either Margrena or Jessyla prompted him with another question. Before he knew it, he could see that it was getting late.

"Oh . . . I've talked far too long, and I really should be going."

"You didn't talk too long at all," said Margrena. "We're the ones who insisted on asking all the questions. You were very patient. I am surprised that your uncle didn't see that you were really a black."

"Uncle was good at heart, but he did tend to see things as he wanted to. I think he had trouble seeing just how evil some of the whites had become because he didn't want to. Also . . . he was very much against the women of Westwind, and I never knew why. He wouldn't talk about it, and when he didn't want to talk about something, it wasn't talked about."

"That's awful," declared Jessyla.

"Not always," replied Margrena. "There are times when no amount of words will change anything and can only make matters worse. Wisdom is knowing when to talk and when not to." She looked hard at her daughter. "As I believe I've mentioned a few times."

"Yes, you have," replied Jessyla sweetly.

Too sweetly, Beltur thought.

"Jessyla . . ."

"Yes, Mother."

"I really should be leaving. I didn't tell Athaal and Meldryn where I was going."

"I'm certain they know," replied Margrena, "but you're likely to have a very busy day tomorrow."

Beltur stood and inclined his head to Jessyla. "I can't tell you how much . . . that you came to Athaal's."

She immediately stood.

So did Margrena, who picked up the empty platters and moved toward the kitchen. "Bring in the mugs, would you, Jessyla, once you've seen Beltur off."

"I will, Mother." She walked beside Beltur to the door, but did not open it.

Beltur was very aware of just how close she stood to him. "Thank you . . . for the afternoon." He took her left hand with his right . . . and found she'd taken his left with her right.

"Thank you . . . for being you."

Beltur just stood there, looking into her eyes and holding her hands, aware that she was holding as tightly as he was.

Finally, she said, "I suppose you'd better go."

"I know."

"Be very careful."

"You, too."

Slowly, Jessyla eased her hands from him and opened the door.

Beltur stepped back. "Do take care."

"Me?" She smiled. "You take care."

He stepped outside, looking back, and watching as she closed the door.

As he walked back along Bakers Lane, Beltur couldn't help smiling, for more than a few reasons. He decided not to think about tomorrow . . . for the moment.

L

On the last oneday of harvest, under a hazy sky, Athaal and Beltur walked to the Council building together. Beltur did not wear his new tunic and trousers.

"We need to go in the main door," said Athaal.

"I want to see Raymandyl first. Maybe he can tell me something."

"You've got time," replied Athaal with a smile.

Almost as soon as Beltur entered through the north door, the clerk was on his feet pointing toward the south. "All the mages are being assembled in the audience hall. You get there through the main door, not through here."

"Thank you. Ah . . ." Beltur didn't really want to ask whether the clerk had passed on the information that Beltur had given him.

"Oh . . . it's you, Beltur." Raymandyl paused, then said, "I did tell Jhaldrak's assistant what you told me about forging the blades. He didn't look happy. I don't know whether that's good or bad."

"Thank you. I appreciate that. I really do." Beltur paused, then took the medallion from around his neck. "Since I won't be working for the City Patrol . . ."

"Thank you. I'm glad you remembered."

"I almost didn't, but I'm sure you could have found me."

"Best of fortune." Raymandyl paused. "You should do fine."

As Beltur left the north side of the building, he thought over what the clerk had said, and the implication that some mages might not. *Why not?* He had no idea, but didn't doubt Raymandyl's judgment. He hurried toward the main entrance, still hoping that Veroyt—if indeed the assistant to whom Raymandyl had spoken was Veroyt—might have been able to do something. Even before he neared the main door on the west side of the building, he saw a number of men in blue uniforms also heading there and entering. He had the feeling the uniformed men were officers, but they ranged from some who could only be his own age, if that, to men who could easily be Meldryn's age. He saw only one mage amid those men in front of him, not surprisingly, someone he did not know.

As he reached the entrance, a young officer held the door for him and said, "Go ahead, Mage."

"Thank you."

Inside, Beltur found himself in a large foyer, with the uniformed officers heading off to the right.

"All mages assemble in the conference room. All unassigned officers in the audience hall," called out an older man in blue. "Mages in the conference room, officers in the audience hall . . ."

Beltur had no idea where either chamber might be, and he approached the man giving directions. "Which way to the conference room?"

"To the right. Over there, under the plaque with the grain sheaves and the ship."

"Thank you."

As soon as Beltur stepped into the conference room, a modest chamber with an oblong table set in the center and chairs around it, Athaal gestured and pointed to the empty chair beside him, one of only a few remaining.

Beltur immediately joined the older mage and slipped into the empty chair. "Has anything happened yet?"

"No. I think Veroyt's going to be the one talking to us. That means it won't be good. Officers don't want to announce something unpleasant to a group of mages."

Beltur looked around the table. He didn't see either Waensyn or Cohndar. "I don't know anyone here, except you."

"That tells you some of those who aren't here."

Beltur sat and waited. Two more mages of an indiscriminate age—older than Beltur and not yet graying—entered and sat at the conference table. No one talked. Beltur counted those around the table and came up with fourteen, only two of whom seemed to be close to his age. He didn't sense anyone he couldn't see, but then, among a group of mages there wasn't much point in using a concealment.

When the city chimes began to strike the glass, Veroyt walked through the door, closed it behind himself, and made his way to the end of the table without a chair. He stopped and looked over the group, fourteen men in black close-seated around the oblong conference table designed for perhaps ten men at most, then began to speak.

"For those few of you I have not met, I'm Veroyt, and I'm the assistant to Councilor Jhaldrak. I'm also the one the Council has chosen to work with Marshal Helthaer's staff to assign mages to duties in support of the defense of Spidlar. It's likely that all of you know much of what I'm about to tell you. I'm going to say it anyway, because not all of you know all of it, and you all should." Veroyt paused. "Early in harvest, the Prefect of Gallos demanded that Gallosian traders be granted free passage along the entire River Gallos, and that Spidlar immediately remove all tariffs on all goods previously tariffed and that there be no tariffs on any goods entering or transiting Spidlar. He refused to grant our traders the same privileges in entering and transiting Gallos. The Council refused his demands, but offered to lower tariffs if the Prefect did the same. The Prefect rejected the Council offer. The Prefect then declared that he would force the issue.

"The Gallosians have amassed a force of over five thousand men. It could be even larger. Over two thousand have created a fortified post some five kays south of the border on the west side of the river. There have been no boats coming down the river for the past six days. Our scouts have reported twenty flatboats tied up just upstream of the Junction Rapids. Many are loaded with what appear to be siege engines of various types, including two large trebuchets. More troopers, both foot and mounted, are on the road to the Gallosian post. We anticipate that the flatboats will begin to travel the rapids in the next day or so, if they have not already started.

"Each of you has been assigned to a duty based on your capabilities, as assessed by Osarus, the Patrol Mage, and by the respected Mage Cohndar. Once I finish this introduction, I will meet with each of you, in turn, in the adjoining study, to discuss those duties. Each of you will also be issued an officer's uniform—except that the tunic will have wide black sleeve cuffs. The reason for this is so that you can't be distinguished from other officers and men from a distance. I understand that most of you can protect yourselves from many weapons, but we don't want the Gallosians knowing where you are, because that will allow them either to attack you individually in force with their mages or to avoid you and attack those of our forces without mages." Veroyt stopped, then asked, "Are there any questions?"

"How long are we expected to serve?"

"Until the Gallosians are defeated and destroyed or until they retreat and are no longer a danger. You will be paid for that time."

"How much?" asked one of the younger blacks.

"Your pay scale is the same as that of officers. More junior mages are paid at the rank of captains, senior mages at the rank of majers."

"How many mages do the Gallosians have?"

"We don't know. We do know that there are at least five very powerful white mages and a number of others."

Beltur wondered if that number had come from him, through Athaal.

When there were no more questions, Veroyt walked to the door that apparently led to the study, then turned. "Mage Caradyn?"

A short man with silver-streaked black hair stood and walked to the study door.

"Do you know him?" asked Beltur.

"Only by name. I've seen him once or twice."

Athaal was the sixth mage called. That suggested to Beltur that Athaal was a far more senior mage than he let on.

When Athaal left the study, he walked back to Beltur. "I'm where I thought I'd be, doing what shielding I can. I have to report. I'll likely see you later." Then he was gone before Beltur could say anything in reply.

Beltur couldn't help but worry as others were called, went to the study, spent some time there, and then left the conference room.

Finally, when there were only three mages left in the conference room—the two who looked younger than Beltur—Veroyt announced "Mage Beltur."

Once he was in the small study, where Veroyt seated himself behind a small table desk, the councilor's assistant looked at Beltur and said, with a smile, "I understand from Clerk Raymandyl that you can't be in two places at once."

"I thought that might be a problem, ser. I'm willing

to do what the Council wants, but the Council wants me to shield an infantry battalion, and the Council wants Jorhan to provide cupridium blades, and he can't forge them without a mage."

Veroyt nodded, then said, "Apparently, according to Meldryn and Athaal, and even Cohndar, you're presently the only mage in Elparta who can do that."

"I wouldn't know that. I do know that we spoiled an awful lot of bronze working out how to make cupridium."

"Jorhan told me that yesterday. It was a long day. He even showed me some lumps of cupridium so hard they can't be worked or even scratched."

Yesterday? The councilor's assistant worked all day on eightday?

"He also said that he could keep making the swords the Council needs so long as you're available to work four to five days out of every eight."

"That's the way we've been working ever since I was called to City Patrol duty."

"So I understand. I brought this up to the councilor. We've come up with a slightly different approach to your duty. You were assigned to the Third Infantry Battalion, but you've been reassigned to the Second Reconnaissance Company to provide shields for them. You can ride, can't you?"

"I'm not the greatest rider, ser, but I did spend half a season riding with my uncle in Gallos this last summer."

"Good. Second Recon is from Kleth. Commanding is Captain Laugreth. They're occupying the warehouse at the east end of the second pier south of the south city gate."

"Those are the first piers upstream of the walls?"

"That's right. You'll report to Captain Laugreth this morning, and he'll brief you. He understands that you'll only be available twice an eightday until the Gallosians arrive, on threeday and sevenday. Once the Gallosians do, you'll sleep with the company, but if the company doesn't have maneuvers, you're to work with the smith. I've told Jorhan to expect you tomorrow. When the Gallosians actually cross our border or begin to attack, you'll be with Recon Two all the time, but by then it will be too late for any more blades to make a difference."

Beltur could definitely see that.

"Captain Laugreth will tell you what he expects. In return, you will tell him whether you can do what he wishes and to what degree and under what circumstances. Is that clear?"

"Yes, ser."

"Before you go there, go to see Androsyt. He's the tailor charged with providing uniforms for the mages. His place is on Tailors Way. You can't miss it. Double doors, brass-bound, and a big 'A' above the doors."

After leaving the Council building, Beltur headed south to Tailors Way and then walked east. Despite Veroyt's directions, he did in fact miss Androsyt's establishment, largely because he'd thought it was on the north side of the street, but when he looked back and saw a man in black step out of a door, he retraced his steps.

No sooner had he stepped inside than a young man stepped forward. "Another mage for a uniform tunic? And your name, ser?"

"Beltur."

"Your assignment?"

"The Second Reconnaissance Company. From Kleth."

The young tailor picked up a sheaf of papers and leafed through it, quickly stopping. "Yes, I have it here. Please stand against the wall outline."

Beltur moved over to where the rough outline of a

figure was painted against the plaster. At one edge was a vertical line of measures in cubits and digits.

The tailor studied Beltur. "You will not be difficult. Shoulders broad, but not too broad. Chest not sunken." In moments the tailor had his cloth tape out and had jotted measurements on the sheet that held Beltur's name. Then he stepped back. "Captain Beltur, your tunic will be ready on threeday afternoon after fourth glass. We close at sixth glass."

Beltur felt slightly dazed at the speed of the measurements. "That soon?"

"We have five seamstresses and a complete workroom for dealing with uniforms."

"Thank you."

"Good day, ser."

It seemed as though Beltur had hardly been in the tailor's before he was leaving. He also had the feeling that the tunic Celinya had made was likely to be better fitted. *But then, you could be wrong.*

He headed toward the south city gate and hoped he could find the right warehouse that held Second Recon Company.

Finding the warehouse itself wasn't difficult, since there was only one warehouse at the end of the second pier, but it was close to three hundred yards long, with doors every thirty yards or so.

Beltur asked of the trooper posted outside the first door, "Second Recon Company?"

"Not here, ser. They're farther down. I don't know where, ser."

Beltur tried four more doors and got essentially the same response. Finally, the trooper guarding the fifth door replied, "Second Recon, ser. Two doors that way."

"Thank you."

When he reached the second door, a set of double

doors already swung wide open, the trooper posted there stiffened as he approached. "Are you Undercaptain Beltur, ser?"

Beltur managed not to frown. He'd thought Veroyt had said he was a captain. "I'm Beltur."

"The captain said you'd be reporting, ser." The trooper turned. "Chaertal! Escort for the undercaptain." Then he turned back. "We're still getting settled here. The mounts will be to the left, what passes for quarters to the right. The captain's watching over setting up the stabling. Chaertal will take you there."

Chaertal hurried up, a fresh-faced ranker likely several years younger than Beltur. "Ser, this way."

Beltur followed the young man into the warehouse, toward the left where a welter of activity was taking place, with men and planks and timbers creating what had to be stalls. In moments, Beltur was standing before the captain, and Chaertal had slipped away.

Laugreth was perhaps ten years older than Beltur and several digits shorter with a well-trimmed short beard somewhat more reddish than his reddish-brown hair. His pale gray eyes assessed Beltur. "You're the mage who helps forge cupridium?"

"Yes, ser."

"Can you ride?"

"Yes, ser. At least I can stay on a horse at a gallop."

Laugreth barked a laugh. "Fair enough. Can you use a sabre?"

"No, ser."

"Can you keep from being struck by one?"

"Yes, ser."

The captain walked over to the edge of the makeshift stall and picked up a short length of wood. "I'm asking again. Can you stop me if I try to hit you with this?"

"Yes, ser."

"Do so." Almost instantly, the captain struck.

The wood cracked against Beltur's shield . . . and then broke in half, the loose section bouncing off the shield.

The captain dropped the remaining length and rubbed the hand he had used with the other. "What if I'd struck you without warning?"

"The same thing. I carry shields whenever I'm outside and awake."

"How many others can you shield?"

"Two others, easily. A third for a very short time."

"They actually assigned someone useful." Laugreth shook his head, as if in disbelief. "What else can you do?"

"I can conceal a small group for a while. That will have limited use, though. They won't be able to see while they're concealed. I can sense figures beyond the concealment, but not details."

"What else?"

"I know the basics of grooming and feeding and watering a mount."

"Have you ever been in a fight or a battle?"

"I've been with armsmen who were attacked by raiders. My job was to shield them." His task had been more than that, but Laugreth wasn't a mage, and Beltur didn't want to reveal his past use of chaos.

Laugreth frowned again. "So you can shield a group, then? Were you mounted?"

"Yes. A small group, perhaps a score, if they're close together."

"On horseback, though?"

Beltur nodded.

"I think we just might get along, Beltur. You're being paid as a captain, but your field rank is that of an undercaptain, and that's how you'll be addressed. Is that clear?"

"Yes, ser."

"Do you know why?"

"I don't know, but I'd guess that's so I don't outrank you or any other officers."

"That's right." Laugreth gestured to an older ranker. "Keep them at it. I'm taking Undercaptain Beltur to meet Undercaptain Zandyr and Undercaptain Gaermyn."

"Yes, ser," replied the ranker.

Laugreth gestured for Beltur to walk beside him and began to speak. "They wanted us to bivouac outside. That wouldn't work. Not with fall and the rains coming. Whatever happens isn't going to be over quickly. And I'm not going to have men and mounts getting sick." He paused. "Do you know Undercaptain Zandyr?"

"No, ser."

"He's from here. He just arrived this morning. The Council insisted that I have an Elpartan undercaptain. His father is a trader here."

Beltur debated a simple answer and decided against it. Not letting the captain know his past could come back to bite him. "I'm fairly new to Elparta, ser. I left Gallos after the Prefect had my uncle killed. Arms-Mage Wyath tried to have me killed as well."

"That would be a good reason for leaving. Do you have any family left there?"

"No, ser. My parents died when I was young. My uncle was my only living relation."

"What did your uncle do to merit such a fate?"

"He was skeptical of Wyath. No more than that."

"I take it you're not exactly fond of either the Prefect or his arms-mage?"

"That would be putting it too kindly."

"Do you know anything useful about any of the Gallosian mages?"

"No, ser. I had almost nothing to do with any of

those remaining, except one, and I don't know if he's alive."

"We could hope. What's the worst they could do?"

"Most of the white mages can throw chaos-fire."

"Can you stop it?"

"It depends on how many are throwing it. I can likely hold my own against most of them for quite some time—one on one. The more there are, the less time I'll be able to hold them off."

"We're a recon company. You likely won't run into many at a time." Laugreth gestured to the two officers who stood waiting some five yards away. "The dark-haired older one is Undercaptain Gaermyn. He's my second. Zandyr is the light-haired one."

"Captain," offered Gaermyn, inclining his head as Laugreth and Beltur halted.

Zandyr merely nodded without speaking.

"Gaermyn, Zandyr, this is Beltur. He's our mage under-captain. He'll only be here twice an eightday until the Gallosians arrive. That's because he'll be working on weapons when he's not here."

"I'm pleased to meet you both," Beltur said, studying the two. Gaermyn was much older, likely a good ten years older than the captain. Although clean-shaven, he had a weathered look, and his hair was shot with silver. Zandyr seemed even younger than Beltur. His smooth face was slightly rounded, and both his dark blue uniform tunic and trousers appeared to be of fine wool and well-tailored to his slender figure. Under his golden-blond hair and eyebrows, his blue eyes appeared guileless.

"Gaermyn," said Laugreth, "if you'd keep those carpenters in line while I brief the undercaptains. Also, send back a squad leader who can fill in the undercaptains on Second Recon. One who's less needed at the moment."

"Yes, ser." With quick nod, the older undercaptain strode away back toward the eastern half of the space.

Laugreth walked over to the north wall of the warehouse. Beltur and Zandyr followed.

"At this point, I don't know what your duties will be." The captain looked at Zandyr. "I understand you know the roads and the terrain south of here across the border in Gallos?"

"I know the road. There's only one main road, and but a handful of side byways. I've traveled it a score of times. I'm not as familiar with the ground more than a kay from the road."

"You haven't traveled that far off the main road, then?"

After a slight hesitation, Zandyr replied, "No, I haven't."

"We'll talk about that later. I need to go over one or two things first. Why do you two think that the Gallosians are attacking right at the end of harvest and beginning of fall? Especially when we usually have heavy rains in the fall and early snows well before winter?" Laugreth looked from Beltur to Zandyr.

"The crops are mostly in," ventured Zandyr, "and the Prefect can call up levies without hurting the harvest and without losing tariffs? Trade falls off by midharvest, and he won't lose any tariffs, but closing the river to trade will cost Elparta and all of Spidlar more than it does Gallos."

"That's likely, but what happens when the river freezes over? That could happen by late fall, and they won't be able to get supplies then."

"Not if they already hold Elparta, ser," suggested Beltur.

"How do you think they'll manage that, Undercaptain Beltur?"

"I don't know, ser. I'd guess that they're relying on their white mages to keep our forces from attacking their siege engines. If they breach the walls, then there won't be much to hold back the chaos-bolts of the mages."

"I thought you black mages could do that."

"We can protect small groups and areas. I don't think there are enough of us to protect an entire city if the walls are breached in a number of places."

"That means that we can't let them get that far," Laugreth turned his eyes on Zandyr, "don't you think, Undercaptain?"

"It would seem that way."

"What does that mean for Second Recon?"

"We're going to have to stop them."

"Your thoughts, Undercaptain Beltur?"

"I know nothing of military tactics, ser, but doesn't it mean that Second Recon will need to find out where the Gallosians appear to be heading before they actually get there, because once they get there and set up fortifications they can use chaos against any attacks?"

"That's correct. That's also why we'll need you sooner than the Council anticipates. Not this eightday, in all likelihood, but after that . . . we'll have to see." Laugreth looked past the two undercaptains toward a ranker who approached. "That's enough from me for right now. Squad Leader Lhestyn will fill you in on the company, its structure and capabilities, and arrange for suitable mounts for each of you, as well as introduce you to all the squad leaders so that they all know who you are. Zandyr, you'll start riding recon patrols on threeday. That's to allow the horses some rest. Beltur, you and Gaermyn and I will need to go over how to mesh tactics and patrols with your capabilities. That will also be on threeday. Lhestyn will take care of you for the rest of the day. Listen carefully to what he has to say." Laugreth turned to the older squad leader. "You know what to do."

"Thank you, ser," said Beltur politely.

Zandyr barely nodded.

"You're welcome, Undercaptains."

"Yes, ser. If you'd accompany me, Undercaptains . . ." The squad leader's voice was level, neither arrogant nor condescending.

Beltur understood what Laugreth hadn't said—that there was a great deal that neither Beltur nor Zandyr knew, and that much of it was what every ranker in the company already understood. He had the feeling, from the momentary look of surprise on the face of the trader's son, that was something that Zandyr still hadn't realized.

Beltur kept his smile to himself.

LI

Twoday morning Jorhan was waiting when Beltur walked into the smithy.

"Councilor's clerk said you'd be here today. I wasn't sure I believed him." Jorhan looked inquiringly at Beltur.

"Threeday and sevenday I have to be with Second Recon Company, until the Gallosians show up in force. Otherwise, I'm supposed to help you." Beltur pulled off his old tunic and hung it on the peg. "What are we working on today?"

"More blades. The Council wants as many as we can do for as long as we can."

"If they want that many, then they'd better pay you, or you won't be able to buy the copper and tin we need."

"They had ten stones' worth of copper here yesterday and two stones' worth of tin." Jorhan offered a twisted smile. "Seems like blades are in short supply. Any kind of sword blade. They want more of the straight-swords first. I spent most of yesterday on the molds."

"You did more than I did. I just did what they told me and found out that no one seems to know when the Gallosians will arrive. It could be in a few days, or in a few eightdays."

"Let's hope it's longer."

Nodding, Beltur moved toward the bellows, even as he wondered how the Council could have even considered not having Jorhan make blades if they were so short of weapons. But there was also the nagging question of just what difference another ten or twenty or even thirty swords might make . . . even cupridium blades.

"The first mold is just about hot enough," said Jorhan. "Bit of a gamble, but I figured someone'd let me know if you weren't coming."

Beltur's first thought was that he wasn't certain he'd trust the Council that much, but then he considered that they'd brought all the copper and tin . . . and traders wouldn't want to waste the metal, especially after Jorhan had showed Veroyt the unworkable cupridium from the first attempts.

The first casting went well, and Beltur felt that he was getting more precise with each blade . . . and that it took less effort. *Or maybe you're getting to be a stronger mage.*

While Jorhan was checking the heat on the second mold, Beltur asked, "What will you do if the Gallosians cross the border and surround the city?"

"That's two 'ifs.' I don't see the Council letting them get that close." Jorhan paused. "If it happens that way, though . . . I guess I'd skedaddle off to Axalt and visit my sister. No way I'd stay here if the Prefect's men were roaming here, trying to live off the land."

"Your sister lives in Axalt?" Beltur knew that, but since he'd heard that from Athaal and not from the smith, he thought it better to ask, especially since Jorhan had mentioned it. That way, he might learn more.

"A merchant from Axalt took a fancy to her, and she liked him. Doesn't happen often, and back then I couldn't support her and Menara. Every now and again, he stops by and brings a letter and some wine and ale. They've got three children, two boys and a girl. I visited them once, but it's a long trip. Not so long as the one you made, that's for sure, but too long for me to do often. Just wanted to make sure she was happy."

"I take it that she is."

"Couldn't be happier. One of the boys'll get my lands and the smithy, but I'm in no hurry to give them up. Might even let him know where the coal is. With a powerful merchant family from Axalt behind him, the traders here won't be able to steal it from him."

"Coal? The coal you burn in the forge?"

Jorhan nodded. "There's a family story about it. My grandfather's great-grandfather was a herder, but they had lands. Parts of those lands were in Gallos back then. Now, they're in Spidlar. His father died in a battle to take Axalt, but one day a mercenary captain showed up and paid to stay at their house. The Prefect had a price on his head, and the assassins followed him. The young fellow—he was barely more than a boy— somehow helped the captain, and they killed all the assassins. The captain found the coal digging graves for the assassins and told the boy to keep it secret. Then the fellow left in the middle of the night and took all the arms and mounts belonging to the men who'd tried to kill him, but left six golds. Those golds let the family buy more sheep, and then in time, my great-grandsire became a smith using the coal." Jorhan laughed. "That's the story, anyway."

"Who was the man?"

"He never knew. Just called him the stranger."

"Do you think it's all true?"

"The coal's there. My grandfather said that his father had planted all the trees so that it'd be harder to find the coal for anyone who didn't know." Jorhan stretched. "We need to get the melt ready."

Beltur walked back to the bellows, thinking. A stranger had asked for help, and then ended up helping Jorhan's ancestor. Beltur himself had asked Margrena and Athaal for help, and he'd been a stranger to them. But what could he do beyond what he'd already done? *You'll figure out something . . . somehow.*

He put his hands on the bellows and began to pump.

By the end of the day, Beltur's hands and arms were sore from all the work with the bellows, and he'd drunk more ale than usual, because he'd worked harder, and almost until fifth glass. Jorhan was in a good mood, most likely because they managed more castings and, just as likely, because it appeared that he wouldn't be called up as a shieldman.

When Beltur reached the southeast city gates, he saw that masons had been working there to reinforce the stonework around the gates. There were also four troopers there as guards, rather than the usual two. One looked hard at Beltur, but a second one said something, and they both nodded as Beltur passed.

What Beltur did notice as he walked north along Bakers Lane was that there were almost no armsmen anywhere. *Because they've been moved out . . . or ordered to stay out of sight?*

Beltur entered the house with some trepidation, even though Athaal had told him that the Council didn't need him for several days, possibly longer, and had said, once again, that Meldryn's greatest use was to bake large quantities of bread. When Beltur heard the voices from the kitchen, he took a deep breath and made his way there.

"How many blades did you forge today?" asked Athaal cheerfully.

"We cast five. Jorhan will be working late on those and probably most of tomorrow as well, since I have to be with Second Recon tomorrow. We'll cast more on fourday—if the Gallosians haven't showed up by then."

"They won't," offered Meldryn. "Not that soon."

"I don't know," said Beltur. "With what you've told me about the late fall weather here, I don't see how they can afford to waste time."

"Maybe they think that it won't take that long," suggested Athaal.

"Everything takes longer than you think," replied Meldryn, "except disaster and failure."

"You're such an optimist, Mel," said Athaal sardonically.

"Realist. Moving five thousand men more than two hundred kays doesn't happen quickly."

"We don't know when they started, and there are already two thousand some ten kays south of us."

"So why doesn't the marshal attack them before more arrive?" asked Meldryn dryly.

"You tell me, O realistic one," asked Athaal, his tone light.

"Because that would make Spidlar the evil aggressor, and then both Certis and Gallos could join in the reprisal and plundering of Spidlar."

"That doesn't make sense," said Beltur quietly. "The

Prefect has already declared that he's going to force Spidlar to accept his terms."

Meldryn shook his head. "It makes great sense, in a convoluted way. The Prefect knows that many people, including the rulers of Suthya, Sarronnyn, Certis, and Montgren, possibly even Lydiar, will regard him as the aggressor if he attacks first. What if all this talk is merely to get Spidlar to attack first? Then the Prefect can declare to all of Candar that he was just trying to get better trade terms, and he had fortified his border with Spidlar because he was worried about those greedy traders of the north who might attack him because they wanted to keep unfair tariffs on his poor traders and merchants. And if we attack first, even knowing that he would attack anyway, that's exactly the way the world would see it, and everyone would unite against us because they could be sure of being on the winning side and profiting from it. That would also ensure that all of them would pay lower tariffs and that the Prefect wouldn't lose as many men or mages."

Beltur's immediate thought was to declare that what Meldryn had said was absurd, but his second thought was that the older mage was absolutely right . . . and that depressed him. "So we have to wait for their attack?"

"Do you think the Council has a choice?" replied Meldryn.

"Not when you put it that way."

"Why don't you get washed up?" suggested Athaal. "Dinner's almost ready."

"Oh . . . I should." As he headed upstairs, Beltur was still mulling over how the political implications had changed a simple tactical suggestion for an easier fight into something much larger and more complex, in a way he would not have even thought about before Meldryn's explanation.

LII

Beltur had to force himself to get up earlier than usual on threeday because Second Recon mustered at sixth glass, a full glass earlier than he'd been used to starting work either at the smithy or as a City Patrol mage. When he left the house, he realized that the air was cooler than it had been on previous mornings. Was autumn in Elparta that much cooler than in Fenard? One way or another, he'd find out.

Somehow, he managed to show up at the warehouse before sixth glass, where he was immediately met by Undercaptain Gaermyn.

"When do you get your uniform, Beltur?"

"This afternoon, any time after fourth glass, ser."

Gaermyn paused. "You haven't served as an armsman, have you?"

"No, ser. Why do you ask?"

"You seem to understand military structure and discipline, unlike . . . some."

Beltur got both messages. "My uncle and father were very formal, and believed in respecting those of higher position and ability." *Mostly, anyway.*

"This is for you." The weathered-looking undercaptain handed Beltur a visored cap seemingly identical to the one he wore.

Immediately, Beltur could see that the bronze insignia above the shiny leather visor was a miniature version of the plaque that had been over the Council conference room where Veroyt had addressed the mages. That—and its use as a visor emblem—strongly suggested it might even be the seal of Spidlar, but Beltur wasn't about to ask. "Thank you, ser."

"Wear it at all times when you're on duty and, after you get your uniform, when you're in full uniform."

Beltur put on the visor cap.

"Now, we'll be mustering the company shortly. The five squads will each line up outside here, with their squad leader in front. All officers will be forward of first squad—that's the squad on the right—and at a right angle so we can see the captain and the squads. You'll see. Just stay with me."

Beltur did just that, following Gaermyn out of the warehouse, and noticing as he did that all the temporary stalls seemed to be in place.

"We've got a durable gelding for you, Beltur. He's solid and doesn't spook easily. Since you'll be doing magery at times, the captain wanted to make sure you had a horse that wasn't high-strung."

"I appreciate that."

"I suspect all of us will benefit from that," replied Gaermyn dryly. "This morning you and I are going to take a ride with first squad. That way you'll get to see what a recon squad does, and you can show the squad what you can do. Then we'll see how we can put the two together."

Zandyr was waiting outside the warehouse and walked on the other side of the senior undercaptain as the three strode toward the east end of the area where the squads had formed up.

"One of you on each side of me," said Gaermyn as he came to a halt.

"I thought we formed up by seniority," said Zandyr.

"We are. Since you and Beltur are both undercaptains who joined the company at the same time, right now, you have equal seniority. The only way to show that in a three-officer grouping is with each of you on a side and with me a pace forward of you."

Beltur immediately moved to Gaermyn's left. Zandyr was markedly slower.

"That's good. Come to attention when I order it."

Beltur had no idea exactly what that meant, but decided he'd just copy what everyone else did.

As the chimes of the city drifted out over the piers, Gaermyn called out, "Company! Attention!"

Beltur immediately copied the erect position taken by all the rankers and waited.

"Squad leaders, report!"

"Squad One, all present and accounted for, ser."

Each squad leader reported the same way, and after the last report, Gaermyn turned to face Captain Laugreth, who had taken a position to the right of the senior undercaptain during the reports. "All squads present and accounted for, ser."

"Very good, Undercaptain. Dismiss them to duties."

"Company! Report to duty stations! Dismissed!" Gaermyn looked to Zandyr. "You report to the captain. He'll be working with you this morning."

"Yes, ser."

Beltur could tell that Zandyr sounded less than pleased. Beltur guessed that being subordinate to an undercaptain who had worked his way up through the ranks bothered him.

"As for you, Beltur, we're headed for the stable, such as it is. You can saddle your own mount, I take it?"

"If the saddle and girth aren't too different from what I'm used to, ser." Beltur doubted there would be much difference, but, if there were, he wanted a reason to explain possible clumsiness.

"I doubt they are. There aren't that many ways to make a useful saddle. Before you saddle up, we need to go over a few basics."

"Yes, ser."

"There are a number of ways an officer or a squad leader can deploy a squad to find out what the marshal or the officer in charge of the evolution needs to know. Techniques and scouting tactics depend on the terrain, the disposition and the weapons of the enemy, the weather, and the time of day. Those are just the obvious ones," concluded Gaermyn. "I can't go over all of them, or when they'll be used. Just keep in mind there are reasons. Don't question a squad leader in front of his rankers, but feel free to inquire, politely and deferentially and out of hearing of the rankers, as to why something is being done a given way. If you were a regular undercaptain, you'd have learned all that earlier. But you're not, and we'll need your abilities long before we could train you as a proper undercaptain. We'll try to give you as much information as possible before we have to deal with the Gallosians."

"I appreciate that, ser."

"First Squad will muster in the open space east of the building. You are to walk your horse outside before you mount. Then ride to where the others will be mustering. The First Squad leader is Vaertaag. I'll tell him to be on the lookout for you. He'll be going over things with the squad before they saddle up. That should give you some extra time with your mount."

"Tharmyn . . . would you show Undercaptain Beltur to his mount?"

"Yes, ser. This way, Undercaptain."

The big brown gelding was a large horse. At least, he looked large to Beltur, certainly larger than the horse he'd ridden in Analeria.

"Does he have a name?"

"Not that any of us know," replied the ranker holding the gelding's bridle, "except maybe Slowpoke."

"Does he have any nasty habits I should know about?"

"Sometimes, when you're saddling him, he puffs up his belly. Just knee him in the gut—here—firmly, but gently. If he doesn't whuff, do it again. He's not mean. To him, it's almost a game. Your saddle and blanket pad are here on the stall rack. Your blanket and ground cloth roll up behind the saddle. Begging your pardon, ser, but don't ever forget them. You can never tell when you might not get back here to sleep. Not in a recon company."

"Thank you."

The saddle looked similar to the one Beltur had used before, except both the pommel and the cantle were a bit higher and thicker, and there were two leather holders off the cantle on each side that held water bottles.

"I've filled the water bottles today," offered the ranker.

"But it's my responsibility from now?" asked Beltur with a smile.

The ranker smiled back. "Yes, ser."

Beltur was glad that he had a little extra time to saddle the gelding.

While Slowpoke was certainly not high-strung, he did need a certain firmness, Beltur immediately discovered when the gelding moved to one side of the stall so that his right shoulder and hindquarters were pressed against the planks. Beltur stepped to that side and tapped his shoulder. Slowpoke didn't move. Beltur thought about using the bridle, but wasn't certain that would get the desired result. Also, there was the question of whether the gelding would make getting the bridle on more difficult in the future.

After a moment, Beltur created a narrow shield between the planks and the gelding. Then he looked at the gelding and said, firmly, pointing to the left, "Move."

As he spoke, he widened the shield, and to prevent Slowpoke from sidling up to the other stall wall, created another shield. Then he shortened both shields to keep the gelding's hindquarters in the middle of the stall so that he could finish saddling the gelding.

While the effort of using the shields was work, and he was beginning to sweat a little, the gelding just stood there as Beltur finished saddling him and then dropped the shields before leading Slowpoke out of the stall and warehouse. Once outside, he mounted and rode along the north side of the former warehouse toward the east.

Once past the end of the warehouse, he saw a group of riders in a loose column of two abreast, with a single rider at the head. Since that was the right number for a squad, he used the reins in order to turn toward the riders, but the gelding kept heading straight. Beltur kept the pressure on the reins and created a small shield alongside the left side of the gelding's head and used it to push Slowpoke's head in the direction he wanted to go. The gelding immediately turned. Beltur wondered how long it might take before he could use just the reins. *Oh, well, it's another kind of shield practice.*

He ended up using shield pressure twice more before he halted opposite the squad leader. Slowpoke did respond to a direct pressure back on the reins to halt, as a flick of the reins would start him, but, as for turning . . .

"Undercaptain Beltur?"

Beltur nodded. "You're Squad Leader Vaertaag?"

"Yes, ser." Vaertaag looked at Beltur. "I see that they gave you the big brown. I thought he was assigned to Undercaptain Zandyr. Did you have . . . any difficulty?"

"He starts and halts easily enough. He does like one side or the other of the stall, and he seems to require a bit more direction," Beltur said dryly. "We're working it out."

"You seemed quite in control. Others have had difficulty with his occasional willfulness."

"He's beginning to understand." *You hope.* Beltur also had the feeling that the choice of his mount had been a test of some sort . . . possibly from Vaertaag's words, one for Zandyr, a way of telling a new officer that there was much he didn't know, but that applied to Beltur, not that Beltur didn't already understand that. The past two seasons had made that very clear.

"I see." Vaertaag nodded. "You've never ridden with a squad like this, I take it?"

"No, I haven't."

"We're not a parade guard or anything like it. We can hold any formation, but that's not our task. We've scouted the approaches to Axalt, and we were the ones who had the first fight with the Suthyans nine years ago. We sent their recon units packing." Vaertaag paused.

"You want to know what I can do for the company. I can keep a squad hidden for as long as you want. You won't be able to see, but I can sense anyone coming. If you don't trust my senses, well, I could leave you unconcealed, and hide the rest of the squad."

The squad leader frowned.

"Let me show you."

Beltur dropped a concealment around himself and Slowpoke. He could sense the horse tense. "Easy, there." After a moment, he lifted the concealment.

Slowpoke shook his head.

"Now, I'll conceal the squad. Tell your men that they'll be surrounded by blackness, but not to move. You stay a yard away from the nearest one."

Beltur waited until Vaertaag had passed the word, then looked at Beltur. "Now what?"

Concentrating, Beltur raised a concealment around the twenty mounts and men. It was the largest he'd ever done, but it was much easier than holding four separate shields. He enjoyed the startled expression on the squad leader's face when his squad seemed to vanish. "They can still hear you."

"Are you there, Khalyst?"

"Yes, ser."

Beltur dropped the concealment. "Now, I'm going to put one around you so your men can see what it looks like, and you'll know what they experienced." He raised his voice. "Troopers, I'm going to conceal your squad leader. He'll be in darkness the way you were."

Beltur held the concealment for the count of twenty, then dropped it.

Vaertaag looked to the closest trooper. "Could you see me?"

"No, Squad Leader. It was like the mage said. You were gone."

"What else can you do?"

"I can shield a small group for a short time. Take out your sabre. Ride to about two yards from me and try to swing it at me. I wouldn't swing too hard."

Vaertaag rode forward and struck. He could barely hold on to the sabre as it bounced back from Beltur's shield. He shook his head, then asked, "What else?"

"I can move, slowly, while concealed. I can sense where objects and people and animals are, but it's like moving on a very dark night." Beltur shrugged. "That's pretty much it."

"Pretty much it?" Vaertaag laughed softly. "An officer like you might come in very useful."

"I've never had any weapons training, and I wouldn't know the first thing about handling a blade. And the concealment has its limits. You can still hear or smell someone under a concealment, if you're close enough." Beltur added the last words because he didn't want the troopers to think the concealment would allow them to get too close without detection.

"Here comes Undercaptain Gaermyn, ser."

Beltur turned in the saddle and watched as the second-in-command rode toward them and then reined up.

"It appeared to me, Undercaptain, that you made the squad disappear, and then did the same to Squad Leader Vaertaag."

"Not disappear, ser. I just concealed them. They were still there, and they could hear anything around them. They just couldn't see. It's like being in a deep black hole with no light."

"It is," affirmed Vaertaag.

"Show me," said Gaermyn.

Beltur immediately surrounded him with a concealment. "You should still be able to hear us."

"I can. You're right, though. It's pitch dark in here."

Beltur lifted the concealment.

Gaermyn shook his head. "I don't know . . ."

"I can sense things and objects, but you have to be a mage to do that. A few healers can, too." Beltur was thinking of Jessyla when he said that. "I could also conceal all of a squad but one person. That was what I was showing the squad leader."

"That might be useful." Gaermyn frowned for a moment. "I'll have to think about that. This morning, we're going to ride south to the border. It's a little more than five kays. Undercaptain Zandyr and Third Squad did that yesterday. We'll be doing a number of patrols like that in the next few days."

Beltur had an immediate thought. "Could we spend a little time practicing moving under a concealment?"

"That might be a very good idea."

In fact, the little time turned into almost a glass, for which Beltur was glad, since Slowpoke was initially hesitant to move in darkness, until Beltur gently prodded him with shields.

Finally, when Gaermyn was satisfied, the older under-captain and Beltur rode at the head of a two-breast column of armsmen, down a road that was scarcely more than a wide path, unlike the wide road that angled to the southwest away from the single pier on the far side of the river.

"Take a good look at the road," ordered Gaermyn. "What do you see?"

"It's barely wide enough for two riders or a single cart, but it's been well-traveled."

"What does that tell you?"

"That it's likely used mainly by herders."

"Why do you think that?"

"The main road is across the river. Also, the ground on the east side of the river south of here is rough and rises steeply from the river. There aren't any large towns, and not much level ground. But people travel the road. The only people I can think of who would live in this direction are herders, maybe a few small growers."

"How do you know about the ground beside the river?"

"That's how I came to Elparta, by flatboat."

Gaermyn nodded. "You're likely right about the road, but check the tracks in the dirt. If there are matched pairs of hooves side by side, you're most likely talking armsmen. A single pair of hoofprints means travelers, and a single horse or ox is most likely someone local. Why am I telling you all this when you won't likely be in command of a squad? Because you never know. Here are a few simple rules. A scout is just to let you know what's immediately ahead. A reconnaissance starts more than a kay from the squad or company. Never send a single rider out on a reconnaissance mission against an armed enemy. Five is usually the minimum. They can be spread, but they all need to be in sight of two others. Why?"

"Because if one gets wounded or killed, the others will know it and can return and let the squad leader or officer know?"

"That's right. Also, they can regroup quickly to deal with a pair or a trio of opposing scouts, or even to keep a larger group from picking them off one by one."

As the squad continued along the dirt road that wound around hills that grew larger as they moved south, Gaermyn's questions and instructions continued, and Beltur tried his best both to listen and to take in the surroundings beyond the road, recalling that the captain had questioned Zandyr on that very point.

Close to noon, Gaermyn called a halt, and turned his mount, raising his voice to address the entire squad and pointing to two cairns of reddish stones, one heaped on each side of the road. "That's the border. It goes roughly east-west from here. If you ride to the rise to the west there, you can see the river."

The rise, Beltur noted, was just an expanse of scattered grass, dirt, and some scraggly bushes, clearly unsuited to growing much or even more than occasional grazing.

"Below the rise," continued Gaermyn, "it's about five hundred yards away across the sand flats. There are pockets of quicksand amid the dry sand. It can be treacherous, especially after times of high water. Right now, it's probably safe enough to ride across except within a few yards of the water." He turned to point eastward. "The hills here get higher and rougher, but it's still possible for armsmen and horsemen to flank the road and attack. I've been told that less than a kay south of the border, the road turns almost due east and continues only another few kays before it comes to an end. If we rode straight ahead, we'd run into rough and rocky ground, and after another few miles, a steep rock escarpment that marks the end of the Border Gorge. That's why the Gallosians have to cross here. It's the only place they can near Elparta. On their side of the border, anyway."

By the time first squad rode back to Elparta and dismounted outside the doors of the converted warehouse, slightly before third glass, Slowpoke was responding to the reins alone. The only question was whether the gelding would remember that the next time Beltur saddled him. Beltur had the feeling he would, especially since he had no trouble while he unsaddled and groomed the gelding. *If not, you can repeat the exercise until he does.*

He had just walked away from the stall when Captain Laugreth appeared.

"Beltur."

"Yes, ser."

"Gaermyn tells me that you demonstrated what your magery could do. He thinks there are times it might be most useful."

"I would think so, ser, but he would know better than I would."

"Come with me. You and the other officers need to hear the latest." Laugreth led the way to a small room where Gaermyn and Zandyr already waited, standing on the far side of a battered round table. Four equally worn and scarred stools were spaced around the table. A single pallet bed stood against the wall, indicating that the captain slept in what doubled as a study.

"Might as well sit down," suggested the captain.

Beltur followed his example, slightly surprised that he wasn't even sore. But then, unlike the time before his first rides in Analeria, he'd been working fairly hard at the smithy, mostly with the bellows, and between that and all the lifting and carrying, he'd been getting a fair amount of exercise.

"The naval marine units won't be coming to Elparta after all," began Laugreth. "Not for a time, if they come at all."

Gaermyn frowned.

Beltur hadn't known that any marine units were expected.

"The Council doesn't believe that sufficient numbers can be gathered in less than two eightdays, and it could take that long for them to travel here."

"They've known about the danger for almost a season, and they're just now thinking about gathering those forces?" Gaermyn shook his head.

"Most of the marines are aboard ships," said Zandyr. "They cannot be gathered until the ships port. Most traders would not wish to leave ships unprotected until they are certain of a Gallosian attack."

"I'm certain the Prefect, or his arms-mage, counted on that," replied Gaermyn dryly.

"The good news," continued the captain, "is that the Chief Councilor of Axalt has conveyed to the Council that they will not allow any forces through their land. That means that they don't want the Viscount of Certis getting involved, and he's unlikely to do so if he has to fight Axalt before he can get to Spidlar."

"What about Suthya?" asked Gaermyn.

"That might be another reason why the Council's reluctant to send all its forces to Elparta. Suthya hasn't forgotten their losses in their ill-considered attempt to take Diev." Laugreth straightened slightly. "Our scouts report that another thousand Gallosian troopers have arrived at their staging base, but there isn't any sign of the flatboats with siege engines yet. Everything we've seen so far suggests that they'll build up their force on the west side of the river, then bring down boats and use them to ferry men and horses across to the east shore."

"Ser?" ventured Beltur. "Undercaptain Gaermyn pointed out how treacherous the east shore is near the border. Can they cross safely farther south, or will they have to come north and cross the border before crossing the river?"

"At the end of the Border Gorge, the banks are solid on both sides. That area is narrow. The old east road doesn't go anywhere near the gorge. That's why I think it's likely that they'll split their forces, with some coming down each side of the river and some using flatboats to travel past the border. We'll have to see." Laugreth paused, then said, "That's all I have. Do you have any more questions? No? Then I'll see you all later." He stood, gesturing for Gaermyn to stay.

Once Zandyr and Beltur were outside and well away from the study, Zandyr turned to Beltur. "You're from Gallos? What do you think?"

"I was never an armsman. All I know is that the Prefect likes to get his way, and he doesn't seem to care who might suffer."

"Why don't you wear a uniform besides the cap?"

"Because it won't be ready until this afternoon. I didn't even know I was going to be a mage undercaptain until oneday."

"Do you know any of the patrol mages?" asked Zandyr.

"There's only one Patrol Mage, and that's Osarus," replied Beltur.

"No . . . I mean the ones who work with city patrollers."

"All mages are required to do some service with the City Patrol, or something similar, for a season every three years. Why?"

"Every mage?"

"That's what the Council clerk told me."

"It has to be a mage who's been doing that recently."

Beltur was afraid of what might be coming next. "What has to be?"

"The mage who detained my cousin in the market."

"Why would he do that?" Beltur was very glad Zandyr wasn't a mage. "And who is your cousin?"

"He treated her like a common thief. Her name is Rhyana. She's the daughter of Trader Eskeld."

"I don't know anything about him." Beltur managed a rueful smile. "But then, I don't know much about any of the traders. I take it your father is a trader?"

"He is. Alizant of the House of Alizant."

Rather repetitive. "What does he trade?"

"He doesn't trade. Those who work for him trade."

"What I meant was for what trading goods is the House of Alizant known? Because I'm new to Elparta, I don't know the various traders and what their houses are usually known for."

"House Alizant is especially known for spices that are rare and difficult to find. Also people come to us for ancient works of art or sculpture. A cupridium bust of one of the emperors of Cyador could bring five thousand golds."

"That much? Because it's cupridium?"

"No." Zandyr shook his head. "Because the devastation of Cyador was so great that almost nothing of worth survived. Not where anyone could find it, anyway. The Accursed Forest covers most of what was Cyador now, and the druids don't let anyone take anything out. A terrible waste, if you ask me. What are they going to do with old art? Decorate their trees?"

Beltur decided not to comment on that. "What spices are the most valuable?"

"Saffron, of course. Grains of paradise, Atlan lemon berries, and Meroweyan pepperpods."

"Lemon berries?"

"It's a little berry that tastes like lemon, but it's not

bitter or acid. They're very hard to find. Only the nomads in eastern Hamor know where to find them, and
they kill outsiders."

"That might make anything rare."

Zandyr shrugged. "If people will pay for it, our traders
can find it."

"How did you end up as an undercaptain?"

"I'm a third son. Father decided I needed some experience as an officer, and he purchased my commission. I was already trained in riding and arms." Zandyr
paused. "You don't carry a sabre."

"Black mages don't. Blades don't usually go with
magery."

"Doesn't that bother you?"

"No."

"But you're an officer."

"A mage-officer. That's different."

"I don't understand."

Beltur raised a concealment, and then stepped back
several paces to the side . . . as quietly as he could.

"Where . . ."

"Here," replied Beltur, dropping the concealment.

"How did you do that?"

"Magery."

"Could you teach me that? I'll pay you."

"I can't. I mean I would if I could, but you have to
have the talent."

"How do you know I don't?" Zandyr's voice was
almost sulking.

"Some people attract order. Some attract chaos. Some
can attract both. It swirls around them. It doesn't swirl
around you."

"That doesn't sound fair."

Beltur repressed a sigh. What could he say? After a
moment, he finally went on. "Different people have different talents. I wouldn't make a good trader. Someone

who's small and thin probably wouldn't make a good blacksmith. Someone afraid of heights won't make a good sailor. You've got the blond hair that the women like. I don't. It's like that."

"Not all women," replied Zandyr, "but I see what you mean." He paused. "Excuse me. I'm supposed to meet my brother at the third pier at fourth glass."

"Is he an officer, too?"

"No. He's leaving to serve as supercargo on one of Father's ships." Zandyr nodded, then turned and hurried off.

Beltur stood there, for several long moments, wondering what exactly to think about the other undercaptain. Neither order nor chaos lingered around Zandyr, and while he seemed more than a bit spoiled by his family's wealth, he didn't seem mean or malicious.

Immediately after fourth glass, Beltur left Second Recon and hurried to Androsyt's to pick up his uniform tunic. He had to wait almost two fifths of a glass because of the older blacks who had arrived before him. And then he was surprised to discover that the tunic came with matching dark blue trousers. He tried them on, and they both fit, almost, but not quite as well as the tunic and trousers from Celinya. Even so, he had an actual uniform.

He dressed again in his everyday garb and carried the tunic and trousers back to the house, where he found Athaal and Meldryn in the kitchen, seemingly cleaning up.

"Laranya couldn't come. Her son was ill again," explained Athaal as he put away a platter.

"I see you got your uniform," said Meldryn.

"I didn't realize it came with trousers."

"Uniform means everything matches," replied Meldryn.

"Did you get yours?" Beltur asked Athaal.

"Mine was ready earlier. I wore it today. I don't have to be up quite as early as you. At least for now."

"Are you doing what you thought you would be?" asked Beltur.

"Not yet. I'm mostly answering questions from the commanders who report to Marshal Helthaer about what white and black mages can do and what they can't. I also have to point out that what each mage can do is different, sometimes just a little, sometimes a lot. That doesn't make them happy. To them an archer is an archer and a lancer a lancer. How did your day go?"

Beltur shrugged. "I did some maneuvers with a squad, and then we rode up to the border on the east side of the river. We studied the terrain there. I got a series of lectures on what officers did on the way out and back, and then the captain had a brief meeting with the undercaptains and told us that the Gallosians had moved another thousand men into the base on the other side of the border."

"So far," said Athaal.

"We can talk about this at dinner," said Meldryn. "It will be much more pleasant with food and ale."

Beltur could agree with that, and he hurried upstairs to set down his uniform and wash up.

LIII

Fourday through sixday, Beltur worked from seventh glass until fifth glass at the smithy with Jorhan. During that time, they cast seventeen more blades, all either straight-swords or sabres, and good workman-like weapons, but without any ornamentation. Jorhan did almost no work beyond the casting, since that was something he could do later without Beltur.

As Beltur pulled on his old and worn tunic and readied himself for the walk back to the city, Jorhan handed him a cloth bag.

"Here's your pay—for now. I owe you more, and I'll pay you when I get paid by the Council."

"Thank you. I don't know if I'll be back on oneday. The Gallosians are moving more troops into their post just across the border." That was something he'd learned from Athaal the evening before.

"I won't count on it, but you'll be welcome if you can come. I've got almost an eightday of finish work on what we cast."

"That was the idea, wasn't it?" replied Beltur with a smile. Left unsaid, he knew, was that such finish work would likely keep Jorhan from being called up as a shieldman, although he felt that had been more threat than a real possibility.

"I'm too old to be a shieldman. I'd ask too many questions. Just take care of yourself. You're the only mage in Candar able to forge cupridium."

Just the only one with the ability who actually tried, most likely. "I'll do my best."

Once he was well away from the smithy, Beltur did look in the bag . . . and found six silvers. He just looked. Even after having paid Athaal and Meldryn the day before, he still had slightly more than two golds in silvers. In some ways, it made absolutely no sense. Starting as a near-copperless mage who had fled for his life, within a season, he'd earned more on his own than he ever had. *But that's all because of Athaal . . . and Meldryn.*

Just because he'd learned how to help forge cupridium, he'd been able to earn more than Athaal did an eightday, and Athaal had worked much longer and harder than Beltur. Somehow . . . it just didn't seem right. He shook his head. "Right" wasn't the correct word or feeling. It just felt somehow unbalanced.

He eased the silvers into his wallet, checked his shields, and continued walking, still trying to work out a way to hold five shields for longer than a few moments.

As he neared the southeast gate, he saw that the masons had completed the stonework reinforcing the gate, which included an iron portcullis behind the iron-sheathed timbered gates. To Beltur, that didn't make much sense. That gate couldn't be hit by a trebuchet fired from the south, and for the Gallosians to get into a position to directly bombard the gate, they would have to have overrun the piers and occupied the lands to the east of the city as well. That would expose a greater part of their flank to an attack. So why would they do that when it would be easier and cost fewer lives to remain back somewhat to the south and batter the walls until they gave in?

Or is this another thing you don't understand?

Beltur was still pondering that when he passed through the gate and turned north on the unnamed wall street. He really didn't want to go anywhere near the market, which had been thronged with people the past few days, even after fourth glass, when usually that late there were fewer sellers and far fewer buyers. *Because they think the city will be besieged and food will be hard to come by?*

He was still thinking about that and wondering what it was that he didn't know when he entered the house and walked directly back to the kitchen, because he'd heard Meldryn and Athaal talking.

"We wondered how late you'd be," said Athaal.

"I told you I'd likely be late. We tried to cast as many blades as possible. I wasn't sure when I'd be able to help Jorhan again."

"Have you heard anything new?" asked Meldryn.

"No, but the market squares have been so crowded, even late in the day. I've been wondering if people know something we don't."

"That's always possible," observed Athaal.

"I'd wager many are buying dried fruits, beans, goods that will last," suggested Meldryn. "Flour, rice if they can get it."

"Are people that worried?" asked Beltur. "The Gallosians are across the border, but they're not that close yet."

"We Elpartans are a cautious people," said Meldryn. "It's what comes of living in a place where food is much harder to come by in winter. Also, by the time it's obvious, there may not be that much left to buy."

"Maybe I should have bought some things," said Beltur. "Except I don't know what you have and don't, and what you need."

"Dried fruit is always good," said Athaal with a grin. "Especially apricots and cherries."

"Good and expensive," retorted Meldryn with a snort.

"Good is always expensive."

"Not when Meldryn bakes it," suggested Beltur.

"That's because we don't pay him," said Athaal.

"When do you start baking bread for the Council?" asked Beltur.

"I already have. They're supposed to deliver another barrel of flour tomorrow."

"Already?" Athaal frowned.

"A barrel only makes around three hundred loaves, and that's about what I can do in a usual day, if I work it right."

"And you don't bake much else," said Athaal.

Three hundred loaves a day sounded like a lot, but when Beltur considered that Second Recon had more than a hundred rankers, squad leaders, and officers, at a loaf a day for each man, Meldryn would only be baking enough for three companies. Even at half a loaf . . .

"How many companies have come from elsewhere to support Elparta?" Beltur asked Athaal.

"I know of ten so far. We've raised twelve. So twenty-two in all."

And the Prefect has more than twice that number?

That shone a whole new light on the crowds in the market square.

LIV

Sevenday was yet another very early morning for Beltur, but he managed to get up, into full uniform, and out of the house in time to reach the huge warehouse east of the second pier that now housed something like eight companies, although Beltur had the impression that there was only one other mounted company, and it wasn't a reconnaissance unit, but mounted heavy infantry. He was even early enough that the rankers hadn't yet begun to form up for the morning muster.

At that moment, Zandyr appeared. "Good morning, Beltur."

"Good morning, Zandyr."

"You look like a real officer now."

"I'm the same as I was on threeday." *Except we forged seventeen more blades.*

"The captain said you were helping to forge cupridium blades. I can't believe it. An officer actually forging blades. That's more like a ranker's job."

"I was carrying out the orders of the Council. I don't actually forge the blades. Jorhan's the smith, and he does that. I'm the one who puts the order-trapped chaos into the molten bronze."

"Oh . . . that's different."

Beltur concealed a grin, adding, "That's in addition to working the bellows and doing other chores."

After the briefest hesitation, the younger under-captain said, "Everyone talks about cupridium as if it's special."

Beltur refrained from frowning. If Zandyr came from a trading house that dealt in valuable old goods, how could he not know something about cupridium? Especially after talking about the value of a cupridium statue from Cyador? "It is. It's harder and tougher than anything except black iron, and it doesn't corrode or rust. They say it lasts forever. Like black iron, it takes a mage and a smith working together to make it. Not many mages are good at it. I understand that very little has been forged anywhere in Candar since the fall of Cyador."

"But blades . . . ?"

"Someone told me that a Cyadoran blade might fetch ten golds."

Zandyr's eyes widened for a moment. "Why did the Cyadorans forge such blades? Just because they fetched such a price?"

"I don't think so. I think it's because a white mage or wizard can't touch an iron blade, not without burning his hands, maybe even killing himself, but they can use a cupridium blade because the order-chaos within the metal is balanced, and it's not in an iron blade. The ancient histories said that some of the great

emperors were also great warriors as well as Magi'i—
that's the old word for men who can handle chaos and
order."

"What's it really like? Cupridium, I mean?"

"It's metal. It's more silvery than bronze, more golden
than iron."

"Do you have a cupridium sabre, then?"

Beltur was glad the other had asked about a sabre
and not just a blade. "No. I wouldn't know what to do
with a sabre."

"I forgot about that."

Forgot about it . . . or couldn't believe it? Beltur knew
he'd mentioned that he didn't have or use a sabre.

At that point Gaermyn walked toward the two.
"Time to form up."

Beltur and Zandyr followed him out to the muster,
which took little more than a tenth of a glass.

After dismissing the company to duties, Captain
Laugreth walked over to the three undercaptains.
"Beltur, you'll accompany me with First Squad on a
reconnaissance south along the east shore of the river.
Zandyr, you'll be working with Gaermyn and Third
and Fourth Squads."

"Yes, ser," replied the undercaptains, close to simultaneously.

When Laugreth motioned, Beltur followed.

"Our scouts haven't sighted Gallosians on this side
of the border, but several herders have reported that
they've seen horsemen they didn't recognize over the
last day or two. That suggests they're sending spies
across the border."

Spies? Beltur had to think about that for a moment.
"They're scouts if they're in uniform and spies if they're
not? Why wouldn't they be in uniform?"

"Because, if they're discovered in uniform, that's an
act of war, and the Council could order an attack on

the Gallosians before they're fully established without our being considered the ones who started the war. If they're spies, that doesn't constitute an act of war, but once war is declared or under way, spies on our lands can be killed immediately."

On the one hand, Beltur could see a certain logic in what the captain said, but on the other, it almost seemed like splitting hairs.

"I'll be bringing maps and taking notes. So if you notice anything of worth, please feel free to bring it to my attention. Now . . . go get saddled up. We'll form up to the east of the barracks building, as you've been doing."

That was the first time Beltur had heard the warehouse referred to as the barracks building, although that was certainly what it had become. "Yes, ser."

Despite his efforts to saddle up quickly, prolonged by the fact that he almost forgot the blanket and ground cloth, he was among the last to join First Squad, although the captain wasn't there yet. Part of that was the time it took him to clean out his water bottles and get them refilled. He did use a bit of order to make sure there wasn't any chaos in the water.

As soon as Beltur rode to the waiting squad and reined up, Vaertaag immediately reported, "First Squad present and ready, ser."

Beltur hesitated only a moment before saying, "Thank you, Squad Leader."

Moments later, Captain Laugreth reined up and Vaertaag glanced meaningfully at Beltur.

"First Squad present and ready, Captain." Beltur didn't hesitate that long.

"Very good, Undercaptain."

While Beltur was thankful he had arrived just before the captain, that might have been because Laugreth had delayed his arrival so that he wouldn't seem to be waiting on a junior undercaptain. *Which is most likely.*

Laugreth looked to Vaertaag. "We'll be taking the old east road south to the border. Have your men keep an eye out for anything unusual."

"Yes, ser."

Laugreth turned his mount, motioning for Beltur to move up beside him. "First Squad, forward!"

As they rode away from the barracks, Beltur noticed the end of what looked to be a rolled section of paper sticking out of a leather pouch fastened to a tie on the front of the captain's saddle pommel and realized that it had to be a map.

"If there are Gallosian armsmen and skirmishers out ahead of us," said Laugreth, "they'll either withdraw or immediately loose arrows in hopes of forcing us back or weakening us enough that they can attack successfully. Can you shield us quickly enough to prevent casualties?"

"If I have a few moments' warning and know from what direction the shafts are coming," replied Beltur. "I can't maintain a large shield all the time, though."

"That's understandable. Most shield walls can only be held for a while." The captain turned in the saddle. "Did you hear that, Vaertaag?"

"Yes, ser. The undercaptain needs to know that shafts have been loosed and where they're coming from."

The captain set a steady pace, not quite a fast walk, but definitely not a slow one, for the first glass, until the squad was probably within two kays of the border. At that point, he ordered out scouts to ride on the higher ground on each side of the road so that they could report on whether they saw any Gallosians or others on or near the river or the rolling ground to the east of the road.

After the squad had covered another half kay, the scout on the river side called down from the rise where he rode, "Ser, it looks like there are flatboats ahead on the south side of the river."

"Beltur, ride up there with me."

While Beltur had no idea what he might be able to add, he immediately replied, "Yes, ser," and followed the captain off the road and up the low rise to the top, little more than two or three yards above the road, but high enough to provide a clear view of the River Gallos. He reined up beside the captain and looked south where, close to a kay away, right about where Beltur thought the border might be, it was obvious that flatboats were pulled halfway onto the west shore.

"I count ten flatboats there," said Laugreth. "How many do you see?"

Beltur counted twice before replying. "Ten, ser." His eyes drifted back toward the east shore. After a moment, he frowned. He squinted, then concentrated, confirming with his senses what he'd seen—partly— with his eyes. He was about to speak when the captain did.

"They could cross with anywhere from five hundred to a thousand armsmen. There are tents, it looks like, beyond the west bank of the river."

"There's one other thing, ser," ventured Beltur. "There's a flatboat on this side of the river, maybe a hundred yards north of the ones on the west side. It's almost hidden behind those rocks sticking up."

After several moments, the captain murmured, "I see it. Can you tell if there are any armsmen anywhere nearby?"

Beltur tried to sense whether there were men near the half-concealed flatboat. "There are a few men with the boat. Three . . . maybe four. Not any more than that."

"That means the men they carried across have moved

away from the river. They can't have come north, or we
would have seen them or their tracks. There's no reason
for them to head south. They likely moved east and
then north, most likely along the border." Laugreth
turned to the scout. "Keep your eyes open for any sign
of the Gallosians."

"Yes, ser."

The captain turned his mount toward the road and
the waiting squad and headed down the rise. Beltur followed.

Once they were back on the road, the captain called
out to the scout riding along the road to the east, "Keep
an eye out for Gallosians."

"Yes, ser."

Beltur doubted that he'd ridden more than a hundred
yards when he began to sense riders, although it was
hard to determine too much. After another hundred
yards, he finally said, "Captain . . . there are riders
about half a kay to the southeast of us. They're moving
back toward the river."

"How many?"

"That's hard to tell. At least twice as many as we've
got. Maybe more."

"Is there anyone closer? Outriders? Scouts?"

"Not that I can tell."

"Are they on our side of the border?"

"I can't tell that. They're close to the border, as well
as I can sense."

"We'll keep moving. Can you let me know if those
riders move north?"

"Yes, ser. They're still moving west toward the river."

After riding about a fifth of a glass longer, at the top
of a gentle rise in the road, Beltur could see the border
cairns. Just beyond the cairns was a force of armsmen
in dark gray uniforms. Beltur frowned. The gate guards
in Fenard had worn black and black leathers, and Pacek

and the armsmen that had accompanied Beltur and his uncle to Analeria had worn faded light gray. Had they just been wearing their uniforms so long that they'd faded from dark gray to light gray? Beltur almost shook his head and returned his attention to the Gallosians.

One group was positioned on the road facing the border. The remainder seemed to be riding westward toward the river.

"Squad! Halt!"

For several moments, the captain said nothing. Finally, he spoke. "So far, it looks like they're staying on their side of the border. Do you know anything different, Beltur?"

"I can't sense anyone nearby that's across the border. There's another rider much farther east, but I can't tell from here which side of the border he's on."

"How much farther east?

"About a kay. It could be a little less. There are a lot of trees there. It's hard to tell." Beltur paused. "There's also what seems to be a path or a road heading east, and one heading north, maybe a little northeast."

"We'll stay here and watch for a while. Keep track of that rider if you can."

"Yes, ser."

"Squad! Stand down."

As Beltur and the squad watched the Gallosians, they moved back to the west and the riverbank, where they began to drag the flatboat upstream. For a moment, Beltur wondered why, but almost immediately recognized that was so that the Gallosians wouldn't cross into Spidlarian territory on the return to the west side of the river.

Almost a glass passed before the first contingent entered the flatboat and headed for the western bank of the river. During that time, Beltur continued to sense the presence of the single rider, who had not moved all that much.

At that point, Laugreth turned to the squad leader. "Vaertaag, select four men to remain and watch the Gallosians. They'll be relieved in three glasses. If there's any movement across the border, one is to report immediately, the others to withdraw slowly and keep watching."

"Yes, ser."

"There's no point in the entire squad waiting and watching."

Less than a tenth of a glass later, the rest of the squad was riding back north along the narrow road. So, Beltur realized, was the rider he'd been sensing, and the rider was slowly getting closer to the squad, along the path that did not quite parallel the old east road on which the squad was riding.

Beltur extended his senses again. Finally, he turned in the saddle. "Ser, that rider? He's moving north and getting closer to us."

"You can tell that?"

"Yes, ser."

"Maybe we should see if we can trap him. Let me know if he gets closer."

Beltur took that to mean when the rider was much closer, since he was still more than half a kay east of the squad.

By the time half a glass had passed, the distance had closed considerably. "Ser, I think he must be on a path that's nearing the road. He's maybe only three hundred yards east of us, over that low ridge there."

"Vaertaag . . . send three men back and over the ridge. Make certain they're quiet and that they get behind the rider. He might just be a weary traveler, but I have my doubts. Just have them keep well back of him for now."

"Yes, ser. Until we're in a position to confront him?"

Laugreth nodded. "If the path he's on is the one I think it is, it will join the main road in less than a kay. We'll pick up our pace just a little so that we arrive first."

While Beltur hadn't even noticed where the path joined the road, before long it was clear that Laugreth had been right.

As they neared the junction, the captain asked, "Can you conceal the squad while we wait for this traveler? It would make it easier."

"I can if you don't mind being in the darkness for a while. Everyone will have to be quiet. The concealment won't hide sounds or voices."

"Recon troopers are good at that. Where is he?"

"Just about a hundred yards up and around a bend."

"We need to get into position."

"How close do you want him before I lift the concealment?"

"As close as possible . . . or when he suspects something and tries to get away."

Beltur nodded.

Laugreth set up the squad facing the path and spread so that the rider couldn't spur his mount and ride around the Spidlarian force.

Then Beltur raised the concealment.

Almost a third of a glass passed before the single rider neared the hidden Spidlarian force. He was less than twenty yards away when he reined up.

Beltur decided not to wait, and dropped the concealment. The slender man wore faded grays and a battered gray leather jacket.

"Welcome to Gallos, stranger," said Laugreth.

The rider turned his mount and started back up the path, but when he saw the three troopers coming down, he turned toward the trees on the slope to the east.

Not wanting the man to escape, Beltur threw a containment around the fleeing rider, but also recalling what had happened in Analeria when he'd used shields against a charging horse, Beltur kept the containment just around the upper part of the rider's body. Even so, Beltur was almost yanked out of his saddle for a moment. When he regained his balance and seat, he was relieved to see that the rider was stretched on the ground. He was less relieved when he saw that one leg was at an angle that it should not have been.

"How did you do that?" asked the captain.

"I just used part of a shield. I couldn't have held the shield long against a galloping horse. I didn't do him any favors from the way his leg looks."

"It was likely easier on him than the troopers would have been," replied Laugreth, urging his mount forward.

By the time Beltur and Laugreth reached the fallen rider, Beltur saw that the three trailing rankers had captured the rider's mount and were leading it back down the path. Beltur looked down at the figure in nondescript gray. "Can someone splint his leg?"

"Tiegan can," offered Vaertaag. "Is it worth it?"

Beltur looked to Laugreth.

"He's likely a spy, and spies in wartime . . ."

"Are we at war yet?" asked Beltur.

"You'd better have Tiegan splint it," said Laugreth before turning back to Beltur.

Beltur dismounted, handing Slowpoke's reins to a ranker who had eased his mount forward, and walked toward the suspected Gallosian. He let his senses run over the leg, then waited while Tiegan straightened and splinted the leg. When the ranker moved away, Beltur eased slight bits of order into the places where there was wound chaos. "Try not to move it much. I think it will heal."

"Does it matter?" The man's voice was bitter.

"It might," said Beltur, stepping back and then re-mounting.

Two rankers helped the captive back onto his mount, but not before removing a blade from the pack behind the saddle, and handing it to the captain.

Laugreth looked over the weapon and then nodded to Beltur. "You might be right. They were careful." He handed the blade to Vaertaag. "That's a Suthyan bravo's blade." He looked at the captive. "We know better, but it's best to stick to the letter of the military code, especially since we're not at war. Yet."

Once the squad was headed back toward Elparta, Beltur glanced back. Two rankers rode beside the injured man, and one held the reins to his mount. "You think he's a spy?"

"Don't you?"

"It's likely."

"If he hadn't tried to run, he'd have ended up in the same place, but without a broken leg." Laugreth paused, then asked, "Are you a healer, too?"

"No, ser. I know a little about it. I don't know how to splint a leg and set a bone the way Tiegan did. What I did might make healing easier." Beltur wasn't about to mention that he'd been reading about healing. Reading wasn't the same as actually healing. "Why did he try to ride away from us?"

"Because someone told him we'd kill him on sight. We wouldn't have. Not without trying to find out what he knows."

"I doubt he knows much more than we do," suggested Beltur.

"You're probably right. He was sent out to find out what he could."

"Just as we've sent out scouts?"

"Of course. Ours have been more careful and discreet. So far, they've all returned. But then, they've had more training and experience. That's one advantage we'll have when the fighting really starts."

"If I might ask, where are we at a disadvantage?"

"They have more troopers, and they have chaos-mages."

"What about siege engines?"

"If it comes to that, we'll likely be hard-pressed."

"Because for the Gallosians to use them, they'll have to have surrounded the city?"

"More or less."

That was what Beltur had already thought.

Once they returned to the barracks, sometime after second glass, the captive and presumptive scout was escorted to see Majer Jenklaar, the battalion commander, and Beltur groomed and stabled Slowpoke. As he finished, he turned to see one of the battalion ostlers standing outside the stall. "Yes?"

"Have you had any trouble with him, ser?"

"Outside of a little stubbornness the first day, no, I haven't. Why?"

"I just wondered, ser."

"Has he been a problem in the past?"

"He hasn't been that good in responding to the bridle, ser."

Beltur had the feeling there was more than that. "Is there anything more I should know?"

"Oh, no, ser. Not so long as he does what you need."

Beltur couldn't help but be curious, but saw no point in pressing the matter since the ostler wasn't about to say much more, if anything, than he'd already said.

He patted Slowpoke on the shoulder, saying, "I'll see you later," and then closed the stall door and headed for the barracks side of the company spaces.

He wasn't sure what he should be doing, or where

he should go, but he figured that if he happened to be in plain sight, either the captain or Gaermyn would find him.

In only moments, the senior undercaptain appeared. "Beltur, the captain said that you had captured a spy from more than thirty yards away with your magery."

"Shields, ser. I just put a shield around him so he couldn't go anywhere. The rankers actually captured him and escorted him back. And it was only about twenty yards. I don't know that I could have done it at thirty yards."

"That's still a good piece of work."

"Thank you, ser."

"What else can you do?"

"You and the captain have seen just about everything. Mostly, it's just using shields in some way or another. A concealment's really just a different kind of shield."

"He said you could sense the Gallosians almost a kay away."

"That was because there weren't any other people around. If there was a battle, I couldn't tell who was who, just a lot of people. I don't sense the people so much as the order and chaos they manifest."

"Can you recognize individuals that way?"

"Only people I've met a few times and paid attention to." Beltur wasn't about to mention that he could pick out mages and healers from other people, even if he didn't know them. That was volunteering too much and could easily lead where he really didn't want to go, not after barely escaping Wyath and his supporters.

In the end, Beltur spent almost a glass going over and back over what he could and could not do with his abilities before Gaermyn finally decided he'd learned all he could, or all that Beltur was able to tell him.

Not long after that, just before fourth glass, when

Beltur was thinking of leaving, he saw the captain striding toward him.

"Just a moment, Beltur."

"Yes, ser?"

"After what occurred today, you need to be with the company all the time from now on. You didn't bring any gear today, did you?"

"No, ser."

"Then . . . be here early tomorrow with your gear. You and Undercaptain Zandyr will share quarters."

"Tomorrow?"

"I know it's eightday, but if the Gallosians want to surprise us, it will likely be on an eightday. There aren't likely to be any days off from here on."

"Yes, ser." Beltur wasn't totally surprised, but he would have liked to have spent a few glasses with Jessyla on eightday. *But there's no reason why you couldn't stop by her house on the way home.* "Is it all right if I leave now, then, so that I can get ready to be here early tomorrow."

"Go ahead. You did a good job today. I want you to know that."

"Thank you, ser. I did the best I could. I still have things to learn."

"We all do. The officers who keep learning are the ones who are most likely to survive and prosper." Laugreth smiled. "You can go."

Beltur nodded politely, and then headed toward the south gate. From there, he made his way directly to Grenara's house.

Jessyla opened the door, smiling. "I knew it would be you."

"You did? How?"

"I just did. You look handsome in that uniform."

"He does indeed," added Margrena from behind her daughter. "Can you come in, Beltur?"

"Just for a bit. I just got off duty and came here from there."

"I'm glad you did," said Jessyla, stepping back and opening the door wider.

Margrena looked at Beltur, almost puzzled. "You're wearing what looks like an officer's uniform."

"I am. I'm a mage undercaptain. All of the mages are officers. I'm about as junior as they come."

"Is that better or worse?" asked Jessyla.

"Better. I'm afraid I'd make a terrible ranker. As a junior officer who doesn't have to command anyone, I can't make as many mistakes."

"You look a little worn, Beltur," said Margrena. "Have you eaten?"

"Not since breakfast."

"Just come into the kitchen. Grenara won't mind."

"That's because she's not here," added Jessyla.

"I wouldn't want to impose . . ."

"Nonsense," said Margrena. "We can get you a little something."

"If it wouldn't be too much . . ."

"Just go to the kitchen," said Jessyla, closing the door.

"There's something I have to tell you," Beltur began as he walked through the parlor toward the kitchen. "From now on, it looks like I'm going to be spending most, if not all, of my time with Second Recon. I've been ordered to report full-time tomorrow morning."

"Are the Gallosians that close?" asked Margrena.

"I was riding a patrol with the captain and a squad today, and we ran across a company of Gallosians. They'd used a flatboat to cross to the east side of the river, and there were ten more flatboats on the west side where there were lots of tents. They were just short of the border with Spidlar. We also captured a spy. At least, the captain thought he was a spy."

"Did you?" asked Jessyla, motioning for him to sit down on the bench at one side of the kitchen table.

"I'm afraid so. He tried to get away and broke his leg."

"How . . ."

"It was my doing. I held him with a shield, and he fell off his horse and came down wrong on one leg. I did have them splint it, and I made sure there wasn't any wound chaos."

"Was he armed?"

"He had a sword hidden in his duffel."

"That sounds like a spy," declared Jessyla.

"Here you go," said Margrena, setting a mug of cider before him, along with a small wedge of cheese and a chunk of bread.

"Thank you." Beltur took a swallow of the warmish cider. It still tasted good. "Are you two still healing for the Council?"

"For the moment," replied Margrena. "Once the fighting starts, though . . ."

"How soon will that be?" asked Jessyla.

"I don't know. The captain thinks it will be any time."

"You will take care of yourself, won't you?"

Beltur could hear and sense the concern. "I'll do my best." He paused, then added, "That is . . . if you don't overdo it on the healing." He looked to Margrena. "Both of you."

Jessyla grinned, then said to Beltur, "Thank you."

Margrena merely shook her head.

"What's it like, being an officer?"

"It's not much different, in some ways, from being a City Patrol mage. It's a matter of watching and using shields, and listening to someone who knows more than I do. And trying not to make mistakes. And coaxing a stubborn horse into doing what he's supposed to . . ."

In describing some of what he did, in between bites of

cheese and bread, and swallows of cider, Beltur tried to keep what he said cheerful, worried as he was, after having seen so many Gallosians.

When he finished, he smiled. "I suppose I should go. I've got to get my gear together, and tell Athaal and Meldryn."

"They don't know?" asked Margrena.

"I just found out this afternoon, and I came here first . . ." Beltur tried not to flush. "I didn't know if you'd be here, but I wanted to tell you myself."

"I can see where—" began Margrena.

"Mother," said Jessyla firmly.

Beltur eased to his feet. "Thank you both, again."

"We were glad to see you," said Margrena.

"Since you do have to go," Jessyla took Beltur's arm, "I'll see you out."

They walked to the front door. Jessyla did not open it, but took Beltur's hand. "Please, please, be careful."

"If you will."

They just stood there holding hands.

"Food is getting expensive, isn't it?" he finally asked.

"It's not . . ." Jessyla smiled. "There's no point in trying to hide that from you . . . or anything. Yes, it is. We've worried."

"I thought so." He fumbled in his wallet with his free hand, then slipped her three silvers. "It's not much, but I'll get fed. No one's going out of their way to feed you and your mother, I think."

"You don't have to . . ."

"I want to. You and your mother saved my life. This is little enough compared to that, and it's something I can do. It's something I want to do." His eyes caught hers, and neither one of them moved.

Finally, Jessyla murmured, "I never thought . . ."

"There's lots we never thought," he said gently. "I'd better go." *Before I do something very improper.*

"I know. I do know."

Beltur did blush, and saw that she had as well, but he stepped back, not wanting to, but knowing that some things couldn't be rushed.

LV

On eightday morning, Beltur left Meldryn and Athaal's house carrying a small duffel he had borrowed from Meldryn. In the duffel were spare smallclothes, his razor, a small towel and a blanket, both also borrowed, and his oldest trousers, along with some soap chips and a few other items. As he walked through the cool and gray early morning, along an almost deserted Bakers Lane, he realized that it was the last day of harvest and that tomorrow would be the first day of fall.

In less than half a season, his entire life had changed. He'd gone from being a marginally competent white mage to a largely black mage with stronger, if limited, capabilities, from living in Fenard with his uncle to living in Elparta with men he hadn't even known two seasons before, and from, in effect, serving the Prefect of Gallos to becoming a mage undercaptain opposing him. And those were just the largest changes.

When he reached the warehouse barracks, well before sixth glass, he made his way to the small cubby that held the duty squad leader and a messenger.

"Yes, ser?" asked Nobryn, a junior squad leader whose name Beltur struggled to recall.

"The captain told me to report here permanently. I just thought I'd let you know."

"Yes, ser. Undercaptain Gaermyn told me to expect

you, ser. He said you're sharing quarters with Under-captain Zandyr. Do you know where they are?"

"I can find them, thank you."

"Yes, ser."

Beltur only made one wrong turn in getting to his "quarters," which consisted of two narrow pallet beds formed of planks and set in a space two and a half yards long, and perhaps two wide with crude plank walls on two sides, the rear being the original wall. There was no door, just a canvas drop cloth, rolled up and tied for the moment.

Zandyr stood as Beltur entered, duffel in hand.

"Good morning," offered Beltur.

Zandyr nodded. "The quarters aren't much, except they're dry, and we're not sleeping in the mud."

"There's something to be said for that." Beltur slid his duffel under the bed. "Have you heard anything new since yesterday?"

"The main Gallosian force is supposedly two days away. I'm not sure how accurate that is, but that's what Senior Undercaptain Gaermyn said."

"He likely knows as much as anyone," replied Beltur, adding quickly, "Did your brother get off all right?"

"My brother?"

"The one you said was going off to serve on one of your father's ships."

"Oh, Alastyn. He left on fourday. He'll be in Kleth by now."

"Where will his ship be going?"

"Swartheld. That's in Hamor."

Beltur ignored the condescension of the unnecessary explanation. "Will he get to Cigoerne? I understand that's the city founded by the heirs to Cyador."

"It is? What do they trade?"

"Except for shimmersilk, I don't know." Beltur wouldn't even have known that, except for his occa-

sional forays into the market squares in Fenard, trips
that seemed so very long ago.

"Couldn't be that much. Father hasn't mentioned
Cigoerne." Zandyr bent over and picked up his visor
cap. He smoothed his not-quite-too-long blond hair and
then carefully put on the cap. "We might as well go out
while the rankers form up for muster."

Beltur nodded, then walked beside Zandyr in the direction of the wide warehouse doors that served Second
Recon.

Once more, after muster, the officers met around the
circular table in Laugreth's makeshift study. The captain cleared his throat, then began.

"There haven't been any more Gallosians coming
down the river. There's still a company of foot on the
east side of the river. The scout we caught yesterday
denies that he's Gallosian. He'd do that either way. He
hasn't said very much. He admitted seeing the Gallosians, but he claims the reason he was on the side path
was because he wanted to avoid them."

"Is it possible he's not?" asked Zandyr.

"About as possible as the river freezing over tonight.
That's not our problem. Today, I'll be taking Beltur and
Second Squad back toward the border to see what else
we can find out."

"If we already have scouts . . . ?"

Beltur could see Zandyr's confusion.

"Because the scouts have trouble seeing what they
can't see," replied Laugreth. "Undercaptain Beltur can
use magery to find what's hidden. The only problem is
that there's only one of him."

Zandyr seemed only slightly less confused.

Laugreth gave a quick look to Gaermyn and continued. "Undercaptain Zandyr, you'll be working with Undercaptain Gaermyn today. Are there any questions?
Good. Dismissed."

Less than half a glass later, Beltur was riding to join Second Squad.

Chaeryn, Second Squad leader, reported as Beltur reined up. "Second Squad ready, ser."

"Very good, Chaeryn." Beltur smiled. "Did Vaertaag let you know what I can and can't do?"

"He told all of the other squad leaders what you've done so far, ser."

"I don't know if we'll be doing any of that today, have you and your men been briefed on what happens if I raise a concealment—that they'll be in total darkness and that a concealment doesn't hide sounds or smells?"

"Yes, ser."

"Good. I just wanted to make sure." Beltur paused, then asked, "Is there anything I should have heard, and didn't?"

Chaeryn offered a faint smile. "I wouldn't know that, ser."

Beltur smiled back. "You can't blame a very new officer for trying."

"How are you doing with Slowpoke, ser?"

"He was a little stubborn the first day. Since then, he's been fine. He just needed a little gentle convincing." Beltur wasn't about to say more. He'd just been fortunate that what he'd tried had worked. It just as easily might not have.

Laugreth rode up, a good fifth of a glass later.

Although it was well past the time Beltur had expected, he simply reported, "Second Squad ready, Captain."

"Thank you, Undercaptain, Squad Leader. Let's head out."

Beltur got the impression that Laugreth was less than perfectly pleased, both from the not-quite-preoccupied tone of his voice and from a hint of chaos swirling around the captain.

After they had ridden almost a kay, Laugreth turned in the saddle and asked in a quiet voice, "How are you getting along?"

"With Recon Two, ser? You and Undercaptain Gaermyn, and the squad leaders would know better than I do. I'm just trying to do what you need and not make any terrible mistakes."

Laugreth laughed. "Your best characteristic is that you know you don't know much about Recon Two or regular armsmen. It takes some junior undercaptains a while to learn that. Some never do."

Those words told Beltur why the captain had been preoccupied, and the way Laugreth had broached the subject also indicated that Laugreth wanted to let Beltur know without mentioning Zandyr's name. "I've never had either the burden or privilege of position, ser, and I barely escaped the wrath of the Prefect. I try to be very aware of what I don't know." Beltur grinned. "That's not too hard, because there's a great deal I don't know."

"You'll learn." Laugreth nodded.

When they had ridden another two kays or so, the captain asked, "Can you tell if there are any Gallosians ahead of us?"

Beltur concentrated. After a time, he said, "There are horses and men near the border, but it's too far for me to tell where exactly they are."

Beltur judged that he'd ridden another half kay before he could get a much better sense of the armsmen. "I think there's about a company right near the river, and most of them are very close together. There are also three men just about on the border, from what I can tell, on a hill just back from the river."

Laugreth smiled. "Those are our scouts. Are there any others to the east of the Gallosians by the river?"

"There aren't any that I can sense, ser. But I wouldn't

know if they're more than two kays away, maybe three. Should I be looking for anything besides men or horses?"

"They're likely only to bring across mounted or foot units."

What else could they bring? That was Beltur's first thought, but he realized that there were supply wagons and, of course, the siege engines. "Because the road is too narrow, ser?"

"Partly. Also it's too hilly and steep in places for supply wagons, but especially for the wagons carrying parts of the siege engines. I don't think they try to bring those across until they've crossed the border and have set up a post on the flatter ground closer to Elparta. That's something the marshal will want to stop before they can bring in too many armsmen. But the Gallosian marshal will probably try to stage as many troopers as they can on their side of the border. Then they'll quickly move one force to the east side and march down the east road here as quickly as possible while their main force advances on the west side. Their goal would be to take and hold the flatter land south of the piers on both sides of the river."

"If they don't want us to know, they could do that well before dawn in the morning, couldn't they?" asked Beltur.

"That's why we have scouts from Fifth Squad posted here all the time. If it looks like they're starting to ferry lots of men or men and mounts, they'll report, and the marshal will decide what forces to use against them. Even if they used ten flatboats, it would take more than a glass, possibly two, to get everyone across, and they'd still be bunched together on the road."

"But so would we, wouldn't we?"

"We don't have to go anywhere. We just have to stop

them, and that's easier in rocky and hilly ground. On wide open ground, it's the other way around."

After another kay of riding, as they came around a gentle curve, Beltur could see the stone cairns on the road marking the border, perhaps three hundred yards ahead. He could also sense someone approaching.

"One of the scouts is headed this way, ser. Well, toward the road. That's if those three are our scouts."

"How close is he?"

"About a hundred yards ahead, coming down that slope on the west side of the road with the single small juniper by the clump of bushes."

"We'll ride to meet him."

When the squad neared the slope that Beltur had described, Laugreth called out, "Squad! Halt!" He turned in the saddle. "We'll wait here."

Within moments, a man scrambled down the last yards of the slope on foot toward the road. "Captain, ser! Salaatyr here."

Laugreth rode over toward him, and Beltur followed, wanting to hear what Salaatyr might have to say.

"They've got close to a company on this side, ser. It looks to us like they're building a rough ramp out of stones and sand and dirt and deepening a spot at the edge of the river."

"How wide a ramp?"

"Could be maybe four, five yards wide. They haven't filled in a lot of the middle part yet. Must have twenty, thirty men lugging buckets of gravel and small rocks."

"Could we see it from the hilltop there?"

"Yes, ser."

Laugreth looked to Beltur. "Come with me." Then he dismounted and handed his mount's reins to a ranker.

Beltur did the same, and the two of them followed

the scout up the slope. Beltur almost slipped several times in sandy graveled patches between the grass and scraggly bushes.

At the top of the rise, two other scouts waited. Beltur caught sight of their mounts farther down the slope, but out of sight of the Gallosians.

"You see, ser?" said Salaatyr.

The captain nodded and turned to Beltur. "Can you tell me anything more about it?"

Beltur concentrated. After a short time he said, "It feels solid around the edges and next to the water. That side near the water is straight up and down. I can't really tell much more than that."

"How deep is the water there?"

"I can't tell you. Water blocks what I can sense."

"Do they have a mage or wizard down there?"

"No, ser. Not that I can sense."

Laugreth studied the riverbank for a time, then turned to the scouts. "If they start ferrying troopers, especially mounted troopers, one of you is to let me know immediately."

"Yes, ser."

"Or if they start bringing siege engines or anything like that."

Salaatyr nodded.

"We're heading back to let Majer Jenklaar know." Laugreth turned and started down the back side of the hill.

Beltur once more followed, trying to be careful as to where he put his boots.

Once they returned to the narrow road, Laugreth mounted and turned to Chaeryn. "We're heading back. We can't do anything more here at the moment, and the majer needs to hear about this."

Beltur mounted and then followed the captain as he

rode to what had been the rear of the squad. Behind Beltur was the squad leader.

"You don't sense any more troopers or mounts anywhere, do you?" asked Laugreth as the squad began the ride back to Elparta.

"No, ser."

"For now, that's good. It won't last. They're going to be bringing mounted foot or lancers or some kind of mounted armsmen. That ramp is so that they can get the horses off easily. They'll have a ramp mounted inside the flatboats as well. It will take them at least the rest of the day to finish that. It might take longer, but they're not doing all that work as a diversion."

Beltur wondered about that. Building a ramp took work, but it didn't cost lives. It also might make a diversion more effective, and from what Laugreth had pointed out, it would certainly make ferrying troopers and mounts faster. At the same time, he wondered why he hadn't sensed any white mages. He knew that some of them could certainly do what he'd done without any real risk.

LVI

When Beltur went to bed on eightday night in the cramped quarters, the other undercaptain was nowhere to be seen. When Beltur woke early on oneday, Zandyr was sound asleep in the other narrow pallet bed, and Beltur had a vague recollection of Zandyr returning sometime in the darkness.

Washing up and shaving was more than a little

inconvenient, given that the area set aside for that for officers was essentially at the back of the warehouse with water barrels and taps, and a long communal trough with a drainage pipe, not to mention its proximity to the officers' jakes.

Better than sleeping on the ground and washing in a stream, but definitely not as pleasant or convenient as my quarters with Athaal and Meldryn.

Eating wasn't much better. All the officers quartered in the huge warehouse had a single mess, if it could have been called that, in a corner of the west end of the building. The cheesed eggs were barely warm and tough, and Beltur absently wondered how anyone could make eggs that chewy. The toast was cold and just short of being burned. The ale was at least passable, and Beltur saved some in the chipped mug for the last, in order to rinse away the off taste of the food.

As he stood to leave, he caught sight of Athaal at another table, with two other mage officers, neither of whom Beltur recognized. He would have liked to have gone over and said a few words to Athaal, but the three looked very intent . . . and Beltur worried about being late to muster.

After muster, Beltur and Zandyr walked back toward the captain's study together.

"You were out late last night," Beltur said.

"Not that late. Besides, I knew nothing was going to happen today."

"You don't think so?"

"You said yesterday that the Gallosians hadn't finished building that docking ramp. They won't attack until they can cross the river easily on their side of the border. That means tomorrow at the earliest, possibly threeday, and more likely fourday."

"Unless they try something else," Beltur pointed out.

"They won't. There's no other easy crossing point in Gallos."

While Beltur had heard that before, it seemed to him that relying on an enemy to always do the expected could be dangerous if it became a habit. "You think they're that predictable?"

"It's not being predictable when there aren't any other practical options." Zandyr smiled knowingly.

Which suggests that a way to surprise people is to come up with practical options when people think there aren't any. Unfortunately, Beltur couldn't think of any at the moment. Nor had he thought of any by the time the four officers sat in the small study and the captain began the morning briefing.

"First off, we're going to be more shorthanded here than the marshal planned on. The Council decided to hold two battalions in reserve in Kleth. If the Council had a reason for such a decision, Commander Vaernaak didn't share it with Majer Jenklaar. The majer was quite clear about that. The Gallosians are still working on that flatboat ramp. They're making it wider and likely won't finish until late today."

Zandyr nodded as if he had expected that.

"That may be, Zandyr, but you'll accompany me and Fourth Squad on another recon of the east river road. I don't expect much difference, but you need to see the Gallosian positions and the possibilities for where they'll go when they do attack."

"Yes, ser."

"Beltur, today you'll do some maneuvers and practice with Gaermyn and Third Squad. I want you to familiarize them more with concealments. Gaermyn will also familiarize you with how various maneuvers can be used. That's in the unlikely event you find yourself in command of a squad. It can't hurt."

What bothered Beltur about Laugreth's matter-of-fact words was the implication that, while Beltur's being in command was unlikely, it was a definite possibility. His second thought was that was exactly the point the captain had wanted to make.

"All of this could change within glasses." Laugreth looked directly at Zandyr and added, "So . . . it might be for the best if none of you were out late at night from now on. We might have to head out before dawn."

"Yes, ser." Beltur joined Zandyr in acknowledging the de facto command, although he had no intention of being out anywhere.

"That's all. Go mount up." Laugreth stood, followed by the three undercaptains.

Beltur and Zandyr walked toward the stables together.

Once they were well away from the study, Zandyr did speak, if in a low but intense tone. "What difference does it make if I'm out a little late? I can still do what the captain wants." He glared, not quite looking at Beltur.

"We can't do what he wants if we're not here."

"He's not going to send squads up the northeast road in pitch darkness." Zandyr shook his head.

Beltur decided against pointing out that such a maneuver was possible if a mage were helping guide such a squad. "Not if he can help it, but he might not have that choice."

"The Gallosians aren't going to attack over hilly narrow roads in pitch darkness. That wouldn't make sense."

How often does war make sense to anyone fighting it? Beltur still couldn't see why the Prefect wanted a war over tariffs. Even if he conquered Spidlaria, how could he ever recover the golds spent if he wanted to lower river tariffs in Spidlar? Or was that just a pretext? *How many of the reasons people give for their actions are just pretexts?*

Beltur mulled over those thoughts after he left Zandyr and as he saddled Slowpoke and then rode out to join Gaermyn and Third Squad.

Two glasses later, Beltur at least knew the different commands that he'd be expected to use if he ever found himself in command of a squad, although he couldn't conceive of a time when he'd ever have to wheel a column, except on a parade ground, and that was highly unlikely, given that he was essentially only a temporary officer, and that probably only until the fighting ended, however it did. He didn't want to think of the rather unpleasant possibilities for himself if matters ended catastrophically for Spidlar.

On the other hand, all of Third Squad had experienced the complete darkness of a concealment as well as seeing part of their squad appear to vanish, yet still be able to hear commands or other sounds.

Gaermyn then suggested practicing riding under a concealment. That took more than a glass to work out how to keep riders and mounts in a straight line, a maneuver that required, paradoxically, staggering riders so that each pair was close enough to the pair in front to be able to follow their lead.

As he and Gaermyn rode back toward the temporary barracks and stables, the older undercaptain cleared his throat.

"Yes, ser?"

"Have you talked much to Undercaptain Zandyr?"

"Some. He doesn't think the Gallosians will attack before tomorrow, perhaps not even until fourday."

"That could be. It also could be that's what they want us to believe. Has he said anything else . . . of interest?"

"No, ser. He did tell me his brother just left to serve in some capacity on one of his father's ships, and he said that the temporary barracks were better than sleeping in the rain. We really haven't talked that much. Oh, and he asked about cupridium blades. He was very interested in how much they cost."

"He sounds very much like a trader's son."

"I wouldn't know, ser. He's the first one I've met."

"You're not missing much." Gaermyn shook his head. "If the Gallosians don't attack tomorrow, I'll have you work with another squad, most likely Fifth." He paused. "One other bit of advice. Sleep when you can. Once the fighting starts you never know when you'll next get the chance."

"I'll keep that in mind."

"I need to check on something. I'll see you later." Gaermyn turned his mount.

Beltur kept riding toward the stables.

LVII

Immediately after muster on twoday morning, Beltur and the two other undercaptains sat around the small table in the captain's makeshift study, listening as Laugreth briefed them.

"The scouts have reported two heavy infantry companies beginning to cross the river from the main Gallosian position to the east side. We've been ordered to watch them closely and to engage them, if necessary, to keep them from flanking the south piers. Third Recon will be joining us within a glass of the time we're in position." Laugreth delivered the words evenly.

Beltur had the definite feeling that the captain wasn't particularly pleased. Then part of that might have been because Zandyr had once again been rather later in getting to bed—at least late enough that Beltur had had no idea exactly when it had been. To Beltur's right, Zandyr shifted his weight on the stool where he sat, and then shifted it again.

Gaermyn raised his eyebrows.

"You have a question, Undercaptain?"

"We're a recon company, ser."

"You'd like to know why we're being dispatched?" The captain smiled. "No one's explained that to me. In fact, I was told not to ask for an explanation. It might be that our men have bows as well as blades. Or that moving any of the forces the marshal has mustered on the west side of the river to the eastern bank would take time and boats. We're outnumbered as it is. What if the two Gallosian companies are a feint? What happens once the marshal removes a company or more from the main force on the western side of the river?"

Beltur understood what Laugreth wasn't saying—that if the Gallosians established a position close to the piers they could shift all their forces to the east side of the river and then move on the city. If the Prefect's forces took the piers they could use their siege engines at very close range.

Gaermyn nodded, slowly, with a sour expression. "So we have to act like mounted infantry and archers all in one."

"Who else?" asked the captain sardonically. "Gaermyn, you'll have rearguard with Fifth Squad. Zandyr, you'll ride at the head of Third Squad. Beltur, you'll be with me and First Squad. That may change." Laugreth offered a tight smile. "Any other questions?"

"No, ser." All three undercaptains uttered the same acknowledgment close to simultaneously.

Once they had left the captain's study, Zandyr eased up beside Beltur as the two walked toward the stables. "We're a recon company. We're not lancers, and the men don't carry the shields of the heavy foot." After an instant, he added, "Not that some of them might not be better suited to just hauling shields."

Beltur didn't want to even acknowledge Zandyr's last comment. Instead, he replied evenly, "I imagine Majer Jenklaar, Commander Vaernaak, and Marshal Helthaer all know what the company can do."

"It doesn't make sense," said the younger undercaptain in a voice barely above a murmur. "Why would they order that?"

"It could be because they think the alternatives are worse. We're not getting the naval marines, and we haven't gotten all the troopers the marshal counted on. The captain mentioned that yesterday. I think it's worse than that." The last was just a guess, but one Beltur had suspected for some time.

"Why do you think that? Magery?" Zandyr's last word was clearly deprecating.

"Have you seen any more armsmen recently? Have there been any boats ferrying troopers from Elparta across the river to join the marshal's forces on the west bank?"

"But the Council said that all available forces . . ."

"I believe the Council once said something about naval marines, didn't it?"

"That was different."

"Was it?" Beltur asked, rather than more bluntly pointing out what he thought—that some traders didn't want to commit troopers to defend Elparta, either because they didn't want to weaken Kleth or Spidlaria, or because they didn't want to spend the golds, or possibly even because they wanted to do nothing to draw the Prefect's wrath in the event that Gallos prevailed.

"It was. There must be some mistake." Shaking his head, Zandyr strode away.

Beltur knew there was a great deal he didn't know and likely never would, but after seeing Zandyr's reaction, he had to question the younger undercaptain's powers of observation. *Or maybe he just believes everything his father told him about how wonderful all traders are.*

Beltur straightened as he sensed someone approaching behind him, then turned and waited as Gaermyn neared.

"Young Zandyr didn't look too happy."

"He had some concerns about why we're being sent against heavy infantry. I suggested that the marshal didn't have as many armsmen as he thought necessary to stop the Gallosians. He didn't like the possibility that the Council's orders for additional forces might not have been heeded."

"They never are," replied Gaermyn. "That was one reason why the trouble with Suthya lasted so long. Wasn't that the Suthyans were that tough. It was that we never had enough armsmen to finish them off. We only got more troopers when foreign traders refused to port at Diev because the fighting was so near to the harbor."

That scarcely surprised Beltur, although it wasn't something he'd heard before. "How good are our rankers as archers?"

"Good enough. That's not the problem. We don't carry enough shafts for long encounters. Ten for each man. If they've got mages, they could stop a lot of those shafts . . . and more. Giving us more shafts would short another company."

Beltur understood that as well.

At the entrance to the stable, the two separated, and Beltur made his way to the stall, where he saddled the big brown gelding, then led him outside. He looked the gelding in the eye. "This is going to be a long day, big fellow." Then he patted Slowpoke on the shoulder, mounted, and rode eastward toward the area that served as the marshaling ground. When he reined up beside Vaertaag at the head of First Squad, surprisingly, Zandyr had not even reached Third Squad.

"Good morning, ser."

"Good morning, Vaertaag. Do you think this morning will be the morning that the Gallosians attack?"

"You'd have to ask them, ser." Vaertaag grinned. "But I wouldn't be surprised."

Both turned in the saddle and watched as the captain rode up.

"Company ready, ser," declared Vaertaag.

"Company! Forward!" ordered the captain.

Once they were on the road south, with scouts out ahead, Laugreth turned to Beltur. "Gaermyn tells me that Undercaptain Zandyr wasn't pleased to learn the normal condition of Spidlarian armed forces."

"Something like that, ser."

"That sometimes happens with the youngest son."

Beltur understood that as well, because he had the feeling that much of Zandyr's behavior lay in the fact that he was a younger son.

"Can you tell anything about the Gallosians yet?"

"No, ser. Nothing except that there aren't large numbers of people or animals anywhere close to us . . . to the south, that is."

Beltur judged that they'd ridden slightly over two kays when he began to sense the mixtures of order and chaos that indicated larger living things, mostly men, but also horses. He was about to report that when Laugreth turned in the saddle.

"Can you tell where the Gallosians are?"

"No, ser," replied Beltur. "Only that there's a mass of people to the south of us . . . and maybe a bit east. Mostly foot."

"East? Already? How far?"

"It's too far for me to tell."

"Let me know when you can."

"Yes, ser." Beltur understood why the captain wanted to know, but he also knew from previous reconnaissance that there wasn't any way for Second Recon to get to where the Gallosians were and appeared to be moving other than by taking the old east road that Recon Two was already on.

By the time they had ridden another half kay, Beltur was getting a far better sense of the Gallosians' position. He also realized one other thing. There was definitely a white mage accompanying them, riding with the handful of men who had to be officers.

"Captain."

"Yes?"

"I don't think the Gallosians are a feint. At least, not a complete feint. There are two full companies, if not more, and there's a white mage with them."

"Can you tell if there are more crossing the river?"

"Not from this distance. The water makes it difficult." *Not as bad as rain, but still hard.* "There are only a few men on the east shore, though."

"What about the white wizard?"

"I don't think he's one of the most powerful ones, unless he's shielding himself more fully, and that takes more effort." *A great deal more.* Beltur had been required to learn that to become a white, but holding a total concealment that blocked order, chaos, and light was exhausting, even for strong mages, although merely damping order and chaos was considerably less tiring. He did have the feeling, based on what he had learned from Athaal and on his own, that it was far easier for blacks to shield order and chaos and to hold those broader concealments. He didn't know for certain, because, he realized, he hadn't tried since he'd come to Elparta. *It's something you should have tried.*

He repressed a sigh. Once again, he'd realized something later than he should have, but now wasn't the time to try that out, not when he might need every bit of magely strength he possessed.

He kept riding, for perhaps close to a kay before he reported once more to the captain. "There's a company set up about where the road reaches the border, and another company, possibly two, moving east along that other path."

"Frig," muttered Laugreth, almost but not quite inaudibly, before saying clearly, "They're trying to avoid us, or sending those companies far enough east to draw us away from the river road. If we don't follow, then they'll be in a position to flank us whenever they want. That means we either have to attack the one company to get to the others, or climb hills on our side of the border. We can't afford to attack. Not now."

"They're mostly on foot, I think," Beltur pointed out.

"Do they have any wagons?"

"Not that I can tell."

"Then the scouts were right about that. We might be able to stay with them until they decide what to do."

"Do you think they'll cross the border?" asked Beltur.

"They'll cross the border. It has to be soon, or they'll be turning back before long. The only question is when they'll decide." Laugreth turned in the saddle, looking back at Vaertaag. "We need to send a message to Third Recon. Tell them that we're shadowing a Gallosian company. Tell them that I recommend that they continue to the border on this road because another Gallosian company is drawn up just on the other side of the border here."

"Yes, ser."

Beltur noted that the squad leader didn't question whether Second Recon could successfully shadow the

Gallosians, and in what seemed like moments, a single rider headed back north toward Elparta.

Laugreth then shifted his weight in the saddle and looked at Beltur. "If we want to stay close to the Gallosians, we're going to have to shadow them single file. If they have two companies, they'll outnumber us. We can't get too close, but we also don't want them getting to another road heading north while we're still in the hills. That would allow them to get around us. If we drop back to the flatter land around Elparta, we won't have any idea where they are, and they could even double back and strike Third Recon."

"Yes, ser."

"How close do you have to be in order to know what they're doing?"

"No more than two kays. One kay is much better. If they get into a thick forest . . . it might be less than that. And if there's heavy rain, it might be only a few hundred yards." Beltur was guessing about that because he simply didn't have enough experience.

The captain nodded slowly, then turned to Vaertaag. "Send back that I need Undercaptain Gaermyn."

"Yes, ser."

Before long, Gaermyn reined up beside the captain and Beltur.

"Here's what Beltur has discovered about the Gallosians on our side of the river . . ." When Laugreth finished explaining the situation, he just waited.

"Stringing out the company might not be the best way to handle it, ser."

"One squad, then," replied Laugreth, "and pull back the rest of the company to, say, where that other path forks from the river road?"

"To begin with. Then, if the Gallosians cross the border farther to the east, we can pull back and make better time heading east across the flatter lands north of the more rugged hills."

"And if they double back, the rest of the company can simply move south again to reinforce Third Recon."

"Yes, ser." Gaermyn smiled grimly. "I don't think they'll double back. They'll want to spread us out. Whatever they intend has to be quick because they're carrying whatever food they have in their packs."

"But if we don't spread, they'll reinforce their flankers and attack on all fronts. If we do, then they'll concentrate on our weakest point and try to smash through it."

"That's the way I see it."

What both officers didn't mention, Beltur noted, was that such a strategy was eminently possible because the Spidlarians were heavily outnumbered.

"Beltur will have to go with you and the recon squad," said Laugreth. "Which squad do you want to take?"

"Fifth Squad."

Before long, the riders of Fifth Squad were moving eastward up the slope beside the east river road, with Beltur directly behind Gaermyn and only a single scout riding ahead of them.

When they reached the top of the first hill, Gaermyn asked, "Can you tell how far away the Gallosians are?"

"Not exactly, ser. The ones we're shadowing . . . I'd say we've closed a little on them. I'd guess it might be a kay and a half."

Another half glass passed, and Fifth Squad was coming down a rough gully barely wide enough for two horses, although they were still riding single file. Once the squad was in a small valley, perhaps half a kay across, filled with sparse browning grass and scattered scrubby bushes, Gaermyn glanced back. "Are they still moving east?"

"They're not moving at all, ser. Just a little while ago, they stopped. No one seems to be turning back west."

"Let me know if that happens. How far?"

"Around a kay. I'd judge they're about two hills beyond the slope ahead of us at the east end."

"At this rate, we might be able to get in sight of them by early afternoon . . . if the ground doesn't get that much more rugged."

Fifth Squad was halfway across the valley when Beltur noticed a change in what the Gallosians were doing. "Ser . . . they're marching again. Now they're moving almost straight north, and they seem to be moving faster. I think they might have found a road or a long valley."

"Frig . . ." muttered Gaermyn. "Can you find an easier way north so that we can get ahead of them?"

Beltur concentrated. After a time, he finally said, "If we turn and head north right now, once we get over that ridge there, the one at the north end of the valley, riding will be easier than heading east, but it feels like it's very steep on the other side of the ridge. When we reach the north end of the valley, we might be better heading southwest over the western part of the ridge we just crossed."

Gaermyn studied the rocky escarpment to the north. "If the other side is steeper than this side, we don't even want to try it. Looks like we don't have much choice if we want to stay between them and Elparta." He turned his mount and called out, "This way."

In the end, it took Fifth Squad more than a glass to get out of the valley and then down to a stretch of rolling hills. Although the northern end of the ridge bordering the small valley on the west wasn't as steep as the rock-strewn slope that Beltur had pointed out, it was sandy, with spots where the footing, for both men and mounts, was treacherous, and in several places, everyone had to dismount and walk their horses.

By the time all of Fifth Squad was riding north along

the crest of one of the rolling hills, the sun was almost at its zenith, a white orb in a green-blue sky that didn't offer as much heat as the bright light suggested, especially given that Fifth Squad was riding into a brisk wind.

"What about the Gallosians now?" asked Gaermyn.

"They're about a kay east of us and a little south of us."

"After all that we went through, we gained on them?"

"They've taken more breaks than we have."

The older undercaptain frowned. "I don't like that. They have to have crossed the border into Spidlar by now, and they're slowing down? Why would they do that?"

The realization hit Beltur hard. "Ah . . . it might be that their white mage has been sensing us. He'd know that we only have a squad. They might be waiting to see what we do."

"Can he sense you?"

"I don't know. Blacks are harder to sense from a distance because they don't have any free chaos around them, and some whites are order-blind."

"You're saying it's likely he can sense us, but not you?"

"If he can sense you, he can sense me. He just might not be able to sense that I'm a mage."

Gaermyn nodded slowly. "Then . . . if we travel on, as if we don't know about them, we can see what they do. We're about five kays south of the narrow road that wanders along the foot of the hills to the southeast of Elparta and likely ten kays from the main road between Elparta and Axalt. I'd wager they'll make for the hill road and move toward Elparta. They'll likely want to take the road less traveled because they won't be so obvious. If they do that, we can call in the rest of the company and set up an ambush. If they don't move west toward Elparta, we may just have to post scouts to watch them and withdraw to Elparta ourselves."

That made sense to Beltur, because the marshal likely wouldn't want one or two companies held away from where the main attack might come.

For the next half glass, Fifth Squad kept riding, but at a measured walk aimed at tiring their mounts as little as possible. Beltur kept sensing the Gallosians who had remained in one place for close to a quarter glass before resuming their northward progress on a track that looked to be what Gaermyn had suggested.

Another fifth of a glass passed, and when Beltur reported that the Gallosians were continuing, Gaermyn dispatched a rider with a report to the captain.

After that, he turned to Beltur. "Can you tell if we're nearing the road that borders the hills?"

"No, ser. I can tell that beyond the hills ahead, on the far side, the ground is much flatter."

"How far would you say?"

"A kay and a half. That's just a guess."

Gaermyn smiled. "So far, so good. The Gallosians are still behind us?"

"Yes, ser."

"We'll head more to the northwest, away from them, as if we don't know about them. I'd like a bit more space between us right now."

Beltur could see that, for a number of reasons.

Slightly less than a glass later, Fifth Squad reined up on the south side of the hill road, a way barely wider than a path that was even narrower than the east river road. Beltur had already reported that the Gallosians had stopped earlier, about two kays east of Fifth Squad, seemingly on the back side of the last hill before coming to the hill road.

Gaermyn dispatched one rider to the top of the rise in the road to the east, and another to the south. Then the squad dismounted and settled down to wait, letting the horses graze on the sparse late-season grass.

A short while later, the senior undercaptain asked, "Are the Gallosians still there?"

"They are. They've made camp or bivouac, I think. They have a few fires lit."

"They might stay there one night. That's likely all. They can't forage that much here. It's mostly grasslands, and the locals haven't brought their flocks this far south quite yet."

A good two glasses passed before the scout posted to the south rode back and reported. "The rest of the company is only a kay away, ser."

"Just Second Recon?"

"Yes, ser."

Less than a third of a glass later, the remainder of the company neared Fifth Squad. Accompanying the captain and the other four squads of Second Recon was a single large wagon, drawn by two horses. The captain rode immediately to Gaermyn.

"Supplies?" asked Gaermyn.

"Extra blankets, too," replied Laugreth.

"How did you manage that?"

"By telling the majer that we needed them so that we didn't tire out the men and their mounts riding back to keep track of two companies of heavy infantry. The Gallosians now have three companies on the east side of the river. Two foot and one mounted. They were still ferrying more when we left."

"You went straight back to the pier, didn't you?" Gaermyn's words weren't really a question.

The captain nodded. "The more I thought about it, the more I thought it likely something like this would happen. I did post riders where any messenger you sent could be intercepted. Your message confirmed that, but we were ready to move out. Where are those two companies?"

"Beltur says they're two kays east of here . . ." Gaermyn went on to describe what had happened.

When the undercaptain finished, Laugreth nodded. "We'll post scouts a little north of where you have them now. The Gallosians will stay where they are tonight. Then, if they don't see any of our forces, they'll form up well before dawn and move west, trying to get as close as they can to Elparta. It's almost certain that the Gallosians will send a force down the river road at the same time. The scouts with Third Recon say that they think there is a white wizard with the force on the east bank. Third Recon will harass them and inflict what casualties they can as they pull back closer to Elparta. They'll have to be very careful in how they do that."

"Dirt is a very good protector against chaos-fire," Beltur said. "As long as you keep it between you and the chaos. If they can loft it and there's no mage to block it . . ."

"Then we lose men."

Beltur nodded.

"What's happening on the west side of the river?" asked Gaermyn.

"The same as on the east side, but with more men. They'll try to take the flat land upstream of the piers, then bring down the siege engines and hold them there while the forces on the east side try to push us back to the piers. That's my guess." Laugreth shrugged. "We can't do much about that. We're to keep those heavy infantry companies from flanking the piers."

"Just us?"

The captain laughed. "Why not? We're only outnumbered two to one, and we have archers and a mage. Also, I've had the rest of the company practice riding blind, the way you told me you'd practiced. The rankers weren't too pleased with being told to close their eyes, but I think we got most of the problems straightened out."

Beltur managed not to apologize for not thinking about that. He just nodded. "I hope we don't have to do that with a whole company."

"Hope isn't much help in trying new maneuvers," replied Laugreth.

"Yes, ser." Beltur suddenly felt like someone had dropped several stones' weight of bronze on his shoulders.

"For the moment," Laugreth continued, "we should get everyone fed."

Gaermyn nodded.

Beltur looked eastward toward the Gallosian forces he could sense, but had never seen.

LVIII

Even with two blankets, Beltur awoke shivering twice during the night, thinking more than once before he fell back into a continually disturbed slumber that it was only early fall. Breakfast was cold bread and cheese, but with halfway decent ale, eaten in darkness well before dawn, but after Beltur had dealt with Slowpoke. Whether it was the food, the ale, or just walking around, Beltur began to feel better as he finished eating.

Zandyr, who had eaten without saying more than a few words, finally said to Beltur, "Do you think the Gallosians will really attack?"

"By crossing into Spidlar with armsmen, they already have."

"No . . . I mean attack us, Second Recon."

"If they're headed toward Elparta, we'll probably be the ones doing the attacking. That's what the captain was saying last night." *Didn't he or Gaermyn tell Zandyr?*

"Gaermyn said something about Third Squad standing in reserve after the first attack."

Beltur doubted that Gaermyn had been that vague, but only replied, "He probably was referring to any attack we make."

"Why would we attack? They outnumber us."

"Because we'll have to fight them sooner or later. If we attack first, and they don't expect it, we can gain an advantage. It also might slow them down."

"I can't believe I asked to be assigned to a reconnaissance company."

"Why did you?" Beltur managed to keep his sense of wry amusement out of his voice.

"Because Rhyana and Aliza thought I'd distinguish myself better there."

"You've told me about Rhyana, but you haven't mentioned Aliza."

"Aliza's my sister. She's going to be consorted to the elder son of Trader Chaeltyn once this unpleasantness is over."

Beltur was very glad it was dark enough that Zandyr didn't pick up on his momentary shock at Chaeltyn's name. *Are all the traders' offspring like that?*

At that moment, Laugreth appeared. "Time to mount up. The Gallosians are forming up and look to be headed toward us. Beltur, you'll be with me and Second Squad. Zandyr, you and Third Squad will withdraw with the rest of the company to the second ambush position. Undercaptain Gaermyn will fill you in on what you're to do."

Beltur was more than glad that he'd already arranged his gear and saddled Slowpoke before breakfast.

Zandyr did not move.

After a moment, Laugreth said firmly, "Undercaptain Zandyr, you'd best see to your squad."

"Yes, ser." Zandyr turned and headed toward the tie-lines that held the horses.

"Beltur . . . ?"

"Yes, ser?"

"I've been thinking. There's not much chance of ambushing the Gallosians if that white mage can sense us. Can you keep a squad from being detected by their white mage?"

Beltur frowned, then said, "If they're very close together and it's not for more than a glass or two . . . I *think* I can. It's not something I've done much."

"Could you tell if he's sensing us?"

"Maybe some mages can. I can't. I can tell if the Gallosians change direction, though."

"That should give us enough time to withdraw, then, if they do detect us." Laugreth shook his head. "This is all new."

Why? "You haven't used mages before?"

"No. The Suthyans don't like whites, and they don't have that many blacks, and they didn't use them. So the Council didn't think it was necessary. Now . . . with the Gallosians having so many whites, without using black mages to counter their whites, even the Council had to admit that using mages was necessary. So I've been told."

Beltur accepted what Laugreth said, even while he wondered why the Council had been so late to see the need. It wasn't as though magery hadn't been used in the past. That was how Nylan had defeated the Gallosians and Saryn the Black had become the first Tyrant of Sarronnyn.

"We'll just have to get into position and see if you can make it work."

"Yes, ser." Beltur wasn't looking forward to holding that sort of concealment, especially since he'd have to do it from the moment Second Squad rode away from the rest of the company.

Nearly half a glass later, Second Squad rode up the back side of a hill close to a kay east of where Second Recon had spent the night, guided through the darkness in part by Beltur. He didn't feel more than a slight strain from holding the shield that blocked detection of order and chaos. He wasn't holding a concealment, since there wasn't any point in that yet and it would have tired him more. Even so, he still worried.

So did the captain.

Beltur could tell that when Laugreth asked for the third time since they'd set out, "Where are the Gallosians?"

"They're now about a glass away. They seem to be on the road, and they have three scouts out ahead, two on foot and one mounted. The mounted scout is on the hilly side of the road, a bit farther away from the column than the other two."

"They're thinking about a possible ambush. We'll have to loose arrows before they know we're here. Otherwise, they'll lift their shields overhead."

"How effective will that be?"

"Too effective," replied the captain dryly.

Beltur kept his senses searching. While there were tiny flickers of order and chaos from small creatures and possibly a fox, and farther away what might have been a mountain cat, the only concentration of order and chaos was that surrounding the oncoming Gallosians.

Beltur kept sensing and watching. He could see slightly more than he had been able to, but whether that was because dawn was nearing or because his eyes were getting more used to the darkness, he couldn't tell.

The lead scout was still some three hundred yards away when Beltur said, "It's time to raise a concealment. I can just barely see the mounted scout."

"Do it."

Darkness enfolded Second Squad.

Beltur murmured to the captain, "The lead scout is two hundred yards to the east . . . not coming up the slope . . . first rank about three hundred yards back from him . . ."

When the mounted scout rode past the concealed Squad Two, less than fifty yards below Beltur, Beltur managed not to give a sigh of relief . . . or to say anything until the rider was more than a hundred yards west of him. ". . . scout passed by . . . now a hundred yards west . . . first rank a little less than two hundred yards away . . ."

"Let me know when they're abreast of us."

"Yes, ser."

Beltur found it hard to believe that they were so close to the Gallosians . . . and yet undiscovered. *But when they do find out, their mage will be very close. Very close.*

Finally, Beltur murmured, "The first mounted officers and the mage are riding past. Do you want me to drop the concealment now?"

"In a moment."

Beltur wondered why Laugreth wanted to wait still longer, but said nothing, waiting . . . and waiting, until it seemed as though a good third of the Gallosian rankers had passed them.

"Drop it now."

Beltur did. He immediately saw the long column of marchers, even the occasional glint of starlight on weapons or armor.

"Loose shafts! Now!"

Beltur still held the limited concealment to block the sensing of order and chaos.

The slightest hissing of arrows filled the air around Beltur as the rankers fired into the mass. Almost immediately, he could feel wound chaos from below, possibly some men who were dying, but that wasn't certain.

With a blast of light, a chaos-bolt arched from the front of the Gallosian formation, angling toward Second Squad.

How did he know where we are? Beltur threw up his regular shield, in time for the chaos-fire to spray across the hillside some fifteen yards below the squad.

"Hold your shafts!" ordered Laugreth. "On me!" He turned his mount and headed southwest across the upper slope of the hill. Beltur had to use his boot heels to get Slowpoke to move faster and match the fast trot of the captain.

Even as Beltur deflected another firebolt, he kept wondering how the other mage had known where Second Squad had been. *Except he didn't know until after the first three or four volleys of arrows struck the column.*

Laugreth led the squad over the back side of the slope before turning back onto a westward track.

Beltur didn't have to deflect the last firebolt that dropped onto the north side of the hill behind where Second Squad was riding.

"What are they doing?" demanded the captain.

"They've halted, ser."

"Good." After several moments, Laugreth spoke again. "How did that wizard find out where we were?"

"I don't think he sensed us . . . not exactly. That last firebolt wasn't anywhere close. Maybe he saw us when I dropped the concealment."

"He was well past us," the captain pointed out.

Then how . . . Abruptly, Beltur understood. "He sensed what wasn't there."

"What wasn't there?"

"When I shielded our order and chaos from him—or any mage—that meant he couldn't sense anything at all where we were. There's always some background order and chaos from small animals and what's in the grass. It's very low, but it's there. He started seeking out where there wasn't anything at all and then aimed the first two firebolts there. But when we started moving he couldn't figure that out quickly enough." Beltur shook his head. Yet another thing he really hadn't thought through. *You just don't have enough experience.*

As the first hint of dawn seeped up from the east, Laugreth asked, "Do you have any idea what sort of casualties they took?"

"No, ser. I do know that a number of the arrows hit their armsmen."

"It sounds like their mage will detect another attack like this."

"He might not. Not if you put the squad just over the top of a hill out of direct sight. He wouldn't be able to sense that there wasn't anything there because there would be background chaos and order in front of us and behind us, and the absence of order and chaos wouldn't stand out the way it did on an open hillside. It would be very hard to find us—until the men moved to the hilltop and loosed shafts."

After a moment, Laugreth said, "We might as well try."

As Second Squad moved west along the back side of the hills, the faint gray light on the eastern horizon began to strengthen. After the squad had ridden close to another kay, the captain positioned the squad just below the south side of a hill with enough of a curve that the squad couldn't be seen from either the road or farther east. Then he turned to Beltur. "Can you keep us concealed until they get here?"

"Keeping the white wizard from sensing us shouldn't be that hard. Holding a visual concealment once they or their scouts get close enough to see us will be harder, but I can do that." *You think.*

"Have they resumed their march?"

"They have. They're about half a kay north now."

Laugreth nodded. "It looks like they're moving to be in position for an attack on Elparta or on our forces outside the city. Let me know when their scouts are within a few hundred yards."

"Yes, ser."

Just about the time the white disk of the sun had cleared the horizon, Beltur again turned to the captain. "The Gallosian scouts are about two hundred yards north. The mounted scout is high enough on the slope above the road that he'll be able to see us soon if I don't raise the concealment."

"Raise it."

Darkness replaced the dim light around Squad Two.

"We don't want to attack until the middle of the column is below us. That should make it harder for them."

"Yes, ser." Beltur could feel that his shoulders were tight, and that his head was beginning to ache. *You can do this. They're only a few hundred yards away.* He shrugged several times, trying to loosen the tightness, even as he tracked the oncoming Gallosians and the white mage. Each moment that passed felt like a glass. That was the way it seemed, anyway, but the mounted scout passed without noticing the Spidlarian force, and eventually Beltur could say, "The middle of the column is almost even with us."

"Drop the concealment," ordered the captain quietly.

Beltur did, and the early sunlight flooded over the squad. He had to blink several times before his eyes adjusted to what seemed like a harsh glare.

"Squad! Bows ready! Forward!"

As soon as the rankers reached the crest of the hill, Laugreth first ordered, "Halt!" and then, after just a hint of a pause, "Loose shafts!"

The first arrows had barely struck the second company of infantry when a chaos-bolt flared directly toward the squad. Beltur deflected it, but noted that some of the Gallosians had already lifted their shields in an effort to block the shafts that sheeted down on them.

A second chaos-bolt followed the first.

Beltur felt the strain on his shields as he managed to block it.

"Withdraw! On me!"

Beltur managed to keep Slowpoke beside the captain as Laugreth led the squad over the top of the hill and then toward the southwest. At that moment, another chaos-bolt slammed into Beltur's shields with enough force that it rocked him in the saddle, and a wave of pain needles ripped through him. Yet, at the same time, Beltur had the feeling that the last firebolt hadn't been nearly as strong as the ones before.

Good thing it wasn't. His shield against direct chaos was gone, and he could barely hold on to the blocking shield as the squad continued, slowly moving away from the Gallosians, who had barely slowed after the second attack, although Beltur had sensed wound chaos among the armsmen, until he'd had to deflect the last chaos-bolt, after which he wasn't able to sense much of anything. Even his vision was blurred, as flashes of light flickered before his eyes, and he was definitely feeling very light-headed. He swallowed to force down the bile in his throat, and he seemed to be having trouble hearing because what Laugreth was saying seemed both far and distant, and some words were missing.

". . . you . . . right . . . ? Undercaptain!"

"Sorry, ser. I don't think I can do any more for a while."

"That's probably for the best. I doubt we could get away with a third attack, anyway."

Beltur finally had to drop even the chaos/order-blocking shield. "I can't hold any shields right now."

"We definitely aren't trying a third attack."

Beltur would have sighed, except it was taking all his effort and strength even to stay in the saddle.

Second Squad caught up with the rest of Second Recon sometime just before eighth glass. The rest of the company was halted, but whether that had been planned or Gaermyn had just ordered a stop to rest the mounts, Beltur didn't know, and the captain didn't say.

Instead, as soon as Second Squad reined up, Laugreth turned and said, "Squad Leader, send a ranker to get a water bottle full of ale for Undercaptain Beltur."

Chaeryn must have looked askance, because Laugreth added, "Blocking all those firebolts exhausted him, and we just might need his shields again before long."

"Yes, ser."

As a rider headed toward the single supply wagon, Gaermyn rode to meet the captain, then reined up beside him. "How did it go?"

"There are two companies of heavy infantry. They're well-disciplined, and they have a white wizard. We inflicted casualties, but how many we couldn't remain to determine. Beltur kept the white mage from seeing us until we loosed shafts from the hills overlooking the road, but after that, the mage was quick to throw firebolts at us. They're good enough with their shields that an archery attack, even by the whole company, won't stop them."

"Do they have pikes?"

"No. They've got the straight-swords that are longer than a sabre, though. I could see that."

"If . . . if we have to stop them, the only thing that might break their formation is a charge, but that would cost us . . ." Gaermyn broke off.

Beltur listened, but he had trouble concentrating and following the words.

"They don't have any supply wagons," said Laugreth. "If they're not planning on attacking, they'll have to start foraging."

"That won't be as hard on the herders as it might be. Most of the flocks are still north."

"It'll be hard enough. Have there been any messages?"

"Just one. We're supposed to delay the Gallosians as much as we can without taking excessive casualties."

The captain snorted. "That's helpful."

"What else could the majer say?"

At that moment, the ranker returned and handed a water bottle to Beltur. "Ser." For a moment, he paused, then added, "Begging your pardon, ser, you'd best drink some of this."

Beltur realized he hadn't even reached for the water bottle. "Thank you." He extended a hand and took it, then carefully pulled the cork and took a small swallow.

After drinking, if slowly at first, the entire bottle of ale, Beltur could at least see straight, and the light-headedness was gone, although he'd scarcely heard any of what else had passed between Laugreth and Gaermyn.

"Did that help?" asked Laugreth.

"Yes, ser. But I can still only sense about half as far. I *might* be able to block one of those chaos-bolts right now."

"Do you think their white wizard feels the same way?"

"Ah . . . his last chaos-bolt wasn't as strong as the others, but other than that, I couldn't say."

"That's something. It suggests that he can't throw chaos all day." The captain glanced back over his shoulder, looking east at the hill road, then turned back to Beltur. "Can you sense the Gallosians?"

"No, ser, but I can only sense about a kay right now."

"What about our scouts?" asked Laugreth.

"Second Squad is all they've seen so far," replied Gaermyn, "but foot don't raise dust the way a mounted company does."

Laugreth turned back to the older undercaptain. "We'll rest our horses for just a bit longer, and then we'll withdraw for another kay and take stock. There's a taller hill about that far, and we'll be able to see all the eastern approaches to Elparta from there. We'll send a report to the majer once we're in position."

"That's only two kays from the piers," Gaermyn pointed out.

"That's close enough that we can request reinforcements if we need to."

Beltur understood what Laugreth hadn't said—that the captain didn't see much point in losing lightly armed recon troopers against heavy infantry.

"There's one other thing," Laugreth added, turning back to Beltur. "We'll need to make sure you have extra ale from here on. We're going to need your shields."

Beltur nodded, just hoping he didn't have to do much of anything soon.

LIX

By noon on threeday, Second Recon was in position on the hill that Laugreth had described, only about a kay east of the river road. Beltur realized that he could actually see the lower hills on the south side of the road to Axalt, the same hills that backed Jorhan's smithy, slightly more than a kay to the north.

After having eaten some stale bread and hard cheese, and drinking more ale, Beltur was feeling close to recovered from the morning's efforts. He sat on the east side of the hill some ten yards below the crest on a ledge of red sandstone, really more of a protrusion that was just wide enough for sitting and long enough for perhaps three or four people side by side. The sunlight wasn't all that warm, but felt good, since there was barely a hint of a breeze.

Zandyr stood at the end of the ledge. "How long before the Gallosians attack, do you think?"

"They should have come into sight by now. So they've stopped or headed somewhere else."

"There's nowhere else for them to go, except Axalt."

"That's not likely. Two companies would just get trapped in the canyon, and then they'd be slaughtered." That had happened to the Prefect's grandsire, Beltur knew. "It's more likely that they've stopped or withdrawn to the south to join up with another Gallosian force for an attack somewhere else." Beltur didn't think that was likely, either, but it was possible, he supposed.

Zandyr sidled away without saying more, and that was fine with Beltur.

A short time later, Beltur thought he saw a puff of

dust to the east on the hill road. He tried to sense that far, only to find that all he could determine was that a single horse and rider approached. Finally, by squinting, he could just barely make out the man and mount, one of the scouts earlier dispatched by the captain.

Beltur stood and made his way down the hill toward where he saw Laugreth and Gaermyn standing and waiting.

By the time the scout reined up by the two officers, it was closer to first glass than noon, and Beltur had positioned himself where he could overhear the scout's report without being too obvious. He could have moved closer under a concealment, but that, somehow, felt wrong.

". . . Gallosians have started raiding the local steads for forage . . . why they haven't moved that far west yet . . . not burning or pillaging so far as I could tell, ser . . . They did take a wagon and a mule . . ."

To Beltur, that suggested that an immediate attack was unlikely. He remained silent and in the background until Laugreth dismissed the scout. Then he eased toward the other two officers, where he stopped and waited.

"You heard all that, Beltur?" Gaermyn's words were not quite a question.

"Yes, ser."

"What do you think?" asked the captain.

"Something's changed or the infantry commander isn't very smart. They wouldn't have sent two companies into Spidlar without support and supplies if they'd meant them to stay for long, would they?" Beltur stopped when he realized he was essentially saying what the captain told him earlier.

"I wouldn't wager on a stupid commander," replied Laugreth. "It's more likely that something else didn't work out. It could be that they were trying to pull more than one company away from the city. Or they've been told to wait to attack until the Gallosians advance somewhere else. It looks like they want to tie us up here for now."

"Have you heard from the majer, ser?" Beltur had thought to ask more, but decided against it for the moment as he saw Zandyr approaching.

"Only orders to hold here and keep the Gallosians at bay as long as possible and to let him know if we need support." Laugreth offered a tight smile. "That's a way of saying he doesn't have many reinforcements available."

"That's a waste. We shouldn't be used against heavy infantry," said Gaermyn.

"We both know that. So does the majer. Probably the commander does as well. He just might not have an infantry company or two to replace us at the moment. Or he needs them more somewhere else."

"So we just sit here and wait?" asked Zandyr.

"It's usually better to wait until you can figure out where you're needed and for what, rather than go riding off in what might be the wrong direction," said Gaermyn dryly. "Besides, we'd lose too many men in a direct attack on heavy infantry when they're expecting it. Right now, they're definitely looking out for us to attack."

Zandyr opened his mouth, then quickly closed it.

"When do you think it's likely we'll hear from the majer, ser?" asked Beltur.

"Either when he needs us desperately or after the fighting stops today," replied Laugreth. "It will stop for a time because the Gallosians can't have moved enough men across the river yet. Not with the number of flatboats they have. Even if they brought more flatboats downstream it would take time." He smiled politely. "I need to send a report to the majer."

"Yes, ser," replied Beltur, immediately turning and beginning to head back up the hill.

"Can you sense farther from up higher?" asked Gaermyn.

Beltur stopped and half turned. "A little better, I think. I'm still not sensing as well as I was. So it's hard to tell."

Gaermyn nodded.

Beltur resumed walking.

"It still seems stupid to wait and do nothing," murmured Zandyr as he followed the mage away from the two more senior officers.

"If we move, what happens when the Gallosians march around us straight to Elparta and attack? From where we are we can see any approach to the city. I imagine that's why the captain picked this hill."

"Our scouts know where the Gallosians are."

"Our scouts know where some Gallosians are. What if they've split up, or another company has joined them?"

"Aren't you supposed to be able to discover that?"

"Only if they're close." Beltur didn't bother to look at Zandyr.

Zandyr took several more steps, but when Beltur didn't say anything or look in his direction, he stopped. Beltur walked back to the ledge and sat down. He still couldn't sense much farther than he had before the scout had reported. But he did like the sunlight and being a little away from the rest of the company.

Three glasses passed. During that time Beltur walked up to the top of the hill and then back down, ate some more stale bread and cheese, drank another bottle of ale, and finally went to the tie-line and checked on Slowpoke, who had grazed away all the scrubby grass within reach.

When he sensed a single uniformed rider coming

from the direction of Elparta, he immediately headed down to tell the captain. By the time the rider arrived, all four officers were waiting as the ranker, wearing a messenger's sash, handed the dispatch to Laugreth.

No one said anything while the captain broke the seal and began to read.

Finally, Laugreth looked up. "The Gallosians crossed the border on the west side of the river. They pushed north to within a kay and a half of Elparta and stopped."

"Why did they stop?" asked Zandyr before the captain could say more.

"Because that's where the solid flat land begins on the east side of the river," replied Laugreth impatiently. "You might let me finish, Undercaptain Zandyr."

"Yes, ser."

Laugreth cleared his throat and continued, "They also made an attack at the same time on the east side of the river, but the marshal stopped them before they advanced a little more than a kay. The Gallosians are now landing more armsmen on the east side. That includes lancers and heavy infantry and some white wizards. The marshal judges that they'll try to advance tomorrow to drive as far north as their forces on the west side. Then they'll move forward slowly on both sides of the river until they hold enough ground close to the walls to bring up their siege engines. They've been using their mages against any units that don't have a black to shield them. The casualties from mage-fire have been significant. The dispatch doesn't say how significant. We're to be replaced within the next glass, but we're not to leave our position until Eighth Foot arrives. We'll receive orders once we return."

Gaermyn nodded, as if to agree with Second Recon's replacement by a foot company.

The captain turned to Beltur. "How do you think they'll use their mages against ours?"

"They'll try to concentrate on ours by bringing two or three mages against just one of ours. Since blacks can't throw chaos, the whites only have to shield against arrows. Some of them would have trouble with iron arrows or iron bolts from crossbows, but just an iron arrowhead wouldn't be enough. I don't know if we even have any iron arrows."

"Have you told anyone about the idea of iron arrows?"

"Some of the other mages," admitted Beltur. "I hadn't thought about that. I'm sorry."

"That's something I can pass on immediately. Do you have any idea how many of those whites they have?"

"I know of six or seven strong whites. I wouldn't be surprised if Wyath has at least twice that."

"That many?"

"There were always many more whites than blacks in Gallos," Beltur pointed out. "Fenard is probably four times the size of Elparta, and there are lots of towns in Gallos. Aren't there more blacks in Spidlaria?"

"I grew up there," said Gaermyn. "I never saw many. Didn't see many in Kleth, either. I don't know why."

"Do you have any ideas about that?" Laugreth asked Zandyr.

"I've never been to Spidlaria, ser."

"That's not something we can do anything about. Go get the men ready to move out." Laugreth looked to Beltur. "Do you sense any Gallosians ... or our replacements?"

"No, ser."

"Carry on. I need to send back a quick response with the courier."

As Laugreth turned, Beltur again felt that he'd slipped up, that he should have mentioned that iron arrows could sometimes affect white mages, but it was something he'd thought was more common knowledge.

Common to mages, but with so few wars involving
mages in recent years . . . ?

He shook his head and started toward the tie-line and
Slowpoke.

LX

Beltur and Second Recon were awakened well before
dawn on fourday morning, but Beltur had no idea
what lay in store for them, because the captain had
departed to meet with the majer as soon as the company had returned to the warehouse barracks late on
threeday afternoon. The barracks were also largely
empty except for Second Recon and a single company
of foot. As he finished eating a cold breakfast quickly
with Zandyr, Beltur thought he saw Cohndar and
Waensyn at a table in the poorly lighted corner of the
mess. He wasn't about to go over and greet either.

"Have you heard anything?" asked Zandyr as the two
junior officers walked from the mess toward the mustering area in the near darkness.

"You know what I do. I never saw the captain after
he went to meet with the majer. Gaermyn didn't know
anything last night." Beltur didn't mention that he'd
taken the captain's advice and gone to sleep as early as
he could.

"I asked Viltaar—he's a junior undercaptain with the
foot. That's because his father's barely a trader. He
didn't know anything, either."

"Did he have anything else to say?"

"Nothing of interest, except that he agrees with me

about the lack of respect we get from the rankers. I can see why they don't respect him, though."

Beltur was glad it was dark enough that Zandyr couldn't see Beltur's face clearly.

Gaermyn was already outside and roughly in position.

"Do you know what we'll be doing?" Zandyr asked.

"The captain will brief us quickly after muster."

"Thank you, ser," replied Beltur quickly and politely.

"But about what?" pressed Zandyr.

"You'll find out then, Undercaptain. We're about to form up." Gaermyn's voice was more tired than cold.

Muster was quick, and the rankers were dismissed to duties. Scarcely more than moments later, once again, the four officers sat on stools in the captain's study around the small table, the small makeshift chamber lit by a single small brass lamp that smoked slightly.

Laugreth began, "Our mission is simple. We're to use our abilities to get behind the Gallosians on the east side of the river and then make rear attacks on whatever Gallosian force appears vulnerable. These attacks are to inflict as many casualties as possible with as little loss as possible. The aim is to keep the enemy off-balance and unable to advance. We've been provided considerably more arrows, enough that each ranker will have two score. There are also a few iron shafts for possible use against white wizards. Those are limited and will remain with First Squad so that Undercaptain Beltur can help direct their use.

"Our scouts have discovered that so far the Gallosians are not using the narrower way that branches off the main east river road and heads more to the east. We will begin by taking that way as far as we can. You're each to pick up field rations at the stable and make sure your water bottles are full. Keep the extra blankets.

We'll mount up as soon as we finish here. Beltur and I will be with First Squad. Gaermyn with Fifth Squad, and Zandyr with Third Squad. Any questions?"

The last words were spoken with a tone that suggested there shouldn't be questions, so much so, Beltur noted, that even Zandyr joined in the murmured, "No, ser."

"Dismissed." Laugreth immediately stood.

Beltur lagged slightly in leaving the study, letting Zandyr walk beside Gaermyn. Then he ducked back to the cubby he shared with Zandyr to recover his water bottles, which he took to the mess and had the mess ranker fill with ale. After that, he hurried to the stables.

At the entrance stood a ranker beside a stack of cylindrical supply duffels, who immediately addressed Beltur. "Undercaptain, ser, you get two extra water bottles. They have ale in them. Captain's orders."

"Thank you." Beltur took both the proffered duffel and the two water bottles, which were already in a leather holder, clearly designed to fasten to his saddle.

The ranker nodded acknowledgment.

Beltur walked carefully toward Slowpoke's stall, sensing as much as seeing, given the bare handful of lamps in the stables. Even in the gloom, he had little problem in saddling the big brown gelding, and even figured out the attachment of the extra water bottles. *Practice in the dark helps.* He shook his head. Who would ever have thought he'd turn out to be an undercaptain, even a temporary one, in a war against the land in which he'd grown up?

With Slowpoke saddled and his gear in place, Beltur led the gelding outside. There he mounted and rode eastward where he again sensed more than saw that Second Recon was forming up. He reined up beside Vaertaag at the head of First Squad.

"First Squad, ready to ride, ser."

"Very good, Squad Leader. I imagine the captain will be here soon." Beltur couldn't imagine that Laugreth wouldn't be. He glanced to the east, but there was but the faintest glow on the horizon.

As soon as Laugreth reined up, Beltur reported, "First Squad, ready to ride, ser."

"So are the other squads. You can sense the way until we get more light, Undercaptain?"

"Yes, ser. I can lead the way."

"Then do so." Laugreth raised his voice. "Company! Forward!"

Leading the company wasn't difficult, but it felt strange to Beltur, to say the least, as he guided Slowpoke to the east river road, a way far more traveled, and widened by that travel, over just an eightday.

By the time Beltur had ridden about a kay, but not to where the narrower road forked off, the sky had turned greenish-gray, bright enough that he could see clearly. He still could not sense any armsmen, although he had a vague feeling that there were quite a number beyond what he could discern. Within riding another hundred yards or so, that feeling turned into a definite sense of more armsmen than he could possibly have counted, at least five hundred, most likely Spidlarian troopers, in position to hold back the Gallosians.

"Ser . . . our forces are ahead. I'd say a kay and a half."

"Are there any on the side path?"

Beltur concentrated for a moment. "Yes, ser. There's a squad at the fork, and there seem to be some on the slopes overlooking the path about as far away as the other troopers. Two squads, I'd guess, but it's hard to tell exactly."

"What about farther than that?"

"I can't tell. The side road angles more to the east and farther away."

"Let me know when you can sense more." Laugreth turned. "Send out two outriders. Just a hundred yards ahead. Tell them to take the east fork when the narrow road joins this one."

"Yes, ser."

Beltur watched and kept riding as the two rankers went past.

Although the hills on the east side of the road blocked a direct view of the actual sunrise, a slow flood of slightly orange-tinged white light that replaced the greenish blue of the sky occurred as Second Recon approached the fork where the narrower path-like road angled to the south-southeast from the main road.

Two troopers stood at the fork, and Laugreth reined up short of them. "Have you seen any sign of Gallosians, Squad Leader?"

"No, ser."

"Very good."

"Ser . . ."

"I know. This leads away from the main line of battle, but it's where the marshal's sending us." With a brief smile, Laugreth urged his mount forward.

After riding another half kay, Beltur could sense the nearest Gallosians and immediately raised a shield to block anyone sensing his own order and chaos, but just around himself. That didn't take all that much effort, and he was going to need all the strength he could muster before the day was over. Then he said, "Ser, there's a Gallosian force on the road, just beyond where our armsmen are posted on the slopes above it. A company, I think, about a kay ahead." More important to Beltur was the fact that he didn't sense a white mage anywhere near the Gallosians, although he thought there were several farther to the west, seemingly amid the leading edge of the Gallosian troopers.

"Foot or mounted?"

"It must be mixed. There are men on foot and those mounted."

"Do any of them have shields or pikes?"

"I can't tell. At this distance, I can only make out the outlines of the ground and living things."

"Why the ground?"

"Things live in it."

"How close do you think we can get before they could see us?"

Beltur studied the narrow road that curved slightly several hundred yards ahead. Then he concentrated on sensing what lay beyond that. Finally, he turned in the saddle and looked at the captain. "Possibly another three or four hundred yards beyond where the road curves."

"That would leave us open for a half kay." Laugreth paused. "What about moving into the hills before they can see us?"

"The slopes seem open and rough. I could put a concealment around the company, and we could stay on the road."

"That would take us close to the Gallosians. Then what? We can't fight inside a concealment."

Beltur frowned. There was something . . . something about the captain's words. Then he smiled. "You've just answered your own question. In a way, that is. We could advance on the road under a concealment. When we get near enough to attack, I lift the concealment, for just a few moments, and then drop it around the Gallosians. They won't be able to do much within a concealment. That would give us time to ready an attack, or avoid them, or fire arrows into where they were. Even loosing some shafts into a company that can't see might cause some confusion."

"Where did you come up with that?" Laugreth shook his head. "I know—from my words." He hesitated.

600 L. E. MODESITT, JR.

"They have mages, too. Do you think they might expect something like that?"

"I don't know. I've never heard of a concealment being used that way, but it's possible. That doesn't change
the fact that they wouldn't be able to see."

"They could still charge toward us and break out of
the concealment . . . or they could withdraw."

"Or . . ." mused Beltur, "I could throw a concealment
around them before I lift the one around us, and tell you
where the Gallosians are. That way, they wouldn't even
know how big a force they faced . . . or where to go. I
don't think the company ahead has a white wizard,
either."

"We'd waste shafts that way," said Laugreth.

"What if we fired two volleys at them, and then I
dropped the concealment for two or three counts, and
then the men fired two more volleys? The Gallosians
might be confused enough not even to see where
we are."

"That sounds like the best plan . . . but if they have
pikemen with shield bearers, the arrows wouldn't do
much good and we couldn't charge them directly. Can
you tell about the ground on each side of the road?"

"It slopes, but it's not as steep on the sides. It's more
like a big bowl. The sides are where the horses and
riders are."

"It might be better to attack the mounted armsmen
first, and then sweep around the foot and strike from
the flanks. Could you keep the foot in the dark the
whole time, and do a separate concealment for the
sides?"

Beltur shook his head. "That would mean switching
from one concealment to three, one on each side and
one in the middle. I *might* be able to include the foot
and the mounted on one side, with a separate concealment for the mounted on the other side."

"Let me think about that."

The two continued riding for another twenty yards before the captain spoke.

"We'll attack the mounted riders on the east side first, then swing around to flank the foot. That way, the remaining mounted armsmen would have to ride over their own foot to get at us directly. We'll hit those on foot that we can and then just keep going. That will get us behind them and create more confusion than if we stayed and fought. Then if they come after us, you can drop a concealment over them, and we can pick them off if they pursue us once they come out of the concealment."

"That sounds better."

"It also fits better with what the marshal wants because we'll be behind their lines." Laugreth hesitated, then added, "More to the east than I'd like, but we've gone through rough terrain before." He raised an arm. "Company! Halt! Squad leaders and officers forward! Pass it back."

Beltur reined up and waited beside the captain while Gaermyn, Zandyr, and the five squad leaders rode forward. He leaned forward in the saddle and patted Slowpoke on the shoulder, wondering what his uncle would have thought of his situation. Given what his uncle had thought of Wyath, Beltur would like to have thought he would have approved . . . or at least understood. *Except he'd worry that he hadn't protected me enough.* That was something Beltur was only coming to understand, that his uncle had cared about Beltur more deeply than he'd ever let on. *And you'll never be able to tell him that.*

"Are you all right, Beltur?" asked Laugreth.

Beltur swallowed. "I'm fine. I was just thinking." He could tell Laugreth was dubious.

"You're sure? If you can't do this . . ."

"Oh, that's not a problem. It really isn't."

Something in Beltur's tone of voice must have convinced the captain, because he turned his eyes to the approaching riders. Once the other six were circled around, all still mounted, Laugreth began. "There's a mixed Gallosian force up ahead, less than a kay away. It's roughly the size of a company but is half foot and half mounted. The foot may have pikes. That's why we're going to attack in a different way . . ." He went on to describe the approach to the Gallosians and the attack, as well as the handling of moving under a concealment, ending by saying, "Our objective is to get behind the Gallosian lines where we can attack vulnerable units. We're not to engage in direct and prolonged combat. This attack is designed to conform to those objectives." He looked across the various faces, ending with Gaermyn.

"Do they have a white wizard?" asked the senior undercaptain.

"There's no sign of one," replied Beltur.

Gaermyn nodded and looked back at Laugreth.

"Return to your squads. A moment, Undercaptain Gaermyn, if you would."

Once Zandyr and the squad leaders had left, although Vaertaag had merely eased his mount several yards away and back in front of First Squad, Laugreth said, "You're concerned?"

"Do we know what other Gallosian units are nearby?"

Laugreth nodded to Beltur.

"The closest unit to the Gallosians is a Spidlarian squad on the hilltop to the west of the road, slightly north of the Gallosians. There are no Gallosian forces within half a kay of the force we'll be attacking. Beyond that, I can't tell."

Gaermyn smiled wryly. "Fair enough. That's all I had, ser."

"We'll try not to leave you a mess to ride through," said Laugreth.

"Appreciated, ser." Gaermyn nodded and turned his mount.

Beltur couldn't help but wonder why the senior undercaptain hadn't just asked the question when all the others were present. *What aren't you seeing?*

Laugreth didn't answer Beltur's unspoken question, but waited a time before ordering, "Company! Forward!"

The two rode without speaking until they neared the curve in the road, when Beltur said, "We can ride about halfway around this curve, about to where that clump of bushes is, before I should conceal us."

"Is the road straight beyond the curve?"

"Yes, ser."

"That makes sense. The Gallosians would want as much notice as possible. How much farther could we go before you do the concealment? I don't like to have the men ride a corner blind."

"I can't tell until we get closer, ser. I'll make it as late as I can."

As he rode into the beginning of the curve in the road, Beltur again checked the Gallosians. "Ser, from what I can tell, the Gallosians are still only in the same three formations. They're not tight. Not yet, anyway."

"That's good for us. Tell me immediately if that changes."

"Yes, ser." Beltur supposed that the loose formations made a sort of sense, since the distance from where the road straightened to where they were positioned on the top of a gentle rise was a good five hundred yards. Then he frowned, belatedly realizing that a horse in a walk wouldn't take that long to cover the distance, and that was why the company would walk until the lead riders were just under a hundred and fifty yards away, when Beltur would drop the concealment and Recon Two would charge the units on the left, most of whom weren't even mounted. At least, it seemed that way to Beltur.

As he rode around the last yards of the curve in the narrow road, Beltur kept his eyes forward looking for any hint of the Gallosians, then created the concealment when he saw a glint of light on something metallic. "The Gallosians are still where they were, ser. Straight ahead up the road."

At about two hundred yards from the enemy, Beltur could sense rapid movement. "I think they've spotted something, ser. We're at two hundred yards."

"Drop the concealment."

Light flooded over Beltur, although he was actually in shadow from the hills to the east, which made adjusting to the comparative glare easier. He could see Gallosians running toward the middle of the road, some with shields, others with pikes.

"Company! Charge! On me!" thundered Laugreth.

Beltur had to use his boot heels to get Slowpoke moving, but in moments, or so it seemed to Beltur, the big gelding had caught up to Laugreth, and Beltur had to rein him back slightly, since the last thing he wanted was to be leading a charge. He extended his personal shields just a bit so that they totally covered Slowpoke. *And they call him Slowpoke?* Beltur smiled at the vagrant thought even as he concentrated on holding position.

Ahead, the Gallosians on the road were hurrying to set pikes and shields.

Beltur glanced to the east, where half the Gallosian

mounted unit seemed to be still scrambling into the saddle.

"Sabres! Ready!"

About fifteen yards from the tips of those pikes that had been raised, Laugreth shouted, "Left! Now!"

First Squad swung onto the sloping ground beside the road, headed straight toward the Gallosian riders; then, almost before Beltur could react, they had smashed through the thin line and were cutting across the back of the east side of the foot, behind the pikes and almost directly across the shieldmen, and a mixture of dull thuds, thumps, scraping of sabres on metal or something hard, as well as shouts and screams, rose around Beltur. Even with the shields he carried, he could feel the impacts, if in a muffled way.

As First Squad turned to follow the road on the gentle slope away from the Gallosian position, Beltur glanced back, but all he could see were the troopers immediately behind him.

Once First Squad had covered several hundred yards, Laugreth slowed the company to a walk, but did not bring it to a halt until Fifth Squad was a good kay from the Gallosian position. He looked to Beltur and said, "No one's following us. Not yet, anyway."

Before that long, the five squad leaders rode forward. Beltur noticed that neither Gaermyn nor Zandyr joined them. *So Gaermyn can watch the road in case the Gallosians do decide to pursue?*

"Squad leaders, report," ordered Laugreth quietly.

"First Squad, one wounded, not seriously."

"Second Squad, one lost. Dargaal was unseated. We couldn't see what happened."

"Third Squad, one wounded, one missing."

"Fourth Squad, one wounded, broken arm."

"Fifth Squad, no casualties."

Three wounded and two missing. Was that good or bad . . . or expected? Beltur had no idea.

"You all handled that well, especially after riding blind." The captain looked to Nobryn, the Fifth Squad leader. "You were the last through. Could you tell what sort of casualties we inflicted?"

"Hard to tell, Captain. I saw at least four of their cavalry unhorsed and injured and maybe a half score of foot laid out, but how bad they were hurt I couldn't say. We did some damage. Two of my men say they cut down pikemen. There might have been more."

"You don't think so?"

"They were running around like headless fowl, ser. Who could tell?"

"Return to your squads. Nobryn, tell Undercaptain Gaermyn I'd like to see him as we ride. We need to keep moving just in case the Gallosians change their mind."

"Yes, ser."

"Company! Forward!" Laugreth didn't offer any explanations to Beltur, but just kept studying the hills on the right side of the road, apparently comparing them to a small map he had pulled out of his tunic.

Beltur judged that he'd ridden almost a half kay before Gaermyn rode up, a slightly grim expression on his face. Beltur reined up slightly to allow Gaermyn to ride beside the captain, but he stayed as close as he could to listen to what the two had to say.

"Sorry, ser. I had to take care of something. It couldn't wait."

"Wounded man or the undercaptain?"

"Both."

"I hope it's the last time."

"It just might be."

Beltur could see the captain nod and wondered what Zandyr had done . . . or hadn't.

"We've got rough maps of the land here," said Laugreth. "If we follow this path that calls itself a road for another half kay, we could cut over a low ridge and pick up an even worse old path back toward the river. Years back it was a mining road. We'd get almost to the river, just under those red cliffs."

Gaermyn frowned. "How did you find that out?"

"Talked to everyone I could. There were some old deeds in the Council building, too. One of the maps was attached to it. I borrowed it."

"If the Council knew . . ."

"If we win, I'll return it. If we don't, the Council will have much more to worry about."

Gaermyn shook his head. "You think there is really a way to that old road."

"We might have to make our way. There used to be a path that connected, but something happened back in the time of Relyn. Seems like part of a hill collapsed and filled it with rocks. Too rough for horses, and the mine had already played out. No one could tell me where that place was. It could be kays to the east, and we don't want to ride that far and then double back."

"I can see that, ser. When we get to the river, then what?"

"We'll figure that out when we do."

Gaermyn raised his eyebrows. "I've heard that before."

"You might have." Laugreth smiled.

The weathered undercaptain shook his head.

A third of a glass later, at around seventh glass, the captain called a halt and turned to Gaermyn. "This might work. I'll let you know."

Then he and two rankers rode up a slope on the south side of the road, which had gradually turned so that it was definitely headed southeast and away from the river and whatever fighting was occurring. The slope looked barely passable, as opposed to those others they had ridden past that had appeared impassable to Beltur.

"Do you know what the captain has in mind, ser?"

"No, but it will be black angel frigging difficult, and if it works, it'll cost the Gallosians dear."

Left unsaid was what it might cost the company if what the captain had in mind did not work.

A good half glass passed before one of the rankers rode back, halting some twenty yards up the slope.

"Undercaptain, ser, the captain's found a way to the other road."

Gaermyn nodded and turned to Beltur. "You'll lead First Squad, Undercaptain."

"Yes, ser." Beltur could see that Gaermyn needed to bring up the rear and make certain the rest of the company was in good order. *And watch over Zandyr?*

"Company! Forward."

Although Beltur worried that Slowpoke might have trouble because of his size, the big gelding was surprisingly agile as he led the way up the slope at an angle. When Beltur neared the ranker, the man turned his mount.

"This way, ser."

Getting to the top of the rise wasn't that hard, but when he reached the crest and looked to the south, Beltur could see that going down the far side was going to be tricky, because the slope was sandy and rocky, not to mention fairly steep.

"You'll have to angle back toward that scrubby pine, ser, and then keep going until you see a clearing off to the left. That's where the captain is. He'll point the way to the old road."

"Thank you." The fact that the captain had apparently found the old road was reassuring, but Beltur had to swallow as Slowpoke started down the slope. He let the gelding set his own pace, but was ready to rein him back if necessary. Beltur very much hoped that it wouldn't be necessary.

Going down the sandy decline was nerve-racking for Beltur, but when he looked at the almost sheer drops on the backside of the other hills, he could see that Laugreth had picked the only possible route. Beyond the weathered and scrawny pine tree, the ground became less sandy, although in one place Slowpoke's hooves clattered on flat red rock. Finally, after what seemed to be more than a glass, but could only have been a fraction of that, the ground before Beltur leveled out, and he could see what looked to be a clearing ahead, the way to it barely marked by the slight bending in the knee-high, autumn-tan grass that showed the faintest trace of previous riders. Beltur could sense a single horse and rider ahead.

He kept riding and finally could make out Laugreth.

"From here, we'll have to walk the horses through that gap." The captain pointed to his right, where Beltur saw a narrow opening in the redstone cliff. "It's just wide enough for them without a rider. The old road is at the other end of the gap. Khalyst is waiting there. Just form up and wait. I didn't see any tracks on the old road, but it wouldn't hurt for you to see if you sense anyone else around."

"Yes, ser."

Leading Slowpoke through the narrow gap in the rock was far less nerve-racking than coming down the sandy and rocky slope had been, and before long Beltur stood on what had once likely been a well-traveled road, because the surface was still comparatively level. He glanced down to see that the roadbed looked to be crushed rock, and he wondered what they had mined that had resulted in such a durable road—and why it had not been used in years.

Remembering what the captain had said, Beltur did

his best to sense whether any Gallosians were nearby, but he could detect no one and no large animals, except those belonging to Second Recon.

A half glass passed, and all of First and Second Squad had come through the gap and formed up along the road, which was fringed by low scraggly bushes of a sort Beltur didn't recognize. Another half glass passed before the last rider—the captain—led his mount out onto the road. The three undercaptains waited, all holding their mounts.

"We'll take a break here. Then we'll ride to the river." Laugreth blotted his forehead with the back of his sleeve.

Beltur took one of the water bottles filled with ale, uncorked it, and took a long swallow, then another. He hadn't realized how thirsty he was.

Beside him stood Zandyr, who drank whatever was in his bottle, then said, "That skirmish with the Gallosians seemed easy. If they're all like that—"

"They won't be," interrupted Gaermyn. "They were well away from the fighting. They knew there were Spidlarian troopers on the hillside watching them, and they were watching the squad up there, figuring any change in their position would let them know if anyone was coming. Also, it was early. Most officers wouldn't expect an attack on a road well away from the main lines at sixth glass in the morning. If that trailing ranker in Third Squad hadn't blundered out of the concealment, we would have had them at even more of a disadvantage." The older undercaptain glanced at Zandyr, but kept talking. "You can't blame them entirely for not being ready. Their captain didn't want them worn out and kept them in a loose formation. He must have figured they'd have time to mount. By tomorrow at the latest most of the Gallosians will know what we did. It won't be that easy again."

"It might be once or twice more," said Laugreth, "but we can't count on it. They also didn't have a mage there, and we couldn't have done what we did if they had had one." He looked to Beltur. "Isn't that right?" His words were barely a question.

"Yes, ser. We couldn't have gotten nearly that close without being detected, and the Gallosians have quite a few mages."

"A word with you, Zandyr," said Gaermyn quietly, handing the reins of his mount to a ranker and walking along the road away from First Squad.

After Gaermyn had drawn Zandyr aside, Laugreth turned directly to Beltur. "For someone who doesn't carry a weapon, you can be deadly."

Beltur hadn't the faintest idea what the captain meant.

"You and your gelding plowed aside three or four of the Gallosians, and I don't think most of them will be fighting anytime soon."

"I was just trying to stay with you and First Squad, ser."

"Could you break through a shield wall that way?"

"I might be able to, but I couldn't make the shield much wider." Beltur suspected he could, but he wouldn't be able to hold a wider shield all that long, and he certainly didn't want to be caught in the middle of a fight with no shields at all. He had no doubts that, without shields, he'd be dead very quickly.

"So doing that would be a way to break through a line to get clear of a fight?"

"That . . . or in a glancing attack like we just did."

Laugreth nodded. "Thank you."

The calculating look in the captain's eyes made Beltur uneasy. He uncorked the water bottle and took another swallow before recorking it and checking over Slowpoke. It wouldn't be that long before he had to mount up again.

LXI

While the old road toward the river was in surprisingly good condition, at least for travel by horse, there were enough small gullies, caused by years of rainfall, that it would have been impassable to a wagon. Even so, the road was better and faster than trying to cross hills and occasional thickets, despite the fact that it wound so much that Second Recon likely traveled almost ten kays to cover the five that a vulcrow would have flown to the collapsed mine entrance less than half a kay from the east bank of the River Gallos. To the north, in the direction of Elparta, the hills were even more rugged than Beltur recalled, although he'd only seen them once, and that was from a flatboat.

After the mounts and rankers were settled in, the captain gathered the officers together in a flat area against the high redstone cliffs.

Beltur glanced skyward, taking in the high clouds coming in from the northwest, wondering if they would just drift past or whether they foreshadowed rain. From what he had learned from Athaal, and what he could sense, the clouds didn't seem to have much rain . . . and there wasn't the split between order and chaos that he'd sensed in the thunderclouds in Analeria. But . . . farther away, the clouds looked darker and thicker. He quickly shifted his gaze as the captain cleared his throat.

"We can't do that much more today," said Laugreth. "The mounts need rest and water. There's some grass here. Not as much as I'd like, but it will do. I've sent scouts north along what looks to be a footpath. We

can't be much more than a kay from where the Gallosians built that ramp to carry mounts across the river."
He looked to Beltur.

"We're either farther than that, or they've moved north, ser. There are some armsmen and a few mounts at the edge of the river about a kay and a half north of us. That's what I sense, anyway, but it might be because it's been a long day."

"We'll see what the scouts report, and our evolutions tomorrow will be based on where the Gallosians are. Since there's no one near us, it's clear that they don't know where we are, and that will give us some leeway in what we can do . . ."

From there, the captain turned his words to the more mundane details of watches and sentries.

Once Laugreth and Gaermyn left to inspect the camp, Zandyr turned to Beltur.

"What does the captain have against me?"

Beltur wasn't about to address that question, not directly. "What do you mean?"

"Both the captain and Gaermyn have blamed me because that ranker rode out of the concealment before the attack on the Gallosians. I didn't have anything to do with his stupidity."

"Who was the ranker?"

"I don't know his name. Waggel or something. He's just a ranker."

Beltur barely managed to keep from wincing. "What did they say?"

"That it was all my fault. They didn't say it that way, of course. They politely suggested that I needed to give more attention to detail. As politely as their type can ever manage. It was all an excuse to suggest I wasn't doing my job. They didn't want me here. They don't respect me. They don't like traders. They don't like anyone but armsmen."

"Your family's business is trade. Their business is the use of arms. Different skills are required."

"They don't say things like that to you."

"Not in public. I've never heard what they said to you. I don't imagine you've heard what they've said to me."

Zandyr shook his head. "I'll be glad when this war's over. Then we'll see."

"That might be a while." *Especially if the Gallosians take Elparta.* Beltur could see the Gallosians withdrawing if they were defeated at Elparta, particularly with winter approaching, but that might only be for the winter. And if they took Elparta before then, it would certainly be a much longer fight, one way or the other.

"It won't be." Zandyr shook his head. "You'll see." He turned and strode off in the direction of the river.

Beltur stood there for several moments, not really seeing anything, until he realized a trooper had appeared—Squad Leader Vaertaag.

"Ser?"

"Yes, Vaertaag, is there something I can do?" Not that Beltur thought there was anything he could do, but he didn't know what else to say.

"Ser . . . it's about your mount."

Beltur stiffened. "Is there anything wrong with him?"

"Oh, no, ser. Nothing like that." Vaertaag didn't quite meet Beltur's eyes. "How are you finding him?"

"I had a little trouble the first few days, but we're doing well now. The way he handled that sandy slope and all the rough terrain, I couldn't have asked for a better horse."

"We're all glad to hear that, ser. I thought it was that way, but I did want to make sure."

"No. I'm very happy with him."

"Thank you, ser." Vaertaag nodded.

After the squad leader left, Beltur allowed himself a smile. He had a very good idea what that had been all about. He almost felt sorry for Zandyr. *Almost.*

Almost two glasses later, after an evening meal of very hard biscuits and cheese, washed down with water, water in Beltur's case that he had filled his empty bottle with and then treated with order and chaos, since he was trying to save the remaining ale, Laugreth gathered both officers and squad leaders.

He looked at Beltur and began. "You were right, Undercaptain. The Gallosians have largely abandoned their initial bridgehead on this side of the river. It appears as though they have advanced closer to Elparta. There's little more than a squad posted by that ramp they built earlier. The scouts could see tracks, and even a number of wagon ruts." After a pause, he went on. "We've got quite a task ahead of us. There is a footpath along the river. It's just wide enough for a single horse at a time. That won't be a problem, since the Gallosians seem to have left, except for that single squad, and they aren't even watching the path. First Squad will lead, with Undercaptain Beltur near the front, so that he can conceal us, if necessary, once we reach the landing area. We'll secure that as quickly as possible and then move on."

The captain held up a hand, as if to forestall any comments or questions. "I'm concerned that the Gallosians appear to have moved so far in a single day, but it appears that they have been stopped well short of the city and the piers, because the scouts could see a line of fires, probably cookfires, somewhat more than a kay south of the piers. We should be able to move fairly quickly once we get to the rock ramp. We might even be able to take the river road part of the way. We need to do something that will give the Gallosians something to think about. That means a rear attack on the Gallosians, but what sort of attack will depend on how they're drawn up."

Beltur could see Zandyr shifting his weight as if he wanted to question something, but didn't want to upset the captain.

Laugreth obviously saw the same thing, because he added after a moment of silence, "Some of you might question what a single company can do against thousands. We don't have to win the battle or any battle by ourselves. Our task is to unbalance them so that will give our main force the opportunity to push the Gallosians back or inflict massive casualties on them. That's all for now. Get as good a night's sleep as you can. We'll be moving out early."

Beltur stood there mulling over what the captain had said and thinking about what else he might be able to do to make the company more effective . . . and to keep casualties low, especially given that he was a mage still very inexperienced in combat. He didn't even notice Zandyr approach until the other coughed.

"Beltur?"

"Oh . . . I didn't see you. I was thinking."

"Do you think attacking the Gallosians from behind is really such a good idea?"

"Do you have a better one?"

"Why do we have to attack? What difference can one company make against a score or more? Except to get killed?"

Zandyr's questions didn't exactly surprise Beltur, since he'd asked himself one similar, and he offered the only response he had found acceptable. "What if everyone in each company felt that way?"

"But they're all together. We're out here by ourselves."

"What difference does that make?"

Zandyr's face twisted in disbelief. "You're just like

them. Except swords and arrows won't kill you. What do you care for anyone else?"

"Swords and arrows will kill me if I'm too exhausted to hold shields. Mages can certainly be killed. My uncle was a mage. He still died at the hands of the Gallosians. I almost did. Does it matter whether it's arrows or swords or chaos-bolts that can kill you?"

"You don't understand. It's different." Zandyr glared at Beltur, then said again, "It's different." Then he turned and walked away.

Is it different? Beltur couldn't have voiced a reason why his situation was no different from Zandyr's, but whether the trader's son knew it or not, what force or weapon killed someone mattered little to them in the end. They were dead.

And Beltur had to find some way so it didn't turn out like that.

LXII

Fiveday morning came early. Even in the dim light before dawn, Beltur could tell that the clouds he'd seen the evening before had become thicker and darker and somewhat lower, but certainly not low enough for rain in the next few glasses. While the rankers were eating, the captain gathered the officers and squad leaders.

"We need to do what we can with the fewest losses possible. Every man is valuable." Laugreth paused. "Some of you might not know. Nueltyr died last night. He didn't want anyone to know how badly he was hurt." Laugreth paused. "We need to keep the casualties as low as possible to get through this. That's why we need to surprise the Gallosian squad holding the boat ramp. We'll have to get close without being seen. They'll have a sentry near the end of the footpath. They did yesterday. Our scouts can take care of him. That leaves the problem of getting enough men through the low point between the hills where the footpath ends and onto flatter ground. There's about fifty yards between the footpath and the ramp. The Gallosians are set up east of the ramp, by maybe sixty yards. Even with a sentry positioned near the footpath, someone will be watching." The captain looked to Beltur.

"I can do a concealment, but they'll have to move out quietly and form up by touch."

Laugreth frowned. "A tight double file might do it. When we're ready, you could drop the concealment, and the other squads could move after us quickly. If we're discovered, drop the concealment and we'll hold the ground around the end of the footpath until we out-number them."

"You want me to lead the way straight north from the end of the path to just east of the ramp, and have them form on me?" Beltur didn't worry about his doing the leading. That was much easier for him than following him would be for Laugreth and the rankers.

"That should work. If we can even get out half a squad before they hear us, we should be all right, be-cause we'll be mounted, and they're all foot." With that, the captain nodded. "Get ready to form up."

A glass later, Beltur stood on the narrow footpath, one hand on Slowpoke's reins, waiting for Laugreth, just in front of him, who had called a halt. From what Beltur could sense, the lead scouts were less than a hun-dred yards in front of the captain, perhaps fifty yards from the sentry that they stalked.

Moments later, the captain appeared out of the pre-dawn gloom. "How many men do they have?"

"About a squad. Most are around the cookfire. The scouts are closing on the sentry." Beltur could sense the two scouts nearing the sentry, an increase in order and chaos, and then what felt like a puff of black mist. He swallowed as he realized what that indicated. After a long moment, he said, "The sentry's dead."

"You can tell that?"

"I didn't know I could. I've never been sensing some-one when they died." He realized that he hadn't even sensed his uncle's death because he'd been so preoccu-pied with escaping from Wyath and the Prefect, and a brief spasm of guilt gripped him. He shook his head. *Not now . . . not now.*

"We need to get moving then." Laugreth turned.

Beltur tugged on Slowpoke's reins and put one boot in front of the other, trying to be as quiet as possible as he trudged along the narrow sandy path in the gloom that should have lightened more than it had with the approach of dawn. Then it dawned on him. *The clouds are heavy enough and low enough to block the early sunlight.*

A tenth of a glass later or so, Laugreth stopped and murmured back to Beltur, "The end of the footpath is right past that heap of rocks on the left. Just before you get there, the Gallosians could see you."

"I'll drop the concealment over the area from there to the stone ramp. Then Slowpoke and I will move past you. That way the men don't have to worry about where they're going until they're on level ground."

"Good." The captain continued on, leading his mount.

Beltur kept his eyes on Laugreth, and as soon as the captain neared the rock pile, he put the concealment in place, then moved ahead, keeping an arm out. The moment his hand vanished, he murmured, "Captain?"

"Go around on the left."

Beltur did, using his senses to guide Slowpoke past the captain and his horse, then moved as quietly as he could toward the stone ramp, trying to sense those behind him as well as the Gallosians around the cookfire. Laugreth followed. Beltur could barely hear a few words drifting his way, but he didn't sense any sudden movements. When he neared the stone ramp and turned Slowpoke, he murmured, "In position at the ramp."

"Mount up quietly."

Beltur did so, waiting, hoping that the Gallosians didn't hear the occasional click of a hoof on a stone, but no one seemed to notice . . . not until most of the first file was in position and two rankers had moved up behind Beltur and Laugreth.

Then one of the Gallosians called out, "Where's Landret?"

"Landret!"

"I hear riders!"

"Drop the concealment," ordered Laugreth.

Beltur did so, glancing to his right as he did so, and seeing the first ten riders forming a line abreast.

"First Squad! Blades ready! Forward!"

Not having a blade, Beltur merely made certain his shield was solid and urged Slowpoke forward.

The Gallosians around the cookfire scattered, running at full speed into the hills south of the fire. Not a one even tried to lift a blade.

"Hold up!" shouted Laugreth.

In less than half a glass, all of First Squad was off the footpath and in formation east of the slowly dying cookfire.

Gaermyn rode up to Laugreth. "We got the uniform from the sentry and a couple of tunics from the Gallosians that ran. They left a few things."

"Good. We might need them."

"More than might, ser."

"You're probably right."

While half listening to his senior officers, Beltur was already trying to sense where the Gallosian forces might be, but he could tell immediately that most of them were farther than a kay to the north, and that meant they were likely little more than a kay and a half from the south piers of Elparta. Even so, that wasn't close enough for siege machines, even a trebuchet.

"Beltur, are there any other Gallosians nearby, within a kay or less?"

"No, ser. Not on this side of the river. It's hard to tell, across water, but there are at least two companies on the west bank across from us."

"We'll be gone before they can get here. What about on the river road?"

"There are companies everywhere farther north. I think the closest are those posted about where the narrow road we took yesterday branches off."

"That's about a kay and a half." Laugreth nodded, as if confirming something for himself. "We'll take the river road. At least for a time."

From the flatboat ramp to the stone cairns that marked the border on the river road, the most obvious signs that the Gallosians had been there were the proliferation of horse dung and tracks of men and mounts in the dust and sand created by the passage of a considerable number of both. Roughly half a kay farther on, that changed, with the blue-clad bodies of Spidlarian rankers strewn here and there, occasional dead horses, gouges in the hillside created by mounted riders either charging or fleeing, and a faint but increasing odor of death and incipient decomposition, a smell that would have been far more redolent had it been full summer rather than a comparatively cool autumn.

Beltur lost track of the bodies before it struck him that he hadn't seen any fallen in the gray and black of

Gallos. "The Gallosians took care of their dead, but
not ours." Beltur was slightly surprised to find himself
saying he was a Spidlarian. *But you're certainly not a
Gallosian.* Still . . .

"That surprises you?" asked Laugreth. "They just
loot our men. They probably loot their own before
burying or burning them, whatever they do."

Beltur realized he hadn't the faintest idea what happened to the bodies of fallen Gallosians. Then he sensed
something. "There's a Gallosian squad about four or
five hundred yards ahead, around that next bend in the
road."

"Are there any others nearby?"

"Not for almost half a kay. There's another group,
maybe two or three squads, perhaps as a rearguard for
the companies holding the fork in the road."

"Frig . . ." muttered the captain. "That's to be expected, but . . ." He shook his head. "We'll have to do
something about that." He turned in the saddle. "Vaertaag, send someone to tell Undercaptain Gaermyn I
need to see him."

"Yes, ser."

"Beltur, the first squad is on a rise in the road, I presume, and where it's straight for a ways in our direction?"

"It feels that way, but that's the part of the road that
curves more. I can't say exactly, but the straight part of
the road might only be a hundred yards long or so. The
road swings east right behind the squad."

"How sharp is the curve?"

"They probably couldn't see who was on the road
behind them for more than fifty yards."

"What about the rearguard? How far are they from
the rest of the Gallosians?"

"Two or three hundred yards. I think they're on top
of another rise."

"What about the main body?"

"A little less than three companies, but that's more of a feel. They're about as far as I can sense."

"They're being cautious, and that's going to make it harder for us. Then, if we can pull this off, it might work to our advantage. It might also take some pressure off the companies directly defending Elparta."

Beltur was glad Laugreth felt that way, even if he didn't yet understand what the captain had in mind.

Before that long, Gaermyn rode up and eased his mount in beside that of Laugreth. Again, Beltur dropped back and listened as they kept riding.

"You need that diversion we talked about?" asked Gaermyn.

"We may need two. Beltur tells me that there's a recon squad around the curve ahead, some four hundred yards ahead. Then another half kay beyond that are two more squads acting as a rearguard. I was thinking that you could have Fifth Squad circle around behind the recon squad, and then we'd have three troopers in Gallosian uniforms riding toward the Gallosians."

"What about cover? There aren't that many trees. It's mostly bushes and grass and sand and rocks."

"The road curves. If you go some fifty yards farther north past them, you ought to be able to form up without being seen. The rest of us would follow the three, but under a concealment. That would get us close enough to attack in force, or in as much force as four abreast will allow."

"Four abreast?"

"The road is straight there, and a bit wider."

"How will we know when Fifth Squad . . ." Gaermyn broke off. "Beltur can tell us?"

"We'll be close enough that I can," Beltur quickly said.

"It might be hard on Fifth Squad," observed Gaermyn. "We can't afford to let any of the Gallosians escape."

624   L. E. MODESITT, JR.

"Then you want to lead them?"

"It might be best."

"Then we'll do it that way. We'll advance another hundred yards or so, then wait until Fifth Squad is in position. Tell the rankers in the Gallosian uniforms to put them on over their own tunics so that they can strip them away immediately."

Gaermyn nodded and then turned his mount back down the road, easing past the oncoming rankers.

"Any change with the Gallosians?" asked Laugreth.

"No, ser."

After riding not quite a hundred yards farther, the captain called a halt, allowing the men to dismount and stretch their legs, but also asking Beltur to let him know if anyone else appeared to be approaching. A short time later, Fifth Squad rode forward and then moved up the eastern slope and out of sight.

Beltur kept the captain informed of where the squad was, but it was almost a glass later when he said, "Fifth Squad is in position, ser."

"Mount up!" Laugreth turned to the three rankers in Gallosian uniforms. "Just ride slowly, as if you're exhausted and maybe wounded. The moment you hear me shout 'Company!' you go to the east side of the road and strip off those Gallosian uniforms. Is that clear?"

"Yes, ser."

"Once you're back in uniform, then you can look for Gallosians. Not until. Now, put yourselves about five yards in front of us. Undercaptain Beltur won't drop the concealment over the company until we're close to where the Gallosians can see us. Even if you can't see us, you can hear any command I give." Laugreth gestured to the three. Once they were in position, he called out, "Company! Forward!"

As the three decoy riders neared the end of the bend in the road, Laugreth turned to Beltur. "Any change?"

"No, ser."

"How are they formed up?"

"Some at the edge of the road aren't mounted. It's hard to tell about the others in the road because they're close together." When men and mounts were packed tightly, it was difficult for Beltur to sense separations. Men could have been standing beside their horses or be mounted.

"They wouldn't be across the road and holding mounts. Probably half are mounted while the others are standing by."

Beltur realized he should have come to that conclusion. *But you've had to learn a great deal in a very short time.* That thought made him feel like he was looking for an excuse, and he didn't like that.

Just before Beltur and the captain reached the point where the bend in the road began to straighten, he dropped the concealment over the first two squads. The other two squads wouldn't be around the bend far enough to be visible to the Gallosians until the three decoys were within fifty yards or so.

He kept trying to determine what the Gallosians were doing, but he didn't sense anything different even after he'd ridden almost another hundred yards. Still none of the Gallosians in the rear on the side of the road had mounted up. When Beltur felt he was less than a hundred yards away, he extended the concealment farther behind him to cover the two trailing squads.

When the three decoys were perhaps thirty-five yards from the reconnaissance squad, one of the Gallosians called out, "What happened to you three?"

"Spidlarians . . . whole company of them . . ."

"Back there? They're folding like limp plaques. Likely story. Prefect doesn't like deserters."

". . . not deserters . . . you'll see . . ."

"Squad Leader, he talks funny! They're not ours!"

"Company!" shouted Laugreth.

That was the loudest voice Beltur had ever heard from the captain, and he immediately dropped the concealment.

"Charge!"

Beltur strengthened his personal shield and charged with the captain, the shield propelled by Slowpoke throwing aside one Gallosian as the trooper attempted to slash at him. Then, knowing that he was just getting in the way, Beltur moved Slowpoke to the side of the road and watched as the Spidlarians chopped down the surrounded and surprised Gallosians, even as he understood that if any of the Gallosians escaped, Recon Two would suffer far greater casualties in the next confrontation. He winced as each death sent a puff of black mist over him, a mist that no one else could see or sense. At the same time, he realized that he hadn't sensed anything like that when he'd been in Analeria. *Why not?* Because all the chaos loosed by his uncle and Sydon had obscured it? *Or because you weren't sensitive enough to it then?*

As a result of the narrowness of the road and the close quarters, the skirmish likely took a good half glass, but the Gallosians had little chance. The close quarters didn't totally favor Recon Two, either, and Beltur saw at least two troopers go down, and several others took slashing cuts. At least, it looked that way to him.

When the carnage was over, Laugreth simply said, "Strip the Gallosian bodies and leave them. Take what mounts we need."

While that happened and two rankers recovered the personal effects of the dead Spidlarians, Recon Two moved on another two hundred yards north and stood down, both to rest and to tend to the wounded.

Beltur finished off his third bottle of ale, then turned

over Slowpoke to a ranker and walked to join the other officers. As he neared Laugreth, he glanced skyward, sensing rather than seeing, given the clouds, that it was close to midday. He only had to wait a few moments before Gaermyn and Zandyr joined him and the captain.

"That went fairly well," offered Laugreth. "We won't use the same decoy plan for dealing with the rearguard. So we'll just get close enough for Fifth Squad to take to the hills and circle behind the rearguard. Fifth Squad will remain concealed on the back side of the hill until we attack. This time, we'll attack in reverse order, with Fourth Squad leading. Gaermyn, I want you to have Fifth Squad loose shafts at the rear of the Gallosian forces. They'll be bunched up, and you should have good targets. If some of them try to charge you, pick them off as you can, but don't let them close with you. Circle back to rejoin the company if you need to."

"We won't need that," declared Gaermyn.

"I expect not . . . but . . ."

"Yes, ser."

Beltur almost smiled at the way Gaermyn's seeming acquiescence was anything but agreement.

Laugreth's smile was both amused and resigned. "I'll leave it to your judgment, Undercaptain."

"Yes, ser."

Almost a glass passed before Beltur reported that Fifth Squad appeared to be in position and the company resumed its progress northward toward the Gallosian rearguard, which, so far as Beltur could tell, was still in the same position it had been all day.

"Beltur?"

"Yes, ser."

"When we charge, I want you to stay on the road and just take that big gelding as far as you can go as fast as you can go without breaking his leg or unhorsing yourself. That way, Fourth Squad can take full advantage of your shields."

For a moment, Beltur didn't quite understand. Then he understood all too well. "Yes, ser." After a moment, he added, "If they get packed together, even Slowpoke can't push his way through."

"Then hold tight. We'll get to you." After a pause, Laugreth asked, "How long before we're in sight of the Gallosian rearguard?"

"Another three hundred yards."

Covering those three hundred yards seemed to take forever, except the next three hundred felt even longer.

"We're close to fifty yards, ser," Beltur was finally able to say.

"Company!"

Beltur dropped the concealment and glanced toward the Gallosians some fifty yards away, all in good formation, unlike the recon squad, although he thought several of the Gallosians did look surprised.

"Charge!"

Beltur urged Slowpoke forward, not holding him back, and the big gelding gathered speed in a way Beltur hadn't felt before, almost as if he knew he had to be at full speed. Beltur leaned forward nearly against the gelding's neck, trying be one with his mount.

One of the Gallosians tried to move his mount and slash. Beltur didn't even feel that impact on his shields, but he certainly felt the glancing impact on his shields as Slowpoke slammed between two other mounted Gallosians and kept going. More riders scattered, or were pushed aside, but the big gelding finally slowed, and Beltur reined him up when he found there was no one in front of him. He started to turn Slowpoke when two Gallosian riders spurring their mounts galloped past him, followed by several others.

He looked back south at the milling mass of gray and

blue uniforms, only to realize there were few gray uniforms left. After a moment, he rode toward the riders of Second Recon. He reined up short, aware that he could do little. Instead, he tried to sense whether more Gallosians were heading toward him, but the only movement was that of the handful or so of fleeing Gallosians.

When he again studied the road, he saw that several rankers were going over the bodies of the fallen, several of whom had arrows protruding. The rankers were removing the shafts, carefully, apparently to save and possibly reuse those they could, as well as weapons and coins.

"Make it quick!" snapped Laugreth, who quickly rode toward Beltur, stopping just short.

"Are more Gallosians headed this way?"

"No, ser. Not yet."

Laugreth turned in the saddle as Gaermyn neared. "How many?"

"Just one dead. Five wounded. Not many escaped, from what I could tell," said Gaermyn. "Less than half a squad. What about their wounded?"

"We'll take their mounts. Leave them. We'll move north to behind the next hill. Have the men finish stripping the bodies of weapons and coins. We might not have much time. Leave the bodies. Bring the horses that you can. Have Nobryn and Fifth Squad make tracks on the road and then head back south before he goes into the woods. Make sure they get rid of tracks pointing into the hills."

"Yes, ser."

"Then we'll move up like we planned and wait on the back side of that hill. If anyone gets close, Beltur can do a concealment. We'll just wait." The captain turned back to Beltur. "If you see any Gallosians coming south, throw a concealment around Fifth Squad and

yourself. Then you ease back behind the hill and hold
the concealment on Fifth Squad until they're out of
sight. Do you understand?"

"Yes, ser. That's so that they can create tracks south,
to give the Gallosians the idea that the whole company
withdrew after meeting up with the Gallosian rearguard."

"That's right. Then once the new rearguard is established, with us already inside them, we'll just slip out
around the curve below and head for the main body."

Beltur watched from the hillside as Fifth Squad milled
around on the road, and then rode back south for several hundred yards, possibly more because they were
out of sight. A good half glass later, he could see Nobryn leading a line of riders, single file, coming around
the west side of the hill south of the one behind which
the remainder of Second Recon waited.

He kept looking north, wondering when the Gallosians would return. From what he could tell, Fifth
Squad would be in position with the rest of the company before the Gallosians would be in sight. Half a
glass passed, and Fifth Squad had returned to position
with the company.

Beltur still could sense no movement from the Gallosians. What he did sense was the faintest hint of a
white mage, something he hadn't felt before. "Ser, the
Gallosians aren't moving."

"They're going to force us to come to them."

Beltur said nothing. He just waited and drank from
his last water bottle filled with ale while Laugreth and
Gaermyn talked quietly in voices so low that he could
hear nothing.

Finally, the captain rode over to Beltur. "How many
Gallosians are there?"

"Still more than two companies I think. Less than
three. They have a white mage."

"Can you tell how they're drawn up?"

"Not really, ser. They're on both sides of where the road forks, and a few are on the narrow road we took before. There are more in the hills on each side of the roads."

"Can you and that big gelding do what you did to the rearguard? Just plow through?"

"We can try, ser. Against two or three companies, I don't know how far we'll be able to go."

"We really don't want a pitched battle with two or three companies. If you can widen your shield a little, I think we can cut our way through."

"They do have a white mage there, ser." Beltur wanted to make certain the captain understood that.

"Where is he?"

"In the middle, on the west side, probably on a slope from what I can tell. That's to allow him to see over both roads so that he can throw chaos-bolts. He's got troopers around him as well."

"If you lead the charge again, won't he concentrate on you?"

"He might, but he's high enough above the road that I can't charge him directly. At least, I don't think I can."

"Won't your shields deflect chaos-bolts? They did before."

"For a while. But if my shields hold, he'll just aim farther back and burn the rankers beyond my shields. The stronger he is, the smaller my shields have to be."

"Then what do you suggest?"

"Aim the attack at the point closest to him."

"The road is so narrow that we really can't do that."

Beltur thought for a moment. "Is there a ranker who can loose those iron-shafted arrows at the wizard, or close enough that he'll think they'll hit him?"

"What do you have in mind, Undercaptain?"

"If I take a small group that starts loosing arrows at

him, he'll aim chaos-bolts at me. They'll have to use the iron arrows though."

"Those aren't much good beyond a hundred yards, if that."

"We'll be closer than that. We'll have to be for them to do any good." That was another guess on Beltur's part, but they had to be close so that the wizard didn't have much time to react. "Hopefully, my shields will splash the chaos on any Gallosians near us, which might open things up behind us. It will also keep him from doing as much damage to the rest of the company."

"You think so?"

"I'd like to think so."

Laugreth laughed softly. "So would I." He turned in the saddle. "Gaermyn . . . you heard the undercaptain. Do you have someone who can shoot that well during an attack?"

"Most of them."

"We'll put one on each side of the undercaptain, and he can lead the way."

With those words from the captain, Beltur decided to cloak himself from order and chaos. He didn't see much point in cloaking the entire company, since the Gallosians had to know where they were, but the last thing he wanted was for the white wizard to know exactly where he was.

"This way, Beltur." Laugreth led the way to where Fourth Squad had formed up, then waited for the other squads to take their positions.

Finally, he ordered, "Company, forward!"

The first hundred yards were slightly downhill, the next hundred near-level, at which point Beltur dropped a concealment over the company, just before the company reached where the road dropped down a gradual slope to the fork in the road. That was where Recon Two would have come into sight without the concealment. The Gallosian wizard might well be telling company captains where Recon Two happened to be, but without seeing the company, the Gallosians might be reluctant to loose shafts, if indeed they even had archers.

The first Gallosian units were still almost two hundred yards away when Beltur sensed something else. "Captain . . . the first units are pikemen and shieldmen."

"Can you knock the first rank aside?"

Beltur kept his sigh to himself. "I can try." *What else will he want? And how long can you keep doing this?* Yet, how could he not try? Elparta had taken him in when Gallos had thrown him out . . . and then there was Jessyla. If Elparta fell . . .

He shook his head, knowing the captain couldn't see him.

They rode another hundred yards in silence and darkness. By then, he could hear the Gallosians.

". . . out there a couple hundred yards . . ."

"Pikes! Stand by. Shields! Ready."

"They know we're here," said Laugreth.

"The white wizard told them, but they don't know exactly where. How close do you want to be when I drop the concealment?"

"Thirty yards, unless they loose arrows before that."

Beltur forced himself to wait as the distance decreased, and the comments from the Gallosians became clearer.

". . . hear hooves . . ."

". . . got to be close . . ."

"Why are we waiting?"

Beltur had a last-moment idea. "Just before I drop the concealment, I'm going to extend it over the front ranks of the Gallosians."

"Fine. Let me know."

Beltur said nothing until they were around forty

yards. "Extending concealment. Forty yards." He smiled at the surprise from the Gallosians.

". . . can't see . . ."

". . . frigging mage blinded us . . ."

". . . where are the bastards?"

"Thirty yards," declared Beltur.

"Company!"

Beltur dropped the concealment.

"Charge!"

Beltur urged Slowpoke on, just hoping that the gelding wouldn't spook at the pikes, then decided to extend his shields another few yards so that the shield would knock them away before they looked that close to Slowpoke. He also angled the gelding slightly between two pikes.

Even so the impact on his shield felt as though he'd been hit with a blunt timber, and he immediately contracted his shield to just in front of Slowpoke, but wide enough to cover the rankers riding closely beside him on each side. Once through the pikemen and shield bearers, Slowpoke and the shield plowed aside several footmen with spears.

Beltur guided the gelding slightly to the left, angling more toward the mage.

HHISSST!

Chaos-fire splattered away from the shield, and a wave of heat flared across Beltur, no worse than midsummer in Fenard, but definitely warmer than fall in Elparta. A second chaos-bolt followed the first as footmen scattered away from Beltur. It created more heat, like a fire close up.

Beltur forced himself to look beyond the Gallosian rankers ahead, using sight and senses to locate the white wizard. "See the five men on the knoll to the left! The one in the middle is the white wizard. Start loosing shafts! The iron ones!"

A third chaos-bolt slammed into Beltur's shield, and the heat felt like he'd passed through an oven. He could sense iron shafts heading toward the mage, then saw reddish flares as the shafts bounced off the wizard's shields.

"More shafts! Now!" Beltur could see they were less than forty yards from the knoll and the wizard. Without quite knowing why, he put order on the arrowheads being nocked by the two rankers.

That shaft flared against the wizard's shields, and Beltur could sense that something had happened. The same effect occurred with the next shaft! "Again!"

He added more order to the next pair of shafts . . . and to the third pair.

At that moment, he began to feel light-headed, and he just hung on for a moment.

Abruptly, chaos flared from the knoll and five Gallosians turned into charcoaled figures.

How much order did you put there? Even that question made his head ache, or ache more.

Beltur could barely hang on to his shield and dropped it just to cover himself and Slowpoke, but by then no one seemed to be near him and the two rankers. He slowed the gelding to a fast walk, but kept moving. He didn't want to be close to the fighting because he could feel his shields all slipping away.

Then he was swaying in the saddle.

"Catch him, Dobryn!"

Those were the last words he heard before the blackness, tinged with flecks of white-hot chaos, flowed over him.

LXIII

When Beltur woke, his head was splitting, and he lay
on his back on a narrow pallet bed. Flashes of light
flicked in front of his eyes. They didn't come from the
small oil lamp suspended from a spike in the wall.

"Where . . ."

"You're all right, ser. You're at the barracks. The
healer said you'd be all right in a while, but you're not
to do any more magely stuff. Not for a while." A
younger ranker stood by the plank wall that confirmed
to Beltur that he was indeed in the barracks, possibly
in his own temporary bed.

"The healer? What healer?" Beltur's throat was dry,
and his voice rasped with each word.

"Older blond woman. She seemed to know you."

Margrena, then. Another thought crossed his mind.
"When is it?"

"After sixth glass. It's still fiveday, ser."

"Thank you."

"There's stuff here for you to eat and drink, ser. Especially drink. You're supposed to do that as soon as
you can."

Beltur had to roll onto his side and brace himself on
the side of the narrow bed in order to sit up. The ranker
stepped forward and handed Beltur a mug. Beltur found
his hands were shaking so much that he had to use both
of them to hold the mug and take a small swallow of
the ale. After several swallows, his mouth and throat
didn't feel so dry, and there weren't quite so many
flicker-flashes breaking up what he could see. His hands
also stopped shaking. Mostly.

"How did the company do?" he finally asked.

"We lost eight in the last fight, ser. Five wounded. Ryhsyn likely won't make it. Would have been a lot more if we hadn't broken through."

"I'm sorry to hear that."

"You've got nothing to be sorry about, ser. Would have been a lot worse if you hadn't opened them up so we could get through." The ranker paused. "You be all right, now, ser? Captain said I was to tell him when you woke."

"I won't go anywhere." That was true enough. Beltur scarcely felt like moving.

After the ranker hurried off, Beltur drank more of the ale, and then ate some of the sweet bread and the pearapple that had been left for him. By the time he finished, most of the light flickers had stopped, and the throbbing in his head had subsided to a dull ache, and the last of the tremors in his hands seemed to have stopped. On the other hand, he was even more aware of the soreness in his thighs, chest, neck, and shoulders, soreness that might show up as bruises before that long.

He couldn't sense anything, not even faintly and only a few yards away. Yet he wasn't totally surprised when the captain walked into the small space and looked at him. The captain's uniform was splotched in places, as if he'd wiped away blood and other matter. Beltur might have been able to sense that, if he'd been able to sense anything.

"You look a lot better than when they carted you in here, Undercaptain."

"I imagine so, ser. I don't remember much after we rode past where the Gallosian mage was."

"You and the two rankers almost made it to our lines before you collapsed."

Beltur definitely didn't remember that. "How are the men?" he asked cautiously.

638 L. E. MODESITT, JR.

"Fifteen dead, so far. Another eleven wounded."

Beltur winced. That was a quarter of the company.

"The majer thinks we worked wonders." Laugreth's voice was dry. "It depends on how you look at it."

Beltur didn't say anything.

"After two days of real fighting, we're less than eight-tenths of full strength. Just two days. On the other hand, we've effectively removed almost three companies of Gallosians. To the majer and the marshal, our casualties are acceptable."

"Twenty-six men." Beltur didn't know what else to say.

"Six of them look to recover fully. One will likely die. The other four . . . with luck and a good healer . . ." Laugreth paused. "I understand about shields. I've seen your concealments. What else did you do?"

"I did what you ordered, ser. I shielded Slowpoke, and we broke through the pikes and shields, and then we rode toward the mage on the knoll. I just had the rankers shoot iron shafts at the mage."

"That's what your rankers said. But you must have done something more. I talked to the majer. Other companies have loosed iron shafts at mages, and they just get knocked down."

"That happened at first, but we got really close . . . and I added a little order to the shafts." Beltur suspected he'd added too much order, and that was what had exhausted him. Or part of it.

"That was what I thought. I asked some of the mages if that could be done. None of them think order can be added to iron except when it's being forged."

"Then I don't know what I did. That's what I thought I did."

"I told the one of them . . . Cohndar, he said he was the head mage, what I saw, and he said that you must have been using chaos."

"I definitely didn't use chaos," said Beltur. "If I'd added chaos to iron shafts, both rankers would have burned to death."

"They would have?"

"That's what happened to the Gallosian mage. When all that ordered iron hit the chaos of his shield, everything exploded."

"Then . . . why . . . ?"

"I'm a black mage, but I'm not like Cohndar and some of the others. I don't know why."

"There was another mage there, Waensor or something."

"Most likely Waensyn. He's not exactly fond of me."

"He muttered something . . . well . . . about you being . . . sort of a mongrel mage."

"He's said that before."

Laugreth smiled. "I couldn't help but tell him that the mongrel dogs I've known were usually the smartest and always the most loyal. Loyalty and intelligence make them useful."

"I'm sure he appreciated that," replied Beltur sardonically.

"What does he have against you? Did you take his girl or something?"

That startled Beltur. "His girl?" *Jessyla? How could he think that?* "She was never even interested in him."

The captain laughed. "It's good to see that."

"See what, ser?"

"You're thinking about a woman even when you look like wild horses ran you down." Laugreth smiled, if for a moment. "Are you sure you're all right? I need to look in on the others."

"I think I will be." Before the captain could leave, Beltur asked, "How close are the Gallosians?"

"They haven't been able to advance today, and we've pushed them back in places."

"What about siege engines?"

"There's no sign of them yet." The captain stepped back. "You're supposed to take it easy for a while. I'll check with you tomorrow morning."

Beltur sat on the edge of the pallet bed and finished the last of the bread, as well as the ale. He was debating what to do next, when a woman in healer greens and holding a pitcher stepped into the space. It took him a moment to recognize her. "Margrena. The ranker said you were here."

"I'd have expected order exhaustion from Jessyla, but not from a full mage."

"How is she?"

"She's fine. I need to watch her. She tends to give too much of her own order." Margrena looked hard at Beltur. "What in the Rational Stars did you do? You didn't get so order-depleted just by holding shields and smashing an entire company."

"I didn't do that. We just broke through the shield wall and pikes."

The healer shook her head. "Your captain said that you and that horse that no one else can really control killed or wounded something like fifty Gallosians in your last charge. He said he'd never seen something like that before."

"I didn't see much at all. I was just trying to break through so that we could get back, and then I had to hold a shield against a white wizard's chaos-bolts," Beltur admitted.

"You were shielding others and wielding off chaos? Don't you know what that can do to you?"

"It's exhausting. I know that."

"When a chaos-bolt hits your shield, you lose a bit of order. You don't notice it like that. It just feels harder to hold the shield, but it draws order, and if you don't have enough free order around you, it will draw order right out of you."

"I didn't know that."

"You wouldn't have. White mages have that problem with chaos, not order."

Beltur nodded slowly, then asked, "You said you were worried about Jessyla. How is she?"

"She's fine. She's showed more sense than you did."

"It didn't seem that I had much choice at the time."

"You likely didn't. That's why you need to think things out before you get into such a situation." Margrena's expression softened. "Unhappily, the knowledge to see things in advance comes with experience, and experience is a costly tutor."

Beltur was beginning to understand that even more.

"You drank all the ale?"

"I did. I also ate the bread and pearapple."

"Very good. Here's a pitcher of ale. Drink another mug before you go anywhere or do anything. Don't use any order or chaos, not even for shields. Not until you've had a good night's sleep. If you do even a fraction of what you did today with order or chaos in the next day or so, it could kill you."

The seriousness in Margrena's words froze Beltur for a moment.

"I told the captain that, too. By tomorrow, you *might* be able to do a very few things. Carefully. If you get light-headed or dizzy or feel weak, stop. No matter how little you think you're doing." She handed Beltur the pitcher. "I need to go. They said they were bringing in more wounded. Drink some more ale right now. I know I'm repeating myself. You're young enough you need to hear things more than once."

"Yes, Healer." Beltur managed a smile, then immediately refilled his mug.

Margrena shook her head.

Beltur thought he saw a hint of a smile as she turned away.

He'd drunk another half mug of ale by the time Zandyr stepped into the makeshift cubicle. Other than some wrinkles and creases, his uniform looked almost untouched, and his hair was brushed into place.

"You're alive, I see." The blond undercaptain sat on the end of his bed.

"Mostly, anyway," bantered Beltur.

"I heard you fainted after you charged the mage."

Beltur just looked at Zandyr for a long moment. "You might see it that way. It wasn't what happened."

"What did happen, then?"

"The best way I can explain it"—*to you anyway*—"is to say that attacking the mage was like being thrown into a stone wall from the saddle at full gallop." Beltur wasn't about to explain about order and chaos and the effect of the loss of either. Besides, he felt like he'd hit a stone wall.

"Why is that?"

Because Zandyr actually looked puzzled, Beltur replied, "Because white wizards have shields. You can't see them, but they're there. My shields hit his." That was a total falsehood, but Beltur didn't care. It was true in a roundabout fashion, since two mages, one aided by a few volleys of iron-shafted arrows, had clashed, and one was dead, and the other, apparently, had come much closer to that than he'd ever intended.

"Oh . . . like two lancers charging each other."

"Not quite, but it's close enough. It's not something that I'd want to do again."

"But the Gallosians have more white wizards. What else can you do?"

"That's a very good question. Right now, I don't know." Beltur just hoped he could find a better way to deal with another mage. "I'll think about that tomorrow." He yawned.

"You're tired, aren't you?"

You just realized that? Beltur nodded, then leaned down and slipped the mug, pitcher, and empty platter under the bed before easing himself flat on the narrow pallet, wincing at the aches in his legs and buttocks. *You're going to be very sore tomorrow.*

As he drifted toward sleep, he recalled the words of the captain, about mongrels being the smartest and most loyal of dogs . . . and useful. *Like tools.*

LXIV

When Beltur woke on sixday, he was indeed sore in more places than he could easily count. Zandyr was nowhere to be seen, and Beltur wondered if he'd even spent the night there.

Beltur found it was an effort to wash up and shave, and every step seemed to remind him of another muscle he didn't realize he had. He did feel somewhat better after cleaning up. He even wiped off his uniform with a damp rag. Unlike the captain's uniform, his was only dusty, especially below the knees. He was faintly surprised that Second Recon hadn't been awakened early and sent off somewhere, despite what the captain had said, but he made his way to the mess, trying his best to walk normally, despite his aches and bruises. As he entered the modest chamber that held little besides benches and tables, and the rough stoves at one end, he was surprised to see Athaal, sitting alone at one end of a crude plank table.

"What are you doing here?" asked Beltur.

Athaal looked up, clearly surprised. "What happened to you? You're so order-depleted I didn't even realize it was you. Go get something to eat, and some ale. Then we can talk."

"I'll just be a moment," Beltur managed, even as he wondered if he looked as bad as Athaal had suggested. He did get a full platter of something that resembled an egg and mutton hash, a small loaf of bread, and a mug of ale, all of which he carried back to where Athaal sat, finishing up his own breakfast. He sat down and took a swallow of the ale, then looked at the older mage.

"You asked why I'm here. I've been reassigned to provide shields to Commander Vaernaak, as necessary. Since the Gallosians are so close, Marshal Helthaer has moved his command center inside the walls where he doesn't need that kind of protection. Vaernaak is the field commander. Now . . . what happened to you?"

"I'm with Second Recon—"

"That's the company that smashed through the Gallosians on the east flank. You had something to do with that. You had to have. I should have remembered you were with them. They had a mage out there." Athaal frowned. "You didn't use chaos, did you?" He shook his head and said, before Beltur could reply, "You couldn't have. There's no sign of it around you. What did you do?"

"I used shields and had two rankers fire iron-shafted arrows at the mage, with just a touch of order on them." Beltur shrugged. "I passed out and they carried me back here. Margrena did something, I think. Anyway, she told me if I used any more order in the next few days that someone would be burying me. Not quite like that, but she was very clear. Oh . . . and when the captain told Cohndar what I'd done, Cohndar didn't believe it.

He said that I must have used chaos." Beltur took another swallow of ale.

"You couldn't muster that amount of chaos if your life, or even Jessyla's, depended on it. He should have known that."

"I almost mustered too much order," replied Beltur as wryly as he could, taking a bite of the barely warm egg hash.

"I can tell that. But how did you destroy the mage?"

"I thought I told you. I linked order to the iron shafts. It took a bunch of them, but the rankers kept firing—we got really close—and finally the ordered iron broke through his shields and there was a big flare. I only remember hanging on to Slowpoke for a few moments after that."

"Slowpoke?"

"My horse. Well, the one I've been riding."

Athaal took a swallow from his own mug before replying. "You know there are very few mages that can add more order to iron. It's already order-saturated."

"I didn't know that. It didn't seem that different from adding it to the bronze."

The bearded mage frowned, then smiled. "I hadn't thought of that. I'll make sure Cohndar knows."

It won't make him any happier with me. "Thank you."

"You're not going back into the fighting today?"

"I don't know. I don't think so. We'd have been awakened early, I think."

"You're in no shape to do any magery."

"Margrena made that very clear."

"Beltur . . . listen to her, if you won't listen to me."

"What am I supposed to do if the majer or the commander orders Second Recon out into the field? Sit there on Slowpoke and hold what shields I can? Hoping that the Gallosian mages don't target me?"

For a long moment, Athaal did not reply. Finally, he said, "That's all any of us can do, when we can't do any magery."

"I'm sorry. I'm not angry at you, but I don't have to like the situation."

"I understand." Athaal smiled sadly. "I don't think any of us do."

"How is Meldryn? Do you know?"

"He was fine, the last time I saw him. Now that I'm looking after the commander, I haven't been able to get away. Mel grumbled some about the wear on the ovens from all the bread the Council wants, but it keeps the silvers coming."

"You'll probably see him before I do. Give him my best."

"I will." Athaal set his mug on the table. "I need to go. The commander will be heading out on an inspection tour before long."

"You be careful."

"I'll do my best. That's all any of us can do."

After Athaal had left the mess, Beltur wondered if now was the only time the older mage had ever really been in a situation where events were largely beyond his control. *You've been there, and every time you think you're getting some control, something happens.* But maybe that was just life.

Beltur finished off the last of the hash, bread, and ale and headed back to where Second Recon would muster. Muster was quick and almost perfunctory, with the captain announcing that no evolutions were scheduled, but that the company was on standby, in the event that it was needed. After muster, the officers met around the small table in the captain's makeshift study.

Laugreth immediately said, "We're still on standby. That means all of us are to remain here in case Recon Two is needed." He paused and looked at Zandyr. "That includes all officers. I hope that we aren't needed today, but those are the orders. The Gallosians don't seem to be making a push. At least so far this morning. They appear to be regrouping and moving more men to the eastern side of the river." He offered a wintry smile. "The majer told me they moved another two companies to the fork in the river road. Those were the two companies we encountered earlier. They've pulled back to reinforce the force we broke through. The majer doesn't know if they've replaced the mage."

"Why is that, ser?" asked Zandyr, respectfully.

"The majer didn't say." Laugreth looked to Beltur. "Do you have any idea?"

"Mages look like anyone else from a distance. The Gallosians seem to be doing the same thing as we are with mages and putting them in uniform. White doesn't look that different from light gray, anyway. That means that only a mage can tell if another mage is there . . . and only if the mage isn't using special shields to hide himself."

"You knew where the Gallosian mage was." Zandyr's tone was not quite accusatory.

"I don't think he was the strongest of white mages. He also might have been one who couldn't do those kinds of shields. Every mage I've ever met has talents a little bit different from every other mage. Sometimes, a great deal different."

"That doesn't seem very efficient."

"War and magery aren't like trading," said Gaermyn. "A barrel of flour or oats is a barrel of oats. Every armsman is a bit different from every other one. So is every captain and undercaptain. It makes sense that mages are as well."

Laugreth cleared his throat, then continued. "We should get a little respite unless the Gallosians mount an immediate attack. The past two days have put quite a load on both the men and the horses. I let the majer know that. I also told him we physically couldn't do what we did yesterday for at least several days. He wasn't happy, but he understands. I doubt the commander or the marshal would understand or care."

At those words, Gaermyn frowned.

Beltur had the feeling that the weathered undercaptain agreed with the captain's words, but didn't think Laugreth should have uttered them before junior undercaptains. *Or is he concerned for some other reason ... because Zandyr might say something to his father?* Or was his father even that close to the council and the marshal? There was so much Beltur didn't know and hadn't had time to learn.

"Beltur," continued the captain, "you said that you didn't think the mage you and the rankers faced was as strong as others. Were you suggesting something?"

"Yes, ser. I can't do what we did against a stronger mage and a larger force. I didn't have any shields at the end and could barely stay in the saddle. That white mage wasn't one of the stronger ones, either. Not compared to some that the Prefect has." He really didn't know that, but he recalled his feelings of powerlessness during those terrible moments in the palace of the Prefect, and the aura of power around Wyath and the others. The mage he and the two rankers had killed hadn't seemed to show that range of power.

"He threw almost a score of firebolts."

Beltur didn't recall nearly that many. "I've seen the most powerful mages once, and I barely escaped with my life. This one didn't seem nearly that strong. If we go against another mage, one that's stronger, we're going to need to try something else."

"You've been right so far ... and I wouldn't want to destroy the company ... or lose you. But I wonder if you're not underestimating yourself."

"I couldn't answer that, ser. I only know what happened out there yesterday and what I've faced before."

Laugreth smiled faintly. "That's as fair an answer as I could expect. That's all." He stood.

As Beltur stood and began to leave, he noticed that Gaermyn was also departing, when usually the older undercaptain remained, at least for a few moments.

Zandyr eased past Beltur without speaking and hurried off. That bothered Beltur. Was Zandyr trying to get away before Gaermyn or the captain reprimanded him or thought of some duty for him?

Beltur and Gaermyn walked in the general direction of the stables. Gaermyn spoke quietly. "I'm curious, Beltur. You don't have to answer me, if you'd rather not, but can other mages do what you did yesterday?"

"I don't know how to answer that, ser. Part of that is because I've known so few mages well. I'd think so, but every mage is a bit different from every other mage. I know that my shields are stronger than some mages', but I believe others' are as strong. I put some order on the iron-shafted arrows, and I found out this morning from one of the mages I do know that not many black mages can do that, and no white mages would ever try it. It's far too dangerous for them. Most mages can do concealments, the ones that shield the troopers from sight. I don't know if my abilities there are greater or lesser than the stronger black mages. As for sensing things, I'd guess that I'm maybe a little more sensitive than most blacks, and almost all blacks are more sensitive than whites."

Gaermyn frowned. "Why is that?"

"When you're sensing, you're really trying to pick up the patterns of both order and chaos. White mages have trouble sensing smaller bits of order, and those bits give you a better feel of what you can't see, because under a concealment no one can see anything."

The older undercaptain nodded. "I'll have to think about all that. I'd like you to as well. The Gallosians aren't going to give us that much of a break. Once they get regrouped, they'll push to get close enough to use siege engines and trebuchets."

"I can see that, ser." Beltur hadn't thought otherwise.

Gaermyn nodded. "Until later." Then he turned away.

Beltur kept walking toward the stables. He wanted to see how Slowpoke was, and to make sure the gelding had been properly groomed, fed, and watered. Those were things he could do without worrying . . . too much.

LXV

By midmorning on sixday, Beltur had visited Slowpoke and spent some time currying him, talking as he did. He doubted the gelding understood a word, but it was clear he enjoyed the attention, and Beltur really didn't have any other way to show his appreciation. When he finished, he persuaded one of the stableboys to give him more oats, which he fed to Slowpoke, who definitely liked them.

Then Beltur walked from the stables back toward the mess, looking for a place to sit down, also hoping he could cadge some bread and ale. As he entered the mess, the only officers he saw were Zandyr and another undercaptain, standing beside one of the plank tables. Zandyr was gesturing in a most animated fashion as he talked. Beltur would have like to have raised a concealment and eased closer, but he recalled exactly what Margrena had said and decided he didn't want to know that badly what Zandyr was so exercised about.

Instead, he angled toward the cooking area, where he saw one of the rankers who appeared not to be actively engaged, and asked, "Might I get some bread and ale?"

"Ser?"

"Bread and ale?"

"Oh, yes, ser. The bread might be a bit stale."

"That's fine."

In moments, Beltur had a mug of ale and a largish loaf of bread, which he took to a table behind Zandyr, who was still talking and who had not even looked in Beltur's direction. He listened, picking up fragments of what Zandyr and the other undercaptain said, as he sipped the ale and slowly chewed morsels of the bread.

"... rankers ... no respect ... smirk when they think I'm not looking ... stupid to think I can't see ..."

"It could be they don't care," said the other undercaptain.

"... they're going to care. So will the captain ... worse that he defers to ... old undercaptain. He's the captain ..."

"... think ... he's being kind to an old undercaptain ... won't ever be ..."

"... shouldn't be ... condescending ... arrogant ..."

"... shouldn't be saying ... even here ..."

"... treat mage better ... lowborn ... mage or not ... rides with one of them ..."

"... because he's a mage ... knows magery ..."

"... doesn't matter ... can't treat ... this way ... insufferable ..."

"... is what it is, Zandyr ... war won't last forever ... need to go now ..."

"... walk out with you ..."

Beltur didn't know whether to smile ruefully or shake his head as Zandyr left with the other undercaptain, never having once looked around the mess, not in the time that Beltur had been there. But then, Beltur had been the only other officer there.

He took his time finishing the bread and ale, then returned the mug and made his way back to his space, glad that Zandyr wasn't there. He eased onto the pallet bed gingerly.

Before long, his eyes closed.

When Beltur woke again, it was close to mid-afternoon. As he slowly rose, he became very much aware—again—of how many places on his body were sore. *Because your shield distributed all those blows and impacts across your frame?*

Once he was on his feet and had moved around a little, he decided he was feeling somewhat better, provided he didn't bump or touch his upper arms. Even so, the muscles in his thighs and buttocks continued to remind him that he'd done something to them. One encouraging sign was that he could sense order and chaos patterns, almost a kay to the south, but the patterns in the crowded areas to the north, behind the walls were still just a jumble.

Before long he made his way to the captain's study, not really expecting to find Laugreth there, and he didn't. But Gaermyn was there, seated at the conference table and looking at maps.

"How are you feeling, Beltur."

"Better, ser."

"You're still pale."

Beltur just nodded. "Has anything happened with the Gallosians?"

"Scouts from Third Recon reported that four more companies arrived from Gallos. Three foot and one mounted. They're being ferried from the west side of the river to the east. They probably won't attack today. Tomorrow . . . who knows? I'd doubt it, but they might position troopers for an attack the next day."

"You think they'd attack on eightday?"

"They might well, if they thought they'd catch us off guard." Gaermyn paused. "I'll let you know if anything changes."

"Yes, ser." Beltur understood that Gaermyn needed to get back to whatever he was working out with the maps. "I'm not going anywhere." Not that he was allowed to or that he really had the strength.

He walked slowly back to his bunking area and sat down on the bed. He thought about reading, but his head still throbbed intermittently, and he had nothing to read. So he settled back on the pallet bed and tried to think about what he could do differently, or better, the next time he and Recon Two encountered a white wizard.

He didn't get too far before he dozed off.

How long he dozed he wasn't certain but he woke when he heard faint steps, and he immediately sat up . . . and winced as he was reminded of all the aches and soreness. He immediately forgot those when he saw who stood there.

Deep and dark circles ringed Jessyla's eyes, still intense green, but clearly tired, and even without trying, Beltur could sense her order levels were far too low. He tried not to show his concern. "You've been working hard, haven't you?"

"Too hard, Mother says."

He gestured to the other bed. "You need to sit down." He paused, then added, "You need to rest." *More than I do.*

"It's hard to do that. There are so many." She eased onto the other bed, directly across from Beltur, and looked directly at him. "She wouldn't let me see you yesterday. She said you'd be all right, and that I'd need every bit of order just to get through yesterday and today."

"She let you come to see me so you wouldn't try to heal any more troopers."

"She didn't say that, but . . ." Jessyla smiled faintly. ". . . she didn't have to." She moistened her lips. "You . . . it was very close . . . yesterday, Mother said."

"Closer than I knew. She told me not to use any order for anything. I could tell she meant it."

"Why did you do it?"

"I didn't know how much order I was using. It's hard to tell when people are trying to kill you and a white mage is throwing chaos-bolts at you, and when everyone around you will die if you don't hold some shields."

"I . . . think . . . that was what was . . . supposed to happen."

"That I wouldn't know and would do too much?"

She nodded. "I had this feeling . . . when Mother told me. I went and asked Athaal if any other mages were assisting the other reconnaissance companies. None of them are. They're all with heavy foot companies. Or they're shielding important officers."

"I didn't know that." Beltur couldn't say that it surprised him.

"You don't look that surprised."

"Now that you've told me, it makes sense. I'm pretty sure that Athaal doesn't have as strong a shield as I do, and I can do more things with order at the same time than he can. I've never said anything, but I saw his expression when he heard that I'd held four separate shields at once, and he admitted it later."

"You're not angry? You should be furious. Cohndar and Waensyn set you up to die out there."

"I've known all along that neither of them liked me. I didn't think they were quite that bad." *But you should have.* Except he couldn't believe that Cohndar would risk the lives of other Spidlarian troopers and officers just to see him dead. "I think I know why Waensyn doesn't." He looked directly at Jessyla. "I think you do, too."

"I can't stand him. Weasels and vulcrows are honorable compared to him. Mother thinks so, too. You have to be more careful from now on."

"I don't know about careful. I'm going to have to be more effective without using as much order. I can't very well just walk away. Then they'd have every reason in the world to get rid of me. The Prefect and Arms-Mage of Gallos already want me dead. The last thing I need is the Council thinking the same thing, and if word got out that two lands wanted me dead, how long would I last somewhere else . . . unless I hid and lived as a laborer . . . or worse. I can't do that." *Not now that I've known you.*

"Why do little people make life so difficult?" demanded Jessyla.

"Because they're little people." *Because they can't stand the thought of someone they want to look down on as being better . . . or not worshipping them . . . or . . .*

"You *have* to take care." She leaned forward and took his hands. "You have to."

Beltur managed a grin. "Only if you promise to."

Jessyla started to say something, then laughed, shaking her head.

"What is it?" Beltur was totally confused. *Why was what you said so funny?*

"Mother . . . That's what . . . who . . ."

What did Margrena have to do with it?

When Beltur didn't speak immediately, Jessyla went on. "Don't you see? Why else did she want us to see each other?"

Beltur finally did. He just shook his head, still holding Jessyla's hands, knowing that neither of them could afford to do more.

LXVI

Sevenday began much the same as sixday had, except Beltur woke in somewhat less pain, but with more soreness and stiffness. Some of that passed after he had a full breakfast, and he felt a little less stiff after muster as he and Zandyr walked toward the captain's study.

Once the four officers were seated around the small table, Laugreth offered a crooked smile. "We've been assigned an actual recon mission today. Locals have been saying they saw a few Gallosian troopers on the road to Axalt, some five to six kays east of the city walls. Recon Three is still at full strength. We're not. So we're to head out and see what we can find. We're not to engage any superior force, but if we encounter one, we're to delay the Gallosians as much as possible without incurring significant casualties." Laugreth paused. "The majer didn't define what he meant by significant."

Beltur was afraid he understood what the captain wasn't saying, or at least the fact that the majer was sending the weakest company to scout, because the strongest one might be needed to reinforce any weak point in the Spidlarian lines.

Laugreth looked to Beltur. "You're not back to full strength. What exactly are you able to do?"

That was a question Beltur didn't want to answer, because he was anything but certain. He also knew he had to give the best reply that he could. "I could sense a Gallosian force at a little over a kay. I could hold a concealment over a squad for perhaps half a glass. I can't shield anyone right now for more than a few moments." Beltur wasn't about to point out that he likely could—and would—shield himself. "The longer I don't have to do any of that the more I should be able to do."

"Should?"

"I've never been that close to dying before," said Beltur. "I don't know how fast I'll recover and how strong I'll be."

Gaermyn looked surprised.

Laugreth didn't. He just nodded and said, "One of the senior healers told me that. We've already lost one mage from something similar."

Beltur wondered if he'd known the mage who died. He also wondered why Margrena had told Laugreth and not him.

"Pardon me . . ." interjected Gaermyn. "I knew you were exhausted, and the rankers had to keep you in the saddle, but . . ."

"It's a little like bleeding to death. All of us have order and chaos in our bodies. Both are necessary. If a mage loses too much of either, he will die, just as a man who loses too much blood will die. It takes a great deal of order to hold a shield, especially against chaos-bolts. The chaos-bolt and the order in the shield combine and explode." Margrena hadn't told him that part, but he'd seen and felt it. "That destroys the force of both, but after a time it drains order from me. If I hadn't kept holding the shield on fiveday, we'd have died immediately." His explanation was an oversimplification, but true for all that, and he wasn't about to mention that he'd actually been without shields at the end.

Laugreth nodded. "It's not just exhaustion. Think of it as the same as exhaustion and a huge loss of blood." He looked, not at Gaermyn, but Zandyr, then back to Beltur. "Mount up immediately. We need to be riding out in less than half a glass. That's all." He stood.

Immediately after that dismissal, Beltur rounded up

his water bottles, all four of them and made his way to the mess area.

The ranker there took one look at the black cuffs on Beltur's uniform and filled all four, then said, "Best of luck, ser."

"Thank you." Beltur just hoped he didn't need luck.

As he was walking into the stable area, Gaermyn walked up beside him.

"I didn't realize . . ." offered the older officer.

"There's no reason you'd know." Beltur laughed softly. "I didn't even realize all of that until afterward. I wasn't trained as an arms-mage, and helping forge cupridium is very different from what I had to do on five-day." *And what you're going to have to keep doing, if you want to stay alive.*

"Does Zandyr talk to you very much?"

"Usually only in passing. One of the few things he wanted to know was why I was forging cupridium. He seemed more surprised at how valuable it is than why it was useful to white wizards."

"I have to say that I don't know that, either."

"A truly strong white can't handle iron, especially bare-handed, without pain, sometimes burns, and in rare cases, a slight wound from an iron weapon can kill whites. They can handle a cupridium blade. That's also why their knives and razors are bronze or cupridium. Cupridium is actually just order-and-chaos-reinforced bronze, but the order locks the chaos within the metal." Beltur laughed softly. "That's probably more than you wanted to know."

"Of course. That's why all the iron-shafted arrows. I'd thought they were more to get through the mage's shields."

"That, too."

"Thank you. I'll see you in a bit." Gaermyn turned, presumably toward where his mount was stalled.

Beltur wondered why Gaermyn was interested in what Zandyr had to say, beyond the obvious fact that both Gaermyn and Laugreth had concerns about the blond undercaptain.

A stableboy hurried toward Beltur as he neared Slowpoke's stall. "I gave him a few more oats this morning, ser."

Beltur smiled, knowing the youth was hoping for something, but that was fine with him. He dug a copper from his belt wallet. "Thank you. I'd offer more, but undercaptains don't get paid that much, and I haven't even been paid yet."

The youth grinned in return as he took the copper. "You know he's one of the biggest horses in the stable?"

"I hadn't looked, but it's a good thing for me that he is." At the stableboy's quizzical look, Beltur added, "He's gotten me out of some tight situations." *Even if you've been the one to put you both there.*

Beltur didn't dawdle in saddling Slowpoke, but he didn't rush, either. He didn't see any point in using any more energy than he needed, at least not until he was back to full strength. He hoped that it wouldn't be too long.

Even though he was deliberate, he and Slowpoke arrived and took their place at the head of First Squad just before Zandyr appeared and eased his mount in front of Third Squad.

Almost at that exact moment, the captain ordered, "Company! Forward!"

Once the company was well away from the piers, Beltur asked, "Have you heard anything else, ser?"

"The Gallosians moved some of their forces on the other side of the river even farther to the west."

"To try and spread us out?"

"That's what the majer thinks. He's probably right, but that would only help us. The fall crops have already been harvested, and the large growers have moved or sold their harvest. That just means we face fewer troopers attacking Elparta."

"Are there enough small growers to supply the Gallosians?"

"I doubt it will matter. If we hold them off until the snows begin to fall, there won't be enough to supply them through the winter, even if they raid all the holdings."

Beltur couldn't help but think that it would matter very much to the smallholders. "Then the Gallosians need to attack before long."

"It would seem that way to me, but I'm just a captain."

There wasn't much Beltur could say to that, and he didn't.

In less than a third of a glass, Second Recon was on the road to Axalt, riding east. Before long, Beltur could make out Jorhan's house and smithy. While the house was shuttered, as was every dwelling that Beltur had passed, a thin trail of smoke rose from the smithy, a faint white line against the cool and clear green-blue sky. Beltur hoped that meant Jorhan was still smithing and not carrying a shield for the Spidlarian forces, unlikely as that might be.

"Can you sense any forces?" asked Laugreth.

"Not yet, ser."

"The way you say that . . . Is this a feeling on your part that there might be some farther away?"

"No, ser." *I wish it were.* "I just can't tell beyond that."

"Let me know if you do sense anything."

"Yes, ser."

They rode almost another two kays, and as Beltur was capping his water bottle after taking several swallows of ale, he began to sense something. "Ser?"

"Yes?"

"There aren't any large groups. There are four riders near the road about a kay ahead, just to the east of it. On a rise, I think."

"Four riders. That's more likely scouts than locals." Laugreth glanced at Beltur. "Are you able to conceal a squad for a bit? Once we get close. Not right now."

"I should be able to for a while."

"Then you and I will accompany Second Squad, and we'll move out in front of the rest of the company. You'll tell me when you think we're getting close enough that they're likely to see us."

"I can do that."

"Company! Halt!" Laugreth turned. "Vaertaag, send someone to inform Undercaptain Gaermyn he's needed up here."

"Yes, ser."

Before that long, Gaermyn reined up beside the captain. "Ser?"

"Beltur's sensed four riders up ahead. I don't want Beltur trying to conceal the entire company. So I'm going to take Beltur and Second Squad and see what we can find out. You're to give us about half a kay head start and then follow. Hold the separation, as well as you can, since we'll go under a concealment at some point."

"Yes, ser. Should I give Undercaptain Zandyr the rearguard."

"Just for now."

"Yes, ser."

Before long, Laugreth, Beltur, and Squad Leader Chaeryn led Second Squad along the road, into a breeze blowing out of the east, a wind much cooler than Beltur had felt before in Spidlar. He scanned the horizon but could see no sign of clouds.

"Where are those riders now?" Laugreth asked after they had covered another three hundred yards.

"They haven't moved. I'd judge they're about half a kay beyond where the road curves around that hill on the left. They're back from the road, possibly in woods or an orchard. They might be on a rise or low hill."

"That suggests they're scouts. They could see anyone coming for a distance." Laugreth frowned. "Do you sense anyone else? Any other force?"

"No, ser. I'd thought to raise a concealment just before we'd come into their sight."

"Good." Laugreth turned in the saddle. "Squad Leader. Pass it back that we'll be entering a concealment just before the road straightens around the next bend. Have them go to a staggered formation so they can hold position."

"Yes, ser."

The road was relatively exposed, with harvested fields and pastures on the north side, and undulating gentle slopes to the south. The lower slopes beside the road held rows of bushes, redberry, Beltur thought, with trees above them.

"With all these redberry bushes . . . ?" Beltur offered.

"You wonder why no one seems to drink it here?" asked Laugreth.

"That thought had occurred to me."

"I'm told that's because most of the redberries are dried and added to ship's rations so that the sailors don't get mouth rot. The Hamorians use lemons for that, but it's far too cold for lemons and limes here. You can use greenberries the same way, but if you've ever tried to chew a greenberry, you'd see why no one does."

Beltur nodded, although he'd never heard of greenberries.

As they neared where the road straightened after the curve around the hill, Beltur said, "It's time for the concealment."

"Go ahead."

Beltur placed the concealment over the squad, then checked on the four riders. "The riders are moving toward the road."

"Quickly or slowly?"

"At a walk."

"We'll keep moving and see what happens."

After perhaps a tenth of a glass, Beltur said, "They've reached the road, and they're heading east."

"How far away are they?"

"Three hundred yards."

"Drop the concealment. Let's see who they are."

Beltur dropped the concealment and immediately could see that the four riders ahead of them all wore gray uniforms.

At the appearance of the Spidlarian squad, all four riders spurred their mounts into a gallop.

"Let them go. There's no point in wearing out the horses chasing them." Laugreth turned to Beltur. "Are there any other groups of riders near?"

"There might be another four. They're directly south of us. A little farther than a kay. Maybe a kay and a half. It's hard to tell."

"They'll be on the hill road we took before. Can you tell which way they're headed?"

"No, ser. I don't think they're moving."

"Squad! Halt!" After a moment, the captain added, "We'll just let the rest of the company catch up and see what the other Gallosian scouts are doing."

Beltur nodded, then pulled out his water bottle and took a long swallow of ale.

By the time the rest of the company joined them, it was clear that the other four riders were headed east as well.

"We'll go east for another two kays and see what we find . . . or don't. Then we'll head back. We don't want to get too far from Elparta."

Slightly less than a glass later, Laugreth called another halt after Beltur could sense no groups of riders anywhere.

"This is as far as we go." The captain smiled sourly. "We've only seen four Gallosian scouts, and we're more than six kays from Elparta."

Once Second Recon turned and headed back along the road toward Elparta, Beltur took another swallow of ale from his water bottle, thinking that despite what was turning into an uneventful day in the saddle, he was beginning to be able to sense farther away than he had been able to do that morning. "We don't have much to report."

"That's not all bad," replied Laugreth. "Would you really have wanted to face two companies the way we did the last time we were here out east?" Without waiting for a reply, he went on. "I'll report to the majer that there are certainly Gallosian scouts east of Elparta. I'll tell him that they turn and gallop for the hills at the first sight of any Spidlarian unit, and that we could find no traces of any significant Gallosian forces anywhere near the Axalt road. Also no signs of raiding or pillaging." He laughed humorlessly. "That's not out of honor, but because there's precious little left here to pillage, not right after the Council tariffs have to be paid and when most of the herders have left their flocks in the north."

"Even with the chance that they'll be trapped there if the fighting drags out or there's an early snow?"

"Most sheep can survive snow. They don't survive being slaughtered."

Beltur could see that. He just nodded and took another swallow of ale.

LXVII

Meoryt, the duty squad leader, roused Beltur and Zandyr out of sleep well before dawn on eightday. "The Gallosians are attacking. Second Recon is to form up immediately."

Beltur was halfway dressed before Zandyr struggled into a sitting position on the side of his pallet bed.

"Attacking on eightday before dawn," muttered Zandyr. "Uncivilized barbarians."

"It doesn't matter whether it's uncivilized," replied Beltur, pulling on his boots. "It only matters whether it works."

Zandyr was still struggling into his uniform when Beltur hurried to the mess with his water bottles. He got all four filled and stuffed a loaf of bread into his tunic before hurrying off to saddle Slowpoke. Even with his stop at the mess he was mounted and reined up in front of First Squad before several of the rankers appeared. As usual, Zandyr was almost the last one in place, again barely getting into position with Third Squad before the captain appeared.

"Company! Forward!" ordered Laugreth, who then lowered his voice and turned to Beltur. "We're headed to the river road to reinforce the foot company that's about a kay south of the end of the piers. Let me know if there are any Gallosians nearby."

After several moments, Beltur replied, "I don't sense anyone between us and the foot company." When Laugreth said nothing, Beltur uncorked his first water bottle and took a long swallow of ale. He wasn't that hungry; so he didn't eat any of the bread.

The eastern sky was just beginning to gray when Second Recon neared the rear of the foot company holding position on the river road and reined up.

"The Gallosians are four hundred yards south," Beltur reported. "They're not moving."

"How many are there?"

"At least two companies, possibly three, but they're split into three groups with about a hundred yards between each. The closest is on the road to the south. There's another group just up the fork to the east. The third is on a ridge west of the middle group."

A single rider moved out of the gloom toward Laugreth. "Chelstaat, Captain, Eighth Foot out of Kleth."

"Laugreth, Second Recon. We're here to support you, if necessary. The Gallosians are attacking about a kay to the southwest. Have you seen any movement here?"

"No. So far as we can tell there are three forces south of us. It's hard to tell how many."

"About three companies in all," replied Laugreth. "Do you have any archers?"

"No. We have a squad of shield and pike, and the rest are heavy foot. What about you?"

"We're standard recon. Sabres and bows."

"The commander must have sent you to make sure we don't get flanked."

"The majer didn't say."

"Do they ever?"

"Not often." Laugreth punctuated the words with a laugh. "We'll leave one squad at the ready, and have the others stand down until there's any sign of movement from the Gallosians."

"Good with us. If we learn anything, I'll send word."

From the exchange between the two captains, and what he could see in the dim light, and sense, Beltur had the feeling that Captain Chelstaat was more like Gaermyn—older and tough. He'd probably worked his way up all the way from ranker to captain. That also raised again the question of how Laugreth had become a company commander.

"Vaertaag," ordered the captain, "have First Squad stand down. Pass the word that Third Squad and Undercaptain Zandyr will be the ready squad for the next glass. Second, Fourth, and Fifth Squads are to stand down as well."

"Yes, ser."

"You don't expect an attack in the next glass, ser?" Beltur asked quietly.

"I think it's the least likely then. But I want you to keep sensing what the Gallosians are doing. If I'm wrong, you need to let me know immediately." Laugreth dismounted and led his horse to the side of the road.

"Yes, ser." Beltur followed the captain's example. After tying Slowpoke to a short but stout pinyon, he felt his stomach growl. Rather than take out the bread immediately, he said, "I brought a large loaf of bread. Would you like some?"

Laugreth laughed. "For a mage, you've got an armsman's common sense. No, I won't, but that's because I did the same thing. So neither of us has to feel guilty or worry about sharing. I do thank you for the courtesy, though."

Beltur didn't wait to sample the bread. It was still warm in the middle, and he felt a great deal better after eating about a third of the loaf. He had needed to eat more than he'd realized, because he could now sense farther away. That was a mixed blessing because he could now discern, barely, the fighting taking place about a kay and a half to the southwest . . . and the continuing puffs of dark black mist that indicated death after death.

"Ser? The Gallosians to the south of us haven't

moved, but the fighting to the southwest is fierce. Lots of men are dying."

"Ours or theirs? Can you tell?"

"No, ser." Beltur concentrated. "Those fighting seem to be staying in pretty much the same place, from what I can tell."

"That usually means a large number of casualties."

That made sense to Beltur. He took another swallow from his water bottle, then finally asked the question he'd pondered earlier. "Might I ask how you came to be a Recon officer?"

"You can. I'll even answer. It's no secret. I'm the youngest of four sons. My father is a merchanter, not wealthy enough to be a trader. I was never interested in trade, but I liked learning about blades and bows, weapons of all sorts. My father couldn't afford a commission for me in any of the Spidlarian regulars, but he had some friends, and he managed an apprentice squad leader position for me in the naval marines—the ones who protect the cargoes on ships. I was good enough that I became a squad leader after five years. Then the Suthyans attacked Diev. Rather, they tried to. My ship was in port there, and the Council ordered us to reinforce the troopers there while they mustered and sent more armsmen. We were assigned to support Second Recon. In the fighting, the company undercaptain was killed, and so was the First Squad leader. That wasn't surprising for a number of reasons I'm not going to explain and one that I will. We were greatly outnumbered at first, until armsmen the Council sent finally arrived. I was foolish enough to take over temporarily, and fortunate enough to survive. After that small war was over, I was offered a commission as undercaptain, in part because the senior squad leader and the other squad leaders pressed for me. I took it. If I had to fight,

I preferred to do it in Spidlar, and the Council wasn't likely to start any wars. Starting wars is bad for trade. When the captain was promoted to majer five years later, I made captain."

"The senior squad leader wasn't Undercaptain Gaermyn, was it?"

"How did you come to that conclusion?"

"I couldn't say, except that it made sense. I had the feeling he came up the long way."

"He did, indeed. Best undercaptain in Spidlar, I'd say."

Which was likely one of the reasons why Laugreth was a good captain, Beltur suspected.

Before Beltur could have asked another question, not that he had intended to, Laugreth asked, "What about the Gallosians to the southwest?"

"It's about the same, ser. They're still fighting, and men are still dying. I can't sense that they've moved much."

"And the ones on the road to the south?"

"They haven't moved either."

A good glass passed, and Third Squad stood down, with Fourth Squad becoming the ready squad. Just after that happened, Beltur began to sense a change in the more distant fighting. At first, there were far fewer bursts of the black death mists. Then, there were almost none. After that, he began to sense a growing separation of the two masses of order and chaos.

"Ser, the Gallosians to the southwest are pulling back and the fighting seems mostly to have stopped."

"Is there any other movement toward Elparta anywhere?"

"Not where I can sense it, and right now I can sense all the way to the river and almost two kays to the south."

"Keep a close watch. They might be pulling back to support an attack somewhere else. I'm going to let Captain Chelstaat know."

While Laugreth strode away toward the foot lines, Beltur continued to try to sense for any sign of a possible attack, but all he could determine was that the Gallosians were withdrawing to a position in line with the Gallosian units that had not attacked. He ate some more bread and had a few more swallows of ale . . . and waited.

When the captain returned, he asked Beltur, "Is there any change?"

"The Gallosian companies that were fighting have withdrawn to what looks to be their previous position. I can't sense anyone else moving forward. Not yet anyway."

"They probably won't attack again today. They picked what looked to be the weakest spot and tried to surprise us. The next attack, whenever it comes, will likely be in full force on all our positions, or full force between our positions."

"When do you think that will be?"

"Whenever they think we'll least expect it," replied Laugreth dryly. "I'm going to talk with Gaermyn. If anything changes, let me know immediately."

"Yes, ser."

A half glass passed. The captain returned but said little. Another half glass went by, and Fifth Squad became the ready squad. At ninth glass, First Squad took over, and at noon, Second Squad relieved First Squad. During those nearly three glasses, neither Beltur nor the foot scouts could discern any sign of Gallosian movement.

Just after Third Squad relieved Second Squad, Beltur finally sensed some movement. "The Gallosians on the river road are moving back, ser. So are the groups on each side."

"All three of them?"

"Yes, ser."

"I'll let Chelstaat know."

While Laugreth strode toward the foot company, Beltur kept checking, but the Gallosians continued to move back.

Less than a glass later, the Gallosian forces that had faced Eighth Foot and Second Recon had halted and established a new position half a kay south of their previous location. At third glass, a messenger arrived with orders for Second Recon to return to the piers.

Laugreth lost no time in having the company mount up and begin the ride back.

"Did the orders say why or what might be next?" asked Beltur once the company was riding north on the river road.

"I'm just to report to the majer immediately upon our return," replied the captain. "If I learn anything, I'll let you and Gaermyn know."

"Yes, ser." Beltur doubted that the captain had omitted Zandyr accidentally, but he wasn't about to ask about that. He'd sensed from the beginning that Laugreth did little other than intentionally.

"Vaertaag, pass the word," ordered Laugreth. "All squads to mount up and prepare to return to Elparta."

"Yes, ser."

Beltur took out another water bottle and took a quick swallow of ale, before untying Slowpoke. While he was more than glad that Second Recon had not been required to fight, he had no doubts that the Gallosian withdrawal was only temporary before another onslaught.

LXVIII

Despite the ale and bread, Beltur's stomach felt empty by the time he'd unsaddled and groomed Slowpoke, and he made his way to the mess, where he found the cooks serving any officer who appeared. What they offered was mutton slices and boiled potatoes slathered with a thick brown gravy.

To Beltur, it didn't matter in the slightest. The meal was hot, and he was famished. He'd only taken a few bites and a swallow of ale when Zandyr dropped onto the bench across from Beltur and waited to be served.

"I wondered where you went so quickly," offered the younger officer, watching as a server immediately appeared with a platter and a mug.

"I was hungry."

Zandyr looked at the platter with an expression of disgust. "I was, too, until they served me this."

"It's not bad. I wouldn't let it get cold, though." Beltur took another mouthful of gravied potatoes.

Zandyr looked again at his fare. "Better than cold bread and cheese, I suppose. I'll be glad when it's all over, and we can go back to eating real food."

Beltur nodded, although he'd certainly eaten worse in his life, much of it that he'd had to cook himself for his uncle and Sydon, not to mention more cold meals than he wanted to count. *But you never went hungry at Uncle's house.*

After several more bites and a swallow of ale, Zandyr looked directly at Beltur. "Did you see what they did to me today?"

"Who did what?" asked Beltur, actually puzzled, because the only slight he'd heard was something the younger undercaptain couldn't have heard.

"You didn't see? You really didn't? How could you not have seen?"

"I'm confused," Beltur admitted. "All we did today was stand by as reserves in case the Gallosians tried a flank attack."

"Exactly!" Zandyr set his mug on the table with a thump. "And they treated me just like a squad leader. A squad leader. I'm an undercaptain, not a frigging squad leader."

"I didn't see that." Beltur also didn't see that it had happened that way. Zandyr had been in charge of Third Squad. *What else was the captain supposed to do? Turn over command of the company to Zandyr when the captain was still right there?*

"It happened just that way." Zandyr shook his head. "They can't do that to me. They can't. Just wait until this war is over. Then they'll see."

"We're junior undercaptains," Beltur pointed out. "That means we have to obey orders." *Even orders we might question . . . unless they're completely mad, and neither Gaermyn nor Laugreth has ever given orders like that.*

"There's such a thing as courtesy and respect. We deserve some respect. From the rankers, and especially from the captain."

"That's true, but I haven't seen any lack of respect." *Perhaps some doubt at the beginning, but no outright disrespect.*

"That's because you're a mage. They worry about that. They think they don't have to respect me because I'm a very junior son of a trader. Well . . . they're wrong."

"Have you talked to the captain about this?"

"He won't listen. And Gaermyn's worse. I can tell by the way he looks at me."

"One way or another, the fighting can't last into winter," Beltur said evenly, trying to calm Zandyr. "The Gallosians will have to withdraw by then." *If they haven't taken the city.* If they had, Zandyr and Beltur's problems would be far worse than a supposed lack of respect.

"What if they don't?"

"If they haven't taken Elparta by then, they'll starve and freeze. You should know. Doesn't the snow get at least a yard or two deep everywhere, and doesn't the river freeze over?"

Zandyr opened his mouth, then shut it. After a moment, he said, "That's true. And the snows start even before winter." He stopped again. "But we're still eight-days from the first snow. That's usually halfway through fall. That means I have to put up with them for at least another four eightdays. Four full eightdays."

Beltur wanted to sigh. He did not.

Abruptly, Zandyr rose, leaving half his meal untouched. "I'll see you later."

Taken off-guard, Beltur barely managed to say, "Until later." He watched as Zandyr hurried out of the mess. Then he finished the last of his ale.

He was about to stand and leave the mess when he saw four officers walk in, one of whom was definitely older with white hair. It took him a moment to realize that they were all mage officers . . . and the white-haired one was Cohndar. He thought that the black-haired and bearded officer was Waensyn, but he couldn't be certain because the mage had seated himself with his back to Beltur. None of them so much as glanced in his direction.

Beltur wondered if he could shield both his order and chaos and use a concealment to get close to the four mage officers. He smiled. *Why not?* It also might tell him just how good his concealments were, and if they discovered him, he could simply claim he was testing his shields in a setting where the results wouldn't be fatal. *And that's not a bad idea in itself.*

He looked around, and convinced that no one was paying attention to him, he raised both kinds of concealments, then stood and eased toward the four mage officers, getting only close enough to be able to hear, and standing to the side while they were served. Once the servers finished, he edged slightly closer, but kept his back to the rough plank wall.

"It's hot. That's about all," said one of the two mages Beltur hadn't recognized.

"What do you expect in Elparta?" replied the other unknown mage. "To get the best food, you have to eat in Kleth or Spidlaria." After a pause, he asked, "How was the food in Fenard?"

"Too often spoiled," replied Waensyn, with the arrogance that Beltur had hated from the moment he'd met the mage. "There were too many white mages, and their chaos taints the more subtle flavors, almost anywhere you eat."

"You blacks didn't favor inns where the whites didn't go?"

"There never were that many blacks in Fenard, and some of those weren't real blacks . . . but more like mongrels."

"I believe you've mentioned that."

"It's true."

"It is indeed," added Cohndar. "That's why I recommended that a particular mongrel be assigned to a reconnaissance company. They're mongrel companies, anyway. He's been able to work with a smith to forge cupridium. That takes a certain untutored strength with metals and shields."

"Definitely untutored in other areas as well," said Waensyn with a snort. "Look at which blacks here have supported him."

L. E. MODESITT, JR.

"He may be untutored in those areas," replied one of the unknown mages, "but we need all the strength and shields possible against the whites."

"He's strong in some areas," said Cohndar, "but without understanding in many. He almost died from order depletion the other day. He wasn't even up against one of the stronger whites. That weakling Athaal told me so."

"That may be," conceded the unknown with the deeper voice, "but he did defeat that mage, and that's one less to worry about."

"Perhaps we should make sure that he has a chance to prove himself against stronger mages," suggested Waensyn. "If he's successful, that will prove his worth."

"You don't like him very much, do you?"

"He's a pleasant enough fellow. I don't like what he stands for. His uncle was a white, and he handles order effectively, but he's not even an honest gray."

"So you want to be sure he's in the middle of every battle?"

"Why not? If he takes out some of the whites, we're that much better. If he survives, he'll have earned the right to be called a black and stay in Elparta," replied Waensyn.

"Even as what you call a mongrel?" asked the deeper-voiced unknown.

No one spoke for a moment.

"What if that doesn't work?" asked the lighter-voiced unknown. "If the reconnaissance company takes more casualties, then the commander won't use them except as a last resort . . ."

"I can take care of that," replied Cohndar.

"What about Athaal? He's protective of the mongrel."

"Leave Athaal alone. Jhaldrak's people like him, and

he'll never be a problem. Not with his . . . partner. Besides, we all like good pies and the like."

Beltur winced at the round of laughter and decided to ease back from the group before he was discovered or gave himself away. And he just might if he didn't move, after the contempt he'd heard from several of the mages about Athaal and Meldryn.

He didn't breathe easily until he was in the corridor outside the mess and alone enough that he released the concealment. Still . . . he'd proved that he could conceal himself from other mages, even when he was fairly close.

He'd also confirmed just how much of an enemy Waensyn was, and how contemptuous he was of Athaal and Meldryn. Paradoxically, he felt the same way about Waensyn as apparently those at the table felt about him—that every black mage possible was needed to repulse the Gallosians.

As he walked away from the mess, he couldn't help but shake his head. *Will they ever think of you except as a mongrel?*

LXIX

On oneday, Beltur woke early, half anticipating he would be awakened because the Gallosians had mounted a massive attack. That never happened, and he lay in the darkness thinking. While he'd been dismayed by the conversation between Cohndar and Waensyn and the other two blacks that he'd never met, the depth of Waensyn's dislike and Cohndar's support of Waensyn hadn't exactly been a surprise. In some ways, what Zandyr had said bothered him more. Almost a glass passed before he rose and made his way to the mess, carrying his water bottles. Without quite knowing why, he ate quickly and then carried the water bottles filled with ale and a loaf of bread to the stable, where he made ready his gear before returning to muster.

The Second Recon muster was brief, but, before dismissing the company, the captain announced, "We'll be riding out shortly. All squads form up immediately east of the barracks. Officers to me."

Once all three undercaptains faced Laugreth, he announced, "The Gallosians are loading foot onto flatboats, and they're concentrating forces as if they intend to attack along the east side of the river. Some of you may have noticed that we've had very little rain in the last two eightdays, and the water levels of the river have dropped."

Beltur could see the puzzled expression on Zandyr's face.

So could Laugreth, because he looked at the junior undercaptain and said, not quite condescendingly, "The water's been low enough long enough that the mud has dried. That means they can advance along the river in greater force than before or if they tried the river road or through the hills." His eyes moved back to Beltur. "We'll be supporting the foot being sent south to block any advance along the east bank. Form up as usual. That's all."

As Beltur hurried toward the stables, he silently congratulated himself on already having taken care of the water bottles and managing to snare a small loaf of bread. He saddled Slowpoke quickly, led the gelding out of the stables, mounted and rode to where the company was forming up. Thinking about all that Zandyr had said the night before, he eased toward Third Squad, halting where it was unlikely anyone would ride into him and Slowpoke, but close enough to watch the squad and listen.

Several rankers glanced back toward the barracks building, although Squad Leader Meoryt did not, instead surveying each of the few remaining rankers as they rode up and joined up.

When Zandyr appeared outside the stable end of the barracks and mounted, several rankers stiffened.

". . . comes the fancy undercaptain," murmured someone.

"Quiet in the ranks," said Meoryt firmly. "None of that."

There were more mutters, but Beltur could not hear them, and he eased Slowpoke forward and toward First Squad, where he reined up beside Vaertaag. "Have you heard anything more about what's happening, Squad Leader?"

"No, ser. Some think the graycoats will make a big push. That has to happen sooner or later."

"They're massing as if they'll put most of their forces on the east bank of the river. That's what the captain said."

"Makes sense. What about us, ser?"

"We'll likely be sent to reinforce some foot company." Beltur didn't want to make that as an absolute statement, just in case the orders had changed.

"Could be worse." Vaertaag's tone of voice suggested the opposite.

Beltur nodded, his thoughts going to the last fight and the problems he'd had with the white mage. If the Gallosians had enough whites to put one out on the flank, they were certain to have one or more supporting the main attack. *What if your rankers can't get or use a bow because we're in some sort of melee?* After a moment more of thought, in which he recalled the order-based catapult he'd used in Analeria, he turned to the squad leader. "Vaertaag . . . it might be very helpful if I had two of those iron-shafted arrows."

"Would you need a bow, ser?"

"No . . . just the arrows. I have a way to deliver them." *At least at short range.*

"Very good, ser."

Seemingly, within moments, Vaertaag handed two of the arrows to Beltur, who fitted them into one of the water bottle holders, where he could reach them quickly. He'd just finished that when the captain reined up beside the squad leader.

"Getting last-moment orders from the majer." Laugreth turned to Vaertaag. "We'll ride past the end of the first pier and then move onto the dried mudflats once we're past the pier channel. Eleventh Foot should be a good kay upstream, if not a bit farther. They're supposed to be digging in about a hundred yards behind the armsmen holding the line. We're to take a position where we can attack on either the rougher ground east of the riverbank or along the mudflats."

"Yes, ser."

"Company! Forward!" ordered the captain.

Beltur urged Slowpoke up beside the captain. "I didn't want to ask in the open, but is Eleventh Foot digging in because of the firebolts of the white mages?"

"I wasn't told," replied Laugreth. "Why do you think that?"

"Because chaos-bolts can't burn through earth or rock." For a moment, Beltur wondered why the captain hadn't recalled that, but then remembered that none of the Spidlarians had fought against forces with chaos-mages before. Still . . . if someone had known enough to order the foot behind earthworks, why hadn't they told Laugreth that? All of that—and the fact that the

Gallosians had mages—reminded him, again, to raise a shield blocking any detection of order and chaos.

"That makes sense for the Eleventh. Any position that would allow us to survey both the mudflats and the ground immediately east of the riverbank would put us in an exposed position . . . unless . . ." Laugreth looked to Beltur.

"I can sense large movements of armsmen."

"Then we'll see what position is the most favorable when we get nearer. Can you tell if the Gallosians are attacking?"

Beltur concentrated. "Not yet. They must have close to ten companies within five hundred yards of the river. And there are more behind them."

"How far?"

"A hundred yards."

"That's so they can take advantage of any weakness."

The sun was rising above the rocky outcrops several hundred yards to the east of the river by the time Beltur saw a line of troopers ahead.

"There's Eleventh Foot," declared Laugreth. "There are three other companies farther east."

Beltur surveyed the terrain. The troopers were setting up behind a low embankment running across the middle of what was a point, more like a protrusion of higher ground, that extended perhaps twenty yards into the river and was possibly fifty yards wide, not counting almost ten yards of dried mud at the edge of the water, more in some places, less in others.

"There's enough space to the left, just north of that line of bushes." Beltur pointed. "That's about the only place that's not totally exposed. East of there, the ground is flat, rocky, and uneven. It's only about two hundred and fifty yards from the end of the bushes to the base of those rocky bluffs."

"Is there any way to get up on top of that bluff?"

"Not from anywhere near here, especially not on horseback, from what I can sense." While a white wizard might be able to fling chaos-bolts from the top of the outcropped bluffs, some ten yards higher than the ground immediately beneath, Beltur doubted that the Gallosians would risk having a mage climb up there with no way to withdraw—or advance—quickly.

"Company! On me!" ordered Laugreth.

In short order, Second Recon was positioned behind the highest part of the embankment, largely out of sight from the south.

"Have the Gallosians started to advance?" asked the captain once he was satisfied with the way the company was drawn up.

"Not yet."

Over the next half glass or so, Laugreth asked the same question, and Beltur's reply was the same. In between replies, he took several swallows of ale from his first water bottle.

Then, Beltur sensed both chaos and movement, and a single black mist point, farther back in the Spidlarian force, but to the east, almost in the middle of the uneven ground between the riverbank and the bluffs. Where the death occurred suggested the victim had been hit by an arrow. "They've started the attack. It feels like they loosed a raft of shafts, and then charged."

"Where are their white wizards?"

"I can sense two—one on each side of the advance, more toward the rear. So far they're not doing anything." To Beltur, that made sense. If the Gallosian foot could advance without tiring the whites, then they could be saved for when the advance ran into trouble.

Laugreth turned to Vaertaag. "Pass the word. The Gallosians have started their attack."

"Yes, ser."

For the next half glass or so, the line of battle didn't

seem to change, but the number of deaths continued to rise; then slowly Beltur began to definitely sense the chaos of fighting build as the defending Spidlarians were being forced back, although he couldn't see over the low rise behind the top of which the Eleventh Foot waited. He also had lost track of the number of points of black death mists that flared and faded along the uneven line of battle.

He turned to Laugreth. "The Gallosians are pushing back the middle of the front line. They're losing more men than we are—I think—but they keep coming."

"When you have superior numbers, you can do that."

Then Beltur sensed something else. "Ser! They're bringing horse along the mudflats."

"How far away are they?"

"No more than two hundred yards. They're almost upon the first line of foot next to the river."

"First Squad, Second Squad, at the ready! Undercaptain Gaermyn to the fore!"

Just two squads? Beltur wasn't about to voice the question, instead saying, "The Gallosians are breaking through the middle of the first foot line."

"If we don't stop the mounted attack, the Eleventh won't be able to hold the flank that long, either." Laugreth raised his arm, then lowered it, and urged his mount forward, heading west toward the dried mudflats and the river. Once the two squads reached the flats, he looked to the south.

Even from the saddle, Beltur could barely see over the somewhat higher ground in the middle of the section of ground extending eastward into the water, ground on which foot troopers crouched behind low piles of rock, sand, and earth. He could make out riders still a hundred yards away.

Beltur wondered if the captain would ask for a concealment, which Beltur didn't think wise, given the irregularity of the mudflats and the nearness of the river, but Laugreth had obviously thought the same, because he didn't even ask.

"Four front!" ordered Laugreth, staying on the mud-flats. "Forward!"

Beltur could see what he thought the captain had in mind—to position the two squads on the south side of the point, with enough space so that they could charge the oncoming Gallosians with what would almost be a flank attack.

Just past the tip of the point, Laugreth called a halt, most likely because the Gallosian riders were still almost a hundred yards away and because attacking them earlier would minimize the effect of the charge because the two forces would meet head-to-head, rather than having the Second Recon squads charging into both the front and side of the Gallosian force.

As he waited for the Gallosians to draw closer, Beltur quickly tried to sense what was happening in the middle of the attack, farther to the southeast. He winced, because, while the number of deaths, mostly Gallosian from what he could tell, seemed to be increasing, the Gallosians were moving inexorably forward.

Time passed so slowly that it felt as though a glass had passed before Laugreth raised his arm, then dropped it. "Charge!"

Beltur couldn't help but notice that the captain lagged just slightly, letting Vaertaag and Beltur take the lead. Until he noticed that, Beltur had felt almost selfish in limiting his shields to himself and Slowpoke, but his last battle had made his own limitations all too clear, even if most of Second Recon had no idea of his weaknesses.

As Slowpoke neared the gray-clad riders, Beltur re-alized that they all carried small shields as well as blades and wore iron helmets. *Heavy mounted!* He just held tight with his knees and let Slowpoke plow through the column and partway up the actual bank of the river before turning the gelding and charging back, if at an angle toward the Gallosian lines so that he wouldn't strike any of the Second Recon rankers.

At least one Gallosian slashed at Beltur with enough force that Beltur could feel it on his shields, if momentarily, but the shields, propelled by Slowpoke, hit the Gallosian with enough force that the man was unhorsed and flung sideways into the river. Slowpoke went into the water almost knee-deep, and for a moment Beltur was afraid the gelding would stumble and go down in the water. Instead, it felt as if Slowpoke almost shrugged his massive shoulders and turned, charging out of the water and knocking two other Gallosians out of the way.

Not knowing what else to do, Beltur guided the gelding along the shore edge of the mudflats to where the south side of the point began and turned him, looking to see where he might help. All he could make out was a tangle of blue and gray uniforms, but most of those remaining mounted were blue, to Beltur's surprise. Then the remaining Gallosians broke off the engagement and withdrew.

"Back to the point! On me!" ordered Laugreth.

Beltur immediately urged Slowpoke toward the captain. As he glanced back toward where the fighting had been, he saw at least four figures in blue sprawled on the mudflats, two lying partway into the river. There were far more bodies in gray.

Once the two squads were re-formed on the point, again in the same formation from which they had attacked, with the two officers mounted side by side, Laugreth asked, "What's happening with the Gallosian attack?"

"I think Eleventh Foot moved up and reinforced the front line. Almost no one's dying, and I don't sense any movement. But the entire Gallosian force is another hundred yards north. There's no one withdrawing, and there are more troopers moving north behind them."

"Then they're regrouping for another attack. Their mounted likely won't do that again," said Laugreth. "Not that way. Now that they know you're here . . ."

"They may not know that," said Beltur. "I'm order/ chaos shielded."

"They won't?"

Beltur shook his head.

"I did notice your shields weren't as broad."

"I'm trying to use as little order as possible. I don't want to collapse in the middle of a fight again. Order/ chaos shielding doesn't take as much effort, and it should make it hard for any of their mages to sense me. They could still see what I'm doing, but they're not close enough for that yet." Beltur eased his first water bottle out and finished the last of the ale in it.

"They still might try something different." Laugreth paused. "Then again, from what you've told me, they aren't doing that with their foot. They're just going to try to keep cutting us down. They can lose twice as many men as us in getting close to the piers and still have enough left to set up siege engines and protect them."

To Beltur that meant the Spidlarians had to kill at least three Gallosians for every Spidlarian who fell. He had the feeling there was something wrong with that calculation, but he couldn't grasp what it was, perhaps because a second thought came to the fore. *All over tariffs? How can anyone really win?* Almost absently, he uncorked the second bottle of ale and took a swallow, realizing that, if he didn't survive, none of that mattered. And his situation wouldn't be that much better if he survived but the Gallosians won.

Then he sensed that a much larger mounted force was heading north along the mudflats, just as another mass of Gallosian foot began to move forward. "More heavy mounted heading our way, ser."

"Ser!" called someone. "There are flatboats headed toward the point. They're filled with armsmen."

Beltur could immediately see that if the flatboats landed on the north side of the point, they'd be behind the line Eleventh Foot held, as well as behind First and Second Squads, but if the two squads retreated to deal with the troopers on the flatboats, the combination of Gallosian foot and mounted might override Eleventh Foot, and then cut off the two squads.

"Send for Undercaptain Zandyr and Third Squad!" shouted Laugreth.

Beltur's eyes checked the flatboats, still several hundred yards upstream and moving slowly, and then the oncoming riders, still moving at a walk and almost as far away.

In a short time, Zandyr and Third Squad appeared, and Zandyr immediately rode over to where the captain waited.

Laugreth pointed. "Those flatboats are likely going to try to ground themselves behind First and Second Squads. If they can land troopers there, they'll force the foot on the point to defend against them. The armsmen in front of Eleventh Foot are already being forced back. You and Third Squad need to cut down as many of those troopers landing as possible."

"Yes, ser!"

"Hold back until the first armsmen start to climb out onto the shore. Then attack. Don't get your mounts into the water. Catch the Gallosians just as they reach shore. Don't let your men get caught flat. And keep moving!"

Once Zandyr rode back to Third Squad, Laugreth

turned to Vaertaag. "Send word to Undercaptain Gaermyn that he's to reinforce whatever force appears to need the support of Fourth and Fifth Squads the most."

"Yes, ser."

Laugreth turned back to Beltur. "If all of the company were here, we'd just get in each other's way. The flats aren't that wide, and the banks above the flats are too steep for safe maneuvering in too many places."

That sounded reasonable to Beltur, although he also understood that it could have been totally unreasonable, and he wouldn't have known the difference. Still, on the narrow flats south of the point, the two squads had stopped and thrown back a larger force. *Once.* But could the two squads do it again . . . and possibly a third time? Beltur had the feeling that the Gallosians would attack until they couldn't anymore.

"We'll lead Second Squad on the next charge," Laugreth said, before turning to Vaertaag. "First Squad will follow Second this time. Undercaptain Beltur and I will still lead."

"Yes, ser."

Raising his voice, Laugreth ordered, "Second Squad! To the fore!"

As he waited with the captain for the squads to re-form, Beltur glanced in the general direction of the white disk that was the sun . . . and was surprised to see that it was high in the sky, around ninth glass, he judged.

Although he didn't feel that hungry, he broke off a chunk of bread and ate it, then took several swallows of ale. By the time he finished, Second Squad was in position, and the Gallosians were moving north on the mudflats, less than a hundred yards from where the last encounter had taken place. Beltur studied the flats and the edge of the river, not liking what he saw. There were bodies, mostly of men, although there were several fallen horses as well.

"About all those bodies, ser?"

"I'm glad you noticed that. We'll have to let them come a bit farther north, but just enough that some of their riders will be dealing with the fallen."

Beltur waited and watched, moistening his lips, and glancing to the river, but the flatboats seemed barely to crawl through the water toward the point. He looked back to the mudflats, where the Gallosians moved ever closer. Beyond the flats, he could see and sense the continuing conflict—and the growing numbers of deaths indicated by the black mists only he or another mage could sense.

Laugreth waited until the Gallosians were some twenty yards farther north than they had been on the previous advance before he raised his arm, then dropped it. "Charge!"

Beltur couldn't help but notice that, once again, Laugreth lagged just slightly, letting Squad Leader Chaeryn and Beltur take the lead.

Beltur leaned forward in the saddle more than he had earlier, which allowed him to reduce the size of his shields somewhat. He hoped that would reduce the effort it would take Slowpoke to make his way through the lead riders of the Gallosian heavy mounted, as well as the number of blows transmitted to his body through the shields.

Slowpoke didn't seem any slower as he approached the column, the leading riders of which had begun to swing west where the mudflats followed the curve of the point. The big gelding slammed aside two riders and threw yet another Gallosian into a fourth before he reached the slope of the bank, where he half jumped over something. Beltur barely managed to stay in the saddle, but recovered to turn Slowpoke, slowing him considerably, enough that one of the Gallosians swung a vicious cut at Beltur, only to look stunned as his sabre bounced away. That surprise turned to shock as a ranker in blue slashed him across the neck from the other side.

Beltur turned Slowpoke south along the edge of the mudflats, where there looked to be fewer bodies on the ground. He let Slowpoke run for almost fifty yards before turning him, using his shields to move and occasionally unhorse Gallosians. Then he let the gelding walk back north along the flats less than a yard from the water. Men in gray slashed at him, and their sabres rebounded from his shields. He and Slowpoke managed to unhorse one, possibly two, even while walking, but as they reached where the attack had begun, Beltur had to turn Slowpoke east to get him around the mass of bodies sprawled there, some of which wore the dark blue of Spidlar.

As he moved Slowpoke along the flats toward the point, he thought he saw that one of the flatboats had grounded near the end of the point, but all he could make out was a mass of riders in blue. *Zandyr and Third Squad.* He just hoped that they could repulse or at least hold off the attackers.

Somewhere a horn sounded, and before long the only riders on the flats around the point were those in blue. Beltur finally made out Laugreth and angled Slowpoke toward the captain, where he reined up and watched and listened as the captain issued orders.

"Get the wounded back to the far side of the point where we mustered by the hill. Make it quick with the bodies." Laugreth looked to Beltur. "Are they readying another attack?"

"It doesn't look like it yet."

"We'll only last for another charge," said Laugreth. "Almost half of Second Squad is dead or wounded. If you hadn't upset and unhorsed so many of them it would have been much worse."

"I didn't know what else to do," Beltur admitted. "Slowpoke couldn't keep charging, not with all the fallen. He would have stumbled or broken a leg."

"You did what was necessary. Where are the Gallosian foot?" asked the captain. "I don't see many near the riverbank or just beyond."

Beltur hadn't thought to check, but then, he'd been somewhat occupied. After several moments, he said, "They've withdrawn perhaps two hundred yards. They seem to be regrouping."

"What about the heavy mounted?"

"It looks like they're still regrouping."

Laugreth nodded slowly, then asked, "Can you extend your shields across the mudflats for just a moment if we have to charge the Gallosians?"

"Maybe for a moment or two. Not for very long." Beltur might have been able to do more, but then, he'd thought he could do more before, and he'd been wrong . . . and fortunate to survive.

Laugreth nodded. "Then we'll attack."

"After all the casualties?" asked Beltur in surprise.

"We aren't going to carry it through. We'll just strike their front, knock them back, and then withdraw around the point. We can't fight where we fought before, but, after we withdraw, if we have to, we can loft arrows into them while they're on the flats around the point, and then hit them once they're at the end of the point." He paused. "We'll have to leave Third Squad on the point because they've still got a flatboat anchored out there, and they'll try to land troopers if we don't leave a force."

Beltur glanced back at the point. There was no flatboat there. He looked back upstream. There was indeed another flatboat less than half a kay away. *What happened to the one that tried to land troopers?* He finally located it—apparently grounded downstream several hundred yards from the point, but on the west bank of the river. The troopers remaining in it weren't going to be a problem for Second Recon. For other Spidlarian units, but not Second Recon. *That might be selfish, but at the moment, you have the right to be selfish.*

"We'll have to consolidate First and Second Squad into one body, and with the losses to both squads . . ." Laugreth shook his head. "We also lost Chaeryn on the last attack."

Beltur didn't recall seeing Chaeryn go down, but then he didn't recall much except what had happened around him, and some of that was blurred because it had happened so quickly.

"Squads One and Two! Form up!" After a moment Laugreth asked, "Are they still regrouping?"

"Yes, ser, but they look less chaotic."

"Then we need to get moving. Squads! Forward!"

This time Laugreth was in the fore, if immediately beside Beltur, as the combined squads moved at a quick walk through the fallen and then southward on the dried mudflats toward the Gallosian mounted.

Beltur still couldn't sense any Gallosian foot near the water, but it appeared that they were massing and trying to push forward across the ground closer to the bluffs, where the Spidlarian forces seemed to be giving ground. *You can't worry about that now.*

Once the squads were past most of the fallen and re-formed, Laugreth increased the pace. Then, when they were less than fifty yards from the mounted Gallosians, he ordered, "Charge!"

The first ranks of the Gallosian mounted looked surprised, at the very least, to see the Spidlarian force speeding toward them. Those in the front closed ranks and drew weapons, but they didn't move, even as the distance narrowed between the two forces.

When Beltur was less than ten yards from the Gallosians, he began to sense a buildup of chaos somewhere to his left. Then a huge chaos-bolt arched skyward and then downward toward the front ranks of the charging squad, seeming straight toward Beltur, who almost instinctively extended his shields in an effort to deflect the heat and chaos from himself and the leading riders.

The chaos-fire splashed across the unseen shield and then flared back across the front ranks of the Gallosians, turning perhaps half a score into blackened and instantly charred figures. Then the Gallosian formation seemed to splinter as riders tried to escape.

"Squads! Withdraw!" ordered Laugreth. "Withdraw! Now!"

For a moment, Beltur thought he might have trouble with Slowpoke, but the gelding slowed, and Beltur turned him, contracting his shields somewhat, and hoping that another chaos-blast wasn't forthcoming. He thought that the white wizard who had thrown it was on a knoll a hundred yards east, just below the rocky bluffs.

He kept glancing back, but no more chaos flew in his direction.

"Why didn't that white mage throw more chaos?" asked Laugreth. "Was it because we were withdrawing, and he thought that we'd been the ones who'd been burned and were retreating?"

"I don't know, ser," replied Beltur, glancing past the mass of riders now in front of him toward the point.

"Frig!" swore the captain. "That other flatboat has grounded on the point. We need to get back there." He guided his mount to the edge of the water. "Coming past! On your left!"

Beltur just followed the captain, shrinking his shields close to himself and Slowpoke so that he didn't inadvertently unhorse any of their own rankers.

By the time they began the turn to the west along the

south side of the point, Laugreth and Beltur were again in the van, and Beltur could see that the armsmen scrambling out of the flatboat seemed endless. Only half of Third Squad remained mounted and trying to stem the flow of attackers from the boat.

Beltur wondered where Fourth and Fifth Squads were, but as he rounded the tip of the point he saw why they weren't there. Gaermyn and his squads were engaged in a melee in support of the middle of the Eleventh Foot. *That was where the Gallosian foot went.*

Beltur's eyes went back to the grounded flatboat. Possibly one in three of the attackers carried a staff-like weapon that had a spear-like point at the end with an ax blade below the point. On the other side of the pole from the blade was an iron hook.

"They've got halberds! Get them before they can form up!" shouted Laugreth.

Beltur wondered what in the Rational Stars such an unwieldy-looking weapon was for until he saw one of the men with it slash a horse's neck, then jerk a ranker out of the saddle with the hook. He also saw that the men with the weapons were forming into a squad. *If they get formed up . . .* He didn't finish the thought, but urged Slowpoke toward the group, riding ahead of Laugreth and the two combined squads toward the rapidly forming Gallosian squad.

"Third Squad! Clear the way!" he yelled, angling Slowpoke to try to cross the front of the halberd squad.

Even so, he knocked aside one Spidlarian ranker before he expanded his shields slightly and cut across the front rank of the halberd carriers. Slowpoke's momentum carried him a good thirty yards farther along the mudflats on the north side of the point before Beltur could slow the gelding and then turn. By the time he did, the flatboat had pushed off and the remaining rankers of the first three squads were dispatching the surviving Gallosians.

Beltur glanced back toward the rise in the middle of the point and then farther east.

The fighting was dying out, and the Gallosians seemed to be withdrawing, at least for the moment. Beltur reined up, uncertain of what he could or should do.

Possibly a glass passed before there were no more Gallosians standing, or anywhere near, so far as Beltur could sense. Beltur looked at the sun, well past midafternoon. *How can it be that late?*

A ranker rode toward Beltur, leading a mount with a body draped over the saddle and roughly tied in place. As the rider neared, Beltur swallowed. The body had wavy blond hair. Beltur looked dumbly at Zandyr, seeing the level but deep slash across the side of his neck.

"Ser," the ranker said to Beltur, "the undercaptain says his body has to go back to his people. His father's a councilor or something."

"What happened?"

"I don't know, ser. We lost half the squad fighting the bastards coming off the boats. Excuse me, ser."

"Carry on." Beltur nodded, still thinking about Zandyr. He'd been so enthusiastic about taking on the flatboats . . . and now, like that, he was dead.

Beltur wasn't certain how much time passed before Laugreth issued another order. "Company! Stand down. For now. The Gallosians have withdrawn half a kay or more."

Beltur dismounted and stood beside Slowpoke, eating the last of his bread, interspersed with swallows from his next-to-last water bottle. He didn't even remember finishing the ale in the second bottle.

Almost absently, he watched as Laugreth sent off a

ranker as a messenger. Then he drank more ale. He almost didn't notice as Gaermyn appeared at his elbow. "Oh, ser . . . I didn't see you."

"At least you're standing today."

"I tried to be more careful."

"It would have been a lot worse, the captain said, if you hadn't broken that halberd squad."

"I've never seen a halberd before. It just seemed . . . what had to be done."

"Keeping the boat from landing all those troopers was likely what turned things."

"From what little I saw, your support of the foot did that," Beltur replied.

"We would have been flanked and slaughtered if they'd been able to land all the troopers on those two big flatboats. Let's say it took all of us."

Beltur could accept that.

Sometime after fourth glass, a messenger delivered a dispatch to the captain, who read it, then motioned for Gaermyn and Beltur to join him. "Because of our losses, we've been recalled. Third Recon will be taking our place, if it's necessary."

Beltur rode back toward the piers and the barracks, again beside the captain. Finally, after they had ridden for a time, he said, "Zandyr . . . I was surprised . . . I just didn't think . . ."

"At first, you never do," replied Laugreth. "But it's war. People die. The only thing is that they die in different ways . . . and for different reasons. Some get burned by chaos. Some get unhorsed and trampled. Some die with a single slash or cut, and some strangely live through a score of wounds. But some people die. That's war."

All those deaths because the Prefect wants more golds, and the Council doesn't want to pay them? Was that enough reason for rankers, or Zandyr, to die? And

Beltur also had to admit that he'd never really liked Zandyr. That only made it worse, in a way.

Neither he nor Laugreth had much to say on the ride back, and once the captain dismissed the company to stabling and quarters, Beltur rode to the stables, where he dismounted and led Slowpoke to his stall. Beltur could hardly see straight after grooming Slowpoke, but the feeling came from physical exhaustion, rather than from having too little order left. At least, that was the way it felt, since he didn't have any flashes of light across his vision. Just before he left the stall, he saw the two iron arrows, still in place in the holder.

He had no doubts that, sooner or later, he'd need them.

When he finally washed up and collapsed on his bunk, he still couldn't help but think about Zandyr. There had been something . . . something. But he couldn't remember what it might be before his eyes closed.

LXX

Chaos-bolts rained down on Beltur, so many of them that each one burned as it struck his shields. Trying to escape the deluge of chaos before his shields collapsed, he bent close to Slowpoke's neck and urged him to sprint at an angle to the oncoming Gallosian heavy mounted riders so that the white wizards couldn't keep throwing chaos-bolts without incinerating their own troopers . . . but the chaos-bolts kept coming as Slowpoke charged past the endless line of Gallosian riders, as each was charred into a blackened set of bones that collapsed.

Ahead, he could see a figure in blue, slashing wildly at other men in the blue of Spidlar . . . and there was something all too familiar about the blond officer . . . and the flaming bloody slash across his neck—

Beltur woke with a start, sweat streaming down his face, the salt burning the corners of his eyes. He glanced around, half seeing, half sensing the other pallet bed— empty—thinking that Zandyr must have stayed out late again . . . *Except he's dead.*

Shuddering, Beltur sat up and swung his legs over the side of the pallet bed, then half wiped, half blotted the worst of the sweat out of his eyes, still trying to escape the ominous sense of dread that his nightmare had occasioned.

There hadn't been that many chaos-bolts. Does that mean that there will be?

Beltur could have snorted at the stupidity of that question. He didn't. He just blotted away more sweat, despite the cool, almost chill air in the small space.

He could understand why he'd dreamed of fiery chaos-bolts, but why had he dreamed of a flaming bloody slash across Zandyr's neck? Why was the slash flaming, and not just bloody? *What was that all about?*

After several moments, he suddenly understood what his dream had been trying to tell him. Zandyr hadn't been fighting mounted Gallosians, but footmen with blades and shields, bucklers really, or foot with halberds. But the slash across his neck had been level and deep. If he'd been killed in the melee on the mudflats, how could a footman have made a slash that deep and level—unless Zandyr had practically been lying against the neck of his mount? Any wound from a halberd would still have been angled.

A level slash . . . Beltur shuddered at what that meant.

LXXI

Although Beltur finally did get back to sleep, when he awoke on twoday morning, he couldn't totally shake the feeling of foreboding that the nightmare had conveyed. Given that foreboding, he decided to take no chances and had the mess fill his water bottles with ale at breakfast. He also managed to get a loaf of bread and immediately secreted the ale and bread in his gear in the stable before making his way to the morning muster.

Even though he had seen the carnage of the previous day, it was a shock for him to survey the squads lined up at muster. If he counted correctly, there were only about sixty men in formation when the captain stepped forward. *Sixty . . . out of over a hundred.*

After Gaermyn announced that all men were present or accounted for, Laugreth paused, then announced, "We've been assigned to patrol the Axalt road again today. There have been isolated Gallosian units observed. Dismissed to mount up."

As the rankers and squad leaders headed for their mounts, Laugreth walked over to Gaermyn and Beltur, where he addressed Beltur. "You'll still ride with me at the head of First Squad. You may go and saddle up." Then he turned to Gaermyn. "I'll need a few words with you about today."

"Yes, ser," answered Gaermyn.

As he headed for the stabling area, Beltur wondered exactly what the captain had to say to Gaermyn, but whether he'd ever find out was another question.

He'd just finished saddling Slowpoke, who seemed no

worse for the wear of the previous day, when he heard
a voice behind him.

"Undercaptain."

Beltur looked up to see Laugreth standing just outside the stall.

"Yes, ser?" Beltur could sense that Laugreth was
less than pleased, and he wondered what he'd done
wrong. "What is it?" He walked over to the captain and
waited.

Laugreth handed him a sealed envelope. "Your orders. I understand you're being assigned to the command staff. I'm assured it's temporary." The captain
paused. "Temporary for as long as the fighting lasts."

"But . . . why? I never asked . . ."

Laugreth frowned. "It was suggested . . ."

"Never, ser. I've never even spoken to anyone about
wanting to leave or serve in another way."

"You've been as straight with me as any captain
could wish. Why would anyone suggest that you requested a change of duty?"

"The only thing I can think of is that I'm not exactly
in the favor of the senior mage here."

Laugreth smiled. It wasn't exactly a friendly smile,
but Beltur knew it wasn't directed at him. "Would you
mind, Undercaptain, if you didn't happen to receive
whatever is in this envelope until after today's evolutions."

Beltur understood. "I wasn't aware that you even had
anything for me."

"Good. You must have left to form up before I could
reach you."

"Yes, ser."

Laugreth grinned. "Then get out of here. We have a
road patrol to undertake."

In moments, the captain was gone.

As Beltur led Slowpoke outside, he wondered about

the purported orders. He didn't see how it could have been anything but Cohndar's doing. But why would Cohndar want him transferred away from the dangers posed to Second Recon to a position that Athaal had indicated was merely shielding high-ranking officers? That didn't seem to make sense, and that meant Cohndar had something else in mind. Beltur was certain he wouldn't like it when he found out.

By the same token, the captain had clearly wanted Beltur to go on the road patrol. *But why?* Was it simply that Second Recon had taken so many casualties, and Laugreth wanted Beltur's ability to sense Gallosians at a distance for as long as possible to minimize possible losses? Or did the captain also have enemies? Did he believe that Second Recon was being given the most dangerous missions? But a road patrol was almost a rest compared to what Second Recon had been doing.

Once outside, Beltur mounted and then rode and joined the company at the head of First Squad, noting that the wind was definitely out of the north and cool. Laugreth appeared shortly and ordered the company to move out without saying a word to Beltur.

Beltur waited another third of a glass before speaking. "Do you know if anyone saw a company of Gallosians or just more scouts?"

"Only a few uniformed Gallosians, but someone on the Council was worried because there are wagons with valuable cargo coming from Axalt. The trader apparently insisted on a company. I'd guess that Commander Vaernaak told Majer Jenklaar to pick the company he could spare most."

"Because we're the most understrength?"

"The majer didn't say that."

"So we're to ride east and make certain the wagons or caravan or whatever isn't raided, and escort them safely back to Elparta."

"I don't think the majer would be upset if that occurred."

"But no one is about to issue an order like that?"

Laugreth laughed softly. "Do they have to?"

Beltur understood that as well. If anything happened to the trader's shipment, Second Recon would take the blame. "We might be fortunate and have a pleasant ride."

"That's possible. Even likely."

Beltur nodded. The majer hadn't had to say it. "Captain . . . ?"

"Yes?"

"There's one other thing. I've been thinking. About Zandyr. There was a level slash across his neck . . ."

"It's almost too bad you're a mage, Undercaptain. You could become an outstanding officer, even without lifting a blade."

For a moment, Beltur didn't understand what Laugreth's comment had to do with the half question Beltur had posed. Instead of saying anything, he nodded and waited.

"Not all wounds come from the enemy, Undercaptain," Laugreth said quietly.

"But . . . who . . ." Beltur didn't even have to shake his head. He understood why all too well.

"I think you understand." Laugreth shrugged, fatalistically. "It could have been any one of twenty. No one will say anything. Rankers judge their officers. They know enough that they can respect an officer they don't like. Those they respect, they'll often die for. They'll accept those they merely dislike. Those officers who belittle them and worse . . . and who don't listen or learn . . . well, it's not a good idea for an officer who's hated and who seems incompetent to lead his men into a bloody battle. You've already seen the difference. Rankers rushed to support you. The fact you demon-near died didn't hurt, either, because it was clear part of the reason for that was because you were protecting the rankers beside you."

"I just did what had to be—"

"You did what you should have done. Good officers do. Let's leave it at that, shall we? And appreciate the fact that we're all getting a bit of a rest."

Since Laugreth's words were anything but a question, Beltur did.

Three glasses later and almost ten kays east of Elparta, Beltur had not even sensed a Gallosian. Shortly after that, Second Recon encountered a line of wagons, led by two mounted guards, both of whom appeared relieved at the sight of Spidlarian uniforms.

Beltur accompanied Laugreth as he rode over to the lead wagon and reined up.

"Thank the Rational Stars you're Spidlarians," said the bearded wagon master. "We worried about Gallosians or raiders."

"You've got quite a line of wagons here," said Beltur. "They've goods for Trader Eskeld?"

"Oh, no, ser, Trader Alizant."

"Spices, then."

"Yes, ser."

"I can see why you're concerned."

"We couldn't bring them through Gallos."

"No, you couldn't," said Laugreth.

Beltur thought the captain hid a smile.

"We'll escort you to Elparta," said Laugreth.

"The trader would appreciate that. We'd appreciate it even more."

The captain nodded, then turned his mount. Once they were away from the wagons, and Laugreth had sent Gaermyn and Fifth Squad to ride rearguard, he turned to Beltur. "As you said, a pleasant ride to finish out an uneventful day. Possibly the last one for a while."

"You think the Gallosians will step up their attacks?"

"They'll have to if they want to have any chance of taking Elparta before the weather turns bad." Laugreth gestured toward the north, where dark clouds were beginning to creep over the horizon. "Those suggest rain, or at least showers, tonight or tomorrow. They'll pass, but in a few days, there will be more. That's what fall is like."

As he and Laugreth escorted the wagons back along the road, Beltur couldn't help but think about the incredible irony of Second Recon being the company to escort Alizant's precious spices back to Elparta. He also wondered if that had any bearing on Laugreth wanting Beltur to ride with Second Recon, except he doubted that Majer Jenklaar had ever mentioned what trader's wagons were involved.

After escorting the wagons to the northeast gate, Second Recon returned to the piers, where Laugreth dismissed the company to quarters.

Beltur had finished stabling and grooming Slowpoke and was leaving the stabling area, when he saw Laugreth walking toward him, an envelope in hand, most likely the very same envelope that the captain had carried that morning.

"Yes, Captain?"

"Here are your orders, Undercaptain. I can only say Second Recon will miss you, and that having you serve was a pleasure. Since your duties will require a mount, you will remain responsible for Slowpoke." Laugreth smiled. "Besides, you two belong together."

"And you'll have to find another difficult horse for arrogant junior undercaptains?"

"I haven't the faintest idea what you mean, Undercaptain." But Laugreth was still smiling when he turned and left.

LXXII

The orders were indeed a transfer from Second Reconnaissance Company, but what Laugreth hadn't said, or possibly known, was the specific wording:

> ... You are to report to Majer Nakken, Chief of Staff for Marshal Helthaer, for further assignment as directed by and necessary ...

Beltur still wondered why Laugreth had not wanted him to have the orders until after the road patrol, especially since Laugreth had been taking a risk in not delivering them. *Except he changed his mind after you told him you hadn't requested any transfer. Was he trying to protect you, to give you another day's rest?*

Beltur nodded. That was likely just another example of why the rankers and squad leaders had wanted him as an officer.

After a moment, Beltur took a deep breath, then set out.

Finding Majer Nakken wasn't so much difficult as time-consuming and required Beltur to ask at least a half score officers and rankers where the majer was to be located. By half past fourth glass, he finally found himself sitting on a rough plank bench against the wall of the converted warehouse near the westernmost doorway. An older squad leader sat at a table outside a closed door, one of the few actual doors Beltur had seen since he'd arrived.

The door opened and two captains walked out, and

a thin graying man with a majer's insignia on the collar of his rumpled blue uniform stood in the doorway and motioned to Beltur. "Come on in, Undercaptain. Close the door after you."

By the time Beltur had entered the small room that held little besides a wide table desk, two chests, and four straight-backed chairs, one behind the desk, and three in front of it, the majer was seated and motioned to the chairs.

Beltur sat down and waited.

"I thought you received orders this morning, Undercaptain."

"No, ser. I received them right after Second Recon returned from patrol this afternoon. I immediately came to find you."

"What patrol was this?"

"We were ordered to patrol the Axalt road because of reports of Gallosians."

"Did you find any?"

"No, ser. We did end up escorting a trader's wagons back to Elparta. I understand the wagons carried spices."

Nakken said nothing.

Neither did Beltur.

Finally, the majer said, "It's a wonder there aren't more delays. In your case, it wasn't critical." He paused, then went on, "As you will discover, Undercaptain, there are already two other command mages, and you would be the third mage in the battlefield command group, after Captain Athaal and Undercaptain Lhadoraak. I believe you know Captain Athaal?"

"I do, ser."

"Excellent. You might ask why Commander Vaernaak needs three black mages in the command group. The answer is that he doesn't. You will be assigned to support a specific unit as soon as it arrives, which will be sometime tomorrow. Senior Mage Cohndar felt that you would be the best possible mage officer for this duty. You have already managed to destroy one of the Gallosian mages, I understand?"

"It took the help of archers with iron arrows, and the support of a full squad, but we managed it, ser."

"You'll have even more impressive support in this unit. For tomorrow, you will support Majer Waeltur, as necessary, and as he sees fit. You will report to the briefing room next door at sixth glass tomorrow. You'll be summoned earlier, if necessary."

"Can you tell me about this unit, ser?"

"You'll find out when it's appropriate." Nakken stood. "That's all for now."

Beltur stood. "Yes, ser."

Then he made his way out, careful to close the door behind himself.

After the majer's terse words about the delay in Beltur's arrival, Beltur wondered again why exactly Laugreth had wanted him with Second Recon for another day.

He'd taken no more than a score of steps in the direction of the officers' mess when he saw a familiar figure hurrying toward him. "Athaal!"

"I thought you were going to be here this morning."

"The orders didn't get to me until after we returned from patrolling the Axalt road. Majer Nakken wasn't pleased about that, but it wasn't my doing." *Not entirely, anyway.*

Athaal half turned and gestured to the fine-featured blond mage beside him. "Beltur, this is Lhadoraak. You might recall—"

"I do." Beltur smiled at Lhadoraak. "He's spoken most favorably of you." His smile turned into a grin. "And your daughter."

Lhadoraak offered a rueful but humorous smile in

return. "Taelya makes a far better impression on people than I do, I fear."

"We might as well go to the mess together," said Athaal. "You haven't eaten yet, have you?"

"No. It took me a while to find the majer, and then I had to wait."

"Undercaptains, even mage undercaptains, always have to wait," said Lhadoraak cheerfully.

As the three walked toward the officers' mess, Beltur studied the blond mage, sensing almost immediately that while Lhadoraak was definitely black, he didn't have the "depth" of blackness or order that Athaal had. *Is that why he was assigned to the command group?*

Once in the mess, the three sat down at one end of an empty table.

Almost immediately a ranker appeared with three mugs of ale. "The fare will be here in a few moments, sers."

"Thank you," replied Athaal warmly.

After a moment, Lhadoraak looked to Beltur. "Athaal says that you've been involved in a lot of action."

"More than I ever thought," admitted Beltur.

"Were there many deaths in your company?"

"Almost half the company is either dead or wounded."

"That many?" asked Athaal, clearly surprised. "I had no idea."

"How can you stand that many deaths?" asked Lhadoraak. "Or don't you sense them?"

"Sense them? Every death creates what feels like a cold black mist. That's how I sense them, anyway."

"But you've been so much closer to them than I have," said Lhadoraak.

"I've had to ride at the front to shield others," replied Beltur. "Trying to stay in position and hold shields against arrows, blades, and chaos-bolts kept me occupied."

Athaal laughed softly. "Beltur's quite sensitive, Lhadoraak. He could likely be a healer. But he's been forced to be more practical than we have. I suspect that surviving as an orphaned black, raised by a white uncle in Fenard, has had something to do with that." The black-bearded mage gestured. "If I'm not mistaken, here comes our food."

Two rankers arrived with three platters, setting one down in front of each mage. Each platter contained what looked to be mutton slices covered with a cream sauce, accompanied by thoroughly fried lace potatoes, and a small loaf of bread.

Beltur was glad that the cream sauce had been liberally applied to the mutton, especially given how crusty the lace potatoes looked.

"It's a good thing I like mutton," said Lhadoraak wryly.

"Does Taelya still like it?" asked Athaal.

"She likes most foods that are warm. She'll eat cold meats, but they're not her favorites." Lhadoraak smiled. "I told her that Uncle Athaal ate mutton cold, and she asked me how that could be when all the ovens were always hot."

"How old is she?" asked Beltur, knowing only the little Athaal had mentioned.

"She's almost seven. Tulya and I can't believe it."

Beltur just nodded, since his mouth was full. He was hungrier than he'd realized, and while the lace potatoes were every bit as crusty as he'd suspected, with the cream sauce they were more than palatable.

"This is definitely not up to Meldryn's standards," Lhadoraak said after a time, "but at least it's hot."

For a time, none of the three spoke.

Finally, Beltur said, "Has the majer or the commander said anything about what might happen tomorrow?"

"The only time we ever hear anything is at the morning briefing," replied Lhadoraak. "This morning, Majer Nakken said that he thought the Gallosians might attack tomorrow."

"What will you do if they do?"

"Stay with the commander and shield him," replied Athaal. "He likes to be close enough to see what's happening."

"So far, the Gallosians haven't gotten close enough that we were needed," added Lhadoraak.

"Let's hope it stays that way," replied Beltur.

"You'll excuse me if I leave," said Lhadoraak apologetically as he stood up, "but I told Felsyn that I'd meet him at half before sixth glass."

"We won't hold you," replied Athaal. "How is he?"

"He's not happy. You know why."

"I understand Cohndar said his shields weren't strong enough for him to support a fighting force. I don't always agree with Cohndar, but I do in this case. There's little point in losing all Felsyn knows for no gain."

"He doesn't see it that way."

"Maybe you can convince him. I couldn't."

"I haven't been able to so far. I'll see you both in the morning." With a nod, Lhadoraak turned and walked out of the mess.

"What do you think of him?" asked Athaal.

"He seems cheerful and pleasant enough. I never asked you about how you helped his daughter. I wondered because . . . well . . ." Beltur didn't quite know how to say what he meant tactfully.

"Because I don't sense order and chaos in small enough pieces for healing? I don't. It actually took both me and Grenara."

"Jessyla told me she didn't do healing anymore. Or not often."

"That's because she doesn't have enough order to do

it all the time. What about Lhadoraak? What do you think?"

"Like I said, he seems nice and good at heart. He's not that strong a black. Not as strong as you are. You'd never said much about him. You mentioned once you needed to take a present to little Taelya, that you thought of her as the only niece you'd ever have . . ."

"Or nephew," replied Athaal. "Unless, of course, you consort a certain young healer . . ."

Beltur found himself blushing. "I don't know if . . ."

"She'll have you. So will Margrena. Especially now."

But what will Cohndar and Waensyn say or do about a mongrel mage consorting such a beautiful redhead? "There's a small problem with that," Beltur managed to say dryly. "I don't seem to be the most fortunate in escaping the Prefect and his arms-mages. Until that's resolved . . ."

"The Gallosians didn't bring as many whites as you suggested they might have."

"How many are there? Do you know?"

Athaal shook his head. "Not for certain. Anywhere from six to eight. Less the one you managed to kill."

"It only took me, rankers with iron-shafted arrows, and an attack by an entire company, and I almost didn't make it, according to Margrena."

"But you did. That's what's important."

"I still worry."

"If the commander's men can bring enough iron to bear, even the strongest white mage can be brought down . . . or at least forced to withdraw."

"I'd settle for all of them withdrawing." Beltur kept his voice light, even as he wondered, *Would you . . . after all that's happened?* "But given the way Wyath treated Uncle Kaerylt, they won't withdraw unless we or the weather force that." He paused, then asked, "There aren't any blacks that are weather mages, are there?"

"There are legends . . . but I've never heard of one who could actually call storms. Years back, when I was a boy, supposedly Norodyn could sometimes call a lightning bolt from a thunderstorm." Athaal shrugged. "Even that wouldn't be much use. I don't see the Gallosians starting a battle in a thunderstorm." He drained the last of the ale from his mug. "We'd better go. You still could use some sleep . . . or at least some rest."

Beltur wasn't about to dispute Athaal on that. So he rose from the table. "I'll see you in the morning."

"Let's hope it's not too early." Athaal stood as well.

Beltur nodded, and the two walked from the mess.

LXXIII

A ranker—Beltur didn't know who—awakened him in the gloom before dawn on threeday. "Majer Waeltur requests you report to the briefing room immediately."

Feeling a definite sense of foreboding, Beltur scrambled into his uniform and headed for the briefing room, where he tried to slip inside unnoticed by the officers standing around an oblong table on which a large map was laid out.

The tall majer, presumably Waeltur, turned and immediately addressed Beltur. "Do you have a mount, Undercaptain?"

"Yes, ser."

"Good. Have your horse saddled and wait for me with your mount outside the second door as soon as you can. This briefing won't take long."

With that, the majer turned back to the captains around the table.

Beltur immediately left, stopping by what passed for his quarters and grabbing his water bottles before heading to the mess, where he had them filled and took two loaves of bread. *Not exactly the best breakfast.* But the majer and events hadn't left him much choice, and trying to do any sort of extended magery on an empty stomach was worse than foolish.

He quickly saddled Slowpoke and then walked him outside and to the second door, where a ranker stood, holding another horse. "Is that for Majer Waeltur?"

"Yes, ser."

"Good. Thank you." Beltur took a deep breath, then took out one of the water bottles and took a long swallow, and ate a large chunk of bread, still warm. He had just taken a second swallow of ale and was about to take another when he saw Waeltur hurry out the door. He corked the water bottle and replaced it in the holder.

"Mount up, Undercaptain."

Beltur did so and brought Slowpoke up alongside the majer as Waeltur urged his mount eastward along the front of the converted warehouse in the darkness. The stars offered some little light, but Beltur was relying far more on sensing than seeing.

"I understand you mages can shield two or three men against almost anything or a larger group briefly." The majer did not look at Beltur.

"Yes, ser. If you're thinking about chaos-bolts, shielding a larger group would have to be very brief, just long enough to divert it."

"The problem we have is that the white wizards keep us on the defensive. Our men can stay behind earthworks so that the whites can't use their firebolts. Only when the Gallosians attack and engage can our men fight without having large numbers wiped out at once by the white chaos. That means that we can't advance on them without taking heavy casualties. You and

Captain Waensyn seem to be the only mages with shields strong enough to stand up to that chaos. Waensyn is assigned to support Majer Jenklaar."

"You'd like to see if we could attack one of the whites, ser?"

"We won't be able to stop them if we can't remove at least a few of their mages. They're moving most of their foot near the river to take advantage of the mudflats. They saw how effective the Second Reconnaissance Company was on the flats the day before yesterday. That was your company, wasn't it?"

"Yes, ser."

"Could you lead a foot company the same way?"

"Not on foot, ser. My mount provides much of the force behind moving the shields and shoving men aside."

"I hadn't thought of that. What about leading while mounted?"

Beltur thought for a moment. "Wouldn't I stand out and cause more chaos-bolts to be directed at us?" He paused. "I could do it on horseback, if I concealed just myself. That way the men would just look like another group of troopers. Now, they wouldn't be able to see me, but they could hear me."

"Let me think about that, Undercaptain."

Less than a third of a glass later, Waeltur and Beltur reined up not all that far from where Second Recon had been posted two days earlier, except several hundred yards closer to Elparta, which suggested that the Gallosians were slowly but steadily advancing toward the city.

As gray light seeped over the sky from the east, a dull light that suffused the heavy clouds that covered the sky, Beltur couldn't help but wonder why the Gallosians were attacking if there was a chance of rain. *Or do they believe that the rain will hamper us just as much as them . . . or since they have more armsmen, rain might even favor them?*

In that light, Beltur didn't know what to think. He just remained in the saddle, holding the reins to the majer's mount while Waeltur talked to several captains about the movement of various companies, based on what the scouts had reported about the Gallosian buildup.

Then, some two hundred yards to the south, Beltur both saw and sensed movement, and gray-clad men began to move forward. Before all that long, the clash and interplay of battle, and the accompanying interactions of order and chaos, were increasingly marked by black death mists.

Beside Beltur, the majer watched, occasionally receiving messages from either riders or rankers on foot, and less frequently dispatching orders or messages. The line of battle didn't seem to move all that much for a time.

Then Beltur noticed something. "Majer, the Gallosians are massing a larger force behind the river point."

"I can't see anything there."

"I can sense that. It might be as many as three companies."

"We'll see."

Half a glass later, a mass of Gallosian troopers swarmed over the rise on the point and began to push the entire right flank of Majer Waeltur's companies back. While Beltur could sense a white wizard moving forward, amid a squad of riders, the white had not loosed any chaos-bolts.

"They're attacking now, ser, and they've got a white wizard behind them."

"I see that. Why don't you do something about it?"

"Is that an order, ser?" Beltur managed to keep his voice even.

"Yes. Make yourself useful."

"Very well, ser. I'll see what I can do about slowing that attack." Beltur eased Slowpoke away from the majer, then raised a concealment, making certain that he also shielded himself fully so as not to reveal his presence to the white wizard, before riding to the riverbank and then guiding Slowpoke onto the mudflats.

He kept moving, looking eastward while steadily moving south toward the advancing Gallosians until he found a squad of foot being gathered by an undercaptain, who said little, and then darted down the line to the east. Something about the situation bothered Beltur and he moved on until he found a squad leader crouched down behind a crude earthworks less than fifty yards from the oncoming Gallosians. Without dropping the concealment, he listened.

"When those Gallie-bastards come over the top . . . don't let them take another cubit . . . not even a digit. Otherwise they'll be pushing us back into the water . . ."

Beltur dropped the concealment.

One of the rankers just pointed, and the squad leader turned. "Ah . . . ser . . . I didn't see you."

"You weren't supposed to. How close do the Gallosians have to be for you to engage with them quickly enough that the mage behind them can't drop a chaosbolt on you?"

The squad leader frowned.

"Just answer me."

"Five yards, maybe a little more."

Beltur nodded. "All right. I'm going to disappear. I'm still here. You can hear me." With that he lifted a tight concealment, just around himself. "When the Gallosians are maybe ten yards away I'm going to attack them. The best I can do is knock them down and disrupt their advance. It's up to you and your men to take care of them after that. If we can breach their attack line, I'll become visible, and you're to follow me. I'll be able to offer some cover and to keep any firebolts off you. Is that clear?"

"Yes, ser."

"Good. Now we wait."

Beltur reached down and patted Slowpoke on the shoulder. Then he took out a chunk of bread and ate it, and followed that with several long swallows of ale, even as he sensed the Gallosians nearing, cutting their way through the Spidlarian troopers some fifteen yards in front of the squad he'd commandeered. *The squad you think you've commandeered.*

"They're about fifteen yards south of us," he said to the squad leader.

At that moment, a chaos-bolt arched from the white mage and splattered some forty yards to the southeast, spraying across a half score of Spidlarian troopers who'd been charging toward the Gallosians.

At almost the same time, thunder rumbled out of the north. Since he was within a concealment, Beltur hadn't seen the lightning flash, but he had the feeling that it had been well north of the fighting, at least a kay . . . and there was still no rain falling. He didn't even smell rain, although he could sense, as he had before, order within the clouds overhead and behind him, being confined by clumps of chaos . . . or perhaps the order was confining the chaos. Either way, there was power there, but the power overhead was still diffuse. He needed far more chaos and far more violent flows or swirls of that chaos before there could be lightning . . . or before he could even help it along.

Then the Gallosians burst through the remaining Spidlarian troopers and moved quickly forward. Most had blades and small circular shields, as well as helmets.

"I'm moving! Stand ready to attack." Beltur urged Slowpoke forward at what might have been a fast trot and aimed him at an angle to the oncoming Gallosians.

Just before he reached the first attacker, he extended his shields. The first three Gallosians went down without even knowing what had hit them. So did several more, before Beltur turned the gelding and angled back across the attackers. Before long all he could do was have Slowpoke move at a fast walk. Even so, the force of the unseen shields disrupted the attackers enough that the Spidlarian squad was able to cut through the attackers, following Beltur's unseen lead.

Then several adjacent squads joined the attack.

Beltur sensed the chaos-bolt as soon as it left the white mage, and was ready with a containment that catapulted it back into the Gallosians in front of him, widening and deepening the gap in the Gallosian advance.

A second chaos-bolt followed the first, and, again, Beltur flung it back into the Gallosians, wincing at the massive black mists that followed it, far, far more than the first had occasioned.

He kept Slowpoke moving, not too fast, because he was working off senses, rather than sight, but still disrupting the Gallosians.

Then Beltur heard more rumbling across the sky, much closer, and with enough power that he could feel pressure against his shields for a moment. His head ached suddenly, if slightly, and even more when he managed to catch and return the next chaos-bolt, one that was far weaker than the previous one.

He wondered about that, but only for a moment, when he both heard and felt the rain. He dropped the concealment, to see that what had to be ice-cold sheets of water poured from the overhead clouds, clouds that were almost black, with the chaos within them as violent as he'd ever sensed. In an instant, he was soaked through by water like ice.

Beltur searched for the white wizard, mostly with his

senses, now limited to only a few hundred yards. *Should you try it?* He smiled grimly. The storm was close enough and low enough that Beltur could sense the cold but slender links of order confining the chaos, and see when they were pushed aside, and the raging chaos departed in a single flash.

As the next flux of chaos built, Beltur began to ready a special containment, but not so much a containment as an order-bounded tube, similar to the order-bounding within the thunderstorm.

Just as the storm's order released that chaos, Beltur order-channeled it down that order-tube toward the white mage. Strong as that mage's shields were, they were no match for the lightning.

A reddish-white globe of order and chaos flared out, and for an instant swept away even the downpour—but only for an instant before a flood of lukewarm water flooded over Beltur, followed in turn by more and more icy water.

Lightning flashed in all directions, and Beltur's head ached so much that he could barely see, and he was having trouble holding just simple shields. Slowly, he turned Slowpoke back north, making his way back to where the majer had been.

Waeltur wasn't there.

So Beltur rode farther back to where he thought the command companies might be.

"There he is!" shouted someone.

Two rankers rode toward him.

"The majer's looking for you, ser."

Beltur nodded and followed the rankers for another fifty yards, where they stopped. He looked and saw the majer, with two foot captains on one side of the majer and his mount.

Waeltur gestured impatiently for Beltur to join him, and no sooner had Beltur reined up than the majer demanded, "Were you the one who started that breach in the Gallosian line?"

"Yes, ser. You told me to make myself useful."

"You did. That was masterful, I have to say. And just as we get a break where we could really hit them hard, this frigging storm drops on us. Like the Rational Stars were tempting us, and then snatching victory from us." Waeltur shook his head. "What a frigging mess!"

"What about the Gallosians?"

"They're already well back to their previous positions, if not farther. They can't use their mages in this. Captain Athaal thinks one of them was hit by lightning. That's a small consolation."

"If you wouldn't mind, ser, I'd like to return to the barracks. Out there . . . that was hard work."

"If you think . . ." Waeltur seemed ready to protest, but after he looked hard at Beltur he nodded.

"Thank you, ser. Someone can summon me if the Gallosians return." Beltur doubted that they would. From what little he could sense, the storm clouds seemed to stretch endlessly toward to the north. He didn't even wait for the majer to say anything more. He just turned Slowpoke and began to ride back toward the stable . . . and the makeshift barracks.

Back at the stables, he did his best to groom and clean Slowpoke before trudging to the mess. The rankers on duty didn't even question him as he sat down, although it was midday. Someone handed him a mug, and another provided a plate of something like warm mutton hash. Beltur didn't care. He ate it all, ignoring the dampness of his uniform.

He was about to rise when Athaal, comparatively dry, except for his trousers below the knees, sat down across from him. Beltur waited for Athaal to speak. He scarcely felt like talking, since his head still ached, and his eyes burned.

"I thought I'd find you here. Or sound asleep in your quarters."

"That comes next."

"Waeltur is furious. He makes a mad dog look calm. That's behind a calm front. He's just about ready to gut Majer Nakken."

"What did Nakken do?" Beltur didn't pretend to understand.

"He never told Waeltur what you'd done with Second Reconnaissance."

Beltur just looked at Athaal for a moment, realizing that he'd never made the connection. Second Recon had reported to Majer Jenklaar, and for whatever reason, Jenklaar hadn't shared that knowledge with Waeltur. Finally, Beltur asked, "Do Jenklaar and Waeltur get along?"

"I've gotten the impression that they don't."

Beltur could only shake his head, very slowly. It still throbbed some.

"You did something out there, didn't you?" said Athaal quietly.

"Why do you say that?"

"A lightning bolt hit one of their mages. There was more order around it. You were nearby. That's what I overheard when Waeltur was pointing out to the commander what an opportunity we had missed because he didn't know what you could do." Athaal smiled. "The commander pointed out it might not have gone all that well anyway, because of the storm."

"You didn't say anything about the lightning?"

Athaal shook his head. "As I told you, we can't count on storms, or the weather, to help us out. Not with winter still eightdays away. If they thought any of us could call the lightning, they'd want to know why we couldn't do it any time clouds are in the sky."

"And right overhead, less than a few hundred yards away," added Beltur.

"You need to get out of that wet uniform and get some sleep . . . or some rest, if you can't sleep." Athaal stood.

So did Beltur. At least his legs weren't shaky. Sleep sounded awfully good.

LXXIV

Beltur slept most of the threeday afternoon, and then until sixth glass on fourday. The storm subsided from torrents to a lighter but steady rainfall that dwindled into a cold drizzle on fourday. By midafternoon on fourday, the sun was out, but the air was cool, and the ground, despite its sandy nature south of Elparta, still sloppy. The rain had fallen as snow on the heights of the Easthorns, according to scouts. Neither force showed any inclination to resume hostilities on fiveday morning.

In midafternoon, Beltur, along with Athaal, Lhadoraak, and Waensyn, was summoned to a meeting of the command staff in the briefing room. Waensyn stood close to Majer Jenklaar. Majer Waeltur nodded politely to Beltur but did not motion him nearer.

Once all the officers were gathered, Commander Vaernaak, followed by Cohndar, entered and stood on the far side of the oblong table. Cohndar took a position several steps to the side.

"Our scouts have reported that the Gallosians are preparing for what appears to be a major attack. While I would have anticipated that they would wait until the ground is firmer, they apparently feel that it will be solid enough tomorrow. Also, the early snows on the

Easthorns will likely already have reminded them that they are running out of time."

"What if they don't attack, but just keep preparing to attack?" asked Waeltur.

"So far they've never let us have more than a day or so between attacks, and they keep pressing on. If we just keep defending and giving ground, we'll be bled dry . . . and before winter comes." As if to forestall any objection, Vaernaak held up a hand. "Spare me any vain hopes based on the idea that winter often comes sooner. It may indeed come sooner, but it doesn't come in a rush. We got a cold rain, and now it's sunny. In a few more days we *might* get a light snow or a heavy snow, and it will melt, and there will be sunny days before there is another snow, and after that, more sunny days, if not quite so many. Do you think that the Prefect's commanders will just do nothing on those days? If you might recall, we're only in the second eightday of fall. Even if winter comes four eightdays early . . ." After a long pause, the commander finished, "I trust you all understand."

Beltur certainly did, and he'd seen Athaal nod as well, if almost reluctantly.

"We have a plan to deal with that attack, and with their mages," added the commander. "I do not intend to go into that plan until just before the Gallosians launch such an attack, but I am pleased to report that we have two more companies of foot and a special mounted unit of naval marines. They were supposed to arrive late on threeday, but because of the rain, they arrived late yesterday."

A marine mounted unit? wondered Beltur. *Why do naval marines need horses?*

"We would have preferred the marines to be here sooner, but it's a long ride from Spidlaria. The unit is larger than a squad, with thirty marines. Ten are lancers.

Ten are armed as mounted infantry, and ten carry special crossbows that shoot quarrels of ordered-iron . . ."

Beltur couldn't help but notice that Cohndar frowned, if momentarily. *Because he didn't think it could be done, or because the commander is contradicting what he has said before?*

". . . This unit will be deployed for maximum effect. Marine Captain Toeraan, Majer Waeltur, Majer Jenklaar, and I will meet here at fourth glass to complete the planning for that deployment. Plan to be awake by fourth glass tomorrow morning. The mess will open at fourth glass, and the morning briefing will begin at fifth glass. That is all for now."

As he filed out of the room behind Athaal, Beltur had no doubts about who would be commanding him by morning on sixday . . . and why he'd been included in the meeting in the first place. Once outside in the wide corridor, Beltur noted that Cohndar and Waensyn had already hurried off out of sight.

"That's strange," said Lhadoraak. "Cohndar and Waensyn left in a hurry, and they didn't even look in our direction at the briefing."

"Not in our direction," said Beltur. "My direction."

"I can't believe that."

"It appears to be true, regretfully," said Athaal. "There might be a bit of jealousy involved. There often is when someone assumes that they're perfect."

"He can't believe that Jessyla would be right for him. She's far too direct," said Lhadoraak. "Consorting her would destroy them both."

"He appears to be of a different opinion," replied Athaal.

"But . . . he's always been so pleasant to me."

"He can be very pleasant," agreed Athaal matter-of-factly.

Lhadoraak started to say something, then paused. Finally, he said, "You don't often say something you don't mean. Or did you mean it just that way?"

"He can be very pleasant . . . when matters go in the fashion he wishes."

"You're saying I should be careful," said Lhadoraak.

"Watchful, anyway."

"Thank you."

"Is Felsyn better?" asked Beltur quickly.

"He's much better," replied the blond mage. "But he shouldn't be anywhere near the fighting. I think he's beginning to understand that. He's been telling me techniques, and cautioning me."

Athaal smiled. "He's got a good heart. He can also tell who doesn't. He'd never say anything, but you can tell . . . if you watch and listen."

Beltur had the definite feeling that while Athaal looked at him, the words were meant as much for Lhadoraak.

"You've said that before," said Lhadoraak.

"I just might have." Athaal laughed softly. "I have been known to repeat myself."

"Speaking of Felsyn," replied Lhadoraak, "I really should look in on him."

"Tell him about the meeting and who was there. That will make him feel better," said Athaal.

"That I will."

Beltur nodded slowly as the blond mage hurried away. "Lhadoraak wants to believe the best about everyone, doesn't he?"

"Shouldn't we all?" replied Athaal. "At least until they prove unworthy of that trust?"

Beltur had to agree. He also had to admire the way Athaal had maneuvered Lhadoraak into perhaps thinking differently about Waensyn. *That's something else you could learn from him.*

LXXV

Beltur woke early on sixday, even before the ranker appeared to rouse him, with a certain feeling of foreboding, a feeling that he'd tried to disregard, and hadn't been able to, since he'd felt that foreboding every morning since Zandyr's death. *Because his death made it clear that death can come from anywhere?* Yet nothing that terrible had yet occurred. *So far.* Then again, Beltur reflected, the mess with the storm and the lightning on threeday could have gone so much worse. He definitely didn't want to dwell on that.

He hurried to the officers' mess and began to eat warmish cheesed eggs and to sip ale that seemed more bitter than usual, fearing that he'd need as much nourishment as possible before the day was done. He was seated alone when Athaal joined him.

"You're looking pensive," offered the older mage.

"It might be the weather."

"Maybe it's because you haven't seen Jessyla lately." Athaal smiled.

"That could be," Beltur admitted, "but it's not just that."

"What else happened on threeday? That you didn't tell me?"

"With Majer Waeltur?" Beltur shook his head, then took another bite. "Not really anything. Except that it could have been so much worse."

"Then what? You still thinking about the reconnaissance company losses?"

"With nearly half the company dead or wounded,

wouldn't you be? Not to mention the most junior undercaptain."

"You didn't mention that."

"He was arrogant and condescending, but he died in a horrible way, not even understanding why."

"Is there any really sensible reason for war?" replied Athaal. "I'm just as glad I haven't seen what you have. We only had to shield against arrows and a few chaos-bolts on threeday. They weren't that strong because we were hundreds of yards back."

"Are you ready for the commander's briefing?" asked Beltur, finishing off the last of his ale. "Or haven't you eaten?"

"I ate earlier. I do worry that the commander's rushing things."

"You think that Vaernaak's wrong and that we could use the weather more to our advantage?"

"No. It's not that . . ." Athaal paused, then said, "He's right. If we keep fighting battles where we keep losing men and ground, even though it's only a little each day, pretty soon the fact that winter is coming won't matter."

"Because they'll be able to take Elparta before the snows get deep?"

"I have to say I worry about that. So does Meldryn."

Beltur nodded, then stood. "If you'll excuse me, I need to take care of a few things."

Athaal raised his eyebrows.

"To get my water bottles filled with ale and check on Slowpoke."

"Slowpoke?"

"My horse, remember?" Beltur was more than certain he'd mentioned Slowpoke to Athaal. Did that mean that Athaal was more worried than he was letting on?

"Oh . . . yes. Were you the one who named him?"

"I suppose so. Some of the rankers called him that, but it wasn't his name. He's not slow, but he was slow to respond to the reins when I first rode him. We worked that out. He's the reason why I'm still here."

"I doubt he's the only reason." Athaal smiled. "You'd better take care of him."

"You take care of yourself," returned Beltur. "Those chaos-bolts could get closer."

"I'll say the same to you. You're in a lot more danger than I am. Besides, I've got Lhadoraak with me. You're out there alone."

Beltur managed a smile as he answered. "I've got Slowpoke."

Athaal shook his head ruefully.

Beltur practically had to run to do all that he needed and still get to the briefing room just before fifth glass. Lhadoraak and Athaal were waiting outside.

Lhadoraak kept looking at the door, finally saying, "We might as well go in." He turned and stepped through the door into the rough plank-walled chamber where the commander had briefed them the day before.

Athaal and Beltur followed.

Beltur was surprised that so few officers were inside, just Majer Jenklaar and Majer Waeltur, as well as a captain in a uniform Beltur hadn't seen before, and Cohndar, who did not look directly at any of the other three mages.

Vaernaak appeared as the chimes struck, closing the door behind himself and walking to the far side of the oblong table, which was empty of anything, including maps.

"Now that you all are here, including Senior Mage Cohndar," began Vaernaak, "it is time to go over matters so that you all know the general plan for today. The Gallosians are readying a massive attack. This is not a surprise. We've known that they would have to do this at some point or withdraw with winter coming on. They will attempt to find a weak point in our lines. We will actually provide that point for them. When they finally concentrate on that point, we will rally and attack fiercely. If that succeeds, then we will take the fight to the Gallosian command units. If it does not, then we will use the alternative battle plan, involving the naval marine unit and Fifteenth and Eighteenth Foot. In either event, the naval marines and Fifteenth and Eighteenth Foot will take a position due south of the piers, roughly a kay from here, half a kay south of the pier channel, but behind the battle line of the main forces. All three units will be under the operational control of Captain Toeraan. They will hold that position and not join in the general advance being led jointly by Majer Waeltur and Majer Jenklaar. Captain Toeraan will be directly under my orders for this operation. His force will engage when and as required by how the battle develops. Because the naval marine unit has a particular objective, Mage Undercaptain Beltur will be assigned to protect it in all operations from this point on." The commander inclined his head in Beltur's direction.

Beltur definitely noticed the faint smile that crossed Cohndar's lips.

"Mage Captain Waensyn will be supporting Majer Jenklaar in order to facilitate the counterattack and subsequent events. Mages Athaal and Lhadoraak will protect the command group from chaos-bolts and other possible magely attacks." Vaernaak smiled tightly. "That is all. To your respective duties." He turned and strode out.

Beltur couldn't help wondering why the very short briefing had even been necessary. *Because Vaernaak believes in briefings? Or because Marshal Helthaer insisted on it? Or for some other reason?* Beltur felt like shrugging, but didn't. Instead he walked over to the naval marine officer.

"Captain, Undercaptain Beltur."

Toeraan studied Beltur for a moment before speaking. "Majer Waeltur told me you looked most unprepossessing and not to be deceived by that. We can talk later. We need to get moving."

"Where will you be forming up, Captain?" asked Beltur.

"We're already formed up at the end of the first pier. I'd appreciate your being there as soon as possible."

"Yes, ser." Beltur inclined his head, glad that he'd already taken care of the ale and bread.

After leaving Toeraan, Beltur hurried to the stable, quickly saddled Slowpoke, led him out into the chill air, and mounted. Once he was outside, he could see just the hint of gray light beginning to ooze over the eastern horizon into a dawn that was cold and clear, not quite cold enough for his breath to steam, but chill enough that he felt it should have, especially given the stiff and frigid wind blowing directly out of the north. He could see the naval marine unit as soon as he reached the end of the barracks building, and he guided Slowpoke along the stone-paved road that bordered the pier channel, then rode directly to the marine rankers in their bluish-green uniforms.

He didn't see Toeraan, but scanned the rankers in front until he saw the one with the squad leader's insignia and reined up in front of him. "Squad Leader, I'm Mage Undercaptain Beltur. I've been assigned to your unit until further notice."

"Yes, ser. Captain Toeraan said we'd be getting a mage officer." There was a pause, before the weathered-looking squad leader said, "Ser . . . might I ask what your duties have been so far?"

"I've been with Second Recon. Over the past eight-day, we fought most days there was fighting. At present, the company is at half strength from deaths and casualties. Someone here might recall Captain Laugreth. He was once a naval marine. I believe he fought the Suthyans at Diev."

"He was your captain, ser?"

"He was."

"Thank you, ser."

Beltur had the definite feeling that naval marines were skeptical of both regular troopers and mages, but that the mention of Laugreth had at least tempered that slightly.

At that moment, Toeraan rode up and studied Beltur, as if he hadn't seen him before. Then he said, "Laugreth said I was fortunate to have you."

Beltur couldn't have said he was surprised that Toeraan had found Laugreth, or the other way around. "I was fortunate to have him and Undercaptain Gaermyn to learn from, ser."

"He didn't mention Gaermyn. He's with Second Recon?"

"Yes, ser."

Since Toeraan said nothing more, Beltur asked, "What, exactly, will we be doing, and what do you require of me?"

"All I'll say at this point, Undercaptain," offered Toeraan, "is that Marshal Helthaer and Commander Vaernaak both noticed that the strongest white mages and a well-reinforced halberd company are always directly behind the middle of the main Gallosian attack, wherever that attack may be."

"That's likely the Gallosian command group, then."

"If it's not, it's quite a waste of mages and men," replied Toeraan. "We'll just have to see if that turns out to be accurate when the time comes."

That didn't even come close to answering the question.

"About my duties . . ."

"Once we're in position."

Beltur understood that Toeraan wasn't about to say more. *Why not? It's not as though anyone could do anything with that information. Or does Vaernaak suspect that someone is relaying information to the Gallosians?*

"We'll talk more on the way. The two foot companies are already in position." Toeraan gestured for Beltur to ride beside him, and then urged his mount forward, behind two outriders who had moved ahead without a word from the captain.

Beltur immediately raised his second shield, the one that concealed his order and chaos. The last thing he wanted was for the Gallosian whites to know he was there, and especially where he was.

Toeraan didn't say another word until the marines were riding along the south side of the pier channel, skirting the area where the companies comprising Commander Vaernaak's reserves and command group were formed up. "They ought to be farther forward." After a moment, the marine captain added, "I'd have them farther south."

"You think they're forming too close to the pier channel?"

"Closer than I'd have chosen, but I'm not the commander." Toeraan paused, then said, "Laugreth told me you can sense the movements of troopers from a distance."

"Depending on the weather and how much magery I've had to do, sometimes as far away as two kays on open ground, less than a kay in a town or city. Much less in heavy rain. I can only tell the general movement of forces, not of individual armsmen."

"He also said you can shield yourself and a few men close to you."

"Only a very few. I can also divert chaos-bolts for a time, but I can't do that for long while I'm holding much in the way of shields."

Toeraan nodded. "So you might be able to lead a wedge toward a specific unit and keep away chaos-fire?"

"That depends on how many mages are throwing chaos-bolts. If your men can loose iron quarrels at the white wizards, that would help."

"Senior Mage Cohndar said that might help when we attack the command group."

"How will we be able to get to them?"

"That's what the commander's battle plan is all about. You'll see."

Beltur certainly hoped he would. For all his doubts, Toeraan's calm certainty was partly reassuring. Beltur couldn't see the hard-bitten captain agreeing to something that didn't have any chance of succeeding, but he also worried about the details of the overall plan he didn't know, especially after Toeraan's observations about the positioning of the reserve forces. *Then again, you're not exactly a military strategist.*

Just as Commander Vaernaak had outlined, when Beltur and the naval marines rode up to join the two foot companies, they were already in position close to a half kay south of the first pier, with the right flank of the foot on the bank of the river, since the mudflats were once again covered by water, no doubt as a result of the rain and snow that had fallen earlier both on Spidlar and on the Easthorns.

Beltur could sense that fighting had already broken out across the entire Spidlarian line, with more and more Gallosians surging forward as if to push back the defenders by sheer numbers. "Ser, the Gallosians have attacked everywhere." He couldn't help but wonder if there weren't so many attackers that they might be getting in each other's way, at least in some places.

"We'll be ready long before we're needed." The tone of Toeraan's reply suggested that he wasn't all that concerned that the naval marines hadn't completed moving into position. "There's no sense in rushing before there's any need. Just let me know if any Gallosian units look like they might break through."

"Yes, ser."

Then, to Beltur's surprise, Toeraan ordered the naval marines to dismount and stand down, after which he turned to Beltur and said, "It's going to be quite a while before we're needed, and the horses need to be as fresh as possible."

With a battle already under way only a few hundred yards away, it would be some time before the marines would be needed? Beltur just hoped that what Toeraan and the commander had planned would work out . . . or at least not lead to catastrophe.

Beltur dismounted as well, but he kept sensing what was happening, yet all that he could determine was that, while the number of deaths kept rising, neither the Gallosians nor the Spidlarians seemed to be gaining ground, possibly in part because the footing wasn't as sure as it had been before the two days of rain.

A half glass passed, then perhaps a glass, and both forces still seemed mired as midmorning approached and then passed. Beltur was surprised that the foot companies under the command of Majer Jenklaar, the ones whose rear ranks were less than a hundred yards in front of Toeraan's force, hadn't advanced, because it seemed to him that they outnumbered the Gallosians and that on that part of the battlefield, the Gallosians were taking far heavier casualties. He could sense Waensyn, to the northeast of the naval marines, but not at the rear, which suggested that Jenklaar wasn't there, either.

Beltur took a long swallow of ale, then another, before recorking the water bottle.

Several moments after that, Beltur could sense that the Spidlarian companies on the east were being pressed back. "The eastern companies are being pushed back, ser."

"Slowly or quickly?"

"Slowly, so far."

Beltur could sense more and more Gallosians pressing into the eastern attack on the weakening Spidlarian defenders. "They're still giving ground, slowly."

"Let me know when they stiffen or withdraw more quickly."

Beltur kept sensing, trying not to wince at the growing number of deaths, so many that the area where the heaviest fighting was taking place seemed covered with black mist. As the white sun neared its zenith, that changed, and Beltur announced, "Our troopers are counterattacking from the west. They're digging into the side of the Gallosians."

Beltur could tell that by the increase in the number of men dying, with the flares of the black death mists increasing even more in the area just west of the redstone bluffs. There were comparatively fewer deaths along the irregular line of battle to the south of Toeraan's command. Again, that puzzled Beltur, because it seemed that the foot in front of the naval marines could have advanced.

"Let me know how the Gallosians are responding as soon as you can tell."

The counterattack kept up, for another half glass or so, then seemed to grind to a halt, and Beltur passed that on to Toeraan.

"It won't be long now," declared Toeraan.

Long for what? Our attack? Something else? More out of nervousness than anything else, Beltur got out his water bottle and took several more swallows of ale.

Except what happened next wasn't quite what Beltur expected, because, almost at the same time, troopers all across the forefront of the counterattack began to withdraw, as if they had been overwhelmed by the mass of Gallosians. "Ser, the counterattack looks like it's collapsing."

"Is that just on the east side . . . or everywhere?"

"Just on the east side."

"Marines! Mount up!"

Beltur was in the saddle almost as fast as the marines.

"Undercaptain, tell me when the withdrawing troopers stop, and where they are."

"Yes, ser."

"Are the troopers in front of us, and immediately to our south, holding fast?"

Beltur had to concentrate for several moments. "They seem to be, ser. There aren't all that many Gallosians in front of the right side of Majer Jenklaar's force."

"Excellent."

Beltur continued to follow the withdrawing Spidlarian units, and began to breathe easier when he saw they seemed to be re-forming. Then he frowned. Those troopers were creating a line of defense to hold off the pursuing Gallosians, and the two white mages that supported them, but that line was less than a hundred yards from the leading edge of the foot companies shielding the command group . . . and there wasn't that much distance between the command group and the pier channel immediately to the north. If the Gallosians broke the Spidlarian line on the east, they could trap the command group between the channel and the river. "Majer Waeltur's forces are almost as far back as the command group, and there are two white wizards in the

Gallosian forces pressing him. If the majer's forces don't hold on the east side, the Gallosians might overwhelm the commander and his companies."

"We can't worry about that now. Has the Gallosian command group moved forward?"

"No, ser."

"How strongly are they supported? Can you tell?"

"Three companies, maybe four."

"How are they set up?"

"A rough semicircle," said Beltur, adding, "There are three white wizards there. The white wizards are behind the troopers. I think the ground there is a little higher."

"If it isn't, they're idiots, and I haven't seen any evidence of that so far. Is there largely open ground between the Gallosians in front of us and those troopers around the Gallosian command?"

"Yes, ser. Only a little over a hundred yards, though."

"Then it's time for us to attack the command group." Toeraan raised an arm. "You and the lancers are in the lead. I'll be right behind you. I do mean right behind. Aim yourself straight for the center of the command group. Start at a fast walk."

Beltur straightened himself in the saddle. He wasn't about to extend his shields until the last possible moment.

"Banners up!" After a moment came the command, "Forward."

Beltur wondered about the banners. Weren't they just calling unnecessary attention to Beltur and the marines? *Or is that the point?*

Pushing aside those questions, Beltur urged Slowpoke forward, then had to rein him back slightly. He had the feeling that the gelding wanted to go into a full charge. "Not yet, big fellow. Not yet." He had no idea how much Slowpoke understood, but he felt that somehow the gelding did. *That just might be your imagination.*

"Faster now!" ordered Toeraan as the Spidlarian troopers scrambled out of the way of the oncoming mounted marines. Beltur urged Slowpoke into what he thought might be a fast trot as he neared the Gallosian troopers, then extended his shields just to the trooper on each side.

The Gallosian armsmen looked up in surprise as they saw the wedge of naval marines bearing down on them, led by Beltur and the line of lancers whose weapons glinted in the cold light of midday autumn, sweeping out of the north with the wind at their backs.

Some Gallosians ran. A few tried to stand up to the marine lancers, totally in vain.

Although the Gallosians were several ranks deep, if not deeper, the surprise of the mounted attack—and Slowpoke's power propelling Beltur's shields—cleared a path through the Gallosians, a path followed by the two foot companies. Even without trying, Beltur could sense that.

"More to your left!" ordered Toeraan. "Toward the black and silver banner! Slow to a walk on the open ground so the foot can keep up."

Beltur obediently reined Slowpoke back. As he kept moving, he studied the massed force now less than a hundred yards away, a force that was slowly turning toward the oncoming marines and Spidlarians. The front line of that Gallosian force consisted of shieldmen alternating with troopers bearing halberds. Somewhere behind them on a slightly higher rise, Beltur could sense three white mages. So far he didn't sense any building chaos, but he had no doubts that chaos-bolts would be aimed at the naval marines once they drew closer to the Gallosian command group.

Almost absently, Beltur realized the idea behind Vaernaak's plan. By attacking the command group, Toeraan was effectively immobilizing the Gallosian reserves, and keeping half of the white mages occupied—and only using one black mage in the process. And if Majer Jenklaar's forces could pivot fast enough to strike the rear of the Gallosians who had pursued the "retreating" Spidlarians, then the bulk of the Gallosian force would be trapped.

If Jenklaar can make it work . . . if the troopers at the edge of the pier channel hold . . . if you can keep these whites occupied . . . So many "ifs." Beltur forced himself to concentrate on anticipating the firebolts to come, hoping he could again use a separate shield to catch each one and catapult it back into the Gallosian ranks.

He was close to fifty yards from the halberdmen and shieldmen when the first chaos-bolt arched over the ranks of waiting Gallosians. Beltur was ready, quickly forming a containment around the chaos-bolt and order-catapulting it straight at the point in the shields where he and the naval marines would likely strike.

Then, two other chaos-bolts flared toward him—or rather toward where his temporary shield had captured the first chaos-bolt. Beltur could only manage to fling one back, this time directly behind where the first one had struck, but he could only block the second one, and late enough that a wave of heat flared over him momentarily.

Thirty yards to go.

"Charge!" ordered Toeraan.

Beltur urged Slowpoke into a run, but not a headlong gallop, managing to deflect another chaos-bolt into the Gallosians, but not really aiming it. *If you can get into their armsmen, the whites can't use firebolts without destroying more of their own men.*

No sooner had Beltur thought that than he saw a chaos-bolt arching far higher, showing that the whites had realized that as well and were targeting the foot troopers following the mounted marines. Beltur diverted that one, roughly to the southeast part of the Gallosian reserves, and tried to concentrate on catching the next one as soon as it rose.

He just managed to drop it around the white who had flung it when Slowpoke—and Beltur's shields—crashed over charred bodies and through the line of Gallosians behind those bodies.

Then there were blades and halberds swinging and flying everywhere. Beltur contracted his shields and let Slowpoke move forward at his own pace, aware dimly of the blades slamming against his shields as he struggled to watch for chaos-bolts and redirect them, all the while trying to move to where he was closer to the nearest white mage.

Yet another chaos-bolt flared toward the advancing Spidlarian foot. Once more, all Beltur could do was shield it away from the troopers somewhere into the Gallosian foot to the east of where he struggled through the mass of armsmen, all of whom seemed to be beating at him with one sort of weapon or another. The continued impacts on his shields were getting more and more painful.

Somewhere behind him, he heard Toeraan shout out, "Fire at the silver banner! The silver banner!"

Beltur turned his head to the right, belatedly sensing a white wizard not ten yards away, one whose shields flared with each impact of an iron quarrel as chaos and order flared into ravening fire. For just a moment, Beltur froze, trying to remember what he should do. Then he grabbed the ordered iron arrow from where it had rested in the water bottle holder for days. He forced more order into it and threw it in the direction of the mage, using more order to catapult it at the white. With the combination of iron quarrels and Beltur's over-ordered iron arrow, the mage's shields collapsed. In that instant, a look of total dismay crossed the face of the angular and graying white mage that Beltur had met once. Then a flash of fire flared where Naeron had been, consuming both mage and mount.

With that flash of flame came a hammer blow that struck Beltur's shields, shaking him so violently that he barely remained in the saddle. A sharp and somehow brilliant needle of pure pain knifed through his eyes.

For a moment, all he could do was to hold on to his shields as pain and tears blurred his vision. He managed to straighten up, vaguely aware that there seemed to be fewer Gallosians striking at him or Slowpoke. After a time, he could finally sense that one of the remaining mages and a group of riders were rapidly withdrawing. He could also sense another white mage still throwing chaos-bolts, albeit much smaller ones, and that mage was more to the east, surrounded by a diminished shield wall.

As soon as Beltur turned toward the other mage, a chaos-bolt flared toward him. So surprised was Beltur that he barely was able to deflect it into a scattered group of Gallosians.

By the time the next chaos-bolt flew toward him, Beltur was ready and flung it back at the other mage. Then several iron quarrels flew toward the mage, each one impacting his shields, with the resulting fiery explosions ripping through the nearby Gallosian armsmen, who abruptly broke away from the mage. Beltur didn't want to use the last iron arrow, although he couldn't have said why, and he urged Slowpoke forward toward the other mage. The mage wheeled his mount and spurred it into a headlong gallop to the south, despite the uneven nature of the ground.

Beltur immediately decided against chasing two white mages single-handedly and turned Slowpoke back toward where the center of the command group had been, then reined up as he realized that there was little he could do as the Eighteenth and Fifteenth Foot were essentially slaughtering the Gallosian troopers who had not been able to withdraw.

"Undercaptain!" shouted someone. "Beltur!"

Beltur had to look around for a moment before he could make out Toeraan in front of some fifteen, possibly twenty naval marines. He urged Slowpoke toward the group, then reined up short of the captain.

"What's happening with the commander's forces?" demanded Toeraan. "There's not much we can add here. The Gallosian commander fled. Or maybe he was killed and his second fled. It doesn't matter."

Beltur's head throbbed slightly as he concentrated. "The Gallosians, I think, are surrounded, but there aren't that many troopers left between them and the pier channel."

"I was afraid of that. Let's see what we can do." Toeraan signaled and the marines turned their mounts, leaving the Spidlarian foot to finish off the Gallosian reserves, while heading back north toward where the fighting still continued, a melee that was killing a number of troopers every moment, or so it seemed to Beltur from the black death mists that seemed to blanket the air near the pier channel.

Even from almost four hundred yards away, Beltur could see a firebolt arching northward, indicating to Beltur that one of the white mages was still trying to attack the Spidlarian commander. After a moment, another chaos-bolt flew southeast, as if the other mage was trying to flame his way out of the troopers who surrounded him.

How long has that been going on? How long can Athaal and Lhadoraak hold out? Beltur urged Slowpoke into a faster walk. He didn't dare move any faster, not with all the bodies and discarded weapons lying everywhere. At the same time, he had to wonder where

Waensyn was, and what he was doing, since, if he happened to be protecting Majer Jenklaar, he couldn't be that far from either of the remaining white mages.

"I'm going to need help if we have to deal with those white mages," Beltur told Toeraan.

"What do you need?"

"Do you have any crossbows and quarrels left?"

Toeraan glanced back, seeming to count. "Six with crossbows. I don't know how many quarrels."

"Once we find the first mage, I'll need them to aim quarrels at him. Each one that hits his shields will weaken him. That will keep him from doing more damage until I can get close enough."

"What will you do?"

"I've got one ordered iron arrow left. If I can deliver it with enough force . . ."

"Was that what you did to the one back there?"

"Yes."

"I thought black mages couldn't attack. Only defend."

"I've been called a black mongrel," Beltur replied sardonically, belatedly remembering to take out his water bottle. He didn't realize that his hands were shaking until he dropped the cork, and nearly the bottle. He took several swallows. After a few moments, he thought his hands were a bit steadier, and he pulled the cork from the empty first bottle and used it on the half-empty third bottle.

As Beltur and the marines neared the rear of Majer Jenklaar's force, Beltur finally located the nearer white mage, who was less than fifty yards ahead, and using his shields, his mount, and small chaos-bolts to burn his way and that of half a score of mounted Gallosians through the Spidlarian foot. "There he is! The one in gray on the chestnut. The air around him sparkles!" Beltur supposed that was the free chaos and minute embers left from the firebolts. "Don't fire at him yet. We have to get closer."

The Spidlarian foot quickly moved out of the way of the oncoming naval marines, but that might not be for the best, Beltur realized, because if he and the marines couldn't stop the mage, that opening would allow the white a greater chance of escape.

And you don't want that to happen. Every one that escapes might be back next year ... and seeking revenge.

When the white mage noticed the riders heading toward him, he flung a firebolt directly at Beltur, not necessarily because he thought Beltur was a mage, but because Beltur had taken the lead in an effort to stop the mages and to keep the Gallosians from overrunning the command group—and Athaal and Lhadoraak.

Beltur contained the firebolt and flung it back against the white's shields, where the chaos splattered and then consumed the nearest pair of Gallosians. That scarcely deterred the white wizard, who flared a narrower bolt, again directly at Beltur. Once more Beltur returned the chaos-bolt, but this time, the white did something and the chaos flared harmlessly into the air.

This one's more powerful and skilled. Beltur grabbed the iron arrow, but decided he needed to be closer. "Have them start firing at him," he told Toeraan.

"Target the mage on the chestnut! Now!" ordered the marine captain.

The first iron bolt slammed into the mage's shields, and fire spurted from them.

Both Spidlarians and the remaining mounted Gallosians edged away from the mage as the same thing happened with the second quarrel. And the third and fourth.

Beltur was less than twenty yards away, and he could see that, while those spurts of fire were smaller, they weren't that much smaller. He kept Slowpoke moving, close enough that he could see the mage's face, but he didn't recognize the man.

At that moment, the mage launched what looked like a massive dart of chaos full-force at Beltur.

Beltur could only deflect it into the ground between them, and steam rose in a misty curtain that obscured Beltur's view of the other mage. Even so, he decided he was close enough. He shrouded the iron arrow with order and order-catapulted it at the other mage.

The other's shield flared a golden red, then vanished, but the mage remained untouched.

Beltur urged Slowpoke forward. The white turned his mount to avoid the oncoming gelding. Beltur extended his shields to touch the white.

There was a brief scream and a flare of yellowish red . . . and the mage vanished, leaving the chestnut largely untouched except for a blackened saddle.

Beltur's shields had held, but his head was aching as he looked back to the west, where he saw yet another chaos-bolt flaring into the ground in front of the command group, turning one shieldman into a momentarily flaring and then charcoaled figure.

Then another wave of chaos seared away more Spidlarian troopers, leaving only a handful of defenders between the white and his escorts and Lhadoraak and Athaal, both mounted and flanking Commander Vaernaak.

Beltur cast his senses around. *Where the frig is Waensyn?* He could only sense that the other black mage was to the south, and even farther from the command group than Beltur himself was.

Even from more than fifty yards away, Beltur could sense that Lhadoraak's shields were failing. So could the white mage, because he pressed his mount toward Lhadoraak, a line of chaos in front of him like a lance.

Beltur strained, throwing a containment across fifty yards, capturing and holding that chaos, but unable to do more, trying to hold on as light flashes flickered across his vision, trying to block any chaos from striking Athaal, Lhadoraak, or the commander.

Then, as the white mage continued forward, Athaal drove his mount forward, putting himself and his shields between the oncoming mage and Lhadoraak and Vaernaak. Athaal's shields struck those of the chaos-mage, and a sheet of fire flared up—but away from Lhadoraak.

Beltur struggled to keep an order wall on the north side of the containment that held the captured containment, holding it as chaos washed over the mage ... and then back over Athaal ...

No! Not Athaal ...

Blackness rose up and smashed Beltur down.

LXXVI

Chaos washed over Beltur like a river of fire, and just as the pain was so great he would have screamed, had he been able, cold order quenched the heat. But the chill of order soon seeped into his bones, and he would have shivered uncontrollably, had he been able, before the heat of chaos thawed him out, and then the river of fire began to scorch him once more ...

"Beltur ..."

He thought he recognized the voice ... but he couldn't say just whose voice it might be.

"You need to open your eyes," the voice insisted.

He did, slowly, except pain lanced through them, and he closed them quickly.

A cool hand touched his forehead, and his forehead and eyes tingled. "Try opening them again."

Beltur tried once more, gingerly. There were still needles of light pricking at his eyes, but they were bearable. Sitting on a stool beside his bed was Margrena.

"No, I'm not Jessyla. I couldn't let her do your healing."

Couldn't . . . For a moment, Beltur just didn't understand.

"You both might have died . . ."

"Both?"

"That's a danger when two people are as close as you two are."

"Close?" *When we haven't even kissed?*

"Closeness isn't just what your bodies do, Beltur."

Beltur didn't want to think about that. "What day is it? What happened?"

"It's eightday. You don't know what happened? You were there at the end, Lhadoraak said."

"I know I took out two white mages, but then Commander Vaernaak and Athaal and Lhadoraak were in trouble, and it took forever to get there, and by then . . ." Beltur winced as he recalled the ball of order and chaos flame that had consumed Athaal and the last white mage . . . all because Athaal likely hadn't wanted the young girl he regarded as his niece to be fatherless. "I couldn't get close enough to do enough, and Athaal put himself in front of Lhadoraak, and then there were order and chaos explosions everywhere. I don't remember anything after that."

"I'll tell you what I know in a moment." She helped Beltur into a sitting position, half propped against the wall, and handed him a mug. "It's ale. Drink it."

He took several small sips, then a swallow.

"Most mages don't survive two rounds of order depletion. It might help if you didn't make it a practice. For Jessyla's sake, if not for yours."

"Athaal did so much for me . . . I couldn't not try." He found himself half laughing, half crying. "Is that what mongrels do . . . try to give everything to protect those who take them in?"

"That's why Jessyla loves you. That's why Athaal did what he did, for you, for Lhadoraak, for me, for Jessyla. No matter what Cohndar and Waensyn think, some of us are mongrels at heart. Athaal understood that. You don't think he and Meldryn aren't mongrels as well?"

After several moments, Beltur stopped shuddering. "I'm sorry."

"You don't have anything to be sorry for. Drink some more ale. You don't want Jessyla to see you like this."

Beltur took another swallow of ale.

Margrena didn't say anything.

Neither did Beltur, but he worried about Jessyla. Had she been so order-depleted that they both could have died? Slowly, he drank more ale.

"You only look half-dead now," said Margrena dryly, rising from the stool. "A few others want to see you. I'll be back later. And don't even think about magery."

Beltur had several more small swallows of ale before another figure stepped into the gloom of the quarters, one he hadn't expected—Laugreth. "Captain . . ."

"At ease," replied Laugreth dryly. "I've seen you look worse. I've also seen you look a lot better. I thought I'd stop by. Toeraan and the naval marines—what's left of them—are already on their way down the river to Spidlaria."

"Down the river?"

"With the Gallosians beaten and skulking back to Fenard, the traders wanted their cargoes protected again.

At times, you have to wonder." An ironic smile crossed Laugreth's lips, then vanished. "Toeraan told me that you're most of the reason why we won . . . if you can call a battle with over two thousand casualties a victory. That's ours. We didn't count theirs."

"They're gone?"

"They're gone. They even left their siege engines behind. Good thing they never got close enough to the walls to use them. Even with all those white wizards. They had eight of them. The way we figured it out, you got rid of four of them. Another got hit by lightning."

"Three . . . Athaal took out the last one." Beltur wasn't about to claim the mage struck down by the lightning bolt.

"The other black, the one who died defending the commander?"

"That was Athaal."

"You did something to help him, Toeraan said."

"I tried. I couldn't do enough. I wasn't close enough. I just couldn't get there in time."

Laugreth straightened. "I always thought you'd make a good officer. I was right. I might see you around. I might not . . . but if you ever want to be an undercaptain again, let me know." He nodded, respectfully, then turned.

Beltur just remained propped up on the bed. After all the deaths he'd sensed, remaining an undercaptain was about the last thought on his mind. But the fact that Laugreth had come to see him confirmed Beltur's feelings about the captain.

Before that long, but after Beltur had finished the last of the ale in the mug, a fine-featured, blond, and very tired-looking black mage appeared.

"Margrena told me you finally roused. We were all worried about you. It just . . . wouldn't have been right."

"It wasn't right about Athaal." Beltur tried to keep

the bitterness out of his voice. *Neither of you should have been there.* That wasn't something he'd ever say, but it was still true.

"No . . . it wasn't. War isn't fair."

Life sometimes isn't fair. But Beltur just nodded.

"I owe my life to you and Athaal."

"To Athaal. He's the one who put himself and his shields between you and that white."

Lhadoraak shook his head. "It took both of you. I could sense the shield you cast that held back all that chaos. Athaal couldn't have done that. I couldn't, either. My shields were almost gone after all the chaos-bolts the whites threw at the commander. They just kept coming . . . and coming."

"I think that last mage was the strongest." Beltur wasn't certain of that, only that the last white had been very strong. *But it's best that he was the strongest.* For more than a few reasons, even if Beltur was in no shape to explain why.

"You're tired. You need to rest."

"So do you. And take care of Taelya." *Athaal would have wanted that.*

Lhadoraak swallowed, then shook his head. "I'll . . . I'll see you later." He hurried off, as if he didn't want Beltur to see how he felt.

Just when Beltur was thinking of lying back and dozing off, if he could, another man in blue appeared, in the blue of the Council. It took Beltur a moment to recognize Veroyt.

"I'm here on behalf of Councilor Jhaldrak and the entire Council. The Council wanted you to know how much they appreciated all you and the other black mages did for Spidlar in defeating the Gallosians."

"Especially Athaal," Beltur added.

Veroyt nodded. "Lhadoraak said you tried to save him."

"I couldn't get there soon enough." Beltur paused. "Does Meldryn know?"

"I told him myself. It was quite a blow. They were together more than twenty years." After a pause, Veroyt added, "He asked how you were. I told him what happened, and that you'd been injured, but were expected to recover."

"Thank you."

"You're welcome." Veroyt shifted his weight from one boot to the other. "If there's anything else I can do?"

"Right now, I can't think of anything. I know where to find you." Beltur managed a smile he didn't feel. "Thank you for coming."

"I was glad to do it." Veroyt paused. "Now that the fighting's over, what are you going to do?"

"Go back to smithing cupridium. What else?" *What else is there for a mongrel mage?*

"That must be interesting."

Beltur nodded. "It's good work." *What else can you say?*

"Until later."

Beltur wondered how many others Veroyt had to visit. He didn't envy the councilor's assistant.

Did he really want to go back to forging cupridium? He was still musing over that when he heard footsteps and vaguely sensed someone coming.

"I said I'd be back. I brought someone."

Beltur looked up as Margrena stepped into the makeshift quarters, but his eyes instantly shifted to the red-haired healer with blood on her sleeves, dark circles under her eyes, and a smile meant for him.

In a way, we're both mongrels.

And that was the way it should be . . . for once.